Formal Sentential Entailment

Charles F. Kielkopf
The Ohio State University

University Press of America™

University Press of America™
division of
R.F. Publishing, Inc.
4710 Auth Place, S.E., Washington, D.C. 20023

Printed in the United States of America

0–8191–0313–6

CONTENTS

PREFACE

The author started to plan a text on entailment systems when he began preparing for his logic seminar for the Spring Quarter 1973 at The Ohio State University. There was a genuine need for a text at that time. N.D. Belnap's excellent monograph [1960a] would have been a fine introductory text. Indeed much of Parts III and IV of this work are developments from his monograph. Unfortunately, Belnap's monograph was very difficult to obtain. The author was unaware of the plans of A.R. Anderson and Belnap to produce a book Entailment which Princeton published in 1975. As far as he knew the literature on entailment was scattered throughout the logic and philosophic journals of the world. The author's intent, however, was not merely to produce a text on entailment systems. He wanted to survey all entailment systems and to show that they were all defective in some way or another. Material implication is inadequate to symbolize most conditionals and classical logical implication has its odd features. Still one is reluctant to admit that what he has been teaching for several years is wrong. So, to avoid teaching with a guilty conscience, the plan was to show that no other system of logic is better than that which is currently taught as formal sentential logic.

Work with the literature has converted the author. There is still the belief that the area needs a text. Hopefully, there will be a text nearly as good as Hughes' and Cresswell's excellent modal logic text. There is still the belief that the text should be more than a mere presentation and development of systems. The present work does have extensive portions on evaluating systems and the evaluation of systems. A glance through the table of contents will show that this is also a work in the philosophy of logic. There is still the belief, although as shaky as before, that what is currently taught as formal logic should continue to be taught. At least there should not be any change in the typical first two logic courses. The conversion has been to the conviction that there is a formal connection between premisses and conclusion of some valid arguments which is better than logical implication and that the theorems of the Anderson and Belnap system E of entailment give the truths about this special formal connection. This special connection is called entailment. The case for the conversion is given in the text along with the survey of many alternative systems.

The belief that the current teaching of logic should remain the same can be reconciled with the conversion. Even if some valid arguments do not support an entailment between the premisses and conclusion, they are still valid and validity is an important feature. So it is important to learn to recognize validity. Thirdly, and with some embarrassment, it has to be admitted that classical logic is used in this book to talk about systems. Of course, entailment systems should be taught; but only as a third or possibly second course in logic. In so far as this book is suitable for logic courses, it is intended for such advanced courses in non-classical logic.

Most of what is worthwhile in this book has come from others. If I have failed to give proper credit for a result, the failure was unintentional. There is no claim that there are any results which are not already in the literature. I cannot list here all of those from whom I borrowed. Nevertheless, I borrowed so much from N.D. Belnap Jr. , J.M. Dunn, R.K. Meyer, and R. Routley that I must give them special acknowledgment. It must also be brought out that R.G. Wolf of Southern Illinois University at Edwardsville provides an extraordinarily valuable service to people working on the search for the right logic or logics by circulating literature. I sincerely appreciate the support of the Ohio State University in awarding me a research duty quarter for Fall 1974 and three grants-in-aid for preparation of material.

The typescript for this University Press of America edition has been prepared by the author; so he is responsible for all errors. Hopefully, there will not be too many errors. The author would sincerely appreciate notice of errors from readers. Send them to the Department of Philosophy at The Ohio State University, Columbus, Ohio 43214. In due time, then, a list of errata will be available.

Columbus, Ohio
July 1977

Notational Preface

In this Preface our goal is twofold. First we present the notation of the formal languages of most of the systems of sentential logic which we study. Secondly, we want to develop terminology for talking about formal languages. Readers familiar with literature on entailment systems and relevance preserving logics may skip this Preface and refer to it only upon finding eccentric usages in the text.

The formal languages which are the objects of our study are, as usual, called *object languages* and we talk about them in what is called a *metalanguage*. Our metalanguage is English supplemented with special signs for referring to items of the object languages. We add to English every sign and finite sequence of signs from the object languages as names of these signs and sequences of signs. So each sign and finite sequence of signs from object languages can be used as an *autonomous name*, i.e., as a name of itself. Thus p and $(p \supset q)$ may be object language signs as well as names for object language signs. However, if there is danger of confusion between signs and names of signs, we place single quotes around a sign or sequence of signs to serve as a name of the quoted sign or sequence of signs. An example of using quoted signs as names is the sentence: 'p' and '$(p \supset q)$' may be object language signs as well as names for object language signs. When signs such as p, $\supset$, and $\rightarrow$ are used in our metalanguage they name themselves and their object language occurrence is *mentioned*, i.e., talked about. However, when a sign or sequence of signs is presented in an object language it is *used*. We also enrich English with p_i, where i is a natural number, as variables ranging over what we call below sentential variables. Further English is enriched with A,B,C, and D with subscripts and other devices such as primes for referring to sequences of object language signs. As we proceed we will introduce, frequently without comment, symbols into our metalanguage.

In this book we study many different systems; not all will be in the full language characterized below. As we study the various systems, we will note the fragments of the following language which are used in the respective systems. The *punctuation marks* are the left and right parentheses: (,). The *sentential signs* are *sentential variables*; p,q,r, and p_i for any natural number i; and two sentential constants: t and f. There are three classes of *logical signs*. There are *truth-functional signs*: $\sim, \wedge, \vee, \supset, \equiv$. There are *modal signs*: $\Diamond, \Box, ⥽$. There are *entailment* and *relevance preserving signs*: $\rightarrow$, $\circ$, +, $\Rightarrow$. $\leftrightarrow$, $\Leftrightarrow$. The chart below gives all of the well-formed formulas or *wffs*. with their intended interpretation or interpretations.

Wffs. with intended interpretations and readings,

Formulas	Interpretations,
Atomic formulas	
1) t	1) An obvious necessary truth such as o = o or (o = o or o ≠ o).
2) f	2) An obvious necessary falsehood such as o ≠ o or (o = o and o ≠ o).
3) A sentential variable by itself,	3) Sentences of a natural language which are true or false, Also elements of matrices; and especially elements of a 2-element matrix whose elements are T (the true) and F (the false),

Molecular formulas

If A and B are wffs., the following are wffs.

1) $\sim(A)$	1) It is not the case that A.
2) $(A \wedge B)$	2) A and B.
3) $(A \vee B)$	3) A or B.
4) $(A \supset B)$	4) If A, then B. Also:A materially implies B. It is frequently abbreviates: $(\sim(A) \vee B)$.
5) $(A \equiv B)$	5) A if and only if B. Also: A is materially equivalent to B. It abbreviates $(A \supset B) \wedge (B \supset A)$.
6) $\Diamond(A)$	6) It is possible that A.
7) $\Box(A)$	7) It is necessary that A.
8) $(A \rightarrow\!\!\!\!\!\!\; \ni B)$	8) A strictly implies B. It usually abbreviates: $\Box(A \supset B)$.
9) $(A \equiv B)$	9) A is strictly equivalent to B. It abbreviates $(A \rightarrow\!\!\!\!\!\!\; \ni B) \wedge (B \rightarrow\!\!\!\!\!\!\; \ni A)$
10) $(A \rightarrow B)$	10) A entails B. Also A relevantly implies B. But 'entails' and 'relevantly implies' are not synonymous. In some systems $(A \rightarrow B)$ cannot accurately be read as: A entails B.
11) $(A \circ B)$	11) A is intensionally conjoined with B. Also: A is consistent with B, and A is cotenable with B. It usually abbreviates $\sim((A \rightarrow \sim(B))$.

12) (A+B) — 12) A is intensionally disjoined with B. It usually abbreviates $(\sim(A)\rightarrow B)$. Because $\rightarrow$ changes meaning from system to system, so do intensional conjunction and disjunction.

13) $(A\leftrightarrow B)$ — 13) A and B mutually entail each other. A and B are equivalent. It abbreviates $((A\rightarrow B)\wedge(B\rightarrow A))$.

14) $(A\Rightarrow B)$ — 14) A strictly and relevantly implies B. It abbreviates $\Box(A\rightarrow B)$.

15) $(A\Leftrightarrow B)$ — 15) Abbreviates $(A\Rightarrow B)\wedge(B\Rightarrow A)$,

A useful notion is the notion of <u>subformula.</u> Each wff. is a subformula of itself. If a molecular wff. C is formed from wffs. A and B, then A and B are subformulas of C. The relation of being-a-subformula-of is transitive. The paired parentheses introduced with each logical sign mark its <u>scope</u>. Further we say that the formation rule for each of the logical signs shows what it is for the logical sign to be the <u>principal logical sign</u> or <u>principal connective</u> of a formula. (Here 'connective' does not have that special sense which it is given in II.1. So,here we should give warning that we occasionally use 'connective' to mean 'logical sign',or in the terminology of II.1, 'functor.')

We enrich our metalanguage with all the schemas for talking about object language formulas. To specify the schemas which have been added to English proceed as follows. First stipulate that a p_i or a schema letter by itself is a well formed schema. Then regard A and B as autonomous names and the logical signs as autonomous names. The fifteen rules for molecular formulas can be regarded as rules giving well-formed-schemas. Of course, in our enriched English we also have any finite sequence of symbols used in schemas. Analogous to what we did for formulas we can define subschemas.

None of the systems we study have all of the logical signs as basic or primitive. So we want to abbreviate complex formulas and schemas. We depart from standard practice by allowing new signs to be introduced into the object language by definition and by abbreviations of object language formulas; the new formulas and abbreviations are genuine object language formulas. For instance,if a system has only $\sim$ and $\vee$ as primitive, we accept the definition: $(A\supset B) =_{df} (\sim(A) \vee B)$ as telling us that in the object language $(\sim(p) \vee q)$ is a wff. which is abbreviated by a new wff. $(p\supset q)$. We do not take the definition as telling us only that the schema $(A\supset B)$ denotes exactly the same wffs. as those denoted by $(\sim(A) \vee B)$. After we present some standard abbreviations, we will consider reasons for, and consequences of, allowing object languages to be augmented by definitions and abbreviations.

It is convenient to adopt conventions for eliminating parentheses. We follow quite closely the conventions of Church [1956]. We frequently delete the parentheses marking the scope of a logical sign. The unary signs: $\sim, \Diamond, \Box$ have as their scope the shortest wff. on their right when their scope marking parentheses are deleted. The binary signs, without scope markers, have their parentheses replaced according to the following precedence ordering where 'has precedence over' means 'has larger scope than.'

$\Leftrightarrow, \Rightarrow, \leftrightarrow, \longrightarrow, +, \circ,$ ≣ , ⥽ , $\equiv, \supset, \vee, \wedge$

Examples illustrate these precedence conventions for restoring parentheses.

$A \longrightarrow B$ ≣ $B \equiv C \supset A$ gives $(A \longrightarrow (B$ ≣ $(B \equiv (C \supset A))))$.
$A \vee B$ ≣ $B \supset A \wedge B$ gives $((A \vee B)$ ≣ $(B \supset (A \wedge B)))$.
$\Box p \vee q \longrightarrow \sim \Box \sim p$ gives $((\Box(p) \vee q) \longrightarrow \sim(\Box(\sim(p))))$.

In a formula or subformula parentheses are restored to a series of the same logical signs by association to the left.

$A \longrightarrow B \longrightarrow B \longrightarrow A$ gives $(((A \longrightarrow B) \longrightarrow B) \longrightarrow A)$.
$p \longrightarrow p \vee q \vee r$ gives $(p \longrightarrow ((p \vee q) \vee r))$.

Frequently we use a dot . in place of a pair of parenthese marking a scope. A pair of parentheses is restored from a dot by the following convention. Replace the dot with a left parenthesis (; pair this left parenthesis with a new right parenthesis). The new right parenthesis goes on the immediate left of the first right parenthesis which is not already paired with a left parenthesis and which is to the right of the dot. If there is no such paired right parenthesis to the right of the dot, the new right parenthesis goes on the far right of the formula.

$A \longrightarrow .B \longrightarrow .B \longrightarrow A$ gives $A \longrightarrow (B \longrightarrow (B \longrightarrow A))$.
$(A \longrightarrow .B \longrightarrow B) \longrightarrow .A \longrightarrow B$ gives $(A \longrightarrow (B \longrightarrow B)) \longrightarrow (A \longrightarrow B)$.

We tolerate alteration of object languages by abbreviations and introduction of new signs for two reasons. First, when we present object language formulas for illustrative purposes we want, of course, our illustration to be clear. But formulas in primitive notation are often very complex visual patterns. For instance, if a language has only $\sim$ and $\vee$ as primitive some of its formulas may look like a bunch of worms. Second, most of our talk about object languages is by use of schemas. We get a very inaccurate picture of these object languages if their formulas are very different in appearance from frequently used schemas. Furthermore, allowing alteration of object languages allows them to share a feature with natural languages which, of course, are altered by definitions and conventions. Nevertheless, despite our tolerance of new logical signs, we designate some of a languages logical signs as primitive to bring out relations between logical signs as well as to simplify mathematical inductions on the length of formulas.

Our tolerance of alteration of object languages by definition and convention requires, as Church observes in footnote 108 of his [1956], an addition to usual rules of proof, viz., rules for selecting theorems or theses. ('Proof,' 'thesis,' and 'theorem' will be defined later in this Preface.) We need a rule saying that a defined formula may replace the formula which it defines, and conversely. To state such a rule we introduce some metalinguistic signs which are helpful for talking of replacements. Let F(A) represent a formula with A as a subformula. Let F(B/A) represent a formula just like F(A) except that some occurrences of A in F(A) have been replaced with B. We now have the following rule.

Rule of Replacement for Defined Terms in Object Languages,

If $A =_{df} B$, from F(A) infer F(B/A) and From F(B) infer F(A/B). Also if the following are wffs., they are theses. $F(A) \longleftrightarrow F(B/A)$ and $F(B) \longleftrightarrow F(A/B)$.

When we use such a rule we simply write 'by definition,' or <u>Def</u>. and occasionally cite the definition used. We must admit that this use of definitions is tantamount to adding equivalences as axioms to axiom systems.

We ought to note that definitions abbreviating schemas also require a rule of replacement. For instance, in a system whose primitive logical signs are only $\sim$ and $\wedge$ we may say that we have shown $(A \supset A)$ is a theorem schema because for talk about this system we have defined the schema $(A \supset B)$ as $\sim((A \wedge \sim(B)))$ and have shown that $\sim((A \wedge \sim(A)))$ is a theorem schema. So, analogous to what we did for talk of replacement in object languages, we introduce Sc(B/A) to represent the schema obtained from the schema Sc(A) by replacing some occurrence of subschema A in Sc(A) with schema B. We can have, then, the following rule for replacement of defined terms in schemas. We never explicitly cite this rule. We present this rule here only to call attention to the fact that we do follow such a rule.

Rule of Replacement for Defined Terms in Schemas,

If $A =_{df} B$, then Sc(A) is a thesis schema iff. Sc(B/A) is a thesis schema, and Sc(B) is a thesis schema iff. Sc(A/B) is. Also $Sc(A) \longrightarrow Sc(B/A)$, $Sc(B/A) \longrightarrow Sc(A)$, $Sc(B) \longrightarrow Sc(A/B)$, $Sc(A/B) \longrightarrow Sc(B)$, and $Sc(A/B) \longleftrightarrow Sc(B/A)$ are thesis schemas.

As is obvious, we are using 'iff.' to abbreviate 'if and only if.' In passing, let us note that we do not introduce a meta-metalanguage. We simply use our enriched English to talk of itself.

Before discussing processes of selecting a subset of formulas of a formal language as theses, we present a list of definitions which we use throughout this study.

Some definitions,

Truth-functional formula	A wff. containing only sentential variables and constants and truth-functional signs.
zdf. (0-degree formula)	A truth-functional formula,
fde. (1st-degree entailment)	A wff. $(A \longrightarrow B)$ where A and B are both zdfs..

We now define <u>degree of a formula</u>. A zdf. has 0-degree. If the degree of A is m, the degree of $\sim A$ is m while the degree of $\Diamond A$ and $\Box A$ is m+1. If the maximum degree from A and B is m, the degree of $A \wedge B$, $A \vee B$, $A \supset B$, and $A \equiv B$ is also m, while the degree of $A \rightarrow\!\!\!\!\!\!\exists\, B$ and $A \longrightarrow B$ is m+1. The degree of $A \Longrightarrow B$ is that of $\Box(A \longrightarrow B)$, the degree of $A + B$ is that of $\sim A \longrightarrow B$, and the degree of $A \circ B$ is that of $\sim(A \longrightarrow \sim B)$.

fdf. (1st. degree formula)	
full entailment language	A language with $\longrightarrow$ as a primitive or defined sign in which there are no restrictions on the degree of the formulas admitted as wffs..
full entailment system	A system in a full entailment language,
nested entailment	An $\longrightarrow$ in the scope of an $\longrightarrow$,
classical formula	A zdf.
classical tautology	A zdf. which is a standard two-value tautology,
tautology	Wffs. of any degree which can be obtained from classical tautologies by uniformly substituting wffs. for variables, viz., substitution instances of classical tautologies,
variable	Sentential variable

One of the most significant issues encountered in a study of formal languages is the selection of a subset of a language's wffs. as the wffs. which cannot become false sentences upon replacing variables with natural language sentences which are true or false and by giving the logical signs their intended reading. A method for making such a selection is called <u>a system</u>. The wffs. selected are called <u>theses</u> of the system. If two methods of selection select the same wffs. as theses we call the systems <u>equivalent systems</u>. However, we frequently talk as if equivalent systems were identical, i.e., we frequently talk as if systems were identified by their theses. When we talk as if systems were identified by their theses, we may say that different but equivalent systems, eg., different axiomatizations which have the same theorems, are *different versions of the same system.* Systems in different languages may even be called equivalent if they have the same theses after both languages are enriched so that they have the same logical signs. If the method of selection is the syntactical method of giving axioms and rules of proof, the theses are called *theorems*; otherwise they are merely called theses. But we do call theorems theses too. Because this Preface is on notation, we focus our attention on the axiomatic method.

We present axiom systems by presenting finitely many axiom schemas and finitely many rules of proof. Axiom systems are identified by their axiom schemas and their basic or primitive rules of proof. (We cannot be so precise about identity conditions for non-axiomatic systems because we cannot express the identity conditions in terms of syntactic features.) An *axiom schema* is a schema which by virtue of being designated axiomatic tells us that every wff. obtained by substituting wffs. uniformly for schema letters is an axiom. A wff. is *substituted uniformly for a schema letter in a schema* if the wff. is substituted for each occurrence of the schema letter. We frequently call axiom schemas axioms although, strictly speaking, only their object language substitution instances are axioms. Of course, if we give a system with axiom schemas the system has infinitely many axioms.

Because we use axiom schemas we do not need to give a rule of uniform substitution for variables as a basic rule. Nevertheless, we should admit that we use a procedure which could be called: A rule of uniform substitution for schema letters in schemas. Let us adapt notation from sections 10 and 12 of Church's [1956] for presenting uniform substitution rules. Let Msub.(A,B,C) denote the schema obtained from schema C by substituting schema B for each occurrence of schema letter A in schema C. Similarly, let Osub.(p_i,B,C) denote the wff. obtained from wff. C by substituting wff. B for each occurrence of variable p_i in wff. C. We follow the procedure that we denote axioms or theorems with Msub.(A,B,C) if we denote axioms or theorems with C. Thus if we have $A \rightarrow B \rightarrow . C \rightarrow A \rightarrow . C \rightarrow B$ as an axiom schema we have $A_1 \supset A_2 \rightarrow B \rightarrow . C \rightarrow . A_1 \supset A_2 \rightarrow . C \rightarrow B$ as an axiom schema. We do not use this Msub.(A,B,C) notation; at most we give the reader a few hints how to determine how the substitution instance of a schema has been obtained. We introduce the Msub.(A,B,C) notation to show a similarity between presenting an axiom system with axiom schema and presenting it with finitely many object language wffs. as axioms.

To select other formulas as theorems, after axioms have

been given, basic or primitive rules of proof must be given. As Belnap points out on pp. 11-12 of [1960a], there are object rules of proof and meta-rules of proof. Object rules are presented by presenting finitely many schemas as premiss schemas and a single schema as the conclusion schema. Often the premiss schemas are presented on the left of $\vdash$ with the conclusion schema on the right. Occasionally the $\vdash$ will be tagged to indicate the system which is being used. But the context usually allows us to use an untagged $\vdash$. A typical object rule is Transitivity for $\rightarrow$: $A\rightarrow B, B\rightarrow C \vdash A\rightarrow C$. Sometimes, though, it is more natural to state rules in the forms: From $A_1,\ldots,A_n$ infer B or $A_1,\ldots,A_n$; so B. In a full entailment language we have schemas for material implications, strict implications, and entailments associated with object rules. The associated material implication, strict implication, and entailment schemas are obtained by conjoining the premiss schemas with $\wedge$, placing $\supset$, $\prec$, or $\rightarrow$ on the right of this conjunction, and then placing the conclusion schema on the far right. Meta-rules do not give us the unrestricted **permission** to infer a B from $A_1,\ldots A_n$. Meta-rules only tell us that we can infer that B is a thesis if $A_1,\ldots,A_n$ are all theses. Typical meta-rules are uniform substitution for variables: If $\vdash$ C, then $\vdash$ Osub.(p_i,B,C), and Necessitation: If $\vdash$ A, then $\vdash \Box$A. A system may have both object and meta-rules as primitive rules of proof.

A proof in an axiom system S is a finite sequence of wffs. Pr. such that each member of Pr. is either an axiom of S or a consequence of predecessors in Pr. by use of primitive rules of S. A last member of a proof in S is a theorem of S. We prefix $\vdash_S$ or plain $\vdash$ to wffs. to assert that the wff. is a theorem of S. If Γ is a set of wffs. there is a deduction or derivation of B from Γ in S if there is a finite sequence of wffs. Der. such that each member of Der. is an axiom of S, a member of Γ , or is obtained from predecessors in Der. by primitive rules of S, and the last member of Der. is B. If Γ is finite, we say that 'From Γ, infer B' is a derived rule of S, and frequently use $\Gamma \vdash_S$ B or $\Gamma \vdash$ B to say that this is a derived rule. Let us call derivations deductions only when all members of Γ are theorems of S. If Γ is finite, there is a deduction of B from Γ , and if $\vdash_S$ B, then 'From Γ, infer B' is an admissible rule of S. The distinguishing feature of admissible rules is that they guarantee only to take us from theorems to theorems. The typical way to present a rule which is only admissible is as a meta-rule: If $\vdash$ A, then $\vdash$ B, where A is the conjunction of the members of Γ . Of course, all primitve meta-rules are admissible rules; but usually meta-rules are not derived rules. For example, a rule of uniform substitution for variables would not be a derived rule in any useful sentential logic.

We will be using the familiar notation of set-theory in our metalanguage. We use $\in$ for 'belongs to,' $\cap$ for intersection, $\cup$ for union, and $\subseteq$ for inclusion. However, we will not use the notation of set-theory in presenting derived rules although strictly speaking we should. For instance, we use $A \vdash B$ instead of $\{A\} \vdash B$. We also may regard a proof as a deduction from the null set, $\emptyset$, of premisses.

In the course of this study we will be interested in derivations on which restrictions are placed. These restrictions will be introduced and explained at the appropriate places.

Because we work with axiom schema, we do not actually present proofs or derivations. We present proof schemas, derivation schemas, and abbreviations of these. A derivation schema DerS. of schema B from a set of schemas Γ is a finite sequence of schemas $A_1, \ldots, A_n$ such that each A_i is a member of Γ, an instance of an axiom schema obtained by uniform substitution for schema letters, or is obtained from predecessors in DerS. by use of primitive rules as if they applied to schemas as well as wffs., and A_n is B. If Γ is finite, we use $\Gamma \vdash B$ to say that there is a derived rule schema. If Γ is $\emptyset$ we say that B is a theorem schema, i.e., $\vdash B$. If every member of Γ is a theorem schema we say that we have a deduction schema and again assert $\vdash B$. We call deduction schemas proof schemas, as we do any sequence of schemas which leads to a $\vdash B$. We abbreviate these derivation and proof schemas by deleting steps, used of substitution instances of previously proved theorem schemas, and derived rules. These abbreviated derivation schemas could appropriately be called 'sketches of how to obtain a proof,' although we label them proofs.

We close this Notational Preface with a list of schemas and rule schemas which have standard names. There is no claim that this list is complete. When only a schema $A \to B$ is listed a rule is also implicitly listed. The implicitly listed rule is $A \vdash B$; the rule is named 'rule of N' where N is the name of the $A \to B$. Thus if $A \to B \to . \sim B \to \sim A$ is named Contraposition, $A \to B \vdash \sim B \to \sim A$ is called the 'Rule of Contraposition.' On this list, we use $\to$ for implication. If desired, new schema names can be obtained by replacing $\to$ with $\dashv$ or $\supset$ and modifying name with 'for strict implication' or 'for material implication.' Thus 'Contraposition for strict implication' would name $A \dashv B \dashv . \sim B \dashv \sim A$. If a rule is given the associated entailment is very often given the name of the rule. For instance, the schema $A \wedge (A \to B) \to B$ may be called Modus Ponens.

Names and abbreviations	Schemas
Absorption Abs.	$A \rightarrow B \rightarrow . A \rightarrow A \wedge B$
Addition Add.	$A \rightarrow . A \vee B$, $B \rightarrow . A \vee B$
Adjunction, Rule-β, Adj.	$A, B \vdash A \wedge B$
And-elimination, $\wedge$-elim.	$A \rightarrow B \wedge C \rightarrow . (A \rightarrow B) \wedge (A \rightarrow C)$
And-introduction, $\wedge$-intro.	$(A \rightarrow B) \wedge (A \rightarrow C) \rightarrow . A \rightarrow . B \wedge C$
Antilogism	$A \wedge B \rightarrow C \rightarrow . A \wedge \sim C \rightarrow \sim B$
Aristotles' Thesis	$\sim (A \rightarrow \sim A)$
Assertion	$A \rightarrow . A \rightarrow B \rightarrow B$
Association, Assoc.	$A \wedge (B \wedge C) \leftrightarrow (A \wedge B) \wedge C$ $A \vee (B \vee C) \leftrightarrow (A \vee B) \vee C$
Boethius' Thesis	$A \rightarrow B \rightarrow \sim (A \rightarrow \sim B)$
Commutation	$A \wedge B \leftrightarrow B \wedge A$, $A \vee B \leftrightarrow B \vee A$
Composition, Comp. Consequent composition	Same as $\wedge$-intro.
Constructive Dilemma CD	$(A \vee B), (A \rightarrow C), (B \rightarrow D) \vdash C \vee D$
Contraction	$A \rightarrow (A \rightarrow B) \rightarrow . A \rightarrow B$
Contraposition, Contra.	$A \rightarrow B \rightarrow . \sim B \rightarrow \sim A$
Demorgan Equivalences, DM	$\sim (A \wedge B) \leftrightarrow \sim A \vee \sim B$ $\sim (A \vee B) \leftrightarrow \sim A \wedge \sim B$
Destructive Dilemma	$A \rightarrow B$, $C \rightarrow D$, $\sim B \vee \sim D \vdash \sim A \vee \sim C$
Disjunctive Syllogism, DS Occasionally identified with MD below,	$\sim A, A \vee B \vdash B$
Distribution, Dist.	$A \wedge (B \vee C) \leftrightarrow A \wedge B \vee A \wedge C$ $A \vee (B \wedge C) \leftrightarrow (A \vee B) \wedge (A \vee C)$
Double Negation, Dbl. Neg.	$\sim\sim A \leftrightarrow A$
Excluded middle	$A \vee \sim A$
Exportation, Exp.	$A \wedge B \rightarrow C \rightarrow . A \rightarrow . B \rightarrow C$
Factor	$A \rightarrow B \rightarrow . A \wedge C \rightarrow . B \wedge C$

Let $\mathrm{Comm}(A_1 \wedge, \ldots, \wedge A_n)$ represent some rearrangement of the conjuncts A_i. Similary let $\mathrm{Comm}(A_1 \vee, \ldots, \vee A_n)$ represent some rearrangement of the disjuncts A_i.

General Commutativity Gen. Comm.	$A_1 \wedge, \ldots, \wedge A_n \leftrightarrow \mathrm{Comm}(A_1 \wedge, \ldots, \wedge A_n)$ $A_1 \vee, \ldots, \vee A_n \leftrightarrow \mathrm{Comm}(A_1 \vee, \ldots, \vee A_n)$

Schema list continued

Let Assoc($A_1 \wedge \ldots \wedge A_n$) and Assoc($A_1 \vee \ldots \vee A_n$) represent any rearrangement of parentheses in the n-member conjunction and n-member disjunction which still gives a wff..

General Associativity Gen. Assoc.	$A_1 \wedge \ldots \wedge A_n$---Assoc($A_1 \wedge \ldots \wedge A_n$) $A_1 \vee \ldots \vee A_n$---Assoc($A_1 \vee \ldots \vee A_n$)
Rule-γ	See MD and DS.
Identity	$A \rightarrow A$ and also $A \leftrightarrow A$
Importation	$(A \rightarrow .B \rightarrow C) \rightarrow .A \wedge B \rightarrow C$
Material Detachment, MD See Rule-γ and DS	$A, A \supset B \vdash B$ $A, \sim A \vee B \vdash B$
Modus Ponens, MP, Rule-α	$A, A \rightarrow B \vdash B$
Modus Tollens, MT	$A \rightarrow B, \sim B \vdash \sim A$
Necessitation, Nec.	If $\vdash A$, then $\vdash \Box A$.
Permutation, Perm.	$(A \rightarrow .B \rightarrow C) \rightarrow .B \rightarrow .A \rightarrow C$
Prefixing, Prefix. Frequently in rule form,	$A \rightarrow B \rightarrow .C \rightarrow A \rightarrow .C \rightarrow B$
Premiss addition	$A \rightarrow B \rightarrow .A \wedge C \rightarrow B$
Simplification, Simp.	$A \wedge B \rightarrow A, \quad A \wedge B \rightarrow B$
Strict Detachment, Str. D	$A, A \dashv B \vdash B$
Suffixing, Suf. Frequently in rule form,	$A \rightarrow B \rightarrow .B \rightarrow C \rightarrow .A \rightarrow C$
Summation Also $\vee$-elimination	$(A \rightarrow B) \wedge (C \rightarrow B) \rightarrow .\ A \vee C \rightarrow B$
Syllogism	See Transitivity
Transitivity, Trans. Frequently in rule form,	$(A \rightarrow B) \wedge (B \rightarrow C) \rightarrow .A \rightarrow C$
Transposition	Another word for Contraposition,
Tautology	$A \leftrightarrow A \wedge A, \quad A \leftrightarrow A \vee A$
Weak Assertion	$A \wedge (A \rightarrow B) \rightarrow B$

We now begin our study by considering two features of standard or classical logic which have stimulated it.

PART I

I.1 The Lewis derivations, oddities which provoked this study vs. the so-called paradoxes of material and strict implication.

In this Section we present what can be called the Lewis derivations and their connection with the two claims which have provoked a search for an entailment connection. We also contrast our concerns in this study with worries about the so-called paradoxes of material and strict implication. In the next two sections we develop in more detail reasons for rejecting the two provocative claims supported by the Lewis derivations.

Two claims have provoked this study. They are the claims that both ' $A \wedge \sim A$ entails B' and ' A entails $B \vee \sim B$ ' are true. In Section I.4 we discuss use of 'entails'. Here consider the following two claims using the term 'formally correct'. 'Formally correct' will be identified with 'is an entailment'.

C1: Any argument of the form: $A \wedge \sim A$, so B, is formally correct.

C2: Any argument of the form: A, so $B \vee \sim B$, is formally correct.

An argument is formally correct if it is as good as it can be on formal considerations alone. If we reject a formally correct argument, we have to reject it on some material consideration such as:the premisses being false, terms used equivocally, the premisses being irrelevant to the conclusion, or the conclusion being trivial. Note in passing that a goal of this study is to build a case that considerations of relevance between premisses and a conclusion can, on occasion, be formal considerations. Of course, no criterion for applying 'formally correct' has been given at this stage of the study. Hopefully, we can conclude with such a criterion. Here we have only presupposed that we do have an idea of appraising an argument on purely formal grounds. This presupposition is justified because we do have the idea of appraising an argument as formally valid. Perhaps only formal validity suffices to make an argument as good as it can be on formal considerations alone. Nevertheless our notion of formally correct leaves open the possibility that more than formal validity is needed to make an argument as good as an argument can be on formal considerations alone.

What makes the above two claims plausible? A fundamental reason for saying that such arguments are formally correct is that arguments of these forms are formally valid and, as we also say, these forms themselves are formally valid. In this study, 'formal validity ' and 'deductive validity' mean when applied to argument forms that it is impossible that the premisses be interpreted as true and the conclusion as false. Strictly speaking, a schema of an inference is formally valid if it becomes a valid argument form by uninformaly replacing each distinct schema letter with a distinct variable. But we speak of schemas being valid by speaking as if they were argument forms. When applied to an argument these terms mean that the argument has a valid form. We dismiss immediately a suggestion that an argument could be formally correct but not formally valid. For us formal validity is a necessary condition for formal correctness. As important as formal validity is, we soon find that formal validity does not guarantee a very intimate link between premisses and a valid conclusion from those premisses. Early in our study of formal validty we realize that a necessary truth is a valid conclusion from any premisses and any conclusion is a valid conclusion from necessary falsehoods. So, for formal correctness we hope that there is a more intimate connection between the premisses and a conclusion than mere formal validity. It has been claimed that there is a more intimate connection between the premisses and conclusions of the kind of arguments cited in C1 and C2 than mere formal validity. It is claimed that the conclusions can be derived from the premisses by acceptable rules and deductive practices. Formal derivability or deducibility is being suggested as the formal factor which added to formal validity constitues formal correctness. For the basis of such a suggestion we turn to pp. 250-51 of Lewis' and Langford's [1932].

First let us consider the argument that an arbitrarily selected B can be derived from an explicitly contradictory $A \wedge \sim A$. We consider three versions of this familiar derivation in order to make clearer what we have to reject to reject the derivation.

Lewis Derivation I.

i)	$A \wedge \sim A$	Hypothesis (Hyp.)
ii)	A	Simplification on (i) (Simp.)
iii)	$\sim A$	Simp. on (i)
iv)	$\sim A \vee B$	Addition on (iii) (Add.)
v)	B	Material Detachment, MD, on (ii) and (iv).

If at (iv) we had added B to A, we would have used Disjunctive Syllogism, DS, to detach B from $A \vee B$ by use of $\sim A$. So, we can consider either MD or DS as having crucial use in Derivation I.

If we reject Derivation I we certainly have to reject some generally accepted deductive practices or deduction rules. An example of rejecting a deductive practice is rejection of use of contradictions as hypotheses. An example of rejecting a deductive rule is to claim that MD,DS, or Add. is not a proper rule. It is, of course, perfectly clear that we cannot charge that these rejected practices or rules lead to formal invalidity. A case, then, has to be made that they suffer from some formal defect different form formal invalidity. Hopefully, a case can be made that they are formally incorrect in the way in which the inference from $A \wedge \sim A$ to B is formally incorrect, if the inference is indeed formally incorrect.

In the preceding paragraph we expressed a hope to discover a single sense of 'formally correct' which applies to rules, practices, whole arguments, and immediate or basic inferences. There is a hope that the notion of 'formally correct' can be nearly as succinct as that of 'formally valid.' Despite our desire for simplicity, we should not be satisfied with a sense of formal correctness in which a rule is classed as formally incorrect merely because it is used in a derivation of a conclusion from certain premisses, we consider the argument formally incorrect, and can find no other rule which we are willing to reject. For instance, it is unsatisfactory to reject the rule MD or the rule DS merely because it is the only rule in Derivation I which we are willing to give up. If we classify DS as formally incorrect we hope to be able to specify that DS is defective in exactly the same way as the rule: From $A \wedge \sim A$, infer B, is defective. But this way of being defective should not be anything as question begging as: Is used to go from $A \wedge \sim A$ to B. We have to be prepared to accept the fact that maybe only a very complicated characterization tells us what formal correctness is. Maybe the only homogenous sense of 'formally correct' will be defined in terms of corresponding to the rules and theorems of some formal system. Hence, our search for the formally correct arguments may become primarily a search for a formal system of sentential logic which meets certain adequacy conditions to be discussed in Section I.6.

A technique to help insure that we find a single sense in which defective moves in the Lewis derivation are defective is to convert as many of the moves as possible into schemas which can be read as statements that a certain argument form is formally correct, i.e., as statements that a certain entailment holds. When the derivation is rewritten as a series of entailment claims,which are true or false, the rejection of an intermediate line is the rejection of the same kind of logical thing as the last line. Thus it is likely that the rejection of the intermediate line will be for the same kind of reason as that for rejecting the last line. The last line will say: $A \wedge \sim A$, so B is a formally correct inference.

In Lewis Derivation II below $A \rightarrow B$ may be read as 'there is a formally correct inference from A to B' or as 'A entails B.'

Lewis Derivation II

i) $A \wedge \sim A \rightarrow A$ Simp.
ii) $A \wedge \sim A \rightarrow \sim A$ Simp.
iii) $\sim A \rightarrow . \sim A \vee B$ Add.
iv) $(A \wedge \sim A \rightarrow \sim A) \wedge (\sim A \rightarrow . \sim A \vee B) \rightarrow . A \wedge \sim A \rightarrow . \sim A \vee B$
Transitivity (Trans.)
v) $(A \wedge \sim A \rightarrow \sim A) \wedge (\sim A \rightarrow . \sim A \vee B)$
Adjunction (Adj.) of (ii) and (iii).
vi) $A \wedge \sim A \rightarrow . \sim A \vee B$ Modus Ponens MP, (iv) and (v).
vii) $(A \wedge \sim A \rightarrow A) \wedge (A \wedge \sim A \rightarrow . \sim A \vee B) \rightarrow .$
$. A \wedge \sim A \rightarrow . A \wedge (\sim A \vee B)$ Composition Comp;
viii) $(A \wedge \sim A \rightarrow A) \wedge (A \wedge \sim A \rightarrow . \sim A \vee B)$ Adj. of (i) and (vi).
ix) $A \wedge \sim A \rightarrow . A \wedge (\sim A \vee B)$ MP on (vii) and (viii).
x) $A \wedge (\sim A \vee B) \rightarrow B$ MD as an entailment claim.
xi) $(A \wedge \sim A \rightarrow . A \wedge (\sim A \vee B) \wedge (A\ (\sim A \vee B) \rightarrow B) \rightarrow .$
$. A \wedge \sim A \rightarrow B$ Trans.
xii) $(A \wedge \sim A \rightarrow . A \wedge (\sim A \vee B)) \wedge (A \wedge (\sim A \vee B) \rightarrow B)$ Adj. (x), (xi).
xiii) $A \wedge \sim A \rightarrow B$ MP on (xi) and (xii).

Derivation II may be regarded as a deduction of $A \wedge \sim A \rightarrow B$ in an axiom system whose basic rules of proof are MP and Adj.. For our immediate purposes the interest of the above deduction is that if we reject the last line we have to reject one of the previous lines. We simply will not consider rejecting MP or Adj. . Since all of the lines are $A \rightarrow B$ claims, rejection of an intermediate line is a rejection of the same kind of logical thing as is rejection of $A \wedge \sim A \rightarrow B$. In Derivation I, we initially rejected a whole derivation and then moved to rejecting a single step in the derivation. But for Derivation II our initial rejection and secondary rejection are both of entailment claims. Hence, if we reject line (x) to avoid accepting line (xiii) we have to do so on some general grounds for rejecting entailment claims. We cannot have as these general grounds the charge that the antecedent and the consequent share no schema letter and hence have instances in which the antecedent and consequent share no variables. In every schema down to (xiii) antecedents and consequents share schema letters. Indeed, an advantage of Derivation II is that it forces us to develop a basis for rejecting entailment claims for deeper reason that that the antecedent and consequent share no variables, viz. are in a very clear formal sense irrelevant to one another.

A case can be made that there is a basis for doubting the intelligibility of lines (iv),(vii),and (xi). These lines contain $\rightarrow$'s within the scope of $\rightarrow$'s. It does seem odd to say that a formally correct argument is obtained by a formally correct argument from a formally correct argument. It seems that there would be an argument whose premisses are arguments! In later sections we will defend use of such nested $\rightarrow$'s. Here let us modify Derivation II to eliminate use of nested $\rightarrow$'s. We can use Trans. and Consequent Composition in rule form to get Derivation III below.

Lewis Derivation III

i) $A \wedge \sim A \rightarrow A$	Simp.
ii) $A \wedge \sim A \rightarrow \sim A$	Simp.
iii) $\sim A \rightarrow . \sim A \vee B$	Add.
iv) $A \wedge \sim A \rightarrow . \sim A \vee B$	Trans. (ii) and (iii).
v) $A \wedge \sim A \rightarrow . A \wedge (\sim A \vee B)$	Comp. on (i) and (iv).
vi) $A \wedge (\sim A \vee B) \rightarrow B$	MD
vii) $A \wedge \sim A \rightarrow B$	Trans. on (v) and (vi).

Derivation III can be presented in an fde. system. Because we will require Transitivity for $\rightarrow$ and Comp. as rules, Derivation III is as suitable for our purposes as Derivation II. Let us repeat that our purpose is to require ourselves to reject an entailment claim different from $A \wedge \sim A \rightarrow B$ and to justify that rejection on the basis of some general considerations for rejecting entailment claims. In a later section, we explain, if we do not defend, our resolution not even to consider seriously a rejection of Transitivity. Here consider how Derivation III is especially suitable for our purpose. Derivation III makes it clear that the basic problem which stimulated this study is independent of use/mention worries involved with use of nested $\rightarrow$'s. Indeed, we get a variant of Derivation III by merely replacing the $\rightarrow$'s with $\vdash$'s, where $\vdash$ need only indicate a formally correct argument from zdfs. to a zdf.. Derivation III brings out that the issue raised by the derivability of an arbitrary B from any $A \wedge \sim A$ is an issue about which first degree entailment claims to accept and to reject. Consequently, we begin our search for the right entailment system in Part II by searching for the right fde. system. So, Derivation III is what we refer to as the first Lewis derivation although he did not give it exactly in this form. It is the one which we react to.

Observe, in passing, that our recasting of the Lewis derivation so that we have to reject an entailment claim in order to reject: $A \wedge \sim A$, so B, as a formally correct inference allows us to retain the rejected entailments in weaker forms. For example, consider the rejection of MD in the form: $A \wedge (\sim A \vee B) \rightarrow B$. Rejection of $A \wedge (\sim A \vee B) \rightarrow B$ will not in all systems involve rejection of $A, \sim A \vee B \vdash B$ as a basic or derived rule. Also rejection of MD as an entailment need not involve rejection of MD as a strict implication $A \wedge (\sim A \vee B) ⥽ B$ nor the rejection of MD as a material implication $A \wedge (\sim A \vee B) \supset B$. But acceptance of MD as an entailment will bring acceptance of it as a rule, and usually acceptance of MD as a strict and as a material implication. Here it is appropriate to note that we will accept $A \wedge (\sim A \vee B) \supset B$ and even $A \wedge \sim A \supset B$ because we will accept all classical tautologies.

Before turning to a consideration of the second Lewis derivation which provoked this study, let us consider one of the so-called paradoxes of strict implication and one of the so-called paradoxes of material implication. Let us consider one of the paradoxes of strict implication which is discussed by Lewis on pp. 174-75 of [1932]. Consider $\sim \Diamond A ⥽ . A ⥽ B$ which is their formula 19.74 presented here as a schema. Call this schema 'the paradox of impossibility' although we may be uncomfortable calling it a paradox in light of Lewis' p. 175 correct observation that such formulas express slightly surprising truths about deductive validity. Indeed we will accept a thesis stronger than Lewis' 19.74. Consider the following derivation which we will accept.

Derivation IV

i)	$\Diamond(A \wedge \sim B) \rightarrow \Diamond A$	Any adequate representation for 'it is possible' should give such a thesis. This is an entailment version of Lewis' 19.01.
ii)	$\sim \Diamond A \rightarrow . \sim \Diamond (A \wedge \sim B)$	Contraposition (Contra.) on (i).
iii)	$\sim \Diamond A \rightarrow . A ⥽ B$	Use of $A ⥽ B =_{df} \sim \Diamond (A \wedge \sim B)$ in (ii).
iv)	$\sim \Diamond A ⥽ . A ⥽ B$	Infer $A ⥽ B$ from $A \rightarrow B$.

The move from (iii) to (iv) merely reflects our position that a necessary condition for formal correctness is formal validity. In Derivation IV we intend $A ⥽ B$ to represent 'there is a formally valid argument from A to B.' Because of our acceptance of (iii) and this move we can be said to accept a stronger version of the paradox of impossibility, although line (iii) does not really express a paradox. Line (iii) tells us that from the form of a claim that a formula A cannot be true, i.e., is impossible, we can conclude by the best possible formal reasoning a claim of the form $A \wedge \sim B$ cannot be true. Really, line (iii) is no more paradoxical than line (i). Line (i) tells us that the best possible formal reasoning can take us from a form asserting a conjunction is possible to a form asserting that one of the conjuncts is possible. If (iii) is not paradoxical, (iv) is not. Line (iv) tells us that it is not possible that a form A is impossible while a form $A \wedge \sim B$ is possible.

A genuine paradox of impossibility is expressed by $\sim\Diamond A \rightarrow . A \rightarrow B$. This genuine paradox tells us that we can conclude from the form of a claim that A is impossible, by the best possible formal reasoning, that we can go from the form of A to the form of any claim whatsoever by the best possible formal reasoning. The following rather famous objection in the entailment literature is best interpreted as an objection to what we have just called a genuine paradox of impossibility. The following quotation is from p. 23 of Anderson's and Belnap's [1962a] and it is repeated in section 3 of their [1975].

> Imagine, if you can, a situation as follows. A mathematician writes a paper on Banach spaces, and after proving a couple of theorems he concludes with a conjecture. As a footnote to the conjecture, he writes: " In addition to its intrinsic interest, this conjecture has connections with other parts of mathematics which might not immediately occur to the reader. For example, if the conjecture is true, then the first order functional calculus is complete, whereas if it is false, then it implies that Fermat's last conjecture is correct." The editor replies that the paper is obviously acceptable, but he finds no connection whatever between the conjecture and "the other parts of mathematics." and none is indicated in the footnote. So, the mathematician replies," Well, I was using 'if...then__' and 'implies' in the way logicians have claimed I was: the first order functional calculus _is_ complete, and necessarily so, so anything implies that fact—and if the conjecture is false, it is presumably impossible, and hence implies anything. And if you object to this usage, it is simply because you have not understood the technical sense of 'if...then__' worked out so nicely for us by logicians" And to this the editor counters: " I _understand_ the technical bit all right, but it is simply not correct. In spite of what logicians say about us, the standards mainained by this journal require that the antecedent of an 'if...then___' statement must be _relevant_ to the conclusion drawn.

Anderson's and Belnap's mathematician is portrayed as reasoning in the following way where C represents his conjecture. He accepts C or $\sim C$ and presumably on philosophical grounds accepts $\sim\Diamond C$ from matematical $\sim C$. His philosophical grounds are that if a mathematical proposition is false it is necessarily false. He then uses the genuine paradox of impossibility to conclude (C$\rightarrow$Fermat's last conjecture is correct) from $\sim\Diamond C$. (Later we will note how he used what we call a genuine paradox of necessity to conclude (C$\rightarrow$the first order functional calculus is complete)).

There would have been no odd claim, only a trivial claim, if the mathematician had only observed that if the conjecture were impossible then $\sim\Diamond$(C and Fermat's last conjecture is not correct), i.e., (C ⥽ Fermat's last conjecture is correct). The odd and, indeed, false claim is that the best possible formal reasoning, the kind acceptable in the journal, can be used to go from C to the correctness of Fermat's last conjecture.

Note that the genuine paradox of impossibility is stronger than the paradoxical entailment claim which concludes Derivation III. In any system with $\Diamond$ in its language as a basic or defined logical sign $\sim\Diamond(A\wedge\sim A)$ should be a thesis. So if a system with $\Diamond$ also had the genuine paradox of impossibility as a thesis, it would by use of MP have $A\wedge\sim A\longrightarrow B$ as a thesis. However, systems may have $A\wedge\sim A\longrightarrow B$ as a thesis without having $\sim\Diamond A\longrightarrow.A\longrightarrow B$ as a thesis. Of course, systems without $\Diamond$ can have $\vdash A\wedge\sim A\longrightarrow B$ without $\vdash \sim\Diamond A\longrightarrow.A\longrightarrow B$. But of more interest will be the systems of Emch [1936a,b] and Vredenduin [1939] which we discuss at the end of Part II. These systems have $\Diamond$, $\vdash A\wedge\sim A\longrightarrow B$ but lack $\sim\Diamond A\longrightarrow.A\longrightarrow B$ as a theorem although having it as a wff.. In the next Section we will argue that $A\wedge\sim A\longrightarrow B$ is unacceptable as a thesis; let alone the stronger genuine paradox of impossibility.

The so-called paradoxes of material implication are not of primary concern here. In particular, we not bothered by having $\sim A\supset.A\supset B$ as a thesis. We want all tautologous schemas as thesis schemas and $\sim A\supset.A\supset B$ is simply the tautologous schema $\sim A$ **v.** $\sim A$ **v** B. We should be bothered if we had $\sim A\longrightarrow.A\longrightarrow B$ as a thesis. We should even be bothered if we had $\sim$A ⥽ .A ⥽ B as a thesis. We cannot give a formally valid argument that there is a formally valid argument from a false claim to any claim whatsoever.

However, although we are not worried about the paradoxes of strict and material implication we are not suggesting that we can dispense with such worries because we will use $\longrightarrow$ to symbolize all 'if__then__' claims or conditionals. We intend to use $\longrightarrow$ to symbolize the best possible formal implication. Hence, once we get a logic for $\longrightarrow$, it may turn out that $\longrightarrow$ is not the best symbolization for many natural language conditionals. Maybe ⥽ and $\supset$ will have their uses. We do have an interest in getting a suitable symbolization for conditional sentences in our natural languages; it is simply that our main interest here is not in getting suitable symbolizations for all conditionals. In passing, though, we will note that the $\longrightarrow$ of system R, which is discussed in Part IV, is a far better symbolization for many conditionals than either ⥽ or $\supset$. Of course, if the only signs which we had for symbolizing conditionals were ⥽ and $\supset$, the so-called paradoxes of strict and material implication would indeed be paradoxical. They would be paradoxical because we would then be forced to use one of them to symbolize entailment or to admit that entailment is expressed in natural languages with a kind of conditional or implication which cannot be symbolized without having inaccurate theses about it arise from the symbolization.

Consider now the second Lewis derivation from p.251 of [1932]. Again we modify the derivation. Again we use $\rightarrow$ instead of $-\!\!\exists$. Lewis would use $-\!\!\exists$ where we use $\rightarrow$. But because Lewis intended $-\!\!\exists$ to symbolize the best formal implication we are not distorting his intentions by our use of $\rightarrow$. We also modify this derivation to focus attention upon its crucial step. The crucial step is use of a principle of Suppression of necessary truths. We can here regard this suppression principle as: From $A \wedge C \rightarrow B$ infer $A \rightarrow B$ if C is asserted in some way to be a necessary truth or C is asserted in such a way that it shows itself to be a necessary truth. Examples of asserting C to be a necessary truth are asserting $\vdash$ C or $\Box$C. An example of C's being asserted in such a way to show that it is a necessary truth is C's being asserted and C's being a tautology with D and $\sim$D as disjuncts of C. We are justified in focusing attention on Suppression of necessary truths in Lewis' second derivation. If we look at his p. 251 derivation, we find it begins with his theorem 18.9: $p -\!\!\exists (p \wedge q \vee p \wedge \sim q)$. We find that the proof of 18.9 uses his theorem 18.61: $\Box p \wedge (p \wedge q -\!\!\exists r) -\!\!\exists . q -\!\!\exists r$. So, if we take the $-\!\!\exists$ as representing the best possible formal connection, as does Lewis, 18.61 is a thesis which permits Suppression of necessary truths. In our presentation of the second Lewis derivation we need, however, use Suppression only in the rule form: From $A \wedge (D \vee \sim D) \rightarrow B$ infer $A \rightarrow B$. We give two formulations of the second Lewis derivation which we call Lewis Derivation V and Lewis Derivation VI.

Lewis Derivation V

i)	$A \wedge (B \vee \sim B) \rightarrow . B \vee \sim B$	Simp.
ii)	$A \rightarrow . B \vee \sim B$	Suppression on (i).

Derivation V is ridiculously simple. Still, Derivation V suffices to bring out the crucial step in an argument designed to show that a necessary truth, at least an explicit tautology, follows in the best possible formal way from any claim whatsoever.

Of course, Suppression of necessary truths from the premisses of a valid argument leaves a valid argument. Thus, if the $\rightarrow$ of Derivation V were only $-\!\!\exists$, as it is for Lewis, line (ii) would be perfectly acceptable. Lewis did not make any mistake about what was in his system.

In light of our revisions of the first Lewis derivation so that we make what we reject as leading to an undesirable entailment claim be itself an entailment claim, it seems that we should revise V so the the Suppression rule occurs as an entailment claim. (Recall that, in light of Derivations II and III, we are considering rejecting MD and DS only in the strong form of entailment claims;not necessarily as rules.) But the acceptability of Simp. and Derivation V make it clear that Suppression has to be rejected even in rule form if there is something unacceptable about line (ii) of V. However, we still have to be careful not to say that the rule of Suppression is incorrect simply because it allows Derivation V. Our efforts to show why Suppression is a defective rule may well lead to a consideration of why it is unacceptable as an entailment claim.

A second way of presenting the second Lewis derivation calls attention to how Suppression may be used to suppress the premiss which is used to get the conclusion. So, with Suppression we may end up with an $A \longrightarrow B$ which says that we get B from A in the best possible formal way and yet A has not been used to get B. The notion of 'getting from' is not yet clear. A requirement that the antecedent be used to get the consequent will be explicated by the restricted derivations of Part IV, Sections 3,4, and 5. Here we want only to hint that Suppression is going to lead to a search for a connection which holds between an antecedent and consequent which are not only relevant to one another but are such that the consequent is gotten from the antecedent.

Lewis Derivation VI

i)	$B \vee \sim B \longrightarrow .B \vee \sim B$	Identity
ii)	$A \wedge (B \vee \sim B) \longrightarrow .B \vee \sim B$	Premiss addition on (i).
iii)	$A \longrightarrow .B \vee \sim B$	Suppression on (ii).

Derivation VI makes it clear that A was not used to get $B \vee \sim B$.

Before moving to the next Section in which we consider why we should reject $A \wedge \sim A \longrightarrow B$ and $A \longrightarrow .B \vee \sim B$ as theses about entailment, let us briefly compare $A \longrightarrow .B \vee \sim B$ with a so-called paradox of strict implication: □A ⥽ .B ⥽ A, and a so-called paradox of material implication: $A \supset .B \supset A$. We could call □A ⥽ .B ⥽ A the paradox of necessity although it is not a genuine paradox because it is a truth about validity. Similarly, there is nothing paradoxical about having $A \supset .B \supset A$, i.e., the tautology $\sim A \vee .\sim B \vee A$, as a thesis. These schemas would be paradoxical in a system which offered no device besides ⥽ and $\supset$ for symbolizing implications. But even in this case, the schemas are not at fault; it is the system as a whole which is at fault by failing to provide an adequate way to symbolize the best possible formal implication. However, there is a genuine paradox of necessity, viz., having $\Box A \rightarrow . B \rightarrow A$ as a thesis. Anderson's and Belnap's mathematician, presumably on philosophical grounds, moves to $\Box$(The first order functional calculus is complete) from the fact that it is complete. Then by use of MP with the following instance of the genuine paradox of necessity: $\Box$(The first order functional calculus is complete) $\rightarrow$.C$\rightarrow$The first order functional calculus is complete, he concludes the counter-intuitive: C$\rightarrow$The first order functional calculus is complete. In addition note that any system with $\Box$ would likely have $\vdash \Box(B \vee \sim B)$. So in almost any system with $\rightarrow$ and $\Box$, the genuine paradox of necessity is going to yield $\vdash A \rightarrow . B \vee \sim B$.

But why do we object to $A \wedge \sim A \rightarrow B$ and $A \rightarrow . B \vee \sim B$?

I.2 Rejection of $A \wedge \sim A \rightarrow B$ and $A \rightarrow . B \vee \sim B$ as theses about entailment and rejection of: $A \wedge \sim A$ so B, and: A so $B \vee \sim B$ as being the best possible formal inferences.

The arrow: $\rightarrow$, is to represent the best possible formal logical implication, viz., formal entailment. An $A \rightarrow B$ is to be asserted only if the inference from A to B is the best possible formal kind of argument. Hence, we focus our attention on rejecting the rules $A \wedge \sim A$ so B and A so $B \vee \sim B$. Fallacies of formal relevance occur in these two inferences. We detect two types of formal fallacy of relevance. First, these forms allow inference from premisses to conclusions which are totally irrelevant to what the premisses are about. There is a formal fallacy of content irrelevance. Second, the conclusions of these inferences do not seem to have been obtained by means of some special formal link with the premisses. There is a formal fallacy of derivational irrelevance.

If we accept these two inferences as formally correct, we have to accept the following two natural language arguments, in which the premisses and conclusion are totally irrelevant to one another, as being as good as arguments can be on formal grounds.

A) Philadelphia is in Pennsylvania and Philadelphia is not in Pennsylvania, so 2+2=4.

B) 2+2=4, so Philadelphia is in Pennsylvania or Philadelphia is not in Pennsylvania.

Undoubtedly, (A) and (B) are formally valid. Yet our knowledge of English tells us that the premisses and conclusions are totally irrelevant to one another. This recognition of irrelevance based on our knowledge of a natural language is material knowledge; not knowledge of formal matters. Thus, it may be suggested that it is a material consideration, rather than a formal consideration, which marks the above two arguments as defective despite their formal validity. However, we do not need to rely on material considerations to object to arguments (A) and (B). We can object to the forms on the basis of which (A) and (B) are certified as formally valid. They are instances of the forms: $p \wedge \sim p$ so q, and: q so $p \vee \sim p$, and (A) and (B) are certified as formally valid by virtue of possessing such forms. We can say of these forms that they can be instantiated to natural language sentences which are totally irrelevant to one another, if any sentences are totally irrelevant to one another. Possibly in a formal language, such as that of set-theory where every sentence contains the ϵ membership predicate, no two sentences are totally irrelevant to one another. But in natural languages there certainly are sentences totally irrelevant to one another such as the claims about the location of Philadelphia and 2+2=4. It is the formal feature of lack of a common variable in both premiss and conclusion forms which enables us to determine that both: $p\wedge\sim p$ so q, and q so $p \vee \sim p$ have materially defective instances such as (A) and (B). So we can and should reject the formally valid $p\wedge\sim p$ so q, and q so $p \vee \sim p$ as formally correct because we can determine on formal grounds, given the material truth that some sentences are totally irrelevant to one another, that these forms admit what can be called oddities of relevance if not fallacies of irrelevance. To a large extent, the present study is an investigation of the consequences of making, where possible, evaluation of an argument on the basis of relevance between premisses and conclusion a formal matter rather than a mere material consideration. For the sake of greater objectivity in argument assessment it is desirable that tests for relevance be formal tests.

Since it is object language formulas such as $p\wedge\sim p$ and q which have natural language sentences as their interpretation, it was proper that we talked of $p\wedge\sim p$ so q and q so $p \vee \sim p$ in the preceding paragraph rather than of schemas. However, we may talk of schemas when we properly should be talking of formulas; we simply regard each schema letter as a sentential variable. Thus we charge $A\wedge\sim A$ so B, and $A \longrightarrow A \longrightarrow . B \longrightarrow B$ with a failure to have a common variable in premisses and conclusion or in antecedent and consequent. We make such charges despite the fact that, strictly speaking, the schemas do not contain sentential variables.

A second reason for rejecting these two formally valid arguments as formally correct arguments is that their formal validity is not due to any formal connection between the premiss and conclusion. The inference form: $A\wedge\sim A$ so B, is valid solely because of the form of the premiss; the conclusion could be of any form. The fact thatB can be of any form and the way B is obtained from $A\wedge\sim A$ in the first Lewis derivation, viz., disjoined onto $\sim A$ and then detached by MD, suggest strongly that B is not obtained from $A\wedge\sim A$. Indeed $C\wedge\sim C$ would do as well as $A\wedge\sim A$. Similarly, A so $B \vee \sim B$ is formally valid solely because of the form of the conclusion; the premiss may be of any form. It seems inaccurate to say that $B \vee \sim B$ is obtained by formal manipulation of A. In the second Lewis derivation $B \vee \sim B$ is obtained from an aribtrarily selected A by exploiting only formal features of only $B \vee \sim B$. So, if formal validity were our highest mark for formal correctness, we would have to give the highest marks for formal correctness to arguments in which the particular premisses given were not used, let alone needed, to derive the conclusion. We do not consider in any detail this second reason for rejecting these two formally valid argument forms until we have developed systems in which we can talk about derivations in which the premisses have been genuinely used used to get the conclusion. Without having such restricted derivations, talk of having derivations in which we genuinely use the premisses is obscure due to lack of illustrations of what is being talked of.

Let us say of formulas and inferences, and derivatively of schemas and inferernce schemas, that they suffer from formal content irrelevance if the have natural language instances in which the premisses or antededent is totally irrelevant to the conclusion or consequent. We also call formal content irrelevance variable sharing irrelevance because lack of a variable common to premisses (antedent) and conclusion (consequent) is what allows instances in which there is total content irrelevance. Let us say that rules and entailment claims, and derivatively schemas and inference schemas, in which the consequent (conclusion) is not genuinely derived from the antecedent (premisses) involve derivational fallacies of relevance. In Part IV, where we present prefixing devices for keeping track of what is used to get what in a derivation, we also call some derivational fallacies of relevance prefixing fallacies.

Formal content irrelevance is a glaring formal defect. Nevertheless to those who reject the instances where premisses have total content irrelevance to the conclusion as formally correct arguments, content irrelevance is regarded only as a symptom of deeper mistakes about entailment. To be sure, we will not accept any rule or schema which has variable sharing irrelevance. However, when we seem to be committed to variable sharing irrelevance, as in the case of the Lewis derivations, we go back to reject a claim or rule which has led to this irrelevance but which does not itself suffer from this irrelevance. We have to give a reason for rejecting this claim or rule which has led to the fallacy of irrelevance. The reason should not be merely that the rejected claim suffers from content irrelevance itself because it can be used to derive a claim or rule explicitly containing variable sharing irrelevance. We need to diagnose some deeper formal logic defect embodied in the claims or rules which we reject such as MD or Suppression. A major problem of defending an entailment system is to state clearly what these other formal defects are and then to show that they are really defects and really formal defects.

Let us now consider and reject a suggestion that we do not bother to search for a logical implication more restricted than strict implication but that we simply use variable sharing as a criterion for selecting correct formal implications from the merely valid ones.

I.3 Our demand for a transitive $\rightarrow$.

In this Section, we consider and dismiss a suggestion that we do not look for a formal implication relation between A and B which is more strict than that relation between A and B in which the inference from A to B is formally valid. The suggestion is that we simply develop a criterion for selecting that proper subset of the logical implications which are the best possible formally valid implications.

Let us develop the suggestion in more detail. Without digressing into an investigation of what makes a connection an implication, we say that an implication is a <u>discursive implication</u> if it is transitive. A logically implies B, where this means that the inference form A to B is formally valid, viz., strict implication, is a discursive implication. There are non-discursive implications. For instance, A obviously implies B is not transitive. We choose the name 'discursive implication' to indicate that discursive implications meet a necessary condition for being that connection, that implication, which holds between the premisses and the last conclusion of a derivation as well as between the premisses and the intermediate conclusions.

The suggestion is that we accept logical implication as our discursive implication but that we discriminate amongst the logical implications. We are advised to develop a criterion for selecting a proper subset of the logical implications. Members of this subset will not admit of instances where the antecedent is totally irrelevant to the conclusion and the logical implication involves some formal connection between the antecedent and the consequent. This proper subset of the logical implications may be called the set of formally correct implications or the entailments. If it turns out that logical implication restricted to just the implications in the subset is transitive, that is fine; but there is no demand that there be such transitivity. In Part II we will find this suggestion made in many forms because we regard any specification of entailment which leaves it as non-transitive as embodying this suggestion. In this Section, we consider and dismiss some general considerations in favor of this suggestion. We touch on the issue again when we consider specific criteria for making the discrimination amongst the logical implications. Indeed it is a suggestion that we can never completely dismiss. If our attempt to find a proper subset of the logical implications which is also a set of discursive implications leads to too many oddities, we must be prepared to accept some form of the suggestion now under consideration.

We consider two reasons in favor of the suggestion. The

first is a simplicity consideration. It goes as follows. Two problems were cited as being presented by the alleged thesishood of $A \wedge \sim A \longrightarrow B$ and $B \longrightarrow . A \vee \sim A$ and with the corresponding inference rules. First they allowed us to certify as formally correct arguments in which the premisses were totally irrelevant to the conclusion. Second, they allow us to certify as formally correct inferences in which the conclusion was not genuinely obtained from the premisses. We complained that there should be a formal way to detect these defective argumentforms and schemas. So, the response to the complaint is: Concern yourself with only solving the problem at hand, viz., finding a formal way of detecting forms and schemas which also have the features lamented in $A \wedge \sim A \longrightarrow B$ and $B \longrightarrow . A \vee \sim A$. The suggestion solution goes on that it may not be difficult to develop such a criterion. For clearly a necessary condition for avoiding the first defect is that premisses (antencedent) and conclusion (consequent) share a variable. Indeed variable sharing suffices to avoid the defect of having instances in which the premisses are totally irrelevant to the conclusion. And certainly checking an argument form for variable sharing is about the simplest formal relevance test imaginable. So, if we had worried only about the first kind of defect we trivially have a criterion for selecting what could be called the formally correct formally valid implications from the merely formally valid ones.

When confronted with the suggestion under consideration, it is tempting to take correction of content irrelevance as the only kind of correction with which we need to be concerned It is easy to assume that if antecedent and consequent share a variable, the antecedent must have been used in some way to bring the variable into the consequent.. However, consideration of the fact that only a minor change in Derivations II and III of Section I.1 are needed to obtain $A \wedge \sim A \longrightarrow . A \wedge B$ suffice to destroy that assumption. We do not need the A from $A \wedge \sim A$ to get the A occurring in $A \wedge B$; the whole conjunction $A \wedge B$ can be used as plain B in these derivations. So our hypothetical suggestors do have to suggest that we concern ourselves with the more complicated task of detecting a formal feature of those formally valid inferences in which the premisses are not genuinely used to get the conclusion. Of course, part of the difficulty in such a task lies in the imprecision of 'genuinely get.' Hence, those who try to develop such a criterion for 'genuinely get' have to make a case that they have a significant sense of 'genuinely get,' and this may be as difficult as developing a system for a transitive $\longrightarrow$. Still, even though we can dismiss the secondary suggestion that it is easy to find such a criterion, we must concede that search for such a criterion is relevant to the problems raised in Sections I.1 and I.2. We need to show that we should not content ourselves with such a criterion even if one could be found.

Derivation III of I.1 provides the basis for the second argument that we should content ourselves with merely finding a criterion for those formally valid argument forms which do not allow instances in which the premisses are totally irrelevant to the conclusion and in which the premiss is relevant to getting the conclusion and that we should not seek for a new discursive implication. The argument amounts to the observation that no line of Derivation III corresponds to an inference which allows total irrelevance and instead each line corresponds to an inference in which the premisses are actually used to get the conclusion. So it seems that Transitivity is the only candidate for rejection. Here it may be noted that we do have non-transitive implications such as obviously implies. (Obvious implications are selected from the logical implications by means of some psychological criterion which does not guarantee transitivity.) Why shouldn't an implication which we may wish to label 'relevantly implies' also be non-transitive? Why should relevance transfer from implication to implication if obviousness does not so transfer?

We dismiss the suggestion that we ignore Transitivity for the following reasons. First, it has not been shown that there cannot be a discursive implication stricter than logical implication. Admittedly the second argument for the suggestion reveals that we will have to find fault with some logical implications which seem as good as formal inferences can be, viz., some lines of Derivation III of I.1. Still it has not yet been shown that we cannot make a good case for rejecting some line of Derivation III. In Section III.5 we make a case that MD or DS can be rejected. Secondly, the suggestion violates what we call in Section I.5 a <u>normative intuition</u>. If a criterion is found, then we segregate logical implications into two groups: the good and the not-so-good. It seems that we <u>ought</u> to be able to restrict ourselves to using only the good logical inferences in our discursive reasoning. If there is a proper subset of the logical implications which are better than the rest of the logical implications, why shouldn't we restrict ourselves to using only these best ones when we want our formal reasoning to be at its best? Note also that the kind of criterion suggested will not discriminate amongst the logical implications on the basis of some external feature such as being obvious to some people or even obvious to all people. The criterion will discriminate amongst logical implications on the basis of some formal feature which they have independently of anything outside the formulas.

Examples of internal or instrinsic features of formulas are variable sharing between antecedent and consequent and haviing a formally consistent antecedent. It seems that such internal features which mark the best possible formal implications ought to be carried along in the best possible formal reasoning since what happens outside the formulas does not affect these good features. (As we will see the formal features cited as examples of internal features do not mark off a transitive implication.) We admit, though, that our search for entailment is primarily in pursuit of fulfilling this norm. We will discuss the role of norms in logic in I.5. But next let us discuss a bit the use of the word 'entails.'

I.4 The term 'entailment,' formal vs. material entailment.

Our goal in this Section is to baptize the implication for which we are seeking as what has been called in recent history entailment. We also emphasize that we are searching for a formal entailment as opposed to what can be called material entailment. In passing we distinguish between an entailment and what can be called a relevant implication.

As we resolved in the previous Section, we shall look for a formal discursive (transitive) implication which is stricter than formal logical implication and which is based on some formal connection between antecedent and consequent which is different from that formal connection which gives formal validity. A formal inference is an entailment when it is formally valid and suffers none of the defects alluded to in I.2, or as we say: is as good as it can be on formal grounds, i.e., formally correct. An implication is put forth as an entailment claim when it is claimed that the inference from the antecedent to the consequent is formally correct.

An entailment claim is a claim that there is a logical connection between the antecedent and the consequent; indeed the best kind of logical connection. Thus, the $\rightarrow$ which we introduce may not adequately serve for symbolizing non-logical implications even if we want those non-logical connections to hold necessarily in some non-logical sense on 'necessary.' For instance, if we are dissatisfied with $\supset$ or any $-\!3$ for symbolizing non-logical implications because they require us to accept odd claims of the form $A \wedge {\sim}A \supset B$ and $A \wedge {\sim}A -\!3\, B$ as implications of this kind, we still cannot use the $\rightarrow$ of entailment for symoblizing non-logical implication. One may object to the thesishood of $A \wedge {\sim}A \supset B$ and $A \wedge {\sim}A -\!3\, B$ because such thesishood says that the kind of implication being symbolized holds even if the content of the antecedent is totally irrelevant to the content of the consequent. So, our search for an entailment sign $\rightarrow$. will not provide a symbol for what we can call relevant implication. A minimal condition for a relevant implication is that any thesis of the form $A \rightarrow_r B$, where $\rightarrow_r$ symbolizes relevant implication, has a variable common to A and B.

G.E. Moore introduced 'entailment' into current logical discussions when he wrote the following on p.291 of [1920].

> We require, first of all, some term to express the <u>converse</u> of that relation which we assert to hold between a particular proposition q and a particular

proposition p, when we assert that q follows from or is deducible from p. Let us use the term "entails" to express the converse of this relation. We shall then be able to say truly that "p entails q" when and only when we are able to say truly that "q follows from p" or " is deducible from p," in the sense in which the conclusion of a syllogism in Barbara follows from the two premisses taken as one conjunctive proposition; or in which the proposition "This is colored" follows from "This is red." "p entails q" will be related to "q follows from p" in the same way in which "A is greater than B" is related to "B is less than A."

In the essay from which the preceding quotation is taken, Moore seemed to identify 'entails' with what we have been calling 'logically implies.' But in [1944] he distinguished logical implication from entailment on p. 153 of a reprinted version of the 1944 essay.

I feel no doubt that Russell was here using "implies" not in this "special" sense, but in one of the senses which the word can properly bear in English; nor yet that he was using it in that one among its common senses, in which p cannot be truly said to imply q, unless the proposition that q is false is inconsistent or incompatible with the proposition that p is true; unless it is impossible that p should be true and q false; unless if p is true q must be true too—is necessarily true too. In other words, "implies" is being used in such a sense that a necessary condition for its being true that p implies q is that it shall be self-contradictory to assert that p is true but q is false. But I do not think that it is being used in such a sense that the fact that it would be self-contradictory to assert that p is true but q is false is a sufficient condition for its being true that p implies q. I doubt if there is any common sense of "implies" such that this is a sufficient condition. For, of course, the assertion that p is true but q false will necessarily be self-contradictory, if the assertion that p is true is by itself self-contradictory, or the assertion that q is false is by itself self-contradictory. But I do not think that in ordinary language "implies" is ever so used that in all cases where this is so, it would be true to say that p implies q.

Owing to the ambiguity of the word "implies," I think it is often desirable where, as here, we are concerned with what it expresses when used with that particular one among its common meanings which I have tried to describe (though,of course, I have not attempted to define it), to use another word instead, as a synonym for "implies" when used in this particular way. And I shall do that now. I shall use the word "entails."

Moore has made well our point that there is a type of implication stricter than logical implication; and we follow him by using 'entails.' However, we do not follow him in doubting whether there is an implication of the kind which we have called logical implication or strict implication. Possibly, non-technical use finds no place for logical implication. But logicians use the notion of logical implication and we are concerned with whether or not this technical sense is the best possible technical sense for a formal implication. Also of interest is Moore's example of 'This is red' entailing 'This is colored.' This example leads us to distinguish between formal and material entailment.

Let us say that an implication in a natural language is a formal entailment if replacement of its simplest sentences with sentential variables and replacement of its 'if_then_' with a $\longrightarrow$ gives an entailment thesis. We also call theses and thesis schemas formal entailments. Thus, 'If John loves Mary and Mary loves John, then John loves Mary' is a formal entailment because $p \wedge q \longrightarrow p$ is a thesis. And we also call $p \wedge q \longrightarrow p$ and $A \wedge B \longrightarrow A$ formal entailments. In brief, since we are concerned only with sentential logic, we say that a natural language implication is a formal entailment if its truth can be based solely on the meaning of the terms which are the intended readings of the logical signs listed in our Notational Preface, i.e., the so-called logical signs. We also say that inferences whose corresponding implications are formal entailments are themselves formal entailments. What we call formal entailments, Parry in [1968] called structural entailments.

If the truth of a natural language implication can be based solely upon the meaning of non-logical terms, we call it an <u>intensional</u> or <u>material entailment.</u> For example, 'If John is a boy, then John is a male' is true by virtue of the meaning of 'boy' and 'male.' If a natural language implication is true because it is self-evident or in some way recognized as necessarily true but not because of formal considerations or meaning of non-logical terms, we also grant that it is a material entailment. In other words we concede that there may be synthetic apriori entailment truths. Perhaps, 'If it is red, then it is not green' is such a synthetic apriori entailment truth. Recognition of material entailments depends upon material knowledge of the meaning of non-logical terms or upon some insight into the subject matter of what the alleged synthetic apriori truth is about; thus the name material entailment. MATERIAL ENTAILMENT HAS NO SIGNIFICANT RELATION TO SO-CALLED MATERIAL IMPLICATION.

In this work, by 'entailment' we mean 'formal entailment.' We are looking for a transitive implication which can be called 'formal entailment' and we will claim only to have discovered theses about formal entailment. Thus if $A \twoheadrightarrow B$ symbolizes a material entailment we will not claim that $A \wedge C \twoheadrightarrow B$ is also a material entailment even if we accept $A \twoheadrightarrow B \twoheadrightarrow . A \wedge C \twoheadrightarrow B$ as a thesis when $\twoheadrightarrow$ symbolizes formal entailment. In short, we are not looking for a logic for material entailment.

It is plausible to hold that formal and material entailments form exclusive clases, If the truth of a natural language implication can be shown by solely formal considerations, it isn't clear that we should say that its truth depends upon the meaning of the non-logical terms or the nature or essence of the things talked about even if the meanings of the non-logical terms or the natures of the things talked about suffice to make the implication true. For instance, we should not say that the meaning of 'boy' and 'male' make 'If he is a boy and he is a male, then he is a male' true. The implication is true by virtue of having the Simplification form. Similarly, we should not, or at least it is not clear that we should, say 'If it is red and it is not green, then it is not green' is a synthetic apriori truth. Also some formal entailments such as $A \twoheadrightarrow A$ and Simplification do not seem to be material entailments. So, we can make the two classes exclusive by stipulating that if an entailment is formal, it is not material.

Our non-eccentric stipulation that being a formal entailment prevents an implication from also being a material entailment will help us appreciate views of people such as Blanshard in [1939] and Strawson in [1948] who reject $A \twoheadrightarrow A$ as well as the views of people such as E.J. Nelson who in [1930] rejected Simplification. These people can be regarded as making correct claims about material entailment. Any implication of the form $A \twoheadrightarrow A$ is not a material entailment because it is first a formal entailment and its being a formal entailment precludes it from being a material entailment. Also our rigid separation of the two classes enables us to dismiss their claims as relevant to our concerns about formal entailment. In addition we can dismiss some early attempts to get a logic for entailment such as Baylis' [1931] because they are explicitly concerned with entailments based on the meaning of non-logical terms. There may be a need for a logic of non-formal entailments as well as a need for a logical interconnecting material and formal entailments. If we here let $\twoheadrightarrow\!\!\!\!\!\rightarrow$ symblize material entailment, we can say that we have just been arguing that $A \twoheadrightarrow B \twoheadrightarrow\!\!\!\!\!\rightarrow . A \twoheadrightarrow\!\!\!\!\!\rightarrow B$ should be a thesis of such an interconnecting logic. We have also suggested that neither $A \twoheadrightarrow\!\!\!\!\!\rightarrow A$ nor $A \wedge B \twoheadrightarrow\!\!\!\!\!\rightarrow A$ should be theses of such an interconnecting logic. However, we are not concerned here with developing any kind of logic for such a material $\twoheadrightarrow\!\!\!\!\!\rightarrow$.

Let us close with a few remarks about the word 'material' and about intuition. It is misleading to call non-formal entailments 'material entailments' because this terminology may suggest that they can be adequately symbolized with the so-called material implication sign $\supset$. We are not making any such suggestion; we want only to suggest that the truth of non-formal entailments is determined by consideration of some non-formal material, eg., meaning connections. It may be better to call material entailments 'intensional entailments.' However, formal logics of formal entailment are also called intensional because the truth of an entailment formula is not determined solely by assignment of values: True and False, to the simplest formulas, viz., the variables, in it. Also the truth of a formal entailment does depend upon the meanings of the logical terms in it. So, we do not want to say that formal entailments are non-intensional. So, we are not going to use 'intensional' to label any kind of implication. It may seem that a distinguishing mark of what we have here been calling material entailments is that we need intuition to determine their truth. The intuition would be of meaning connections or into the essence or nature of the things talked about. It may seem that only consideration of syntax is required to determine the truth of formal entailment claims; this seems especially true when we are talking of determining which formulas express theses. However, we see in the next section that intuitions play a crucial role in determining what are the true formal entailment claims.

I.5 The role of intuition in our investigations, informative and normative intuitions.

In this Section we clarify how we will be using 'intuition.' This clarification will give the epistemological perspective underlying this work although there is no justification of this epistemology. There are two kinds of inuitions: informative intuitions and normative intuitions. Almost always when we talk of intuition, we will be talking about what below are called normative intuitions. For instance, a remark beginning 'It is counterintuitive that. . .' will be about normative intuitions.

First consider informative intuitions. An informative intuition is the recognition that what a sentence says is what must be true, i.e., cannot be otherwise. For instance, one may have informative intuitions about claims of Elementary Arithmetic and basic Euclidena Geometry. Some may have an informative intuition that no homogenously red surface can be simultaneously a homogenously green surface. It is an informative intuition which leads us to say that B has to be a theorem of a system if the system has $A \rightarrow B$ and A as theorems in addition to Modus Ponens as a rule of proof. There is no claim that everyone has the same informative intuitions. It may take much preparation before we get an informative intuition; some may never get certain intuitions despite considerable effort. For instance, it may take quite a bit of reflection before we see that the end formula of a sequence of formulas has to be a theorem of the system under consideration. In the preceding sentence 'see' means 'have an informative intuition.' Needless to say, in proofs of metatheorems it may take even more time and effort to see that the theorem holds. Fortunately, there is not much disagreement on informative intuitions. Consider the vast areas of agreement in arithemetic and geometry. Even where people disagree about which systems are correct, they agree on what must hold in the different systems.

An informative intuition is indispensable for accepting a proof. People are dishonest if they claim to accept a proof or to follow a proof when they do not have, as a result of the proof, a recognition that what is said to be proved cannot be otherwise. Some of us can recall politely but dishonestly nodding assent at mathematical or logical lectures when asked whether or not we accept a proof which is being given as a proof. You are dishonest or a plagarist if you present a proof when the considerations which you are calling a proof did not lead you to recognize that the conclusion could not be otherwise. Many of us, in an effort to be honest, can recall how when re-presenting a proof which we worked out earlier we had to struggle to regain that recognition of necessity which we had when we first worked out the proof.

Nevertheless, as indispensable as these psychological states are for proof receiving and proof giving, any reference to them is entirely unnecessary and highly undesirable in any proof receiving or giving. If you want to get yourself to see that a claim must be true, it is, of course, irrelevant to tell yourself that you see it. Certainly, it does not help others to recognize that such and such must hold by telling them that you see it or that they see it. In a proof it is important to lay out considerations such as verbal arguments, sequences of formulas, and diagrams which bring ourselves and others to see what is supposed to be seen. The informative intuition is only the inner state of accepting the proof. Saying that such a state is present by locutions such as 'we see,' 'it is self-evident that,' or 'it is obvious that' are neither necessary nor sufficient for the occurrence of such a state. It is highly undesirable to refer to an intuition in the course of giving a proof because such a reference is likely to suggest that informative intuitions are a special nonsensuous vision into a realm where what holds holds of necessity. In the final epistemology of formal sciences we may have to admit that there is such a special faculty and such a special realm. In this work there is no consideration of the epistemological issues. Here we accept the phenomenological fact that an indispensable factor in successful and honest proof giving is that the givers and receivers attain certain psychological states despite the fact that the occurrence of these psychological states provides no evidence for what is proved. But since reference to these psychological states is unnecessary and misleading we rarely talk of informative intuitions. Occasionally we slip into skipping parts of proofs by use of remarks such as 'it is obvious that,' and ' it is easily seen that.' Sometimes such remarks are made solely for stylistic reasons. For instance, there is less likelihood of confusing schema letter A with a capitalized indefinite article if we begin a sentence with ' It is obvious that A follows from. . ,' instead of " A follows from . . .' Again, though, it must be emphasized that not talking of informative intuitions is not to deny that in all proofs and proof sketches we need an informative intuition of what we prove and with our proof we are trying to cause such an intuition in the reader who does not already have such a psychological state. The preceding view of informative intuition is developed more fully in the author's [197_d] and in sections 32-46 of his Wittgenstein book [1970].

We will, though, talk a great deal of what we call

normative intuitions. For instance, on intuitive grounds we already rejected any non-discursive implication as being the best possible formal implication. In our survey of systems, other failures to satisfy our intuitions will be cited. Here our interest is to discuss what it is like not to satisfy our intuitions when we are talking of normative intuitions. When we reject a relation as not being entailment, we do not do so because we have had some insight into what entailment really is. Indeed when we reject a non-discursive implication as entailment we do not do so with that psychological conviction, viz., on the basis of an informative intuition, with which we know that a certain implication is not transitive. We have instead the ideal that there ought to be a connection between an antecedent and a consequent which is suitable for discursive reasoning reasoning but which does not hold between $A \wedge \sim A$ and an arbitrarily selected B nor between an arbitrarily selected B and $A \vee \sim A$. We do not know that there is any such connection which satisfies all that we think that it ought to satisfy. We acknowledge that we are trying to discover a system which satisfies some clear, some vague, and even some, as yet, unrecognized ideals. Possibly 'invent' would be a more suitable word than 'discover' in the preceding sentence. We are not reporting some discovery by means of a special insight nor what we have been convinced of by a proof when we claim that such and such is or is not intuitive. With such claims we are telling about what we want and do not want in a system of logic. Of course, saying what we want and do not want is of little or no interest. Just as in the case of informative intuition, biographical remarks are unnnecessary and misleading. What we shall do when talking about the acceptability or unacceptability of systems is to lay out considerations which will make what what we want desirable to the reader and what we do not want undesirable to the reader, i.e., intuitively acceptable or intuitively unacceptable to the reader. Indeed this is the way we argued in I.2. Our remarks on getting a discursive implication more restricted than logical implication have been directed towards causing a desire for such an implication.

We hasten to add, though, that we do not mean desirable for some practical purpose. For instance, we do not consider whether a different logic would be more useful for engineering or more easily taught. We are not saying that practical concerns are irrelevant for accepting a system. We simply will not be offering any practical considerations. Considerations that such and such is desirable are addressed to whether or not it corresponds with some ideal, which may be quite vague, and some ideals, which may even be incompatible. We argue as we do in daily life when we argue that abortion is wrong because it is a desecration of what it is to be a human female regardless of the utility of abortion or that slavery is an assault on human dignity regardless of how efficient and useful a system of slavery may be. Hence, we talk here of normative intuitions because the ultimate test for an entailment system is how well it corresponds with such ideals.

It is the case with these logical ideals as it is with aspects of our moral and aesthetic ideals; they may develop and later be lost, be vague, inarticulate, and incompatible. You may lack certain logical intuitions,viz., ideals, but attention to considerations advanced to show that a system meets an ideal can develop in you the ideal. For instance, attention to systems designed to show that the Lewis derivations are not the best formal inferences may develop in you the ideal that there ought to be developed a system for a better logic than that used in the Lewis derivations. Such attention can develop in someone associated ideals such as the ideal that Suppression of necessarily true premisses is highly undesirable. Similarly, attention to aesthetic controversy can develop taste in someone. Admittedly, normative intuitions are vague. They are vague in the sense of being partial. We have, let us say, an intuition that some formally valid inferences simply are not as good as formal inferences can be. We also,let us say, have an intuition that there is a discursive implication more restricted than logical implication. Still we may not have any clear idea of what else has to be left out or put into a system to attain these two basic ideals. Indeed there may be no system that satisfies all of our basic ideals and the additional ideals we develop in pursuit of the basic ideals. It may be that even if we can satisfy our basic ideals with a system, we have to accept so much which violates recently acquired ideals that we lose some of our basic ideals. But before these features of systems, which are now ideals over and above the basic one, were accepted we may not even have had any thought of them. We really should not be too surprised that normative ideals may be incapable of realization due to mutual incompatibility; they are like wishes and we can wish for the impossible. (What would be terrible is incompatible informative intutuitions. And we admit that we cannot say that it is impossible that there be incompatible informative intuitions.) Also the degree or ranking of normative intuitions is vague. We may hold that some features of standard logical implication are undesirable. Still if we move to consideration of two other systems one of which has three mildly disagreeable features while the other has only one very disagreeable feature we may be unable to choose between the three systems now under consideration. In general, the intuitions which guide us in the selection of logical theses have the importance for logic which moral intuitions have for daily life and the logical intuitions suffer from pretty much the same defects as the moral ones.

The preceding paragraph suggests that we are adopting a relativistic or, indeed, a radically subjectivist view of logic. Nonetheless we are not subjectivists about what is in a particular system; nor are we subjectivists about what is the right system to select. What is true of a system, viz., metatheorems about it, is true independently of our ideals or practical concerns. The way to discover and to show what is true of a system is to develop proofs. We admit that metatheorems about a system depend upon the logic used in the metalanguage and that the logic used is a matter of choice. Still, we have the following objective matter: Given logic L for metalanguage M of system S such and such is true of S. We do not want to argue that formal systems are in some platonic heaven waiting to be discovered and investigated by users of various logics. Our doctrine of informative intuition may provide a basis for avoiding platonism. However, we are not worried in this investigation about speaking in a way which suggests platonism. If platonism is true, such talk is certainly harmless. If platonism is false, this talk can be phased out in whatever way it will be phased out of other talk of formal sciences. Except for the suggestion that practical considerations guide our choice of a system, the following quotations from Lewis' and Langford's [1932] express our position on the objectivity of formal systems. On p. 259 we read the following.

> The number of relations which can validly give rise to inference is indefinitely large. At least their number is so great that it is practically impossible for our human minds to be observant of them all, or even aware of them. Thus, practically, it is necessary that we make our inferences upon observation of some chosen one— or at least some chosen few— of these relations. This choice will, of course, be determined, in part at least, by conformity to our capacities, our bent of mind, and our characteristic intellectual purposes. Thus logic as the canon of deductive inference must necessarily be something which, in addition to being absolutely determined, is pragmatically determined.

To say that they are "absolutely determined" is to say that what is in them is necessarily in them. On the next page

Lewis and Langford write the following.

> Thus there are an indefinitely large number of 'logics,' or possible canons of inference, everyone of which is true throughout and states true laws of inference. If our intellectual habits and interests were slightly different, we might choose some other than the logic of tradtitional deduction to be our guide.

We are in the process of changing our intellectual habits. At least we have been trying to provoke ourselves to change them. But we are going to let our, hopefully modified, intellectual habits be the sole guide in selecting a new canon of deductive inference.

We can say that informative intuitions bring recognition of what the systems are and that normative intuitions tell us which system to select. However, simply because the choice of a system depends upon our preferences does not make the choice subjective in the sense that each person will make a different choice and that each person is justified in making the choice which he makes. Just because what people eat depends upon their tastes does not mean some will eat fecal matter; let alone that anyone is justified in eating it. Certainly, many if not all, can have the same logical tastes. Of even more interest, of course, is the objectivity of the arguments for and against accepting particular systems. Facts are layed out and comments are made upon these facts to make a case about the desirability, or lack of it, for a particular system. This is as rational and objective as we can get about matters of preference. Arguments are given, evidence is weighed, ideals are modified, and we are even willing to compromise. (But we do not in this case try to maximize utility.) We concede the unpalatable possibility that relativism about logic is justifiable. If we can be justified in holding ideals which cannot be simultaneously realized, then presumably we can be justified in holding incompatible logical ideals. If we have such incompatible but justifiable logical ideals, we will need to select more than one of the many logical systems as satisfying our ideals. Although what-is cannot present us with contradictions, the author fears that that the world may be absurd in the sense that morality can present us with irremovable inconsistencies. If the world is absurd we could have irreconciable but irremovable obligations. So, it is feared that we have to accept as correct incompatible systems of logic. So, if the world is absurd relativism in logic is maybe correct. Still the hope guiding this book is that the world is not so absurd that there is not one and only one correct logic.

We close this Section with a remark about the organization of this book. This book is primarily an argument for the selection of a system which most adequately satisfies some ideals presented in the next Section. The argument proceeds by surveying several systems which fail to meet these ideals. Hence, this book can be used to survey much of what has been done in an attempt to present the correct entailment system or systems. We study systems which we ultimately reject for at least two reasons over and above the reason that it is good to offer a comprehensive survey. First, we must admit that we are not so confident in our ideals that we cannot be enticed to to give them up upon seeing realization of other ideals. Objectivity in choosing requires carefull attention and even openess to alternatives against which we have a bias. Secondly, the undesirable features of the system we choose may not seem so bad once we see that the system as a whole is better than several alternatives.

I.6 Adequacy conditions for entailment systems with special attention to some conditions of Belnap.

In this Section we bring together several of the norms appealed to in the appraisal of entailment systems. We do not present all of the norms used because some of them presuppose special techniques and others apply only to particular systems; and it is best to develop those special norms while using the technique or appraising the particular system. We thereby realize more clearly how norms develop. We do not give extensive arguments for accepting these norms. Most of the conditions required are already required by standard or classical logic. We are assuming that there are already strong normative intuitions supporting classical logic, or supporting at least most aspects of classical logic. What requires extensive defense are departures from classical logic such as not requiring Modus Ponens for $\supset$, i.e., Material Detachment, and not requiring that $\supset$ be transitive. In general, it is deviations from classical logic which need defense. We begin by adapting Belnap's thirteen adequacy conditions from his [1960a]. We then present rules and theses which should be in any adquate entailment system. We label the Belnap conditions with $C_n, n \leq 13$, and other conditions with $C_m, m > 13$.

C1. An acceptable system must have the rule: $A \longrightarrow B / \vdash \sim(A \wedge \sim B)$, i.e., $\sim A \vee B$ or $A \supset B$, provided $\sim(A \wedge \sim B)$, $\sim A \vee B$, and $A \supset B$ are wffs..

We add the well-formedness condition because there are systems in which only fde. formulas are wffs.. For the systems in languages in which $\sim(A \wedge \sim B)$ etc. are not wffs., we require that the system have this rule if its language is enriched to include zdfs..

For those who reject the suggestion that material implication is any kind of implication because they realize that $A \supset B$ is merely an abbreviated disjunction, plausibility is not given to C1 by advertizing it as a requirement that a strong implication $A \longrightarrow B$ yield the weak implication $A \supset B$. However, C1 becomes very plausible when we realize that it only requires us to assert that the conditions for falsifying any implication from A from to B do not obtain if we assert $A \longrightarrow B$.

C2. An acceptable system cannot have a rule: $\sim(A \wedge \sim B) / \vdash A \longrightarrow B$.

$A \longrightarrow B$ would not be significantly different from $A \supset B$ if we did not impose C2. We do not want to assert that B can be formally derived from A simply because, as a matter of fact, we do not have A and $\sim B$, i.e., lack the facts which would provide an actual counterexample to $A \longrightarrow B$.

C3. An acceptable system must have a rule: $A \rightarrow B / \vdash \Box(A \supset B)$, i.e., $A \dashv B$, provided $\Box$ occurs as a primitive or defined sign in the language and there are truth functional signs.

Of course, the $\Box$ must behave as a genuine necessity sign. In Section II.2 we set down conditions for a $\Box$ to be a genuine necessity sign. C3 reflects our position that an entailment is at least formally valid and that we have to say that it is formally valid if our language allows us to assert the occurrence of formal validity. Although we may have very strong normative intuitions favoring C3 when stated in this general way, our normative intuitions may falter when we confront a $\Box$ on which some definite conditions have been imposed. For instance, if $\Box A$ is defined as $\sim A \rightarrow A$, it may turn out that we are disinclined to accept C3 for a $\Box$ so defined. Indeed, we use C3 as an adequacy condition for the introduction or definition of $\Box$. Similarly, C4 can be regarded as giving adequacy conditions for necessity in an entailment system.

C4. An acceptable system cannot have a rule of the form: $\Box(A \supset B) / \vdash A \rightarrow B$.

Of course, C4 simply reflects our goal of distinguishing entailment from logical implication.

In Sections I.1 and I.2 C5 and C7 have been defended. Because C6 requires some discussion, we present C7 before C6.

C5. An acceptable entailment system cannot have any of the following as theses or any of the following schemas as thesis schemas.
$p \wedge \sim p \rightarrow q$, $p \rightarrow .q \vee \sim q$, $p \rightarrow .q \rightarrow p$, $\sim p \rightarrow .p \rightarrow q$
$\Box p \rightarrow .q \rightarrow p$, and $\Box \sim p \rightarrow .p \rightarrow q$.
$A \wedge \sim A \rightarrow B$, $A \rightarrow .B \vee \sim B$, $A \rightarrow .B \rightarrow A$, $\sim A \rightarrow .A \rightarrow B$,
$\Box A \rightarrow .B \rightarrow A$, and $\Box \sim A \rightarrow .A \rightarrow B$.

C7. If $A \rightarrow B$ is a thesis, then A and B share at least one sentential variable.

Condition C7 is sometimes called "the weak relevance condition" to contrast it with relevance conditions on derivations which are presented in Part IV. We also say that formulas violating C7 violate variable sharing relevance and that systems with a thesis violating C7 violate variable sharing relevance.

C6. An acceptable system cannot have any thesis of the form: $A \rightarrow .B \rightarrow C$, where A is a zdf. .

Condition C6 is supposed to protect us against so-called modal fallacies. We need to discuss the need for such protection. See section 22.1.2 by J.A. Coffa in Anderson and Belnap [1975] for another discussion.

On pp. 7 - 8 of his [1960a], Belnap acknowledges that he does not have strong normative intuitions in favor of C6. The Routleys in their [1969] have some harsh things to say about principles allegedly underlying C6; especially as these principles are presented in Anderson's and Belnap's [1962b]. The Routleys show that neither DC1 nor DC2 below justify C6. They label the principles with DC because they are interpretations of a more general principle called the Distribution of Contingency. The general principle of Distribution of Contingency is: If A entails B, then if A is contingent B is also contingent. Such a general principle is suggested on p. 30 of Anderson's and Belnap;s [1962b]. Under the supposition that true entailments are necessary truths, DC1 and DC2 are two ways of applying general DC to systems. Modified versions of the Routleys' DC1 and DC2 are as follows.

DC1. An acceptable system cannot have any thesis of the form $A \rightarrow B$ in which A is contingent and B is a necessary truth.

DC2. An acceptable system cannot have any thesis of the form $A \rightarrow . B \rightarrow C$ in which A is contingent.

The Routleys state DC1 as "No contingent proposition entails a necessary proposition" and DC2 as "No contingent proposition entails and entailment." Regardless of how we state them, DC1 and DC2 are too strict. We want to accept Simplification. Certainly $A \rightarrow A$ is a necessary truth and so is $A \vee \sim A$. If B is a single variable both $B \wedge (A \vee \sim A)$ and $B \wedge (A \rightarrow A)$ are contingent. Now $B \wedge (A \vee \sim A) \rightarrow . A \vee \sim A$ is a counterexample to DC1 while $B \wedge (A \rightarrow A) \rightarrow . A \rightarrow A$ is a counterexample to both DC1 and DC2. (Belnap accepted counterexamples to DC2 on p.6 of his [1960a].) In light of these counterexamples, we cannot accept general DC and its specifications in DC1 and DC2 as justifying C6. It simply is not wrong, and certainly not a "fallacy of modality," to get an entailment or some necessary truth from a contingent truth by use of the best possible formal reasoning.

The Routleys also show us that attempts to modify general DC,Distribution of Contingency, to read: If A entails B and A is <u>purely contingent</u> then B is contingent, easily leads to trivilization of DC. The danger is that we take 'A is purely contingent' as 'A does not entail any necessary truth or entailment.' So, it seems that attempts to modify DC are unprofitable. At least we shall not pursue such attempts. In leaving consideration of DC, note that DC would not suffice to justify C6 anyway. Zdfs. can be necessary truths and C6 prohibits having a thesis such as $p \vee \sim p \rightarrow . p \rightarrow p$. We can however speak in favor of C6; but our support is not based on DC.

We do have vague normative intuitions that we cannot get an 'ought' from and 'is' and a 'must' from an 'is.' Upon reflection we may develop an even weaker and even more vague normative intutition that we cannot get an 'entails' from an 'is' because entailment claims are claims of what must be. It is difficult to find out just how, if at all, these norms are realized. If we stay with logical implication as our best implication, they simply are not realized. For instance, it is raining and it is not raining logically implies the sixth commandment. If we consider material entailments, the Routleys point out that we have to accept that we can get necessary truths and entailment claims from 'is' premisses of the form 'X proved S' where S is a necessary truth or an entailment claim. Similarly, E. Morscher in [1972] points out that we can get an 'ought' from such 'is' premisses. (Very likely the material entailment schemas 'X proved S⟶S' and 'X knows S⟶S' would be converted into formal entailments in any reasonable formal logic for proving and knowing even if 'X proved S' and 'X knows S' are contingent, or 'is' claims.) Nevertheless we adopt the position that these norms have some realization. A system which satisfies C6 can be regarded favorably because it thereby gives precision and a realization to these norms as applied to 'entails.' So to speak, it is not some deeper principles which justify C6. Rather C6 supports and clarifies the principles likely to be adduced to support C6. We may grow to appreciate C6 by seeing other pleasing features of systems satisfying C6. Also it helps to look at C6 as giving a sense to a position that entailment symbolized by ⟶ is a new primitive logical notion because ⟶ cannot be obtained from any truth functional signs.

Condition C8 does not suggest any deep issues as did C6. C8 merely lays down conditions for rejecting certain formulas as theses given that certain other formulas have been rejected as theses. Let us use ⊣ for 'is not a thesis' and also for 'is not a thesis schema.'

C8. If ⊢ A⟶B but ⊣B, then ⊣A. If ⊣A or ⊣B, then ⊣A∧B. If A is obtained from B by uniform variable substitution and A is not a thesis ⊣B.

Of course, C8 also tells us that any adequate system must have Modus Ponens, Adjunction, and uniform substitution for variables as meta-rules or admissible rules. Our normative intuitions for features of classical logic support C8.

Belnp's C9,C12, and C13 give less clear guidance than his C10 and C11. So, we present his C9,C12, and C13 while we are presenting conditions which require discussion.

C9. If A is an axiom, A is true.

We not only require that axioms be true, or at least apparently true, upon the intended reading for the logical signs; we also require that the axioms be valid and the rules of proof preserve validity in a significant sense of 'validity.' More will be said about validity in the next Section on matrix semantics and in Part V on model structure semantics. Here we cite being a classical two-value tautology as an example of a type of validity. Although various senses of 'validity' can be precisely defined, 'significant sense of validity' cannot be. One has to appeal to normative intuitions to get agreement on what is a significant sense of validity for a system. We add the validity condition to the truth requirement because we want our axioms and theorems to be necessarily true in some specifiable sense of 'necessary.' However, C9 is precise enough to be a requirement of consistency in the sense that no adequate system can have A and $\sim$A as theses. We are precise enough about truth to know that not both A and $\sim$A can be true in any significant sense of 'true.' Thus C9 enables us to reject what Meyer and Routley in [197_j] call Dialectical Logic.

C12. A theory of entailment should be defined in a natural way.

Obviously with a word such as 'natural' C12 does not give very precise guidance. Helpfully, Belnap mentions two types of conditions which provide naturalness in an entailment system over and above requiring "the system should be easy to handle, that in constructing proofs one whould be able to see where one is going and where one has been." He requires "that in so far as possible axioms and rules governing the used of a certain symbol should be separable from those governing the use of other symbols, and that relations between symbols should grow out of their properties stated separately."

This last remark quoted from Belnap calls attention to an area of intensive research which is ignored in this study. We do not concern ourselves with the issues of finding for a given system just the axioms which give theorems containing a proper subset of the system's basic logical signs. Hence, although we do get just the axioms for a system E which give all but only the E theorems with $\longrightarrow$, we are not here interested in isolating the so-called pure implicational fragments of axiom systems. In general, we can say that we are not interested here in showing that certain extensions of a system are conservative extensions or in proving Separation theorems. If we let So_n denote some axiom system with n logical signs $o_1, \ldots, o_n$ and So_{n+1} a system just like So_n

except for a new logical sign o_{n+1} and some axioms containing the new logical sign, So_{n+1} is a <u>conservative extension</u> of So_n if for any A containing only logical signs from $o_1, \ldots, o_n$, A is a theorem of So_n iff. A is a theorem of So_{n+1}. Separation theorems state that certain systems are conservative extensions of other systems. See A.R. Anderson [1963] for formulation of some problems about conservative extensions. For some literature on this topic see R.K. Meyer's [1970c],[1973a],[1973b],[1973c], L. Maksimowa's [1971], and Meyer's and Routley's [1974].

Our present dismissal of the problem of proving Separation theorems does not indicate a belief that the issues involved are unimportant or uninteresting. We do get a more precise idea of the meaning of a logical sign if we can specify exactly what are the theses containing only it as a logical sign. For instance, we do have a better idea of what a $\longrightarrow$ means if we can say that the necessary truths involving it are the theorems of these axioms where the axioms and theorems have $\longrightarrow$ as the only logical sign. These theses containing only $\longrightarrow$ give, if you will, the pure essence of $\longrightarrow$. Also it is interesting and important for understanding the interconnection of our ideas to know that certain systems cannot be separated from others. Our excuse for not considering this issue, over and above the general excuse that we cannot study everything, is that it is of more importance to discover the right system. Once we have the right system, we may turn to trying to understand more fully its logical signs and their interconnections. However, we must admit that our conviction that we have the right system may be diminished if we find out that it cannot be well axiomatized. On p. 274 of their [1974] Meyer and Routley say "A system is <u>well-axiomatized</u> if it is a conservative extension of all its important fragments." They immediately note that this definition requires what we have called normative intuitions to judge whether or not a system is well axiomatized. They do go on, though, to make a good case that the systems with which we will be most concerned are well axiomatized. These systems are E, R, and NR.

In his remarks on C12, Belnap adds that Gentzen style presentations of a system are exemplars of presentations in which each logical sign is introduced separately. Since we are not concerned with this issue we shall not consider Gentzen style presentations in this study. For some literature on Gentzen style presentations, see Chapter IV sections 5,6, and 7 of Belnap's [1960a],Anderson's and Belnap's [1963], Belnap's, Dunn's, and Gupta's [197_], Meyer's and Routley's [1974], and now Anderson's and Belnap's [1975].

However, Belnap suggests an aspect of naturalness which we will consider. He wrote "Though the requirement of naturalness does not suggest that no constants be introduced by definition, it does tend to suggest that entailment be taken as primitive. And not only is taking entailment as primitive more natural, but it is also likely that our intuitions concerning entailment are clearer than our intuitions concerning some other candidates for primitives, e.g., some intensional sense of 'or'." We interpret Belnap as talking about normative intuitions. We agree that entailment, i.e., a logical sign whose intended reading is "entails' should be primitive. In particular, we do not think that entailment should be defined as the necessity of some kind of implication. For instance, we have some normative intuitions against defining entailment as $\Box(A \longrightarrow B)$, i.e., $A \Longrightarrow B$, where $\longrightarrow$ is some implication which we do not consider to be entailment, e.g., a relevant implication. It seems that the intended reading for this will be 'it is necessary in the sense in which entailments, as opposed to mere logical implications, are necessary that__.' Here we do not want $\Box(A \longrightarrow B)$ to mean that it is impossible that A be true and B be false. So, it seems that such a definition of 'entailment' presupposes a fairly well understood notion of entailment; that fairly well understood notion of entailment should be presented first. In general, we think that because of the vast number of systems for $\Box$, necessity should, whenever possible, be a defined symbol. There simply is not a single sense of necessity about which we have some clear intuitions. So, we take C12 as directing us to prefer an entailment system with entailment as a primitive. This will be our major reason for preferring system E to NR.

C13. A theory of entailment ought to be as strong as is consistent with its fundamental aims.

The fundamental aims of a theory of entailment are to develop a system for a transitive $\longrightarrow$ in which no $A \longrightarrow B$ thesis suffers from content or derivational irrelevance as discussed in Section I.2. C13 advises us to try to reject only the oddities due to treating formal logical implication as the best possible formal implication. To be sure, C13 does not thereby give very prescise advice. Here we cite only four bits of advice which we take from C13. If we use a different symbol from either $\supset$ or $\dashv$ to symbolize entailment, neither use of $\supset$ nor $\dashv$ produce oddities about entailment. So, C13 advises us to keep all classical tautologies as theses and to have a subsystem for $\dashv$. Certainly a derivation of B from $A_1, \ldots, A_n$ in which none of the A_i are used is not a formally correct derivation of B from $A_1, \ldots, A_n$. Nevertheless we may be restricting the notion of derivation too much if we demand that a formally correct derivation of B from $A_1,\ldots,A_n$ use each A_i. So, C13 advises us to try to develop a notion of derivation which requires the use of some but not all of the premisses. If we develop a significant notion of validity which is narrower than logical validity, C13 advises us to try for semantical completeness in the sense that A is a thesis iff. A is valid in this significant sense. In exercise 8 of V.1 we present R.K. Meyer's notion of coherence. In their [1976] Meyer and R.G. Wolf require that "Any propositional logic which is a satisfactory formalization of entailment should be coherent." They offer this requirement as a specification of C13. At this stage we take this requirement only as having C13 advise us to have all true entailments as theses and only true entailments as theses.

Condition C10 is closely related to C9 and the notion of semantical completeness discussed above. To present our adaptation of Belnap's C10 we use $A_1,\ldots A_n \models B$ to say that the inference from $A_1,\ldots,A_n$ to B is valid where the sense of 'valid' can be specified in the context. Plain $\models B$ says that B is valid.

C10. $A_1,\ldots,A_n \vdash$ iff. $A_1,\ldots,A_n \models B$ if we have an acceptable sense of 'valid' for inferences.

Certainly we want our accepted derivations to correspond to valid inferences if we can develop an acceptable notion of valid inference when we depart from the notion of logically valid inference. Sometimes C10 is said to require strong semantical completeness or argument completeness. Belnap calls C11 below the coherence condition. We say that a system is rule normal if it satisfies C11. For us C11 is a very important condition.

C11. $A_1,\ldots,A_n \vdash B$ iff. $\vdash A_1 \wedge,\ldots,\wedge A_n \longrightarrow B$, provided the conjunction $A_1 \wedge,\ldots,\wedge A_n$ is a wff..

Certainly if we assert that $A_1 \wedge,\ldots,\wedge A_n$ entails B, we want to be able to derive B from $A_1,\ldots,A_n$. Similarly, it seems that we should be able to assert that $A_1 \wedge,\ldots,\wedge A_n$ entails B if we can derive B from $A_1,\ldots,A_n$. At least we have to justify a practice of allowing a derivation which we are not prepared to assert to be the best kind of formal reasoning, viz., an entailment. If we have a non-normal rule, viz., a rule $A_1,\ldots,A_n \vdash B$ for which we do not accept the corresponding $\vdash A_1 \wedge,\ldots,\wedge A_n \longrightarrow B$, we have a case in which we accept some formal reasoning which we will not assert to be the best possible formal reasoning. To us the oddity of having a rule which is not accepted as the best kind of formal reasoning makes fulfillment of C11 mandatory.

We now present some adequacy conditions over and above those of Belnap.

C14. Any adequate entailment system must have the following rules as primitive or derived if expressible about the language of the system.

We label these rules with R. followed by a numeral and we will frequently refer to them by use of theses R-labels. At the left of rules we list some names or signs also used to refer to them. See the Notational Preface for other labels.

R1. $A, A \longrightarrow B \vdash B$	MP (α)
R2. $A, B \vdash A \wedge B$	Adj. (β)
R3. $A \longrightarrow B, A \longrightarrow C \vdash A \longrightarrow . B \wedge C$	Comp.,and-intro.
R4. $A \longrightarrow . B \wedge C \vdash A \longrightarrow B$ $A \longrightarrow . B \wedge C \vdash A \longrightarrow C$	Consequent Simplification, and-elim
R5. $A \longrightarrow C, B \longrightarrow C \vdash A \vee B \longrightarrow C$	or-elim.
R6. $A \vee B \longrightarrow C \vdash A \longrightarrow C$ $A \vee B \longrightarrow C \vdash B \longrightarrow C$	Antecedent Simplification, Simplification of Disjunctive Antecedents,SDA
R7. $A \longrightarrow B, B \longrightarrow C \vdash A \longrightarrow C$	Trans.
R8. $A \longrightarrow B \vdash \sim B \longrightarrow \sim A$	Contra.
R9. $A \longrightarrow B \vdash A \wedge C \longrightarrow B$	Prem. Add.
R10. From $\vdash A \longrightarrow B$ and $\vdash B \longrightarrow A$, infer $\vdash F(B/A)$ from $\vdash F(A)$.	Repl.

Presumably there already is a bias in favor of these rules since they hold for classical logic. Still some comments are in order. Despite their fundamental character R1 and R2 are not applicable to all systems. For instance, R1 and R2 do not apply to systems with only fde. formulas. A simple reading of R3 and R4 seems to be the best argument in their support. R5 and R6 help bring out that our reasoning from a disjunction is what can be called 'reasoning from the disjuncts' as opposed to what can be called 'reasoning from the disjunction as a unit.' Let us briefly elaborate upon this distinction.

An example of reasoning from a disjunction as a unit is as follows. John can go to the ball game or John can go to the movies; so, John has two choices. This could also be called 'reasoning from the fact that there is a disjunction.' In our example neither disjunct logically implies that John has two choices; let alone entails it. Perhaps a distinguishing mark of reasoning from a disjunction of A and B taken as a unit would be to have the rule: From $(A \pm B) \longrightarrow C$ infer both $\sim(A \longrightarrow C)$ and $\sim(B \longrightarrow C)$ where $\pm$ indicates that a disjunction is to be taken as a unit. We shall not explore such a disjunctive sign in this work. We will not take disjunctions as units. Still a brief digression pointing out a reason for rejecting MD, i.e., Modus Ponens for $\supset$, and an observation on the difference between MP for $\longrightarrow$ and so-called MP for $\supset$ are useful for appreciating this idea of taking a compound formula as a unit. The premisses: A,($\sim$A v B) of an MD inference give us two cases to consider which we here represent as the disjunction $A\wedge\sim A \vee A\wedge B$. If we want to get B from this disjunction, our rules rules R5 and R6 tell us that we have $A\wedge\sim A \vee A\wedge B\longrightarrow B$ iff. we have both $A\wedge B\longrightarrow B$ and $A\wedge\sim A\longrightarrow B$. Typically,use of $A\wedge\sim A\longrightarrow B$ is glossed over with the misleading remark that we do not have to consider the case that the disjunct $A\vee\sim A$ occurs. This remark is misleading because A,($\sim$A v B) do give the case of $A\wedge\sim A$. So, if we are using currently standard reasoning the more accurate claim to make is that the $A\wedge\sim A$ case entails B because the explicit contradiction entails, by current standards, any formula. So, in currently standard reasoning $A\wedge\sim A\longrightarrow B$ is used in getting B from A,($\sim$A v B) by MD,and use of R5 and R6 makes explicit that in use of MD the disjunction is not treated as a unit and that $A\wedge\sim A\longrightarrow B$ is used as a result. Of course, if we have an adequate entailment system we cannot use $A\wedge\sim A\longrightarrow B$. Perhaps we may say that Modus Ponens for $\supset$ fails because we do not reason from A and the unit ($A\supset B$) to B; instead we reason from A and the disjunct $\sim$A from ($\sim$ A v B) to B and from A and the disjunct B to B. On the other hand, in genuine Modus Ponens, viz., $A, A\longrightarrow B\vdash B$, we reason from A and the unit $A\longrightarrow B$ to B. In genuine MP we do not reason from A and the antecedent of $A\longrightarrow B$ taken apart from the consequent B;nor do we reason from A and the consequent of $A\longrightarrow B$ taken apart from the antecedent. In genuine MP, the implication is taken as a unit.

We will say no more here about our resolve to require transitivity for $\longrightarrow$. So much reasoning in mathematics and logical theory uses Contraposition that we should be reluctant to deny that Contraposition embodies the best kind of formal reasoning. Also Contraposition did not play a role in the paradoxical derivations of I.l. Hence, we have nothing against Contraposition. It is important to be confident in our requirement of Contraposition because our main reason for rejecting Parry's system in Part II is that it lacks Contraposition. R9 gets support from its reasonableness in classical logic. Also R9 reveals that we cannot require that the best possible reasoning use all of the premisses given. R10 demands a type of extensionality for for $\longrightarrow$ contexts. Thus even if $\sim$(A v B) and $\sim A\wedge\sim B$ have different meanings they can replace one another if they are provably entailment equivalent. But the extensionality is restricted because we can have $\Box(A\equiv B)$ as a thesis for an A and a B which cannot always replace one another. For instance, we will see that the system E has $\Box(p\wedge\sim p\equiv q\wedge\sim q)$ as a theorem although $q\wedge\sim q$ cannot replace $p\wedge\sim p$ in the theorem $p\wedge\sim p\longrightarrow p$.

C15. Any adequate entailment system must have the following as thesis schemas.

1. $A\longrightarrow A$	Identity
2. $A\wedge B\longrightarrow B$ and $A\wedge B\longrightarrow A$	Simp.
3. $A\longrightarrow .A\vee B$ and $B\longrightarrow .A\vee B$	Add.
4. $A\longrightarrow\sim\sim A$	Dbl. neg.
5. $\sim\sim A\longrightarrow A$	Dbl. neg.
6. $A\wedge(B\vee C)\longrightarrow .A\wedge B\vee A\wedge C$	Dist.
7. $A\wedge B\vee A\wedge C\longrightarrow .A\wedge(B\vee C)$	Dist.
8. $A\vee(B\wedge C)\longrightarrow .(A\vee B)\wedge(A\vee C)$	Dist.
9. $(A\vee B)\wedge(A\vee C)\longrightarrow .A\vee(B\wedge C)$	Dist.
10. $\sim(A\vee B)\longrightarrow .\sim A\wedge\sim B$	De. M.
11. $\sim A\wedge\sim B\longrightarrow .\sim(A\vee B)$	De. M.
12 $\sim(A\wedge B)\longrightarrow .\sim A\vee\sim B$	De. M.
13 $\sim A\vee\sim B\longrightarrow .\sim(A\wedge B)$	De. M.

And also General Commutativity for $\wedge$ and $\vee$ as well as General Associativity for $\wedge$ and $\vee$ must hold.

Since we accept C11 each of the above schemas gives a rule. In this work we will not give proofs of General Communativity and Associativity for $\wedge$ and $\vee$. One can consult Copi [1967] pp. 238-240 for nice proofs of these general principles. Rules R3 through R7 with schemas 2 and 3 above give Communativity and Associativity for $\wedge$ and $\vee$; then see Copi for the general cases. Here, though, we are more interested in why we should require these schemas than in deriving consequences from them. We allow our normative intuitions in support of classical logic to provide support for schemas 6 through 13. Acceptance of schemas 4 and 5 is borrowed from classical logic and reveals our resolve not to concern ourselves with worries about Double Negation and so-called Intuitionistic Logic. (One can consult Heyting [1956] for an introduction to Intuitionistic Logic which does not have $\sim\sim A\longrightarrow A$ as a thesis schema.) Acceptance of schema 1 brings out that an entailment may be trivial. To have an entailment we do not need to uncover or in some way bring the conclusion out of the premiss. Once we drop a normative intuition that entailments have to bring out something in some way lying within the premisses, there can be no objection to the totally safe inference to A from itself. Simplification seems to be a paradigm of entailment. Certainly, a conjunction entails, brings along with itself, each of its conjuncts. Still, a pioneer in the search for entailment rejected Simplification. In Part IV we will consider E.J. Nelson's system which rejects Simplification.

Let us suggest that our acceptance of Simplification reveals that we do not reason from a conjunction as a unit; instead we reason from a conjunction by reasoning from its conjuncts. If one treats a conjunction as a single unit, rejection of Simplification may not be too odd. To reason from A and B as a unit could be to reason from that fact that A is conjoined with B. From the claim that A is conjoined with $\sim$A we can conclude that there is an explicit contradiction; but we cannot conclude either A or $\sim$A from a claim that A is conjoined with $\sim$A. We, though, treat $A \wedge \sim A$ in such a way that we can conclude both A and $\sim$A from the conjunction. So, just as with the case of 'or' our ways of treating 'and' may not cover all ways of interpreting 'and.' We may be a bit unhappy with the Addition schemas. According to the Addition theses we have to accept the following as an example of the best possible formal reasoning. 2+2=4;so, 2+2=4 or R.M. Nixon was the first U.S. President to resign. There is, to be sure, not total irrelevance between the premiss and the conclusion. But half of the conclusion is totally irrelevant to the premiss. So, acceptance of Addition is acceptance that parts of the conclusion may be totally irrelevant to the premiss even in the best possible formal argument and that consequently the best possible formal arguments may have conclusions which are ridiculous. However, we accept Addition for systematic reasons. We have it primarily as a consequence of Simplification and Contraposition. If we did not have to accept Addition as such a consequence, we would be happy with Parry's system which rejects Addition.

We now supplement Belnap's C5 with another condition stipulating that an adequate entailment system cannot have certain rules.

C16. No adequate entailment system can have the following as rules.

Antilogism	$A \wedge B \longrightarrow C \vdash A \wedge \sim C \longrightarrow \sim B$
Exportation	$A \wedge B \longrightarrow C \vdash A \longrightarrow . B \longrightarrow C$
Boethius' Rule	$A \longrightarrow B \vdash \sim (A \longrightarrow \sim B)$
Suppression of Necessary Truths	

$$\vdash A,\ \vdash A \wedge B \longrightarrow C; \text{so, } \vdash B \longrightarrow C.$$

$$\vdash A,\ A, B \vdash C; \text{ so, } B \vdash C.$$

$$\Box A,\ A \wedge B \vdash C; \text{ so } B \vdash C.$$

These rules become unacceptable if used with what we have already accepted. Antilogism with Simplification immediately gives $\vdash A \wedge \sim A \longrightarrow \sim B$ from which it is easy to get a thesis schema $A \wedge \sim A \longrightarrow B$. We need to derive some consequences of our rules and theses from C14 and C15 to derive the formally objectionable $A\wedge\sim A\longrightarrow B$ by use of Exportation. So, here we observe that just because we can get C from $A\wedge B$ by the best possible formal argument, there is little plausibility to the claim that from A we can get, by the best possible formal argument, the result that the best possible formal argument will take us from B to C. For instance, it is implausible to hold that just because 2+2=4 and R.M. Nixon was the first U.S. President to resign entails that 2+2=4, we can conclude that 2+2=4 entails that R.M. Nixon was the first U.S. President to resign entails that 2+2=4. Boethius' Rule, as J. Bode pointed out in his thesis [1973], immediately gives an inconsistent system if the system has the instances of Simplification: $A\wedge\sim A\longrightarrow A$ and $A\wedge\sim A\longrightarrow \sim A$. Suppression of Necessary truths is intuitively undesirable Indeed the tolerance of such suppression in classical logic was the main stimulus to search for a new logic which acted on this author. After all, if we use A to get C from B, we cannot say that we got C from B alone even if A is necessarily true. In an entailment claim everything used to get the conclusion must be cited. An exercise below brings out how Suppression gives undesirable schemas as theses.

We suggest a few exercises before leaving our listing of adequacy conditions and moving on to our introduction to how we will talk of matrix semantics.

Exercises I.6

1. Use rules and theses of C14 and C15 to establish the following. $A\wedge(B\wedge C)\longleftrightarrow A\wedge(B\wedge C)$, $A \vee (B \vee C)\longleftrightarrow (A \vee B) \vee C$, $A\wedge B\longleftrightarrow B\wedge A$, $A \vee B\longleftrightarrow B \vee A$, $A\wedge A\longleftrightarrow A$, and $A \vee A\longleftrightarrow A$.
2. Use Antilogism to get $A\wedge\sim A\longrightarrow B$.
3. With Exportation and Importation: $A\longrightarrow .B\longrightarrow C \vdash A\wedge B\longrightarrow C$, get $A\wedge\sim A\longrightarrow B$.
4. Get $B\longrightarrow .A \vee\sim A$ from the second suppression schema cited. Use C11.

I.7 Matrix semantics, an introduction.

The purpose of this section is to introduce the notion of matrix and matrix interpretation or valuation of the formulas of a language. In the course of this introduction, we introduce notions such as: homomorphism, isomorphism, Lindenbaum matrix, filter, lattice, and world-matrix. Despite assuming familiarity with the set-theoretic notions of ordered tuple and function or operation, this section is very unsophisticated but is,hopefully, helpful to readers unfamiliar with the notions introduced. This section is not an introduction to algebraic semantics. Readers interested in pursuing a study of algebraic semantics can consult works such as Meyer's and Routley's [1972d], Dunn's excellent dissertation [1966], and Dunn's section 18 and 28.2 in Anderson's and Belnap's [1975].

A matrix, which will be labelled with cursive capital letters with subscripts and suffixes, can always be regarded as an ordered triple: $\langle M,D,O\rangle$. In such a triple M is a set of objects, D is a non-empty subset of M, and O is a finite set of basic operation on M. D is the set of <u>designated elements</u>. The elements of M are frequently called <u>values</u>. Frequently, a matrix will be presented as an ordered n-tuple by calling attention to other subsets of M and by citing the members of O. Thus we may present the standard (classical) truth tables $\mathcal{C}$o as the ordered triple: $\langle \{T,F\},\{T\},\{\wedge,\vee,\bar{\ }\}\rangle$ or as the ordered quintuple: $\langle \{T,F\},\{T\},\wedge,\vee,\bar{\ }\rangle$, where $\wedge$, $\vee$, and $\bar{\ }$ are operations interpreting respectively the $\wedge$, $\vee$, and $\sim$ of formal languages. Of course, mere citation of $\wedge$, $\vee$, and $\bar{\ }$ does not tell us what these operations on M are. So, part of presenting a matrix is specifying what the operations are. In the case of a small M such as $\{T,F\}$ we can say what the operations are by displaying a set of ordered pairs for unary operations, a set of ordered triples for binary operations, and, in general, a set of ordered n+1 tuples for an n-ary operation. For instance, we could display the following set of ordered triples as the operation labelled by $\wedge$.

$\{\langle TTT\rangle, \langle TFF\rangle, \langle FTF\rangle, \langle FFF\rangle\}$

In the above set of ordered triples the rightmost member of each triple is the result of applying the operation to the first two members. In this work we will not tell what operations are by displaying sets of ordered n-tuples. Frequently, though, we will tell what operations are by displaying computation tables which, in effect, present sets of ordered n-tuples. So, let us illustrate how tables are to be used.

The operation denoted by $\bar{\ }$, which will always be a unary operation interpreting $\sim$, can be presented on a two column table with the left column being a list of the elements of M and the right column listing the result of applying $\bar{\ }$ to the element of M listed on its immediate left. Binary operations are presented with square tables of n+1 rows and columns if M has n elements. In the upper left hand corner the sign of the operation is displayed, in the leftmost column the elements of M are listed, and on the top row the elements of M are listed in the same order as in the leftmost column. The intersection of a row and a column gives the result of applying the operation, whose sign is in the upper lefthand corner, to the ordered pair consisting of the entry from the leftmost column and the topmost row. In this work we consider only unary and binary operations on matrices. Examples are the best way to clarify the notion of computation tables which are sometimes called matrix tables. The first example is the familiar classical truth table while the second is simply the tables for a three-value matrix. In these examples $\rightarrow$ denotes another basic matrix operation.

Example 1.

	$-$
T	F
F	T

$\wedge$	T	F
T	T	F
F	F	F

$\vee$	T	F
T	T	T
F	T	F

$\rightarrow$	T	F
T	T	F
F	T	T

Example 2.

	$-$
+1	-1
0	0
-1	+1

$\wedge$	+1	0	-1
+1	+1	0	-1
0	0	0	-1
-1	-1	-1	-1

$\vee$	+1	0	-1
+1	+1	+1	+1
0	+1	0	-1
-1	+1	0	-1

$\rightarrow$	+1	0	-1
+1	+1	-1	-1
0	+1	0	-1
-1	+1	+1	+1

In these two examples we would have presented matrices if we would have specified which elements were designated, eg., $\{T\}$ for Example 1 and $\{0,+1\}$ for Example 2.

We also present operations by means of computation rules. For instance in Example 2 above we could have ordered the elements by a less than relation $\prec$ so that $-1 \prec 0 \prec +1$. We could then give computation rules as follows.

$a \wedge b = \min(a,b)$, $a \vee b = \max(a,b)$, $\bar{a}$ is as on the table in Example 2, $a \rightarrow b = \max(\bar{a},b)$ if $a \preceq b$, but $a \rightarrow b = \min(\bar{a},b)$ if $b \prec a$.

In the above example of computation rules min and max, of course, refer to minimum and maximun under the given ordering.

This example of computation rules shows that we use a, b, c, d, with and without subscripts, as variables for referring to matrix elements. These rules also show that we use signs for matrix operations on signs referring to matrix elements as we use similar signs on sentential variables and schema letters.

Of course, if M has infinitely many elements or if we want to characterize a type of matrix instead of a single matrix, we need to present operations by means of computation rules. Because computation rules usually involve reference to an ordering of the elements of the M, we should review the notions of total and partial ordering.

A two-place relation Rxy is a partial ordering of a set M if R is transitive, anti-symmetric, i.e., Rab and Rba only if $a = b$, and for some $a, b \in M$ Rab holds. If R is reflexive and partially orders M, R is a reflexive partial order of M. If R partially orders M and for any $a, b \in M$ either Rab or Rba, then R totally orders M or, as we also say, R linearly orders M. We use $<$ for a non-reflexive partial order and $\leq$ for a reflexive partial order. We explicitly state when we want $\leq$ to be a total order. When $<$ and $\leq$ express standard arithmetical 'less than' and 'less than or equal to' the context, hopefully, will make it clear that we are using the standard arithmetic notions.

Let us now give two more examples of matrices to illustrate presenting a type of matrix and to illustrate getting a particular matrix of a certain type.

Example 3.

Let us say that a matrix $\langle M, D, \wedge, \vee, \bar{\ }, \rightarrow \rangle$ is a finite classical matrix if it meets the following conditions. M is a finite totally ordered set with a least element, which we label F, a greatest element, which we label T, and D consists of the members of M which are different from F. If $a \in D$, then $\bar{a} = F$, $\bar{F} = T$, $a \wedge b = \min(a, b)$, $a \vee b = \max(a, b)$ and $a \rightarrow b = \max(\bar{a}, b)$.

Our next example is a particular five-value classical matrix.

Example 4.

Let $M = \{F, 1, 2, 3, T\}$ with $F < 1 < 2 < 3 < T$ and $D = \{1, 2, 3, T\}$. The tables are as below.

	‾
T	F
3	F
2	F
1	F
F	T

∧	T	3	2	1	F
T	T	3	2	1	F
3	3	3	2	1	F
2	2	2	2	1	F
1	1	1	1	1	F
F	F	F	F	F	F

∨	T	3	2	1	F
T	T	T	T	T	T
3	T	3	3	3	3
2	T	3	2	2	2
1	T	3	2	1	1
F	T	3	2	1	F

→	T	3	2	1	F
T	T	3	2	1	F
3	T	3	2	1	F
2	T	3	2	1	F
1	T	3	2	1	F
F	T	T	T	T	T

Because no discrimination has been made amongst the designated values in regard to some being "truer" than others, these tables show why we call the matrices of Example 3 'classical.' All of the designated values can be identified with T. All values designated can be identified with T because there is a homomorphism between any finite classical matrix and the classical matrix of Example 1 which maps all of the designated elements to the T of Example 1.

With the use of 'homomorphism' it is appropriate to review the notions of homomorphism and isomorphism. A function h on a set M onto a set M' is a homomorphism with respect to an operation $\boxtimes$ if $h(a \boxtimes b) = h(a) \boxtimes' h(b)$, where $\boxtimes'$ is the operation on M' corresponding to $\boxtimes$. The definition can easily be extended to cover several operations. A homomorphism is an isomorphism if it is a one-to-one function on M onto M'. As an example of a homomorphism consider the matrices of Examples 1 and 4 and the mapping h on M of Example 4 onto the M of Example 1, viz., $\{T,F\}$, such that $h(F) = F$ and $h(a) = T$ if $a \in D$. You can verify that $h(\bar{a}) = \overline{h(a)}$, $h(a \wedge b) = h(a) \wedge h(b)$, $h(a \vee b) = h(a) \vee h(b)$, and $h(a \rightarrow b) = h(a) \rightarrow h(b)$.

In a matrix new operations can be defined in terms of basic operations. Thus an operation $a \supset b$ could be defined as $\bar{a} \vee b$ or $\overline{(\bar{a} \wedge b)}$. We do not want to suggest, though, that only $\wedge$, $\vee$, $\bar{\ }$, and $\rightarrow$ are basic operations. There may be a need to introduce other basic operations such as $\Box$. What operations are needed is determined by the basic logical signs of the language to be interpreted. In general, we have a basic matrix operation sign corresponding to each basic logical sign, and for us the operation signs look very much like the logical signs. We need the sign used with variables to tell whether it is a matrix operation sign or a logical sign. Note that we use matrix element variables with operator signs to designate operations. Thus $\bar{a}$ and $a \wedge b$ are used to denote operations.

What is it to interpret a language by use of a matrix or by use of a type of matrix? We can look at logical signs as operations on the wffs. of a language into the wffs. of the language. For simplicity's sake let us confine our attention to: $\wedge$, $\vee$, $\sim$, $\supset$, $\rightarrow$, and $\leftrightarrow$. For instance, the logical sign $\wedge$ can be looked at as the operation which takes us from the ordered pairs of wffs. $\langle A,B \rangle$ to exactly one other wff. for each pair, viz., $A \wedge B$. Once we regard logical signs as standing for such syntactic operations, it makes sense to interpret them as operations on a matrix because logical signs, after all, are operations. So, the first step in interpreting a language by means of a matrix is to correlate each logical sign (logical operation) with a matrix sign (matrix operation). In general, we correlate a logical sign with a matrix sign which looks just like it except $\sim$ is correlated with $\bar{\ }$. So, we have given, once and for all, the instructions for interpreting logical signs on matrices. Henceforth, we talk only of interpreting sentential variables and sentential constants to interpret the formulas of a language. Of course, punctuation marks are not to be interpreted and we are considering only languages for sentential logic. A language is interpreted on a matrix $\mathfrak{M}$ by assigning each variable and constant in the language to exactly one element of M. We also talk of interpreting only the formulas in a proper subset of the wffs. of a language by assigning each variable occurring anywhere in the formulas of the subset exactly one element of M. To be precise we should use a function sign i() for such an interpretation function for variables and sentential constants. Once we have interpreted a language each formula in the language, or part of the language, being interpreted is assigned a matrix element as a value. To be precise we should use another type of function sign v() to represent the assigning of values to all formulas. The function i() is properly called the <u>interpretation.</u> and v() is properly called the <u>valuation</u>. The valuation developed from an interpretation is what interests us most. We get a valuation on a matrix $\mathfrak{M}$ in the following recursive way after we have interpreted each variable and sentential constant.

MATRIX VALUATION RULES given an interpretation i()

i) v(p) = i(p) for each sentential variable p.
ii) v(c) = i(c) if c is a sentential constant.
iii) $v(A \wedge B) = v(A) \wedge v(B)$
iv) $v(A \vee B) = v(A) \vee v(B)$
v) $v(\sim A) = \overline{v(A)}$
vi) $v(A \supset B) = v(A) \supset v(B)$
vii) $v(A \rightarrow B) = v(A) \rightarrow v(B)$
viii) $v(A \leftrightarrow B) = v(A) \leftrightarrow v(B)$.

Similarly, if we had formulas of the form $\Box A$, $v(\Box A)$ would be $\Box v(A)$. The first two clauses of the definition of a typical v() reveal that the interpretation function can be, in practice, disregarded. We will disregard the interpretation function in our talk of interpreting a language and then assigning values to all the formulas. We will simply talk of a valuation v() as both an interpretation and as a valuation. Note, in passing, that a valuation of a set of formulas is a homomorphism on the set of formulas into the M of a matrix $\mathfrak{M}$.

Properly speaking, we interpret formulas by interpreting variables and sentential constants; then formulas receive values. However, because we deal with schemas so much more than with formulas, we talk of interpreting schemas and sets of schemas. When we talk of interpreting schemas and sets of schemas, we proceed as if schema letters were variables and as if names of sentential constants were sentential constants. We,then, assign values to schemas as if they were wffs.. So, we will say such things as 'v(A) = +1' as well as 'v(p) = +1.'

We now define some semantic terms for matrix interpretations. Formula <u>A is satisfied by a valuation</u>, or interpretation, <u>v() on $\mathfrak{M}$</u> if $v(A) \in D$ for $D \in \mathfrak{M}$. A set of formulas <u>Γ is simultaneously satisfied by v() on $\mathfrak{M}$</u> if v() satisfies each A such that $A \in \Gamma$. Formula *A is valid on $\mathfrak{M}$* if A is satisfied by every v() on $\mathfrak{M}$. If A is valid on $\mathfrak{M}$ we say that *A is a thesis of $\mathfrak{M}$* or that *A is an $\mathfrak{M}$-thesis*. If no v() on $\mathfrak{M}$ satisfies A, we say that *A is $\mathfrak{M}$-inconsistent*. If no v() on $\mathfrak{M}$ simultaneously satisfies Γ, we say that *Γ is $\mathfrak{M}$-inconsistent*. A formula *A is interpreted, or receives a valuation, on a kind of matrix K* if A is interpreted on a matrix of this kind. A formula *A is valid for a kind of matrix K* if A is valid on every matrix of kind K. Thus $p \rightarrow . q \rightarrow p$ is valid on finite classical matrices, as you can check by noting that $\max(\overline{v(p)}, \max(\overline{v(q)}, v(p)))$ is never the F, i.e., the least element, of a finite classical matrix. If A is valid on a kind of matrix, we say that A is a thesis for that kind of matrix. Thus we talk of Sugihara-theses and Parry-theses to talk of formulas valid on these kinds of matrices. We even *give systems semantically* rather than axiomatically by specifying that a certain system is exactly the formulas valid on this matrix or exactly the formulas valid on this kind of matrix.

We are especially concerned, though, with interpretations or valuations of systems axiomatically given. A *matrix $\mathfrak{M}$ is suitable for a system S* if all theorems of S are valid on $\mathfrak{M}$. If $\mathfrak{M}$ is suitable for system S, we sometimes talk of $\mathfrak{M}$ as an *S-matrix*. It should be noted that a matrix $\mathfrak{M}$ can be an S-matrix and an S'-matrix where S and S' are different systems. Thus the matrix of Example 2 is an S0-matrix for Halldén's system of Section II.19 and an SA-matrix for Sugihara's system SA of Section II.20. A *matrix $\mathfrak{M}$ is characteristic for a system S* if the theorems of S are exactly the theses of $\mathfrak{M}$. Thus, as is well known, the classical two-value matrix is characteristic for classical sentential logic. It should be noted that a system can have two distinct characteristic matrices. For instance, recall that there is a homomorphism of the classical matrix of Example 4 to the classical matrix of Example 1. This homomorphism which takes all values different from F to the T of the classical matrix of Example 1 shows that if a formula is valid on the matrix of Example 4 it is also valid on the classical two-valued matrix, i.e., is a tautology. One can verify that all tautologies are valid on the matrix of Example 4. So, both matrices are characteristic for classical sentential logic. Of course, if a characteristic matrix $\mathfrak{M}$ for S is finite, *$\mathfrak{M}$ is a finite characteristic matrix for S.* The great value of having a finite characteristic matrix for a system S is that possession of such a matrix enables us to determine in finitely many steps whether or not a given formula is a theorem of the system, viz., it provides *a decision procedure for provability in S*, i.e., theoremhood in S.

The notions of suitability and characteristic extend to

kinds of matrices. A kind of matrix K is suitable for an axiom system S if every matrix of kind K is suitable for S. A kind of matrix K is characteristic for an axiom system S if the theses of this kind of matrix are exactly the theorems of S. In this case, a negative definition is more illuminating. A kind of matrix K is characteristic for axiom system S if K is suitable for S and for every non-theorem B of S there is a $\mathfrak{M}$ of kind K such that $v(B) \notin D$, $D \in \mathfrak{M}$, for some v() on $\mathfrak{M}$. Thus, as is brought out in an exercise, finite classical matrices are characteristic for an axiom system whose theorems are exactly the classical two-value tautologies. If a system S has a characteristic kind of matrix, then S has a feature which is similar to what is called the finite model property; but which is still different from the finite model property. A system S has the finite model property if for every non-theorem B of S there is an $\mathfrak{M}$ with a finite M such that B is not valid on $\mathfrak{M}$. It should be noted that the finite model property does not, by itself, guarantee that we can decide in finitely many steps whether or not a given formula B is a theorem of S. We may not know of any bounds on the size of the M's we may need to consider.

We can now call attention to Lindenbaum's interesting observation that every system S which admits uniform substitution for variables in theses has a characteristic matrix. Define system S's Lindenbaum matrix $\mathfrak{M}$s as follows. Let Ms be the formulas of the language of S, let Ds be the theses of S, and let Os be the primitve operator signs of S's language. Let us make the following our first theorem.

Theorem I of I.7: For any system S whose theses are closed under uniform variable substitution, its Lindenbaum matrix $\mathfrak{M}$s is characteristic.

By way of proof consider the following. $\mathfrak{M}$s is suitable for S because if we take any thesis A of S and let a v() on $\mathfrak{M}$s assign elements of Ms to variables of A, v() assigns A to a result of uniform variable substitution in A,which result we label As. By hypothesis As is a thesis of S if A is a thesis of S; hence As, viz., v(A), is in Ds. On the other hand, if B is a non-thesis of S, there is a v() on $\mathfrak{M}$s which maps B to a non-designated element, viz., the v() which maps B to itself by mapping each variable occurring in B to itself.

Lindenbaum's observation is significant for at least two reasons. First, it dramatizes limitations of the use of matrices. Second, it suggests the valuable idea of taking formulas as the elements of matrices, although the author is not sure that Lindenbaum introduced this idea.

Attention to the first reason provides the occasion for

defining some terms applicable to the designated elements of matrices. We have just seen that showing that a system S has a suitable matrix does not suffice to show that S is consistent in the sense that not both B and $\sim$B are theses of S. Also having a matrix suitable for it does not show that S is consistent in the senses of not having every wff. as a thesis and not having a single variable as a thesis. But we will be concerned with negation consistency for a system S, viz., not having both B and $\sim$B as theses. If a system S had both B and $\sim$B as theses, both B and $\sim$B would be in the Ds of its $\mathfrak{M}$s. In this case both v(B) and v($\sim$B),i.e.,$\overline{v(B)}$, would be in Ds. Thus a matrix can have both $\underset{\sim}{a}$ and $\overline{\underset{\sim}{a}}$ in its D. If a matrix has both an $\underset{\sim}{a}$ and $\overline{\underset{\sim}{a}}$ in its D, it is an inconsistent matrix. In the case of finite matrices one can tell by inspection whether or not they are consistent. But in the case of a Lindenbaum matrix it is no easier to determine the consistency of $\mathfrak{M}$s than it is to determine the consistency of S. We can, though, show that a system S is negation consistent by showing that there is a suitable consistent matrix for S.

However, it is not only for the sake of consistency proofs that we like consistent matrices. We often want to think of the designated elements as good truth-values, i.e., we frequently want to think of assigning a formula a designated value as interpreting the formula as true in some sense of 'true' or as true to some degree. Correspondingly, we want to think of the non-designated elements as bad truth-values. Thus we like to think that showing that a formula is valid on a matrix shows in some way that the formula is true on all interpretations of a certain kind. Of course, these desires are irrelevant to the mathematical tasks of showing that a matrix is suitable for a system, etc.. These desires, though, are relevant to the significance we attribute to matrix interpretations. So, let us consider features of D which make designated elements into what we can, according to our normative intuitions about truth, call truth-values of the true variety.

If designated values are to be truth-values and $\overline{}$ is to represent negation, we want a consistent matrix. Also we would want a complete matrix. A matrix $\mathfrak{M}$ is complete if for each $\underset{\sim}{a}$ in M either $\underset{\sim}{a} \in$ D or $\overline{\underset{\sim}{a}} \in$ D. Completeness, with consistency, divides the values of M into the designated, the "trues," and the undesignated, the "falses." We certainly want Modus Ponens to preserve truth in the following way: If $\underset{\sim}{a} \in$ D and $\underset{\sim}{a} \rightarrow \underset{\sim}{b} \in$ D, then $\underset{\sim}{b} \in$ D. We also want a conjunction to be interpreted as true if both conjuncts are interpreted as true and a disjunction to be interpreted as true if a single disjunct is true. Our decision in I.6 that we not take disjunctions as a unit leads us to hold that if a disjunction is true, then at least one disjunct is true. So, our normative intuitions about truth, our intended interpretation of the matrix operation signs: $\wedge$, v, and $\rightarrow$, together with our desire that members of D be "trues," lead us to desire that D of a matrix with $\wedge$, v, and $\rightarrow$ be a prime filter. D is a filter on $\mathfrak{M}$ with $\wedge$, v, and $\rightarrow$ if the following three conditions are met. Here $\wedge$, v, and $\rightarrow$ need not be basic.

Conditions for Designated elements to be a filter

i) If $\underset{\sim}{a} \in D$ and $\underset{\sim}{a} \rightarrow \underset{\sim}{b} \in D$, then $\underset{\sim}{b} \in D$
ii) If $\underset{\sim}{a} \in D$ and $\underset{\sim}{b} \in D$, then $\underset{\sim}{a} \wedge \underset{\sim}{b} \in D$
iii) If $\underset{\sim}{a} \in D$, then $\underset{\sim}{a} \vee \underset{\sim}{b} \in D$ and if $\underset{\sim}{b} \in D$, then $\underset{\sim}{a} \vee \underset{\sim}{b} \in D$.

If condition (iv) below is met D is a prime filter on $\mathfrak{M}$.

iv) If $\underset{\sim}{a} \vee \underset{\sim}{b} \in D$, then $\underset{\sim}{a} \in D$ or $\underset{\sim}{b} \in D$.

We also want $A \leftrightarrow B$ to be interpreted as saying at least that A and B have the same truth-value. Thus our intuitions about truth require a fifth condition.

v) $a \leftrightarrow b \in D$ iff. $a = b$.

In recognition of a notion of J.C.C. McKinsey in [1941] we say that a matrix is McKinsey normal if it meets conditions (i),(ii), (iii), and (v). We call a matrix normal if it is consistent, complete, its D is a prime filter, and it meets condition (v).

Shortly, we will note that our intuitions lead us to prefer matrices whose $\wedge$ and v parts form a lattice. First, though, let us remark on the second reason for saying that Lindenbaum's observation is significant.

When the elements of a matrix are formulas it is not plausible to regard the elements as truth-values. Nevertheless, such matrices can be extremely useful for showing that a certain kind of complete and consistent matrix is characteristic for a system S. Call the kind of matrix: K-matrices. Assume that we have shown that every K-matrix is suitable for S and are dealing with the, usually more difficult task of showing that every non-theorem B of S is not valid on some K-matrix. Because K-matrices are assumed to be consistent and complete, we can show $v(B) \notin D$ by showing that $\overline{v(B)} \in D$ where $\overline{v(B)} = V(\sim B)$. So, we want to show that $\{\sim B\}$ is simultaneously satisfied on some K-matrix. A typical procedure, due to Lindenbaum, is to show that $\{\sim B\}$ can be extended to a maximal S-consistent set of formulas Δ. Δ is a maximal S-consistent set of formulas if every theorem of S is in Δ, there is no A such that both A and $\sim A$ belong to Δ, and for every A in the language of S either $A \in \Delta$ or $\sim A \in \Delta$. Then one defines a matrix $\mathcal{K}$ where M of $\mathcal{K}$ is the set of formulas and the D of $\mathcal{K}$ is Δ. The formulas of the language are then given the so-called canonical valuation or interpretation. The canonical valuation maps each formula to itself by mapping each variable to itself. Obviously, the formulas satisfied by the canonical valuation are exactly the members of Δ, which contains $\sim$B Of course, more work still has to be done to show that $\sim$B is satisfied on a K-matrix; one has to show that $\mathcal{K}$ is a K-matrix. It is not a trivial task to show that such a $\mathcal{K}$ is a K-matrix. In II.10 exercises will bring out how J.M. Dunn uses a modification of such a procedure to show that Parry-matrices are characteristic for a version of the system called Analytic Implication.

While we are considering using formulas as elements of matrices it is useful to note that we can use equivalence classes of formulas as elements of matrices to get the so-called <u>Lindenbaum Algebra</u> for a system. Here we will restrict our attention to axiom systems in which $\leftrightarrow$ is reflexive, symmetric, and transitive, i.e., $\leftrightarrow$ is an equivalence relation between formulas. We define the equivalence class of formula A as follows: $[A] =_{df} \{B: \vdash_S B \leftrightarrow A\}$. Define the Lindenbaum Algebra, which is a matrix, as follows. $M = \{[A]: A \text{ is a wff.}\}$ $D = \{[A]: \vdash_S A\}$. The operations are the following. $[A] \wedge [B] = [A \wedge B]$, $[A] \vee [B] = [A \vee B]$, $\overline{[A]} = [\sim A]$, and $[A] \rightarrow [B] = [A \rightarrow B]$. We will return to a consideration of Lindenbaum Algebras when we discuss at the end of III.6 R.Meyer's and R. Wolf's suggestion that an adequacy condition for an entailment system is that the system should not have a finite characteristic matrix. It can recognize only finitely many distinct propostions if it has a finite characteristic matrix!

Several of the matrices which we use have an ordering of their elements which makes them into lattices with their $\wedge$ and $\vee$. So, we characterize lattices and cite some results about them. There is no pretense here of studying lattices; we simply adapt Curry's synopsis of lattice theory from pp.131-39 of his [1963]. Birkhoff [1948] is the standard reference for lattice theory. Dubish [1964], 18.1 and 18.2 of Anderson's and Belnap's [1975], and Szász [1963] are also helpful. Identifying a matrix, or part of it, as a lattice simplifies arguments about the matrix; especially in regard to arguing that a matrix is suitable for a system.

When presenting lattices, we mean reflexive partial ordering when talking of partial ordering. A <u>set M partially ordered by $\leq$ constitutes</u> a lattice with the two operations <u>$\wedge$ (meet)</u> and <u>$\vee$ (join)</u> under the following six conditions. L7 makes it <u>a distributive lattice</u>.

L1. $a \wedge b \leq a$
L2. $a \wedge b \leq b$
L3. If $c \leq a$ and $c \leq b$, then $c \leq a \wedge b$
L4. $a \leq a \vee b$
L5. $b \leq a \vee b$
L6 If $a \leq c$ and $b \leq c$, then $a \vee b \leq c$
L7. $a \wedge (b \vee c) \leq (a \wedge b) \vee c$.

Lattice law L3 tells us that $a \wedge b$ is <u>the greatest lower bound of a and b under $\leq$</u>. Law L6 tells us that $a \vee b$ is <u>the least upper bound of a and b under $\leq$</u>. Since $\wedge$ and $\vee$ are operations on M $a \wedge b$ and $a \vee b$ exist in M for each a and b in M, i.e., any two elements meet and join. Let us further specify that if a partially ordered set M has only one operation, or we pay attention to only one of its operations, and it meets the first three lattice laws, then <u>M is a semi-lattice with that operation.</u>

So-called Hasse diagrams are useful to represent lattices. Let us illustrate uses of these diagrams with Diagrams D1, D2, and D3 below. On these diagrams the arrow represents the transitive $\leq$ and lack of an arrow represents no relation of $\leq$. Thus on D1 below we have: $-3 \leq -1$ and $-2 \leq -1$ but no relation between -2 and -3.

D1

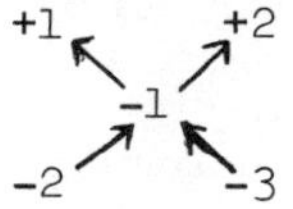

D2

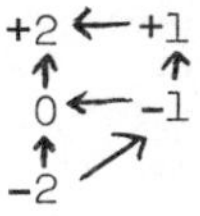

D3

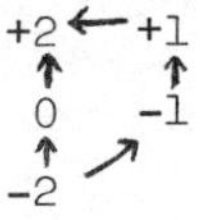

Diagram D1 does not portray a lattice because -2 and -3 do not meet below; nor do +2 and +1 join above. Consider, though, D2 to get a picture of a lattice. Let us use D2 to practice getting a table to represent the operations of a lattice. We compute, from a diagram, the meet of two elements by starting at the two elements and tracing the arrows down until we first meet. Thus on D2, +2 meets +1 at +1 while 0 meets +1 at -1. We compute, from a diagram, the join of two elements by starting at the two elements and tracing the arrows up until we first join. Thus on D2, 0 and +1 join at +2 while 0 and -1 join at 0. Practice on computing meets and joins from a diagram can be obtained by verifying that the following two operation tables list the computations obtained from D2. This little exercise will show how $\wedge$ and $\vee$ tables for a matrix can be read off from a diagram.

$\wedge$	+2	+1	0	-1	-2
+2	+2	+1	0	-1	-2
+1	+1	+1	-1	-1	-2
0	0	-1	0	-1	-2
-1	-1	-1	-1	-1	-2
-2	-2	-2	-2	-2	-2

$\vee$	+2	+1	0	-1	-2
+2	+2	+2	+2	+2	+2
+1	+2	+1	+2	+1	+1
0	+2	+2	0	0	0
-1	+2	+1	0	-1	-1
-2	+2	+1	0	-1	-2

Distributivity is difficult to read off from a diagram. You may have to check through the cases to verify that $a \wedge (b \vee c) \leq (a \wedge b) \vee c$. Here it is interesting to point out that we can get a non-distributive lattice by simply dropping $-1 \leq 0$ from the lattice of D2 to get the lattice represented by D3. One can check that on D3 that $+1\wedge(0 \vee -1) \neq (+1\wedge 0) \vee -1$ and that $+1\wedge(0 \vee -1) \neq (+1\wedge 0) \vee (+1\wedge -1)$. So the matrix whose $\wedge$ and $\vee$ could be represented by D3 may be of interest to those who want to show that Distributivity is independent of some other axioms by showing that a matrix obtained from D3 is suitable for the system consisting of the axioms over and above Distributivity.

Before turning to a discussion of what we will call world-matrices, we simply list some lattice laws from Curry. These laws are especially helpful if we know that a matrix is a lattice with its $\wedge$ and $\vee$. Henceforth, if a matrix is a lattice with its $\wedge$ and $\vee$, we simply call the matrix a lattice. If, in addition, we know that $a \longrightarrow b \in D$ iff. $a \leq b$, these lattice laws enable us to tell at a glance whether certain formulas and schemas are valid and whether certain rules preserve validity on the matrix. The formulas are those obtained by replacing matrix variables with sentential variables and $\leq$ with $\longrightarrow$ of logic and = with $\longleftrightarrow$. Rules come from the 'if_then_' sentences in the lattice laws. In the following laws $a = b$ is $a \leq b$ and $b \leq a$, and * indicates the need for L7.

L8. $a \leq a\wedge a$

L9. $a\wedge b \leq b\wedge a$

L10. If $a \leq b$, then $a\wedge c \leq b\wedge c$

L11. If $a \leq b$, then $a\wedge c \leq b\wedge c$

L12. $a\wedge(b\wedge c) = (a\wedge b)\wedge c$

L13. $a\wedge a = a$

L14. $a \leq b$ iff. $a = a\wedge b$

L15. $a \vee a = a$

L16. $a \vee b = b \vee a$

L17. $a \vee (b \vee c) = (a \vee b) \vee c$

L18. $a\wedge(a \vee b) = a$

L19. $a \vee (a\wedge b) = a$

L20. $a = a\wedge b$ iff. $b = a \vee b$

L21. $a\wedge b \vee a\wedge c \leq a\wedge(b \vee c)$

L22. $a \vee (b\wedge c) \leq (a \vee b)\wedge(a \vee c)$

*L23. $a\wedge(b \vee c) \leq a\wedge b \vee a\wedge c$

*L24. $(a \vee b)\wedge(a \vee c) \leq a \vee (b\wedge c)$

The preceding claim that we can read-off validity results from lattice laws deserves some illustration. Consider $A\longrightarrow .A\wedge A$ and L8 above. On any matrix interpretation $A\longrightarrow .A\wedge A$ goes to: $v(A)\longrightarrow .V(A)\wedge v(A)$. If this matrix is a lattice L8 tells us that $v(A) \leq .v(A)\wedge v(A)$. So, if on this matrix $a \leq b$ suffices to give $a\longrightarrow b \in D$, we have the validity of $A\longrightarrow .A\wedge A$ on this matrix. The converse condition: if $a\longrightarrow b \in D$ then $a \leq b$, is useful for showing that rules preserve designation. Consider L10. Assume that $v(A)\longrightarrow v(B) \in D$ on a matrix. So, then $v(A) \leq v(B)$ and L10 tells us that $v(A\wedge C) \leq v(B\wedge C)$. Then use of the condition: $a \leq b$ implies $a\longrightarrow b \in D$ gives us $v(A\wedge C)\longrightarrow v(B\wedge C) \in D$

In light of the preceding illutstrations we present the following theorem and corollaries. The theorem is of especial interest for the fde. fragment of system E.

Theorem II of I.7: If matrix $\mathfrak{M}$ is a lattice and $v(A\longrightarrow B) \in D$ iff. $v(A) \leq v(B)$, then $A\wedge B\longrightarrow A$, $A\wedge B\longrightarrow B$, $A\longrightarrow .A \vee B$, $B\longrightarrow .A \vee B$ are valid on $\mathfrak{M}$ and the following rules preserve

designation: $A \rightarrow B, A \rightarrow C \vdash A \rightarrow B \wedge C$, (Comp.), $A \rightarrow C$
$B \rightarrow C \vdash A \vee B \rightarrow C$ (or-elim.), $A \rightarrow B$, $B \rightarrow C \vdash A \rightarrow C$;
and if $\mathfrak{M}$ is distributive $A \wedge (B \vee C) \rightarrow . A \wedge B \vee C$ is
valid.

In light of the preceding illustrations a proof can be provided by consideration of the lattice axioms. The transitivity of $\leq$ guarantees the rule of Transitivity.

We draw two corollaries whose proofs are left as exercises.

Corollary 1 of II of I.7: Under the conditions of the theorem if, if $\underset{\sim}{a} \in D$ and $\underset{\sim}{a} \leq \underset{\sim}{b}$ then $\underset{\sim}{b} \in D$, then Modus Ponens preserves designation.

Corollary 2 of II of I.7: Under the conditions of the theorem if, if $\underset{\sim}{a} \in D$ and $\underset{\sim}{b} \in D$ then $\underset{\sim}{a} \wedge \underset{\sim}{b} \in D$, then Adj. preserves designation.

Because the conditions of Theorem II include $\underset{\sim}{a} \rightarrow \underset{\sim}{b} \in D$ iff. $\underset{\sim}{a} \leq \underset{\sim}{b}$, note that the conditions added in the two corollaries are conditions making D a filter. One could formulate theorems to the effect that under the conditions of Theorem II formulas corresponding to lattice laws of the $\underset{\sim}{a} \leq \underset{\sim}{b}$ form are valid and that L10, L11, L14, and L20 give designation preserving rules. Instead, let us turn our attention to what we call world-matrices.

The elements of a world-matrix are obtained from a set of n points or worlds at which formulas are assigned the values T or F, or values from some two member set such as $\{1,0\}$. There may be infinitely many points, but we present this topic as if n were always finite. We take one of these points and label it w_0; and regard w_0 as the first point or first world under a well-ordering of the points. I.e., we talk of the first point w_0 and a next point w_1 and so on. You may want to think of w_0 as the actual world although such pictorial thinking is not essential and may be misleading. Given an ordering of these points there a 2^n ordered n-tuples corresponding to the ways of mapping the n points into $\{T, F\}$; and we can talk of the w_i-place in these ordered n-tuples. These 2^n ordered n-tuples of $\{T,F\}$, or $\{1,0\}$, constitute the elements of a world-matrix. The n points or worlds <u>do not</u> constitute the elements of a world-matrix! The n-tuples are ordered according to the following principle: $\underset{\sim}{a} \leq \underset{\sim}{b}$ iff. every place at which $\underset{\sim}{a}$ has a T $\underset{\sim}{b}$ has a T. The $\wedge$ and $\vee$ operations are defined as follows. $\underset{\sim}{a} \wedge \underset{\sim}{b}$ is the ordered n-tuple which has T at a place iff. both $\underset{\sim}{a}$ and $\underset{\sim}{b}$ have T at that place. $\underset{\sim}{a} \vee \underset{\sim}{b}$ is the ordered n-tuple which has T at a place iff. either $\underset{\sim}{a}$ or $\underset{\sim}{b}$ has T at that place. Because $\underset{\sim}{a} \wedge \underset{\sim}{b}$ and $\underset{\sim}{a} \vee \underset{\sim}{b}$ give ordered n-tuples, the set of 2^n ordered n-tuples is closed under these operations. We now present a useful theorem.

Theorem III of I.7: A world-matrix is a distributive lattice.

For proof we show only that lattice law L7, distributivity, holds. We show that if $a \wedge (b \vee c)$ has T at a place P then $(a \wedge b) \vee c$ also has T at place P. If $a \wedge (b \vee c)$ has T at place P, then both a and $b \vee c$ have T at P, and consequently b has T at P or c has T at P. If c has T at P, then $(a \wedge b) \vee c$ has T at P. If b has T at P, then $a \wedge b$ has T at P because we assumed that a has T at P; and consequently $(a \wedge b) \vee c$ has T at place P.

We often call elements of a world matrix with T or 1 in the first place positive elements; and label them with +m for some integer m. The other n-tuples are then called negative elements and are labelled accordingly. Often the postive elements are the designated elements for a world-matrix;but not always. Always, though, the designated elements D of a world-matrix has the following features.

Features of D of a world-matrix:

i) If $a \in D$ and $a \leq b$, then $b \in D$.
ii) If $a \in D$ and $b \in D$, then $a \wedge b \in D$.
iii) If $a \in D$ or $b \in D$, then $a \vee b \in D$.

iv)If $\rightarrow$ is **introduced** as either a defined or new operation on a world-matrix, we require that $a \rightarrow b \in D$ iff. $a \leq b$. At the end of Section V.1 we will explain why we place this requirement on $a \rightarrow b \in D$. This requirement on $a \rightarrow b \in D$ gives us the following two lemmas whose proofs we leave as exercises.

Lemma 1 of I.7: D on a world-matrix is a filter.

Lemma 2 of I.7: On a world-matrix, if $a \rightarrow b \in D$ and $b \rightarrow a \in D$, then $a = b$.

From these two lemmas we get the McKinsey normality of world-matrices.

Theorem IV of I.7: A world-matrix is McKinsey normal.

Negation $\overline{}$ is not defined in only one way on world-matrices. There is classical negation on a world-matrix. If we use classical negation on a world-matrix $\overline{a}$ is the ordered n-tuple which has T wherever a had F and has F wherever a had T. Classical negation is a special case of negation due to imperfect consistency. We obtain a negation due to imperfect consistency from a one-to-one mapping * of the worlds onto itself so that $w_i{**} = w_i$. Typically $w_o = w_o{*}$; but it is permissible that $w_i{*} = w_j$ where $i \neq j$. Given this mapping $\overline{a}$ is the ordered n-tuple which has T at the w_i-th place iff. a has F at the $w_i{*}$-th place. Classical negation comes from the mapping which sets $w_i = w_i^*$ for all w_i. As we will see, we have classical negation when the consistency is "perfect." We will be especially concerned with non-classical negations due to imperfect consistency. We have such a non-classical negation when there is a mapping * such that for some w_i, $w_i \neq w_i^*$. We say that such a negation is standard if it comes from a one-to-one * that sets $w_o = w_o^*$. We will be primarily concerned with standard negation. (Standard negation comes from normal model structures in the sense of V.3.)

If we say that an ordered n-tuple of T's and F's, or 1's and 0's, is positive if it has T at its w_o-th place and negative otherwise, take all positive elements as designated elements, and have a standard negation due to imperfect consistency; then the resulting world-matrix is normal and its designated elements form a prime filter. This, just mentioned result, can be a corollary of a more general theorem. We may select other worlds in addition to w_o for special consideration. Let us call these worlds selected for special consideration P-worlds or P-points. We can generalize the notion of positive element to: a P-positive element is an element which has T at all P-points. We can generalize the notion of standard negation due to imperfect consistency to: a P-standard negation due to imperfect consistency comes from a one-to-one * mapping such that $w_p = w_p^*$ for all P-points p. (This mysterious talk of P-worlds or P-points may be clarified by Part V where we talk of model structures with several 0-points or "actual"-worlds.) If we now specify that the designated elements are supposed to be the P-positive elements of a matrix, it is fairly easy to prove that such a D satisfies conditions (i) to (iii) for being the D of a world-matrix. This D would also be complete because either $\underset{\sim}{a}$ or $\overline{\underset{\sim}{a}}$ would have T at all P-point places. This D would also be consistent because $w_p = w_p^*$ guarantees that no element $\underset{\sim}{a}$ and its negation $\overline{\underset{\sim}{a}}$ have T at all P-point places. But what about condition (iv) for being the D of a world-matrix?

When we want D on a world-matrix to be the P-positive elements we need to stipulate two conditions on $\underset{\sim}{a} \longrightarrow \underset{\sim}{b}$ to guarantee that $\underset{\sim}{a} \longrightarrow \underset{\sim}{b} \in D$ iff. $\underset{\sim}{a} \leq \underset{\sim}{b}$. These conditions will be better motivated at the end of V.1. Nevertheless we will try to motivate these conditions here. The first condition is that $\underset{\sim}{a} \longrightarrow \underset{\sim}{b}$ has to be so defined that $\underset{\sim}{a} \longrightarrow \underset{\sim}{b}$ has an F at the place of some P-point if $\underset{\sim}{a} \not\leq \underset{\sim}{b}$. What motivates this condition? To say that $\underset{\sim}{a} \longrightarrow \underset{\sim}{b}$ has an F at the place of some P-point is to say that some $A \longrightarrow B$ interpreted as $\underset{\sim}{a} \longrightarrow \underset{\sim}{b}$ is False. To say that $A \longrightarrow B$ is False is to say that in some world A is True while B is False. But if A is True in a world w_i while B is False in w_i, then the world-matrix value assigned to A, viz., a, has T at w_i while the world-matrix value assigned to B, viz., b, has F at w_i; and these are just the conditions for saying that $a \not\leq b$. So, certainly $a \not\leq b$ should suffice for $a \rightarrow b \notin D$, viz., $a \rightarrow b$ to have F at the place of some P-point. The second condition is that $a \leq b$ has to guarantee us that $a \rightarrow b$ has T at the place of all P-points. The motivation for this condition is that an $A \rightarrow B$ should be true if there is no world in which it has a counterexample. Of course, these two conditions are simply requiring that $a \rightarrow b$ be defined so that $a \rightarrow b \in D$ iff. $a \leq b$; so, if we satisfy these two conditions we satisfy condition (iv) for being the D of a world-matrix.

In light of the preceding observations and Theorem IV we get the following general result.

> Theorem V of I.7: If the negation introduced on a world-matrix $\mathfrak{M}$ is P-standard negation due to imperfect consistency and the designated elements are the P-positive elements, then $\mathfrak{M}$ is McKinsey normal besides being complete and consistent.

If there is a plurality of P-points, the D on a world-matrix may not be a prime filter. Consider typical world - matrix elements: $\langle TFF \rangle$ and $\langle FTF \rangle$ from a system of three worlds or points. Let's say that the left two values in the ordered triples come from P-points. Now $\langle TFF \rangle \vee \langle FTF \rangle$ is the P-positive element $\langle TTF \rangle$ and hence belongs to D. But neither $\langle TFF \rangle$ nor $\langle FTF \rangle$ are P-positive elements and hence neither belongs to D. However, the situation is different if there is only one P-point and the D consists of the positive elements. Assume that $a \vee b$ is positive, viz., has T at the w_0-place, and that $a \vee b \in D$. For $a \vee b$ to get T at the w_0-place either a has to have had a T at the w_0-place or b has to have had a T at the w_0-place. So, either a or b is in D if D contains all the positive elements. Hence, we have the following corollary of Theorem V.

> Corollary of V of I.7: If the negation introduced on a world-matrix $\mathfrak{M}$ is standard negation due to imperfect consistency and the designated elements are the positive elements, then $\mathfrak{M}$ is normal.

Some examples of world-matrices to clarify the notion will present matrix tables and lattice diagrams useful throughout this study.

We label elements of finite world-matrices with integers preceded by + and - signs. We always apply the + signs in the same way. We order the n-tuples alphabetically with T, or whatever is used for T, as the first letter and F, or some surrogate, as the second letter. We label the first positive element with +(n-1) and the last positive element +0.

If element a's label is +m we label $\bar{a}$ with -m. However, because we have different kinds of negation, the -m labels do not always have the same referents on matrices with the same elements. Thus we may have two matrices whose elements are the eight ordered triples from {T,F}. On both +2 labels ⟨TTF⟩. But on one, where negation is classical -2 labels ⟨FFT⟩, while on the other, where negation is non-classical -2 labels ⟨FTF⟩ because the non-classical negation comes from a * such that $w_2{}^* = w_3$ and $w_3{}^* = w_2$. Henceforth, we will delete the corners: ⟨ ⟩, from the ordered n-tuples of T's and F's.

Our first example of a world-matrix is the so-called Smiley matrix $\mathcal{Sm}$ adapted from Routley's [1972a].

Example 5, Smiley's $\mathcal{Sm}$,

We have two worlds or points $\{w_o, w_1\}$; so, the elements of $\mathcal{Sm}$ are: TT,TF,FT, and FF which are labelled +1,+0,-0, and -1 respectively. The sole designated element is +1. The elements are ordered as on the lattice diagram D4.

D4

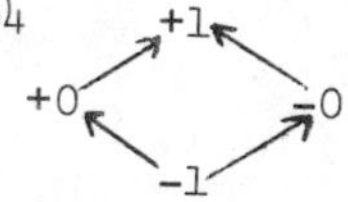

From D4 we can read off the following tables for ∧ and ∨. To insure that $a \rightarrow b$ is defined so that $a \rightarrow b \in D$ iff. $a \leq b$ we set $a \rightarrow b$ = +1 if $a \leq b$ and set $a \rightarrow b$ = -1 otherwise.

∧	+1	+0	-0	-1
+1	+1	+0	-0	-1
+0	+0	+0	-1	-1
-0	-0	-1	-0	-1
-1	-1	-1	-1	-1

∨	+1	+0	-0	-1
+1	+1	+1	+1	+1
+0	+1	+0	+1	+0
-0	+1	+1	-0	-0
-1	+1	+0	-0	-1

→	+1	+0	-0	-1
+1	+1	-1	-1	-1
+0	+1	+1	-1	-1
-0	+1	-1	+1	-1
-1	+1	+1	+1	+1

Negation on Smiley's matrix is not standard. The * mapping is: $w_o{}^* = w_1$ and $w_1{}^* = w_o$. The following tables portray the computation of the negation operation on $\mathcal{Sm}$. We put T in the w_o-place for $\bar{a}$ iff. there is an F in the w_1-place for a on that row. Similarly, we put T in the w_1-place of $\bar{a}$ iff. there is an F in the w_o-place of a on that row.

	w_o	w_1
+1	T	T
+0	T	F
-0	F	T
-1	F	F

—	w_o	w_1
-1	F	F
+0	T	F
-0	F	T
+1	T	T

We will now develop the ∧, ∨, and — portions for matrices with standard negation based on three worlds $\{w_o, w_1, w_2\}$.

If we have the three worlds $\{w_0, w_1, w_2\}$ we have the following eight elements for world-matrices: TTT,TTF,TFT,TFF,FTT,FTF, FFT, and FFF. As agreed upon the first four listed are labelled +3,+2,+1, and +0 respectively. The labelling for the remaining four depends upon the treatment of negation. If we use classical negation the remaining four elements are labelled -0,-1,-2, and -3 in the order listed. Lattice diagram D5 portrays the ordering of the elements when they are labelled according to classical negation.

D5.

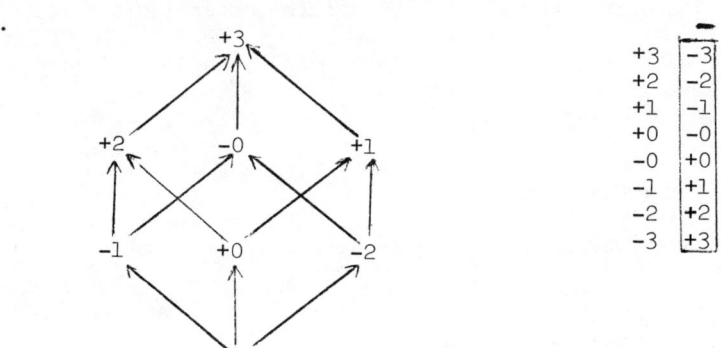

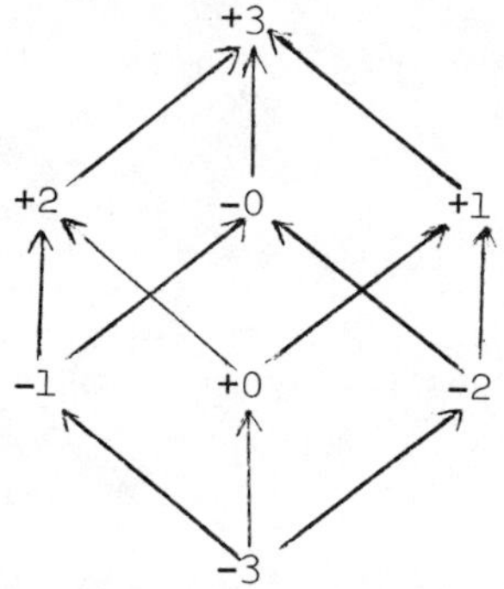

	$-$
+3	-3
+2	-2
+1	-1
+0	-0
-0	+0
-1	+1
-2	+2
-3	+3

Tables for $\wedge$ and **v** can easily be read off from the diagram D5. The negation table is on the right of the diagram. We could have a world-matrix without any $\longrightarrow$ from the D5 operations for $\wedge$ and **v** and the negation as charted above. We also could get what we could call a matrix for classical $\longrightarrow$ by defining $a \longrightarrow b$ as $\bar{a}$ **v** b and taking +3 as the sole designated element. We could call such a matrix $\mathfrak{E}$ c for eight element classical world-matrix. In II.3 we will build a world-matrix for modal systems on the above by treating $\dashrightarrow$ as $\longrightarrow$.

If we switch to a non-classical negation by having $w_0 = w_0^*$ but $w_1^* = w_2$ and $w_2^* = w_1$, we again label FTT -0 and FFF with -3 but we now re-label FFT with -1 and FTF with -2. Lattice diagram D6 enables us to read off the $\wedge$ and **v** tables of Belnap's $\mathfrak{M}_0$. The $\wedge$ and **v** tables are below.

$\wedge$	+3	+2	+1	+0	-0	-1	-2	-3
+3	+3	+2	+1	+0	-0	-1	-2	-3
+2	+2	+2	+0	+0	-2	-3	-2	-3
+1	+1	+0	+1	+0	-1	-1	-3	-3
+0	+0	+0	+0	+0	-3	-3	-3	-3
-0	-0	-2	-1	-3	-0	-1	-2	-3
-1	-1	-3	-1	-3	-1	-1	-3	-3
-2	-2	-2	-3	-3	-2	-3	-2	-3
-3	-3	-3	-3	-3	-3	-3	-3	-3

v	+3	+2	+1	+0	-0	-1	-2	-3
+3	+3	+3	+3	+3	+3	+3	+3	+3
+2	+3	+2	+3	+2	+3	+3	+2	+2
+1	+3	+3	+1	+1	+3	+1	+3	+1
+0	+3	+2	+1	+0	+3	+1	+2	+0
-0	+3	+3	+3	+3	-0	-0	-0	-0
-1	+3	+3	+1	+1	-0	-1	-0	-1
-2	+3	+2	+3	+2	-0	-0	-2	-2
-3	+3	+2	+1	+0	-0	-1	-2	-3

The intended $\longrightarrow$ table for $\mathfrak{M}_0$ is in III.4.

D6 Lattice diagram for $\mathfrak{M}_o$.

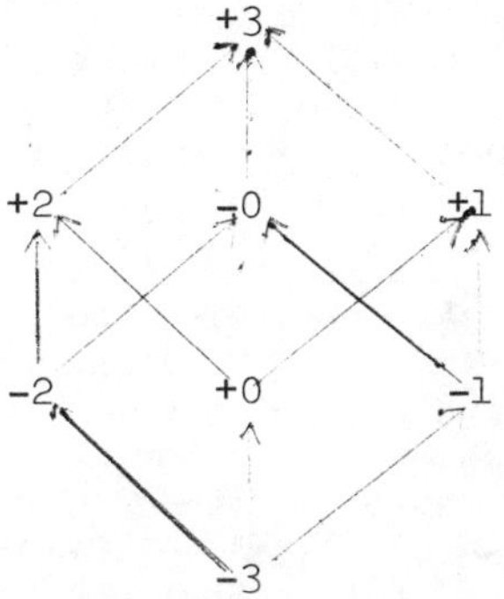

Negation for $\mathfrak{M}_o$.

w_o	w_1	w_2		$-$	w_o	w_1	w_2
T	T	T	+3	-3	F	F	F
T	T	F	+2	-2	F	T	F
T	F	T	+1	-1	F	F	T
T	T	T	+0	-0	F	T	T
F	T	T	-0	+0	T	F	F
F	F	T	-1	+1	T	F	T
F	T	F	-2	+2	T	T	F
F	F	F	-3	+3	T	T	T

We picture how the ordered triples look on the negation table to show how the values in the w_1-place are obtained by looking at the w_2-place and conversely. For instance, consider how we get -1 from +1. To get TFT we put F in the first place because $w_o^* = w_o$. In the second place, the w_1-place, we put an F because we look to the w_2-place of +1 and see a T. In the w_2-place we put a T because we see a F in the w_1-place of +1.

Belnap's $\mathfrak{M}_o$ is presented in several papers; originally in Belnap's [1960a]. It is also presented in Belnap's [1967a], Anderson's and Belnap's [1962a], and in their [1975]. We borrow from R. Routley's explanation of $\mathfrak{M}_o$'s $\wedge$, $\vee$, and $-$ tables from his [1972a].

In closing our introduction to matrices, we should mention that we rarely carry out any of the details of showing that a matrix or kind of matrix is suitable for a system.

Exercises I.7

1. Interpret $A \vee \sim A$, $A \wedge \sim A$, $A \longrightarrow A$, $A \wedge \sim A \longrightarrow B$, $A \longrightarrow A \longrightarrow . B \longrightarrow B$, and $\sim(A \longrightarrow A) \longrightarrow . B \longrightarrow B$ on the matrix of Example 2. Which are valid? Which are satisfiable? Have $D = \{+1, 0\}$.

2. Is the matrix of Example 2 suitable for classical sentential logic with $\longrightarrow$ interpreting $\supset$ and $D = +1, 0$. What if we set $D = \{+1\}$?

3. Are finite classical matrices normal? Do their $\wedge$, $\vee$, and operations form a Boolean algebra with T as a 1 and F as a 0?

4. Show that finite classical matrices are characteristic for the classical tautologies, given that classical truth-tables are characteristic for them.

5. Get tables for a non-distributive $\wedge$ and $\vee$ from diagram D3.

Exercises I.7 continued

6. Consider D5; use it and the negation table to get the $\wedge$, $\vee$, and $^{-}$ operations, let D be the positive elements, and let $\underline{a} \longrightarrow b$ be $\bar{\underline{a}} \vee \underline{b}$. Do we get a world-matrix? We have stipulated that $a \longrightarrow \underline{b} \in D$ iff. $\underline{a} \leq \underline{b}$ as a condition for a world-matrix.

7. Form a matrix $\mathfrak{M}_s$ from the $\wedge$, $\vee$, and $^{-}$ tables for $\mathfrak{M}_0$ by defining $\underline{a} \longrightarrow b$ as $\bar{\underline{a}} \vee \underline{b}$ if $\underline{a} \leq \underline{b}$ and $\bar{a} \wedge \underline{b}$ otherwise and by setting D equal to the positive elements. Make the $\longrightarrow$ table for $\mathfrak{M}_s$ and compare it with the $\longrightarrow$ table from exercise 6 above. On $\mathfrak{M}_s$ which of the following are valid? $A \longrightarrow . B \vee \sim B$, $A \wedge \sim A \longrightarrow B$, $(A \longrightarrow B) \vee (B \longrightarrow A)$, $A \longrightarrow A \longrightarrow . B \longrightarrow B$, $A \longrightarrow . B \longrightarrow B$, $A \longrightarrow . A \longrightarrow A$, $\sim(A \longrightarrow A) \longrightarrow . B \longrightarrow B$. We label this matrix with $\mathfrak{M}_s$ because it is a Sugihara matrix in the sense of II.21.

8. Consider Lattice laws L10 and L11. We want to show that these laws do not require us to validate $A \longrightarrow B \longrightarrow . A \wedge C \longrightarrow . B \wedge C$ (Factor) on all world-matrices. (In IV.10 we give reasons for wanting to reject Factor as leading to violations of the variable sharing condition C7.) Consider $\mathfrak{M}_s$ above. Set $v(A) = +2$, $v(B) = -0$, and $v(C) = +1$. With this valuation is $v(A \longrightarrow B) \leq v(A \wedge C \longrightarrow B \wedge C)$?

I.8 Normal Form Section, systems meeting certain minimal conditions, MA systems, have every zdf. entailment equivalent to certain normal forms; conditions are given for a system to have every classical tautology as a thesis.

At various places in this work we make use of the facts that in certain kinds of system every formula, and especially zdfs., are equivalent to certain conjunctive and disjunctive normal forms. These results are of especial help in our Part II study of Parry's system and Part III study of Anderson's and Belnap's system of Tautological Entailments. In light of condition C13 it is also important to give sufficient conditions for a system to have all classical tautologies as theses. In this Section we, then, specify conditions for formulas to have certain normal forms and for systems to have all classical tautologies as theses. Some useful references for the normal form material are sections 3 and 6 of Hilbert's and Ackermann's [1928,1950] and Appendix A of Copi's [1967].

In the rest of this Section we talk of systems; but it should be emphasized that we are not requiring that systems be axiomatically given. For definiteness' sake, we say that <u>A is entailment equivalent to B in system S</u> if either $A \longrightarrow B$ and $B \longrightarrow A$ are both theses of S or if $(A \longrightarrow B) \wedge (B \longrightarrow A)$, i.e., $A \longleftrightarrow B$, is a thesis of S. <u>A is strictly equivalent to B in S</u> if $\Box(A \equiv B)$, i.e., $A \equiv B$, is a thesis of S. <u>A is materially equivalent to B in S</u> if $A \equiv B$ is a thesis of S. We are primarily concerned with entailment equivalents and not at all with strict equivalents. Our immediate goal is to show that in every system which we call minimally adequate, every MA system, each zdf. is entailment equivalent to a conjunctive normal form as well as to a disjunctive normal form.

An <u>MA system</u> has a $\longrightarrow$, has all zdfs. at least as proper subformulas in its language, $A \supset B$ can be replaced with $\sim A \vee B$, and $A \equiv B$ can be replaced with $(A \supset B) \wedge (B \supset A)$. Note that zdfs. need not be wffs. in an MA system; an fde. system can be an MA system. An MA system also has Rule Transitivity for $\longrightarrow$, viz., R7, a rule of replacement for entailment equivalents, viz., R10, and theses (4) through (13) of C15 together with General Communativity and Associativity for $\wedge$ and $\vee$. It is not required that an MA system have Identity, Simplification, or Addition as thesis schemas! Some additional terminology is useful here and elsewhere. An <u>atom</u> is a sentential variable or the negation of a sentential variable. When we are indifferent as to whether an atom is a plain p_i or a $\sim p_i$, we use $/p_i/$ to refer to the atom. A <u>primitive conjunction</u> is an atom or a conjunction of atoms. A <u>primitive disjunction</u> is an atom or a disjunction of atoms. A primitive conjunction with a variable and its negation as atoms is a contradictory primitive conjunction. A primitive disjunction with a variable and its negation as atoms is a tautologous primitive disjunction. A conjunctive normal form is a primitive disjunction or a conjunction of primitive disjunctions. Thus $\sim p$, q, $\sim p \wedge q$, $\sim p \vee q$, and $(\sim p \vee q) \wedge (q \vee r)$ are conjunctive normal forms but $(\sim p \wedge q) \vee \sim p$ is not. A disjunctive normal form is a primitive conjunction or a disjunction of primitive conjunctions. Thus $\sim p$, q, $\sim p \wedge q$, and $(\sim p \wedge q) \vee (q \wedge r)$ are disjunctive normal forms but $(\sim p \vee q) \wedge \sim p$ is not. A distinguishing mark of a conjunctive normal form is that $\wedge$, $\vee$, and $\sim$ are the only logical signs, $\sim$ applies only to variables, and $\vee$ occurs only between atoms. It is the same for a disjunctive normal form except that $\wedge$ occurs only between atoms. We call a formula, or subformula, with $\wedge$, $\vee$, and $\sim$ as its only logical signs reduced if $\sim$ applies only to variables. We now present two useful lemmas whose proof we leave as exercises except for a sketch of half of the proof of the first lemma.

Lemma 1 of I.8: If F is a reduced formula, F is a conjunctive normal form iff. F has no subformula of the form $B \vee (C \wedge D)$ or $(C \wedge D) \vee E$.

For proof we only show by induction on the length of F that F is in a conjunctive normal form if F has no such subformulas. If F is of the shortest length it has no such subformulas and is a conjunctive normal form because F is a single variable. For induction assume that if reduced F1 and F2 shorter than F have no subformulas of the specified forms they are conjunctive normal forms. If F is of the form $\sim$F1, F1 must be a single variable if F is to be of reduced form. If F1 is a single variable, $\sim$F1 is a conjunctive normal form. If F is of the form $F1 \wedge F2$, the induction assumption, the definition of 'conjunctive normal form,' and the fact that F is reduced imply that F, a conjunction of conjunctive normal forms, is itself a conjunctive normal form. If F is of the form $F1 \vee F2$, F1 and F2 must be primitive disjunctions if F is to be a reduced formula and have no subformula of the specified kind. But if F is a disjunction of primitive disjunctions F is a conjunctive normal form.

Lemma 2. of I.8: If F is a reduced formula, F is a disjunctive normal form iff. F has no subformula of the form $B \wedge (C \vee D)$ or $(C \vee D) \wedge E$.

A third lemma shows that every zdf. in an MA system is entailment equivalent to a reduced formula.

Lemma 3 of I.8: In an MA system the following program applied to a zdf. A and formulas obtained from A by the program produces a formula A^r which is entailment equivalent to A.

Let presentation of the program serve as a proof of the lemma.

i) Replace leftmost $C \equiv B$ in A with $(\sim C \vee B)(\sim B \vee C)$.

ii) Repeat (i) on all formulas obtained by (i) until all $C \equiv B$ are removed.

iii) Replace leftmost $C \supset B$ with $\sim C \vee B$.

iv) Repeat (iii) on all formulas obtained by (iii) until all $C \supset B$ are replaced.

v) Replace leftmost $\sim(C \vee B)$ with $\sim C \wedge \sim B$.

vi) Repeat (v) until all $\sim(C \vee B)$ are replaced.

vii) Replace leftmost $\sim(C \wedge B)$ with $\sim C \vee \sim B$.

viii) Repeat (vii) until all $\sim(C \wedge B)$ are replaced.

ix) Return to (v). If there are now some $\sim(C \vee B)$ begin again with (v). If there are no $\sim(C \vee B)$, move to (x).

x) Replace leftmost $\sim\sim B$ with B and repeat until $\sim$ applies only to variables.

Use of the program of Lemma 3 gives any two people the same reduced form for a formula A. Of course, there are other programs for getting reduced forms, e.g., starting with the rightmost subformulas of a certain type. It is messy to formulate and to prove a lemma that any two such would yield entailment equivalent reduced forms. Fortunately, we do not need to prove such a lemma.

We need two other lemmas to get the theorems that in a MA system each zdf. is entailment equivalent to a conjunctive normal form as well as to a disjunctive normal form.

Lemma 4 of I.8: If A^r is a reduced form of A, the following program reduces A^r to a conjunctive normal form A^c which is entailment equivalent to A^r.

In A^r and in formulas obtained from A^r by this program, replace $B \vee (C \wedge D)$ with $(B \vee C) \wedge (B \vee D)$ from left to right. Repeat until there are no subformulas of the form $B \vee (C \wedge D)$. From left to right replace all $(C \wedge D) \vee E$ with $(E \vee C) \wedge (E \vee D)$ where E as a result of previous work is not a conjunction. Repeat until all $B \vee (C \wedge D)$ and $(C \wedge D) \vee E$ are replaced.

For proof note that the replacements required by the program give entailment equivalents in MA systems; and since the program removes all $B \vee (C \wedge D)$ and $(C \wedge D) \vee E$ from a reduced formula we get, by Lemma 1, a conjunctive normal form.

Lemma 5 of I.8: If A^r is a reduced form of A, the following program reduces A^r to a disjunctive normal form A^d which is entailment equivalent to A^r.

The program for Lemma 5 is as follows. In A^r and in formulas obtained from A^r by this program, replace $B \wedge (C \vee D)$ with $(B \wedge C) \vee (B \wedge D)$ from left to right until there are no subformulas of this form. From left to right replace all $(C \vee D) \wedge E$, where E as a result of previous work will not be a disjunction, with $(E \wedge C) \vee (E \wedge D)$. Repeat until all $B \wedge (C \vee D)$ and $(C \vee D) \wedge E$ are replaced.

The proof for Lemma 5 is similar to that of Lemma 4.

Theorem I of I.8: In an MA system, for any zdf. A there is a conjunctive normal form A^c entailment equivalent to A.

Theorem II of I.8: In an MA system, for any zdf. A there is a disjunctive normal form A^d entailment equivalent to A.

Lemmas 3 and 4 provide a proof for Theorem I while Lemmas 3 and 5 provide a proof for Theorem II.

Let us call a conjunctive or a disjunctive normal form obtained from A by use of the programs of Lemmas 3, 4, and 5 <u>an official left conjunctive normal form of A</u> and <u>an official left disjunctive normal form of A.</u> A few constructions of official left conjunctive and disjunctive normal forms makes it apparent that these forms keep repeated atoms in conjuncts and disjuncts as well as keeping repeated conjuncts and disjuncts. Use of $A \wedge A \longleftrightarrow A$ and $A \vee A \longleftrightarrow A$ could produce shorter normal forms; but we will not use them in construction of normal forms unless we explicitly announce that we will be deleting repeated conjuncts and disjuncts. Use of $A \longleftrightarrow . A \vee (B \wedge \sim B)$ and $A \longleftrightarrow . A \wedge (B \vee \sim B)$ could produce longer normal forms; but these equivalences will definitely not be used because some of the MA systems which we take most seriously do not have these equivalences.

There are at least two types of definition for 'conjunctive normal form of A' and 'disjunctive normal form of A." The first type is system relativized and is based on entailment equivalences in a system S. A conjunctive normal form A^c is <u>a conjunctive normal form of A in S</u> iff. A and A^c are entailment equivalent in S. A similar definition could be given for <u>disjunctive normal form of A in S</u>. The second type of definition uses special normal forms such as official left conjunctive and disjunctive normal forms. As examples of the second type of definition consider the following. A conjunctive normal form A^c is a conjunctive normal form of A iff. A^c differs from the official left conjuctive normal form of A by at most the order and association of conjuncts and by order and association of atoms within conjuncts. A disjunctive normal form A^d is a disjunctive normal form of A iff. A^d differs from the official left disjunctive normal form of A at most by order and association of disjuncts and order and association of atoms within disjuncts. The two types of definitions do have different extensions in some systems. For instance, the system of Tautological Entailments, which we present and promote in Part III, has as theses: both $p \leftrightarrow .(p \vee p) \wedge (p \vee q)$ and $p \leftrightarrow .(p \wedge p) \vee (p \wedge q)$. So by the first type of definition $(p \vee p) \wedge (p \vee q)$ is a conjunctive normal form of p while $(p \wedge p) \vee (p \wedge q)$ is a disjunctive normal form of p. Yet the official left conjunctive and disjunctive normal forms of p are both plain p. Unless we say otherwise we will use the first type of system relativized definition of normal form because such definitions seem to agree more closely with standard usage on these matters. We call conjunctive and disjunctive normal forms which meet the conditions of our example definitions of the second type <u>official normal forms</u>. Note that a formula and its official normal forms have exactly the same variables.

We now give sufficient conditions for an MA system to have every classical tautology as a thesis A sixth lemma reviews an important feature of conjunctive normal forms of classical tautologies.

Lemma 6 of I.8: In an MA system every classical tautology has an official conjunctive normal form in which each conjunct is a tautologous primitive disjunction.

Since a proof of Lemma 6 is easy, we immediately present a third theorem.

Theorem III of I.8: If an MA system which has all zdfs. as wffs. has every tautologous disjunction as a thesis and Adjunction and Modus Ponens as rules, then every classical tautology is a thesis of S.

By way of proof we remark that by Theorem I and Lemma 6 any classical tautology T is entailment equivalent to an official conjunctive normal form T^c consisting solely of tautologous primitive disjunctions connected by $\wedge$. Since by hypothesis each of these tautologous primitve disjunctions is a thesis of S, we can use Adj. to get T^c as a thesis. Then with MP and $T^c \rightarrow T$ we get T as a thesis of S.

A fourth theorem brings out that rather weak conditions suffice for an MA system with Adj. and MP to have every tautologous primitive disjunction as a thesis.

Theorem IV of I.8: If an MA system has $\vdash A \wedge B \rightarrow A$, MP, Adj. and a rule $A \rightarrow B / \vdash \sim A \vee B$, the system has every tautologous primitive disjunction as a thesis.

The proof of Theorem IV is an exercise. Let us close this Section on normal forms by noting that these notions of normal forms can be extended to first degree formulas, fdfs., by including fde.formulas and negations of fde. formulas as atoms. We could define notions such as primitive first degree conjunction and primitive first degree disjunction. We will not develop these notions here.

Exercises 1.8

1. Are any two reduced forms of A symbol-by-symbol identical?

2. Prove Lemmas 1 and 2.

3. With only the resources of an MA system is $(p \wedge q) \vee (\sim p \wedge \sim q)$ a disjunctive normal form of $p \equiv q$? What must be added to an MA system to get it as a normal form of $p \equiv q$?

4. Prove Theorem IV.

5. Develop definitions for first degree conjunctive and disjunctive normal form. See section 19.5 of Anderson's and Belnap's [1975].

PART II

II.1 We devote so much study to fde. systems because fdes. are primary and free from the apparent equivocations in more complex formulas. Belnap's notions of logical signs as: operators, predicates, connectives, or subnectors are introduced. Introduction to Part II,

Our aim in Part II is to present, assess,and to reject several systems of fde. formulas, i.e., fde. systems. As a reminder, we note that an fde. system is a set of theses all of which are fde. formulas. In Part III we present and defend the fde. system of Anderson and Belnap, which is the system of so-called tautological entailments, or as we call it: the TE system. Because the fde. systems we survey are frequently fragments of other systems, we do in Part II present and critically evaluate some full entailment systems. For instance, we study the full systems of W.T. Parry and Sugihara. We also call attention to some systems for first degree formulas, i.e., fdf. systems. However, we criticize systems mostly by reference to their fde. fragment. In this section our aim is to explain why we focus so much attention on fde. systems and to tell how we will present many fde. systems. In passing, we call attention to some illuminating divisions of logical signs made by N.D. Belnap. We introduce Belnap's division of logical signs to discuss use/mention ambiguity problems.

We focus so much attention on fde. systems because fdes. are clearer than any other entailment formulas and they are primary. Their clarity, viz., freedom from any apparent use/mention equivocations makes fdes. such that we can use them even if more complex formulas with a $\longrightarrow$ for entailment are judged to be objectionable. Their primacy makes them such that if we are going to use formulas with a $\longrightarrow$ for entailment, we will use fdes..

As a preliminary to our argument that fdes. are clearer than any other formulas with a $\longrightarrow$, and for their intrinsic interest, we present Belnap's division of logical signs. This division is presented in the Appendix to Anderson's and Belnap's [1975], pp. 473-492; so we will write of it as their division. What we have called logical signs they call functors on p. 475. They define functor as follows. "By a functor is meant a way of transforming a given list of grammatical entities (i.e., a list the members of which are terms, sentences, or functors) into a grammatical entity (i.e., into either a term, a sentence, or a functor). That is to say, a functor is a function -a grammatical function- taking as inputs (arguments) lists of items from one or more grammatical categories and yielding uniquely as output (value) an item of some grammatical category." On p. 477 they go on to characterize four elementary functors. An operator is a functor whose input is terms and whose output is a term. The aritmetic __+___ is an example of an operator.

A *predicate* is a functor whose input is terms but whose output is a sentence. The arithmetic ___ $<$ ___ is an example of a predicate. A *connective* is a functor whose input consists of sentences and whose output is a sentence. The sentence fragments: ___and___, John thinks that___, and It is necessary that___, where the blanks are to be filled with sentences, are examples of connectives. It is important to stress that the blanks are to be filled with sentences if we are to have a connective. For instance, ___and___ is an operator if the blanks are to be filled by terms such as John and Mary. A *subnector* is a functor whose input is a sentence but whose output is a term. Examples of subnectors are putting single quotes around a sentence to make it a term designating itself and placing the word 'that' in front of a sentence to get a that-clause.

We will see that the problems about reading formulas which are frequently called use/mention problems are due to using the same logical sign (functor) in two different ways in the same formula. For example in the formula: $(p \rightarrow .p \vee q) \vee (p \rightarrow p)$, the functor $\vee$ is, as we will point out, interpretable as both an operator and as a connective. It is an operator in its leftmost occurrence and a connective in its second occurrence.

On the author's preferred reading of $\rightarrow$, fde. formulas do not involve any use/mention confusions. We intend to read an fde. $A \rightarrow B$ as the sentence: Formula A entails formula B. It may not hurt to call attention to the obvious fact that if $A \rightarrow B$ is an fde., A and B are zdfs. and not sentences of our natural language. This intended reading distinguishes the functor $\rightarrow$ from the truth functional signs: $\sim$, $\wedge$, $\vee$, $\supset$, and $\equiv$, which are intended to be operators. In fdes. the $\rightarrow$ is a predicate and every occurrence of a truth functional sign is the occurrence of an operator.

We do not interpret truth functional signs in zdfs. as connectives because connectives need sentences as input; but sentential variables are not sentences. Similarly, because sentential variables are the basic items for building zdfs., we do not interpret truth functional signs in zdfs. as the kind of predicate suggested on p. 480 by Anderson and Belnap. For instance __ $\wedge$ __ should not be read as the predicate: __ is true and __ is true because variables, or complexes of variables, fill the blanks. And the variables, and kind of complexes of variables, which fill the blanks in a __ $\wedge$ __ to make a zdf. are neither true nor false. Also because no zdfs. are sentences we do not follow the suggestion on p. 481 and interpret the __ $\rightarrow$ __ in fdes. and elsewhere, as the complex connective: That___entails that___, where the blanks are to be filled by sentences. In III.7 we will expand a bit on reasons for rejecting reading __ $\rightarrow$ __ as the just cited complex connective.

A case can be made that a zdf. A should be read as the term 'the formula A' rather than as 'the sentential form A.' Thus p ⊃ q is read as 'the formula p ⊃ q' and the plain variable p is read as 'the formula p' or even 'the variable p.' Zdfs. are primarily used to represent the forms of sentences; but an assumption underlying formal logic is that we,in a context, can talk about forms of sentences by talking of formulas representing the forms of sentences. In a formal assessment of an argument, we represent what we take to be the form of the argument by presenting formulas which we take to represent the forms of the sentences in the argument. Then by talking about the formulas we assess the argument on some formal standard such as validity. So we prefer to say that in our use of formulas we refer to formulas because it is formulas rather than abstractions such as sentential forms to which we make reference when we use formulas in formally evaluating arguments.

To illustrate the above suggestions about reading formulas: consider: $p \supset (q \wedge r) \longrightarrow .p \supset .q \supset r$. The $\wedge$-sign with variables q and r produces the term 'the formula $q \wedge r$' while the $\supset$-sign with q and r produces the term 'the formula $q \supset r$.' The single variables are terms; so $\supset$ with p and 'the formula $q \wedge r$' and 'the formula $q \supset r$' gives us the terms: 'the formula $p \supset (q \wedge r)$' and 'the formula $p \supset .q \supset r$.' Now the predicate __ $\longrightarrow$ __ applied to these last two terms gives the sentence: The formula $p \supset (q \wedge r)$ entails the formula $p \supset .q \supset r$.

Let us reflect a bit on treating the truth-functional signs (functors) as operators for forming terms for denoting formuals which represent the forms of sentences. An immediate consequence is that zdfs. are neither true nor false because they are terms. For instance, the single variable p is a term for referring to that which we use to represent the form of a simple sentence.; but, of course, the single variable p is itself neither true nor false. Similarly we use p,q,r,$\wedge$,v,and$\sim$to produce the zdf.: $(p \wedge q) \vee \sim r$. But $(p \wedge q) \vee \sim r$ is itself neither true nor false although it can be assigned true or false by familiar truth-table rules. Also the use of p,v,and$\sim$to produce $p \vee \sim p$ does not give a true sentence; but gives instead a term for talking about the form of a sentence which consists of a sentence disjoined with its denial. Certainly on standard truth-tables $p \vee \sim p$ is always assigned True. Nevertheless the fact that $p \vee \sim p$ is always assigned the value True (T) does not make it true. The mere fact that it is we who assign it T or F shows that $p \vee \sim p$ is not true by itself. We are not denying that sentences with the form $p \vee \sim p$ are true; indeed such sentences are necessarily true. Certainly the sentence:J. Carter is the U.S. president in 1978 or J. Carter is not the U.S. president in 1978, is necessarily true. But its form, and terms for talking about its form, need be neither true nor false. We use zdfs. to represent the forms of natural language sentences and structured sets of zdfs. to represent the forms of natural language arguments. Because the forms of natural language sentences are neither true nor false, it is neither surprising nor undesirable that devices for representing these forms and terms for referring to these representatives are neither true nor false. It is amazing though, that so much about sentence forms and the interconnections between sentence forms can be discovered by an analysis of special terms for referring to devices for representing these forms. The zdfs. seem to be pictures of the unobservable sentence forms.

As long as we restrict our formal language to only zdfs. or to only fdes. there are no use/mention problems. However, as we extend our languages problems arise. Let us first consider a language which allows both fdes. and zdfs. but no more complex formulas. Here we have no use/mention problems, but we do have the anomaly that there are two radically different kinds of formulas which can stand alone as independent units, as wffs.. In such a language both p **v** q and p⟶.p **v** q are wffs.. But p **v** q is merely a term while p⟶.p **v** q is a sentence. Still there is no equivocation on the **v**-sign because in both p **v** q and p⟶.p **v** q **v** is used as an operator. Unfortunately, we use the truth-functional signs as both operators and as connectives when we use a language with fdfs.. Consider the fdf.: (p⟶.p **v** q) **v** .q⟶q. The left occurrence of **v** is a use of an operator since it is applied to terms to get the term p **v** q. However, the second occurrence of **v** is a use of a connective because we use it to form a disjunctive sentence from the two sentences p⟶.p **v** q and q⟶q. We say that the left occurrence of **v** is mentioned (talked about) if we read the left disjunct in the disjunctive sentence as: the formula p entails the formula p **v** q. But the second occurrence of **v** is used to form the disjunctive sentence.

Note that to regard there being an equivocation in the just cited fdf., it was not essential that it be regarded as a use/mention equivocation on **v**. If we would have read p **v** q as 'the form p **v** q' we would not be mentioning **v** because we would not be talking about a bit of formal language but would be talking about the form of a sentence. Nevertheless we would be using **v** to form a term on its first occurrence, i.e., using it as an operator,and then using it as a connective on its second occurrence. So the problems are not essentially use/mention problems; they are basically problems of using one and the same functor in different ways in the same formula.

When we move to a full entailment language the multiple uses of the same sign within the same formula become more vivid and more worrisome. Consider the not too complex: ~p⟶.p⟶q. We read this as: the formula ~p entails the formula p⟶q.

Here $p\rightarrow q$ has not been used as a sentence; instead it has been used as a term to denote a formula. Nevertheless, $p\rightarrow q$ by itself is a sentence and it is also a sentence in conjunction with $\sim p\rightarrow.p\rightarrow q$ as in $(\sim p\rightarrow.p\rightarrow q)\wedge(p\rightarrow q)$. So, at least implicitly, some functor has been applied to $p\rightarrow q$ to change it from a sentence into a term when it occurs in:$\sim p\rightarrow.p\rightarrow q$. Immediately, we think of a subnector because subnectors change sentences into terms. But there is no sign in $\sim p\rightarrow.p\rightarrow q$ which indicates an application of a subnector. The left $\rightarrow$ functions as a predicate. The right $\rightarrow$ in $\sim p\rightarrow.p\rightarrow q$ also functions as a predicate to produce the sentence $p\rightarrow q$ from the terms p and q; it is the placement of $p\rightarrow q$ on the right of a $\rightarrow$ which turns it into a term. There is a temptation, which we resist, to augment the symbolism to indicate application of a subnector. For instance, we are tempted to introduce single quotes to mark $p\rightarrow q$ as a term in $\sim p\rightarrow.p\rightarrow q$ as follows: $\sim p\rightarrow$'$p\rightarrow q$'. If we were to introduce single quotation marks in this way, we would clearly have to say that $\rightarrow$ was used and mentioned in the same formula. We may also be tempted to introduce some notation for representing the conjunction 'that' because the word 'that' can transform a sentence into a term. Thus we may introduce a sign th. to get: $\sim p\rightarrow$ th.$(p\rightarrow q)$, which would be read as: The formula $\sim p$ entails that the formula p entails the formula q. If we are inclined to introduce notationfor 'that,' we would have to fault the formula: $(\sim p\rightarrow.p\rightarrow q)\wedge(p\rightarrow q)$ for containing an equivocation on $p\rightarrow q$; on the first occurrence it is the term 'that the formula p entails the formula q' while its second occurrence is the sentence 'The formula p entails the formula q.' The above critical remarks have assumed that a functor should get the same reading on all of its occurrences in a single formula. Should we make such an assumption? Such an assumption requires some consideration.

The preceding observations about possible ambiguities in formulas more complex than zdfs. and fdes. whould suffice to raise worries about the legitimacy of using more complex formulas and to provide contentment with the use of zdfs. and fdes., at least if we segregate fdes. from zdfs.. In III.7 we try to eliminate these serious worries. If we do not eliminate these worries about equivocation, we can still safely have an fde. system. Thus we devote so much effort to discovering the correct fde. system.

First degree entailments are also of interest because they correspond to the argument forms of standard sentential logic which is taught in beginning classes. Hence, our stand on which fdes. are true is our stand on which argument forms of classical or standard sentential logic are formally correct as opposed to being merely formally valid. Thus we devote much effort to the study of fde. systems because it is here where we depart most clearly from standard logic.

We can regard the presentation of an fde. system as a presentation of a principle for selecting a subset of the classically tautologous $(A \supset B)$'s. We are told that $A \rightarrow B$ iff. $A \supset B$ is a tautology and $\mathcal{C}(A,B)$, where $\mathcal{C}(A,B)$ stipulates a condition which tautologous $A \supset B$ must meet to be an entailment. Thus, there are at least two ways to appraise an fde. system. We can appraise the tautologies selected and we can appraise the principle for selecting them. It is occasionally difficult to formulate the $\mathcal{C}(A,B)$ selection principle in a way which admits of appraisal. For several systems $\mathcal{C}(A,B)$ is a statement that $A \rightarrow B$ is a theorem of a certain system, is valid on a certain matrix, or has a certain type of normal form. In such cases, assessment of the $\mathcal{C}(A,B)$ is not very illuminating. In some cases, however, we will find that the $\mathcal{C}(A,B)$ principle is very persuasive; in these cases we critically examine the selection principle. Of course, we need to note that we cannot criticize an fde. system for not having the rules of MP and Adj.; with only fdes. there is no need for such rules.

We now turn to a survey of fde. systems. The first two systems are not really two distinct systems and they are not really serious candidates for entailment systems. They are the systems of classical logic and strict implication. We present them to have them available for later reference and to remind ourselves that the search for an entailment relation is not a search for strict implication.

II.2 Classical fdes. and some difficulties in selecting the classical fdf. theses.

An fde. $A \rightarrow B$ is a classical fde. thesis, i.e., a classical fde., iff. $A \supset B$ is a classical tautology. Obviously, we do not want the classical system because both $A \wedge \sim A \rightarrow B$ and $A \rightarrow . B \vee \sim B$ are schemas of classical fdes.. Since we do not want the classical system of fdes. we could move on to consideration of other systems. However, it is profitable to consider some problems involved in selecting the classical fdf. theses. Such a consideration is profitable because it shows how even a classical logician can distinguish between $\supset$ and $\rightarrow$, calls our attention to variables being used as variables as opposed to not being used as variables, motivates axiomatizing modal logic, and gives further evidence of the safety of using only fdes. Those uninterested in fdf. systems may skip to II.4 because the fdes. of modal logic (strict implication) are the same as those of classical logic.

In the remainder of this Section we evaluate four choices for selecting classical fdf. theses. Because fde. $A \rightarrow B$ is a classical thesis iff. $A \supset B$ is a classical tautology, Choice I is the most natural choice.

Choice I: Fdf. F is a classical thesis if zdf. F' obtained by replacing each $A \rightarrow B$ in F with $A \supset B$ is a classical tautology.

Choice I is too broad. With it we select $(A \rightarrow B) \vee (B \rightarrow A)$ and $(A \rightarrow B) \vee (\sim A \rightarrow B)$ as thesis schemas. But, for a $\rightarrow$ which is at least to symbolize logical implication, these two schemas are totally unacceptable. It simply is not true that for any two zdfs. one or the other logically implies the other; let alone logically implies the other in the best possible formal way.

Perhaps the inadequacy of Choice I is due to not taking $(A \rightarrow B)$'s as basic units of fdfs.. In Choice I $(A \rightarrow B)$'s received values on the basis of A and B in as much as the $(A \rightarrow B)$'s were reduced to $(A \supset B)$'s. So, let us try to treat the $(A \rightarrow B)$'s as units which directly receive a value.

Choice II: Fdf. F is a classical thesis if zdf. F' obtained by replacing each distinct $A \rightarrow B$ in F with a different variable but a variable not occurring in F is a classical tautology; or F is a classical fde. .

Choice II has the merit of distinguishing $\rightarrow$ from $\supset$ because by it we do not select $(A \rightarrow B) \vee (B \rightarrow A)$ and $(A \rightarrow B) \vee (\sim A \rightarrow B)$ as thesis schemas. Unfortunately, our selections by Choice II are too narrow because we do not select $(p \rightarrow p) \wedge (q \rightarrow q)$. Certainly, in an fdf. system we want the theses to be closed under Adjunction. Choice II fails to recognize the true A⟶B as necessary truths and the false A⟶B as necessary falsehoods. Because it is not a contingent matter that $p \supset .p \vee q$ is a classical tautology, it is necessarily true that $p \rightarrow .p \vee q$, where $p \rightarrow .p \vee q$ asserts classical fde. entailment. Similarly, because it is not a contingent matter that $(p \vee q) \supset p$ is not a tautology, it is necessarily false that $(p \vee q) \rightarrow p$. So, we consider a third choice which recognizes the necessity of fdes..

Choice III: Fdf. F is a classical thesis if zdf. F' obtained by replacing each classically true fde. in F with $(p \vee \sim p)$ and each classically false fde. in F with $(p \wedge \sim p)$ is a classical tautology.

We cannot recommend Choice III. By use of Choice II we would select the following formulas as theses: $p \rightarrow q \supset .\sim(q \rightarrow p)$, $p \rightarrow q \supset .\sim(p \rightarrow \sim q)$, and $p \rightarrow (p \vee q) \supset \sim(p \rightarrow q)$. We do not reject these formulas as theses simply because they do not, or may not, conform to our normative intuitions. We reject them because theses should be general principles and the three fdfs. just cited are not general principles. They are not general principles because they do not tolerate uniform substitution for their variables. For instance, consider substituting $p \wedge \sim p$ for p and p for q in $p \rightarrow q \supset .\sim(p \rightarrow \sim q)$. By Choice III we do not select $(p \wedge \sim p \rightarrow p) \supset .\sim(p \wedge \sim p \rightarrow \sim p)$. This failure of uniform variable substitution in fdf. theses of Choice III shows that variables may not be used as genuine variables in some fdf. theses of Choice III. However, in fde. theses which are also theses by Choice III variables are always genuine variables. Thus Choice III forces equivocal treatment of variables upon us. In a plain fde. variables can be uniformly replaced by zdfs. but in the context of an fdf. the replacement does not preserve thesishood. One may be tempted to take the plausibility of Choice III together with its failure as just one more reason for using ⟶ only in fdes.. Nevertheless we submit a fourth choice for selecting classical fdf. theses. This fourth choice does not treat classical assertions of A⟶B as a single unit; it treats them as assertions of logical implication which we can regard as as assertions of $\sim\Diamond(A \wedge \sim B)$, viz., assertions of strict implication.

Choice IV: Fdf. F is a classical thesis if F' obtained by replacing each A⟶B in F with A⥽B is a theorem of one of the Lewis systems, S1 through S5.

At first glance, Choice IV seems subject to the criticism that it should require that the systems of modal logic be systems for a $\Box$ and $\Diamond$ which can be interpreted as logical necessity and logical possibility. Our aim here is not to find the right logic for logical necessity. We can be confident, though, that the modal logic for logical necessity will be one whose first degree is that of the Lewis systems. See Carnap [1947] for an argument that S5 is the logic for logical necessity. Then see Pollock [1967] for proof that most reasonable modal logics have the same first degree as the Lewis systems.

So, in the next Section we briefly survey the Lewis modal systems. Although we do not accept their $A \rightarrow\!\!\!\!\!\exists\, B$ as entailment, it is helpful to have the systems presented for reference. Also consideration of these systems show that a classical $A \rightarrow B$, with Choice IV, is not identical with $A \supset B$, because the Lewis systems do not have $A \supset B \rightarrow\!\!\!\!\!\exists\, .A \rightarrow\!\!\!\!\!\exists\, B$.

Exercises II.2

1. Is $(p \rightarrow p) \vee \sim(p \rightarrow p)$ a thesis by Choice II? What about $(p \wedge q \rightarrow p) \wedge (p \wedge q \rightarrow q)$?
2. Is $(p \rightarrow q) \supset . \sim(q \rightarrow p)$ a thesis by Choice III?

II.3 Presentation of the Lewis modal systems, argument that the fde. theses of the Lewis systems are the classical fde. theses, and observation that no adequate entailment → is strict implication in a Lewis modal system.

It would be preposterous to pretend to give even a minimally adequate survey of modal logic in one section. Here we merely present adaptations of C.I. Lewis' axiomatizations of modal systems S1 through S5, cite some theorems and non-theorems of these systems, sketch the argument that the fde. theses of classical logic are those of these modal systems, bolster the case that Choice IV of the previous section is the right choice for a classical logician, and observe that the strict implication, ⥽, of the Lewis modal systems cannot be an adequate entailment, and adequate → . We frequently call these Lewis modal systems S-systems. Details are in Lewis' and Langford's [1932,1959] and Hughes' and Cresswell's excellent modal logic text [1968].

For the S-systems, the primitive functors are ∧, ∼, and ◇. There is no → as either primitive or defined; the role of → is played by ⥽ . So, when we are discussing the S-systems in this section we call A⥽B where A and B are zdfs. an fde.. It is important to emphasize that (A⥽B) is defined as ∼◇(A∧∼B). Indeed the proofs of some theorems require using (A⥽B) in the basic ∼◇(A∧∼B) form. Because strict implication is defined and hence eliminable from the S-systems, the S-systems are best regarded as <u>alethic modal logics</u>, viz., systems of theses about necessity and possibility. The S-systems do not primarily give theses about strict implication; let alone about that very strict implication which we want to call entailment. One is tempted to say that a sign for strict implication is needed in the Lewis modal systems partly because if only ∧, ∼, and ◇ were used the syntax would be like a mess of worms with all of the negation tildes: ∼'s. In the systems presented below v, ⊃, □, and ≡ have their usual definitions. The rules of proof for these S-systems are Adjunction and Strict Detachment (Str.D) or Modus Ponens for Strict Implication. The following axiomatizations are adapted from Appendix II of Lewis and Langford. We use axiom schemas instead of axioms.

The first seven axiom schemas give modal system S1.

s1. A∧B⥽B∧A
s2. A∧B⥽A
s3. A⥽.A∧A
s4. (A∧B)∧C⥽.A∧(B∧C)
s5. A⥽.∼∼A
s6. (A⥽B)∧(B⥽C)⥽.A⥽C
s7. A∧(A⥽B)⥽B

S2 is S1 plus the S2 axiom: $\Diamond(A \wedge B) ⥽ . \Diamond A$.
S3 is S2 plus the S3 axiom: $A ⥽ B ⥽ . \Box A ⥽ \Box B$.
S4 is S3 plus the S4 axiom: $\Box A ⥽ . \Box\Box A$.
S5 is S4 plus the S5 axiom: $\Diamond A ⥽ . \Box\Diamond A$.

In several systems in which $\Diamond$ and $\Box$ are defined functors while a $\rightarrow$ is primitive we will see axioms similar to the S1 axioms except that $⥽$ is replaced with a $\rightarrow$. Our study of Hallden's S0 in Section II.19 and Sugihara's SA in II.20 dramatize how weak these S1 axioms would be if $⥽$ were primitive. If $⥽$ were primitive, these seven S1 axioms would place few conditions on $\sim$, and consequently, few conditions on **v**. However, because $⥽$ is not primitive, but is defined with use of $\sim$, everyone of the S1 axioms places conditions on $\sim$,and, of course, $\Diamond$.

Below are several theorems of S1. A * by a theorem indicates that the Lewis and Langford proof involved using $(A ⥽ B)$ in its $\sim\Diamond(A \wedge \sim B)$ form. So a * indicates where we have to think seriously about adding new axioms to S1-type axioms for a $\rightarrow$ if we want to build an axiom system for entailment on S1-type axioms, viz., axioms which look like the S1 axioms except that $\rightarrow$ replaces $⥽$. The theorem numbers below are those of Lewis and Langford.

12.1. $A ⥽ A$
12.11. $A \equiv A$
12.15. $A \wedge B \equiv B \wedge A$
12.17. $A \wedge B ⥽ B$
12.2*. $\sim A ⥽ B \equiv . \sim B ⥽ A$ (Transposition)
12.25*. $\sim\sim A ⥽ A$ 12.2 is used to get 12.25.
12.44*. $A ⥽ B \equiv . \sim B ⥽ \sim A$ (Contraposition)
12.6*. $(A \wedge B) ⥽ C \equiv . (A \wedge \sim C) ⥽ \sim B$ (Antilogism)
12.77*. $(A ⥽ B) \wedge (B \wedge C ⥽ D) ⥽ . A \wedge C ⥽ D$
12.77*. $(A ⥽ B) \wedge (B ⥽ C) \wedge (C ⥽ D) ⥽ . A ⥽ D$
16.2. $(A ⥽ B) \wedge (A ⥽ C) \wedge (B \wedge C ⥽ B \wedge C) ⥽ . A ⥽ . B \wedge C$

As we noted at the end of I.6 in our discussion of C16, Antilogism with a Simplification thesis such as 12.17 immediately gives $A \wedge \sim A ⥽ B$. And $A \wedge \sim A ⥽ B$ is unacceptable as a thesis if $⥽$ is to represent entailment or any relevance pre serving implication. So, already we realize that S1 and its axiomatic extensions in the same language are not going to give suitable systems for entailment. However, if $⥽$ had been primitive in the S1 axioms, Antilogism would not have been a theorem as we will see when we extend systems with S1-type axioms.

S1 does have an anti-suppression feature which is desirable for entailment. S1 does not have 19.62 which is a S2 theorem.

19.62. $(A \rightarrow B) \wedge (A \rightarrow C) \rightarrow . A \rightarrow . B \wedge C$

At first glance it seems that lack of 19.62 is very undesirable. Shouldn't a system have and-intro. as a thesis? Perhaps S1 should have 19.62. Nevertheless, consideration of 16.2, which is a restricted version of 19.62, reveals a desirable festure of S1. $(B \wedge C \rightarrow . B \wedge C)$ is, of course, a S1 theorem; but $B \wedge C \rightarrow . B \wedge C$ cannot be supressed from the antecedent of 16.2. This inability to suppress theorem conjuncts from the antecedents of certain theorems brings out a desirable feature of S1 and also S2. It reveals that these systems restrict, to some extent, Suppression of Necessary Truths. Lewis and Langford call formulas which are theorems only if a certain theorem T is conjoined with the antecedent 'T principles.' See Lewis and Langford pp. 147-148 and Hughes and Cresswell pp. 228-230 for more on T-principles.

Antilogism may be paradox producing. Still, Antilogism enables easy establishment of an essential link between the fde. theses of the S-systems and classical tautologies. Start with the following instance of Antilogism:

$(A \wedge (A \rightarrow B) \rightarrow B) \rightarrow . A \wedge \sim B \rightarrow . \sim (A \rightarrow B)$.

Use of s7 and Str.D give:

12.8*. $A \wedge \sim B \rightarrow . \sim (A \rightarrow B)$.

By use of Contraposition, Replacement for double negation, and the definition of $A \supset B$ as $\sim (A \wedge \sim B)$, we get:

12.81*. $A \rightarrow B \rightarrow . A \supset B$.

With 12.81 we get the following lemma.

Lemma 1 of II.3: If $A \rightarrow B$ is an fde. theorem of the S-systems, then $A \supset B$ is a classical tautology.

For proof we only drop the hint that one should show that all theorems of an S-system can be interpreted as tautologies by putting the axioms in primitive notation and interpreting $\Diamond$ as an identity operator.

To complete the argument that modal fde. theses and classical fde. theses are identical,except for occurrence of $\rightarrow$ in the modal ones and $\rightarrow$ in the classical ones, we need to show the converse of Lemma 1. This is not a text on modal logic; so we refer the reader to pp. 218-223 for Hughes' and Cresswell's argument that every classical tautology is an S1 theorem and then to pp. 225-226 for their argument that S1 has a restricted form of Necessitation. This restricted Necessitation is: If A is a zdf and $\vdash_{S1} A$, then $\vdash_{S1} \Box A$. These two arguments from Hughes and Cresswell provide a proof for Lemma 2.

Lemma 2 of II.3: If $A \supset B$ is a classical tautology, then $A \rightarrow B$ is a theorem of the S-systems.

Because we identified $(A \supset B)$'s being a classical tautology with $(A \longrightarrow B)$ being a classical fde. thesis, Lemmas 1 and 2 give Theorem I.

Theorem I of II.3: $A \longrightarrow B$ is a classical fde. thesis iff. $A \rightarrow B$ is a theorem of the S-system.

Theorem I provides the basis for a classical logician to make Choice IV of the previous section. In light of Theorem I, Choice IV gives exactly the fde. theses desired. Because the S-systems give the right fde. theses for a classical logician and because all the S-systems have the same truth-functional compounds of fde. theses, viz., the same fdf. theses, Choice IV seems reasonable for a classical logician.

Let us close these remarks about the S-systems with some more observations about theses and non-theses of these systems. Halldén in [1948a] showed that S1 has the so-called paradoxes of necessity and impossibility as material implications. Lewis and Langford use the S2 axiom to show that S2 has the strict implication versions.

19.74. $\sim\Diamond A \rightarrow . A \rightarrow B$
19.75 $\sim\Diamond\sim A \rightarrow . B \rightarrow A$

Lack of the strict implication version of these two theses does not recommend S1. As discussed in Section I.1, the strict implication versions are desirable for an alethic modal logic. Indeed 19.74 and 19.75 are truisms about possibility and necessity. For instance, 19.74 in the form $\sim\Diamond A \rightarrow . \sim\Diamond(A \wedge \sim B)$, is the contrapositive of the S2 axiom. Certainly, the S2 axiom is a truism about possibility. So, S1 is defective as a modal logic by lacking the so-called paradoxes of necessity and impossibility.

Below are the $\rightarrow$, $\Diamond$, and $\Box$ tables for a matrix which we label $\mathfrak{M}$s5. We use $\mathfrak{M}$s5 to call attention to some non-theorems of the S-systems. The elements of $\mathfrak{M}$s5 are the eight elements for a world-matrix as discussed in association with diagram D5 in I.7. The $\wedge$ and $\vee$ tables for $\mathfrak{M}$s5 can be read off from D5. The negation table for $\mathfrak{M}$s5 is on the right of D5.

These tables were obtained by considering the three point (three world) S5 model structure. (See p. 75 of Hughes and Cresswell for information on S5 model structures.) Here we note only that $\Diamond A$ was given T at a world if A were given T at one of the three worlds, $\Box A$ was given T at a world only if A was given T at all three worlds, and $A \rightarrow B$ was given the value of $\Box(\sim A \vee B)$.

S5's ⥽, ◇, and □ tables,

⥽	+3	+2	+1	+0	-0	-1	-2	-3	◇	□
+3	+3	-3	-3	-3	-3	-3	-3	-3	+3	+3
+2	+3	+3	-3	-3	-3	-3	-3	-3	+3	-3
+1	+3	-3	+3	-3	-3	-3	-3	-3	+3	-3
+0	+3	+3	+3	+3	-3	-3	-3	-3	+3	-3
-0	+3	-3	-3	-3	+3	-3	-3	-3	+3	-3
-1	+3	+3	-3	-3	+3	+3	-3	-3	+3	-3
-2	+3	-3	+3	-3	+3	-3	+3	-3	+3	-3
-3	+3	+3	+3	+3	+3	+3	+3	+3	-3	-3

The designated value for $\mathcal{M}$s5 is +3.

We state without proof the following theorem

Theorem II of II.3: $\mathcal{M}$s5 is suitable for the S-systems.

A proof is facilitated by noting that Theorem II of I.7 holds for $\mathcal{M}$s5.

First we note that the S-systems distinguish strict from material implication. Set v(A)=+2 and v(B)=+1 to get v(A ⊃ B ⥽.A ⥽ B)=-3 and v(A ⊃ B ⊃.A ⥽ B)=-2. By setting v(A)=v(C)=+2 and v(B)=+1, we get -3 for the Exportation schema. Set v(A)=+2 and v(B)=+1 to get v(A ⥽ B ∨ B ⥽ A)=-3. Set v(A)=+2 and v(B)=-3 to get v(A ⥽ B ∨ ∼A ⥽ B)=-3. To get v(A ⥽.B ⥽ A)=-3 set v(A)=+2 and v(B)=+1. Set v(A)=+1 and v(B)=-3 to get v(∼A ⥽.A ⥽ B)=-3.

It is interesting to show that these S-systems do not have strict implication analogues of some theorems of system R of relevance implication. See Section IV 10 for a discussion of system R. These observations help explicate the claim that R is a non-modal system. System R is non-modal at least in the sense that R has theorems which would not be theorems if its → were the ⥽ of the modal S-systems. (The strict implication analogue of a formula in the language for system R is obtained by replacing → with ⥽.) Set v(A)=+2, v(B)=+0, and v(C)=+1 to get v(A ⥽(B ⥽ C) ⥽.B ⥽.A ⥽ C)=-3. So, the S-systems do not have Permutation as a thesis schema while R does. R also has the Law of Assertion; but set v(A)=+0 and v(B)=+1 to get v(A ⥽.A ⥽ B ⥽ B)=-3. System R has the modal reducing A ↔.(A → A) → A as a thesis while setting v(A)=+0 shows that the strict implication analogue of this is not a S-system thesis. A ↔.(A → A) → A is modal reducing in the sense that (A → A) → A seems to be a natural definition of □A.

We abruptly close this modal logic section with an apology for its disjointed structure. We have seen, though, that entailment cannot be strict implication in one of the Lewis systems. In Section II.22 we endorse an argument of R.K. Meyer's that no adequate A → B can be defined in terms of modal notions and the truth-functional signs.

Exercises II.3

These exercises refer to Hughes and Cresswell HC and Lewis and Langford LL.

1. Show that even S1 tolerates a kind of Suppression of Necessary truth by having $\Box A \wedge (A \wedge B \prec C) \prec . B \prec C$ as a theorem.
2. Show that if A is a zdf, A is a theorem of S1 iff. $\Box A$ is. See HC pp. 218-226.
3. Show that $\Diamond(A \wedge B) \wedge (A \wedge B \prec A) \prec . \Diamond A$ is a S1 theorem but that the S2 axiom is not a S1 theorem. See Group V of p. 495 of LL, and p.241 of HC.
4. Show that $A \prec B \prec . B \prec C \prec . A \prec C$ is a S3 theorem but that Suffixing is not an S2 theorem. See LL pp.506-507 and HC 241-242.
5. Define AoB as $\Diamond(A \wedge B)$. (See LL 17.01 and 18.3) Here read AoB as "A is consistent with B' instead of as 'A is intensionally conjoined with B.' In S2 are the following theorems? $AoB \prec A$, $AoB \supset A$.
6. See exercise 6 of Section III.6 for an exercise which brings out that none of the S-systems have finite characteristic matrices.
7. Do any of the S-systems have $\Box A \equiv . (A \prec A) \prec A$ as a thesis?

II.4 1st. Section on variable sharing fde. systems, the V_{fde} systems, rejection of V1.

We now turn to consideration of fde. systems which select a proper subset of the classical and strict fde. theses as the genuine fde. theses. We consider first systems which are given by a $\mathcal{C}(A,B)$ condition requiring some type of variable sharing between A and B. It is natural to begin by consideration of such systems since the most obvious formal defect of both $p \wedge \sim p \longrightarrow q$ and $q \longrightarrow . p \vee \sim p$ is that their antecedents and consequents share no variable. In this Section and in the next three, we criticize a variable sharing condition as being sufficient for selecting the genuine fde. theses. Of course, though, we will keep Belnap's C7 of I.6 as a necessary condtion. Admittedly, we do not survey all possible $\mathcal{C}(A,B)$ requiring some kind of variable sharing. There are infinitely many such conditions. As an example of a variable sharing $\mathcal{C}(A,B)$ which we do not study, consider the following.

$A \longrightarrow B$ iff. $A \supset B$ is a classical tautology and a variable has a negated occurrence in A and this same variable has an unnegated occurrence in B.

Here we consider only the following variable sharing conditions on antecedent A and consequent B. We also call these conditions the principles underlying the systems. (i) A and B have exactly the same variables. (ii) A and B have at least one variable in common. (iii) All variables of A are variables of B. (iv) All variables of B are variables of A. If we stayed strictly with the illuminating labelling practice of Anderson's and Belnap's [1975], we would subscript fde. to names of systems coming from these conditions. However, we simply label the systems V1,V2,V3, and V4, where the V indicates that the system is based on a variable sharing principle. The system V4 is the fde. fragment of Parry's system of Analytic Implication; so our study of V4 provides the occasion for surveying and evaluating Parry's system. Before we begin our critical survey of fde. systems, let us remind ourselves that we cannot criticize them for lacking both MP and Adj. . Fde. systems simply do not have MP and Adj. .

Let us now present and reject V1. The theses of V1 are selected by the following principle.

$A \longrightarrow B$ iff. $A \supset B$ is a classical tautology and A and B contain exactly the same variables.

Condition (i) apparently places a severe restriction on the tautologies. Still Rule Transitivity, R7 of I.6's Cl4, holds in V1. For a proof of Transitivity consider the following argument. If $A \supset B$ and $B \supset C$ are tautologies with exactly the same variables in their antecedents and consequents, then $A \supset C$ is a tautology in which A and C have exactly the same variables. So, despite the severity of the condition, V1 passes the first test for having an entailment functor. Also R3, R5, R8(Contraposition), and R10 hold for V1. Unfortunately for V1, R4 (Consequent Simplification) and R6(Antecedent Simplification) fail. V1 has $p \wedge q \longrightarrow . p \wedge q$ but lacks both $p \wedge q \longrightarrow p$ and $p \wedge q \longrightarrow q$ as theses. Similarly, to get a counterexample to R6, we note that V1 has $p \vee q$---.$p \vee q$ as a thesis while lacking both $p \longrightarrow . p \vee q$ and $q \longrightarrow . p \vee q$ as theses. These counterexamples to R4 and R6, of course, reveal that V1 lacks the Simplification and Addition theses of C15 in I.6. The facts that $p \longrightarrow p$ is a thesis but that $p \wedge q \longrightarrow p$ is not show that V1 lacks the Rule R9 of Premiss Addition. When we consider C16 of I.6, we find that V1 has the desirable features of not having Boethius' Rule and not allowing Suppression of necessary truths. The facts that $p \wedge (q \vee \sim q) \longrightarrow . p \wedge (q \vee \sim q)$ is a thesis but that $p \longrightarrow . p \wedge (q \vee \sim q)$ is not a thesis show that V1 does not tolerate Suppression of necessary truths. Also V1 does not admit a Rule of Antilogism.

Enough has been noted to show that V1 lacks too much to be the fde. system for which we are seeking. Also its principle which requires total variable sharing is not a principle which recommends itself. Part of our ideal of formal reasoning is to get something out of the premisses. Our ideal of a formally correct argument is not that the conclusion should be only a rearrangement of exactly the simple sentences occurring in the premisses. It is surprising that V1 has as many desirable features as it does have, given the apparently severe restriction on variable sharing.

Exercises II.4

1. Is the $\longrightarrow$ of the system given by the condition about negated and unnegated occurrences of a variable transitive?
2. Can V1 be given by the following: $A \longrightarrow B$ iff. $A \equiv B$ is a classical tautology and A and B share a variable?
3. In V1 can we infer $B \longrightarrow A$ from $A \longrightarrow B$?
4. Show that Replacement holds for V1.
5. Do Material Detachment and Hypothetical Syllogism for $\supset$ correspond to theses of V1?
6. Show that Antilogism is not an admissible rule of V1.
7. Does V1 have the following? $A \wedge B \longrightarrow C \vdash A \longrightarrow . B \supset C$ and $A \longrightarrow . B \supset C \vdash A \wedge B \longrightarrow C$? Would these rules be desirable?

II.5 2nd. Section on variable sharing fde. systems, rejection of V2.

In this Section, which is mostly exercises for the reader, we reject the system V2 which is given by the following principle.

$A \rightarrow B$ iff. $A \supset B$ is a classical tautology and A and B have a variable in common.

Immediately we note that Rule Transitivity, R7, fails for V2. V2 has $p \rightarrow . p \wedge (q \vee \sim q)$, $p \wedge (q \vee \sim q) \rightarrow . q \vee \sim q$, but lacks $p \rightarrow . q \vee \sim q$. It is surprising that a system which is based on a principle which is a natural blocking of the Lewis formulas is so immediately inadequate as an entailment system. However, failure of Transitivity is its major inadequacy. Exercises bring out that V2 has the theses of C15 and the rules of C14 except, of course, MP, Adj., R7, and R10 which is Replacement of entailment equivalents. A case in which Transitivity fails reveals the failure of Replacement. Let F(A) be $p \wedge (q \vee \sim q) \rightarrow . q \vee \sim q$, A be $p \wedge (q \vee \sim q)$, B be p, and F(B/A) be $p \rightarrow . q \vee \sim q$. One may readily verify that F(A), $A \rightarrow B$, and $B \rightarrow A$ are theses of V2 while F(B/A) is not. In light of the failure of Transtivity and Replacement, we dismiss V2 as a candidate for the correct system of fde. entailment.

Back in I.3, we discussed the suggestion that we only develop a criterion for selecting a subset of the logical implications as being entailments but that we not demand that entailment be a discursive implication. Despite its inadequacy as an entailment system V2's principle is certainly a candidate for such a selection procedure. Although our goal is not to find such a selection procedure, the fact that $r \wedge (p \wedge \sim p) \rightarrow . q \wedge \sim r$ is a thesis of V2 but is not a thesis of the Geach/von Wright system of II.16 is relevant to those who are interested in finding such a selection procedure.

Exercises II.5

1. Does V2 allow Suppression of necessary truths?
2. Does V2 have Antilogism as a rule?
3. Verify that V2 has R3, R4, R5, R6, R8, and R9.
4. Verify, at a glance, that V2 has all the theses of C15.

II.6 3rd. Section on variable sharing fde. systems, rejection of V3.

In this Section, we give brief consideration to, and then reject a system which is based on a rather implausible principle. The system is labelled V3 and is given by the following principle.

$A \rightarrow B$ iff. $A \supset B$ is a classical tautology and all variables of A occur in B.

The principle is implausible because we simply would not say that an argument lacked formal correctness merely because a simple sentence occurring in the premisses failed to occur in the conclusion. Admittedly, there are defects in Material Detachment. But it is odd to fault the argument: John does not work or 2+2=4, John works, so 2+2=4, on the basis that 'John works' does not occur in the conclusion. Certainly the conclusion of a formally correct argument can be about less than the premisses. So, even if we have to settle for a selection procedure, the principle of V3 will not be the selection procedure.

V3 does have Transitivity and Replacement. So the $\rightarrow$ of V3 is a discursive implication. However, we reject V3 because it lacks R4(Consequent Simplification),R8(Contrpostion), R9(Premiss Addition), the Simplification theses, and V3 tolerates Suppression of necessary truths. In regard to Suppression, assume that $A \wedge T \supset B$ is a tautology in which all variables of $A \wedge T$ are variables of B and that T is a tautology. Under these assumptions $A \supset B$ will also be a tautology in which all variables of A are in B; hence $A \rightarrow B$. The interested reader may determine other properties of V3.

Exercises II.6

1. Verify that Transitivity and Replacement hold for V3.
2. Verify that V3 does not have Contraposition.
3. Does V3 have: $A \wedge B \rightarrow C \vdash A \rightarrow . B \supset C$ and $A \rightarrow . B \supset C \vdash A \wedge B \rightarrow C$? Note that if we regard $\rightarrow$ as the connection between premisses and conclusion, these rules are similar to a deduction theorem.
4. Does V3 have Antilogism?

II.7 4th. Section on variable sharing fde. systems, a critical look at V4 or the fde. fragment of Parry's Analytic Implication, 1st section on Dunn/Parry systems.

In this Section, we critically consider, but do not reject, the fde. system based on the following appealing principle.

$A \rightarrow B$ iff. $A \supset B$ is a classical tautology and all variables of B occur in A.

In this Section, we label the system V4 although it is the fde. fragment of Parry's system of Analytic Implication of his [1933] and [1968]. V4 has to be taken the most seriously of the systems which we have considered so far since its principle seems to express an ideal of formal correctness. This principle is Parry's basic principle of analytic implication which on p. 151 of [1968] he espresses as: "No formula with analytic implication as main relation holds universally if it has a free variable occurring in the consequent but not the antecedent." He also calls this his "Proscriptive Principle." This principle certainly seems to express the ideal that in a really good argument the conclusion should be contained in the premisses. But the best way to evaluate this plausible principle is to evaluate the system or systems developed to accord with it. So, in the remainder of this Section we appraise the fde. system, viz., V4, which comes from the Proscriptive Principle. Then we will consider whether being a fragment of Parry's full entailment system or systems makes V4 more, or less, appealing. Consequently, Sections II.7 through II.11 will be an investigation of what can be called the Dunn/Parry systems of entailment.

Our main objection to V4 is that Contraposition, R8, fails. V4 has $p \wedge q \rightarrow p$ but lacks $\sim p \rightarrow \sim(p \wedge q)$. Of course, V4 lacks the Addition theses of C15. But from our discussions in I.6 recall that we had only weak normative intuitions in favor of the Addition theses. Antecedent Simplification, R6, also fails. The system has $p \vee q \rightarrow . p \vee q$ but lacks both $p \rightarrow . p \vee q$ and $q \rightarrow . p \vee q$. The failure of Contraposition and Antecedent Simplification reveals that acceptance of V4 requires alteration of some strong intuitions about negation and disjunction. Consider, now, some merits of V4. It has Transitivity and Replacement. V4 also has the other rules of C14. Also V4 does not tolerate Suppression of necessary truths. It has $p \wedge (q \vee \sim q) \rightarrow . q \vee \sim q$ but lacks $p \rightarrow . q \vee \sim q$. V4 also lacks Antilogism. It has $p \wedge q \rightarrow p$ but not $p \wedge \sim p \rightarrow \sim q$. So, let us look at Parry's full entailment system to see whether it offers sufficient compensation for V4's failure to give us Contraposition.

Here it is interesting to note that F. Johnson in his [197_] develops a subsystem of V4 by requiring that the antecedent be a consistent zdf. . Johnson gives a normal form technique for selecting theses.

Exercises II.7

1. Show that $\rightarrow$ is transitive in V4.
2. Show that Replacement holds for V4.
3. Does V4 have $A \wedge B \rightarrow C \vdash A \rightarrow .B \supset C$ and $A \rightarrow .B \supset C \vdash A \wedge B \rightarrow C$?
4. Does V4 have the rule: $A \rightarrow .T \supset B \vdash A \rightarrow B$ where T is any tautology?

II.8 2nd. section on Dunn/Parry systems, formal development of the full entailment systems ASI,ASI',AI, a bit on AIN.

Parry's Proscriptive Principle: "No formula with analytic implication as main relation holds universally if it has a free variable occurring in the consequent but not the antecedent" expresses the idea of an analytic implication. In this section we appraise the idea of an analytic implication by presenting, developing, and appraising three full entailment systems conforming to Parry's idea of an analytic implication.

Let us begin by presenting the formal apparatus for these systems. The primitive signs are $\wedge$, $\sim$, and $\rightarrow$. $A \vee B$ abbreviates $\sim(\sim A\wedge\sim B)$, $A\supset B$ is $\sim A \vee B$, $\Box A$ is $\sim A\rightarrow A$, and $\leftrightarrow$ has its usual meaning. F(A) indicates a formula with A as a subformula and F(B/A) indicates a formula obtained by replacing some, perhaps none, of the occurrences of A in F(A) with B. Axiom schemas are labelled with Ap for"Parry axiom" and theorems are labelled with Tp.

Ap.1 $A\wedge B\rightarrow .B\wedge A$
Ap.2 $A\rightarrow A\wedge A$
Ap.3 $A\rightarrow .\sim\sim A$
Ap.4 $\sim\sim A\rightarrow A$
Ap.5 $A\wedge(B \vee C)\rightarrow .A\wedge B \vee A\wedge C$
Ap.6 $A \vee (B\wedge\sim B)\rightarrow A$
Ap.7 $(A\rightarrow B)\wedge(B\rightarrow C)\rightarrow .A\rightarrow C$
Ap.8 $A\rightarrow(B\wedge C)\rightarrow .A\rightarrow C$
Ap.9 $(A\rightarrow B)\wedge(C\rightarrow D)\rightarrow .A\wedge C\rightarrow .B\wedge D$
Ap.10 $(A\rightarrow B)\wedge(C\rightarrow D)\rightarrow .A \vee C\rightarrow .B \vee D$
Ap.11 $(A\rightarrow B)\rightarrow .A\supset B$
Ap.12 $(A\leftrightarrow B)\wedge F(A)\rightarrow F(B/A)$
Ap.13 $F(A)\rightarrow .A\rightarrow A$
Ap.14 $A\wedge\sim B\rightarrow .\sim(A\rightarrow B)$

Ap.15 $A\rightarrow .\sim A\rightarrow A$ i.e., $A\rightarrow\Box A$

Ap.16 $(\sim A\rightarrow A)\wedge(A\rightarrow B)\rightarrow .\sim B\rightarrow B$ i.e., $\Box A\wedge(A\rightarrow B)\rightarrow\Box B$.

The rules of proof are Modus Ponens and Adjunction. Derived rules are labelled with Drp..

In developing systems from the above we follow Dunn's [1972] to a great extent. We call the system developed from Ap.1 through Ap.14 ASI for Analytic Strict Implication. We label ASI plus Ap.16 ASI'. We label ASI plus Ap.16 AI for Analytic Implication. We will see that AI contains ASI'. A textual case can be made that Parry's original system is only the first thirteen axioms and Modus Ponens. Clearly, though, the omission of Adj. in Parry's [1933] was a mere oversight. So, Parry's original system could be regarded as the first thirteen axioms,MP. and Adj.. In 29.6.1 of Anderson's and Belnap's [1975] such a system is labelled PAI. Nevertheless we regard ASI' as the system which Parry originally intended to present. In his [1968] Parry suggests adding both Ap.14 and Ap.16 to what he had in fact originally presented. Still ASI is of some interest because it is significantly weaker than ASI' by virtue of not having Ap.16 which is motivated by modal intuitions. Ap.14 is motivated by intuitions about implication and is needed because we cannot be guaranteed of getting the contrapositive of Ap.11. But it is reading ($\sim A \rightarrow A$) as 'necessarily A' which motivates accepting Ap.16. So, ASI has interest as a system whose axioms are motivated only by considerations of entailment and the truth-functional signs. We cannot regard Dunn's AI as a system Parry presents. Ap.15, in effect, eliminates modal distinctions by yielding $A \rightarrow \Box A$. Parry's addtion of Ap.16 suggests that he wanted modal distinctions. Also at the 1974 St. Louis Relevance Logic Congress, Parry explicitly rejected Ap.15. In 29.6.2 of Anderson's and Belnap's [1975] system AI is labelled DAI to indicate its origin with Dunn. Nevertheless, in light of Dunn's completeness proof for AI, which we sketch in II.10, there is a basis for calling AI the system of Analytic Implication.

For other studies of the idea of analytic implication, see Urquhart [1973], K.Fine [1974], and 29.6.1 and .2 of Anderson's and Belnap's [1975]. Urquhart considers a system which he labels AIN for 'Analytic Implication with Necessity.' System AIN is AI plus S4-ish axioms for a new necessity sign. Urquhart presents model structure semantics for AI and AIN. K.Fine presents model structure semantics for ASI'.

In the following development we borrow heavily from Dunn and K. Fine. We avoid as much as possible use of $\vdash$. Plain $\vdash$ means is a theorem of ASI, $\vdash'$ indicates a need for Ap.16 and $\vdash^{+}$ indicates a need for Ap.15. No mark on a theorem or derived rule indicates that we need only ASI to get it, a ' mark indicates that we need Ap.16 to get it, and a + mark indicates that we need Ap. 15 to get it. We frequently omit proofs.

Tp.1 $A \rightarrow A$

Proof

1) $A \rightarrow A \wedge A \rightarrow . A \rightarrow A$	Ap.8
2) $A \rightarrow A \wedge A$	Ap.2
3) $A \rightarrow A$	MP 1,2

Drp.1 $A \leftrightarrow B \vdash F(A) \leftrightarrow F(B/A)$ Repl. R10

Proof

1) $(A \leftrightarrow B) \wedge (F(A) \leftrightarrow F(A) \rightarrow . F(A) \leftrightarrow F(B/A)$	Ap.12
2) $F(A) \leftrightarrow F(A)$	Tp.1,Adj.
3) $A \leftrightarrow B$	Hyp.
4) $(A \leftrightarrow B) \wedge (F(A) \leftrightarrow F(B/A))$	Adj. 2,3
5) $F(A) \rightarrow F(B/A)$	MP 4,1

Tp.2 $A \leftrightarrow A \wedge A$

Tp.3 $A \leftrightarrow \sim\sim A$

Tp.4 $A \leftrightarrow . A \vee A$

A sketch of a proof is as follows. Start with Tp.2 in the form $\sim A \leftrightarrow . \sim A \wedge \sim A$. Use of Ap.12 and Tp.3 gives; $A \leftrightarrow . \sim(\sim A \wedge \sim A)$. Then use of the definition of **v** and the rule of replacement for definitions gives Tp.4.

Tp.5 $A \wedge B \leftrightarrow B \wedge A$

Tp.6 $\sim(A \wedge B) \leftrightarrow (\sim A \vee \sim B)$

As a hint for a proof of Tp.6, use $(\sim A \vee \sim B)$ in the unabbreviated form $\sim(\sim\sim A \wedge \sim\sim B)$

We present the next eight theorems without any hint of proof because we prove analogues of them for system E in III.2.

Tp.7 $A \vee B \leftrightarrow B \vee A$

Tp.8 $\sim(A \vee B) \leftrightarrow . \sim A \wedge \sim B$

Tp.9 $A \wedge (B \wedge C) \leftrightarrow (A \wedge B) \wedge C$

Tp.10 $A \vee (B \vee C) \leftrightarrow (A \vee B) \vee C$

Tp.11 $A \wedge (B \vee C) \leftrightarrow . A \wedge B \vee A \wedge C$

Tp.12 $A \vee (B \wedge C) \leftrightarrow (A \vee B) \wedge (A \vee C)$

Tp.13 $A \wedge B \rightarrow A$

Tp.14 $A \wedge B \rightarrow B$

Drp.2 $A \rightarrow B, B \rightarrow C \vdash A \rightarrow C$ Trans. From Ap.7

Drp.3 $A \rightarrow B \vdash \sim A \vee B$ From Ap.11

Tp.5,7,9, and 10 give us the basis for the following lemma. We call ASI,ASI', and AI Dunn/Parry systems.

Lemma 1 of II.8: General Commutativity and Associativity hold for $\wedge$ and **v** in the Dunn/Parry systems.

See Metatheorem V of Copi's 7.6 in his [1967] for details of a proof. See also our Theorem II of III.2.

Enough has now been established about the Dunn/Parry systems to justify the next lemma.

Lemma 2 of II.8: The Dunn/Parry systems are MA systems in the sense of Section I.8.

Lemma 2 with Tp.13,Drp.3, and Theorems III and IV of I.8 provides a proof of our first theorem.

Theorem I of II.8: Every classical tautology is a theorem of the Dunn/Parry systems. CL indicates use of this theorem.

A third lemma enables us to draw a useful corollary from Theorem I.

Lemma 3 of II.8: Uniform substitution for variables is an admissible rule for the Dunn/Parry systems.

See p. 80 of R. Thomason's [1970] for a proof which can be taken as a model of how to prove lemmas such as lemma 3.

Corollary of Theorem I of II.8: If A is obtained from a classical tautology by uniform substitution for variables, then A is a theorem of the Dunn/Parry systems.

Let us note that the gist of Theorem I was established by Anderson and Belnap in [1959a]. In that brief paper, they showed that every classical tautology is derivable from finitely many tautologous primitive disjunctions by use of two rules which are derivable in ASI. An exercise brings out their result.

We now present some more theorems of ASI.

Tp.15 $A \rightarrow A \leftrightarrow . \sim A \vee A$

Proof sketch

1) $A \rightarrow A \rightarrow . \sim A \vee A$ Ap.11

2) $\sim A \rightarrow . A \rightarrow A$ Ap.13 $F(A) = \sim A$

3) $A \rightarrow . A \rightarrow A$ Ap.13 $F(A) = A$

4) $\sim A \vee A \rightarrow . A \rightarrow A$ Use 2,3 and Ap.10 mainly.

5) $A \leftrightarrow A \leftrightarrow . \sim A \vee A$ Adj. 1,4 and def. of $\leftrightarrow$.

Tp.15 is undesirable because it suggests that, at least in some cases, the entailment between a premiss and conclusion is the same as material implication. There is in this case of $A \rightarrow A$ a sort of reduction of entailment to a truth-functional notion.

Tp.16 $(A \rightarrow A) \wedge (B \rightarrow B) \rightarrow . A \rightarrow B \rightarrow . A \rightarrow B$

Proof sketch

Use of Ap.11 twice, Adj., Ap.9, and Trans. gives:

1) $(A \rightarrow A) \wedge (B \rightarrow B) \rightarrow . (\sim A \vee A) \wedge (\sim B \vee B)$

By use of Ap.5 (Dist.) and Trans. we get:

2) $(\sim A \vee A) \wedge (\sim B \vee B) \rightarrow . \sim A \wedge \sim B \vee \sim A \wedge B \vee A \wedge \sim B \vee A \wedge B$

3) $A \wedge \sim B \rightarrow . \sim (A \rightarrow B)$ Ap.14

4) $\sim A \wedge \sim B \rightarrow . \sim A \wedge \sim B$ Tp.1

5) $\sim A \wedge B \rightarrow . \sim A \wedge B$ Tp.1

6) $A \wedge B \rightarrow . A \wedge B$ Tp.1

Repeated use of Adj. and Ap.10 on 4,5,3,6 gives:

7) $\sim A \wedge \sim B \vee \sim A \wedge B \vee A \wedge \sim B \vee A \wedge B \rightarrow$
$. \sim A \wedge \sim B \vee \sim A \wedge B \vee \sim (A \rightarrow B) \vee A \wedge B$

The trick of this proof has been to get an occurrence of $(A \rightarrow B)$ into a formula entailed by $(A \rightarrow A) \wedge (B \rightarrow B)$ so that Ap.13 can be used.

8) $\sim A \wedge \sim B \vee \sim A \wedge B \vee \sim (A \rightarrow B) \vee A \wedge B \rightarrow$
$. A \rightarrow B \rightarrow . A \rightarrow B$ Ap.13. We have here $F(A \rightarrow B)$.

Now Trans. can be used to connect 1,2,7, and 8 to get the theorem.

Tp.17 $A \wedge (\sim A \vee B) \rightarrow B$ or $A \wedge (A \supset B) \rightarrow B$

Proof

1) $A \wedge (\sim A \vee B) \rightarrow . A \wedge \sim A \vee A \wedge B$ Ap.5

2) $A \wedge \sim A \vee A \wedge B \rightarrow A \wedge B$ Ap.6

Now Trans. on 1,2 gives the theorem.

Replacement with Dbl. Neg. in Tp.17 gives us the thesis version of Disjunctive Syllogism.

Tp.18 $\sim A \wedge (A \vee B) \longrightarrow B$

Immediate consequences of Tp.17 and Tp.18 are the next two derived rules.

Drp.4 $A, (\sim A \vee B) \vdash B$ Material Detachment MD
Drp.5 $\sim A, (A \vee B) \vdash B$ Disjunctive Syllogism DS

With material detachment and the fact that every classical tautology is a theorem of the Dunn/Parry systems, we have the following classical deduction theorem for these systems. We refer to uses of this theorem with CDT.

Theorem II of II.8: If Γ is a set of formulas and $\Gamma, A \vdash B$, then $\Gamma \vdash A \supset B$. Γ may be empty.

For a proof of CDT consult a typical classical logic text such as pp.231-34 of Copi [1967],pp.32-33 of Mendelson [1964], or pp. 68-69 of Thomason [1970].

Before following Dunn in presenting a so-called Analytic Deduction Theorem for system AI, let us develop ASI and ASI' enough to observe that $\Box A$ for ASI' could have been defined as $A \longrightarrow A \longrightarrow A$ instead of as $\sim A \longrightarrow A$. In his presentation, K. Fine defines $\Box A$ as $A \longrightarrow A \longrightarrow A$.

Tp.19 $(\sim A \longrightarrow A) \longleftrightarrow (\sim A \longrightarrow A) \wedge (A \longrightarrow A)$

Proof sketch

Use Tp.14 to go from right to left. An instance of Ap.13 gives: $(\sim A \longrightarrow A) \longrightarrow . A \longrightarrow A$. Use $\sim A \longrightarrow A \longrightarrow . \sim A \longrightarrow A$, Adj.and Ap.9 to get: $(\sim A \longrightarrow A) \wedge (\sim A \longrightarrow A) \longrightarrow . (\sim A \longrightarrow A) \wedge (A \longrightarrow A)$. Now use of Tp.2 and Repl. gives the theorem.

Tp.20 $(\sim A \longrightarrow A) \longrightarrow . (A \longrightarrow A) \longrightarrow A$, $\Box A \longrightarrow . A \longrightarrow A \longrightarrow A$

Proof sketch

Start with Ap.10 in the form:
$(\sim A \longrightarrow A) \wedge (A \longrightarrow A) \longrightarrow . (\sim A \vee A) \longrightarrow A \vee A$. Use Repl. Tp.19, Tp.15, and Tp.4 to get theorem.

Tp.21 $(A \longrightarrow A) \longleftrightarrow (\sim A \longrightarrow \sim A)$

Proof sketch

Equate both to $\sim A \vee A$ and use Repl..

Theorem Tp.21 is significant in a system which does not have Contraposition.

Some lemmas, proved by Dunn to prove the Analytic Deduction Theorem, also help to prove the converse of Tp.20. The first of these lemmas is interesting by itself; it holds for several systems. Let us call this lemma the Atomic Components Lemma. The following proof is adapted from Anderson's and Belnap's [1959b].

Some notation is useful for this lemma and for subsequent work. Let us use $\bigwedge_{i=1}^{n}(p_i \rightarrow p_i)$ to represent the conjunction of the n $(p_i \rightarrow p_i)$. Let us use Lan.(A), the language of A, to stand for the set of variables occurring in A. Let t(A) be $\bigwedge_{i=1}^{n}(p_i \rightarrow p_i)$ when Lan.(A) $=\{p_1,\ldots,p_i\}$. t(A)=t($\sim$A).

Lemma 4 of II.8 (Atomic Components Lemma.)
If Lan.(A) $= \{p_1,\ldots,p_n\}$, then $\bigwedge_{i=1}^{n}(p_i \rightarrow p_i) \rightarrow .A \rightarrow A$.

Proof is by induction on the length of A. In the basis case A is some variable p_i; so both A$\rightarrow$A and t(A) are $p_i \rightarrow p_i$. So, by Tp.1 we have t(A)$\rightarrow$.A$\rightarrow$A. As inductive assumption, assume that for B and C shorter than A both t(B)$\rightarrow$.B$\rightarrow$B and t(C)$\rightarrow$.C$\rightarrow$C are theorems. In case(i) of the inductive step A has the form $\sim$B. By induction assumption we have t(B)$\rightarrow$.B$\rightarrow$B which use of Tp.21 and Repl. turns into what we want, viz., t(B)$\rightarrow$.$\sim$B$\rightarrow\sim$B. In case(ii), A has the form B$\wedge$C. Use of Ap.9, mainly, gives t(B)$\wedge$t(C)$\rightarrow$.B$\wedge$C$\rightarrow$.B$\wedge$C from the induction assumptions for B and C. In case(iii), A has the form B$\rightarrow$C. Again use of Ap.9, mainly, gives t(B)$\wedge$t(C)$\rightarrow$.(B$\rightarrow$B)$\wedge$(C$\rightarrow$C). Now with Tp.16 we get what we want, viz., t(B)$\wedge$t(C)$\rightarrow$.B$\rightarrow$C$\rightarrow$.B$\rightarrow$C.

A consideration of the proof of the Atomic Components Lemma shows that its proof depends upon no special features of the Dunn/Parry systems. Do not worry about the use of Tp.16 whose proof does involve a special feature of the Dunn/Parry systems, viz., Ap.13. In systems with Suffixing and Prefixing an analogue of Tp.16 is readily available. Also we can note that if a system has Premiss Addition as a rule the hypothesis of the lemma can be weakened to: Lan.(A)$\subseteq\{p_1,\ldots,p_n\}$. The Dunn/-Parry systems have a rule of Premiss Addition.

Drp.6 A$\rightarrow$B $\vdash$ A$\wedge$C$\rightarrow$B

We sketch a proof as follows. Start with A$\rightarrow$B as a hypothesis and use C$\rightarrow$C to get (A$\rightarrow$B)$\wedge$(C$\rightarrow$C). Use Ap.9 and MP to get A$\wedge$C$\rightarrow$.B$\wedge$C. Now Tp.13 and Trans. give A$\wedge$C$\rightarrow$B.

In light of Parry's Proscriptive Principle, we should not want Premiss Addition to hold in the thesis form: A$\rightarrow$B$\rightarrow$.A$\wedge$C$\rightarrow$B. We will see that the Dunn/Parry systems do meet the Proscriptive Principle by not having variables in the consequent of a theorem which do not also occur in the antecedent. So, Premiss Addition is a non-normal rule for the Dunn/Parry systems.

Our next lemma is T4 of Dunn's paper but in the notation of Fine's seventh lemma.

Lemma 5 of II.8: If Lan.(B)$\subseteq$ Lan.(A), then $\vdash$A$\rightarrow$.B$\rightarrow$B.

As proof consider the following. Ap.13 gives A$\rightarrow$.$p_i \rightarrow p_i$

for each p_i in Lan.(A). Mainly by use of Ap.9 we now get: $A \rightarrow t(A)$. The hypothesis of this lemma gives the weaker hypothesis for Lemma 4. So, we have $t(A) \rightarrow . B \rightarrow B$. So, Trans. gives $\vdash A \rightarrow . B \rightarrow B$.

Some more development of ASI and ASI' is needed to get our next lemma, which is K.Fine's twelfth lemma.

Drp.7 $A \rightarrow B \vdash A \rightarrow . A \wedge B$ and $A \leftrightarrow . A \wedge B$

To prove this start with $A \rightarrow B$ and conjoin with $A \rightarrow A$ so that Ap.9 can be used.

Drp.8 $A \rightarrow B,\ A \rightarrow C \vdash A \rightarrow . B \wedge C$

Drp.9 $A \rightarrow B \vdash C \rightarrow A \rightarrow . C \rightarrow B$ A rule of Prefixing

To prove this start with $A \rightarrow B$ and use Drp.7 to get $A \leftrightarrow A \wedge B$ which by Repl. in $C \rightarrow A \rightarrow . C \rightarrow A$ gives $C \rightarrow A \rightarrow . C \rightarrow . A \wedge B$. Now use Ap.8 to get $C \rightarrow A \rightarrow . C \rightarrow B$.

To get Tp.22 below start with Ap.11 and $A \rightarrow A$. Then use Ap.9, Dist. and Ap.6.

Tp.22 $A \wedge (A \rightarrow B) \rightarrow B$

We use Ap.16 to get the next derived rule; so we cannot offer it as a rule of ASI.

Drp.'10 $((C \rightarrow C) \wedge (A \rightarrow A)) \rightarrow A \vdash' A \rightarrow A \rightarrow A$

We sketch the following proof. Use Ap.13 to get both $\sim(A \rightarrow A) \rightarrow . A \rightarrow A$ and $\sim(C \rightarrow C) \rightarrow . C \rightarrow C$. Now, mainly, Ap.10 and Tp.8 (DeM) give $((C \rightarrow C) \wedge (A \rightarrow A)) \rightarrow . (C \rightarrow C) \vee (A \rightarrow A)$. Use Ap.13 to get both $(C \rightarrow C) \vee (A \rightarrow A) \rightarrow . A \rightarrow A$ and $(C \rightarrow C) \vee (A \rightarrow A) \rightarrow . C \rightarrow C$ which with Drp.8 give $(C \rightarrow C) \vee (A \rightarrow A) \rightarrow . (C \rightarrow C) \wedge (A \rightarrow A)$. We connect our results by Trans. to get $((C \rightarrow C) \wedge (A \rightarrow A)) \rightarrow . (C \rightarrow C) \wedge (A \rightarrow A)$, which we label (1). Because $\Box D$ abbreviates $(\sim D \rightarrow D)$ we write (1) as below and an instance of Ap.16 as below.

1)	$\Box((C \rightarrow C) \wedge (A \rightarrow A))$	
2)	$\Box((C \rightarrow C) \wedge (A \rightarrow A)) \wedge ((C \rightarrow C) \wedge (A \rightarrow A) \rightarrow A) \rightarrow . \Box A$	Ap.16
3)	$(C \rightarrow C) \wedge (A \rightarrow A) \rightarrow A$	Hyp.
4)	$\Box A$	Adj.1,3 and MP with 3
5)	$\Box A \rightarrow . A \rightarrow A \rightarrow A$	Tp.20
6)	$A \rightarrow A \rightarrow A$	MP 4,5

Lemma 6 of II.8: If Lan.(A) $\subseteq$ Lan.(B) and $\vdash A$, then $\vdash' B \rightarrow A$

The proof strategy is as follows. By induction on the length of proof of A we show that there is a C such that Lan.(C) $\subseteq$ Lan.(A) and $\vdash' C \rightarrow C \rightarrow A$. Because Lan.(C) $\subseteq$ Lan.(B) also, we have $\vdash B \rightarrow . C \rightarrow C$ from Lemma 5. Trans. then gives us $\vdash' B \rightarrow A$. We assume for all cases Lan.(A) $\subseteq$ Lan.(B) and $\vdash A$.

As the basis for the induction A has a one line proof and hence A is an axiom and has a form $C \rightarrow D$. With Drp.9 we get $\vdash C \rightarrow C \rightarrow . C \rightarrow D$ from $\vdash C \rightarrow D$.

As inductive assumption assume that for proofs of C and D which are shorter than the proof of A, if Lan.(C) $\subseteq$ Lan.(B) and Lan.(D) $\subseteq$ Lan.(B) then $\vdash' B \rightarrow C$ and $\vdash' B \rightarrow D$.

We do not need our strategy when $\vdash A$ has been obtained by Adj. from $\vdash C$ and $\vdash D$. Because we have assumed that Lan.(A) $\subseteq$ Lan.(B) we have Lan.(C) $\subseteq$ Lan.(B) and Lan.(D) $\subseteq$ Lan.(B). So the induction assumption gives $\vdash' B \rightarrow C$ and $\vdash' B \rightarrow D$ which by Drp.8 gives $\vdash' B \rightarrow .C \wedge D$, i.e., $\vdash' B \rightarrow A$.

Consider now the case in which $\vdash A$ has been obtained by MP from $\vdash C$ and $\vdash C \rightarrow A$. Clearly Lan.(C) and Lan.($C \rightarrow A$) are both subsets of Lan.($(C \rightarrow C) \wedge (A \rightarrow A)$). So, our induction assumption gives us both $\vdash' (C \rightarrow C) \wedge (A \rightarrow A) \rightarrow C$ and $\vdash' (C \rightarrow C) \wedge (A \rightarrow A) \rightarrow .C \rightarrow A$ which by use of Drp.8 gives us $\vdash' (C \rightarrow C) \wedge (A \rightarrow A) \rightarrow .C \wedge (C \rightarrow A)$. This last formula with Tp.22 yields $\vdash' (C \rightarrow C) \wedge (A \rightarrow A) \rightarrow A$. Now use of Drp.10 takes us to $\vdash' A \rightarrow A \rightarrow A$. Here $A \rightarrow A$ serves as the $C \rightarrow C$ of our proof strategy. So, Lemma 5 gives us $\vdash B \rightarrow .A \rightarrow A$ from Lan.(A) being a subset of Lan.(B). So, we have $\vdash' B \rightarrow A$.

We present two other lemmas which are, in effect, corollaries of Lemma 6. Lemma 7 is Necessitation for ASI'.

Lemma 7 of II.8: If $\vdash A$, then $\vdash' \Box A$, where $\Box A$ is $\sim A \rightarrow A$.

Lemma 8 of II.8: If Lan.(B) $\subseteq$ Lan.(A), then $\vdash' A \leftrightarrow .A \wedge B$.

Let us now turn to showing that ASI' has the converse of Tp.20.

Tp.'23 $(A \rightarrow A) \rightarrow A \rightarrow .\sim A \rightarrow A$

We sketch the following proof. Start with $\vdash A \rightarrow A$ and use Necessitation to get $\vdash' \Box(A \rightarrow A)$. Use Lemma 8 on this last formula to get (1) below as an ASI' theorem.

1) $(A \rightarrow A \rightarrow A) \leftrightarrow . \Box(A \rightarrow A) \wedge (A \rightarrow A \rightarrow A)$

2) $\Box(A \rightarrow A) \wedge (A \rightarrow A \rightarrow A) \rightarrow \Box A$ Ap.16

Now use of Repl. with (1) in (2) gives the theorem.

Adjunction of Tp.20 and Tp.23 gives the following equivalence.

Tp.'24 $(A \rightarrow A \rightarrow A) \leftrightarrow . \sim A \rightarrow A$.

Let us not regret too much that we have had to use Ap.16 because ASI' is the system which Parry most likely really wanted to present.

We are still on our rather leisurely route to proving Dunn's Analytic Deduction Theorem for AI. But we will first establish some results about ASI' among which is the fact that fde. system V4 is a subsystem of ASI'. So, we have some more lemmas and a bit of new notation. Let us use Th(A) as a term for referring to theorems of ASI' which contain the variables of A.

Lemma 9 of II.8: $\Box A \vdash' \mathrm{Th}(A) \rightarrow A$

For a proof start with $\Box A \rightarrow A$ and get $A \rightarrow A \rightarrow A$ by use of Tp.24 and Repl.. Because $\vdash A \rightarrow A$ we have by Lemma 6 that $\vdash' \mathrm{Th}(A) \rightarrow . A \rightarrow A$, which by Trans. with $A \rightarrow A \rightarrow A$ gives $\mathrm{Th}(A) \rightarrow A$.

We leave the proof of the next lemma as an exercise.

Lemma 10 of II.8: For any Th(A), $\mathrm{Th}(A) \rightarrow A \vdash' \Box A$.

Lemma 11 of II.8: If $\Box(A \supset B)$ and $\mathrm{Lan.}(B) \subseteq \mathrm{Lan.}(A)$, then $\vdash' A \rightarrow B$.

We sketch a proof of this interesting lemma,which suggests that $A \rightarrow B$ in ASI' is a kind of strict implication, by presenting the following pattern. Assume $\mathrm{Lan.}(B) \subseteq \mathrm{Lan.}(A)$.

1) $\Box(A \supset B) \vdash' \mathrm{Th}(A,B) \rightarrow . A \supset B$	By Lemma 9 for any theorem with variables of A and B.
2) $\vdash' A \rightarrow \mathrm{Th}(B)$	By Lemma 6, for any theorem with variables of B.
3) $\vdash' A \rightarrow \mathrm{Th}(A)$	By Lemma 6
4) $\vdash' A \rightarrow \mathrm{Th}(A \wedge B)$	By use of Drp.8 on whatever theorems are referred to in 2 and 3.

Now instantiate Th(A,B) to $\mathrm{Th}(A \wedge B)$ in (1) and use (4) to get:

5) $\Box(A \supset B) \vdash' A \rightarrow . A \supset B$

Use now $A \rightarrow A$ and Drp.8 with (5) to get:

6) $\Box(A \supset B) \vdash' A \rightarrow . A \wedge (A \supset B)$	
7) $A \wedge (A \supset B) \rightarrow B$	Tp.17
8) $\Box(A \supset B) \vdash' A \rightarrow B$	Trans. 6,7.

With Theorem I, Lemma 7, and Lemma 11 we get the result that fde. system V4 is included in ASI'.

Theorem III of II.8: If $A \rightarrow B$ is a thesis of V4, $\vdash' A \rightarrow B$.

We do not have a proof that V4 is included in Dunn's ASI; but this is not too bad because ASI is not Parry's original system. We now develop Dunn's AI a bit.

Lemma 12 of II.8: If $\mathrm{Lan.}(A) \subseteq \mathrm{Lan.}(B)$, then $\vdash^{\pm} A \supset . B \rightarrow A$.

To prove this lemma start with A as a hypothesis for use of CDT. With Ap.15 and MP we get $A \vdash^{\pm} {\sim}A \rightarrow A$ which with Tp.24 gives $A \vdash^{\pm} A \rightarrow A \rightarrow A$. By Lemma 5, $\mathrm{Lan.}(A) \subseteq \mathrm{Lan.}(B)$ gives $\vdash B \rightarrow . A \rightarrow A$. Hence, with Trans. we get $A \vdash^{\pm} B \rightarrow A$. Now CDT gives $\vdash^{\pm} A \supset . B \rightarrow A$.

Our next theorem is the long delayed Analytic Deduction

Theorem for AI. Observe that we do not use lemmas whose proof involved Ap.16. We do use Drp.11 below.

Drp.11 $A \rightarrow . A \supset B \vdash A \rightarrow B$

Theorem IV of II.8: If Lan.(B) $\subseteq$ Lan.(A) and $\Gamma, A \vdash^{\pm} B$, then $\Gamma \vdash^{\pm} A \rightarrow B$, where Γ is a set of formulas which may be empty.

To prove this start with $\Gamma, A \vdash^{\pm} B$ and use CDT to get $\Gamma \vdash^{\pm} A \supset B$. Because Lan.(B) $\subseteq$ Lan.(A), Lan.($A \supset B$) $\subseteq$ Lan.(A). So. Lemma 12 gives $\vdash^{\pm} (A \supset B) \supset . A \rightarrow . A \supset B$. So, by MP with $\Gamma \vdash^{\pm} A \supset B$ we get $\Gamma \vdash^{\pm} A \rightarrow . A \supset B$. Now use of Drp.11 gives $\Gamma \vdash^{\pm} A \rightarrow B$.

As our first use of ADT let us follow Urquhart in [1973] **in** showing that ASI' is a subsystem of AI by showing that Ap.16 is a theorem of AI.

Theorem V of II.8: ASI' is a subsystem of AI.

As proof we present the following deduction in AI.

1)	$(\sim A \rightarrow A) \wedge (A \rightarrow B), \sim B \vdash \sim B$	$\Gamma, B \vdash B$
2)	$(\sim A \rightarrow A) \wedge (A \rightarrow B), \sim B \vdash A \vee B$	Simp.,Ap.11
3)	$(\sim A \rightarrow A) \wedge (A \rightarrow B), \sim B \vdash (\sim A \vee B) \wedge \sim B$	Adj. 1,2
4)	$(\sim A \rightarrow A) \wedge (A \rightarrow B), \sim B \vdash \sim A$	DS on 3
5)	$(\sim A \rightarrow A) \wedge (A \rightarrow B), \sim B \vdash \sim A \rightarrow A$	Simp.
6)	$(\sim A \rightarrow A) \wedge (A \rightarrow B), \sim B \vdash A$	MP 4,5
7)	$(\sim A \rightarrow A) \wedge (A \rightarrow B), \sim B \vdash A \rightarrow B$	Simp.
8)	$(\sim A \rightarrow A) \wedge (A \rightarrow B), \sim B \vdash B$	MP 6,7
9)	$(\sim A \rightarrow A) \wedge (A \rightarrow B) \vdash^{\pm} \sim B \rightarrow B$	ADT on 8
10)	$\vdash^{\pm} (\sim A \rightarrow A) \wedge (A \rightarrow B) \rightarrow . \sim B \rightarrow B$	ADT on 9.

This deduction has some interest because it shows how we can work in AI without Modus Tollens.

Theorem III tells us that we have the following corollary.

Corollary of V of II.8: Fde. system V4 is included in AI.

Before presenting some more theorems of AI and ASI', it will help to show that ASI' has what we call an Entailment Theorem. A value of showing that ASI' has an entailment theorem is that when we use ADT in a proof, and the Γ is empty, we establish the theorem for ASI' as well as for AI.

Theorem VI of II.8: If Lan.(B) $\subseteq$ (Lan.(A_1) $\cup , \ldots , \cup$ Lan.(A_n)) and $A_1, \ldots, A_n \vdash B$, then $\vdash A_1 \wedge , \ldots , \wedge A_n \rightarrow B$.

As proof we offer the following. Assume the hypothesis and observe that by CDT we have: $\vdash A_1 \wedge , \ldots , \wedge A_n \supset B$. Use Necessitation, Lemma 7, to get $\vdash \Box (A_1 \wedge , \ldots , \wedge A_n \supset B)$. Now Lemma 11 tells us that we have $\vdash A_1 \wedge , \ldots , \wedge A_n \rightarrow B$.

When we use, or need to use, only the Entailment Theorem, we cite Ent'.

Tp.'25 $\vdash A\wedge B \rightarrow .A \vee \sim B$

Proof sketch

1) $A\wedge B$	Hyp.
2) $A\wedge B \rightarrow A$	Tp.13
3) A	MP 1,2
4) $A \supset .A \vee \sim B$	CL Theorem I
5) $A \vee \sim B$	MD 3,4
6) $A\wedge B \rightarrow .A \vee \sim B$	ENT' 1 to 5

Similarly, we have the following.

Tp.'26 $A\wedge B \rightarrow .A \vee B$

Tp.'27 $A\wedge B \rightarrow .\sim A \vee B$

If A is necessarily true and entails B, should $\sim A$ entail $\sim B$? Consider the next theorem!

Tp.'28 $\Box A\wedge(A \rightarrow B) \rightarrow .\sim A \rightarrow \sim B$

Proof sketch

1) $\Box A$	Hyp.
2) $A \rightarrow B$	Hyp.
3) $\sim A \rightarrow A$	Def. of on 1.
4) $\sim A \rightarrow B$	Trans. 3,2
5) $\sim A \rightarrow .A\wedge B$	Drp. 8 on 3,4
6) $\sim A \rightarrow .A \vee \sim B$	5 with Tp.25
7) $\sim A \rightarrow .\sim A\wedge(A \vee \sim B)$	6, $\sim A \rightarrow \sim A$ with Drp.8.
8) $\sim A \rightarrow .\sim B$	MD on consequent of 7.
9) $\Box A\wedge(A \rightarrow B) \rightarrow .\sim A \rightarrow \sim B$	ENT' 1 to 8

We can use ENT' because Lan.$(\sim A \rightarrow \sim B)$ is included in Lan.$(\Box A\wedge(A \rightarrow B))$.

Because AI has $A \rightarrow .\sim A \rightarrow A$ we can weaken the antecedent of Tp.28 from $\Box A\wedge(A \rightarrow B)$ to mere $A\wedge(A \rightarrow B)$ to get the following unintuitive theorem of AI.

Tp.+29 $A\wedge(A \rightarrow B) \rightarrow .\sim A \rightarrow \sim B$

Let us present a few more theorems of ASI' and AI before commenting on their unintuitive character as theses about entailment. If we use Tp. 26 rather than Tp.25 in the proofs of Tp.28 and Tp.29 we get Tp.30 and Tp.31.

Tp.'30 $\Box A\wedge(A \rightarrow B) \rightarrow .\sim A \rightarrow B$

Tp.+31 $A\wedge(A \rightarrow B) \rightarrow .\sim A \rightarrow B$

As corollaries of Tp.29 and Tp.31 we have the following.

Tp.+32 $(A\wedge B)\wedge(A \rightarrow B) \rightarrow .\sim A \rightarrow \sim B$

Tp.+33 $(A\wedge B)\wedge(A \rightarrow B) \rightarrow .\sim A \rightarrow B$

Tp.+34 $(\sim A\wedge \sim B)\wedge(A \rightarrow B) \rightarrow .A \rightarrow B$

The next AI theorem does seem to express a somewhat odd claim.

Tp.[+] 35 $\sim A \wedge (A \longrightarrow B) \longrightarrow . A \longrightarrow \sim B$

Proof sketch

1)	$\sim A$	Hyp.
2)	$A \longrightarrow B$	Hyp.
3)	$\sim A \supset . \sim (A \wedge B)$	CL
4)	$\sim (A \wedge B)$	MD 1,3
5)	$\sim (A \wedge B) \longrightarrow . (A \wedge B) \longrightarrow \sim (A \wedge B)$	Ap.15
6)	$A \wedge B \longrightarrow . \sim (A \wedge B)$	MP 4,5
7)	$A \longrightarrow . A \wedge B$	From 2 with $A \longrightarrow A$, Drp.8
8)	$A \longrightarrow . \sim (A \wedge B)$	Trans. 7,6
9)	$A \longrightarrow . \sim A \vee \sim B$	De.M on 8
10)	$A \longrightarrow . A \wedge (\sim A \vee \sim B)$	From 9 with $A \longrightarrow A$, Drp.8
11)	$A \longrightarrow \sim B$	MD on consequent of 10
12	$A \wedge (A \longrightarrow B) \longrightarrow . A \longrightarrow . \sim B$	Ent' 1 to 11.

Use Drp.8 with Tp.35 and $\sim A \wedge (A \longrightarrow B) \longrightarrow . A \longrightarrow B$ to get the next theorem.

Tp.[+]36 $\sim A \wedge (A \longrightarrow B) \longrightarrow . A \longrightarrow . B \wedge \sim B$

Use of Ap. 15 can be eliminated from the proof of Tp.35 if we have $\Box A \wedge \Box B$ as part of the antecedent. So, we have the next theorem for ASI'.

Tp.'37 $(\Box A \wedge \Box B) \wedge \sim A \wedge (A \longrightarrow B) \longrightarrow . A \longrightarrow \sim B$

The reader can develop a proof of the next theorem from that for Tp.35.

Tp.[+] 38 $\sim B \wedge (A \longrightarrow B) \longrightarrow . A \longrightarrow \sim B$

The unintuitive character of several of the theorems from 29 on is due to the fact that they suggest that so much can be concluded from the denial of the antecedent of an entailment. Theorem Tp.29 is the worst offender because it seems to express explicitly a fallacy of denying the antecedent. Admittedly the ASI' theorems are not too odd when $\Box A$ is spelled out as $\sim A \longrightarrow A$, e.g., Tp.30 merely becomes a use of Trans.. So, it may be that AI's identification of A with $\Box A$ <u>via</u> Ap.15 is troublesome. Let us confirm this suspicion by observing that AI has genuine paradoxes of impossibility and necessity. (Recall the I.1 discussion of such paradoxes.)

Theorem VII of II.8: If Lan.(B) $\subseteq$ Lan.(A), then $\vdash^{\pm} \Box \sim A \longrightarrow . A \longrightarrow B$.

To prove this start with $\sim A \longrightarrow A$, i.e., $\Box A$, and A as hypotheses; use MP and Adj. to get $A \wedge \sim A$ which with $A \wedge \sim A \supset B$ gives B by MD. Two uses of ADT give the theorem.

Of course, AI has Tp.39 below. So, we have the following corollary which gives a paradox of analytic implication in AI.

Corollary of VII of II.8: If Lan.(B) $\subseteq$ Lan.(A), then
$\vdash^{\pm} \sim A \rightarrow . A \rightarrow B$

Tp.$^{+}$39 $\Box\sim A \leftrightarrow \sim A$ and $\Box A \leftrightarrow A$

Theorem VIII of II.8: If Lan.(B) = Lan.(A), then
$\vdash^{\pm} \Box A \rightarrow . B \rightarrow A$.

To prove this start with $\Box$A and B as hypotheses for ADT. With Tp.39 and $\Box$A we get A which with B by ADT gives $B \rightarrow A$. Another use of ADT gives $\Box A \rightarrow . B \rightarrow A$.

Corollary of VIII of II.8: If Lan.(B) = Lan.(A),then
$\vdash^{\pm} A \rightarrow . B \rightarrow A$.

So, certainly AI does not seem to be a very attractive system. We can also get metalinguistic analogues of Theorems VII and VIII for ASI'; and hence find a type of paradox of impossibility and necessity for ASI'. The analogues are found by comparing $\vdash' \sim A$ with $\Box\sim A$ and $\vdash' A$ with $\Box$A. Lemma 6 is thus the analogue of Theorem VIII.

Theorem IX of II.8: If Lan.(B) $\subseteq$ Lan.(A) and $\vdash' \sim A$, then
$\vdash' A \rightarrow B$.

To prove this start with A which with $\vdash' \sim A$ gives $A \wedge \sim A$. By CL we have $A \wedge \sim A \supset B$ which with MD gives B. So, use of Ent' gives $\vdash' A \rightarrow B$.

With Theorems VII and VIII and their corollaries we readily obtain theorems such as 40 and 41 below.

Tp.$^{+}$40 $(\sim A \vee \sim B) \rightarrow . A \wedge B \rightarrow . \sim B$
Tp.$^{+}$41 $A \wedge B \rightarrow . (\sim A \vee \sim B) \rightarrow A$

Doesn't it seem odd to say that from $(\sim A \vee \sim B)$ we can get a formally correct argument that there is a formally correct argument that there is a formally correct argument from $A \wedge B$ to $\sim B$? Similar considerations cast considerable doubt on Tp.41 as a thesis about entailment. But these are only more doubts about the dubious AI. However, Theorem IX together with the fact that $\sim((A \wedge \sim A) \wedge \sim B)$ is by CL a theorem of the Dunn/Parry systems gives Tp.42.

Tp.'42 $(A \wedge \sim A) \wedge \sim B \rightarrow B$

Tp.42 is almost as bad as $A \wedge \sim A \rightarrow B$ as a thesis about entailment. To be sure Tp.42 does not sanction as formally correct arguments in which the premisses are totally irrelevant to the conclusion. Nevertheless, as consideration of the proof of Theorem IX reveals, Tp.42 sanctions as formally correct arguments in which the conclusion B was obtained from the totally irrelevant $A \wedge \sim A$. The unused $\sim B$ is placed in the premisses only to satisfy the variable sharing relevance condition; $\sim B$ plays no part in getting B. Lemma 6 also gives some theorems which meet the variable sharing condition but which have consequents not really obtained from the antecedent. For instance, take an axiom as the consequent and put the conjunction of the negation of the variables occuring in it as the antecedent. Thus, $\sim A \longrightarrow . A \longrightarrow . \sim\sim A$ is a theorem of ASI'. But we do not use $\sim A$ to get this half of Double Negation.

We should note that, although, conjoing to $A \wedge \sim A$ any formula C with all of the variables of B gives $(A \wedge \sim A) \wedge C \longrightarrow B$ for ASI' and AI, we do not have this result for Dunn's ASI. Indeed, as admitted earlier, we do not have a proof that fde. system V4 is contained in ASI. In particular we do not have a proof that the V4 thesis $(p \wedge \sim p) \wedge \sim q \longrightarrow q$ is a theorem of ASI. So, regret that we have not shown that ASI is a genuine Parry system by virtue of containing V4 could be transformed into satisfaction that ASI lacks some undesirable theses. Still, we leave open the question of whether or not V4 is contained in ASI.

ASI does allow derivations of an arbitrary B from $A \wedge \sim A$ as the author noted in [1975a]. Let us present this undesirable result about the Dunn/Parry systems in a tenth theorem.

Theorem X of II.8: $A \wedge \sim A \vdash B$.

To prove this simply note that CL gives $A \wedge \sim A \supset B$. So, the hypothesis $A \wedge \sim A$ gives B by MD.

These Dunn/Parry systems fail to have $\vdash A \wedge \sim A \longrightarrow B$ only by virtue of failing to have normal rules,viz., by failing to satisfy Cl1. But even to allow a derivation of an arbitrary B from $A \wedge \sim A$ is opposed to our normative intuitions that the derivations which we accept should be formally correct arguments. So, Theorem X provides the grounds for a strong objection to the Dunn/Parry systems.

Before closing this section,let us explain why we do not consider Urquhart's AIN of his [1973]. Urquhart presents AIN as AI plus the following axioms for a primitive necessity sign.

Ap.17 $\Box(A \longrightarrow B) \longrightarrow . \Box A \longrightarrow . \Box B$
Ap.18 $\Box(A \wedge B) \longrightarrow . \Box A \wedge \Box B$
Ap.19 $\Box A \longrightarrow A$
Ap.20 $\Box A \longrightarrow \Box\Box A$
Ap.21 $(A \longrightarrow A) \longrightarrow . \Box(A \longrightarrow A)$

Axiom Ap.12 is changed to read: $(A \longleftrightarrow B) \wedge F(A) \longrightarrow F(B/A)$ if A does not occur in the scope of a $\Box()$ in F(A). A rule of Necessitation is also added.

If we define $A \Longrightarrow B$ as $\Box(A \longrightarrow B)$ for the $\Box()$ of AIN and conjecture that $A \Longrightarrow B$ is the implication which will serve as entailment, we conjecture wrongly. First, from the corollaries of theorems VII and VIII we would get the genuine paradoxes of impossibility and necessity in AIN. With Lan.(B) $\subseteq$ Lan.(A) $\Box \sim A \Longrightarrow . A \Longrightarrow B$ would be a theorem. When Lan.(B) = Lan.(A) we would have $\Box A \Longrightarrow . B \Longrightarrow A$. Secondly, we would run afoul of adequacy condition C12 by taking $\Box$ as primitive and using it to define entailment.

Exercises II.8

1. Show that the following are derived rules of ASI.
   R1: If F(A) is a wff. where A is a specified occurrence of the subformula A and F($\sim\sim$A)is the result of replacing this occurrence of A with $\sim\sim$A, then infer F($\sim\sim$A) from F(A).

   R2: If F($\sim$A) and F($\sim$B) are exactly alike except that F($\sim$B) has $\sim$B in the specified place in which $\sim$A occurs in F($\sim$A), from F($\sim$A) and F($\sim$B) infer F($\sim A \wedge \sim B$) where $\sim A \wedge \sim B$ occurs in the place where $\sim$A occurred in F($\sim$A).

   See Anderson's and Belnap's [1959a] to see how R1 and R2 can be used to get every classical tautology from primitive tautologous disjunctions.

2. a) State and prove Contraposition rules for ASI'and AI.

   b) State and prove a Contraposition theorem for AI.

3. State and prove a rule for ASI' by which we can go from $A \longrightarrow . B \longrightarrow C$ and $C \longrightarrow D$ to $A \longrightarrow . B \longrightarrow D$.

II.9 3rd. section on Dunn/Parry systems, Parry's original matrix $\mathcal{P}$o, non-theorems and non-rules of Dunn/Parry systems.

In this section we present Parry's original matrix $\mathcal{P}$o from [1933]. We use $\mathcal{P}$o to show that the Dunn/Parry systems: ASI,ASI', and AI conform to Parry's Proscriptive Principle that we do not have $\vdash$A$\longrightarrow$B unless Lan.(B)$\subseteq$Lan.(A). $\mathcal{P}$o is shown to be a finite characteristic matrix for fde. system V4. We close by using $\mathcal{P}$o to show that the Dunn/Parry systems lack theses and rules which we may want in an entailment system. In the next section $\mathcal{P}$o is shown to be a Parry-matrix in Dunn's sense of Parry-matrix. Example 1 of the next section explains computation of the tables for $\mathcal{P}$o.

We present $\mathcal{P}$o by presenting its operation tables. The elements are $\{$+2,+1,-1,-2$\}$ and the designated elements are $\{$+2,+1$\}$.

Operation tables for $\mathcal{P}$o.

$-$	
+2	-1
+1	-2
-1	+2
-2	+1

$\wedge$	+2	+1	-1	-2
+2	+2	+1	-1	-2
+1	+1	+1	-2	-2
-1	-1	-2	-1	-2
-2	-2	-2	-2	-2

$\vee$	+2	+1	-1	-2
+2	+2	+1	+2	+1
+1	+1	+1	+1	+1
-1	+2	+1	-1	-2
-2	+1	+1	-2	-2

$\longrightarrow$	+2	+1	-1	-2
+2	+2	-2	-1	-2
+1	+1	+1	-2	-2
-1	+2	-2	+2	-2
-2	+1	+1	+1	+1

We shirk the labor of presenting a proof of our first lemma.

Lemma 1 of II.9: $\mathcal{P}$o is suitable for the Dunn/Parry systems.

We assert as our first theorem that the Dunn/Parry systems conform to Parry's Proscriptive Principle.

Theorem I of II.9: If A$\longrightarrow$B is a theorem of a Dunn/Parry system, then Lan.(B)$\subseteq$Lan.(A).

As proof consider the following. Given Lemma 1, it suffices to show that if A$\longrightarrow$B has a variable occurring in B which does not occur in A, then there is a valuation v() on $\mathcal{P}$o such that v(A$\longrightarrow$B) is -1 or -2. In his [1933] Parry, in effect, suggested assigning a variable in B but not in A -2 while assigning -1 to all other variables of A$\longrightarrow$B. We now merely state two lemmas which claim that under the assignment suggested by Parry A$\longrightarrow$B takes on -1 or -2 because A's value will be +2 or -1 while B's value will be -2 or +1. An induction on the length of A establishes Lemma 2 while an induction on the length of B establishes Lemma 3.

Lemma 2 of II.9: If v(p)=-1 for all variables p in Lan.(A), then v(A)=+2 or v(A)=-1.

Lemma 3 of II.9: If v(p)=-2 for a variable p in Lan.(B), then v(B)=-2 or v(B)=+1.

With lemmas 2 and 3 and the observations that +2→+1=-2, +2→ -2=-2, -1→+1=-2, and -1→ -2=-2 we have a proof of Theorem I.

Recall that fde. A→B is a V4 thesis iff. A⊃B is a classical tautology and Lan.(B)⊆Lan.(A). So, with Theorem I, Theorem III of II.8 which says that V4 ⊆ASI', and the corollary of V of II.8 which says that V4 ⊆AI we can conclude that the fde.theorems of ASI' and AI are exactly the theses of V4 if we establish for ASI' and AI that if A→B is an fde.theorem A⊃B is a classical tautology. We present, then, a fourth lemma which is easily proved by treating → as ⊃ and interpreting the axioms of AI on classical truth tables.

Lemma 4 of II.9: If A→B is an fde. theorem of the Dunn/Parry systems, then A⊃B is a classical tautology.

Theorem II of II.9: A→B is an fde. theorem of ASI' and AI iff. A→B is a thesis of V4.

The next result that $\mathcal{P}_o$ is a finite characteristic matrix for V4 also deserves to be ranked as a theorem.

Theorem III of II.9: $\mathcal{P}_o$ is a finite characteristic matrix for V4.

Lemma 1 and Theorem I serve to prove that $\mathcal{P}_o$ is suitable for V4. To prove the other half we argue that if fde. A→B is not a V4 thesis it is not valid on $\mathcal{P}_o$. If fde. A→B is not a V4 thesis, then either Lan.(B)⊈Lan.(A) or A⊃B is not a classical tautology. In the case that Lan.(B)⊈Lan.(A) use the technique of the proof of Theorem I to invalidate A→B on $\mathcal{P}_o$. In the case that A⊃B is not a tautology, consider a classical valuation which makes A⊃B False,F. In this classical valuation replace T with +2 and F with -1 to get a valuation of A and B on $\mathcal{P}_o$ which assigns A +2 and B -1 and hence A→B -2.

A corollary provides the following semantic characterization of V4.

Corollary of III of II.9: An fde. A→B is a thesis of V4 iff. A→B is valid on $\mathcal{P}_o$.

In the next section, we try to show that the values of $\mathcal{P}_o$ can be so interpreted that being valid on $\mathcal{P}_o$ is a desirable property of a system. However, because we are making a case against the Dunn/Parry systems, and especially against V4, we use the remainder of this section for employing $\mathcal{P}_o$ to show that these systems lack certain desirable theses and rules. We use Ntp. to label non-theorems of the Dunn/Parry systems and Nrp. to label non-rules. On the right,we frequently cite valuations on $\mathcal{P}_o$ which invalidate the formula or rule.

In Section I.6, we admitted that we had only weak normative intuitions in support of Addition. Indeed lacking Addition as a thesis could even be considered meritorious. However, Contraposition was recognized as very desirable. It turns out that rejection of Addition in the Dunn/Parry systems entails rejection of Contraposition even as an admissible rule.

Ntp.1 $A \rightarrow . A \vee B$ $\qquad$ $v(A)=+2, v(B)=+1$.

For all Dunn/Parry systems $\vdash \sim A \wedge \sim B \rightarrow . \sim A$. If we Contrapose $\sim A \wedge \sim B \rightarrow . \sim A$, and use Dbl. Neg., we get Ntp.1. Consequently, we have the following about non-rules.

Nrp.1 $\vdash A \rightarrow B$, then $\vdash \sim B \rightarrow . \sim A$, $\quad A \rightarrow B \vdash \sim B \rightarrow . \sim A$.

We take this failure of Contraposition as one of the most important reasons for not adopting one of the Dunn/Parry systems.

Drp.6 gave the rule of Premiss Addition. But we do not have the corresponding thesis.

Ntp.2 $A \rightarrow B \rightarrow . A \wedge C \rightarrow B$ $\qquad$ $v(A)=v(B)=-1$, $v(C)=+1$.

We take this failure of rule-normality to be a defect in the Dunn/Parry systems.

These Dunn/Parry systems do not have Antecedent Simplification, R6 of Cl4, as even an admissible rule.

Nrp.2 $\vdash A \vee B \rightarrow C$, then $\vdash A \rightarrow C$ and $\vdash B \rightarrow C$.

Consider the fact that $\vdash p \vee q \rightarrow . p \vee q$ but that, because Addition fails, neither $\vdash p \rightarrow . p \vee q$ nor $\vdash q \rightarrow . p \vee q$.

We also do not have either Prefixing or Suffixing as theses. To invalidate these two, follow Parry's suggestion for use in the proofs of lemmas 2 and 3.

Ntp.3 $A \rightarrow B \rightarrow . C \rightarrow A \rightarrow . C \rightarrow B$ $\qquad$ Prefixing
Ntp.4 $A \rightarrow B \rightarrow . B \rightarrow C \rightarrow . A \rightarrow C$ $\qquad$ Suffixing

From Drp.9 we know that we have Prefixing as a rule. So, again we have a non-normal rule. Moreover, we do not even have Suffixing as an admissible rule. We have $\vdash p \wedge q \rightarrow p$. But set $v(p)=v(r)=+2$ and $v(q)=+1$ to invalidate $p \rightarrow r \rightarrow . p \wedge q \rightarrow r$. So, we have Nrp.3.

Nrp.3 $\vdash A \rightarrow B$, then $\vdash B \rightarrow C \rightarrow . A \rightarrow C$.

Some, following a line of thought suggested on p.496 of Lewis' and Langford's [1932] in their rejection of Suffixing for $\prec$, may be pleased with the total failure of Suffixing and the partial failure of Prefixing. The line of thought is that the main $\rightarrow$ in the consequents of both Suffixing and Prefixing is not genuine entailment because inferences from $C \rightarrow A$ to $C \rightarrow B$ and $B \rightarrow C$ to $A \rightarrow C$ are not by themselves even formally valid. Certainly, in general, $C \rightarrow B$ does not follow from $C \rightarrow A$. But, in these discussions we should not neglect formal context. And we are talking of formal context in this study even if we do ignore the informal context. In the contexts, in the formulas, in which $A \rightarrow B$ is given as an antecedent we can go formally from $C \rightarrow A$ to $C \rightarrow B$ and $B \rightarrow C$ to $A \rightarrow C$ by use of the antecedent $A \rightarrow B$. Use of the antecedent $A \rightarrow B$ is use of only the formal context. So, we take Ntp.3 and Npt.4 as revealing undesirable aspects of the Dunn/Parry systems.

In this section we have seen some desirable aspects of the Dunn/Parry systems, eg., the fde. fragment V4 has a finite characteristic matrix. But on the whole we have found these systems to have more demerits than merits.

When it is fairly easy to prove systems consistent, it is easy to fail to state the consistency results. So, we close with the following theorem.

Theorem IV of II.9: The Dunn/Parry systems are consistent in the senses that no variable is a theorem, some formula is not a theorem, and no formula and its negation are theorems.

Exercises II.9

1. Show that Ap.7 and Ap.12 are valid on $\mathcal{P}$o.
2. Show that $A \rightarrow .A \rightarrow B \rightarrow B$ is not a theorem of any of the Dunn/Parry systems.
3. Show that Ap.14 is independent of the other AI axioms to answer a question of Parry's on p.152 of his [1968]. Use the six-value $\sim$ and $\wedge$ tables of Example 3 of the next section and the following $\rightarrow$ table of Meyer. the + elements are designated.

$\rightarrow$	-3	-2	-1	+1	+2	+3
-3	+1	-1	-1	-1	-1	+1
-2	-3	+2	-1	+1	+2	-2
-1	-3	-2	+3	-3	-2	+3
+1	-3	-3	-3	+1	+1	+1
+2	-3	-2	-1	-1	+2	+2
+3	-3	-1	-1	-1	-1	+3

4. Add Contraposition to ASI' as an axiom schema to get ASIc.
   i) Does ASIc have Addition?
   ii) Is the fde. fragment of ASIc the classical fdes.?
   iii) In ASIc do we have $A \supset B \vdash A \rightarrow B$?
   iv) Let AIc be AI with Contraposition. Does AIc have $A \supset B \leftrightarrow .A \rightarrow B$?
5. Prove lemmas 2 and3.

II.10 4th. section on Dunn/Parry systems, Parry-matrices, Dunn's algebraic semantics for AI.

We have tentatively rejected ASI,ASI',AI, and the fde. system V4 as candidates for the system of entailment. Yet these systems have some appeal. If no better systems can be found, we may have to reconsider the Dunn/Parry systems. So, to be prepared, in this section and in the next we present formal semantics for AI and ASI' respectively. We present from [1972] J.M.Dunn's algebraic semantics for AI and K. Fine's model structure semantics for ASI'. In this section, we define Dunn's notion of Parry-matrix, give heuristic synopses of Dunn's proofs that the formulas valid on Parry-matrices are exactly the theorems of AI and that AI is decidable, and comment on what it means to interpret a formula on a Parry-matrix. It is obvious that J.M. Dunn has contributed greatly to the study of systems conforming to Parry's Proscriptive Principle. Nevertheless, there is no reason for thinking that Dunn advocates such systems as the right systems for entailment.

Dunn defines a <u>Parry-matrix</u> $\mathfrak{M}p$ as a quintuple: $\langle D,U,{}^{-},\wedge,\longrightarrow\rangle$. D and U are disjoined but isomorphic semi-lattices under orderings $\leq_d$ and $\leq_u$ respectively.

Recall from I.7 the definition of a semi-lattice. Recall that a set S partially ordered by $\leq$ with a binary operation $\boxtimes$ is a semi-lattice if the following hold. $a\boxtimes b\leq a$, $a\boxtimes b\leq b$, and if $c\leq a$ and $c\leq b$ then $c\leq a\boxtimes b$.

On $\mathfrak{M}p$, D is the set of designated elements and U is the set of undesignated elements. The operation $\overline{a}$, which represents negation, is the union of an isomorphism from D onto U with its inverse. This uniting of isomorphisms gives the double negation equivalence. We are far more interested in a semi-lattice on the union of D and U, $D\cup U$, than we are in those on D and U. On $D\cup U$ define $\leq$ as follows. If $a,b\in D$, then $a\leq b$ iff. $a\leq_d b$. If $a,b\in U$, then $a\leq b$ iff. $a\leq_u b$. If $a\in U$ and $b\in D$, then $a\leq b$ iff. $a\leq_u \overline{b}$. We leave as an exercise a proof that reflexive $\leq$ is transitive and antisymmetric and, hence, that it partially orders $D\cup U$. The operation $a\wedge b$, which represents conjunction, is the greatest lower bound of a and b under $\leq$, i.e., the meet below of a and b. So, there is a semi-lattice on $D\cup U$ with $\wedge$ and $\leq$. The operation $a\longrightarrow b$, which represents what is supposed to be entailment, is computed as follows. If $a\leq b$, then $a\longrightarrow b = \max(a,\overline{a})$ and if $a\not\leq b$, then $a\longrightarrow b = (a\wedge\overline{a})\wedge(b\wedge\overline{b})$. Here max(,) is maximum under the $\leq$ ordering of the semi-lattice on $D\cup U$.

Let us illustrate the notion of Parry-matrix with some examples. Our first example is $\mathcal{P}o$ of the previous section.

Example 1 Parry's original matrix $\mathcal{P}_o$,

Let D = {+2,+1} and U = {-1,-2.} Have $+1 \leq_d +2$ and $-2 \leq_u -1$. The isomorphism f on D onto U such that f(+2)=-1 and f(+1)=-2 has as its inverse f^{-1} an isomorphism such that $f^{-1}(-1)=+2$ and $f^{-1}(-2)=+1$. The union of this isomorphism and its inverse, $f \cup f^{-1}$, is the function representing negation on $\mathcal{P}_o$. With $\bar{a}$ defined, we can determine the order $\leq$. Besides reflexivity for $\leq$, we obviously have $-2 \leq -1$ and $+1 \leq +2$. We also have $-2 \leq +1$ because $\overline{+1} = -2$. But we do not have $-1 \leq +1$. Pictorially, the situation is represented by diagram D1 on which the arrow stands for the transitive, reflexive, and anti-symmetric relation $\leq$.

D1

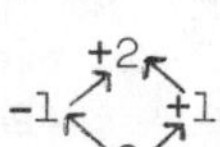

With $a \wedge b$ taken as the greatest lower bound of a and b on D1, the $\wedge$-table for $\mathcal{P}_o$ can be read off from D1. However, to get a table for a **v** b to represent disjunction we need to compute the table for $\overline{(\bar{a} \wedge \bar{b})}$. This new operation a **v** b is not simply the join operation which can be read off of D1. For example, note that on the v-table for $\mathcal{P}_o$ (-1 **v** +1) is not the join of -1 and +1 on D1. As an example of computing $a \longrightarrow b$ consider: $+2 \longrightarrow +1 = (+2 \wedge \overline{+2}) \wedge (+1 \wedge \overline{+1}) = (+2 \wedge -1) \wedge (+1 \wedge -2) = -1 \wedge -2 = -2$.

Example 2

Let D = {+3,+2,+1} and U = {-1,-2,-3} . Let D be ordered as on D2 and U be ordered as on D3.

D2

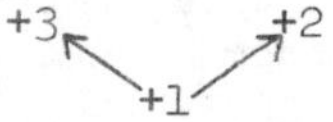

D3

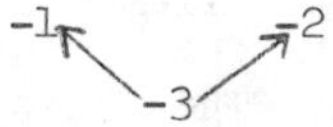

Let f be the isomorphism on D onto U such that f(+3)=-1, f(+2)=-2, and f(+1)=-3. If $\bar{a}$ is $f \cup f^{-1}$, where f^{-1} is the inverse of f, the negation table is as below.

a	+3	+2	+1	-1	-2	-3
$\bar{a}$	-1	-2	-3	+3	+2	+1

The new order $\leq$ is as on diagram D4 below.

D4

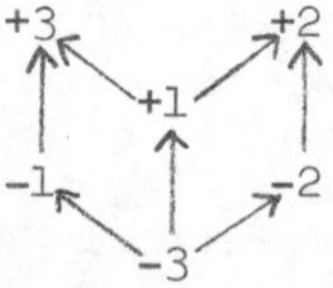

The $\wedge$-table can be obtained from D4 by taking the greatest lower bound of two elements. Thus $-1 \wedge +1 = -3$. The $a \longrightarrow b$ table is, of course, more difficult to compute. But verify that $-2 \longrightarrow +2 = +2$ and that $-1 \longrightarrow +1 = -3$.

Example 3 A non-Parry matrix due to Meyer

Let D and U be as in Example 2 but now let $\leq_d$ and $\leq_u$ be the linear orderings: $+1 \leq_d +2 \leq_d +3$ and $-3 \leq_u -2 \leq_u -1$. The negation table may be as in Example 2. However, the new ordering $\leq$ will be as on D5 below.

D5

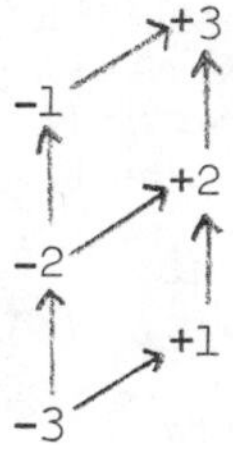

The table is readily obtained from D5 by taking $a \wedge b$ as the meet of a and b. But the $a \longrightarrow b$ table for this matrix is that of exercise 3 in the preceding section. Let /a/ be the absolute or positive value of a. If $/a/ \leq /b/$, compute $a \longrightarrow b$ as on a Parry-matrix but set $a \longrightarrow b = -1$ otherwise. So here $+2 \longrightarrow -1 = -1$ while a genuine Parry-matrix for D5 would give $+2 \longrightarrow -1 = 2$. So, the matrix of this example is not a Parry-matrix.

Recall from I.7 the definitions of such crucial semantic terms such as 'valid,' and 'kind of matrix suitable for a' system. Also recall from I.7 the definition of 'normal matrix.'

Theorem I of II.10: Parry-matrices are normal matrices.

We prove Theorem I by citing three lemmas whose proofs are left mainly as exercises.

Lemma 1 of II.10: The D of a Parry-matrix is consistent and complete.

Lemma 2 of II.10: For a Parry-matrix $a \dashrightarrow b \in D$ iff. $a \leq b$; and so $a \longleftrightarrow b \in D$ iff. $a = b$.

Relevant to a proof of Lemma 2, notice the following. If $a \leq b$, then $a \longrightarrow b = \max(a, \bar{a})$; and for sure $\max(a, \bar{a}) \in D$. If $a \not\leq b$, then $a \longrightarrow b = (a \wedge \bar{a}) \wedge (b \wedge \bar{b})$; and for sure $(a \wedge \bar{a}) \wedge (b \wedge \bar{b})$ sinks down into U.

Lemma 3 of II.10: The D of a Parry-matrix is a prime filter.

As proof for Lemma 3 we offer the following remarks. If $a \in D$ and $a \longrightarrow b \in D$, Lemma 2 tells us that $a \leq b$; so by definition of $\leq$ for a Parry-matrix $b \in D$. The fact that D is by itself a semi-lattice shows that D is closed under $\wedge$. If $a \in D$, $a \vee b \in D$, i.e., $\overline{(\bar{a} \wedge \bar{b})} \in D$. For if $a \in D$, then $\bar{a} \in U$; hence $\bar{a} \wedge \bar{b} \in U$ with the result that $\overline{(\bar{a} \wedge \bar{b})} \in D$. D is prime because if $\overline{(\bar{a} \wedge \bar{b})} \in D$ then $\bar{a} \wedge \bar{b} \in U$ with the result that either $\bar{a} \in U$ or $\bar{b} \in U$. If either $\bar{a} \in U$ or $\bar{b} \in U$, then either $a \in D$ or $b \in D$.

Theorem I together with Theorem II.7 helps to prove Theorem II which is called a correctness or soundness theorem.

In this section $\vdash$ means 'is a theorem of AI.'

Theorem II of II.10: If $\vdash$ A, then A is valid on all Parry-matrices, i.e., A is P-valid.

We verify this theorem only for Ap.15: $A \rightarrow . \sim A \rightarrow A$. If $A \rightarrow . \sim A \rightarrow A \notin D$ for the D of some Parry-matrix, Lemma 2 tells us that $v(A) \not\leq v(\sim A \rightarrow A)$. There are two cases which both lead to contradictions. In the case that $v(\sim A) \leq v(A)$, $v(\sim A \rightarrow A) = \max(v(\sim A), v(A))$. But $v(A) = \max(v(\sim A), v(A))$ when $v(\sim A) \leq v(A)$. So, in this case, we contradict the assumption that $v(A) \not\leq v(\sim A \rightarrow A)$. In the case that $v(\sim A) \not\leq v(A)$, $v(\sim A \rightarrow A)$ becomes $\min(v(A), v(\sim A))$. Now $v(A) = \min(v(A), v(\sim A))$ when it is given that $v(\sim A) \not\leq v(A)$. So, again we contradict the assumption that $v(A) \not\leq v(\sim A \rightarrow A)$.

Because a proof of Theorem II establishes that AI's rules preserve designation, a corollary of Theorem II asserts strong, or argument, soundness for AI.

Corollary of II of II.10: If $\Gamma \vdash$ A, then if v() on a Parry-matrix simultaneously satisfies Γ, then v() satisfies A, i.e., $\Gamma \cup \{\sim A\}$ is Parry-inconsistent.

We now outline Dunn's argument for the strong, or argument, completeness for AI. Formulas valid on all Parry-matrices are called Parry-valid, P-valid, Parry-theses, and P-theses.

Theorem III of II.10: If, for all v() on all Parry-matrices if v() simultaneously satisfies Γ then v() satisfies A, then $\Gamma \vdash$ A. I.e., if $\Gamma \cup \{\sim A\}$ is Parry-inconsistent, then $\Gamma \vdash$ A.

As is usual for a Henkin-style completeness proof, Dunn shows that if it is not the case that $\Gamma \vdash A$, i.e., not-($\Gamma \vdash A$), then there is a v() on some Parry-matrix which simultaneously satisfies $\Gamma \cup \{\sim A\}$. The first step is to show that if not-($\Gamma \vdash A$), then $\Gamma \cup \{\sim A\}$ is consistent in AI in the sense of not yielding an explicit contradiction.

Lemma 4 of II.10: If not-($\Gamma \vdash A$), then $\Gamma \cup \{\sim A\}$ is consistent in the sense that there is no formula B such that $\Gamma \cup \{\sim A\} \vdash B \wedge \sim B$.

For a <u>reductio</u> proof consider that if we had $\Gamma \cup \{\sim A\} \vdash B \wedge \sim B$, then CDT of II.8 we would have $\Gamma \vdash \sim A \supset . B \wedge \sim B$. But then we get $\Gamma \vdash$ A contrary to our assumption not-($\Gamma \vdash$ A).

Of course, the next step is to show that if a set of formulas is consistent in AI, hereafter simply 'consistent,' then there is some v() on some Parry-matrix which simultaneously satisfies it.

Lemma 5 of II.10: If Γ is consistent, Γ is simultaneously satisfied on some Parry-matrix.

To those familiar with Henkin-style completeness proofs, it will be no surprise that the first step towards proving Lemma 5 is Lemma 6. We dispense with any details of a proof of this sixth lemma. The interested reader may consult a Henkin-style completeness proof for classical logic in a text such as Thomason's [1970].

Lemma 6 of II.10: Every consistent set of formulas of AI's language is embeddable within a maximal consistent set of such formulas.

The next step is to build a Parry-matrix from the maximal consistent set so that the maximal consistent set gets simultaneously satisfied by some valuation on this Parry-matrix.

Lemma 7 of II.10: If M is a maximal consistent set of AI formulas, then there is a Parry-matrix $\mathcal{W}$m and a valuation v() on $\mathcal{W}$m such that v() simultaneously satisfies M.

We do not prove this lemma but only make the following heuristic remarks about its proof. Partition the formulas of AI into equivalence classes [A] by specifying that $[A] = \{B: A \leftrightarrow B \in M\}$. These equivalence classes will be the elements of $\mathcal{W}$m. Set $D = \{[A]: A \in M\}$ and set $U = \{[A]: A \notin M\}$. Define operations on the [A] so that: $\overline{[A]} = [\sim A]$, $[A] \wedge [B] = [A \wedge B]$, and $[A] \rightarrow [B] = [A \rightarrow B]$. Specify $[A] \leq [B]$ iff. $A \rightarrow B \in M$. Let $\mathcal{W}m = \langle D, U, \overline{}, \wedge, \rightarrow \rangle$. Most of the labor of this proof is to show that $\mathcal{W}$m is a Parry-matrix. Exercises at the end of this section bring out some of the details of the argument for showing that $\mathcal{W}$m is a genuine Parry-matrix. Assuming that we have shown that $\mathcal{W}$m is a Parry-matrix, we consider the valuation v() on $\mathcal{W}$m such that v(A) = [A]. Obviously, this v() simultaneously satisfies M because $v(A) \in D$ iff. $A \in M$, i.e., $[A] \in D$ iff. A M.

Of course, once we have lemma 4 through 7 we have that if not-($\Gamma \vdash A$) then $\Gamma \cup \{\sim A\}$ is simultaneously satisfiable. Hence, contraposition, which is allowed in the metalanguage for AI, gives Theorem III. Because Γ may be empty we have the following corollary.

Corollary of III of II.10: If $\vdash A$, then A is Parry-valid.

With theorems II and III along with their corollaries we get the next two theorems.

Theorem IV of II.10: $\Gamma \vdash A$ iff. $\Gamma \cup \{\sim A\}$ is Parry-inconsistent.

Theorem V of II.10: $\vdash A$ iff. A is Parry-valid.

Dunn also sketches out how his completeness proof may be modified to obtain a decision procedure for AI. He establishes the following lemma which provides a decision procedure by showing how to tell in finitely many steps whether or not $\{\sim A\}$ is simultaneously satisfiable. If $\{\sim A\}$ is not simultaneously satisfiable $\vdash$ A by Theorem IV.

Lemma 8 of II.10: If $\Gamma \cup \{\sim A\}$ is consistent and Lan.(Γ) $\subseteq$ Lan.(A), then there is a valuation on a Parry-matrix with α or fewer elements which simultaneously satisfies $\Gamma \cup \{\sim A\}$

With n being the number of distinct variables in A

$$\alpha = 2^{2^{2n}}$$

We make only the following heuristic remarks about a proof. Restrict attention to formulas of AI whose variables are contained in Lan.(A). Label this restricted language Wn. When system AI contains only formula of Wn, label it AIn. Embed $\Gamma \cup \{\sim A\}$ in a maximal consistent set of formulas of Wn which is to be labelled Mn . Despite the finitude of Lan.(A), Mn has infinitely many formulas. Also there may be infinitely many [A] where [A] = $\{$B: B $\in$ Wn and A$\longleftrightarrow$B $\in$ Mn$\}$. Even if Lan.(A) contains only a single variable p, there is no guarantee that there are not infintely many non-equivalent formulas in this Wn. Fortunately, if we restrict Wn to formulas with no $\longrightarrow$'s, we have a guarantee that there are only finitely many non-equivalent formulas in the language of Wnz where Wnz is Wn with only zdfs. Indeed, in Wnz there are at most α many non-equivalent formulas. Lemma 2 of II.8 assures us that each formula B of Wnz is provably equivalent to a disjunctive normal form B^d which contains exactly the variables of B. And if there are at most n distinct variables there are at most α many disjunctive normal form.

Why are there only α many disjunctive normal forms if there are only n variables? There are 2n atoms because each variable and its negation make an atom. With 2n atoms we can form 2^{2n} primitive conjunctions, if we count the null conjunction as a primitive conjunction. These 2^{2n} primitive conjunctions make up the disjuncts for disjunctive normal forms. Because disjunctive normal forms are formed by making a selection from these 2^{2n} primitive conjunctions, we can form $2^{2^{2n}}$ distinct disjunctive normal forms, i.e., α many.

Because all theorems belong to maximal consistent sets all B$\longleftrightarrow$$B^d$ $\in$ Mn where B is a zdf..

Now build a Parry-matrix $\mathcal{W}$n with equivalence classes of Wn in the way in which one was built for Lemma 7. In particular let D for $\mathcal{W}$n be the equivalence classes of members

Mn. Similarly to what was done for Lemma 7, define a v() on $\mathcal{W}$n so that v(A) $\in$ D iff. A $\in$ Mn. Matrix $\mathcal{W}$n may have infinitely many elements. But from the preceding remarks we may conclude that there are only finitely many [B] where B is a zdf.. The idea is to get a matrix from $\mathcal{W}$n which uses only the finitely many [B] where B is a zdf.. The first step is to show that there can be a valuation v*() which takes formulas of Wn to [B]'s where B is a zdf. of Wn and v*(A) $\in$ D iff. v(A) $\in$ D. I.e., v*() maps Wn to the at most α many [B]. If A is a zdf. v*() can be just like v(). If v(A$\longrightarrow$B) $\in$ D, let v*(A$\longrightarrow$B) be [p $\vee\sim$p] for some p in Wn and if v(A$\longrightarrow$B) $\notin$ D let v(A$\longrightarrow$B) be [p$\wedge\sim$p]. So, if v() satisfies a formula, so does v*(). Similarly, if v() simultaneously satisfies a set, so does v*(). However, v*() uses only finitely many of $\mathcal{W}$n's elements. So, we have Lemma 8 if we show that we still have a Parry matrix with just the at most α many elements of $\mathcal{W}$n used by v*(). The interested reader should consult Dunn's paper for further details.

Dunn closes his paper with a suggestion on how to interpret values of a Parry matrix. Let us consider this suggestion to see whether being satisfied and being valid on a Parry-matrix corresponds to some normative intuitions we have about logic. Dunn shows that every Parry-matrix is isomorphic to a Parry-matrix whose elements are pairs $\langle X,b\rangle$ where b is a truth value T(true) or F(false) and X is a set of objects. We are to regard X as representing the objects which a claim is about while regarding b as the truth value of the claim about the objects. So, to interpret a variable p by assigning it an $\langle X,b\rangle$ is to interpret p as a true or false claim about some objects. Call the $\langle X,b\rangle$ <u>content/truth values</u> and rules for their combination <u>content/truth rules</u>. On a Parry-matrix with content/truth values as elements, the designated elements are the $\langle X,T\rangle$ ones while the undesignated ones are the $\langle X,F\rangle$ ones. We specify that $\overline{\langle X,b\rangle} = \langle X,\overline{b}\rangle$, where $\overline{T}$ = F and $\overline{F}$ = T. $\langle X,b\rangle \wedge \langle Y,c\rangle = \langle X\cup Y,b\wedge c\rangle$, where T$\wedge$T=T, T$\wedge$F=F, F$\wedge$T=F, and F$\wedge$F=F. For the $\longrightarrow$ operation we specify that $\langle X,b\rangle \rightarrow \langle Y,c\rangle = \langle X\cup Y,T\rangle$ if Y $\subseteq$ X and b is not T while c is F; otherwise $\langle X,b\rangle \rightarrow \langle Y,c\rangle = \langle X\cup Y,F\rangle$. The truth/content rule for $\longrightarrow$ can be regarded as saying that A$\longrightarrow$B holds if A materially implies B and B does not talk of any objects which are not talked about by A.

The content/truth rule for $\longrightarrow$ does seem to capture Parry's Proscriptive Principle. Indeed, a reason for thinking that AI really captures Parry's intentions is that Parry-matrices characterize AI and Parry-matrices are isomorphic to matrices which have the preceding content/truth rule for $\longrightarrow$.

But AI does have Ap.15 which Parry rejects. So, in the next section we consider a semantics for ASI' which, in effect, interprets $A \longrightarrow B$ holding only if A strictly implies B and the content of B is included in the content of A. Most likely the interpretation in terms of strict implication is what Parry wanted. Nevertheless, we must admit that the fact that AI has a semantics which is not only a kind of algebra but which also can be regarded as content and truth value to formulas makes AI more appealing.

But after a more careful consideration should we consider the fact that Parry-matrices can be interpreted as having content/truth values as elements as significant? In particular, should we consider the fact that $\mathcal{P}o$ can be so interpreted as a mark in favor of fde. system V4? We can easily interpret $\mathcal{P}o$. Assume that we have two kinds of claims. The first kind of claim is about no objects at all; their object content is the null set $\emptyset$. Maybe necessary truths and falsehoods are this first kind of claim. The second kind of claim is about all objects; their object content is the universal class V. Maybe empirical truths and falsehoods can be regarded as about everything, as about the world. Now interpret the elements of $\mathcal{P}o$ as follows. $+2 = \langle \emptyset, T \rangle$, $+1 = \langle V, T \rangle$, $-1 = \langle \emptyset, F \rangle$, and $-2 = \langle V, F \rangle$. The content/truth rules give $\mathcal{P}o$. For instance, $+2 \longrightarrow +1$ is $\langle \emptyset, T \rangle \longrightarrow \langle V, T \rangle = \langle V, F \rangle = -2$. At first glance this interpretation for a characteristic matrix for V4 seems to be in favor of V4; V4 has an intelligible semantics.

Upon more careful consideration we realize that the mere fact that some semantics for V4 "makes sense" does not make V4 any better in regard to theses and inaccurate and false claims can make sense. V4 does not have a rule of Contraposition; and that is still our main reason for rejecting V4. A closer look at why V4 does not have Contraposition reveals that the content/truth rules for $\mathcal{P}o$ are not quite what they should be. The content/truth rule for $\overline{}$ is what leads to the failure of Contraposition. The rule $\overline{\langle X, b \rangle} = \langle X, \bar{b} \rangle$ is not really correct. The negation of a claim about objects X is not still a claim about only the objects X. It may be plausible to say that 'Tom is fat' is only about Tom. But 'Tom is not fat' is about far more objects than Tom because it says that Tom is not any of the fact objects. So, we find that the interesting interpretation of semantics for V4 do not compel acceptance of V4.

Some of the exercises may need consultation of Dunn's paper.

Exercises II.10

1. Show that the classical **truth** tables can be regarded as a Parry-matrix.

Exercises II.10

2. Let D = $\{+3,+2,+1\}$ and let U = $\{-1,-2,-3\}$. Let them be ordered as follows. $+1 \nearrow +3 \nwarrow +2$ $\quad -3 \nearrow -1 \nwarrow -2$

   Make $^{-}$, $\wedge$, and $\longrightarrow$ tables for a Parry-matrix.

3. Prove Lemma 6, T20* of Dunn's paper.

4. Let M be a maximal consistent set of AI formulas, show the following. T21* of Dunn's paper.
   i) $A \in M$ iff. $M \vdash A$
   ii) Exactly one of $\{A, \sim A\}$ belong to M.
   iii) $A \vee B \in M$ iff. $A \in M$ or $B \in M$.
   iv) $A \wedge B \in M$ iff. $A \in M$ and $B \in M$.

5. Let M be a maximal consistent set with D and U defined as in the remarks about a proof for Lemma 7.
   i) Show that D and U are disjoined, closed under $\wedge$, and that they fulfill the semi-lattice conditions with $\leq$ defined as $[A] \leq [B]$ iff. $A \longrightarrow B \in M$.
   ii) Show that f below is an isomorphism on D onto U. $f([A]) = \overline{[A]}$. Use Dunn's T24, our Tp.33, to show that order is preserved. Use his T25*: $\sim A \longleftrightarrow \sim B \supset A \longleftrightarrow B$ to show that f is one-to-one.
   iii) Show that if $[A] \in U$ and $[B] \in D$, then $[A] \leq [B]$ iff. $[A] \leq \overline{[B]}$. Here $\leq$ is the order for D, U, and the new matrix $\mathcal{W}$m. Use Dunn's T26: $\sim A \wedge B \wedge (A \longrightarrow B) \longrightarrow . A \longrightarrow \sim B$.
   iv) Show that if $[A] \leq [B]$, then $[A \longrightarrow B] = [A \vee \sim A]$. Use Dunn's T28*: $A \longrightarrow B \supset . A \longrightarrow A \longrightarrow . A \longrightarrow B$.
   v) Show that $\max([A], \overline{[A]}) = [A \vee \sim A]$.
   vi) Show that if $[A] \not\leq [B]$, then $[A \longrightarrow B] = [A \wedge \sim A \wedge B \wedge \sim B]$. Use his T32: $\sim (A \longrightarrow B) \supset . (A \longrightarrow B) \longleftrightarrow (A \wedge \sim A \wedge B \wedge \sim B)$.

6. Show that $(\langle X,b\rangle \wedge \langle X,\bar{b}\rangle) \wedge \langle Y,\bar{c}\rangle \longrightarrow \langle Y,c\rangle$ is always designated.

II.11 Kit Fine's model structure semantics for ASI', a heuristic presentation, 5th. section on Dunn/Parry systems.

In this section we give a heuristic presentation of Kit Fine's model structure semantics for ASI' by adapting Fine's semantics from his [1974a]. This presentation is heuristic because we do not prove soundness and completeness theorems and even dispense with proofs of lemmas. These semantics give a good sense to saying that $A \longrightarrow B$ is a theorem of ASI' if and only if the inference from A to B is valid and the content of B is included in the content of A. These semantics do help to make a persuasive case for acceptance of ASI'. Of course, we are not trying to make a case for ASI'. Still this evidence should be presented to those who are intrigued by ASI' as a candidate for the system of entailment. In applications of these semantics standard quantification logic is used.

An <u>ASI' model structure</u>, an ASI' m.s., is an ordered quadruple: $\langle W,R,I,U \rangle$. We use Msp., with subscripts and superscripts, to refer to ASI' model structures. In a Msp. W is a non-empty set of frameworks for giving a description of how reality could have been. R is a reflexive and transitive relation on W. Read wRv as 'v is accessible from w.' In an Msp. I is a set of sets of contents Iw where there is exactly one Iw for each w in W. In a Msp. U is a set of commutative, associative, and idempotent operations Uw where there is exactly one Uw for each Iw. You may regard the Uw as similar to set-theoretic union except that a Uw unites contents of w. In each Iw, there is a non-empty set Iwb of basic contents. Iw is generated from Iwb by Uw.

We interpret the Iwb as sets of basic assertables for w. For instance, an Iwb may consist of: John loving Mary, all men being mortal, and John being older than Mary. In a description at such a w, unanalyzed assertions or atomic sentences would be: John loves Mary, all men are mortal, and John is older than Mary; other assertions would be compounds built up from these atomic ones by use of $\wedge$, $\vee$, $\sim$, and $\longrightarrow$. Of course, an assertable of w need not be asserted when we give a description at w. For instance, we may assert 'John does not love Mary' when 'John loves Mary' is a basic assertable. What we do at a w by asserting or denying basic assertables and then combining the results by use of $\wedge$, $\vee$, $\sim$, and $\longrightarrow$ is to describe how reality could be, given the limited resources of the basic assertables. To those familiar with R.M. Hare's <u>The Language of Morals</u>, Oxford 1950, these basic assertables will be reminiscient of phrastics.

We want to emphasize that these basic assertables are the basic content of assertions and not what could be called the basic concepts used in assertions. For instance, the basic assertables we cited earlier may use the concepts of loving, humanity, mortality, age, John, and Mary. Our intention is to assign sentential variables to basic assertables of w when interpreting the language of ASI' to develop a description at w. If we had the Iwb consist of basic concepts rather than of basic assertables, we would have to assign each sentence variable to a subset of Iwb rather than to a single member of Iwb because even atomic sentences use more than one concept. A concept interpretation is used by Urquhart in [.973]. We do not follow Urquhart because we do not want even to start to say what a concept is.

We interpret the accessibility relation R as conceivability. If wRv and if an assertion S is given in a description at v, then it is conceivable for anyone giving a description at w that S could be true. This conceivability interpretation not only requires the consistency of any assertion used in a description; it also requires that if wRv, then no assertable used to give a description at v be one which is not available for giving a description at w. So, we explicitly add the condition: If wRv, then $Iv \subseteq Iw$.

To interpret the language of ASI', or a fragment of the language of ASI', by means of an Msp. we take two main steps: we assign content and we assign truth-values. Each sentential variable is assigned by functions c(w,) to a member of Iwb for each Iw in I. This content assignment is then extended to all formulas. The content assignment functions c(w,) are extended to molecular formulas as follows.

$c(w,A) = c(w,p_1)\ Uw,\ldots,Uw\ c(w,p_n)$, where $Lan.(A) = \{p_1,\ldots,p_n\}$.

In other words, the content of A is the content of its sentence letters. In general, c(w,A) is in Iw and not in Iwb. This extension of the c(w,)'s gives Lemma 1 which we state without proof.

Lemma 1 of II.11: For an interpretation on an Msp., we have the following. Remember: read Uw as uniting contents.
$c(w,\sim A) = c(w,A)$
$c(w,A\wedge B) = c(w,A)\ Uw\ c(w,B)$
$c(w,A \vee B) = c(w,A)\ Uw\ c(w,B)$
$c(w,A\rightarrow B) = c(w,A)\ Uw\ c(w,B)$.

For each Iw a relation of content inclusion, $\subseteq w$, can be defined as follows.

If $a \in Iw$ and $b \in Iw$, $a \subseteq w\ b =_{df} a\ Uw\ b = b$.

Thus by Lemma 1, $c(w,A) \subseteq w\ c(w,A\ B)$. Read $c(w,A) \subseteq w\ c(w,B)$ as: Upon this interpretation the content of A in w is included in the content of B in w. We again state without proof a lemma.

Lemma 2 of II.11: [For all interpretations on all w in all Msp., $c(w,A) \subseteq_w c(w,B)$] iff. Lan.(A) $\subseteq$ Lan.(B).

Truth-values are assigned to variables at members of W. But because being true at w is not necessarily to be true, we do not pay attention to the truth-value of formulas at members of W. Instead we consider what is asserted at a w. So, in effect, our next step is to force formulas into descriptions, or as we call them 'set-ups,' at each member of W. We talk of forcing at a point w, $w \in W$, because when we give a description at w we force each formula or its negation to be in the description. The first stage in forcing formulas into a set-up or description at a w, $w \in W$, is to select as the basic assertions some of the sentence variables which have already been assigned by c(w,) a content at w. This first stage is represented by a valuation or assertion function As(,) on $W \times SL$ into a set $\{T,F\}$. Here $W \times SL$ is the set of ordered pairs $\langle w,p_i \rangle$ with $w \in W$ and p_i being a sentence letter(variable) of the language of ASI' or the fragment which we are considering. $As(w,p_i) = T$ represents p_i being selected as a basic assertion to be used in the description at w. The second stage in forcing formulas into a set-up or description Dw at w is building Dw according to the following rules.

Forcing rules for an Msp.

1. $p_i \in Dw$ iff. $As(w,p_i) = T$.
2. $\sim A \in Dw$ iff. $A \notin D$.
3. $A \wedge B \in D$ iff. $A \in Dw$ and $B \in Dw$.
4. $A \longrightarrow B \in Dw$ iff. $(\forall v)(wRv \supset (c(v,B) \subseteq_v c(v,A)))$ and $(\forall v)((wRv \ \& \ A \in Dv) \supset B \in Dv)$.

Rule 4 tells us to make an $A \longrightarrow B$ part of a description if and only if in every conceivable description the content of B will be included in that of A and we cannot conceive of A being true and B being false in any conceivable description.

As an exercise establish that 5 below is a forcing rule.

5. $A \vee B \in Dw$ iff. $A \in Dw$ or $B \in Dw$.

If $A \in Dw$ for some w in some Msp. we say that <u>A has a model</u>. The <u>model</u> consists of the Msp., the content assignment functions and an assertion function. We say that <u>A is Msp. valid</u> if $\sim A$ has no model. Hence, if A is valid $A \in Dw$ for all interpretations on all w in all Msp.. So, we can test A for Msp. validity by assuming $A \notin Dw$ for some w in an Msp.. If we get a contradiction A is Msp. valid; otherwise not. We can show that a schema is not valid by showing that it has an instance which is not valid. The technique used below is intended to be reminiscent of J. Hintikka's model set technique used in his <u>Knowledge and Belief</u>.

Let us illustrate testing for Msp. validity.

Example 1

Show that $A \longrightarrow . A \vee B$ is not Msp. valid. We show that its instance $p \longrightarrow . p \vee q$ is not valid. Assume (i) and show that we can consistently assume it.

i) $p \longrightarrow . p \vee q \notin Dw$ for some w in some Msp. on some interpretation.

Forcing rule 4 gives (ii.1) or (ii.2) with wRv for some $v \in W$ and wRu for some $u \in W$.

ii.1) $c(v, p \vee q) \not\leq_v c(v,p)$

or

ii.2) $p \in Du$ & $(p \vee q) \notin Du$.

Forcing rule 5 tells us that (ii.2) cannot hold. But Lemma 2 tells us that (ii.2) can hold. We simply pick an Msp. with a single member in W but with two elements in Iwb; and assign p and q to distinct elements(contents) of Iwb.

Example 2

Show that Ap.15, the AI axiom, is not Msp. valid. Again we argue that we can consistently assume (i).

i) $p \longrightarrow . \sim p \longrightarrow p \notin Dw$ for some w in some Msp. on some interpretation. Forcing rule 4 gives for some v and u in W wRv and wRu with (ii.1) or (ii.2).

ii.1) $c(v, \sim p \longrightarrow p) \not\leq_v c(v,p)$

or

ii.2) $p \in Du$ & $\sim p \longrightarrow p \notin Du$.

Lemma 1 tells us that we cannot have (ii.1); so we consider that rule 4 tells us (ii.2) gives (iii.1) or (iii.2) with uRx and uRy for x and y in W.

iii.3) $c(x,p) \not\leq_x c(x, \sim p)$

or

iii.2) $\sim p \in Dy$ & $p \notin Dy$.

Lemma 1 tells us that we cannot have (iii.1). But nothing in groups (i) or (ii) forces us to put anything except $\sim p$ in Dy. Hence, we can consistently accept (iii.2); and hence consistently accept (i).

Example 3

Show that ASI' does not have the highly undesirable Tp.29 of Section II.8. We will show that Tp.29 is not Msp. valid. Theorem I of this section will tell us that such an argument suffices to show that it is not an ASI' theorem. Again we assume (i) for some w in a Msp. and use forcing rule 4 to get for some v and u in W wRv and wRu with a(ii.1) or a(ii.2).

i) $p \wedge (p \rightarrow q) \rightarrow . \sim p \rightarrow \sim q \notin Dw$ So,
ii.1) $c(v, \sim p \rightarrow \sim q) \not\subseteq v\ c(v, p \wedge (p \rightarrow q))$
or
ii.2) $p \in Du$ & $(p \rightarrow q) \in Du$ & $\sim p \rightarrow \sim q \notin Du$.

Lemma 1 tells us that we cannot have (ii.1); so we apply rule 4 to the $\sim p \rightarrow \sim q \notin Du$ part of (ii.2) to get (iii.1) or (iii.2) with uRx and uRy for x and y in W.

iii.1) $c(x, \sim q) \not\subseteq x\ c(x, \sim p)$
or
iii.2) $\sim p \in Dy$ & $\sim q \notin Dy$.

Again (iii.1) is not tenable. The facts that $p \rightarrow q \in Du$ and uRx give: $c(x,q) \subseteq x\ c(x,p)$, which with Lemma 1 is inconsistent with (iii.1). But nothing prohibits (iii.2) from being true.

To appreciate the point that (ii.2) does not require us to do anything which which prohibits (iii.2) consider what would happen if the antecedent were $(\sim p \rightarrow p) \wedge (p \rightarrow q)$, i.e., $\Box p \wedge (p \rightarrow q)$, instead of merely $p \wedge (p \rightarrow q)$. If $(\sim p \rightarrow p)$ were in the antecedent, we would have $\sim p \rightarrow p \in Du$; then because uRy and $\sim p \in Dy$, we would have to have $p \in Dy$. But it is inconsistent for us to have $\sim p \in Dy$ and $p \in Dy$ because $\sim p \in Dy$ gives $p \notin Dy$. Of course, the considerations of this paragraph serve to show that Tp.28 is Msp. valid.

Before we give a fourth example we present a third lemma, whose proof is an exercise.

Lemma 3 of II.11: For interpretations on Msp.'s, if $A \leftrightarrow B \in Dw$ then $A \equiv B \in Dv$ for all v such that wRv.

As our fouth example we show that an instance of Ap.12 is Msp. valid. It would take an inductive argument to show that Ap.12 is Msp. valid. In this example we work with a schema and dispense with considerations of content.

Example 4

Show that the schema $(A \leftrightarrow B) \wedge (A \rightarrow . \sim A \rightarrow A) \rightarrow . (B \rightarrow . \sim B \rightarrow B)$, i.e., $(A \leftrightarrow B) \wedge (A \rightarrow \Box A) \rightarrow . B \rightarrow \Box B$, is Msp. valid.

Assume that the formula does not belong in a Dw and get:
i) wRv, $A \leftrightarrow B \in Dv$, $A \rightarrow . \sim A \rightarrow A \in Dv$, but $B \rightarrow . \sim B \rightarrow B \notin Dv$.
From $B \rightarrow . \sim B \rightarrow B \notin Dv$ we get:
ii) vRu, $B \in Du$, but $\sim B \rightarrow B \notin Du$.
From $\sim B \rightarrow B \notin Du$ we get:
iii) uRx, $\sim B \in Dx$ but $B \notin Dx$.
Because of the transitivity of R, vRu and uRx give vRx.
Hence, by Lemma 3 and $A \leftrightarrow B \in Dv$ at (i) we get $A \equiv B \in Dx$.
From $A \equiv B \in Dx$ and $\sim B \in Dx$ we get:

iv) $\sim A \in Dx$ which gives $A \notin Dx$.
From $B \in Du$ and $B \longrightarrow A \in Dv$ with vRu we get:
v) $A \in Du$.
But with $A \in Du$, vRu, and $A \longrightarrow . \sim A \longrightarrow A \in Dv$, we get:
vi) $\sim A \longrightarrow A \in Du$.
But with $\sim A \in Dx$, uRx, and $\sim A \longrightarrow A \in Du$ we get:
vii) $A \in Dx$
And (vii) contradicts what we get from (iv). So, this instance of Ap.12 is Msp. valid.

Hopefully, the preceding examples will show how to establish the soundness theorem for ASI' relative to Msp.'s.

Theorem I of II.11: If A is a ASI' theorem, then A is Msp. valid.

Possibly, Fine's [1974a] will need to be consulted for the completeness theorem.

Theorem II of II.11: (Msp. validity completeness of ASI'.) If A is Msp. valid, then A is a theorem of ASI'.

We close our discussion of Dunn/Parry systems with this announcement of Fine's completeness theorem. Admittedly these semantics help make ASI' appealing. Nevertheless, we still do not accept ASI' because it lacks Contraposition and has $(A \wedge \sim A) \wedge \sim B \longrightarrow B$ as a thesis schema.

Exercises II.11

1. Prove lemmas 1,2, and 3.
2. Show that on any interpretation on a Msp. a Dw is complete and consistent. For no A do both $A \in Dw$ and $\sim A \in Dw$. But for all A, $A \in Dw$ or $\sim A \in Dw$.
3. Show Ap.16 is Msp valid.
4. Show that if R accessibility is made symmetric $\Diamond A \longrightarrow \Box \Diamond A$ is valid.

II.12 1st Section on fde. systems based on principles other than variable sharing principles, critique of a system attributed to Strawson labelled Str. .

We now stop searching among systems based on a principle of variable sharing. To be sure, we continue to require variable sharing as a necessary condition for formal entailment. But variable sharing conditions do not seem to provide sufficient conditions for entailment. So we turn to a consideration of fde. systems based on principles which place restrictions on tautologous $(A \supset B)$'s over and above some condition on the variables in A and in B which condition should at least imply that A and B have a variable in common. These principles seem to go deeper than variable sharing principles because *prima facie* they make an appeal to normative intuitions. The variable sharing principles seem *ad hoc*. One would think that even the variable sharing condition C7 would be a consequence of the principle for selecting the genuine entailments from the tautologous $(A \supset B)$'s. We will consider four systems based on these apparently deeper principles. We first consider a system based on the principle that contradictions and tautologies cannot be terms of an entailment. We label this first system Str. for P.F. Strawson who suggested such a system. Secondly, we consider a system based on an ingenious principle of J. Cleave and S. Körner. We then consider a system based on an epistemological principle of K. Lehrer. Finally, we consider a system based on an extremely appealing principle of P. Geach and G.H. von Wright. We will find all of these systems unacceptable.

As a preliminary to a critique of Str. and to show that Cleave's and Lehrer's systems meet C7, we present Theorem I.

Theorem I of II.12: If $A \supset B$ is a classical tautology in which A and B share no variables, then A is a contradiction or B is a tautology. (Corcoran [1972])

To prove this theorem note that if we have the antecedent of the theorem but the opposite of the consequent there can be a single classical truth table assignment to the variables of A which makes A true and to the variables of B which makes B false; thus contradicting the assumption that $A \supset B$ is a tautology.

In light of Theorem I we can draw the following corollary.

Corollary 1 of Theorem I of II.12: If S is an fde. system which prohibits contradictions and tautologies as terms of its $\longrightarrow$, then S satisfies the variable sharing condition C7.

If there were some general considerations which favored prohibiting tautologies and contradictions as terms of an entailment, Theorem I's corollary would provide a principle for selecting an fde. system. In effect, system Str. is a system selected in accordance with such a principle.

The principle of Str. is as follows.

$A \rightarrow B$ iff. $A \supset B$ is a tautology and neither A is a contradiction nor is B a tautology.

We leave as an exercise an argument that Str. has no contradictions or tautologies as terms of $\rightarrow$ in theses. We call this system Str. after P.F. Strawson who in his [1948] advocated the more general principle that necessary truths and necessary falsehoods cannot be terms of an entailment. Some others who have explicitly rejected necessary truths and falsehoods as terms of entailments are Watling on pp.146-49 of [1958] and S. Körner on p. 158 of [1947]. At the end of this Section and also in the next Section, we will assess this general principle. Now let us assess Str. as an fde. system.

We can immediately observe that Str. does not have $A \rightarrow A$ as a thesis schema because $p \vee \sim p \rightarrow . p \vee \sim p$ is not an Str. thesis. A bit more reflection reveals that Str. has none of the thesis schemas cited in C15 of I.6. The failure of Str. to have any thesis schemas at all can be seen as a consequence of rejecting as true entailments any tautologous $A \supset B$ with contradictory A or tautologous B. Here we will not distinguish between rejecting such an $A \rightarrow B$ as false and rejecting it because it is somehow meaningless.

Theorem II of II.12: If an fde. system S rejects a tautologous $A \supset B$ as a $A \rightarrow B$ if A is a contradiction or B is a tautology, then S does not have uniform substituion for variables as an admissible rule and S has no thesis Schemas.

Proof remarks: One needs only to consider the case where $A \supset B$ is tautologous but both A and B are contingent zdfs.. One can show by induction on the number of variables that A has a contradictory substitution instance. Pick v( ) a classical valuation of A which assigns F (false) to A. Find a contradictory substitution instance of A by substituting $p_i \vee \sim p_i$ for p_i if $v(p_i)$=T and by substituting $(p_j \wedge \sim p_j)$ for p_j if $v(p_j)$=F. Similarly by paying attention to a valuation which assigns T to B we can find a tautologous substitution instance of B. Of course, if we do not have uniform substitution we do not have schemas.

As we argued in support of C8 we think that unifrom variable substitution is an important feature. In a way, the inablility to give thesis schemas and the failure of uniform variable substitution to be an admissible rule reveals that the entailments of Str. are not truly formal entailments in as much as we cannot display the forms of its entailment with schemas. It is not difficult to find instances of the schemas of C15 which are intuitively acceptable, eg., $p\wedge(q \vee \sim q)\rightarrow .q \vee \sim q$. So, it is most unlikely that we will accept Str. Still, let us investigate Str. a bit more to appreciate the disastrous consequences of rejecting necessary truths and falsehoods as terms of entailments.

On the positive side, $\rightarrow$ is transitive in Str. and Contraposition holds. Also R3,R5, and R6 hold. However, R4 fails as is revealed by the fact that $p\rightarrow p\wedge(q \vee \sim q)$ holds while $p\rightarrow .q \vee\sim q$ fails. Premiss Addition, R9, also fails. We have $p\rightarrow p$ but lack $p\wedge\sim p\rightarrow p$. From C16's undesirable features, Str. has Suppression of necessary truths and Boethius' Rule. If T is a tautology and $A\wedge T\rightarrow B$ holds, then both A and B are contingent and $A\supset B$ is a tautlogy; and consequently $A\rightarrow B$ holds in Str.. In regard to the Boethius Rule, note that if $A\supset B$ is a tautoloy and both A and B are contingent, then there will be a classical valuation such that v(A)=T and v($\sim$B)=F. Hence, if $A\rightarrow B$ holds in Str., then $A\rightarrow\sim B$ will fail.

There is no doubt that Str. has too many undesirable features to be accepted. So, let us critically examine some principles which led to Str.. We do not want to reject principles merely because they lead to unacceptable systems. We gain more insight by uncovering defects in the principles. Furthermore, an examination of the principles may reveal them to be so appealing that we revise our normative intuitions on adequacy conditions for entailment theses and rules.

We speak of principles behind Str. because one can hold a broad or narrow version of the principle behind it. The broad version is: No necessary truth or falsehood can be a term of an entailment. The narrow version is: In formal sentential logic no classical contradiction or tautology can be a term of an entailment. An even narrower version says only that no classical contradiction can be a term of an entailment in sentential logic. In[1959], Smilely severely criticizes these principles and we adopt some of his arguments. Of course, the defects of Str. already have shown some of the defects of the narrower versions. Also the fact that the tautologous axioms of standard axiomatizations of classical sentential logic yield some, if not all, of the theorems of classical logic by the best possible formal reasoning suggests that the narrow version is wrong. So, we focus our critique on the broad version. If the broad version is unacceptable, the major reason for accepting the narrow version is eliminated.

A most serious defect in the broad principle is that it makes entailment depend not only upon a connection between antededent and consequent but also upon features which the antecedent and consequent have independently of this connection. It requires entailment to be more than an intimate deducibility connection. On this principle we could have, as far as we know, a perfectly good argument from A to B. But then, without finding any defect in our reasoning, we would have to fault our reasoning, deny that we had an entailment, simply by discovering that B was necessarily true. Secondly, a holder of the broad version has to say that good reasoning in mathematics does not correspond to the best possible reasoning if mathetmatical truths are necessarily true. In particular, a holder of the broad version has to say that a reductio assumption for a mathematical proof has no entailments, if the reductio assumption really is a mathematical impossibility.

Nevertheless, in fairness to Strawson, we need to present and to appraise his rebuttal of the preceding charge that on his principle there are no entailments in mathematical reasoning. We devote the next Section to this epistemological topic.

Exercises II.12

1. Show that Str. has Transitivity and Contraposition.
2. Does Replacement hold in Str.?
3. Does Str. have a rule of Antilogism?
4. Defend Str. against the charge that it has no thesis schemas.
5. Is there any significant difference between Str. and a system Str.' which only forbids contradictions from being terms of an entailment?

II.13 Criticism of the Strawsonian view that mathematical reasoning is not reasoning from necessary truths.

In this Section we present a reconstruction and critique of Strawson's attempted rebuttal in [1948] of the charge that he has to fault all mathematical reasoning if he denies that necessary truths and falsehoods can be terms of an entailment. His rebuttal is based on two claims. The first claim is: Mathematical reasoning from axioms A to a theorem T can be analyzed as reasoning from a sentence 'A is necessary' to a sentence 'T is necessary.' The seccond claim is: A sentence saying that a sentence or formula is necessary is contingent. Let us assess these two claims in order.

In regard to the first claim it is more plausible to try to analyze mathematical reasoning as reasoning from 'A is an axiom' to 'T is a theorem.' The claims of necessity would seem to be based on information that our axioms are necessarily true and that our rules of proof preserve necessity. In this Section, though, let us consider 'A is an axiom' as ' A is necessary and has axiom status in the sytem being used' and ' T is a theorem' as 'T is necessary and has theorem status in the system being used.' Hopefully, in this way we capture Strawson's intentions. What is of most importance, though, is that A be obtained and accepted before T is obtained and accepted by use of A. To obtain and to accept is to prove. Hence, we ignore talk of axioms, theorems, and necessity in favor of 'A is provable' and 'T is provable.' So, the first claim is reconstructed as: Mathematical reasoning from axioms A to theorem T can be analyzed as reasoning from a sentence 'A is provable' to 'T is provable.' For definiteness' sake, assume that we are talking about an axiomatic version of arithmetic such as S. Kleene's on p. 82 of [1950] or E. Mendelson's on p. 103 of [1964].

Certainly it is not obvious that all reasoning in the development of these systems cited is done from metalinguistic sentences of the form: S is provable. From a sentence such as 'S is provable' we can draw a conclusion such as 'S can be used in any subsequent proof as a step in the proof.' We may also be able to get little results which could be called logical corollaries of theorems. In the systems cited we could do the following rather trivial reasoning. S is provable; so $(S \vee R)$ is provable. S is provable and R is provable; so $(S \wedge R)$ is provable. At some time in the development of the system we have to get S or R as theorems. Development of a system is not simply combining claims of provability according to principles of a sentential and quantification logic. Or put it this way: The development of a system, of the type cited, cannot all be done by use of classical sentential and quantificational logic on sentences using the predicate: Provable(A), i.e., $\vdash$A. To develop the system we have to use the axioms to get some of the $\vdash$A's. We occasionally have to use some of the predicates in the axioms; not just the metalinguistic predicate $\vdash$A. If we actually have to use the axioms, as opposed to using $\vdash$A, to get some of the $\vdash$T, Strawson would have to object to the reasoning or say that the reasoning we actually do can be interpreted according to his first claim. If a theorem T is not actually obtained by reasoning from claims of the form $\vdash$A, one wonders how one can move from 'A is provable' to 'T is provable.' Presumably, one would look at the A's and construct a proof in the system to T. Then as a result of having this proof within the system, we could say that the provablity of T is obtainable from the provablity of A. But now the question is: Why not take the proof of T from the A's as being as good as formal reasoning can be? Why say that ideally we have reasoned from 'It is provable that A' when we have actually reasoned from A?

Also on the Strawsonian analysis, how should we regard reductio proofs in mathematics? If we know that the system which we are developing is negation complete, i.e., every sentence or its negation is a theorem, and is consistent, then possibly a reductio assumption ~C can be interpreted as 'C is not provable.' But if we do not know of such completeness and consistency, we have to regard the reductio ~C as plain ~C. And if ~C is necessarily false, as it will be in a good reductio, Strawson will have to fault the reasoning.

We seem to have a solid case that reasoning in formal sciences cannot be analyzed as reasoning from metalinguistic claims of the form 'S is provable,' let alone from sentences of the form 'S is necessary.'

If the first claim is unacceptable, we do not have to worry, in the context of criticizing Strawson's attempted rebuttal, about the correctness of the second claim. Possibly the second claim is correct. At least as long as we do not consider cases, the second claim is plausible. The theory of informative intuition, sketched early in I.5, suggests that the second claim is correct. One suspects that the psychological conditions for our having the necessary truths which we do have could change. So, we cannot claim that our necessary truths are necessarily necessary. But when we consider particular cases it seems unlikely that many of them could fail to be necessary. To be sure 'No bachelors are married' could be a contingent sentence. if usage changed; and we can conceive of what the changes would be like. However, when we consider necessary truths such as those of arithmetic and those saying that a sentence or a formula is a thesis or is provable there seems to be no basis for saying that they could be other than necessary. Consider, for instance, the claim that $p \wedge q \rightarrow p$ is an Str. thesis. No alteration of usage is going to make $p \wedge q$ and p non-contingent formulas. Use of p,q, and $\wedge$ may change; but what $p \wedge q$ and p now stand for will not change. So, no change in usage is going to alter the fact that $p \wedge q \supset p$ is a classical tautology. What is now $p \wedge q \supset p$ is going to stay a classical tautology. So, we can dismiss Strawson's second claim as dubious, if not incorrect.

II.14 Critque of the Cleave/Körner system CK. .

The fde. system presented and criticized in this Section is, surprisingly, even more defective than system Str.. This system was developed by J. Cleave in his [1974]. Cleave acknowledges a debt to S. Körner for some basic ideas. So, we label the system CK.. It is a surprise that CK is more defective than Str. because CK is based on a more subtle principle. The principle behind Str. seemed wrong-headed because it required consideration of the modal status of the antecedent and consequent; not just attention to the connection, or lack of connection, between antecedent and consequent. The principle behind CK is a principle of relevance. Roughly, the principle says that $A \rightarrow B$ holds iff. there is no subformula of $A \supset B$ which is irrelevant to $(A \supset B)$'s being a tautology.

Some terminology is needed to state more precisely the principle behind CK.. We call attention to a particular occurrence of a subformula X of formula F by writing F(X). If this occurrence of X is replaced with $\sim X$, we designate the result of the replacement with $F(\sim X)$. An occurrence of subformula X of formula F is irrelevant in F iff. $F(X) \equiv F(\sim X)$ is a classical tautology. Thus, because $(p \wedge q \supset p) \equiv (p \wedge \sim q \supset p)$ is a classical tautology, q is irrelevant in $p \wedge q \supset p$. The first occurrence of $p \vee \sim p$ in $p \vee \sim p \supset . p \vee \sim p$ is irrelevant because $(p \vee \sim p \supset . p \vee \sim p) \equiv (\sim(p \vee \sim p) \supset . p \vee \sim p)$ is a classical tautology. But the second occurrence of $p \vee \sim p$ is not irrelevant because $(p \vee \sim p \supset . p \vee \sim p) \equiv (p \vee \sim p \supset . \sim(p \vee \sim p))$ is not a classical tautology. A formula F is slack iff. it contains an irrelevant subformula. A formula F is rigid iff. it is not slack. We can now define truth conditions for being an fde. thesis of system CK..

$A \rightarrow B$ is a CK thesis iff. $A \supset B$ is a rigid classical tautology.

In our assessment of CK the first point to note is that CK is a subsystem of Str.. This point is significant enough to be a Theorem in this Section.

Theorem I of II.14: If $A \rightarrow B$ is a CK thesis, then A is not a contradiction and B is not a tautology.

Proof: If A is a contradiction and $A \supset B$ is a tautology, then $A \supset \sim B$ is a tautology; hence $A \supset B$ is not a rigid tautology. If B is a tautology, both $A \supset B$ and $\sim A \supset B$ are tautologies; hence, again, $A \supset B$ is not a rigid tautology.

So, CK has all of the odd features of Str.. But CK is even worse than Str.. Str. at least has some instances of

Simplification as theses. But in CK no formula of the form $A \wedge B \rightarrow A$ is a thesis. Also no formula of the form $A \rightarrow . A \vee B$ is a thesis. But worst of all, as Cleave himself showed, the $\rightarrow$ of CK is not transitive. CK has: $(p \wedge q \vee p \wedge r) \rightarrow p \wedge (q \vee r)$ and $p \wedge (q \vee r) \rightarrow . (p \wedge q) \vee r$. But CK lacks: $(p \wedge q \vee p \wedge r) \rightarrow . (p \wedge q) \vee r$ because both $(p \wedge q \vee p \wedge r) \supset . (p \wedge q) \vee r$ and $(p \wedge q \vee p \wedge \sim r) \supset . (p \wedge q) \vee r$ are classical tautologies.

So we can confidently reject CK as a candidate for the right fde. system. Still, let us briefly assess CK's principle. The weaknesses of CK reveal that the way to insure a special relevance between antecedent and consequent is not to require that every subformula of A and B be relevant to $(A \supset B)$'s being a tautology. We will not pursue modifications of CK such as: $A \rightarrow B$ holds iff. $A \supset B$ is a tautology with no subformula having an irrelevant occurrence only in the antecedent or only in the consequent. We do not pursue such modifications because we believe that relevance to being a tautology is not relevance between A and B.

Exercises II.14

1. Develop a decision procedure for CK. (Edelstein [1976])
2. Show that Contraposition holds in CK..
3. Show that CK has no theses of the form $A \wedge B \rightarrow A$, $A \rightarrow . A \vee B$, and $A \wedge T \rightarrow B$ where T is a tautology.
4. Does CK have: $A \rightarrow B, A \rightarrow C$ then $A \rightarrow B \wedge C$ and $A \rightarrow C, B \rightarrow C$ then $(A \vee B) \rightarrow C$ as admissible rules?
5. Show that if we have $A \vee B \rightarrow C$ then neither $A \rightarrow C$ nor $B \rightarrow C$ hold.
6. Does CK have Replacement?
7. Does CK have Boethius' Rule? Are CK and Str. systems of connexive logic in the sense given in 29.8 of Anderson's and Belnap's [1975]?

II.15 Lehrer's notions of relevant deduction and minimally inconsistent sets, rejection of a quasi fde. system developed from these notions.

In his [1974] Keith Lehrer tried to make precise the following epistemological notion. A relevant deductive argument is an argument in which knowledge of the truth of each and every premiss is needed to establish the truth of the conclusion from the premisses of the argument. We will not explore the epistemological significance of the notion. Our concern is with Lehrer's explication of this notion as a type of first degree entailment. We will show that the formal characterization of his relevant deductive arguments does not select the argument forms we can call the formally correct ones. In this Section schema letters will still denote only zdfs..

An argument form: $A_1, .., A_n$; so, B is a <u>relevant deductive argument form</u> if $\{A_1, ..., A_n, \sim B\}$ is a finite inconsistent set but no proper subset is inconsistent, i.e., in Lehrer's terminology $\{A_1, ..., A_n, \sim B\}$ is a <u>minimally inconsistent set</u>. A <u>relevant deductive argument</u> is an argument with a relevant deductive argument form. Lehrer does not explicitly define an entailment relation; but we can investigate a candidate for entailment corresponding to relevant deductive argument forms. To define an entailment relation corresponding to relevant deductive argument forms we alter our previous practice of regarding the antecedent of $\rightarrow$ as a single formula. Here we regard the antecedents of $\rightarrow$'s as finite sets of zdfs.. Thus we talk of a quasi fde. system. We represent the sets of formulas with formulas and formula schemas separated by commas. A single formula or schema before an $\rightarrow$ represents the unit set of that formula or schema. After defining Lehrer entailment, we will explain our departure from past practice in talking about fde. formulas.

$A_1, A_2, ..., A_n \rightarrow B$ is a <u>Lehrer entailment</u> iff. $A_1 \wedge A_2, .. \wedge A_n \supset B$ is a tautology and $\{A_1, A_2, ..., A_n, \sim B\}$ is a minimally inconsistent set, viz., $A_1, ... A_n$; so, B is a relevant deductive argument.

For Lehrer entailments we cannot treat the premisses of an argument form as a single conjunction which can then be used as an antecedent for $\rightarrow$. We have $\{p \wedge q\} \rightarrow q$ as a Lehrer entailment but lack $\{p, q\} \rightarrow q$. No proper subset of $\{p \wedge q, \sim q\}$ is inconsistent; but the proper subset $\{q, \sim q\}$ of $\{p, q \sim q\}$ is inconsistent. So, from Lehrer's perspective the argument form $A_1 \wedge A_2, ., \wedge A_n$; so, B is different in logically significant ways from the argument form $A_1, A_2, .., A_n$; so, B.

This logical distinction between the two argument forms is certainly unusual. Nevertheless there are some normative intuitions in favor of making this distinction when we are searching for a connection between premisses and conclusion in which we need or use the premisses to get the conclusion. When we get B from $A \wedge B$, we take the unit $A \wedge B$ and pull it apart to get B. When we have premisses $\{A,B\}$, we consider the unit $\{A,B\}$, of course. But we ignore one of the premisses in our selection of B from $\{A,B\}$. So, let us not reject this notion of Lehrer's simply on the basis that it accepts $p \wedge q \longrightarrow q$ but not $p,q \longrightarrow q$. We reject this notion because it does not allow reasoning from contradictions nor reasoning to tautologies. In addition it is not transitive. Lehrer himself points out that this $\longrightarrow$ is not transitive. He has $p, \sim p \vee q \longrightarrow q$, $q \longrightarrow \sim p \vee q$, but lacks $p, \sim p \vee q \longrightarrow . \sim p \vee q$. In a way this system is a subsystem of Str.. To see that it is we close with the following Theorem whose proof is the exercise for this Section.

Theorem I of II.15: If $A_1, \ldots, A_n$ is a Lehrer entailment, no A_i is a contradiction and B is not a tautology.

II.16 The Geach/von Wright system which we label G: presentation, critique, and rejection.

We now consider a system which the author wishes were the right fde. system because the principle of P. Geach and G.H. von Wright which motivates it is so appealing. Geach's version of the principle is that A entails B iff. there is an apriori way of getting to know 'if A then B' which is not a way of getting to know either A or B. The basic idea behind this principle is that we have to pay attention to a connection between A and B to find out that necessarily whenever A holds B holds; we cannot have based our our claim that B holds whenever A holds simply on information about A itself or B itself such as A being necessarily false or B being necessarily true. This principle will be critically examined in II.18 while Section II.17 will be a reconsideration of the issue of the transitivity of entailment. In this Section we examine a system constructed in accordance with this principle. We label this system G for Geach who presents it in [1970] and defends it briefly in [1971]. Geach labels his system ES. A.J.Dale is one of its most severe critics in his [1973]. T. Smilely also considers a system such as G on p.240 of his [1959]. In sections 20.1.1 and 20.1.2 of their [1975] Anderson and Belnap discuss the gist of this principle which they call the WGS criterion. They show that every thesis of E_{fde} meets this criterion. In their 15.1 they make critical observations on the system we call G.

The language of G contains the zdfs. and fdes.. Because we want to make some observations about primitive connectives, we sketch the formation rules for G. The language consists of parentheses, sentential variables, primitive truth functional signs: $\wedge$, $\vee$, $\sim$, $\supset$, and $\equiv$, and the entailment sign $\rightarrow$. The wffs. of G are the smallest set consisting of the zdfs. formed with these primitives and the fdes. made up from these zdfs.. The theses of G are (the members of) the smallest set of G wffs. meeting conditions (a),(b), and (c) below.

a) If A is a classical tautology, A is a thesis of G.
b) If $A \supset B$ is a classical tautology but neither $\sim A$ nor B are classical tautologies, then $A \rightarrow B$ is a G thesis.

However, (b), which is essentially the principle of Str., is not taken as a necessary condition for the thesishood of an $A \rightarrow B$. So he adds a third condition. This third condition is uniform substitution for variables, which was a condition which failed for Str..

c) If A is a wff. of G obtained from a thesis B of G by uniform substitution for a variable of B, A is a thesis of G.

Because our concern is with the fde. formulas of G, we can compress (b) and (c) to give the following condition for G-thesishood of an fde. formula. We merely close Str. under uniform substitution for variables.

A⟶B holds iff. A⊃B is a substitution instance of a tautology A'⊃B' such that neither A' nor B' are tautologies.

We call tautologies A'⊃B' such that neither ~A' nor B' are tautologies G-safe tautologies. We leave as an exercise the details of showing how to list the finitely many wffs. of which a given A B is a substitution instance. Being able to make such a list shows that G is decidable. But specifying how to make such a list is messy. Since we find reasons for rejecting G, we avoid the messy details. So, let us now turn to evaluating G in light of theses and rules which it has and lacks. In this Section the fact that G satisfies variable sharing condition C7 warrants Theorem status.

Theorem I of II.16: If A⟶B is a G thesis, A and B share a variable.

Proof: If A⟶B holds, A⊃B is a substitution in stance of a G-safe tautology A'⊃B'. By Theorem I of II.12 A' and B' share a variable. Hence, any uniform substitution which gives A from A' and B from B' will require A and B to share a subformula and hence to share a variable.

A second Theorem shows that G is rich in theses.

Theorem I of II.16: The thesis schemas of C15 of I.6 are all thesis schemas of G.

Proof: Simply regard each distinct basic schema letter as a distinct sentential variable in those schemas. They, then, are all G-safe tautologies.

Fortunately, G is not so rich in theses that it has all the theses of V2 of II.5. For instance, G lacks the odd r∧(p∧~p)⟶.q∧~r and p⟶.~p v (q v ~q). It also lacks the odd (p∧~p)∧~q⟶q which holds in the Parry/Dunn systems. Admittedly, system G has MD: A∧(~A v B)⟶B, and DS: ~A∧(A v B)⟶B, as thesis schemas. Ultimately we will reject MD and DS; but prima facie they are merits of system G. G also has: A⟶.A∧(B v ~B),which Anderson and Belnap in [1962a] and on pp. 155-56 of [1975] find half as counter intuitive as: A⟶.B v ~B. Ultimately, for systematic reasons, we will concede to Anderson and Belnap that A⟶.A∧(B v~B) should not be an fde. thesis. Still we must admit that to uninstructed normative intuitions A⟶.A (B v~B) seems acceptable. From A we get the A conjunct of the consequent while $B \vee {\sim}B$ cannot provide any reason for rejecting the A which we got from A. At least in the case of $A \rightarrow . A \wedge (B \vee {\sim}B)$ we cannot say that the antecedent is wholly irrelevant to getting the consequent as it is in $p \rightarrow . {\sim}p \vee (q \vee {\sim}q)$. So, we are not able to reject G on the basis of its theses. Unfortunately, G is weak on rules. It lacks some crucial rules and a natural extension has a very undesirable rule. Here it may help to refer back to the list of rules in Cl4 of I.6.

Transitivity, as Geach himself pointed out, fails. We have $p \wedge {\sim}p \rightarrow . {\sim}p \wedge (p \vee q)$ from the G-safe tautology: $p \wedge r \supset . r \wedge (p \vee q)$. We have ${\sim}p \wedge (p \vee q) \rightarrow q$. Transitivity would give $p \wedge {\sim}p \rightarrow q$ which G does not have. Nevertheless Transitivity holds if A,B, and C are contingent formulas. Such restricted Transitivity is not good enough. We want to be able to reason discursively from non-contingent claims with as much propriety as from contingent claims. Although G has Contraposition, it lacks R3,R4,R5, and R6. R4 fails because it has $p \rightarrow . p \wedge (q \vee {\sim}q)$ while lacking $p \rightarrow . q \vee {\sim}q$. A.J. Dale pointed out that G lacks R3. G has $(p \vee q) \wedge {\sim}(p \vee q) \rightarrow p$ from the G-safe $(p \vee q) \wedge {\sim}(r \vee q) \supset p$ and has $(p \vee q) \wedge {\sim}(p \vee q) \rightarrow q$ from the G-safe $(p \vee q) \wedge {\sim}(p \vee r) \supset q$. But G lacks $(p \vee q) \wedge {\sim}(p \vee q) \rightarrow . p \wedge q$. Use DeMorgan's equivalences and Double Negation on the entailments and tautologies in the counterexample to R3 to get a counterexample to R5. Do the same to the counterexample to R4 to get a counterexample to R6.

Dale as well as Smilely point out that a repeated conjunct of an antecedent cannot always be eliminated. We noted in Dale's counterexample to R3 that G lacks $(p \vee q) \wedge {\sim}(p \vee q) \rightarrow . p \wedge q$, which we here abbreviate as $X \rightarrow . p \wedge q$. Dale then observes that G has $((p \vee q) \wedge {\sim}(p \vee q)) \wedge ((p \vee q) \wedge {\sim}(p \vee q) \rightarrow . p \wedge q$, i.e., $X \wedge X \rightarrow . p \wedge q$ from the G-safe $((p \vee q) \wedge {\sim}(r \vee q)) \wedge ((p_1 \vee p_2) \wedge {\sim}(p_1 \vee p_3)) \supset . p \wedge p_2$. Dale also shows that we cannot go from $B \rightarrow . A \vee A$ to $B \rightarrow A$. A counterexample to R5 shows that G lacks $({\sim}p \vee {\sim}q) \rightarrow . (p \vee q) \vee {\sim}(p \vee q)$ although G has both ${\sim}p \rightarrow . (p \vee q) \vee {\sim}(p \vee q)$ and ${\sim}q \rightarrow . (p \vee q) \vee {\sim}(p \vee q)$. But G has ${\sim}p \vee {\sim}q \rightarrow . ((p \vee q) \vee {\sim}(p \vee q)) \vee ((p \vee q) \vee {\sim}(p \vee q))$ from ${\sim}p \vee {\sim}q \supset . ((r \vee q) \vee {\sim}(p \vee q)) \vee ((p_1 \vee p_2) \vee {\sim}(p_1 \vee p_3))$ which is G-safe. Now we can see that Replacement also fails. G has $A \wedge A \rightarrow A$ and $A \rightarrow A \wedge A$ as well as both $A \rightarrow . A \vee A$ and $A \vee A \rightarrow A$.

A further oddity of G, observed by Dale, is that G has $q \rightarrow . (q \supset q) \wedge (q \supset q)$ while lacking $q \rightarrow . q \equiv q$. This is not to say that G lacks $(q \supset q) \wedge (q \supset q) \rightarrow . q \equiv q$ and $q \equiv q \rightarrow . (q \supset q) \wedge (q \supset q)$. G has both from the G-safe tautologies $(p \supset q) \wedge (q \supset p) \supset . p \equiv q$ and $p \equiv q \supset . (p \supset q) \wedge (q \supset p)$. If $\equiv$ is a primitive sign, the only tautologies of which $q \supset . q \equiv q$

is an instance have a tautologous ($p_1 \equiv p_1$) as a consequent. This last noted oddity would vanish if $\equiv$ were defined as usual in terms of $\supset$. If $\equiv$ is not primitive we can start with the G-safe tautology $q \supset .(r \supset q) \wedge (p \supset q)$ and use substitution to get $q \supset .(q \supset q) \wedge (q \supset q)$ which will give $q \supset .q \equiv q$ by definition.

Let us note that G does not allow Suppression of tautologies. Consider that G has $p \wedge (q \vee \sim q) \longrightarrow .q \vee \sim q$ from the G-safe $p \wedge r \longrightarrow r$. But there is a restricted principle of Suppression: If A and B are contingent and T is a tautology, then if we have $A \wedge T \longrightarrow B$ we have $A \longrightarrow B$. In the next Section we will worry about even this restricted version of Suppression.

Despite its weakness on rules, If G had MP for $\longrightarrow$ and Adj., there would be, as the author showed in [1975a], a derivation of q from $p \wedge \sim p$ using only G-theses, MP, and Adj.. We repeat the derivation here. Regard $\longrightarrow$ as $\supset$ to verify that each cited thesis comes from a G-safe tautology.

i)	$p \wedge \sim p$	Hyp.
ii)	$p \wedge \sim p \longrightarrow p$	
iii)	$p \wedge \sim p \longrightarrow \sim p$	
iv)	p	MP (i),(ii)
v)	$p \longrightarrow .p \vee q$	
vi)	$p \vee q$	MP (iv),(v)
vii)	$\sim p$	MP (i),(iii)
viii)	$\sim p \wedge (p \vee q) \longrightarrow q$	
ix)	$\sim p \wedge (p \vee q)$	Adj. (vi),(vii)
x)	q	MP (viii), (ix)

Of course, since $p \wedge \sim p \longrightarrow q$ does not hold in G, the above reasoning does not correspond to a G thesis on entailment. So A, $\sim A \vdash$ B is a non-normal rule for G supplemented with MP and Adj. for zdfs.. One wonders, though, what could make this derivation formally better from the perspective of G. A holder of G should not criticize it on the basis that the hypothesis is a contradiction. To criticize it on such a basis would be to criticize formal reasoning on some basis other than that of a lack of connection between premisses and conclusion. The principle motivating G is that entailment should depend only upon the connection between premisses (antecedent) and conclusion (consequent); we should not have to worry about the modality of the premisses. The suspicion is that G is unacceptable because not only does Transitivity fail but that it can't be used for discursive reasoning even in a limited way because MP and Adj. lead to embarrassments in it.

Enough oddities have been noted to dismiss G as the most likely candidate for the fde. system. However, because the demand for Transitivity looms so large in our arguments and because G's principle is so appealing we consider these two topics in the next two Sections.

Exercises II.16

1. Develop a decision procedure for G.
2. Show that $(p \vee q) \wedge \sim(p \vee q) \longrightarrow . p \wedge q$ is not a G-thesis.
3. Show that Contraposition holds in G.
4. Show that the restricted principle of Suppression holds.
5. Show that MP for $\longrightarrow$ is an admissible rule for G.
6. Show that for zdfs. Adj. is an admissible rule for G.

II.17 The Lewy argument against the Transitivity of entailment, presentation and rejection.

Given the remarks made in Section I.3, it would be dishonest to suggest that these two Sections re-open the question of whether or not entailment is transitive. Instead, we hope to strengthen our resolve to find a transitive implication stricter than strict implication by finding flaws in two arguments that entailment is not transitive. The first argument is made by citing paradigms of entailments and a paradigm non-entailment. Then it is contended that if we assume entailment to be transitive we get the paradigm non-entailment as an entailment from the paradigm entailments. This is the Lewy argument. The force of the Lewy argument comes from the fact that it is about our natural language. It alleges that the entailment which we are trying to represent formally should not be transitive because it is not transitive in natural language. The second case against transitivity is made by developing a plausible general principle explaining why certain paradigm non-entailments, but logical implications, are non-entailments. Systems of entailment constructed in accordance with this principle give a non-transitive entailment. In effect, the second argument is the development of the Geach/von Wright principle. In this Section we show that Lewy does not make a successful case that it is transitivity which leads to trouble. In the next Section we examine and find the Geach/von Wright principle to be less than compelling.

We consider Lewy's argument from his [1958]. The following argument using sentences labelled D,E,and F leads to a sentence $D \longrightarrow F$ which is supposed to be a paradigm of a flase entailment claim despite the fact that it is impossible for D to be True and for E to be false because E is necessarily true. Nevertheless, the other entailment claims made, and each inference made from entailment claims, are supposed to be paradigms of true entailments,or a paradigm of an inference we can make from entailments to entailments. Hence, we are supposed to have a <u>reductio</u> of Transitivity as an inference rule for entailments. Let us see the details of Lewy's argument.

D: Caesar is dead iff. Russell is a brother.

E: Russell is a brother iff. Russell is a male sibling.

F: Caesar is dead iff. Russell is a male sibling.

Lewy suggests reading iff. as material equivalence. Viz., X iff. Y is true in case both X and Y are true or X and Y are both false; and otherwise X iff. Y is false. With iff. read as material equivalence,with 'Russell' understood as referring to Bertrand Russell, and 'Caesar' understood as referring to Julius Caesar, both D and E are true. For Lewy's argument, however, it is not important that we accept D and F as true. But Geach's defense of Lewy's argument requires accepting that D and F are neither necessarily true nor necessarily false. So, certainly, let us grant that D and F are contingent. Let us also admit that E is necessarily true. A claim that E is necessarily true, viz., $\Box E$, is the first premiss of Lewy's <u>reductio</u> argument below. Despite the fact that we ultimately give up Transitivity for material equivalence, let us still accept (ii) and (iii) in the argument below as expressing true entailment claims of our natural language.

i) $\Box E$
ii) $D \wedge E \longrightarrow F$
iii) $D \wedge F \longrightarrow E$
iv) $D \longrightarrow F$ — From (i),(ii) by Suppression of necessary truths.
v) $D \longrightarrow .D\ F$ — From (iv) by Absorption which we will accept.
vi) $D \longrightarrow E$ — From (v) and (iii) by Transitivity.

If we would accept strict implication as explicating entailment, we can agree with Pollock who in his [1966] suggested that Lewy's alleged <u>reductio</u> of Transitivity is rather simply a proof that D does entail E. We must admit that D does strictly imply E because E cannot be false. However, we certainly do not get the analytic truth E from the silly claim D. So, we agree with Lewy that $D \longrightarrow E$ is a paradigm of a false claim of entailment. We have accepted the premisses of the argument leading to $D \longrightarrow E$; so, we have no choice except to reject one of the inference rules. Lewy rejects Transitivity. We reject Suppression of necessary truths. Clearly, if line (ii) is acceptable, it is acceptable because from both D and E together we can get F. In actual reasoning to establish line (ii) E is needed to get F from D. If we drop E from the antecedent of $D \wedge E \longrightarrow F$ simply because we find out that E is necessarily true we violate the guiding idea in entailment studies that the truth of an entailment claim depends on the connection between the antecedent and the consequent. The truth or modal status of the antecedent, consequent, or parts thereof is irrelevant to the connection.

So, because the conclusion of the Lewy argument can be avoided by rejecting a rule other than Transitivity, the Lewy argument is not a conclusive argument that entailment in our natural language is non-transitive. Of course, a more adequate defense of our rejection of Suppression is to develop an acceptable system which does not allow Suppression. We intend to do this. But now let us consider Geach's argument to support the claim that entailment really is non-transitive as Lewy concluded.

II.18 Critique of the Geach/von Wright principle.

P. Geach in his [1958], which is a paper from the same symposium at which Lewy presented the argument of the previous Section, accepts Lewy's claim that entailment is not transitive. Geach gives a concise, fairly precise, and quite persuasive definition of 'entails' so that we can appreciate why entailment is not trnasitive but why it does tolerate Suppression of necessary truths. The definition is basically the one cited at the beginning of our Section II.16. Geach acknowledges that he has adopted his definition from G.H. von Wright's [1957c] which Geach classes as "one of the best papers ever written on entailment." G.H. von Wright's original definition on p. 180 of [1957c] was: " p entails q, if and only if, by means of logic it is possible to come to know the truth of" $p \supset q$ " without coming to know the falsehood of p or the truth of q." Let us examine and criticize this definition.

Von Wright gave his definition to articulate the ideal that in the best possible inference we draw the conclusion from the premisses without regard to the truth-value or modality of the premisses and conclusion. On p. 177 he wrote the following.

> Reviewing the situation and asking ourselves why it is that entailment can be identified neither with material nor strict implication nor with relative necessity, we may answer as follows.
>
> It appears to be the essence of entailment to be a relation between propositions which subsists quite independently of either truth-values or the modal status of the propositions. No account of entailment is satisfactory unless it can do justice to this idea of independence.

On pp. 173-74 von Wright reminded us that our use of _reductio ad absurdum_ proofs, when we know or believe the _reductio_ assumption to be necessarily false, shows that we have the concept of reasoning well from a claim regardless of its truth-value or modal status.

Presumably, if we could come to know by means of logic that whenever A held then B held without knowing that A is false or that B is true, we would do so by recognizing some connection between A and B such A brought B along with it. But this is only a presumption; and even if we recognize some such connection the connection may not be properly classed as entailment. So, we cannot accept von Wright's appealing definition until we find out more exactly what it says and what its consequences are. We follow Geach in his elaboration of the definition.

Geach differs from von Wright in two significant ways. Geach uses apriori instead of 'by means of logic' because it does not seem as if we determine that 'X is red' entails 'X is colored' by means of logic, where 'logic' suggests formal considerations. We should follow Geach in the use of apriori to make it perfectly clear that we are leaving open the question of whether or not there are material entailments, i.e., synthetically necessary entailments, as well as formal entailments. Also Geach specifies that there is an apriori way rather than merely saying "it is possible to come to know." Geach wants to reject any suspicion that it may be merely possible but not true that there is an apriori way of coming to know: if A then B. Nevertheless, Geach does not require that anyone has to know of this apriori way. There can be true entailments which no one knows about. We should also read the definition as telling us that there is an apriori way of getting to know that it is necessary that if A holds then B holds. Let us explicitly exclude saying that someone knows that 'if A then B' is an entailment if someone, only by experience, came to know that as a matter of fact whenever A then B without knowing anything about the truth or falsity of A or B.

Admittedly, the apriori ways of coming to know are not precisely defined. We will not criticize the Geach/von Wright principle merely on the general grounds that apriori is imprecise. We do, however, consider favorably criticisms which exploit the imprecision to show that it is quite plausible to hold that some paradigm non-entailments satisfy the principle. A motive for restricting the apriori ways to those of logic was to avoid the imprecision. It is hopeless, though, to try to characterize precisely the apriori ways. Gödel's Incompleteness Result shows that we cannot precisely characterize the ways of getting to know arithmetic truths, which are presumably paradigms of what is known apriori.For Geach the imprecision of apriori shows that 'entails' will have a family of uses. But we should not take his use of 'family' to have all the connotations of 'family' in Wittgenstein's use of 'family' in his Philosophical Investigations. Geach certainly thinks that any kind of entailment has the kind of property given in his definition. Geach does not want his talk of apriori ways to be construed as committing him to acceptance of a realm of non-empirical objects and a faculty for inspecting such a realm. On p. 166 he writes the following. "Of course the existence of an apriori way of getting to know that p is not to be established by a philosophic inspection of an abstract realm, but simply by proving apriori that p." To be sure a critic can reply that it is not perfectly clear that proving apriori does not involve philosophic inspection of an abstract realm. However, let us not quarrel with Geach over accounts of what there is in order to know entailment truths, i.e., let us not quarrel about the epistemology of entailment. After we discover the system of true entailments, we can worry about the epistemology of entailment. Here the point of interest is that the Geach/von Wright principle cannot be recommended on the basis that it gives an especially appealing epistemology for entailment.

Our main concern is to examine Geach's argument that given his definition of 'entails' it is legitimate to suppress a necessarily true C from a true $A \wedge C \longrightarrow B$ if A and B are contingent. We hope to expose the inadequacy of his definition by showing that the suppression which it allows gives, as formal entailments, entailments which Geach should reject. The following argument is from pp. 166-67 of his [1958] and p. 182 of his <u>Logic Matters</u>. We are given that we have $A \wedge C \longrightarrow B$ and $\Box C$. I.e., we have an <u>apriori</u> way of knowing $A \wedge C \supset B$ holds necessarily without having to know $\sim(A \wedge C)$ or B; and we have an <u>apriori</u> way of knowing C is necessary. From $A \wedge C \longrightarrow B$ we get (i) below because true entailments tell us that we have a good argument.

i) $A, C \vdash B$

ii) $C \vdash A \supset B$ From (i); a deduction theorem for $\supset$.

From $\Box C$ and (ii) we conclude (iii).

iii) $\Box(A \supset B)$

A consideration of what we have done in reaching (iii) reveals that we have used an <u>apriori</u> way of reaching the result that $A \supset B$ holds necessarily without having to find out whether $\sim A$ holds or B holds. So, the consideration allegedly entitles us to assert $A \longrightarrow B$.

Note that in the preceding argument that the Geach definition of 'entails' allows suppression the assumptions that A and B are contingent are not used. Yet such assumptions are crucial because if $q \vee \sim q$ is suppressed from $p \wedge (q \vee \sim q) \longrightarrow . q \vee \sim q$, we get the totally unaccetable $p \longrightarrow . q \vee \sim q$. So, the Geach definition, by allowing suppression as above, is too broad. To support the charge that suppression as used in the above argument is too broad begin with the entailment $(\sim(p \wedge \sim p) \vee q) \wedge (p \wedge \sim p) \longrightarrow q$ as the argument of line (i) below.

i) $(\sim(p \wedge \sim p) \vee q), p \wedge \sim p \vdash q$

ii) $(p \wedge \sim p) \vee q \vdash p \wedge \sim p \supset q$. Deduction theorem for $\supset$.

We now argue that the premiss in line (ii) is necessarily true because it is a substitution instance of the tautology $\sim(s \wedge \sim s) \vee r$. So, as above in the more general argument, we conclude:

iii) $\Box(p \wedge \sim p \supset q)$

So, we have come to know $\Box(p \wedge \sim p \supset q)$ without coming to know that $(p \wedge \sim p)$ is necessarily false. And we did not have to know anything about the contradictoriness of $p \wedge \sim p$ or tautologous of $(\sim(p \wedge \sim p) \vee q)$ to get the first entailment because it is an instance of the G-safe $(\sim r \vee s) \wedge r \rightarrow s$. So, by the Geach definition, we should conclude that we have reached $p \wedge \sim p \rightarrow q$. (Anderson and Belnap in [1962a], A.J. Dale in [1973], J. Pollock in [1965], and P.F. Strawson in [1958] have raised similar considerations to show that the Geach/von Wright principle is too broad.)

Geach's argument for suppression shows how we can go from the information that C is necessarily true and $A \wedge C \supset B$ is necessarily true to a conclusion that $A \supset B$ is necessarily true independently of any consideration of A and B. But knowing that $A \supset B$ is necessarily true, i.e., that A logically implies B is not the same as knowing A entails B. We can now appreciate why the Geach/von Wright principle is inadequate. Recognition of a logical or strict implication from A to B independently of knowledge of $\sim A$ or B does not guarantee that there is a special connection between A and B. The epistemic conditions on recognizing the necessity of an $A \supset B$ only suggest we would have to pay attention to a connection between A and B. Examples have revealed, however, that we can discover the necessity of an $A \supset B$ without discovering the necessity of $\sim A$ or the necessity of B but still without paying attention to a connection between A and B. On the Geach/von Wright principle we pay attention to a connection between our knowledge and A and our knowledge and B; we are not required to pay attention to a connection between A and B by themselves. So, we dismiss the Geach/von Wright principle and its fde. system.

II.19 Halldén's system S0,1st. Section on pseudo subsystems of S2 and S3.

We now assess systems of S. Halldén from [1948b] and T. Sugihara from [1955]. We are primarily concerned with the fde. fragment of these systems. We, nevertheless, have to pay attention to more than the fde. fragment because these systems are presented as what can be called apparent subsystems of S2 because if the $\rightarrow$ in their axioms were taken as the $\dashv$ of S2 their axioms would be S2 axioms. But they are only apparent sybsystems because the $\rightarrow$ in these systems is primitive and is not defined in terms of $\Diamond$, $\wedge$ and $\sim$ as is the $\dashv$ of S2. Recall our discussion of modal primitives from II.3. Halldén is perfectly clear that his system, which he labels S0, is not even a subsystem of S1 because $\rightarrow$ is primitive in S0. Sugihara's definition of $\dashv$ makes it clear that he did not consider has system SA to be a subsystem of S1 or S2. However, these systems are presumably presented in the belief that the axioms of S1 and S2 when expressed with $\dashv$ have the form of theses of entailment. Because they are only apparent or pseudo subsystems of S1,S2 and S3, it is unfortunate that they are labelled S0 and SA because the S in the label suggests that they are in the Lewis S-family of systems. Still, we will use the original labels.

In this Section we assess Halldén's S0 and find it woefully weak. In fairness to Halldén, it should be noted that he did not present S0 as <u>the</u> system of entailment. He presentend it only as a system to be developed into the correct system of entailment. Most of the systems which are considered seriously have all of S0's axioms as theorems or theses. System S0, with its $\rightarrow$ regarded as the $\rightarrow$ of the Dunn/Parry ASI is a subsystem of ASI. System S0 is also a subsystem of system E which we will ultimately defend. Incidentally, it is of interest to note that Halldén thought S0 was somewhat faithful to the ideas of Duncan-Jones in [1935] and that R. Meyer and R.K. Routley develop model structure semantics for S0 in their [197_i]. Duncan-Jones began his paper by writing: " I propose in this paper to use the word entailment for a relation between two propositions p and q when q arises out of the meaning of p." Unfortunately, Jones' formulation is not clear enough to use as a criterion for telling whether Halldén's $p \rightarrow q$ does represent 'q arises out of the meaning of p.' So, we assess Halldén's system as a system of formal entailment rather than as a system for presenting some meaning connection.

For S0 the primitive logical signs are: $\wedge$, $\sim$, and $\rightarrow$. There are four definitions.

D1: $A \vee B =_{df.} \sim(\sim A \wedge \sim B)$

D2: $A \supset B =_{df.} \sim(A \wedge \sim B)$

D3: $A \leftrightarrow B =_{df.} (A \rightarrow B) \wedge (B \rightarrow A)$

D4: $A \circ B =_{df.} \sim(A \rightarrow \sim B)$

The axiom schemas for S0 are below. We will also use these schemas for Sugihara's SA; so we label the schemas with Ahs. for 'Halldén/Sugihara axioms.'

Ahs. 1: $A \wedge B \rightarrow B \wedge A$

Ahs. 2: $A \wedge B \rightarrow A$

Ahs. 3: $A \rightarrow A \wedge A$

Ahs. 4: $(A \wedge B) \wedge C \rightarrow . A \wedge (B \wedge C)$

Ahs. 5: $A \rightarrow \sim\sim A$

Ahs. 6: $(A \rightarrow B)\ (B \rightarrow C) \rightarrow . A \rightarrow C$

Ahs. 7: $A \wedge (A \rightarrow B) \rightarrow B$

The rules are MP for $\rightarrow$, Adj. and Replacement of entailment equivalents.

The most striking feature of these schemas is that only Ahs. 5 places conditions on $\sim$. If $A \rightarrow \sim\sim A$ is all that we are told about $\sim$, we are not guaranteed that $\sim$ can even come close to expressing what we want to say with negation. Part of what we want to express with a negation sign is $\sim\sim A \rightarrow A$, Contraposition, if $A \rightarrow B$ holds, then $\sim A \vee B$ holds, and if $A \wedge \sim B$ holds then $\sim(A \rightarrow B)$ holds. We also want $A \wedge \sim A$ to be a contradiction and hence have $\sim(A \wedge \sim A)$. If we cannot express most, if not all, of these with the $\sim$ of a system, it is best not to consider it as a negation sign. If $\sim$ is not a genuine negation sign, definitions of logical signs using $\sim$ cannot be expected to get their usual meaning. One value of investigating S0 is to uncover the inadequacy of having only $A \rightarrow \sim\sim A$ place conditions on $\sim$.

Before using a matrix of Halldén's to make a case that S0's $\sim$ is not a negation sign, let us compare S0 with some other systems. The fde. fragment of S0 is not included in Str. CK, or Lehrer's system because S0 has $A \rightarrow A$ as a thesis schema. Because the $\rightarrow$ of **S0 is transitive** the $\rightarrow$ of S0 cannot be that of Geach's system.

Halldén presented the two-value matrix given by the tables below, with 1 as the designated element. Let us label the matrix $\mathcal{H}$.

A	B	$A \wedge B$	$\sim A$	$A \vee B$	$A \supset B$	$A \rightarrow B$	$A \leftrightarrow B$	$A \circ B$
1	1	1	1	1	1	1	1	1
1	0	0	1	0	0	0	0	0
0	1	0	0	0	0	1	0	1
0	1	0	0	0	0	1	1	1

An outstanding feature of $\mathcal{H}$ is the treatment of $\sim$ as an identity operator. The reader may check that $\mathcal{H}$ is suitable for S0. $\mathcal{H}$ can be used to show that S0 is consistent in the senses that some formulas are not theorems of S0 and that $p \wedge \sim p$ is not a theorem. $v(p \wedge \sim p)=0$ when $v(p)=0$. However, and unfortunately for the $\sim$ of S0, we cannot use $\mathcal{H}$ to show that S0 is consistent in the sense of not having both an A and $\sim A$ as theorems. For instance, both $\sim(A \rightarrow A)$ and $(A \rightarrow A)$ are valid on $\mathcal{H}$; and hence so is $(A \rightarrow A) \wedge \sim(A \rightarrow A)$. Also consider that $A \rightarrow \sim A$ is valid on $\mathcal{H}$. So we could add $A \rightarrow \sim A$ as an axiom schema to S0 to get S0'. S0' would still be consistent in the sense that $p \wedge \sim p$ is not a theorem. Yet whenever we could prove A in S0' we could also prove $\sim A$. The fact that we would have in S0' $\vdash A$ iff. $\vdash \sim A$ where S0' is consistent dramatizes that the $\sim$ isn't a genuine negation. It's too harmless to be a negation.

A glaring weakness of S0 is that it has no zdfs. as theorems. No classical tautology is a theorem of S0!

Theorem I of II.19: If A is a zdf., then A is not a theorem of S0.

Proof hint: By induction on the length of A, show that $v(A)=0$ if $v(p)=0$ for all p in A.

As a consequence of Theorem I a rule $A \rightarrow B / \vdash A \supset B$ fails. Hence neither $A \rightarrow B \rightarrow . A \supset B$ nor $A \rightarrow B \supset . A \supset B$ are theorem schemas. So, Belnap's C1 is violated. On the other hand $A \wedge \sim B \rightarrow . A \rightarrow B$ is valid on $\mathcal{H}$ and could be added as as axiom schema to S0 without yielding $p \wedge \sim p$. So. Belnap's C2 can be violated in S0. On $\mathcal{H}$ if we set $v(p)=0$ and $v(q)=1$ both $v((p \rightarrow q) \rightarrow (\sim q \rightarrow \sim p))=0$ and $v((p \rightarrow q) \supset (\sim q \rightarrow \sim p))=0$. But not only does Contraposition fail to be a theorem; it also fails even to be an admissible rule. If we have $v(p)=1$ and $v(q)=0$ the contrapositive of the theorem $p \wedge q \rightarrow p$ gets 0.

We have seen enough of S0 to see that its $\sim$ is too weak to express negation. So we turn to a study of Sugihara's SA which is S0 plus an axiom schema for Contraposition. Exercises will bring out further features of S0.

Exercises II.19.

1. Show that S0 is consistent in the sense that for no A do we have $\vdash A$ and $\vdash \sim A$.
2. Verify Parry's observation on p. 153 of [1968] that S0 lacks $\sim\sim A \rightarrow A$. Use the Group I matrix on p. 493 of Lewis' and Langford's [1932] but treat $\sim A$ as follows. $\sim 1 = \sim 2 = 1$, $\sim 3 = 2$, and $\sim 4 = 3$. The tables for $\wedge$ and $\rightarrow$ are as on the next page. $\{1,2\}$ are the designated values.

Exercises II.19 continued

2. (continued)

∧	1	2	3	4
1	1	2	3	4
2	1	2	4	4
3	3	4	3	4
4	4	4	4	4

→	1	2	3	4
1	2	4	4	4
2	2	2	4	4
3	2	4	2	4
4	2	2	2	2

3. Show that the DeMorgan equivalences fail. Note also that S0 could be a subsystem of Intuitionistic logic. See pp. 40-43 of Mendelson [1964].

4. Use the matrix of exercise #2 to show that the fde. fragment of S0 is a proper subset of V4. Consider A ∨ A ⟶ A and p q ∨ p r ⟶ .p ∨ (q ∨ r).
5. Do R3, R5, R6, hold for S0?
6. Show that R4 and R8 hold for S0.
7. Use $\mathcal{H}$ to show that B∘A ⟶ A∘B is not an S0 theorem. Following a suggestion of Parry on p. 153 of [1968] redefine A∘B as ∼(A∧B ⟶ ∼(A∧B)). Show that we now have ⊢ B∘A ⟶ A∘B. But show that if we define ◇A as A∘A ◇A is still ∼(A ⟶ ∼A) on either definition of A∘B.

II.20 1st. Section on Sugihara's systems, The system SA.

This is the first of two Sections on Sugihara's work on SA. Some of the material in these two Sections is covered in 26.9 of Anderson's and Belnap's [1975]. This Section is an investigation of SA with special emphasis on negation and the failure of Distribution. The next Section is an assessment of the theses we get if we take validity on Sugihara matrices as the criterion for thesishood. Although Sugihara suggested the idea of this kind of matrix, a consideration of formulas valid on Sugihara matrices takes us far beyond SA. Still it is well to consider the Sugihara matrix theses here because we will find that we want more that what is given by SA but less than the theses given by Sugihara matrices.

As noted in the previous Section, SA is S0 plus a Contraposition schema $(\sim A \rightarrow B) \rightarrow . \sim B \rightarrow A$ which we will label Asa. 8. Also relabel the axiom schemas of S0 with Asa. instead of Ahs.. We label theorems Tsa.. Instead of Halldén's definitions, Sugihara has Halldén's first three but Sugihara has D4 as $\Diamond A =_{df.} \sim(A \rightarrow \sim A)$ and a D5 which is: $A \exists B =_{df.} \sim \Diamond (A \wedge \sim B)$

Let us call $A \rightarrow A$, which is easily proved in S0, Tsa.1. If we now take Tsa.1 in the form $(\sim A \rightarrow \sim A)$ and use Asa.8 in the form $\sim A \rightarrow \sim A \rightarrow . \sim\sim A \rightarrow A$, MP gives us Tsa.2 which is $\sim\sim A \rightarrow A$. Tsa.3 can be: $\sim\sim A \leftrightarrow A$. From Asa.8 in the form $(\sim\sim A \rightarrow B) \rightarrow . \sim B \rightarrow \sim A$ we get Tsa.4: $A \rightarrow B \rightarrow . \sim B \rightarrow \sim A$, by using Replacement with Tsa.3. With Tsa.3, D4, and Repl. we get the DeMorgan equivalences. Tsa 5: $\sim(A \vee B) \leftrightarrow . \sim A \wedge \sim B$ and Tsa 6: $\sim(A \wedge B) \leftrightarrow . \sim A \vee \sim B$. From Asa. 2 in the form $\sim A \wedge \sim B \rightarrow \sim A$ we can get Tsa.7: $A \rightarrow . A \vee B$. So SA is obviously not a subsystem of any of the Dunn/Parry systems; and of course the fde. fragment of SA is not included in V4. The advantage of having gone beyond the Dunn/Parry systems is that we have a more adequate $\sim$. However, we have lost our guarantee that we can still satisfy the variable sharing condition C7. To re-establish that we still satisfy this variable sharing condition with SA, we give a Theorem whose proof requires a look ahead.

Theorem I of II.20: If $\vdash_{SA} A \rightarrow B$, then A and B share a variable.

Proof remarks: Note that every axiom of SA is a theorem of system E of IV.1 and then see the proof in Theorem I of IV.1 that E satisfies C7.

However, the $\sim$ of SA is not the full negation of classical logic because, as we will see in the next Section, neither MD nor DS hold for SA. Although we too will reject MD and DS, we cannot accept SA because SA is too weak. SA lacks Distribution and it has no zdf. theses. So the $\sim$ of SA is not strong enough to get the classical tautologies. Indeed as the matrix $\mathcal{C}$ below shows the $\sim$ of SA does not give $A \rightarrow B \rightarrow . \sim A \vee B$. So SA fails even C1.

The matrix whose designated value is 2 is given by the tables below.

	$\sim$
2	0
1	1
0	2

$\wedge$	2	1	0
2	2	0	0
1	0	1	0
0	0	0	0

$\rightarrow$	2	1	0
2	2	0	0
1	2	2	0
0	2	2	2

$\vee$	2	1	0
2	2	2	2
1	2	1	2
0	2	2	0

We leave the tedious proof of the next Theorem as an exercise.

Theorem II of II.20. $\mathcal{C}$ is suitable for SA.

$\mathcal{C}$'s suitability for SA allows us Theorem III.

Theorem III of II.20: If A is a zdf.,A is not a theorem of SA.

Proof remarks: By induction on the length of A show that v(A)=1 if v(p)=1 for all variables p in A where the valuation is on $\mathcal{C}$.

Consider the Distribution schema $A \wedge (B \vee C) \rightarrow . A \wedge B \vee A \wedge C$ in the unabbreviated form $A \wedge \sim(\sim B \wedge \sim C) \rightarrow . \sim(\sim(A \wedge B) \wedge \sim(A \wedge C))$ to recognize that Distribution is a thesis about negation. To use $\mathcal{C}$ to invalidate Distribution set v(A)=2,v(B)=2, and v(C)=0. The same assignment invalidates $A \wedge (B \vee C) \rightarrow . B \vee (A \wedge C)$ which is frequently used as an axiom schema to give Distribution. To invalidate $A \rightarrow B \rightarrow . \sim A \vee B$ set v(A)=v(B)=1. Theorem III tells us that we do not have $A \vee \sim A$ or $\sim(A \wedge \sim A)$ as theses. Note also that Sugihara's D4 and D5 do not get $A \rightarrow \Diamond A$ and $\Box A \rightarrow \Diamond A$ as theorems where $\Box A$ is $\sim \Diamond \sim A$. To see the failure of these modal formulas set v(A)=1. Note also that these modal formulas are, in part, principles about negation. So we need more than $A \rightarrow \sim\sim A$ and Contraposition to get an adequate negation.

While we are considering $\mathcal{C}$, set v(A)=v(C)=1, v(B)=2, and V(D)=0 to show that the following positive and desirable schemas are not theorem schemas of SA.

$(A \rightarrow B) \wedge (B\ C \rightarrow D) \rightarrow . A \wedge C \rightarrow D$

$(A \rightarrow B) \wedge (A \rightarrow C) \rightarrow . A \rightarrow B \wedge C$

Sugihara realized that SA lacked the schemas which we have cited. Exercises will bring out some of the extensions which he suggested.

Exercises II.20

1. Show that SA is consistent in the sense that for no A do we have both A and $\sim$A as theorems of SA. Is this consistency of SA preserved if we add $A \rightarrow \sim A$ to SA?
2. Show that SA lacks Boethius' thesis.
3. Show that SA lacks R3 and then show that it lacks R5. For R3 consider $A \rightarrow . A \rightarrow A$ and $A \rightarrow A$ as premisses and $A \rightarrow . A \wedge (A \rightarrow A)$ as a conclusion. Note that on matrix $\mathfrak{C}$ that if the premisses of a primitive rule are 2 the conclusion is 2. Show that if SA had R5 it would also have R3.
4. Show that SA has R6.
5. Add Antilogism as an axiom schema to SA to get what Sugihara calls SB. Show that in SB we have: $A \rightarrow B \leftrightarrow . A \rightarrow B$
6. Add Exportation to SA to get what Sugihara calls SC. Show that in SC we have $A \supset B \leftrightarrow . A \rightarrow B$.

II.21 Sugihara matrices, the Sugihara theses, system RM.

In this section we introduce the notion of Sugihara matrix. This section presupposes familiarity with I.7. We investigate some of the desirable and undesirable features of Sugihara theses, viz., formulas valid on all Sugihara matrices. We report R.K. Meyer's result from his [1971d] and now in 29.3.2 of Andersons's and Belnap's [1975] that the Sughiara theses are exactly the theorems of the entailment system RM presented in IV.10. Most of the systems which we consider in Part IV are subsystems of RM. Consequently, with the Sugihara matrices, we have a readily available source of matrices for showing that certain formulas are not theses of interesting systems. The system of Sugihara theses forms an upper bound on the entailment system for which we are searching; we will not want more than the Sugihara theses. Only incidentally do we make some of Sugihara's points about his system SA since SA is too weak to be the system which we want.

The notion of Sugihara matrix is developed by abstracting and taking as defining, features of a matrix γz which Sugihara used to show that SA was free from implication paradoxes. We adapt J.M. Dunn's characterization of Sugihara matrices from his [1970] which Dunn presents in a slightly different way in 29.4 of Anderson's and Belnap's [1975]. A Suihara matrix is an ordered septuple $\langle M, D, U, \wedge, \vee, {}^{-}, \rightarrow \rangle$, where M is a set totally ordered under $\leq$, while D and U are disjoined subsets of M with $M = D \cup U$. The unary operation $^{-}$ is a one-to-one order inverting function on M onto M and for which $\bar{\bar{a}} = a$. The set of designated elements D is the set of a such that $\bar{a} \leq a$. $a \wedge b = \min(a,b)$ under $\leq$ and $a \vee b = \max(a,b)$ under $\leq$. If $a \leq b$, then $a \rightarrow b = \max(\bar{a},b)$, i.e., $\bar{a} \vee b$; but if $a \not\leq b$ then $a \rightarrow b = \min(\bar{a},b)$, i.e., $\bar{a} \wedge b$. One may define $a \leftrightarrow b$ as $(a \rightarrow b) \wedge (b \rightarrow a)$. We now establish some properties of Sugihara matrices.

Theorem I of II.21: Sugihara matrices are McKinsey normal.

We get the theorem from lemmas 1 and 2 below. Readers uninterested in the details of algebraic arguments should skip the following sublemmas.

Sublemma 1 of II.21: If $a \leq b$, then $\bar{b} \leq \bar{a}$.

Sublemma 1 comes from the definition of $^{-}$ as an order inverting mapping. Note that Sublemma 1 brings out a striking difference between the $^{-}$ of Parry matrices and the $^{-}$ of Sugihara matrices. Recall from II.10 that for Parry matrices we had $\bar{a} \leq \bar{b}$ if we had $a < b$.

Sublemma 2 of II.21: If $a \in U$ and $b \in D$, then $a < b$.

As a proof of Sublemma 2 consider the following. If $a \in U$, then $\bar{a} \not\leq a$ because U and D are disjoined and $\bar{a} \leq a$ is the condition for a to be in D. So, $a < \bar{a}$ because $\leq$ is a total ordering. Because $b \in D$, we have $\bar{b} \leq b$. If we now assume for <u>reductio</u> that $a \not< b$, we have $b \leq a$ from the fact that $\leq$ is a total ordering. By the transitivity of $\leq$ $b \leq a$ and $a < \bar{a}$ give $b < \bar{a}$. Sublemma 1 and $\bar{\bar{a}} = a$ give $a < \bar{b}$ from $b < \bar{a}$. Now $a < \bar{b}$ and $\bar{b} \leq b$ with transitivity of $\leq$ give $a < b$ contrary to our <u>reductio</u> assumption.

Sublemma 3 of II.21: If $a \in U$, then $\bar{a} \in D$.

As a proof of Sublemma 3 consider the following. If $a \in U$ then $a \notin D$ because U and D are disjoined. If $a \notin D$, then $\bar{a} \not\leq a$. If $\bar{a} \not\leq a$, then $a < \bar{a}$ by the fact that $\leq$ is a total order. If we now assume for <u>reductio</u> that $\bar{a} \notin D$, we get $\bar{\bar{a}} \not\leq \bar{a}$, i.e., $a \not\leq \bar{a}$, which contradicts $a < \bar{a}$.

Sublemma 4 of II.21: If $a \in U$ and $b \in D$, then $a \rightarrow b \in D$.

As a proof of Sublemma 4 consider the following. The hypothesis of this sublemma and Sublemma 2 give $a < b$. If $a < b$, then $a \rightarrow b = \max(\bar{a}, b)$. Since $\max(\bar{a}, b)$ is either b or $\bar{a}$, $a \rightarrow b \in D$ either by the hypothesis that $b \in D$ or by use of Sublemma 3 to get $\bar{a} \in D$ from the hypothesis that $a \in U$.

Sublemma 5 of II.21: If $a \in D$, $b \in D$, and $a \leq b$, then $a \rightarrow b \in D$.

As a proof of Sublemma 5 consider the following. Assume the hypothesis of the sublemma and $a \rightarrow b \notin D$ for <u>reductio</u>. So, we have assumed that $\max(\bar{a}, b) \notin D$. Since, by hypothesis, $b \in D$, then $\max(\bar{a}, b) = \bar{a}$, which tells us $b < \bar{a}$. From $a \in D$ we have $\bar{a} \leq a$. So, $b < a$ which is contrary to the hypothesis that $a \leq b$.

Sublemma 6 of II.21: If $a \in U$, $b \in U$, and $a \leq b$, then $a \rightarrow b \in D$.

As a proof of Sublemma 6 consider the following. For <u>reductio</u> assume the hypothesis and that $a \rightarrow b \notin D$. $a \rightarrow b \notin D$ with $a \leq b$ tells us that $\max(a, b) \notin D$. Now Sublemma 3 tells us that $a \in U$ and $b \in U$ give us $\bar{a} \in D$ and $\bar{b} \in D$. So, $\max(\bar{a}, b) = b$ and, hence, $\bar{a} < b$. But Sublemma 1 with $a \leq b$ gives us $\bar{b} \leq \bar{a}$. $\bar{b} \leq \bar{a}$ and $\bar{a} < b$ give $\bar{b} < b$. But Sublemma 2 tells us that we cannot have $b \in U$ and $\bar{b} \in D$ with $\bar{b} < b$.

Sublemma 2 tells us that we cannot have the case of $a \in D$, $b \in U$, and $a \leq b$. So, Sublemmas 4,5, and 6 give us a 7th.

Sublemma 7 of II.21: If $a \leq b$, then $a \rightarrow b \in D$.

Sublemma 8 of II.21: If $a \not\leq b$, then $a \rightarrow b \notin D$.

As a proof of Sublemma 8 consider the following. Assume for <u>reductio</u> $a \neq b$ but $a \rightarrow b \in D$. In this case $b < a$ and $\min(\bar{a}, b) = a \rightarrow b$. If $\min(\bar{a}, b) \in D$ and is $\bar{a}$, we have $\bar{\bar{a}} \leq \bar{a}$, i.e., $a \leq \bar{a}$. But $b < a$ and $a \leq \bar{a}$ give $b < \bar{a}$ which contradicts $\min(\bar{a}, b) = \bar{a}$. In case $\min(\bar{a}, b) = b$, we have $b \in D$ and, hence, $\bar{b} \leq b$ by definition of D. From $b \in D$ we get $\bar{b} \leq b$ which with $b < a$ gives $\bar{b} < a$. By Sublemma 1 $\bar{b} < a$ gives $\bar{a} < b$ which conflicts with $\min(\bar{a}, b) = b$. So, we have the sublemma.

Sublemmas 7 and 8 give us the first lemma.

Lemma 1 of II.21: On a Sugihara matrix $a \rightarrow b \in D$ iff. $a \leq b$ and $a \leftrightarrow b$ iff. $a = b$.

Sublemma 5 and Lemma 1 tell us that if $a \in D$ and $a \rightarrow b \in D$, then $b \in D$. Of course, if $a \in D$ and $b \in D$, then $\min(a, b) \in D$, i.e., $a \wedge b \in D$. Sublemma 2 tells us that $\max(a, b) \in D$, i.e., $a \vee b \in D$, if either $a \in D$ or $b \in D$. If neither $a \in D$ nor $b \in D$, then $\max(a, b) \notin D$, i.e., $a \vee b \notin D$. So, we have the following lemma, which with Lemma 1 gives Theorem I.

Lemma 2 of II.21: On a Sugihara matrix D is a prime filter

To show that Sugihara matrices are McKinsey normal we did not need to show that the designated elements on a Sugihara matrix forms a prime filter; we only had to show that D is a filter. But the primeness of D together with the fact that $a \vee \bar{a} \in D$, which can be established with Sublemmas 3 and 4, tells us that Sugihara matrices are complete.

Theorem II of II.21: Sugihara matrices are complete.

An example below will reveal that Sugihara matrices can be inconsistent. But before presenting examples of Sugihara matrices, we offer some results about systems for which Sugihara matrices are suitable and characteristic.

Theorem III of II.21: Sugihara matrices are distributive lattices.

By way of proof we concern ourselves only with the distributivity lattice axiom, L7 of I.7,: $a \wedge (b \vee c) \leq (a \wedge b) \vee c$. Reflect on: $\min(a, \max(b, c)) \leq \max(\min(a, b), c)$, to convince yourself that Sugihara matrices are distributive in their $\wedge$ and $\vee$ parts.

Sugihara matrices get their value for us by being suitable for many of the systems which we study. Our next theorem is invaluable for showing that Sugihara matrices are suitable for subsystems of system RM.

Theorem IV of II.21: Sugihara matrices are suitable for the system RM of Section IV.10.

Theorems I and III and Lemma 1 of this section along with Theorem II of I.7 are useful in a proof of this theorem. But verification of the validity of axiom schemas with nested $\rightarrow$'s involves messy consideration of cases. We consider only the distinguishing axiom schema for RM, viz. $A \rightarrow . A \rightarrow A$. On any Sugihara matrix $v(A) \leq v(A \rightarrow A)$ for the following reason. Certainly, $v(A) \leq v(A)$. So, $v(A \rightarrow A) = \max(\overline{v(A)}, v(A))$. If $\max(\overline{v(A)}, v(A)) = v(A)$, obviously $v(A) \leq v(A \rightarrow A)$. If $\max(\overline{v(A)}, v(A)) = \overline{v(A)}$, then this is because $v(A) \leq \overline{v(A)}$; so, again $v(A) \leq v(A \rightarrow A)$. With Lemma 1 $v(A) \leq v(A \rightarrow A)$ tells that $v(A \rightarrow . A \rightarrow A) \in D$.

Since Sugihara's SA is a subsystem of RM, we have the following corollary.

Corollary of Theorem IV of II.21: Sughihara matrices are suitable for Sugihara's SA.

In the discussion of Example 2 below, the idea of the special type of Sugihara matrices labelled with $\mathcal{S}n$ is explained. Here we simply state without proof Dunn's Theorem 8 of his [1970] which is Meyer's completeness result for RM. Meyer's compelteness result also gives a decision procedure for system RM. Our Theorem V is now corollary 3.1 of 29.3.2 of Anderson's and Belnap's [1975].

Theorem V of II.21: If A contains but n distinct variables, $\vdash_{RM}$ iff. A is valid on $\mathcal{S}n$.

We are not here so much interested in RM theoremhood as we are in Sugihara thesishood. So, after some examples of Sugihara matrices we consider some desirable and, regretably because of the simplicity of working with Sughihara matrices, some undesirable features of the system of Sugihara-theses.

Example 1 of Sugihara matrices

An example of an inconsistent Sugihara matrix can be obtained by letting M be the positive and negative integers <u>including 0</u> in their standard order. Let $\overline{\underline{a}} = -\underline{a}$ and have $-0 = 0$. Let D be the non-negative integers including 0. Since $-0 = 0$ and $\overline{0} = -0$, $\overline{0} \in D$ and $0 \in D$. So, this original matrix of Sugihara's which we call $\mathcal{S}^{-}z$ is inconsistent.

If we have an inconsistent Sugihara matrix we superscript the label for it with $^{-}$ as we just did for $\mathcal{S}^{-}z$. A lemma, whose proof is an exercise, tells us how to make $\mathcal{S}^{-}z$ consistent.

Lemma 3 of II.21: A Sugihara matrix is consistent iff. for no $\underset{\sim}{a}$ does $\underset{\sim}{a} = \bar{\underset{\sim}{a}}$.

Example 2, $\mathcal{S}$z and the $\mathcal{S}$n Sugihara matrices,

$\mathcal{S}$z is the consistent Sugihara matrix obtained by deleting 0 from the M of $\bar{\mathcal{S}}$z. Lemma 3 tells us that $\mathcal{S}$z is consistent. An important feature of $\mathcal{S}$z, z for "zahlen," is that it has no least and no greatest element. We exploit this feature in Theorem VI below.

In general, let $\mathcal{S}$n be the Sugihara matrix obtained by taking as M the integers -n to +n excluding 0 with D as the positive integers. On $\mathcal{S}$n, $\bar{a} = -a$. Let $\bar{\mathcal{S}}_n$ be like $\mathcal{S}_n$ except that $0 \in M$ and $\bar{0} = 0$. Our third example is $\mathcal{S}_2$ which in Dunn [1970] is called M_4. (On $\mathcal{S}$n $\leq$ is arithmetic $\leq$.)

Example 3, Sugihara matrix $\mathcal{S}_2$,

$-$	
+2	-2
+1	-1
-1	+1
-2	+2

$\wedge$	+2	+1	-1	-2
+2	+2	+1	-1	-2
+1	+1	+1	-1	-2
-1	-1	-1	-1	-2
-2	-2	-2	-2	-2

$\vee$	+2	+1	-1	-2
+2	+2	+2	+2	+2
+1	+2	+1	+1	+1
-1	+2	+1	-1	-1
-2	+2	+1	-1	-2

$\rightarrow$	+2	+1	-1	-2
+2	+2	-2	-2	-2
+1	+2	+1	-1	-2
-1	+2	+1	+1	-2
-2	+2	+2	+2	+2

$\mathcal{S}_2$ can be used to show that the entailment form of Material Detachment, viz., $A \wedge (\sim A \vee B) \rightarrow B$, is not a Sugihara thesis schema. Set v(A) = -1 and v(B) = -2.

Our fourth example is $\bar{\mathcal{S}}_1$ which is used in R.K. Meyer's argument, in our Section II.22, that entailment cannot be defined in terms of modal and truth-functional signs. In Dunn's [1970] and in Anderson's and Belnap's [1975], $\bar{\mathcal{S}}_1$ is labelled M_3.

Example 4, Sugihara matrix $\bar{\mathcal{S}}_1$, (M_3), system RM3,

$-$	
+1	-1
0	0
-1	+1

$\wedge$	+1	0	-1
+1	+1	0	-1
0	0	0	-1
-1	-1	-1	-1

$\vee$	+1	0	-1
+1	+1	+1	+1
0	+1	0	0
-1	+1	0	-1

$\rightarrow$	+1	0	-1
+1	+1	-1	-1
0	+1	0	-1
-1	+1	+1	+1

In his [1974b] Meyer has $\bar{\mathcal{S}}_1$ tables for $\underset{\sim}{a} \leftrightarrow \underset{\sim}{b}$ and one for interpreting AoB, viz., $\sim(A \rightarrow \sim B)$.

$\leftrightarrow$	+1	0	-1
+1	+1	-1	-1
0	-1	0	-1
-1	-1	-1	+1

o	+1	0	-1
+1	+1	+1	-1
0	+1	0	-1
-1	-1	-1	-1

On $\bar{\mathcal{S}}_1$, D = {+1, 0}.

We follow Meyer in [1974b] in calling system RM3 the formulas valid on $\bar{\mathcal{S}}_1$. From Dunn's corollary 2 of his [1970] and his Dugundji Formula Theorem of 29.4 in Anderson's and Belnap's [1975] we get the result that RM3 can be axiomatized by adding to system RM uniform substitution for variables and the following Dugundji formula as an axiom.

The Dugundji formula for giving RM3.

$p_1 \leftrightarrow p_2 \vee p_1 \leftrightarrow p_3 \vee p_1 \leftrightarrow p_4 \vee p_2 \leftrightarrow p_3 \vee p_2 \leftrightarrow p_4 \vee p_3 \leftrightarrow p_4$.

Meyer axiomatizes RM3 in 29.12 of Anderson's and Belnap's [1975] by adding $A \rightarrow . \sim A \rightarrow A$, $A \rightarrow . (A \rightarrow B) \rightarrow B$, and $A \vee (A \rightarrow B)$ to system E. See B. Sobocinski [1952] and Z. Parks [1972] for background on RM3. However, we are not interested in axiomatic versions of RM3. When we talk of RM3 we are thinking of it under its semantic haracterization as the set of formulas valid on δ_1. Exercises bring out that even RM3 lacks certain paradoxical formulas as theses.

Sugihara discussed two types of implicational paradoxes. So, let us now turn away from giving examples and show that the system of Sugihara-theses is free from these two types of implicational paradoxes. The first type of a generalization of a weak version of the paradox of impossibility. A weak version of the paradox of impossibility is: $\Box \sim p \supset . p \rightarrow A$, where A is any formula. The second type is a generalization of a weak version of the paradox of necessity, viz., $\Box p \supset . A \rightarrow p$. Halldén showed in [1948a] that even modal system S1 has these paradoxes in the forms: $\Box \sim p \supset . p \prec A$ and $\Box p \supset . A \prec p$. Let f(p) be a formula made up from one use of a single variable such that for any Sugihara matrix there is a v( ) such that $v(f(p)) \in D$. Let t(p) be characterized as f(p) was. It helps to think of f(p) as $\Box \sim p$ and t(p) as $\Box p$. The first type of implicational paradox is to have an f(p) such that $f(p) \supset . p \rightarrow A$ is a thesis. The second type is to have a t(p) such that $t(p) \supset . A \rightarrow p$ is a thesis. Because we are only interested in systems in which $A \rightarrow B$ give $A \supset B$, knowing that a system lacks these weak general paradoxes is knowing that it lacks the strong ones, viz., $f(p) \rightarrow . p \rightarrow A$ and $t(p) \rightarrow . A \rightarrow p$. The schemas for the strong paradoxes are genuinely paradoxical if substitution instances of f(p) and t(p) are theses which contain no variables occurring in A. For instance, if f(p) is $\Box \sim p$, a subsitution instance of it is the thesis $\Box \sim (p \wedge \sim p)$; Modus Ponens then gives $p \wedge \sim p \rightarrow A$.

Let us also call having $A \wedge \sim A \rightarrow B$ and $A \rightarrow . B \vee \sim B$ as theses having implicational paradoxes.

Theorem VI of II.21: The system of Sugihara-theses is free from implicational paradoxes.

As proof consider the following. Use δ_2 to show that $A \wedge \sim A \rightarrow B$ and $A \rightarrow . B \vee \sim B$ are not valid. To invalidate, i.e., to show that $A \wedge \sim A \rightarrow B$ is not valid, set $v(A) = -1$ and set $v(B) = -2$. To invalidate $A \rightarrow . B \vee \sim B$ set $v(A) = +2$ and $v(B) = +1$. Now consider δ_z from Example 2 to borrow a proof from Sugihara. We invalidate $f(p) \supset . p \rightarrow A$ by taking a v() on $\mathcal{S}z$ such that $v(f(p)) \in D$ which the definition of f(p) guarantees. Let A be q which is a variable different from p and let $v(q) = \underset{\sim}{b}$ such that $\underset{\sim}{b} < v(p)$. Because $\mathcal{S}z$ has no least element we are guaranteed that there is such a $\underset{\sim}{b}$. So, by Lemma 1 $v(p \rightarrow q) \notin D$. The consistency of $\mathcal{S}z$ with $f(p) \in D$ gives us $\overline{f(p)} \notin D$. So, $v(f(p) \supset . p \rightarrow q) \notin D$ because $\max(\overline{f(p)}, v(p \rightarrow q)) \notin D$. We invalidate $t(p) \supset . A \rightarrow p$ by choosing a v() on $\mathcal{S}z$ such that $v(t(p)) \in D$. Again let A be a variable q different from p. Because $\mathcal{S}z$ has no greatest element we can set $v(q) = \underset{\sim}{b}$ where $v(p) < \underset{\sim}{b}$. We leave as an exercise the determination that $v(t(p) \supset . A \rightarrow p) \notin D$.

Despite its freedom from the above kind of implicational paradoxes, we cannot accept the system of Sugihara-theses. We cannot even accept its fde. fragment. Our next theorem, which was suggested in Routley's and Meyer's [1973a], reveals the basis for this unacceptability. Two lemmas help with the proof.

Lemma 4 of II.21: If $\underset{\sim}{a} \in D$ and $\underset{\sim}{a} \leq \underset{\sim}{b}$ on a Sugihara matrix, then $\underset{\sim}{b} \in D$.

Lemma 5 of II.21: If $\underset{\sim}{a} = \overline{\underset{\sim}{a}}$ and $\underset{\sim}{b} = \overline{\underset{\sim}{b}}$ on a Sugihara matrix, then $\underset{\sim}{a} = \underset{\sim}{b}$.

Theorem VII of II.21: If B and C are Sugihara-theses, then $\sim B \rightarrow C$ is a Sugihara-thesis.

For proof consider the following. For <u>reductio</u> assume that there is a v() on a Sugihara matrix such that $v(\sim B \rightarrow C) \notin D$. Lemma 1 tells us that $v(C) < \overline{v(B)}$. Because B and C are Sugihara-these by hypothesis, we have $v(B) \in D$ and $v(C) \in D$. Lemma 4 tells us that $v(C) \in D$ with $v(C) < \overline{v(B)}$ gives $\overline{v(B)} \in D$. So, we have $v(B) \in D$ and $\overline{v(B)} \in D$ which a proof of Lemma 3 shows yields $v(B) = \overline{v(B)}$. By Sublemma 1 we get $v(B) < \overline{v(C)}$ from $v(C) < \overline{v(B)}$. So, Lemma 4 tells us that $\overline{v(C)} \in D$ because $\overline{v(C)}$ is greater than v(B) which is in D. So, again the kind of consideration used to establish Lemma 3 shows that $v(C) = \overline{v(C)}$. Now Lemma 5 gives us $\overline{v(B)} = v(C)$ which conflicts with $v(C) < \overline{v(B)}$.

It is easy to establish that $A \vee \sim A$ and $A \rightarrow A$ are Sugihara-theses. So, we have the following corollaries.

Corollary 1 of VII of II.21: $\sim(p \rightarrow p) \rightarrow . q \rightarrow q$ and $p \wedge \sim p \rightarrow . q \vee \sim q$ are Sugihara-theses.

Corollary 2 of VII of II.21: The system of Sugihara-theses violates the variable sharing relevance condition C7 and so does its fde. fragment.

We close this discussion of Sugihara matrices by considering whether being valid on Sugihara matrices gives us any better understanding of what it is to be valid. To consider the value of Sugihara validity we follow the suggestion of Sugihara on p.57 of his paper.

> "To interpret the infinity of values in SA we establish a distinction between statement-values and truth-values. Statement-values are concerned with the contents of statements, while truth-values are concerned with the truth of statements. As there are an infinite number of things, there must be infinite statement-values, while the number of truth-values is two in the classical case."

Of course, Sugihara's suggestion does not apply to finite matrices. In his paper, though, he considered only infinite matrices because, following Dugundji [1940], he showed that no finite matrix would isolate just the Sugihara valid formulas.

Sugihara's suggestion is reminiscient of the II.11 assignments of K. Fine's semantics for ASI'. Although a modification of Sugihara's suggestion had merit in semantics for ASI', it fails to have merit for Sugihara matrices because of the total ordering of the elements of Sugihara matrices. Suppose, as we should, that both 'Snow is white' and '2+2 = 4' are true and that their truth is indicated by their being given designated values. I.e., the variables given to them as content get designated values. Still we have to put these designated values in order by specifying whether the value of 'Snow is white' is more or less than that of '2+2 = 4.' In either case, Lemma 1 forces an unacceptable choice. We must choose to say that either 'Snow is white $\rightarrow$ 2+2 = 4' is true or ' 2+2 = 4 $\rightarrow$ Snow is white' is true. So, we will not try to interpret Sugihara matrix values; we will use Sugihara matrices as an algebraic technique for showing systems lack certain theses.

Exercises II.21

1. Show that classical truth-tables are a Sugihara matrix $\mathcal{S}_1$.
2. Help prove Theorem IV by showing that Suffixing is Sugihara valid.
3. Prove Lemmas 3,4,and 5; while proving Lemma 3 prove that if $\mathbf{a} \in D$ and $\bar{\mathbf{a}} \in D$, then $\mathbf{a} = \bar{\mathbf{a}}$.
4. Use $\mathcal{S}_2$ of Example 3 to invalidate on Sugihara matrices the following. Antilogism, Exportation, Factor, $A \rightarrow A \rightarrow . B \rightarrow B$ and $A \rightarrow B \rightarrow . A \rightarrow . A \wedge B$.

Exercises II.21 continued

5. Show that $A \rightarrow B \vee B \rightarrow A$ is Sugihara valid.

6. Follow Sugihara, who followed Dugundji's procedure of [1940], in showing that SA has no finite characteristic matrix. Consider the non-theorems of the following form.

$$\bigvee_{i=1}^{n} \bigvee_{j=i+1}^{n+1} (p_i \leftrightarrow p_j)$$

The above schema indicates the disjunction of all of the $(p_i \leftrightarrow p_j)$ formable from n+1 variables. Show that such disjunctions are valid in Sugihara matrices with less than n+1 elements.

7. At the beginning of this section we suggested that RM is an upper limit on the acceptable systems. We hope that we have made a case for this suggestion. In the next section we extend this limit to system RM3. Establish the observation that RM is a subsystem of RM3 and then show that the following paradox producing schemas are not thesis schemas of RM3. $A \wedge \sim A \rightarrow B$, $A \rightarrow . B \vee \sim B$, $A \rightarrow . B \rightarrow A$, $\sim A \rightarrow . A \rightarrow B$, $A \rightarrow . B \rightarrow B$, and $A \rightarrow A \rightarrow . B \rightarrow B$.

8. Let z(p,q) represent a zdf. whose only variables are p and q. Show that there is no zdf. z(p,q) such that $z(p,q) \leftrightarrow . p \rightarrow q$ is an RM3 thesis. As induction assumption, try $v(z_1(p,q)) > v(p \rightarrow q)$ and $v(z_2(p,q)) > v(p \rightarrow q)$.

II.22 R.K. Meyer's argument that no relevance implication, and hence, entailment, cannot be a modal notion.

Recall from Section II.3 that we do not get an adequate system for A⟶B by defining A⟶B as ∼◇(A∧∼B), i.e. A⥽B, in one of the Lewis modal systems. In this section a generalization of this result is presented. We present Meyer's argument from [1974b] that an adequate system for A⟶B is lost by extending the system to a modal logic and by defining A⟶B as an M(A,B). In the definition M(A,B) is built up from only alethic modal signs, truth-functional signs, and variables, and M(A,B) meets minimal conditions for being an implication. For greater generality,'an adequate system for A⟶B' is used very broadly so that we class as adequate for A⟶B systems which lack as theses some of the C⟶D formuluas which violate the antecedent/consequent variable sharing relevance condition C7 of I.6. We allow any subsystem of RM3 to be called adequate for A⟶B. Here, then, we talk of relevance preserving A⟶B, viz., relevance implication, instead of only entailment. On analogy with ∼◇(A∧∼B) we could call M(A,B) 'generalized strict implication.' So, Meyer argues that no relevance implication, let alone entailment, is any kind of strict implication. Meyer gives a similar argument in 29.12 of Anderson's and Belnap's [1975].

The gist of Meyer's argument is as follows. Let S be a system with truth-functional signs and ⟶ but no primitive modal signs. Assume that S is adequate for A⟶B. With a view to reducing the relevance implication ⟶ to a modal notion, let us say that we extend S to a modal system Sm in the following way. We add primitive modal signs to S and add enough axioms and rules to make Sm meet at least minimal contions for being an alethic modal logic. Assume that we find an M(A,B) in the language of Sm with which we can identify A⟶B. As a result of such an identification, Sm has a thesis of the form C⟶D which is solely in the language of system S but which was not a thesis of system S. In other words, Sm is not a conservative extension of S. Consequently, acceptance of the modal definition of A⟶B is an admission, contrary to our assumption, that system S was adequate for A⟶B. If S had been adequate for A⟶B, then this C⟶D would have been a thesis of S.

You may try to challenge Meyer's argument by contending that Meyer has shown that we need to extend systems for A⟶B to modal systems or modal logics in order to get all of the A⟶B theses. But such a challenge is very weak unless it is shown on grounds,independent of the fact that the modal definition gives them, that these theses of the A⟶B form are desirable. In addition, we will see that these additional theses are not even theses of the very undemanding system RM3.

A significant reason for placing Meyer's argument here is that we have been considering systems weaker than is desirable, viz., SO and SA. Meyer's result warns us not to try to strengthen these systems by adding modal signs and then equating A⟶B with some modalized truth-function. So, this section gives us additional reasons, to those discussed under C12 in I.6, for not trying to reduce entailment to a modal notion.

Much terminology is used to establish the formal results on which Meyer's argument is based. We begin by specifying conditions for classing a system as adequate for A⟶B to be a relevance implication. Such systems are labelled RI systems. S is an RI system if S has the truth-functional signs, at least the relevance implication signs ⟶ and ⟷, and meets the five conditions below. Note that we are not saying that ⟶ and ⟷ need to be primitive signs. We explicitly add that S does not have either □ or ◇ as primitive signs.

RIc1: The following are thesis schemas of S.
  i) (A⟷B)⟷.(A⟶B)∧(B⟶A)
  ii) (A V B)⟷∼(∼A∧∼B)
  iii) (A⊃ B)⟷∼A v B

RIc2: ⟷ is reflexive, transitive, symmetric, and Repl. holds for it.

RIc3: If $z_1(p)$ and $z_2(p)$ are zdfs. whose sole variable is p, then $z_1(p)$⟷$z_2(p)$ iff. $z_1(p) \equiv z_2(p)$ is a classical tautology.
RIc3 requires acceptance of ∼∼p⟷p.

RIc4: S has uniform substitution for variables as an admissible rule.

RIc5: S is a subsystem of RM3. See Example 4 of II.21.

These conditions for being an RI system are not stronger than anything which we required in I.6. The previous section, especially exercise 7, has been an argument for RIc5. Certainly, RIc3 will not get us into any trouble with variable sharing relevance.

We next specify the conditions for a system to be a minimally adequate modal extension of an RI system for reducing the RI system's relevance implication sign. Such systems are labelled mRI systems. System Sm is a mRI extension of RI system S under the following conditions.

1) The language of S is changed as follows.
   a) A primitive □ (or ◇) is added and ◇A is defined as ∼□∼A (or □A is defined as ∼◇∼A).
   b) ⟶ is eliminated as a primitive sign. But ⟶ is still available for definition and so is ⟶.

In the following M(p) stands for a formula of the language of Sm which contains only modal signs, truth functional signs, and variable p; it contains no $\longrightarrow$. z(p,q) indicates a zdf. whose sole variables are p and q. z(A,B) indicates a formula obtained from z(p,q) by uniform substitution for variables. z(A,B) need not be a zdf.

c) $A \Longrightarrow B$ is introduced as an abbreviation of M(z(A,B)), and $A \Longleftrightarrow B$ is introduced as an abbreviation of $(A \Longrightarrow B) \wedge (B \Longrightarrow A)$.

2) Axioms and rules are added so that Sm becomes at least a minimal modal logic. At least the following hold.

a) Modus Ponens holds for $A \Longrightarrow B$
b) Uniform substitution for variables is an admissible rule.
c) Repl. holds for $A \Longleftrightarrow B$, i.e., if $\vdash_{Sm}$ F(A) and $\vdash_{Sm} A \Longleftrightarrow B$, then $\vdash_{Sm} F(B/A) \Longleftrightarrow F(A)$.
d) $\Box A \Longrightarrow A$.

3) The relevance implication of S is given a modal definition.

Relevance $\longrightarrow$ reducing modal definition:

$p \longrightarrow q =_{df}.$ M(z(p,q))

Note that the modal definition of $\longrightarrow$ gives Repl. for $\longleftrightarrow$ in Sm.

Two lemmas will facilitate proof of the main theorem. We do not give the inductive proof for the first lemma and a proof of the second lemma is exercise 8 of the previous section.

Lemma 1 of II.22: If z(p) is a zdf. whose sole variables is p, then z(p) is truth-functionally equivalent to exactly one of the following: $p, \sim p$, $p \vee \sim p$, or $p \wedge \sim p$.

Lemma 2 of II.22: In RM3 no thesis has the form $p \longrightarrow q \longleftrightarrow .$ z(p,q).

Theorem I of II.22: If RI system S is extended to a mRI system Sm, then there is a thesis $C \longrightarrow D$ of Sm which is solely in the language of S but which is not a thesis of S.

As proof consider the following. If S is so-extended to Sm, the modal definition of $\longrightarrow$ gives $p \longrightarrow q \longleftrightarrow .$M(z(p,q)) as a thesis of Sm. By variable substitution we get as an Sm thesis: $(p \longrightarrow \sim p) \longleftrightarrow$ M(z(p, $\sim$p)). Lemma 1 and RIc3 tell us that z(p, $\sim$p) $\longleftrightarrow$ p, z(p, $\sim$p) $\longleftrightarrow \sim$p, z(p,$\sim$p) $\longleftrightarrow . p \vee \sim p$, or z(p, $\sim$p) $\longleftrightarrow . p \wedge \sim p$ is a thesis of S and hence of Sm. So, by Repl. for $\longleftrightarrow$ we have as a Sm thesis one of the following four from $(p \longrightarrow \sim p) \longleftrightarrow$ M(z(p, $\sim$p)). (1) M(p) $\longleftrightarrow . p \longrightarrow \sim p$, (2) M($\sim$p) $\longleftrightarrow . p \longrightarrow \sim p$. (3) M($p \wedge \sim p$) $\longleftrightarrow . p \longrightarrow \sim p$. and (4) M($p \vee \sim p$) $\longleftrightarrow . p \longrightarrow \sim p$.

We now argue that no matter which of these four is assumed to be a Sm thesis we get as an Sm thesis a formula of the $C \longrightarrow D$ form, solely in the language of S, which is not even an RM3 thesis; hence , this $C \longrightarrow D$ is certainly not a thesis of RI system S.

Assume that (1) is a thesis of Sm. In (1) substitute $z(p,q)$ for variable p, where $z(p,q)$ is the zdf. used in the modal definition of $\longrightarrow$. Such a substitution gives (5) as a Sm thesis.

(5) $M(z(p,q)) \longleftrightarrow . z(p,q) \longrightarrow \sim z(p,q)$

The modal definition of $\longrightarrow$ enables us to replace $M(z(p,q))$ in(5) so that (6) is gotten as a Sm thesis.

(6) $p \longrightarrow q \longleftrightarrow . z(p,q) \longrightarrow \sim z(p,q)$

Now (6) is solely in the language of RI system S. If (6) is not an RM3 thesis, it certainly is not, by RIc5, a thesis of S. So, assume that (6) is a thesis of RM3. If (6) were a RM3 thesis then,(6) together with the RM3 equivalence $\sim p \longleftrightarrow . p \longrightarrow \sim p$ would give (7) as an RM3 thesis.

(7) $p \text{---} q \longleftrightarrow . \sim z(p,q)$

Since $\sim z(p,q)$ is a zdf. whose sole variables are p and q, Lemma 2 tells us that (7) is not a RM3 thesis. So, we cannot assume that (6) is a RM3 thesis;let alone a thesis of S.

Assume that (2) is a thesis of Sm. In(2) substitute $z(p,q)$ for variable p, where $z(p,q)$ is the zdf. used in the modal definition of $\longrightarrow$. Such a substitution gives (8) as a Sm thesis, after use of Double Negation.

(8) $M(z(p,q)) \longleftrightarrow . \sim z(p,q) \longrightarrow z(p,q)$

The modal definition of $\longrightarrow$ enables us to replace $M(z(p,q))$ in (8) with $p \longrightarrow q$ so that (9) is gotten as a Sm thesis.

(9) $p \longrightarrow q \longleftrightarrow . \sim z(p,q) \longrightarrow z(p,q)$

Now (9) is solely in the language of S. If (9) were a RM3 thesis,then (9) together with the RM3 equivalence $p \longleftrightarrow . \sim p \longrightarrow p$ would give (10) as a RM3 thesis.

(10) $p \longrightarrow q \longleftrightarrow z(p,q)$

Lemma 2 tells us that (10) is not a RM3 thesis. So, as in the consideration of (1), we conclude that (9) was not a thesis of the RI system S.

Assume that (3) is a thesis of Sm. Substitute $\sim p$ for p in (3) and use Double Negation to get (11) as a Sm thesis.

(11) $M(p \wedge \sim p) \longleftrightarrow . \sim p \longrightarrow p$

Use (3) with (11) to get as a Sm thesis (12) which is solely in the language of S.

(12) $p \rightarrow \sim p \leftrightarrow . \sim p \rightarrow p$

You can verify that (12) is not a RM3 thesis. So, as before we conclude that (12) was not a thesis of S before its extension to Sm.

Assume that (4) is a thesis of Sm. By a procedure similar to that just used in our consideration of (3), we again end up having to accept as a Sm thesis (12).

So, we have the theorem.

The proof of the theorem entitles us to draw the following corollary.

Corollary of I of II.22: If RI system S is extended to a mRI system Sm, then there is a thesis $C \rightarrow D$ of Sm which is solely in the language of S but which is not even a thesis of RM3.

The significance of this theorem and its corollary deserves emphasis. Even the minimal restraints of the $\rightarrow$ of RM3 are lost if we identify $A \rightarrow B$ with a formula obtained from modal signs and truth-functional signs. It seems that some of the relevance or entailment signs must be taken as primitive. Even in the so-called classical relevance logics of Meyer and Routley in [1973c] and [197_a] there is still a primitive relevance sign.

Exercises II.22

1. Establish that $p \rightarrow \sim p \leftrightarrow . \sim p \rightarrow p$ is not a RM3 thesis.
2. Establish that $p \leftrightarrow . \sim p \rightarrow p$ and $\sim p \leftrightarrow . p \rightarrow \sim p$ are RM3 theses.

II.23 Vrendenduin's system and Emch's system.

This section calls attention to two systems which are not serious candidates but which are of much interest for an understanding of the early history of the effort to develop entailment systems. The systems are those of Vrendenduin [1939] and Emch of [1936a] and [1936b]. Vrendenduin's paper was reviewed by J.C.C. McKinsey in [1939b] and Emch's by E.J. Nelson in [1936a,b]. Recently R. Routley in [1972b] showed that $A ⥽ B$ can be given a reasonable definition in Vrendenduin's system with the result that $A ⥽ B \longleftrightarrow . A \longrightarrow B$ is a thesis. Emch's system is carefully criticized by C.I. Lewis in [1936]. These systems are not serious candidates because they have an unacceptable fde. fragment. Both have $p \wedge {\sim} p \longrightarrow q$ and $p \longrightarrow . q \vee {\sim} q$ as theses. Indeed we regard their motivation as misguided because their concern is primarily to avoid having the strong paradoxes of necessity and possibility as theses, viz., $\Box p \longrightarrow . q \longrightarrow p$ and $\Box {\sim} p \longrightarrow . p \longrightarrow q$. Still we look briefly at the systems for historical interest and to note two dead-ends in the search for entailment. We give a bit more attention to Vrendenduin's system because he did not make the mistake of trying to identify entailment with some modalized truth function; he used a primitive $\longrightarrow$.

It is an anachronism to say that Vrendenduin's system is an extension of Sugihara's SA. Still we can look at Vrendenduin's system as such an extension. We present Vrendenduin's system N as an extension of SA obtained by adding a primitive possibility sign $\diamondplus$ together with some axiom schemas. We label the axiom schemas with N to conform with his presentation. N1 - N7 are the axiom schemas of Halldén's S0. N8 is $\diamondplus (A \wedge B) \longrightarrow \diamondplus A$. N9 - N12 are the rules of SA plus uniform variable substitution while N13 is the Contraposition schema of SA. The remaining six axiom schemas are as follows.

N14. $A \wedge B \longrightarrow C \longrightarrow . A \wedge {\sim} C \longrightarrow {\sim} B$
N15. $A \longrightarrow B \longrightarrow . A \wedge C \longrightarrow . B \wedge C$
N16. $(A \longrightarrow B) \wedge (C \longrightarrow D) \longrightarrow . A \wedge C \longrightarrow . B \wedge D$
N17 $A \longrightarrow \diamondplus A$
N18 $(A \longrightarrow B) \wedge \diamondplus A \longrightarrow \diamondplus B$
N19. $A \longrightarrow B \longrightarrow . {\sim} \diamondplus (A \wedge {\sim} B)$

The special feature of N is that it does not have the converse of N19. To show that N lacks the converse of N19 regard $\diamondplus$ as an identity operator, treat $\longrightarrow$ as $⥽$, and use one of the matrices from Appendix II of Lewis' and Langford's [1932] to show that we do not have $A \supset B ⥽ . A ⥽ B$ in the S-systems. As an exercise one can reconstruct the basis for Routley's observation that N16 can be obtained from N15. Of most importance for the unacceptability of N is the fact that N2 and N14(Antilogism) give $p \wedge {\sim} p \longrightarrow q$ and $p \longrightarrow . q \vee {\sim} q$. So, we do not want even the fde. fragment of Vrendenduin's system N. Still let us take note of Routley's point that N is also unsatisfactory because given a reasonable definition of a new possibility sign $\Diamond$ we get $A \rightarrow B \leftrightarrow . A \strictif B$, where $A \strictif B$ is defined in the usual way in terms of the new possibility sign $\Diamond$; not in terms of $\langle + \rangle$. The reasonable definition of the new possibility sign is Sugihara's D4 from II.20, viz. $\Diamond A =_{df} \sim(A \rightarrow \sim A)$. Exercise 5 of II.20 already brought out that N14 with Sugihara's system gives $A \rightarrow B \leftrightarrow . A \strictif B$. Routley then goes on to show that the defined $\Diamond$ and its corresponding $\strictif$ will be those of system S2. Because S2 has $\Box A \strictif . B \strictif A$ and $\Box \sim A \strictif . A \strictif B$, system N will have by Replacement $\Box A \rightarrow . B \rightarrow A$ and $\Box \sim A \rightarrow . A \rightarrow B$. Here, of course, this $\Box$ is defined in terms of $\Diamond$; not in terms of the idle $\langle + \rangle$. So, N has paradoxes of necessity and impossibility contrary to its intended purpose.

Emch's concern was narrower than ours. He was upset by the paradoxes of necessity and impossibility; especially the paradox of impossibility. He granted, as opposed to us, that anything did follow from an explicit contradiction and more generally from a logical inconsistency. However, he wanted to allow for non-logical impossibility. He cited 'Parrots are not birds' as an example of a sentence expressing non-logical impossibility. Other examples may be: A cube has seven surfaces,' 'A dog became a cat,' or 'The rocket exceeded the speed of light.' Emch would grant that in a sense of 'implies' "Sugar is sweet' is implied by 'Parrots are not birds' because it is impossible that Parrots not be birds and that sugar not be sweet. Nevertheless, Emch would not grant that this is the best possible kind of implication because it is not based on any connection between antecedent and consequent. At least there is apparently no connection. So, Emch's concern was to develop a system L to distinguish these two types of implication. He introduced two primitive possibility signs which we present as $\langle 1 \rangle$ and $\langle 2 \rangle$. $\langle 1 \rangle$ is intended to represent logical possibility while $\langle 2 \rangle$ is intended to represent some restricted sense of 'possibility' such that $\langle 2 \rangle A \rightarrow \langle 1 \rangle A$ but not $\langle 1 \rangle A \rightarrow \langle 2 \rangle A$, where $A \rightarrow B$ is defined as $\sim \langle 1 \rangle (A \wedge \sim B)$. This $\rightarrow$, despite its modal definition, is to represent entailment while $A \strictif B$ which is defined as $\sim \langle 2 \rangle (A \wedge \sim B)$ is to represent the weaker implication. In L, $A \rightarrow B \rightarrow . A \strictif B$ holds but not the converse. Because the truth functional signs, $\langle 1 \rangle$, and $\langle 2 \rangle$ are primitve while $\rightarrow$ and $\strictif$ are defined, Emch has really presented a logic for two kinds of possibility; not an entailment system. Meyer's result of the preceding section applies to Emch's effort. But for historical interest a brief remark on C.I. Lewis' critique of Emch is in order. In discussion of this critique we will ignore talk of quantification of sentential variables which occurred in the original critique.

The upshot of Lewis' critique is that we get the following contradiction between (i) and (iv) below when we try to interpret $\Diamond_1$ and $\Diamond_2$. The intention behind the system gives the basis for (i).

i) No satisfactory interpretation of $\Diamond_1$ is a satisfactory interpretation of $\Diamond_2$.

The contradictory of (i) is a syllogistic conclusion from (ii) and (iii). Line (ii) is established by showing that the theorems of system L without $\Diamond_1$ are exactly the theorems of S2 and by assuming that S2 has a satisfactory interpretation.

ii) Some satisfactory interpretation of S2's $\Diamond$ is a satisfactory interpretation of $\Diamond_2$.

Line (iii) is established by two considerations. The first shows that $\Diamond_1$ can be interpreted as the $\Diamond$ of S2. Lewis showed that the theorems of L without $\Diamond_2$ are exactly the theorems of S2 with $\Diamond_1$ regarded as S2's $\Diamond$. The second consideration is that $\Diamond_1$ should be read as 'logically possible' and $\Diamond_2$ as 'physically possible' and that the intended interpretation of S2's $\Diamond$ is as logical possibility.

iii) All satisfactory interpretations of S2's $\Diamond$ are satisfactory interpretations of $\Diamond_1$.

So, by a syllogism from (ii) and (iii) we get (iv) which contradicts (i).

iv) Some satisfactory interpretation of $\Diamond_1$ is a satisfactory interpretation of $\Diamond_2$.

Emch's system can be defended against Lewis' criticism as Lewis' criticism is presented above. Line (iii) is not well established. Simply because $\Diamond_1$ considered apart from $\Diamond_2$ is naturally regarded as S2's $\Diamond$ is not sufficient reason for concluding that what we say about S2's $\Diamond$ should apply to L's $\Diamond_1$. System L's $\Diamond_1$ is contrasted with L's $\Diamond_2$ whereas S2's $\Diamond$ is not contrasted with another possibility sign in S2. Being systematically connected and disconnected with another possibility sign makes L's $\Diamond_1$ and hence L's $\rightarrow$ significantly different from S2's $\Diamond$ and S2's ⥽.

Nonetheless, the $\Diamond_1$ of L not only allows $p \wedge \sim p \rightarrow q$ and $p \rightarrow . q \vee \sim q$ but also $\Box_1\, p \rightarrow . q \rightarrow p$ and $\Box_1 \sim p \rightarrow . p \rightarrow q$. So, Emch's system L is not what we want. Still L may be of considerable interest to those who are investigating modal logics for multiple senses of 'possibility.'

PART III

III.1 Introduction to Part III, First Section on Anderson's and Belnap's Tautological Entailments;normal form version, a retraction by the author.

Finally we start to develop the system of entailment to be advocated. We begin by presenting its fde. fragment. Using terminology of Anderson and Belnap, we call the fde. theses of this fragment the Tautological Entailments. For short we call this fde. system TE. In Anderson's and Belnap's [1975] system TE is labelled E_{fde} because TE is the fde. fragment of system E. Although E_{fde} is likely to become the official name, we do not call TE E_{fde} to avoid use of subscripts and because TE is the fde. fragment of many other systems. Despite the name it should not be thought that all tautologous $A \supset B$ give Tautological Entailments. Obviously, the tautologous $p \wedge \sim p \supset q$ is not going to be accepted as giving a Tautological Entailment. Since the TE entailments are so crucial we present them in three ways: by a normal form technique, axiomatically, and semantically. We do not present them by use of the illuminating Gentzen sequent calculus of Anderson's and Belnap's [1963] and section 17 of [1975], because of our policy of not dealing with Gentzen type calculi. In this section we give the normal form presentation of the TE system. So, Section I.8 will be most useful. It is messy to prove theorems about the TE entailments when they are selected by use of normal forms. So, we do not prove many theorems about the TE entailments as presented by normal forms. However, the normal form version was one of the earliest in the readily available literature and it does provide a nice decision procedure. Nevertheless a theorem is proved which enables the author to retract his claim that TE is not significantly different from the classical fde. theses.

Also in Part III we extend the TE entailments to a system TEc which is TE plus the classical tautologies. We then extend TEc to a full first degree system TEf. We also struggle with the philosophic issues of justifying our rejection of Material Detachment and Disjunctive Syllogism as fde. theses. We close Part III by arguing that we can and should extend TEf to a full entailment system. In Part IV we develop and defend this full entailment system which is the system E of Anderson and Belnap.

We follow Anderson's and Belnap's [1962a] in presenting the normal form method for selecting the TE entailments. See also 15.1 of their [1975] for a normal form method of selection. The normal form conditions for an fde. formula to be a TE entailment are best presented in two steps. (Recall from I.8 the notions used below; especially 'official normal form' as presented at the end of I.8.) We first tell how to select the explicit TE entailments and then tell how to select TE entailments in general. If A is a primitive conjunction and B is a primitive disjunction, $A \rightarrow B$ is *an explicit TE entailment* iff. A and B share an atom. For instance, $p \rightarrow p$, $p \wedge q \rightarrow . q \vee r$, and $p \wedge \sim p \rightarrow . (p \vee \sim p) \vee q$ are explicit TE entailments. On the other hand, $p \wedge q \rightarrow . \sim q \vee r$, $p \wedge \sim p \rightarrow q$, and $p \vee p \rightarrow p \wedge p$ are not explicit TE entailments although we will see that $p \vee p \rightarrow p \wedge p$ is a TE entailment. $A \rightarrow B$ is *a TE entailment* iff. an official disjunctive normal form of A: $A_1 \vee A_2 \vee, \ldots, \vee A_n$, and an official conjunctive normal form of B: B_1 B_2 $, \ldots ,$ B_m , are such that each $A_i \rightarrow B_j$ is an explicit TE entailment for $1 \leq i \leq n$ and $1 \leq j \leq m$. We can immediately recognize $p \vee p \rightarrow p \wedge p$ as a TE entailment because $p \vee p$ is an official disjunctive normal form of $p \vee p$, $p \wedge p$ an official conjunctive normal form of $p \wedge p$, and $p \rightarrow p$ is an explicit TE entailment.

Consider other examples. The instance of DS: $\sim p \wedge (p \vee q) \rightarrow q$ is not a TE entailment because any official disjunctive normal form of $\sim p \wedge (p \vee q)$ differs only by Commutation from $\sim p \wedge p \vee \sim p \wedge q$; and no such commutation is going to avoid the need to say falsely that $p \wedge \sim p \rightarrow q$ or $\sim p \wedge p \rightarrow q$ is a TE entailment. Now $p \wedge q \vee \sim p \wedge \sim q \rightarrow . p \equiv q$ is a TE entailment. An official conjunctive normal form of $p \equiv q$ is $(\sim p \vee q) \wedge (\sim q \vee p)$ and $p \wedge q \vee \sim p \wedge \sim q \rightarrow . (\sim p \vee q) \wedge (\sim q \vee p)$ can be readily recognized as a TE entailment. However, and surprisingly, $p \equiv q \rightarrow . p \wedge q \vee \sim p \wedge \sim q$ is not a TE entailment. Any official disjunctive normal form of $p \equiv q$ is going to be some reassociation or commutation of: $\sim q \wedge \sim p \vee \sim q \wedge q \vee p \wedge \sim p \vee p \wedge q$, while any official conjunctive normal form of $p \wedge q \vee \sim p \wedge \sim q$ is going to be some reassociation or commutation of:
$(\sim p \vee p) \wedge (\sim p \vee q) \wedge (\sim q \vee p) \wedge (\sim q \vee q)$.
Now $\sim q \wedge q \rightarrow . \sim p \vee p$ and $p \wedge \sim p \rightarrow . \sim q \vee q$ are not explicit TE entailments and no reassociation or commutation is going to alter this. So in the TE system $p \wedge q \vee \sim p \wedge \sim q$ is not a disjunctive normal form of $p \equiv q$!

Let us talk a bit more about normal forms in TE. In particular, let us discuss using 'official normal form' in the definitions. The following are TE theses: $p \rightarrow . (p \vee p) \wedge (p \vee q)$, $(p \vee p) \wedge (p \vee q) \rightarrow p$, $p \rightarrow . p \wedge p \vee p \wedge q$, and $p \wedge p \vee p \wedge q \rightarrow p$. Hence, by our I.8 decision to use the first type of definition of 'normal form', under which normal form N is a normal form of formula F in system S if $N \leftrightarrow F$ is a thesis of S, we have to say that $(p \vee p) \wedge (p \vee q)$ is a conjunctive normal form of p and that $p \wedge p \vee p \wedge q$ is a disjunctive normal form of p in system TE. Yet plain p is p's official conjunctive normal form as well as its official disjunctive normal form. Since formulas have non-official normal forms in TE why, then, did we use official normal forms in our definition of TE entailment? Anderson and Belnap intended to use what are here called official normal forms. Page 13 of their [1962a] shows that they use only the techniques of what we called in I.8 MA systems to get normal forms. Such techniques give official conjunctive and disjunctive normal forms. Their fourth footnote specifies that the normal forms used differ only in order of conjuncts and disjuncts from one another. But it is only official normal forms which differ from one another only in order of conjucts and disjuncts. Of course, the important question is whether we are justified in following Anderson and Belnap. And this is really the question of whether or not the system of TE entailments is the correct fde. system. The way to answer this fundamental question is to determine how well system TE meets the applicable adequacy conditions of I.6 and to consider whether some more general principles justify acceptance of TE. To answer we turn away from the normal form presentation to an axiomatic presentation. In the normal form presentation, it is messy to prove that even $A \longrightarrow A$ and $A \wedge B \longrightarrow A$ are thesis schemas. Also axioms and rules provide motivating considerations for a system; conditions on normal forms can seem very _ad hoc._

But before turning to an axiomatic presentation, let us use the normal form presentation to prove a theorem which has some philosophical interest. This theorem provides a way of representing all classical fde. theses as TE theses. This theorem offers the author an opportunity to correct his interpretation of its significance in his [197_c].

We first present two lemmas which bring out how classical fde. theses can fail to be TE theses.

Lemma 1 of III.1: If $A \longrightarrow B$ is a classical fde. thesis, $A_1 \vee A_2, \ldots, \vee A_n$ an official disjunctive normal form of A, and $B_1 \wedge B_2, \ldots, \wedge B_m$ an official conjunctive normal form of B, then each $A_i \longrightarrow B_j$ is a classical fde. thesis.

By way of proof we make the following remarks. Use the facts that A and B are truth functionally equivalent to any of their normal forms and that if $(A_1 \vee A_2) \supset . B_1 \wedge B_2$ is a tautology then so are: $A_1 \supset B_1$, $A_1 \supset B_2$, $A_2 \supset B_1$, and $A_2 \supset B_2$.

Since all official normal forms are interchangeable for purposes of TE entailments, we can assume that we are talking of official left ones. In the next lemma A_i and B_j are as in Lemma 1, viz., any selected disjunct and any selected conjunct from the normal forms.

Lemma 2 of III.1: If $A \longrightarrow B$ is a classical fde. thesis but not a TE thesis, then there are $A_i \longrightarrow B_j$ such that A_i and B_j share no atoms while A_i has a p and $\sim p$ as conjuncts or there are $A_i \longrightarrow B_j$ but A_i and B_j share no atoms while B_j has a q and $\sim q$ as disjuncts.

By way of proof we make the following remarks. By Lemma 1 we know that each $A_i \supset B_j$ is tautologous. Since A_i is a primitive conjunction while B_j is a primitive disjunction, Theorem I of II.12 gives the lemma.

Theorem I of III.1: If $A \longrightarrow B$ is a classical fde. thesis but not a TE thesis, the following procedure converts it into a TE thesis $Ac \longrightarrow Bc$.

Put A into an official disjunctive normal form: $A_1 \vee A_2, \ldots, \vee A_n$, and B into an official conjunctive normal form: $B_1 \wedge B_2, \ldots, \wedge B_m$. Pick out the $A_i \longrightarrow B_j$ in which A_i and B_j share no atoms; call them segregated cases. Go through the segregated cases. For each A_i which has a /p/ not in B_j disjoin $p \wedge \sim p$ on the right of B. For each B_j which has a /q/ not in A_i conjoin $(q \vee \sim q)$ on the right of A. In this way we get converted A, call it Ac, and converted B, call it Bc.

By way of proof we make the following remarks. By disjoining the $p \wedge \sim p$ on the right of B each conjunct Bc_j of the official left conjunctive normal form of Bc is going to contain p or $\sim p$. Why? First get an official left conjunctive normal form of B. The $p \wedge \sim p$ disjoined on the right will, by Distribution, disjoin p or $\sim p$ with each B_j. Similarly, having $q \vee \sim q$ conjoined on the right of an official left disjunctive normal form of A is going to lead to either q or $\sim q$ being a conjunct of each Ac_i in the official left disjunctive normal form of Ac. But now there will be no $Ac_i \longrightarrow Bc_j$ which fail to share an atom. The $A_i \longrightarrow B_j$ which failed to share an atom but had a p and $\sim p$ in A_i are converted to $Ac_i \longrightarrow Bc_j$ where Bc_j has either p or $\sim p$ and Ac_i keeps both p and $\sim p$ from A_i. Similarly, the $A_i \longrightarrow B_j$ which failed to share an atom but had a q and $\sim q$ in B_j are converted to $Ac_i \longrightarrow Bc_j$ where Ac_i has either q or $\sim q$ and Bc_j has both q and $\sim q$. So, $Ac \longrightarrow Bc$ is a TE thesis.

Let us see an application of the above representation theorem. Consider $p \wedge (\sim p \vee q) \longrightarrow q$ which is not a TE entailment but which by the procedure of the theorem becomes the TE entailment $p \wedge (\sim p \vee q) \longrightarrow q \vee p \wedge \sim p$ which can be readily converted to $p \wedge (\sim p \vee q) \longrightarrow . \sim (p \wedge \sim p) \supset q$. We could call $\sim (p \wedge \sim p)$ an auxiliary antecedent for the consequent of $p \wedge (\sim p \vee q) \longrightarrow q$ which turns $p \wedge (\sim p \vee q) \longrightarrow q$ into a TE entailment. Next consider $p \supset q \longrightarrow . p \supset . p \wedge q$ which fails to be a TE entailment because from $(\sim p \vee q) \longrightarrow . (\sim p \vee p) \wedge (\sim p \vee q)$ we do not have the $A_i \longrightarrow B_j$ which is $q \longrightarrow . (\sim p \vee p)$ as an explicit TE entailment. However, $(p \supset q) \wedge (\sim p \vee p) \longrightarrow . p \supset . p \wedge q$ is a TE entailment. We could call $(\sim p \vee p)$ an auxiliary conjunct for the antecedent.

In his [197_c] the author charged that the TE system is not really a restriction on the system of classical fde. theses.

It was noted that for every classical fde. thesis there is the TE thesis $Ac \longrightarrow Bc$ and that for the classical logician $Ac \longrightarrow Bc$ is not significantly different from its $A \longrightarrow B$ because the classical logician would suppress tautologous conjuncts from Ac and contradictory disjuncts from Bc. But, of course, $Ac \longrightarrow Bc$ is significantly different from $A \longrightarrow B$ for those who have called into question the legitimacy of classical logic. In this work we are questioning the legitimacy of classical logic. So, we cannot take Theorem I as somehow showing that the TE system is really the same as the classical fde. system. We're questioning Suppression especially in this study. However, Theorem I has great value towards showing how the TE system could be taught as the standard logic for schools. All the arguments currently taught to be valid, with the unstated assumption that logical validity is the best possible formal validity, could still be certified as valid in the best possible formal way if supplemented with certain auxiliary formulas as suggested by the procedure of Theorem I. Indeed such a procedure would illuminate how tautologies are needed for inferences. (In regard to needing tautologies for inferences, see the author's [1974].)

Some exercises will help develp an understanding of, and perhaps an appreciation of, the techniques of this section. A first exercise can be proving Theorem II which tells us that the TE entailments satisfy the C7 variable sharing condition.

Theorem II of III.1: If $A \longrightarrow B$ is a TE thesis, A and B share a variable.

Exercises III.1

1. Show that the following are not TE theses.
   $(p \supset q) \wedge (r \supset s) \wedge (p \vee r) \longrightarrow . q \vee s$ Constructive dilemma for $\supset$.
   $(p \supset q) \wedge (q \supset r) \longrightarrow . p \supset r$ Transitivity for $\supset$.
   $p \supset q \longrightarrow . p \wedge r \supset . q \wedge r.$ Factor for $\supset$.
2. Convert the formulas of exercise 1 to TE entailments.
3. Show that $A \longrightarrow {\sim}A$ is a TE entailment iff. A is a classical contradiction.
4. Show that $A \longrightarrow B$ is a classical fde. thesis iff. $A \wedge {\sim}B \longrightarrow . {\sim}(A \wedge {\sim}B)$ is a TE entailment. Does this show that a holder of the system of TE entailments really accepts all classical fde. theses by accepting the <u>reductio</u> <u>ad</u> <u>absurdum</u> version of them, viz., the $\overline{A \wedge {\sim}B \longrightarrow . {\sim}(A \wedge {\sim}B)}$ version of each $A \longrightarrow B$?

III.2 Axiomatic development of the system of tautological entailments, system TE.

A major test for a system of fde. entailments has been whether or not it had the applicable rules and theses cited in adequacy conditions Cl4 and Cl5 of I.6. We have rejected systems based on very plausible principles because the systems did not meet these adequacy conditions very well. Meeting these adequacy conditions or having these structural features is most important; not plausibility of general principles guiding the formation of the systems. Perhaps, the most unintuitive system building principle which we have considered is the normal form method for selecting TE theses. Because these so-called structural features from the adequacy conditions are so important, a natural strategy for developing an acceptable fde. system is to use the schemas of Cl5, restricted to fde. formulas, as axiom schemas and the rules of Cl4, applicable to fde. systems, as primitve rules. In this section we employ this natural strategy. On p. 93 of his [1960a], Belnap calls the system presented in this section system B. Later another basic system has been labelled with B by Meyer and Routley on p. 193 of [1972c]. So, we use TE rather than B. Also note that the system which we here label TE is labelled E_{fde} in Anderson's and Belnap's [1975]. In this section we develop TE to show that it meets the adequacy conditions of Section I.6. We close by showing that system TE contains as theorems all of the TE theses characterized in the preceding section.

This section begins the program for the rest of the book. We build upon TE by augmenting its language, rules, and axioms. So, because we are advocating an extension of TE as the right system of entailment, we will be reflecting on the correctness of the various axioms, rules, and enrichment of the language. We also begin to present the theorems of the system we advocate. In this section we begin to label theorems,i.e., theorem schemas, with plain T. In general, whenever a theorem is labelled with plain T, it is a theorem of system E which is the system to be advocated. Suffixed T's such as T.R and T.RM, are used to indicate that the theorem is a theorem of an extension of E such as system R or system RM but is not a theorem of system E.

The following axiom schemas and rules give system TE. This system is also presented in 15.2 of Anderson's and Belnap's [1975].

A1. $A \wedge B \longrightarrow A$

A2. $A \wedge B \longrightarrow B$

A3. $A \longrightarrow . A \vee B$

A4. $B \longrightarrow . A \vee B$

A5. $A \wedge (B \vee C) \longrightarrow . B \vee (A \wedge C)$

A6. $A \longrightarrow \sim\sim A$

A7. $\sim\sim A \longrightarrow A$

Since TE is an fde. system it has no need for MP or Adj.. TE's rules are the following four.

r1. $A \rightarrow B, B \rightarrow C \vdash A \rightarrow C$ Trans.
r2. $A \rightarrow B, A \rightarrow C \vdash A \rightarrow .B \wedge C$ Comp.
r3. $A \rightarrow C, B \rightarrow C \vdash A \vee B \rightarrow C$ or-elim.
r4. $A \rightarrow B \vdash \sim B \rightarrow \sim A$ Contra.

Because of the present limitation of the formal language, let us define $A \leftrightarrow B$ by giving the following three rules whose use we will cite with 'Def. $\leftrightarrow$.'

$A \rightarrow B, B \rightarrow A \vdash A \leftrightarrow B$
$A \rightarrow B \vdash A \rightarrow B$
$A \rightarrow B \vdash B \rightarrow A$

Except for A5 and the Contraposition rule, the axioms and rules of TE are natural devices for proving TE entailments by building them up from entailments going from a primitive conjunction to one of its atoms. The first two axioms tell us that any primitve conjunction entails any of its atoms. The next two axioms tell us that any primitive disjunction, including the case of a single atom, entails itself disjoined with any other atom. With Transitivity we then get all of the explicit TE entailments if we have general Commutativity and Associativity. With r2 we build up from explicit TE entailments the conjunctive normal forms in the consequents of TE entailments in the normal form version. With r3 we build up the disjunctive normal forms in the antecedents of TE entailments in the normal form version. So axiom system TE will have as theorems all TE entailments in the form in which the antecedent is an official disjunctive normal form and the consequent is an official conjunctive normal form. We get all TE entailments as theorems of TE if we can show that system TE is an MA system in the sense of Section I.8. Schema A5, the double negation axioms, and Contraposition are crucial for showing that TE is an MA system.

The plausibility of TE's axioms and rules, which has already been noted in I.6, makes a case for the system of TE entailments. However, the more difficult case to make is that no more than the theorems of TE should be accepted as fde. entailments. We continually worry about the need for dealing with this more difficult case. We especially worry about our rejection of $p \wedge (\sim p \vee q) \rightarrow q$ and $\sim p \wedge (p \vee q) \rightarrow q$. But at least TE gives us nothing unacceptable.

The development of TE, to which we now turn, will bring out that TE requires the acceptance of nothing logically obnoxious. In this development we use Dr. for'derived rule.' Proofs are frequently left as exercises. We rarely cite sources for proofs; many are in Belnap's [1960a].

Dr.1. $A \longrightarrow B \wedge C \vdash A \longrightarrow B$ and $A \longrightarrow B \wedge C \vdash A \longrightarrow C$ and-elim.

Proof

1) $A \longrightarrow B \wedge C$ hyp.
2) $B \wedge C \longrightarrow B$ A1
3) $A \longrightarrow C$ Trans. (1),(2)

The proof of the other version is similar. When we have a richer language we may cite the move from $A \longrightarrow . B \wedge C$ to $(A \longrightarrow B) \wedge (A \longrightarrow C)$ as a use of Dr.1.

Dr.2. $A \vee B \longrightarrow C \vdash A \longrightarrow C$ and $A \vee B \longrightarrow C \vdash B \longrightarrow C$

Proof

1) $A \vee B \longrightarrow C$ hyp.
2) $A \longrightarrow . A \vee B$ A3
3) $A \longrightarrow C$ Trans. (1),(2)

The proof of the other version is similar. Again we note that we may cite the move from $A \vee B \longrightarrow C$ to $(A \longrightarrow C) \wedge (B \longrightarrow C)$ as a use of Dr.2.

Dr.3. $A \longrightarrow B,\ C \longrightarrow D \vdash A \wedge C \longrightarrow . B \wedge D$

Proof

1) $A \longrightarrow B$ hyp.
2) $A \wedge C \longrightarrow A$ A1
3) $A \wedge C \longrightarrow B$ Trans. (1),(2)
4) $C \longrightarrow D$ hyp.
5) $A \wedge C \longrightarrow C$ A2
6) $A \wedge C \longrightarrow D$ Trans. (5),(4)
7) $A \wedge C \longrightarrow . B \wedge D$ r2 on (3) and (6).

Dr.4. $A \longrightarrow B,\ C \longrightarrow D \vdash A \vee C \longrightarrow . B \vee D$

Proof is similar to Dr.3's. Use A3,A4, and r3 instead of A1,A2, and r2.

We leave proof of the next three derived rules as exercises. When these rules have been derived we have shown that TE has all of the applicable rules , except Replacement, from condition C14 of section I.6.

Dr.5. $A \longrightarrow B,\ C \longrightarrow D \vdash A \wedge C \longrightarrow . B \vee D$
Dr.6. $A \longrightarrow B \vdash A \wedge C \longrightarrow B$
Dr.7. $A \longrightarrow B \vdash A \longrightarrow . B \vee C$.

Let us now note some theorems by only giving a few remarks on their proofs.

T1. $A \longrightarrow A$ Use A6,A7, and Trans.
T2. $A \longleftrightarrow A$ Use Def. $\longleftrightarrow$ with T1.
T3. $A \wedge B \longrightarrow B \wedge A$ Use r2 on A1 and A2.
T4. $B \wedge A \longrightarrow A \wedge B$ Use r2 on A1 and A2.
T5. $A \wedge B \longleftrightarrow B \wedge A$ Use Def. $\longleftrightarrow$ with T3 and T4.
T6. $A \vee B \longrightarrow . B \vee A$ Use A3,A4, and r3.
T7. $B \vee A \longrightarrow . A \vee B$ Use A3,A4, and r3.
T8. $A \vee B \longleftrightarrow . B \vee A$ Use Def. $\longleftrightarrow$ with T6 and T7.

T5 and T8 give the basis for general Commutativity of $\wedge$ and $\mathbf{v}$.

The theorems giving the DeMorgan equivalences deserve more elaboration.

T9. $\sim(A \vee B) \rightarrow . \sim A \wedge \sim B$

Proof

1) $A \rightarrow . A \vee B$	A3
2) $B \rightarrow . A \vee B$	A4
3) $\sim(A \vee B) \rightarrow \sim A$	Contra. on (1)
4) $\sim(A \vee B) \rightarrow \sim B$	Contra. on (2)
5) $\sim(A \vee B) \rightarrow \sim A \wedge \sim B$.	r2 on (3) and (4).

T10. $(\sim A \vee \sim B) \rightarrow . \sim(A \wedge B)$

Proof remarks: A proof is similar to T9's but start with A1 and A2, Contrapose, and use r3.

T11. $\sim A \wedge \sim B \rightarrow . \sim(A \wedge B)$

Proof

1) $A \rightarrow \sim\sim A$	A6
2) $B \rightarrow \sim\sim B$	A6
3) $\sim\sim A \rightarrow . \sim\sim A \vee \sim\sim B$	A3
4) $\sim\sim B \rightarrow . \sim\sim A \vee \sim\sim B$	A4
5) $A \rightarrow . \sim\sim A \vee \sim\sim B$	Trans. (1),(3)
6) $B \rightarrow . \sim\sim A \vee \sim\sim B$	Trans. (2),(4)
7) $A \vee B \rightarrow . \sim\sim A \vee \sim\sim B$	r3 on (5) and (6)
8) $(\sim\sim A \vee \sim\sim B) \rightarrow . \sim(\sim A \wedge \sim B)$.	A version of T10.
9) $A \vee B \rightarrow . \sim(\sim A \wedge \sim B)$	Trans. (7),(8)
10) $\sim\sim(\sim A \wedge \sim B) \rightarrow . \sim(A \vee B)$	Contra. (9)
11) $\sim A \wedge \sim B \rightarrow . \sim\sim(\sim A \wedge \sim B)$	A6
12) $\sim A \wedge \sim B \rightarrow . \sim(A \vee B)$	Trans (11), (10).

T12. $\sim(A \wedge B) \rightarrow . \sim A \vee \sim B$

Proof

1) $\sim\sim A \rightarrow A$	A7
2) $\sim\sim B \rightarrow B$	A7
3) $\sim\sim A \wedge \sim\sim B \rightarrow . A \wedge B$	Dr.3 on (1),(2)
4) $\sim(\sim A \vee \sim B) \rightarrow . \sim\sim A \wedge \sim\sim B$.	A version of T9
5) $\sim(\sim A \vee \sim B) \rightarrow . A \wedge B$	Trans. (4),(3)
6) $\sim(A \wedge B) \rightarrow . \sim\sim(\sim A \vee \sim B)$	Contra. (5)
7) $\sim\sim(\sim A \vee \sim B) \rightarrow . \sim A \vee \sim B$	A7
8) $\sim(A \wedge B) \rightarrow . \sim A \vee \sim B$	Trans. (6),(7).

Now by Def. $\leftrightarrow$ we have the two DeMorgan equivalences.

T13. $\sim(A \vee B) \leftrightarrow . \sim A \wedge \sim B$

T14. $\sim(A \wedge B) \leftrightarrow . \sim A \vee \sim B$

We now work towards the basic Associativity equivalence

T15. $A \wedge (B \wedge C) \rightarrow . (A \wedge B) \wedge C$

Proof

1) $A \wedge (B \wedge C) \rightarrow A$	A1
2) $A \wedge (B \wedge C) \rightarrow . B \wedge C$	A2
3) $B \wedge C \rightarrow B$	A1
4) $A \wedge (B \wedge C) \rightarrow B$	Trans. (2),(3)
5) $B \wedge C \rightarrow C$	A2
6) $A \wedge (B \wedge C) \rightarrow . A \wedge B$	Trans. (2),(5)

Proof of T15 continued

7) $A\wedge(B\wedge C)\longrightarrow.A\wedge B$ r2 on (1) and (4)

8) $A\wedge(B\wedge C)\longrightarrow.(A\wedge B)\wedge C$ r2 on (7),(6).

The proof of T16, the converse of T15, is similar to that of T15.

T16. $(A\wedge B)\wedge C\longrightarrow A\wedge(B\wedge C)$

T17. $(A\wedge B)\wedge C\longleftrightarrow A\wedge(B\wedge C)$ Def. of $\longleftrightarrow$ on T15 and T16.

We state T18 with only the hints that a proof is facilitated by use of A3,A4 in the given versions together with the version: $A \vee B\longrightarrow.(A \vee B) \vee C$ and the version: $C\longrightarrow.(A \vee B) \vee C$, and then use of r3. The proof of T19 is like that of T18.

T18. $A \vee (B \vee C)\longrightarrow.A \vee (B \vee C)$

T19. $(A \vee B) \vee C\longrightarrow.A \vee (B \vee C)$

T20. $(A \vee B) \vee C\longleftrightarrow.A \vee (B \vee C)$ Def. of $\longleftrightarrow$ on T18 and T19.

Before turning to the rather difficult task of establishing the Distributivity equivalences we cite the theorems relevant to the idem-potent equivalences expressed in T23 and in T26.

T21. $A\longrightarrow.A \vee A$

T22. $A \vee A\longrightarrow A$

T23. $A \vee A\longleftrightarrow A$

T24. $A\longrightarrow.A\wedge A$

T25. $A\wedge A\longrightarrow A$

T26 $A\wedge A\longleftrightarrow A$

T27. $(A\wedge B \vee A\wedge C)\longrightarrow.A\wedge(B \vee C)$

Proof

1) $A\wedge B\longrightarrow B$ A2

2) $A\wedge C\longrightarrow C$ A2

3) $(A\wedge B \vee A\wedge C)\longrightarrow.B \vee C$ Dr.4 on (1),(2)

4) $A\wedge B\longrightarrow A$ A1

5) $A\wedge C\longrightarrow A$ A1

6) $(A\wedge B \vee A\wedge C)\longrightarrow A$ r3 on (4),(5)

7) $(A\wedge B \vee A\wedge C)\longrightarrow.A\wedge(B \vee C)$ r2 on (6),(3).

The following proof for T28 has been adapted from Maksimowas' proof of her 2.14 in [1968].

T28. $A\wedge(B \vee C)\longrightarrow.A\wedge B \vee B\wedge C$

Proof

1) $A\wedge(B \vee C)\longrightarrow.B \vee A\wedge C$ A5

2) $B \vee (A\wedge C)\longrightarrow.(A\wedge C) \vee B$ T6

3) $A\wedge(B \vee C)\longrightarrow.(A\wedge C) \vee B$ Trans. (1),(2)

4) $A\wedge(B \vee C)\longrightarrow A$ A1

5) $A\wedge(B \vee C)\longrightarrow.A\wedge((A\wedge C) \vee B)$ r2 on (4),(3)

6) $A\wedge((A\wedge C) \vee B)\longrightarrow.A\wedge C \vee A\wedge B.$ A5 with $A\wedge C$ playing role of B.

7) $A\wedge C \vee A\wedge B\longrightarrow.A\wedge B \vee A\wedge C$ T6

8) $A\wedge((A\wedge C) \vee B)\longrightarrow.A\wedge B \vee A\wedge C$ Trans. (6),(7)

9) $A\wedge(B \vee C)\longrightarrow.A\wedge B \vee A\wedge C.$ Trans. (5),(8).

T29. $A \wedge (B \vee C) \longleftrightarrow . A \wedge B \vee A \wedge C$ Def. $\longleftrightarrow$ on T27 and T28.

T30. $A \vee (B \wedge C) \longleftrightarrow . (A \vee B) \wedge (A \vee C)$

Proof

1)	$A \longrightarrow . A \vee B$	A3
2)	$A \longrightarrow . A \vee C$	A3
3)	$A \longrightarrow . (A \vee B) \wedge (A \vee C)$	r2 on (1), (2)
4)	$B \wedge C \longrightarrow C$	A2
5)	$C \longrightarrow . A \vee C$	A4
6)	$B \wedge C \longrightarrow . A \vee C$	Trans. (4),(5)
7)	$B \wedge C \longrightarrow B$	A1
8)	$B \longrightarrow . A \vee B$	A4
9)	$A \wedge C \longrightarrow . A \vee B$	Trans. (7),(8)
10)	$B \wedge C \longrightarrow . (A \vee B) \wedge (A \vee C)$	r2 on (9),(6)
11)	$A \vee (B \wedge C) \longrightarrow . (A \vee B) \wedge (A \vee C)$	r3 on (3).(10)

T31. $(A \vee B) \wedge (A \vee C) \longrightarrow . A \vee (B \wedge C)$

Proof

1)	$(A \vee B) \wedge (A \vee C) \longrightarrow . A \vee (A \vee B) \wedge C$	A version of A5.
2)	$(A \vee B) \wedge C \longrightarrow . C \wedge (A \vee B)$	T3
3)	$C \wedge (A \vee B) \longrightarrow . A \vee (C \wedge B)$	A5
4)	$C \wedge B \longrightarrow . B \wedge C$	T3
5)	$A \longrightarrow A$	T1
6)	$A \vee (C \wedge B) \longrightarrow . A \vee (B \wedge C)$	Dr.4 (5), (4)
7)	$C \wedge (A \vee B) \longrightarrow . A \vee (B \wedge C)$	Trans.(3),(6)
8)	$(A \vee B) \wedge C \longrightarrow . A \vee (B \wedge C)$	Trans.(2),(7)
9)	$A \longrightarrow . A \vee (B \wedge C)$	A3
10)	$A \vee ((A \vee B) \wedge C) \longrightarrow . A \vee (B \wedge C)$	r3 on (9),(8)
11)	$(A \vee B) \wedge (A \vee C) \longrightarrow . A \vee (B \wedge C)$	Trans. (1),(10).

T32. $(A \vee B) \wedge (A \vee C) \longleftrightarrow . A \vee (B \wedge C)$ Def. $\longleftrightarrow$ on T30,T31.

We now prove that Replacement holds for TE. Some new notation will facilitate a proof of Repl. for the truncated language of TE. Let Z(A) be a zdf. which may have A as a subformula. (We won't explicitly consider cases in which no replacement is made; but still a z(A) need not denote a zdf. with A as a subformula.) Let z(B/A) be a zdf. just like z(A) except that some occurrences of A in z(A) have been replaced by the <u>zdf. B.</u> Below $A \longleftrightarrow B$ is $A \longrightarrow B$ and $B \longrightarrow A$.

Theorem I of III.2: From $A \longrightarrow B$, $B \longrightarrow A$ infer $z(A) \longrightarrow z(B/A)$ and $z(B/A) \longrightarrow z(A)$.

The proof is by induction on the number of logical signs, which are only truth-functional signs, in z(A). Basis of the induction: z(A) has no logical signs. So, z(A) is a variable p and hence A is a variable p. Hence, the premisses are $p \longrightarrow B$ and $B \longrightarrow p$ while $z(A) \longrightarrow z(B/A)$ is $p \longrightarrow B$ and $z(B/A) \longrightarrow z(A)$ is $B \longrightarrow p$. So, we have the basis. Induction assumption: If z1(A) and z2(A) have fewer logical signs than z(A), then $z1(A) \longleftrightarrow z1(B/A)$ and $z2(A) \longleftrightarrow z2(B/A)$ can be inferred from $A \longleftrightarrow B$.

Induction cases:

i) z(A) is zl(A) v z2(A). By induction assumption we have zl(A)$\longrightarrow$zl(B/A) and z2(A)$\longrightarrow$z2(B/A). By Dr.4 we get zl(A) v z2(A)$\longrightarrow$.zl(B/A) **v** zl(B/A). The proof of the converse is similar.

ii) z(A) is zl(A)$\wedge$z2(A). The proof is similar to that of case (i) except that **Dr**.3 is used.

iii) z(A) is $\sim$zl(A). By induction assumption we have: zl(A)$\longleftrightarrow$zl(B/A). Contraposition gives us what we want.

We label uses of Theorem I Repl. . The value of proving Theorem I here is not only that it allows use of Repl. in TE, but also that a proof of a Replacement Theorem for richer languages is already partially completed.

If general Commutativity and Associativity hld for TE, then TE is a MA system in the sense of Section I.8, although it is one of those MA systems with no zdfs. as wffs.. Despite our earlier claim that we will not prove general Commutativity and Associativity, we will at least sketch a prove of these results for $\wedge$ in TE. The sketch is taken from Michael Ikezawa's proof on pp. 238 - 40 of Copi's [1967].

Theorem II of III.2: If $A_1, A_2, \ldots, A_n$ are zdfs., not necessarily different, while F and G are conjunctions using each of the A_i exactly once, then $\vdash_{TE}$ F$\longleftrightarrow$G.

We sketch a proof by induction on the number of conjuncts A_i. The basis holds by default because there is only one conjunct. Assume that the theorem holds for less than n conjuncts. F has a form H$\wedge$I while G has a form J$\wedge$K. We can assume that H and J have a common conjunct A_j. (If J did not share a conjunct with H, we could consider K$\wedge$J instead of J$\wedge$K because H would then share a conjunct with K.) By induction assumption. $\vdash$ H$\longleftrightarrow$.$A_j\wedge$H', where H' is a conjunction of the A_i in H different from A_j. (H' may be empty.) Similarly, we have $\vdash$ J$\longleftrightarrow$.$A_j\wedge$J'. So, by Repl. $\vdash$ F$\longleftrightarrow$.($A_j\wedge$H')$\wedge$I and also $\vdash$ G$\longleftrightarrow$.($A_j\wedge$J')$\wedge$K. By use of T17 and Repl. we get both $\vdash$ F$\longleftrightarrow$.$A_j\wedge$(H'$\wedge$I) and $\vdash$ G$\longleftrightarrow$.$A_j\wedge$(J'$\wedge$K). Here(H'$\wedge$I) and (J'$\wedge$K) contain the same conjuncts. So, by the induction assumption: $\vdash$ (H'$\wedge$I)$\longleftrightarrow$(J'$\wedge$K). With $A_j\longleftrightarrow A_j$ and Dr.3 we get $\vdash$ $A_j\wedge$(H'$\wedge$I)$\longleftrightarrow$.$A_j\wedge$(J'$\wedge$K). With Trans. we get: $\vdash$ F$\longleftrightarrow$G.

The next theorem gives gives general Commutativity and Associativity for **v**. We do not even sketch a proof for it.

Theorem III of III.2: If $A_1, A_2, \ldots, A_n$ are zdfs., not necessarily different, while F and G are disjunctions using each of the A_i exactly once, then $\vdash_{TE}$ F$\longleftrightarrow$G.

Now that we know that TE is an MA system we can use Theorems I and II of Section I.8 to get the fourth theorem of this section, whose proof is easy with Trans., Associativity, and Commutativity.

Theorem IV of III.2: In TE if A^c is an official conjunctive normal form of A and A^d and official disjunctive normal form of A, then $\vdash_{TE} A \longleftrightarrow A^c$ and $\vdash_{TE} A \longleftrightarrow A^d$.

A little lemma on explicit TE entailments helps us to show that every TE entailment is a theorem of system TE. Recall from I.8 that /p/ indicates either p or $\sim$p.

Lemma 1 of III.2: If $A \longrightarrow B$ is an explicit TE entailment, then $\vdash_{TE} A \longrightarrow B$.

For proof assume that we have explicit TE entailment $A \longrightarrow B$. So, A is a $/p_1/ \wedge /p_2/ ,\ldots, \wedge /p_n/$, B is a $/q_1/ \vee /q_2/ \vee,\ldots,\vee /q_m/$, and a $/p_i/$ is identical with a $/q_j/$. By T1 we have then $\vdash /p_i/ \longrightarrow /q_j/$. By use of Dr.6 we conjoin the others atoms in A with $/p_i/$. By use of Dr.7 we disjoin the other atoms in B with $/q_j/$. So, we use Dr.6 and Dr.7 to build up $/p_i/ \longrightarrow /q_j/$ into an explicit TE entailment which differs from $A \longrightarrow B$ only by Commutation and Association.

Theorem V of III.2: If $A \longrightarrow B$ is a TE entailment, $\vdash_{TE} A \longrightarrow B$.

For proof consider the following. If $A \longrightarrow B$ is a TE entailment, there is an official disjunctive normal form A^d of A: $A_1 \vee A_2,\ldots,\vee A_n$, and official conjunctive normal form B^c of B: $B_1 \wedge B_2,\ldots,\wedge B_m$, and each $A_i \longrightarrow B_j$ is an explicit TE entailment. By Lemma 1 we have $\vdash A_i \longrightarrow B_j$ for each $A_i \longrightarrow B_j$. Now m-1 uses of r2 and maybe reassociation gives $\vdash A_i \longrightarrow B^c$ for an A_i. Now do the same so that we get $\vdash A_i \longrightarrow B^c$ for all A_i. Now n-1 uses of r3 and maybe reassociation will give $\vdash A^d \longrightarrow B^c$. Because Theorem IV tells us that in TE $A \longleftrightarrow A^d$ and $B \longleftrightarrow B^c$. So, Repl. gives the theorem.

Theorem V gives completeness of system TE with respect to the TE entailments. Of course extensions of TE will also contain all of the TE entailments. Our major concern, then, about extensions of TE will be whether or not they have more fde. theorems than does system TE. Our last theorem, whose proof is an exercise, shows why we worry whether a system containing the TE entailments has more fde. theorems than the TE entailments. Our concern in the next section is to show that system TE has only TE entailments as theorems.

Theorem VI of III.2: If fde. $A \longrightarrow B$ which is not a TE entailment, is added to TE to give TE*, then TE* has a theorem which violates the variable sharing condition C7.

Exercises III.2

1. Prove all derived rules not proved in the section.
2. Prove all theorems not proved in the section.
3. Prove Theorem III.
4. Prove Theorem VI. You do not need to assume that the added axiom is a logical axiom, viz., that any instance of it is also an axiom.

III.3 The TE entailments are exactly the theorems of system TE, Smiley's matrix $\mathcal{S}m$ is a finite characteristic matrix for TE.

The main goal of this section is to show that all theorems of system TE are TE entailments so that by use of Theorem V of III.2 we can conclude that the TE entailments are exactly the the theorems of system TE. For this purpose we use the so-called Smiley matrix $\mathcal{S}m$ from Example 5 of Section I.7. In addition we establish that $\mathcal{S}m$ is a finite characteristic matrix for TE. The Smiley matrix was presented in R. Routley's [1972a] and in 15.3 of Anderson's and Belnap's [1975] where there is also the result that $\mathcal{S}m$ is a finite characteristic matrix for TE. Please refer back to I.7 Example 5 for $\mathcal{S}m$; take +1 as designated.

In Example 5 of I.7, $\mathcal{S}m$ was exhibited as a world-matrix; hence in light of Theorems II and III of Section I.7 we need only verify that A6 and A7 of TE are $\mathcal{S}m$ valid and that r4 (Contraposition) preserves designation in order to show that $\mathcal{S}m$ is suitable for system TE. On a world-matrix $v(A \rightarrow B) \in D$ iff. $v(A) \leq v(B)$. You can easily check that $v(A) \leq v(\sim\sim A)$ and that $v(\sim\sim A) \leq v(A)$; hence easily check that A6 and A7 are $\mathcal{S}m$ valid. You can easily check that if $v(A) \leq v(B)$ then $\overline{v(B)} \leq \overline{v(A)}$ and thereby verify that r4 preserves designation. So, we have our first theorem.

Theorem I of III.3: $\mathcal{S}m$ is suitable for system TE.

As a result of Theorem I above, and the McKinsey normality of world-matrices which was established in Theorem IV of I.7, we have that if $\vdash A \leftrightarrow B$ then $v(A)=v(B)$ for all v() on $\mathcal{S}m$. So with Theorem IV of III.2 we get a lemma.

Lemma 1 of III.3: For any v() on $\mathcal{S}m$ $v(A \rightarrow B)=v(A^d \rightarrow B^c)$, where A^d is an official disjunctive normal form of A and B^c is an official conjunctive normal form of B.

The next lemma is the crucial one for showing that only TE entailments are theorems of TE. Its proof is adapted from pp. 15-16 of Anderson's and Belnap's [1962a] and from 15.3 of their [1975].

Lemma 2 of III.3: If fde. formula $A \rightarrow B$ is not a TE entailment, there is a v() on $\mathcal{S}m$ such that $v(A \rightarrow B)= -1$

Consider the following remarks by way of proof. If $A \rightarrow B$ is not a TE entailment, there is an A_i from an official disjunctive normal for A^d of A and a conjunct B_j from an official conjunctive normal form B^c of B such that A_i and B_j share no atom. Develop the following kind of valuation v(). If a variable occurs in A_i but not in B_j assign it +0. If a variable occurs unnegated in A_i but negated in B_j assign it +1. If a variable occurs negated in A_i but unnegated in B_j assign it -1. If a variable occurs only in B_j assign it -0. To complete the valuation for $A \longrightarrow B$ assign the variables in A and B which are not in A_i or B_j +1. With this kind of valuation the atoms of the primitive conjunction A_i are assigned either +1 or +0. Hence, $v(A_i)$ is +1 or +0. Consequently, $v(A^d)$ is +1 or +0. By lemma 1, then, v(A) is +1 or +0. Also with this kind of valuation the atoms of the primitive disjunction B_j are -0 or -1. Hence, $v(B_j)$ is -0 or -1. So, $v(B^c)$ is -0 or -1. By lemma 1, v(B) is -0 or -1. The reader can check that: $+1 \longrightarrow 0, +1 \longrightarrow 1, +0 \longrightarrow 0$, and $+0 \longrightarrow 1$ are all -1.

From the suitability of Sm for TE and lemma 2, we know that if an fde. $A \longrightarrow B$ is not a TE entailment it is not a theorem of TE. So, with Theorem V of III.2 we have the next theorem.

Theorem II of III.3: $\vdash_{TE} A \longrightarrow B$ iff. $A \longrightarrow B$ is a TE entailment.

From Theorem II and lemma 2 we know that $A \longrightarrow B$ is not a TE theorem if it is not valid on Sm. So, we have the following corollary.

Corollary of II of III.3: Sm is a finite characteristic matrix for system TE.

We close this section with some observations on proving the consistency of TE and with some observations on the limitations of TE and Sm. Because no negation of a wff. is a wff. of the language of TE, we cannot show that TE is consistent by showing that TE has no wff. and its negation as theorems. Similarly, because no variable is a wff., we cannot show that TE is consistent in the sense of having no single variable as a theorem. But we can show that there are wffs. which are not theorems. Hence, we have our next theorem.

Theorem III of III.3: TE is consistent in the sense that some wff. is not a theorem.

TE's possession of a finite characteristic matrix is desirable because it gives a nice decision procedure. If, in addition, we can find an interpretation of the values of Sm. we may get a better understanding of why only TE entailments correspond to the best formal inferences from zdfs. to zdfs.. Example 5 of Section I.7 started to develop such an interpretation of Sm.. The interpretation will be developed further in Section V.8. So, system V4, the fde. fragment of Parry's ASI', is not superior to TE by virtue of possessing an interpretable finite characteristic matrix. (Recall Section I.9.) However, Sm and TE have limitations. No zdf. is valid on Sm.. Indeed classical tautologies get -1 on Sm.. So the Sm theses do not even meet Belnap's adequacy condition C1 from I.6.

System TE has the same limitations; it has $A \dashrightarrow B$ as a theorem while lacking $A \supset B$ as a theorem because $A \supset B$ is not in its language. In the next section we enrich the language of TE to rectify this limitation.

We close with a theorem to be proved as an exercise.

Theorem IV of III.3: No zdf. is $\mathcal{S}m$ valid.

Exercises III.3

1. Prove theorems III and IV.
2. Is $\mathcal{S}m$ a Sugihara matrix?
3. Is $\mathcal{S}m$ a Parry matrix?
4. Carry out the procedure of lemma 2 for $p \wedge (\sim p \vee q) \rightarrow q$.

III.4 TE plus the classical tautologies: system TEc, $\mathfrak{M}_0$ is a finite characteristic matrix for TEc.

Our goal in this section is to extend TE to TEc, which is TE plus the classical tautologies, so that not only can we conclude $\vdash A \supset B$ from $\vdash A \rightarrow B$ but also so that we have every classical tautology as a theorem. In a classical tautology, if we regard the variables as universally quantified and read $\wedge$, $\vee$, and $\sim$ as intended we have a necessary truth about the sentences which are true or false. So, if zdfs, are wffs., every classical tautology should be a theorem. We show that the theorems of TEc are exactly the TE entailments and the classical tautologies. In addition we show that Belnap's $\mathfrak{M}_0$ is a finite characteristic matrix for Tec. We close by arguing that Material Detachment cannot be a derived rule of TEc although MD is an admissible rule for TEc.

We extend TE to TEc by first augmenting the language of TE to include zdfs. as well as fdes. as wffs.. Now $(p \vee q)$ is a wff. although $\sim(p \rightarrow q)$ and $p \wedge (p \rightarrow q)$ are still not wffs.. To the axioms and rules of TE we add only three rules. We add r5: $A \rightarrow B \vdash \sim A \vee B$, r6: $A, A \rightarrow B \vdash B$, and r7: $A, B \vdash A \wedge B$. In this section $\vdash$ means 'theorem of TEc.' Although r6 and r7 are not full MP and Adj. because we have only fdes. and zdfs. we call them MP, or α, and Adj., or β. For instance, note that Adj. in TEc cannot take us in TEc from $(p \rightarrow p)$ and $(q \rightarrow q)$ to $(p \rightarrow p) \wedge (q \rightarrow q)$.

Since, after Theorem III of III.2, we concluded that TE is an MA system in the sense of Section I.8 we can conclude that TEc is a MA system. So, Theorem IV of I.8 gives us our first lemma of this section.

Lemma 1 of III.4: If A is a classical tautology, then $\vdash A$.

The next lemma can be proved by treating the $\rightarrow$ of TEc as $\supset$. Then show that, with $\rightarrow$ so treated, all theorems of TEc are classical tautologies.

Lemma 2 of III.4: If A is a non-tautologous zdf., then A is not a theorem of TEc.

The first theorem of this section falls out of lemmas 1 and 2.

Theorem I of III.4: If A is a zdf., then $\vdash A$ iff. A is a classical tautology.

Due to the restricted language of TEc, theorems of TEc can only be zdfs. or fdes.. Consequently, in light of Theorem II of III.3, we get Lemma 3 below if we show that no new fde. theorems can be proved in TEc. We can show that if an fde. $A \rightarrow B$ could not be proved in TE it cannot be proved in TEc. Consider how TEc was obtained from TE. No new axioms were added.

Rule r5 takes us to zdfs. from fdes.. Neither MP nor Adj. takes us to fdes. in TEc. So, nothing in TEc will give us an fde. theorem which is not already obtainable in TE. Hence, the following lemma holds.

Lemma 3 of III.4: If fde. A⟶B is not a TE entailment, then A⟶B is not a theorem of TEc.

Now Theorem II of III.3, Theorem I, and Lemma 3 give us a theorem specifying exactly the theorems of TEc.

Theorem II of III.4: ⊢A iff. A is a classical tautology or A is a TE entailment.

Let us now establish that Belnap's 8-value world-matrix is a finite characteristic matrix for TEc. See the discussion about Diagram 6 in Section I.7 for the ∧, ∨, and ‾ tables for matrix $\mathcal{M}$o. The ⟶ is presented below. The designated elements are the positive elements. An interpretation of the computation of the ∧, v, and ‾ tables is in I.7; the rationale for the computation of $\mathcal{M}$o's ⟶ table is in Section V.5.

The ⟶ table for $\mathcal{M}$o:

⟶	+3	+2	+1	+0	-0	-1	-2	-3
+3	+3	-3	-3	-3	-3	-3	-3	-3
+2	+3	+2	-3	-3	-2	-3	-2	-3
+1	+3	-3	+1	-3	-1	-1	-3	-3
+0	+3	+2	+1	+0	-0	-1	-2	-3
-0	+3	-3	-3	-3	+0	-3	-3	-3
-1	+3	-3	+1	-3	+1	+1	-3	-3
-2	+3	+2	-3	-3	+2	-3	+2	-3
-3	+3	+3	+3	+3	+3	+3	+3	+3

D= {+3,+2,+1,+0}

Lemma 4 of III.4: $\mathcal{M}$o is suitable for TEc.

As proof consider the following. By reference to D6 of I.7 and the above ⟶ table it can be verified that v(A⟶B) ∈ D iff. v(A) ≤ v(B). Because $\mathcal{M}$o is a world-matrix Theorem III of I.7 tells us that $\mathcal{M}$o is a distributive lattice. Hence, we get from Theorem II of I.7 that A1 through A5 are $\mathcal{M}$o valid and that r1 through r3 preserve such validity. By Theorem IV of I.7 $\mathcal{M}$o is McKinsey normal; hence MP and Adj. preserve $\mathcal{M}$o validity. One can verify that A6 and A7 are valid and that Contraposition (r7) preserves validity. So, we give serious consideration only to r5. Assume v(A⟶B) ∈ D; so, v(A) ≤ v(B). For <u>reductio</u> assume that v(∼A ∨ B) ∉ D. Theorem V of I.7 tells us that D for $\mathcal{M}$o is a filter. Condition (iii) for filterhood tells us that if v(∼A ∨ B) ∉ D then v(∼A) ∉ D and v(B) ∉ D. The negation table shows that v(A) ∈ D if v(∼A) ∉ D and that v(∼B) ∈ D if v(B) ∉ D. Now the assumption that v(A) ≤ v(B) with v(A) ∈ D gives v(B) ∈ D. But Theorem V of I.7 tells us that $\mathcal{M}$o is normal and hence cannot have both v(B) ∈ D and v($\sim$B) ε D. So, we have the lemma because we cannot assume that r5 fails to preserve validity.

Because Theorem I tells us that all classical tautologies are TEc theorems, Lemma 4 tells us that all classical tautologies are $\mathfrak{M}_o$ valid. However, we should not expect tautologies to take on the value +3 for all assignments to their variables. For instance, if v(p)=+1 and v(q)=+0, v((p $\vee\sim$p)$\wedge$(q $\vee\sim$q))=+0. Also on this assignment a contradiction gets a rather "high" value; v(p$\wedge\sim$p $\vee$ q$\wedge\sim$q)=-0. If we regard +3 as the best of the designated values and -3 as the worst of the undesignated values, we may be tempted to regard the preceding observations as showing that classical tautologies are not the best logical truths and that classical contradictions are not the worst logical falsehoods. But such an interpretation is misleading. Even the paradigm logical truth p$\longrightarrow$p takes on all designated values. It is best not to have any preference amongst the values on the basis that some of them are "truer" or higher. If v(p$\longrightarrow$p)=+0,there is no need to think that there is anything weak about p$\longrightarrow$p. The fault, if there is any fault, lies in the "worlds" of the world-matrix which do not contain all logical truths.

Let us return from the preceding digression to the task of showing that non-theorems of the language of TEc are not $\mathfrak{M}_o$ valid. Since TEc has only zdfs. and fdes. in its language, we carry out the task with two lemmas.

Lemma 5 of III.4: If A is a zdf. which is not a classical tautology, there is a v() on $\mathfrak{M}_o$ such that v(A)=-3.

An inductive argument can be used. Argue by induction on the length of A that if +3 is used as the T and -3 as the F of classical two-value truth tables a falsifying assignment to A on the classical truth tables corresponds to one on $\mathfrak{M}_o$ by which A gets -3.

Lemma 6 of III.4: If fde. A$\longrightarrow$B is not a theorem of TEc, there is a v() on $\mathfrak{M}_o$ such that v(A$\longrightarrow$B)=-3.

As proof consider the following remarks adapted from Anderson's and Belnap's [1962a]. From the facts that TEc is an MA system and that $\mathfrak{M}_o$ is normal establish that v(A$\longrightarrow$B) =v($A^d\longrightarrow B^c$) where A^d is an official disjunctive normal form of A and B^c an official conjunctive normal form of B. As in the proof of Lemma 2 of III.3 conclude that there is an A_i from A^d and a conjunct B_j from B^c such that A_i and B_j share no atom. Construct a valuation on $\mathfrak{M}_o$ for the variables of A$\longrightarrow$B in the following way. (Here 'p occurs' means that /p/ occurs.) If a variable occurs in neither A_i nor B_j, assign it +3. If p occurs in A_i but not in B_j, set v(p)=+1. If p occurs in B_j but not in A_i, set v(p)=+2. If p is an atom in

A_i and $\sim$p is an atom in B_j, set v(p)=+3. If $\sim$p is an atom in A_i and p is an atom in B_j, set v(p)=-3. The last two cases exclude one another because A_i and B_j share no atoms. As an exercise verify that v(A_i) will be:+3,+1, or -1 and that v(B_j) will be: +2,-2, or -3. Verify that v(A^d) will be: +3,+1,-0, or -1 and that v(B^c) will be: +2,+0,-2, or -3. Finally verify that for all sixteen cases v($A^d \rightarrow B^c$)=-3 and hence that v(A$\rightarrow$B)=-3.

We can get our third theorem from lemmas 4,5, and 6.

Theorem III of III.4: $\mathfrak{M}$o is a finite characteristic matrix for TEc.

If we ignore the zdfs. of TEc and the rules added to TE to get TEc, i.e., if we consider TE, lemmas 4 and 6 show us that $\mathfrak{M}$o is characteristic for TE.

Corollary of Theorem III of III.4: $\mathfrak{M}$o is a finite characteristic matrix for TE. (See M. Dunn's third theorem in 18.8 of Anderson's and Belnap's [1975].)

Admittedly, $\mathfrak{M}$o is characteristic for TEc because of the limitations of TEc's language. For instance, the schema $\sim$(A$\rightarrow$A) v (A$\rightarrow$A) is valid on $\mathfrak{M}$o but it is not a theorem schema for TEc. However, $\sim$(A$\rightarrow$A) **v** (A$\rightarrow$A)'s instances are not wffs. of TEc either; so we do not have to worry that these valid instances of $\sim$(A$\rightarrow$A) **v** (A$\rightarrow$A) are not theorems of TEc when we are considering the completeness of TEc. But $\sim$(A$\rightarrow$A) **v** (A$\rightarrow$A) seems to be the schema of a logical truth; and hence it seems that it should be a theorem schema. In the section after the next we will augment the language of TEc to get such schemas as theorem schemas. But let us here consider a bit more about $\mathfrak{M}$o and the place of MD and DS in TEc.

The Anderson and Belnap procedure given in the proof remarks for Lemma 6 has far greater value than simply being a device for showing that $\mathfrak{M}$o is characteristic for TEc. The procedure gives $\mathfrak{M}$o an important role in determining whether or not a system's fde. fragment exceeds the TE entailments. If a system S is an extension of TEc and if $\mathfrak{M}$o is suitable for S, we can use the procedure to show that a non-TE entailment is not a theorem of S. We do not cite Smiley's $\mathcal{Sm}$ for the purpose of identifying systems with TE as their fde. fragment because $\mathcal{Sm}$ is not likely to be suitable for many systems.

Theorem IV of III.4: If S is an extension of TEc and if $\mathfrak{M}$o is suitable for S,then the fde. theorems of S are exactly the TE entailments.

Let us now see that MD and DS,rule γ , are admissible rules for TEc. The following proof makes crucial use of the fact that $\mathfrak{M}$o is characteristic for the system.

Theorem V of III.4: MD and DS in rule form are admissible rules of TEc.

In our sketch of a proof we consider only the case of MD. Assume that we have $\vdash$ A and $\vdash$ ($\sim$A v B). Since $\mathfrak{M}_o$ is suitable for TEc, we have v(A) $\in$ D and v($\sim$A v B) $\in$ D for all v() on $\mathfrak{M}_o$. Hence, because $\mathfrak{M}_o$ is normal, for no v() do we have v($\sim$A) $\in$ D. So, because D of $\mathfrak{M}_o$ is a filter, the fact that v($\sim$A v B) $\in$ D gives us that v(B) $\in$ D for all v() on $\mathfrak{M}_o$. Because $\mathfrak{M}_o$ is characteristic for TEc, the fact that v(B) $\in$ D for all v() on $\mathfrak{M}_o$ gives us $\vdash$ B.

Nevertheless, neither MD nor DS are derived rules of TEc. We could prove this directly but it is far easier to look ahead to the Entailment Theorem for system E in Section IV.4. The Entailment Theorem tells us that if MD and DS were derived rules of TEc, A$\wedge$($\sim$A v B)$\longrightarrow$B and $\sim$A$\wedge$(A v B)$\longrightarrow$B would be theorem schemas of E which they are not. So, we state the following without proof here. (See exercise 5 of IV.4.)

Theorem VI of III.4: MD and DS are not derived rules of TEc.

A further consequence of this Entailment Theorem for E will be that TEc is superior to Geach's G and any of Parry's systems because TEc does not allow a derivation of an arbitrarily selected wff. B from A and $\sim$A. (Recall Sections II.8 and II.16.) We state this corollary of E's Entailment Theorem as a theorem here.

Theorem VII of III.4: Neither A,$\sim$A$\vdash$ B nor A$\vdash$ B v $\sim$B are derived rules of TEc.

However, just because MD and DS are admissible rules for TEc is not a sufficient reason for thinking that we reason well by going from $\vdash$A and $\vdash$ A$\supset$B to $\vdash$ B. We develop this last point in the next section.

Exercises III.4

1. Prove Lemma 2.
2. Can we use Smiley's $\mathfrak{Sm}$ to prove Lemma 3?
3. Let A be any wff. of TEc. If all variables of A are assigned +2 on $\mathfrak{M}_o$ is v(A) always either +2 or -2?
4. Define A$\rightarrow\!\!\exists$B as A$\wedge$$\sim$B$\longrightarrow$.$\sim$(A$\wedge$$\sim$B). With $\rightarrow\!\!\exists$ so defined does TEc meet Belnap's C3 from I.6?
5. With $\rightarrow\!\!\exists$ defined as in (4) above does TEc meet Belnap's C2 and C4? For C4 note that we have $\vdash$ (p$\wedge$$\sim$p)$\wedge$$\sim$q$\longrightarrow$$\sim$((p$\wedge$$\sim$p)$\wedge$$\sim$q)
6. Look ahead to the proof of E's Entailment Theorem in IV.4. Point out that someone cannot say that we still have MD as a derived rule in TEc because in TEc MD applies only to the restricted language of TEc.

III.5 Sketch of a structural theory of meaning to make a case that MD and DS are not based on a meaning connection,

In the previous section we took note of the lowly status of MD (Material Detachment) and DS (Disjunctive Syllogism.) They did not correspond to entailments, they were not derived rules, and although admissible, it was suggested that they not be admitted. Do these rules truly deserve this lowly status? It is crucial to our way of dealing with the Lewis derivations that we show that MD and DS deserve this lowly status. To block Derivation III of I.1 we have to reject MD as an entailment and because we want normal rules we have to reject it as a derived rule. Moreover we do not want to say that the form of the reasoning: A, ($\sim$A $\vee$ B) and so B, is any better simply because A and $\sim$A $\vee$ B happen to be theorems. The move: It is a theorem that A and it is a theorem that $\sim$A $\vee$ B and so it is a theorem that B, is, of course, not MD; and we cannot object to it because it is justified by the admissibility of MD. We should note that in the sequel we talk mostly of MD, but the remarks are readily transferred to DS.

It must be conceded that MD and DS are valid. But, of course, validity is only a necessary condition for formal correctness. Still, it is important to note that we cannot argue against them by considerations of validity. On the other hand we need not abandon hope of finding fault with them on the basis that they are almost universally accepted as good inferences. Empirical facts about what people in general do, or about what a special kind of person does, accept are not decisive for deciding questions of logic. So, if we are not going to appeal to results about validity and facts about acceptance, how are we going to find fault with MD? Our discussion of rules R5 and R6 under C14 back in I.6 made a good case for rejecting MD and DS as entailment theses. But here we want also to reject them as rules. So, a theory of meaning is developed to show that B does not come from the meaning of A and $\sim$A $\vee$ B. We want to show that consideration of what is meant by the uses of 'and,' 'or,' and 'not' normally symbolized by $\wedge$, $\vee$, and $\sim$ show that MD is defective because in a special sense of 'meaning' B is not necessarily contained in the meaning of A and $\sim$A $\vee$ B. The theory, then, is a theory of what is meant by $\wedge$, $\vee$, $\sim$, and what may be called the null connective or implicit assertion sign preceding a sentence. Since the theory is concerned only with what is meant by these terms connecting and applied to sentences, it is called a <u>structural theory of meaning</u>. For purposes of this theory, sentences which are not complex due to an 'and,' 'or,' or 'not' symbolizable with $\wedge$, $\vee$, or $\sim$ are simple sentences. This theory is an adaptation of the Routleys' first degree semantics in their [1972]; their set-ups are here regarded as messages. At the end of this section, the author explains his repudiation of his critque in [1974] of the Routley's valuable contribution.

The phrases such as 'structural meaning' and 'structurally means' are awkward and unfamiliar. Hopefully, though, it will be seen that we are talking about the meaning of 'and,' 'or,' and 'not' familiar to all who have studied at least classical sentential logic. What is structurally meant by a set of sentences is the message form of the message from Σ. A message form of a message from a set of sentences Σ is the form or structure of sets of sentences developed from Σ by the rules to be given below. These rules give the meaning of 'and,' 'or,' and 'not.' (We do not identify the form of a set of sentences with the sentences although there is no claim that forms or structures of sets of sentences can exist apart from sentences.) The sentences with a form or structure of the kind discussed below provide the message from a set of sentences. Messages are what a set of sentences tell us about whatever it is that they are about. The simple sentences and negations of simple sentences are taken as constituting what is really said in a message because the more complex sentences break down into simple sentences or negations of simple sentences. Let us regard a set of sentences as giving a message, or several alternatives of what could be its message, and let us regard the sentences within a message as telling us what is allegedly the case. A comprehensive theory of meaning would have to say what it is for a sentence to be about such-and-such objects and what it is for a sentence to mean that such-and-such is the case. We are not here developing a comphrehensive theory of meaning. So we should emphasize that we do not hold that the only way in which sentences mean is by giving another set of structured sentences. We are simply not developing a theory of sentence meaning beyond specifying how they mean a message.

The preceding paragraph may have suggested that messages are analogous to Carnap's state descriptions in his [1947]. It may have been suggested that a message is a set of sentences consisting of exactly one member from a set of pairs of sentences where these pairs consist of a simple sentence and its negation. Removal of this possible misunderstanding provides a basis for making two fundamental points about the structure of messages. A message may be inconsistent in the sense of containing a sentence and its negation. A message may be incomplete in the sense that it lacks a sentence and its negation, even if this sentence is about that which some other sentences in the message are about. Indeed, a single message may have both S_1 and $\sim S_1$ while lacking both S_2 and $\sim S_2$. For instance, if you have never thought about Nixon's fidelity to his wife but we know that you gave a speech containing both 'Nixon was an able administrator' and 'Nixon was not an able administrator,' we should regard your message as incomplete in regard to Nixon's marital fidelity but inconsistent in regard to Nixon's administrative competence.

Despite the fact that messages are usually incomplete, messages, as we will see, typically contain more sentences than the set of sentences giving them. This is because what we utter, a set of sentences, typically means more than just the sentences uttered, although rarely does it mean something about every aspect of what we are talking about.

Because the theory is about sentences rather than formulas, we will, as above, use S and subscripted S's in presenting the meaning rules which give the structure of messages. We use H's to represent messages and ϵ to symbolize being in a message.

The first rule for specifying the form of the message given by a set of sentences Σ is called <u>the trunk formation rule</u> . Tree diagrams of message forms will explain this name. This rule could also be called 'the meaning what is said rule.' The rule is:

If $S \epsilon \Sigma$, then $S \epsilon H$.

A set of sentences gives us the formal or structural information that its members are in any message from that set. Once we have the sentences of Σ in a message H these sentences tell us the form of H or, as is usual because of 'or,' the forms which H may have. The sentences originally put in H by the trunk formation rule give the form of H, or forms H may have, by giving other sentences which are actually in H or only possibly in H.

The 'and' symbolized by $\wedge$ means 'both.' So an $S_1 \wedge S_2$ in a message gives us the structural information about the message that both S_1 and S_2 are in it. This rule is called <u>$\wedge$-simplification</u> and its offcial statement is:

If $S_1 \wedge S_2 \epsilon H$, then $S_1 \epsilon H$ and $S_2 \epsilon H$.

Disjunctions reveal that a set of sentences may underdetermine what their message is. The 'or' symbolized by **v** means: either this disjunct or that one or both. So an S_1 **v** S_2 in a message gives us the structural information that the message is one with S_1, one with S_2, or one with both S_1 and S_2. Because having S_1 does not preclude having S_2 and having S_2 does not preclude having S_1, the third case is omitted in the official statement of the rule which is called <u>v-branching</u>.

If S_1 **v** $S_2 \epsilon H$, then $S_1 \epsilon H$ or $S_2 \epsilon H$.

Tree diagrams portray how conjunctions tell us to extend a message and how disjunctions offer us alternative versions of a message. The little arrow pointing upwards from the trunk indicates that these sentences may be part of a larger message. The branches represent alternative versions of a message.

Picture 1

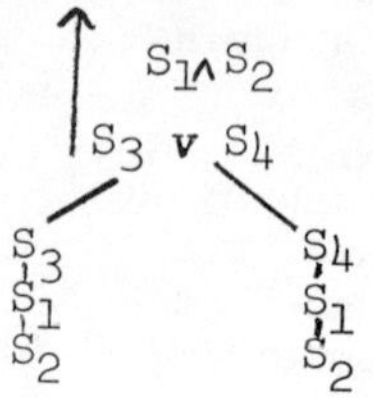

Picture 2

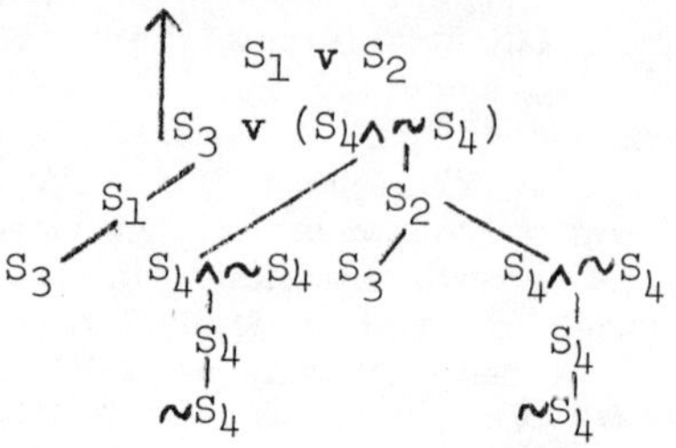

Such tree diagrams will remind some readers of R. Jeffrey's truth-table trees in his [1967]. And we do want to say that conjunctions and disjunctions in messages are to be analyzed in regard to how they say that a message is composed as if their truth-conditions were being given on a truth-table tree. Nevertheless, these meaning-trees are not truth-table trees because they are not being used to lay out the sentences which must be true for a set of sentences to be true. What is structurally meant by a set of sentences is not the truth conditions for the set of sentences. These trees are being used to lay out the message, or what may be the message, from a set of sentences. Hence, because messages may be inconsistent, a perfectly proper branch on a meaning-tree is one with both S_4 and $\sim S_4$. Branches with inconsistencies are rightly closed-off, i.e., discarded, on truth-table trees because such branches cannot represent a way of making all the sentences on the trunk true. On a meaning-tree it would be misleading to eliminate any branch. Branches are there on a meaning-tree to portray our information that there are alternative versions of the message. We are given these alternative versions by a disjunction in the message. Elimination of a branch would be rejection of what is meant by the 'or' in the disjunction and that is exactly what we want to portray. Messages may also remind some readers of J. Hintikka's model sets from his [1962]. However, messages are not model sets because messages can be inconsistent.

The next two rules which involve putting complex sentences into messages make tree diagrams unsuitable for representing message forms. We introduced meaning-trees merely to compare and contrast giving the structural meaning of a set of sentences with giving truth conditions for the set.

Because 'and' means 'both,' we have the rule of <u>$\wedge$ - adjunction.</u>

If $S_1 \in H$ and $S_2 \in H$, then $S_1 \wedge S_2 \in H$.

The rule of $\wedge$-adjunction seems well-justified by the meaning of 'and,' but the next rule of <u>$\vee$-addition</u> may be the most dubious of the theory.

If $S_1 \in H$, then $S_1 \vee S_2 \in H$.

This rule of $\vee$-addition corresponds to a valid inference and even to a TE entailment. But does S_1 gives us the structural information that a message containing S_1 contains $S_1 \vee S_2$ regardless of what S_2 is? There are some reasons for answering affirmatively. The primary function of S_1 in a message is, to be sure, to say that such and such is the case. When we consider a portion of a message we bring the meaning of 'or' to our consideration of the message. So, it is not too implausible to suggest that the occurrence of S_1 in a message and the meaning of 'or' also tell us that the message could be such that it contains S_2 for some S_2 or other. So we can regard S_1 as telling us what $S_1 \wedge (S_1 \vee S_2)$ tells us and hence what $S_1 \vee S_2$ tells us.

The rules of $\wedge$-adjunction and $\vee$-addition will get a negative, and maybe more plausible,formulation after we consider the structural meaning rules for $\sim$. The negative formulation of these two rules shows how they also can be regarded as rules which tell us how to reduce complex information about a message to less complex claims about the structure of the message, and ultimately to the simple sentences and negations of simple sentences which actually make up a message.

The occurrence of $\sim S$ in a message means (structurally) that S is not in the message. Unfortunately, what is meant need not be the case. In particular, $\sim S$ can be in a message even if S is in it. So, how can we represent the structural information that S is not being given when $\sim S$ is being given? The answer is provided by the Routley's in [1972], by R. Routley in his [1972a], and Meyer and R. Routley in several works such as [1973a]. The answer involves associating a complementary message H* with each H. Let us try to motivate use of the H* message.

Assume that we are getting a message from someone who wants us to think that he is honest and rational. If this sender gives us a message with $\sim S$ he wants us to take him as offering a message without S. Since he may, nevertheless, be dishonest or inconsistent we cannot assume that his message with $\sim S$ is in fact the message which he wants $\sim S$ to tell us about. Still $\sim S$ tells us at least that S is not in a message associated with H. Of course, this message is associated with H because sentences fail to be in it on the basis of what is in H. We do not in general know anything about these messages associated with H other than that some of them lack S_i when $\sim S_i \in H$. These * messages are the messages the sender intends us to take him as offering when a negative sentence is sent out.

For simplicity's sake, we regard each H has having a single complement H*. With this simplifying assumption we state the rule of Imperfect Consistency.

If $\sim S \in H$, then $S \notin H^*$. Rule of Imperfect Consistency,

The rule of Imperfect Consistency shows that the absence of a sentence S is structurally meant by $\sim S$ in a message. Because the absence of a sentence can be structurally meant, it is not totally implausible that the absence of a sentence structurally means something, i.e., gives us information about the structure of a message from which it is absent. Absence can mean or indicate. For example, the absence of a third angle tells us that a plane figure is not closed. Let us hypothesize, then, that the absence of affirmining S means that $\sim S$ is not rejected. Of course, not to reject $\sim S$ does not mean (structurally) having $\sim S$ in the message. For instance, if someone never says that he accepted a bribe he has thereby not rejected that he did not take a bribe but, still, he has not affirmed that he did not take a bribe. To get a rule for the absence of sentences, let us first consider what the absence of an S from an H* could tell us. It cannot tell us that $\sim S \in H^*$. unless we assume that messages are complete in the sense of having S or $\sim S$ in them. (It doesn't make any difference that we are focusing our attention on an H* because H*'s are just messages. Furthermore, we are no more entitled to assume that H* messages are complete than we are to assume messages in general are complete.) It is reasonable and simple to interpret S's not being in H* as $\sim S$ not being rejected from H*. I.e., S not being in H* is information that there is a message associated with H* which contains $\sim S$. We do get an indication that $\sim S$ is asserted when S is not asserted; but the indication is not strong enough to assume that $\sim S$ is in the message being delivered. We already have a message associated with H*, viz., H itself. So we will take H as the message associated with H* for purposes of containing the negations of what is not in H*. So we offer the rule which we call Imperfect Completeness.

If $S \notin H^*$, then $\sim S \in H$. Rule of Imperfect Completeness,

The rule of Imperfect Completeness can be taken as a rule about the message H when we consider its contrapositive: If $\sim S \notin H$, then $S \in H^*$. With Imperfect Consistency and Imperfect Completeness H* becomes the message which contains an S iff. $\sim S \notin H$. So we have: $\sim S \in H$ iff. $S \notin H^*$.

Certainly the assumption that there is a single complement for H is primarily a simplification for theoretical purposes. It is not analytically true of 'structural meaning' that there is a single such complement. Indeed, since 'structurally means' is an invented term, there is no basis besides basic logic and stipulation for saying that any claims about it are analytically true. Such stipulated analytic truths are uninteresting. What is of interest, though, is whether or not the theory of meaning is true of what it is supposed to be true of, viz., the uses of 'and,' 'or,' and 'not' symbolized by $\wedge$, $\vee$, and $\sim$. So the real test of whether or not we can assume that there is a single complement of H for both consistency and completeness is whether or not the theory with this assumption agrees with what we mean. We will briefly consider some problems involved in empirically testing this theory. But first we develop the theory a bit more.

In this work we ignore a serious issue raised by the mathematical intuitionists about the legitimacy of double negation. For an introduction see Heyting [1956] for a case that $\sim\sim$S does not mean (structurally) S. We restrict our theory of structural meaning to those of us who do mean S by $\sim\sim$S. We can regard the intuitionists as making a plea that we should not use $\sim\sim$S so that it means S. Their pleas may ultimately convert our normative intuitions. But regarding them as trying to change what we now mean by 'not' is to assume that double negation is, presently, part of the meaning of 'not.' Our theory, then, is at best correct about what is presently meant. So we give a rule of Double Negation as part of our theory. Given that H* is the message such that $S \notin H^*$ iff. $\sim S \in H$, the rule of Double Negation may be given as:

$H^{**} = H$, which yields $\sim\sim S \in H$ iff. $S \in H$.

Let us now summarize our theory by presenting all the rules together. For each message H there is a message H* where H and H* are non-empty sets of sentences structured by the following rules.

The Structural Theory of Meaning,

$S_1 \wedge S_2 \in H$ iff. $S_1 \in H$ and $S_2 \in H$	$\wedge$- normality
$S_1 \vee S_2 \in H$ iff. $S_1 \in H$ or $S_2 \in H$	$\vee$-normality,
$\sim S \in H$ iff. $S \notin H^*$	Imperfect Consistency and Completeness,
$H^{**} = H$	Double Negation,

Observe that all of the rules can be used to reduce complex sentences to less complex ones. Further observe that structural meanings of sets of sentences can be regarded as units, which is a necessary condition for being accepted as objects in an ontology. They can be regarded as units because identity conditions can be given for structural meanings. Let $\Sigma 1$ and $\Sigma 2$ be two sets of sentences with no repetitions within them and with their sentences symbolized with $\wedge$, $\vee$, $\sim$, and simple sentences as 'simple sentence' was used earlier in this section. The structural meaning M1 of $\Sigma 1$ is the structural meaning M2 of $\Sigma 2$ iff. the following two conditions are met.

Identity Conditions for Structural Meanings,

1. There is a one-one function f on the simple sentences in M1 onto the simple sentences of M2.
2. If each $f(S_i)$ in M2 is replaced everywhere in M2 by S_i, then each alternative version with its complement in M2 is an alternative version and complement in M1 and conversely.

Because structural meanings are structured sets of sentences it is not surprising that they have identity conditions. With this definition of 'same meaning' the premisses for an MD: $\{S_1, (\sim S_1 \vee S_2)\}$, have a different structural meaning than the premisses for a DS using the same simple sentences. The MD premisses offer an S_1, $\sim S_1$ and a S_1, S_2 version while the DS premisses offer a S_1, $\sim S_1$ version and a $\sim S_1, S_2$ version. Actually the consequence that MD and DS premisses have different meaning provides some support for our theory. People do think that MD and DS are different kinds of arguments. After all, MD has two affirmative premisses while DS has a negative premiss and an affirmative premiss.

The development of the theory is finished by defining 'entails.' We are here only defining entailment for sentences symbolizable as zdfs.. So, we are only defining first degree entailment. Also, since we only consider finite sets for premisses, we may restrict ourselves to talking of one sentence entailing another.

S_1 entails S_2 iff. it cannot be consistently assumed that there is a message H such that $S_1 \in H$ and $S_2 \notin H$.

This definition tells us that S_1 entails S_2 of the structural meaning of S_2 is, indeed has to be, included in the structural meaning of S_1. This definition satisfies the appealing Geach/von Wright principle of Section II.18 better than Geach's definition of II.16. We do have an <u>apriori</u> way, an analytic technique, of getting to know that a consequent stands in a certain relation to an antecedent which is not a way of getting to know either the consequent or the negation of the antecedent. There is no question here of getting to know anything except whether or not the structural meaning of the alleged consequent has to be in the structural meaning of the antecedent. Here we clearly base entailment solely on a connection, a meaning connection, between antecedent and consequent. The above definition also gives a formal way of determining whether or not an S_1 entails an S_2. We see if we can consistently assume $S_1 \in H$ but $S_2 \notin H$ for some H.

Let us illustrate this formal procedure by showing that MD is defective reasoning because the meaning of the conclusion is not contained in the meaning of the premisses.

Argument that MD is not Based on a Meaning Connection

1 a)	$S_1 \in H$	
b)	$(\sim S_1 \vee S_2) \in H$	Assumption which will be shown to be
c)	$S_2 \notin H$	consistent,
2)	$\sim S_1 \in H.$	v-branching on (1b), (1c) prevents an S_2 version of H.
3)	$S_1 \notin H^*$	Imperfect Consistency on (2),
4)	$\sim S_2 \in H^*$	Imperfect Completeness on (1c),
5)	$\sim S_1 \notin H^*$	Imperfect Consistency on (1a),

We have,above, shown that (1a),(1b), and (1c) can be consistently assumed. We have S_1 and $\sim S_1$ in H; but that is H's inconsistency and not our inconsistency. The only kind of contradiction which we would have to worry about is one saying that a sentence belongs and does not belong to a message. An exercise will show that more uses of the rules will not lead to any contradiction for us.

In light of the theory of structural meaning the above shows that the move from S_1 and $(\sim S_1 \vee S_2)$ to S_2 is not the best possible formal inference. Of course, we have not shown that: S_1, $(\sim S_1 \vee S_2)$ and so S_2, is invalid in the standard sense of 'invalid.' We have only shown that $S_1 \wedge (\sim S_1 \vee S_2)$ does not structurally mean S_2. An invalid bit of reasoning associated with MD would be the following argument about messages. $S_1 \in H, \sim S_1 \in H$ or $S_2 \in H$, and so $S_2 \in H$. This argument about messages is at best an enthymeme with the false missing premiss that messages are consistent, viz., $\sim S \notin H$ or $S \notin H$.

The result that MD is not the best possible formal inference can actually be used as part of the empirical support for the theory of meaning developed here! People could be persuaded that S_1 and $(\sim S_1 \vee S_2)$ do not mean S_2; at least not in the way in which $S_1 \wedge S_2$ does. The task of persuasion is even easier if it is emphasized that there is no need to concede that MD is invalid. You may find it quite natural to accept the following. S_1 and $(\sim S_1 \vee S_2)$ do not explicitly tell us that S_2. If you have these two premisses, you have two cases: $S_1 \wedge \sim S_1$ and $S_1 \wedge S_2$. If you are consistent,you dismiss the first case of $S_1 \wedge \sim S_1$. If you are consistent, you have only the second case which explicitly means S_2. Nevertheless without the factual assumption that you are consistent, you cannot take your S_1 and $(\sim S_1 \vee S_2)$ as meaning S_2.

With the mention of empirical support, it is appropriate to make some more remarks about support of the theory of meaning. In this work there is no presentation of any carefully gathered empirical evidence. There is only the anecdotal evidence from the author's normative semantical intuitions and his speculations. No better empirical support will be provided despite the acceptance of the principle that empirical tests should provide the final evidence for or against the theory of meaning. What, then, justifies neglect of empirical evidence in this work? Empirical evidence plays a curious role in the support of a theory of meaning; the evidence has to be properly developed.

In the long run we cannot say that expression e means M unless a significant number of users of e accept that e means M. But in the short run we can certainly say that people are not really aware of the meaning of what they say. So, simply asking people whether or not e means M will not provide evidence for or against a theoretical claim that e means M. To get people to be able to answer thoughtfully whether or not expression e means M, it may be necessary to explain to them why it is plausible that e does mean M. For instance, if you ask a group of people, e.g., a beginning logic class, whether 'some' means 'at least one,' you may have to explain why it is at least plausible that 'some' means 'at least one.' Such explanations become, in effect, arguments for the theory. Hence, to get thoughtful responses about the predictions of a theory of meaning we have to tell the respondees the theory. This telling of the theory is a "corruption" of the respondees. So, the long run empirical test for a theory of meaning will be whether or not the people who understand it accept it. This acceptance need not be based simply on their linguistic intuitions. Indeed, the acceptance should not be based simply on their linguistic intuitions because these intuitions have been altered by the theory. Hence, the worth of the theory has to be considered; and this involves consideration of features such as simplicity which are generally considered in the acceptance of theories. Consequently, the way to get support for a theory of meaning is to develop it so that it becomes an acceptable theory of what we should take our utterances to mean once we are informed about the theory. Such a development has been the task of this section.

Let us see that the theory does have empirical predictions which, as we noted above, are also linguistic recommendations. It predicts that 'not either___or___' means 'neither__nor___.' If ultimately a significant number of people would not accept this as conforming to their intuitions or would not be reconciled to it because the theory is otherwise desirable, the theory would have very serious evidence against it. An exercise will bring out that $\sim(S_1 \vee S_2)$ and $(\sim S_1 \wedge \sim S_2)$ are such that the structures of the possible messages from them are identical. In Section V.8, we develop this theory a bit further by showing that it converts to a model structure semantics for the system of TE entailments. This conversion of the theory is good for the theory of meaning because it shows that it has a well-defined set of inferences which it predicts to be entailments

Of course, this conversion also helps to support the system of TE entailments if the theory is good.

A closing remark on the author's critique of the Routley's semantics is in order. In his [1974], the author's error was to regard their set-up rules, which are our structural meaning rules, as a device for showing that many classically valid arguments such as MD and DS are invalid. Hence, their set-up rules were regarded as bizarre truth condition rules instead of being regarded as rules for extracting structural meaning from a set of sentences. Hopefully, this section has shown that the rules are plausible as meaning rules and that the classically valid MD is not the best possible formal inference because the meaning of the conclusion is not contained in the meaning of the premisses.

Exercises III.5

1. Show: $\sim\sim S \in H$ iff. $S \in H$ and $\sim S \in H$ iff. $S \notin H^*$ yield $H^{**} = H$.
2. Show: $H^{**} = H$ and $\sim S \in H$ iff. $S \notin H^*$ yield $\sim\sim S \in H$ iff. $S \in H$.
3. Show: if S_1 and $\sim S_1$ both belong to H, neither belongs to H*.
4. Show: $S_1 \wedge (\sim S_1 \vee S_2)$ entails $(S_1 \vee \sim S_1) \supset S_2$.
5. Assume that $\sim(S_1 \vee S_2) \in H$ and break down the assumption as far as the rules take you. Then do the same for $(\sim S_1 \wedge \sim S_2)$ Note that you get identical structures as a result of the break-down.
6. Consider the argument that MD is not based on a meaning connection. To alleviate worries that more uses of the rules would introduce a contradiction for us, assume that S_1 and S_2 are the only simple sentences. We can make this assumption for the sake of getting a counterexample to MD. Specify that $\sim S_2 \in H$ which by Imperfect Consistency gives $S_2 \notin H^*$. So, we have done all that we can with the rules. Regard H as the w1 and H* as the w2 of the Smiley matrix $\mathcal{S}$m discussed in Example 5 of I.7 and in III.3. Regard us as having assigned S_1 +0 and S_2 -1 by the above breakdown. Now argue that this $\mathcal{S}$m valuation shows that we have no worry about saying that a sentence belongs and does not belong in one and the same message.

III.6 Explorations of first degree (fdf.) extensions of TEc, Systems TEc',TEf, and E_{fdf} , remarks on finite characteristic matrices, Dugundji-formulas,

The next section is devoted to settling worries about the intelligibility of the intended reading of the formulas which we have been introducing. In this section we continue our program of progressively enriching the language of the pure fde. system TE. The rationale behind the program is, of course, to monitor extensions of a system's language as well as extensions of its axioms and rules. In the next section we conclude that we can and should develop a full entailment system. Our first concern in this section is to consider some consequences of extending the language of TEc to a language sufficient for a full fdf. system which we label TEc'. Reflection on TEc' shows that we need to do more than enrich the language of TEc to get an adequate fdf. system. Secondly, we introduce a pure fdf. system TEf whose theorems we claim are extactly the zdf. and fdf. theorems of system E which we study and defend in Part IV. To support the claim about TEf we present Dunn's system E_{fdf} from Anderson's and Belnap's [1975]. We close by specifying conditions under which some systems lack a finite characteristic matrix and point out why it may be desirable to lack a finite characteristic matrix.

Let the language of TEc be enriched to include every fdf.. Thus formulas such as $\sim(A\longrightarrow B)$ and $(A\longrightarrow B) \vee \sim(A\longrightarrow B)$ are now wffs. and $A\longleftrightarrow B$ is now definable as $(A\longrightarrow B)\wedge(B\longrightarrow A)$. We call such a language a <u>pure fdf. language</u> although it has zdfs.. Keep the axiom schemas and rules of TEc as they were in Section III.4 except that now there are no restrictions on Adj.. Call the new system TEc'. TEc' is a genuinely different system from TEc because it has different theorems. For example, the conjunction $(A\longrightarrow A)\wedge(A\longrightarrow A)$ and the disjunction $(A\longrightarrow B) \vee \sim(A\longrightarrow B)$ are now theorems. Also, as we will show, TEc' does not have a finite characteristic matrix.

Let us see more precisely how the theorems of TEc' differ from those of TEc. In particular, we are interested in whether or not the material implication analogues of the rules of TEc' are theorems. The condition of rule normality, C11, requires that at least the material implication analogue of rules be theorems. We find that TEc' lacks such rule normality.

Some lemmas about the theorems of TEc' help us to a theorem about a failure of rule normality for TEc'.

Lemma 1 of III.6: If A is a theorem of TEc' and is a zdf. or an fde., then A is a theorem of TEc and is a classical tautology or a TE entailment.

We make the following remarks about a proof. Despite the inflation of the language, the axioms of TEc' are the same as those of TEc. So we can use Lemma 4 of III.4 to show that $\mathfrak{M}_o$ is suitable for TEc'. (Here we have to observe that uniform substitution of fdf. for variables does not destroy $\mathfrak{M}_o$-validity.) So Theorem IV of III.4 tells us that the fde. theorems of TEc' are those of TEc, viz., the TE entailments. Use the technique for proving Lemma 2 of III.4 to show that only classical tautologies are zdf. theorems of TEc'. The inclusion of TEc in TEc' gives us, of course, that all classical tautologies are zdf. theorems of TEc'.

We next give a definition and a second lemma whose proof we leave as an exercise.

A <u>first degree substitution instance of a zdf.</u>. for short: an <u>fd. instance of a zdf.</u>, is a wff. of a pure first degree language obtained by uniform variable substitution in a zdf. or by uniform variable substitution in a previously obtained fd. instance of a zdf..

Lemma 2 of III.6: All fdf. are fd. instances of zdfs..

Lemma 3 of III.6: If A is a TEc' theorem, then A is a theorem of TEc, an fd. instance of a classical tautology, or a conjunction of TEc theorems and fd. instances of classical tautologies.

We make the following remarks about a proof. By Lemma 1 the zdf. and fde. theorems are TEc theorems. The only new wffs. are, by Lemma 2, fd. instances of zdfs.. Divide these new wffs. into four groups. (i) Conjunctions of TEc theorems. (ii) fd. instances of classical tautolgies. (iii) Conjunctions formed from items of groups (i) and (ii). (iv) Wffs. in the language of TEc' but not of the language of TEc and which are not in groups (i),(ii), and (iii). Because we allow uniform substitution for variables, items of group (ii) are theorems. Because we have Adj. the items of groups (i) and (iii) are theorems. A survey of the rules of TEc' shows that none of them except Adj. can lead to an fdf. which is not also an fde.. (This is due to the limitations of the language of TEc'.) An induction on the length of proof will show that such uses of Adj. does not get us out of groups (i) and (iii).

Theorem I of III.6: If $A \supset B$ is the material implication analogue of one of the first six rules of TEc', then $A \supset B$ is not a theorem schema of TEc'.

We make the following remarks about a proof. Consider formulas such as $(\sim(p \rightarrow q) \vee \sim(q \rightarrow r)) \vee (p \rightarrow r)$ for R1 (Trans.) and $((\sim p \vee \sim(p \rightarrow q)) \vee q$ for R6. Use Lemma 3 to conclude that they are not TEc' theorems.

We give a corollary of Theorem I which is really a corollary of Lemma 3. Consider the following rule which is the Rule-TE of Dunn's system E_{fdf}.

Dunn's Rule-TE

If $F_1 \wedge, \ldots, \wedge F_n \rightarrow G$ is a substitution instance of a TE entailment, then $F_1, \ldots, F_n \vdash G$.

This rule is adapted from a formulation on p.207 of Anderson's and Belnap's [1975]. Note that in giving Rule-TE we use a schema which ranges over higher order formulas, viz., $F_1 \wedge, \ldots, \wedge F_n \rightarrow G$. So, although the system for which Rule-TE is a rule may have only zdfs. and fdfs., we refer to formulas with nested $\rightarrow$'s to give the system.

Corollary of Theorem I of III.6: Fdf. system TEc' does not have Rule-TE as a derived rule.

To prove this corollary consider the TE entailment $p \rightarrow . p \vee q$ and its substitution instance $(p \rightarrow . p \vee q) \rightarrow . (p \rightarrow . p \vee q) \vee q$. Lemma 3 tells us that this substitution instance is not a TEc' theorem.

We do not have a matrix to show that schemas such as $(A \rightarrow B) \wedge (B \rightarrow C) \supset . A \rightarrow C$ are not TEc' theorem schemas. So, Theorem I, which is based on Lemma 3, has to suffice as our reason for saying that TEc' is woefully inadequate as an fdf. system because its rules should at least be normal in the weak sense that we get $\vdash A \supset B$ from $A \vdash B$. One way to get an adequate fdf. system is to find an adequate full entailment system and then specify that its fdf. theorems constitute our fdf. system. This is the way which we follow for getting an fdf. system. We specify that the fdf. theorems of system E constitute the correct fdf. system. Nevertheless, we should, it seems, be able to get an adequate fdf. system without committing ourselves to the intelligibility of any higher order formulas than fdfs.. So, we present the following system which is labelled TEf for those who want a full fdf. system without any commitment to higher order formulas.

The language of TEf is the language of TEc'. As axiom schemas, TEf has the seven axiom schemas of TEc' plus the six below. Its rules of proof are only Adj. and MD (Rule-γ). We do not number these new axiom schemas for TEf as axiom schemas because, although they are theorem schemas for system E, they are not axiom schemas for system E. For those who want to stop with the first degree, the TEc axiom schemas may be re-labelled as the first seven TEf axiom schemas and the material implication analogues of the first six TEc' rules may be listed as the six new axiom schemas for TEf.

TEf 8: $(A \rightarrow B) \wedge (B \rightarrow C) \supset . A \rightarrow C$
TEf 9: $(A \rightarrow B) \wedge (A \rightarrow C) \supset . A \rightarrow . B \wedge C$
TEf 10: $(A \rightarrow C) \wedge (B \rightarrow C) \supset . A \vee B \rightarrow C$
TEf 11: $A \rightarrow B \supset . \sim B \rightarrow \sim A$

TEf 12: $A \rightarrow B \supset . \sim A \vee B$
TEf 13: $A \wedge (A \rightarrow B) \supset B$.

With MD (Rule-γ) the first six TEc rules are easily obtained as derived rules of TEf.

Matrix $\mathfrak{M}$o is helpful for proving the following theorem whose proof we leave as an exercise.

Theorem II of III.6: The zdf. theorems of TEf are exactly the classical tautologies and the fde. theorems are exactly the TE entailments.

We are not going to make a case for TEf as the correct set of fdf. theorems despite our claim below that TEf has exactly the fdf. theorems which we accept. We do not make a case for TEf because it gets its theorems in the wrong way. Because TEf has MD there is a derivation in TEf of q from $p \wedge \sim p$. Still, as use of $\mathfrak{M}$o shows, $p \wedge \sim p \rightarrow q$ is not a TEf theorem. So, TEf has relevance failures and non-normal rules. And, as we argued at length in the preceding section, MD is not an acceptable rule. So, we do not accept system TEf. (Here we can note that TEf is essentially Ackermann's system Π' of IV.2 restricted to a pure fdf. language.) We use MD so that we can get a Deduction Theorem for $\supset$ in an fdf. system. Such a Deduction Theorem helps in an argument that TEf is equivalent in theorems to the following fdf. system presented by J. Dunn in section 19.2 of Anderson's and Belnap's [1975]. This system is labelled E_{fdf} because, as can be obtained from sections 18 and 19, Dunn shows that the theorems of E_{fdf} are exactly the fdf. theorems of system E.

System E_{fdf}

Fde. axioms: Each axiom of TE of III.2 (E_{fde}) is an axiom of E_{fdf}

Truth-functional axioms: All wffs. of the form $F \vee \sim F$.

In the following rules F is an arbitrary formula of the fdf. language. Dunn admits that there is redundancy in the rules. We label them with Rd for rules of Dunn.

Rd. 1: $F \vee (A \rightarrow B) \wedge (B \rightarrow C) \vdash F \vee . A \rightarrow C$
Rd. 2: $F \vee (A \rightarrow B) \wedge (A \rightarrow C) \vdash F \vee . A \rightarrow . B \wedge C$
Rd. 3: $F \vee (A \rightarrow C) \wedge (B \rightarrow C) \vdash F \vee . A \vee B \rightarrow C$
Rd. 4: $F \vee (A \rightarrow B) \vdash F \vee (\sim B \rightarrow \sim A)$
Rd. 5: $F \vee \sim (A \rightarrow B) \wedge (C \rightarrow B) \vdash F \vee \sim (A \rightarrow C)$
Rd. 6: $F \vee \sim (A \rightarrow B) \wedge (A \rightarrow C) \vdash F \vee \sim (C \rightarrow B)$
Rd. 7: $F \vee \sim (A \rightarrow . B \wedge C) \vdash F \vee \sim (A \rightarrow B) \vee \sim (A \rightarrow C)$
Rd. 8: $F \vee \sim (A \vee B \rightarrow C) \vdash F \vee \sim (A \rightarrow C) \vee \sim (B \rightarrow C)$
Rd. 9: $F \vee \sim (A \rightarrow B) \vdash F \vee \sim (\sim B \rightarrow \sim A)$
Rd.10: $F \vee (A \wedge (A \rightarrow B)) \vdash F \vee B$
Rd.11: $F \vee (A \wedge \sim B) \vdash F \vee \sim (A \rightarrow B)$

System E_{fdf} also has Rule-TE cited on the previous page.

We leave as a lengthy exercise development of support for the following claim.

Claim: The theorems of TEf are exactly the theorems of E_{fdf}; and hence the theorems of TEf are exactly the fdf. theorems of system E.

We do not get involved in the argument for this claim for at least two reasons. The first is that we are not too interested in fdf. systems by themselves. In the next section we will argue that we can and should use a full entailment language. Thus we can easily get a correct fdf. system by simply specifying that it is the fdf. fragment of the correct full entailment system. Secondly, we are not too happy with either TEf or E_{fdf}. We do not like TEf because it has MD. We do not like E_{fdf} because it has rule-TE. As we remarked when we introduced rule-TE, it does commit us to higher order formulas because we have to look at instances of $F_1 \wedge, \ldots, \wedge F_n \longrightarrow G$ which may be higher order formulas. We leave as an open problem the project of axiomatizing the fdf. fragment of system E without using rules which commit us to higher order formulas and which has only derived rules of E.

Following Theorem III of III.4 we remarked that $\mathfrak{M}_o$ was a finite characteristic matrix for TEc because TEc did not have any fdfs. in its language. We now support this observation by showing that TEc' has no finite characteristic matrix. We then go on to show how this proof can be applied to certain extensions of TEc. This discussion of fdf. systems lacking finite characteristic matrices is appropriate in this section in which we are noting the consequences of enriching a language. It seems a bit remarkable that the mere extension of the language of TEc leads to a system without a finite characteristic matrix.

As a preliminary for the "Dugundji proof," we introduce the notation for special disjunctions which we call Dugundji formulas. We use: $\bigvee_{i=1}^{n-1} (\bigvee_{j=i+1}^{n} p_i \longleftrightarrow p_j)$ to denote a disjunction of the $(n^2-n)/2$ disjuncts of the form $p_i \longleftrightarrow p_j$, where $i \leq 1 \leq n-1$, $2 \leq j \leq n$, and $i < j$ in any $p_i \longleftrightarrow p_j$. Thus if n=4 we have:

$$p_1 \longleftrightarrow p_2 \vee p_1 \longleftrightarrow p_3 \vee p_1 \longleftrightarrow p_4 \vee p_2 \longleftrightarrow p_3 \vee p_2 \longleftrightarrow p_4 \vee p_3 \longleftrightarrow p_4 .$$

The first lemma on this topic makes a rather weak claim.

Lemma 4 of III.6: If a system S has $A \longleftrightarrow A$ as a theorem, then if matrix $\mathfrak{M}$ is suitable for S, v(A) = v(B) is sufficient for $v(A \longrightarrow B) \in D$, where D is the set of designated elements of $\mathfrak{M}$.

We leave the reflections for establishing Lemma 4 as an exercise. We get a proof of the next lemma by realizing that if there are at most n-1 elements in a matrix $\mathfrak{M}$ then at least one disjunct in the Dugundji formula for n-variables is going to have the left and right side assigned the same value on any v( ) on $\mathfrak{M}$.

Then with Lemma 4 we get Lemma 5.

Lemma 5 of III.6: If a system S has A$\leftrightarrow$A as a theorem and if $\mathfrak{M}$ is an m-element matrix with m$<$n which is suitable for S, then the Dugundji formulas for n-variables are valid on $\mathfrak{M}$.

For the next lemma, recall the notion of Sugihara matrix from II.21.

Lemma 6 of III.6: No Dugundji formula with n-variables is valid on a Sugihara matrix with more than n-elements.

To establish Lemma 6 show that for some v() on any such Sugihara matrix every variable in a Dugundji formula with n-variables gets a different value and thus all $p_i \leftrightarrow p_j$ get a non-designated value.

Lemma 7 of III.6: Every consistent Sugihara matrix is suitable for TEc'.

By way of proof we show that MD preserves Sugihara designation and refer to Theorem IV of II.21 because all axioms of TEc' are theorems of RM and Adj. is a rule of RM. Assume v(A)$\in$ D, v($\sim$A v B)$\in$ D, but V(B) $\notin$ D for D on a consistent Sugihara matrix. Since the D of a Sugihara matrix is a prime filter, as Lemma 7 of II.21 tells us, v($\sim$A v B)$\in$ D tells us that v($\sim$A)$\in$ D or v(B)$\in$ D. We cannot have v(B)$\in$ D because we have already assumed the opposite. We cannot have v($\sim$A)$\in$ D because of the assumptions that v(A)$\in$ D and that we have a consistent Sugihara matrix. So, on consistent Sugihara matrices MD preserves validity.

Lemmas 6 and 7 yield an eighth.

Lemma 8 of III.6: No Dugundji formula is a TEc' theorem.

Theorem III of III.6: TEc' has no finite characteristic matrix.

We observe that since A$\leftrightarrow$A is a theorem of TEc', any finite matrix suitable for TEc' will, by Lemma 5, validate a Dugundji formula which, by Lemma 8, is a non-theorem.

Fortunately, our argument for Theorem III entitles us to state a more general result which tells us that the systems seriously considered in Part IV lack finite characteristic matrices.

Theorem IV of III.6: If a system S has A$\leftrightarrow$A as a theorem. the Dugundji formulas are wffs. of its language, and Sugihara matrices are suitable for it, then S has no finite characteristic matrix.

(See Dungundji [1940] for an original result of this kind.)

Should we lament the fact that the systems which we will consider most seriously lack finite characteristic matrices and hence lack one kind of decision procedure? In their [1976] "Two Criteria for Entailment Logics," R. Meyer and R.G. Wolf make a case for the following adequacy condition.

No propositional logic which is a satisfactory formalization of entailment should have a finite characteristic matrix.

The gist of their case is that if a system S has a finite characteristic matrix with n-elements then on any interpretation and valuation of S on this matrix $\mathfrak{M}$, there can be at most n distinct propositions. If two formulas are assigned the same value on $\mathfrak{M}$ we can say that they are interpreted as the same proposition. So, if S has a finite characteristic matrix, it seems that we can interpret it so that itcan say "at most n-things."

The preceding argument is admittedly sketchy; but it at least brings out that it is far from a clear merit for a system to have a finite characteristic matrix.

Exercises III.6

1. How do you prove $(A \rightarrow A) \vee \sim(A \rightarrow A)$ in TEc'?
2. Show that TEf has a Deduction Theorem for $\supset$.
3. Show that the axioms and rules of E_{fdf} are derivable in TEf.
4. Prove Theorem II.
5. Show that if a system has only MP and Adj. as rules we do not need the assumption that we have consistent Sugihara matrices in Lemma 7.
6. Show that the Lewis modal systems of II.3 can be regarded as meeting the conditions of Theorem IV by taking $\prec$ as $\rightarrow$.
7. As a problem rather than as a mere exercise, reconsider the notion of Lindenbaum Algebra from p. 64. Consider the equivalence classes, viz., the [A], as propositions. Give a sense to saying that a system recognizes only finitely many distinct [A]. Then try to show that if a system with a full entailment language has a finite characteristic matrix, it recognizes only finitely many distinct propositions. Perhaps it would be a good idea to start by considering the case of classical sentential logic.

III.7 We can and should use formulas with nested $\longrightarrow$'s.

We have to discuss whether we should restrict our formal language to fdes., fdes. and zdfs., fdfs, or move to a full entailment language. Back in II.1 we suggested problems which arose when we enriched a language beyond fdes.. In this section we want to dismiss such problems. Here it may be well to review II.1; especially the definitions of the types of logical signs or functors. In this section, sources of the arguments for and against the use of nested $\longrightarrow$ will not be cited. The negative arguments have been suggested by the writings of W.V. Quine in works such as his [1953] and Chapter 4 of his [1960]. To some extent, Goddard's and R. Routley's [1966] influenced the arguments in favor of using nested $\longrightarrow$'s. There is no claim of originality for the arguments presented below unless they are exceptionally bad arguments. The general outline of this section is as follows. We first give reasons why every $\longrightarrow$ in a formula should be read in the same way; this is the <u>homogeneity requirement</u>.

The most obvious reason for the homogeneity requirement is that if different occurrences of a sign have to be read differently, then different signs should have been used. Secondly, use of inference rules may be restricted and require one and the same sign to be given two different readings in the course of a derivation. If we allow nested $\longrightarrow$'s we most likley would have a system with both $A\longrightarrow A$ and $A\longrightarrow A\longrightarrow.A\longrightarrow A$ as theorems. Before we allow use of MP from $A\longrightarrow A\longrightarrow.A\longrightarrow A$ and $A\longrightarrow A$ to $A\longrightarrow A$ we should have some guarantee that the $\longrightarrow$ in the antecedent of $A\longrightarrow A\longrightarrow.A\longrightarrow A$ is the same $\longrightarrow$, i.e., has the same reading as, as the $\longrightarrow$ in plain $A\longrightarrow A$ by itself. But if we had developed rules for reading different occurrences of $\longrightarrow$ different, it is likely that that $\longrightarrow$'s in the antecedent and consequent of $A\longrightarrow A\longrightarrow.A\longrightarrow A$ would be read differently than the main $\longrightarrow$ of the formula. Hence, MP should be restricted because the $\longrightarrow$ of $A\longrightarrow A$ by itself is not the $\longrightarrow$ of $A\longrightarrow A$ when $A\longrightarrow A$ is the antecedent of $A\longrightarrow A\longrightarrow.A\longrightarrow A$. If we didn't restrict MP, we may have to change the reading of a $\longrightarrow$ in the consequent of $A\longrightarrow A\longrightarrow.A\longrightarrow A$ after it is detached by MP. Actually, these considerations make the homogeneity requirement so plausible that it hardly needs further comment. Still, for those who want to use nested $\longrightarrow$'s, there are frequent temptations to violate the homogeneity requirement.

To get a homogenous reading for $\longrightarrow$ we do not read $\longrightarrow$ as a connective because we cannot read the $\longrightarrow$ in fdes. as a connective. If __$\longrightarrow$__ were to be read homogenously as a connective the blanks would always have to be filled by sentences. But in fdes. in a formal language the blanks are filled by terms; not sentences. Hence, we do not read $A\longrightarrow B$ as some modified 'if__ then__' connective such as 'If A then,in accordance with the best logical principles, B.' Nor will we read __$\longrightarrow$__ as some connective such as suggested on p. 481 of Anderson's and Belnap's [1975]: That__entails that__, or '__'entails '__.' To the author these two suggested connectives seem to be very artificial connectives with the result that we do not really read them as connectives. They are connectives made by the device of fusing subnectors or operators to a predicate. When we display the form: That__entails that___, we can say that we have a single form which is a connective. But actually we have the subnector 'that__' joined with the predicate __entails__. And we see that there has been only a fusing of a subnector with a predicate when we read a substitution instance. Put the sentence $p \rightarrow p$ into the blanks to get: That $p \rightarrow p$ entails that $p \rightarrow p$. When we read 'That $p \rightarrow p$ entails that $p \rightarrow p$,' we do break it up into 'That $p \rightarrow p$,' 'entails,' and 'that $p \rightarrow p$.' To understand 'That $p \rightarrow p$ entails that $p \rightarrow p$' we do regard ourselves as predicating entailment of 'That $p \rightarrow p$' and 'that $p \rightarrow p$.' There is a similar charge that instances of the alleged unit: '__' entails '__' would actually be understood as the relational predicate __entails___ applied to terms formed by the quote subnectors. To see whether '$p \rightarrow p$' entails '$p \rightarrow p$' is true we look to see whether the entailment relation is reflexive when we refer to $p \rightarrow p$.

We consider only the alternatives of treating the $\rightarrow$ functor as a connective or as a predicate because only on these treatments do $(A \rightarrow B)$'s become sentences. So, since we will not read $\rightarrow$ as a connective, we consider the alternative of reading $\rightarrow$ as a verb such as 'implies,' 'logically implies,' 'yields,' and, of course, 'entails.' When $\rightarrow$ is read as a verb, the contexts such as ___entails___ become predicates.

Are there problems involved with reading $\rightarrow$ homogenously as a verb? There isn't any problem with the English. You may check that in formulas with nested $\rightarrow$'s the $\rightarrow$'s may be read homogenously as a verb such as 'implies,' or 'entails.' So, the arguments against the verb reading do not charge that a verb reading sounds unintelligible. The charge is that there is an equivocation regardless of how natural the verb reading of $\rightarrow$ may sound when nested $\rightarrow$'s are used. Because the arguments against the verb reading, which we respond to, are the same regradless of which verb is used we restrict our attention to 'entails.' So our defense of a verb reading of $\rightarrow$ can also be used to defend a verb reading of a strict implication sign.

When $\rightarrow$ is read as a verb, the __$\rightarrow$__ context can be regarded as a predicate which yields a sentence upon filling the blanks with terms denoting natural language sentences, propositions, statements, or formulas of a formal language. In our discussion we restrict our attention to terms denoting natural language sentences and terms denoting formulas.

Before going on to present and rebut arguments against the verb reading let us remark on why we only consider terms for natural language sentences and formulas. We use terms referring to English sentences and terms referring to formulas because we want to talk of both natural language sentences and formulas as formally entailing and as being formally entailed. So, we want to defend nested 'entails' in natural language as well as in formal languages. In this work we want to avoid considering whether logicians talk of objects such as propositions, assertions, and statements as terms of an entailment or implication relation. We write as if logicians talked of only linguistic items such as sentences and formulas. Possibly what is said about sentences will suggest that sentences are as unusual as what have commonly been called propositions. So our restriction to talk of sentences and formulas cannot be taken as a guarantee that the terms of the entailment relation are some very common-place observable objects. This restriction to sentences and formulas reveals a preference, or wish, that, in the last analysis, the terms of the entailment relation will be shown to be very ordinary objects. However, no theory of the nature of the relata of the entailment relation is developed in this logical investigation. After a logician presents the theses and metatheorems of an allegedly correct system of entailment, it is the job of the metaphysician to develop a theory of what kinds of things stand in the entailment relation presented by the system. Because ultimately metaphysics legislates over logic, a logician may have to alter the system presented if there can be no satisfactory metaphysical account of the terms of the entailment relation of the system. But here we do not worry about the metaphysical presuppositions of the system of entailment being presented in this book; that crucial work is a task for another volume.

We now turn to weighing arguments. The basis of the arguments against the verb reading are that if a $\rightarrow$ occurs in one of the terms that fill the blanks in __$\rightarrow$___ it has a different meaning, because it is mentioned (talked about), than the $\rightarrow$ in the main __$\rightarrow$__ which is used as opposed to mentioned. Hence, the mentioned $\rightarrow$'s should not be given the same reading as the used $\rightarrow$ because that is equivocation.

The first argument against nested $\rightarrow$'s,
The Pedant's Argument,

The Pedant's Argument charges that formulas such as: $p \rightarrow p \rightarrow .p \rightarrow p$ are notationally defective because there is no explicit distinction between used and mentioned parts. In this formula the antecedent and the consequent are mentioned because $p \rightarrow p$ is being used as a name of itself. The pedant type suggests that there should be some device, such as use of single quotation marks, to show that a subnector has been applied to $p \rightarrow p$ to make it into a term standing for $p \rightarrow p$. Thus we should have '$p \rightarrow p$' $\rightarrow$ '$p \rightarrow p$' instead of plain $p \rightarrow p \rightarrow .p \rightarrow p$. More generally: if we are to have a notation adequate to reveal what is being done with nested $\rightarrow$'s we need to supplement our notation with a device such as the quoting device.

We reject the suggestion of the Pendant's Argument. The suggested supplement would not be an insignificant additon which' merely makes formulas more perspicuous; it would require restatement of MP and possibly its restrict, as we noted at the beginning of this section. Of course, we need to explain how we can reject the suggestion of the Pedant's Argument.

We grant that the antecedent and consequent of the main $\rightarrow$ in $p \rightarrow p \rightarrow . p \rightarrow p$ are mentioned on our choice of a verb reading for 'entails.' Interpreting the two $p \rightarrow p$ components of $p \rightarrow p \rightarrow . p \rightarrow p$ as mentioned seems to be the explanation of how the two $p \rightarrow p$ sentences get converted into terms to make a single sentence with the middle $\rightarrow$ in $p \rightarrow p \rightarrow . p \rightarrow p$. We grant that in a natural language we may sometimes need a device,such as the use of single quotation marks, to show that we are talking about a word, or words, rather than using them. For example, if we want to say that the word 'four' is bigger than the word 'six,' we cannot simply say that four is bigger than six. We need not grant, though, that we have to introduce single quotes, or some such device, into a formal language to avoid confusing use with mention. The placement of an $A \rightarrow B$ in a wff. shows whether it is used or mentioned. If you wanted to put in single quotes to indicate that an $A \rightarrow B$ is mentioned you could do the following. When an $A \rightarrow B$ occurs on the immediate right or left of the $\rightarrow$ in a subformula whose main sign is $\rightarrow$ and which is not in the scope of any other $\rightarrow$, place ' ' around $A \rightarrow B$. For instance, you could put quotes in $p \rightarrow q \rightarrow . p \rightarrow p \rightarrow . p \rightarrow . q \vee p$ as follows: $'p \rightarrow q' \rightarrow '. p \rightarrow p \rightarrow . p \rightarrow . q \vee p'$. There would not be quotes around $p \rightarrow p$ and $p \rightarrow . q \vee p$ in the consequent because the $\rightarrow$ connecting them is in the scope of another $\rightarrow$. But if $p \rightarrow p \rightarrow . p \rightarrow . q \vee p$ is detached quotes would be put in to get; $'p \rightarrow p' \rightarrow 'p \rightarrow . q \vee p'$. So, if the Pedant's Argument only says that we need quotes to avoid confusion of use with mention, we can dismiss the Pendant's Argument. Nevertheless, a more serious issue is raised.

The serious issue arises from the fact that when an $A \rightarrow B$ is mentioned it is a term, i.e., namelike; when an $A \rightarrow B$ is used it is a sentence. How can a name and a sentence be two occurrences of the same linguistic unit without equivocation? So let us turn to rebutting the serious charges that we are using linguistic units equivocally, regardless of whether we need quotes to tell when we employ the same sign in different ways.

The second argument which we try to rebut charges that mentioning an $A \rightarrow B$ is really employment of a different symbol or expression than using this $A \rightarrow B$ even if they look identical. We call this "the two languages argument" because it is based on the assumption that a used and mentioned sign are not in the same language.

The Two Languages Argument,

1. When we mention a symbol, eg., a formula, we speak in a metalanguage ML about an object language L and the mention of a symbol is the employment of a term of ML to talk of a symbol of L.

2. No term of ML is a symbol of L because ML and L are two different languages.

   Indeed, even if an expression e is employed to name itself, i.e., employed as autonomous name, expression e as an autonomous name is a different symbol from e used for whatever else e is used for.

So,3: When an A⟶B is employed to mention A⟶B it is a metalinguistic term which is not any symbol of the object language.

Prima facie the second premiss is false. Certainly, it seems that different languages can share symbols. Nevertheless, we focus attention on premiss (1) because it leads to discussion of interesting issues. In a natural language it is clear that occasionally we employ some of it to talk of parts of it. For example we say: 'Four' has four letters. But it is far from clear that our natural languages are split into two languages: an object language and a metalanguage. Indeed it seems obviously false. " 'Four' has four letters" is as much an English sentence as " Four has three factors." Furthermore, a single sentence may be about language and non-linguistic subjects. Consider: 'Forty' is an easy word to spell but forty is a turning point in a man's life. So, we can dismiss reasoning from generalities about two languages. The real issue is: Can an occurrence of a symbol employed to name a symbol, and especially to name itself, be regarded as an occurrence of the same symbol as one not employed to name a symbol or some kind of linguistic unit?

To simplify discussion of the issue just raised at the end of the preceding paragraph we, despite our view that quotes are not needed to distinguis use from mention, talk of quoted expressions and symbols instead of: occurrences of symbols employed to name symbols. By a quoted expression we mean the expression within the quotes; not the expression and the quotes. For instance in 'dog' the word dog is the quoted expression. The third argument against nested ⟶'s which we try to rebut gets to the real issue.

The One Word Argument,

1. A quoted expression is part of a new linguistic unit which is a new word in the language; it becomes a kind of letter.

   Thus just as 'dog' does not occur as a word in the word 'doggerel,' the word 'dog' does not occur as a word in the new word 'The dog bit me.' The occurrence of 'dog' in 'The dog bit me' is to be considered as if it were a new letter for the spelling of a new word.

2. Sentences have a multiplicity of words.

So,3: A quoted sentence cannot be an employment of the same symbol or expression as an occurrence of the sentence itself because the sentence itself has a multiplicity lacking in the quoted sentence.

Thus a mentioned or quoted 'p entails q' does not have any words or terms in it while a used 'p entails q' has the word 'entails' in it. Also, according to this view, $p \longrightarrow p$ in the antecedent of $p \longrightarrow p \longrightarrow . p \longrightarrow p$ is only a letter in a term while $p \longrightarrow p$ by itself is a sentence. So, the two occurrences of $p \longrightarrow p$ are not at all the same and, consequently, use of MP seems of doubtful legitimacy.

Let us not quarrel with the second premiss of the One Word Argument. The attack on the first premiss has been influenced by Goddard and R. Routley; but they should not be blammed for any of the weaknesses in the following attack. Goddard and Routley remind us that there is what can be called semantic quoting or, if you prefer, semantic mentioning. In semantic quoting we mention a sentence to cite a bit of language in whose meaning we are interested. For instance, a man may ask: Which will impress my wife more 'I have been given a raise' or 'I have been promoted'? Another example is: The gist of what he said was 'I do not understand quantum mechanics.' In these quoted sentences, the occurrence of words such as 'raise,' 'promoted,' and 'quantum mechanics' are crucial for understanding what was said. The quoted sentences cannot be regarded as one big word whose component words have been transformed into a kind of letter by virtue of being in a mentioned sentence. Even in cases where we quote a sentence or sentence-like string of words to refer to a sentence or such a string of words, we are interested in the internal structure of what is mentioned. Thus in " 'The dog bit me' were the exact words he uttered" we are interested in the occurrence of the word 'dog' just as we are interested in the occurrence of the non-word 'og' in " 'Th og bit me' were the sounds that he uttered." So, even when we quote for syntactical observations we are interested in the words within quoted sentences as words. Mention of an entailment formula by employment of the The formula____ device is very much like quoting to cite someone's exact words because for formal entailment an exact presentation of the formulas is crucial for determining the truth or falsity of entailment claims. But, as we just contended, mentioning to cite exact words does not obliterate the word mulitplicity of the quoted sentence. Hence, we dismiss the One Word Argument.

We next present and dismiss summarily two more arguments that a quoted and a used sentence cannot be employment of the same sentence. Perhaps these arguments will have to be examined more carefully on another occasion. We call them The Can't Quantify in Argument and The Can't Substitute for Identicals Argument.

The Can't Quantify-in Argument,

The gist of this argument is as follows. If a used sentence and a quoted sentence were employment of the same sentence then if a term has reference in one of the occurrences that term has the same reference in the other occurrence. If a term has the same reference in a used and mentioned employment of a sentence and the used and mention occurrences are in the same sentence, then we should be able to existentially quantify over both occurrences of the term where the quantifier has a referential interpretation. (See Belnap and Dunn [1968a] for a preliminary discussion of referential vs. substitutional quantification.) But such quantification cannot be performed without going from a true sentence to a false one. Consider: John is out and John's secretary said 'John is out.' This sentence could well be true. But $(\exists x)$(x is out and x's secretary said 'x is out) could under the same conditions be false. No secretary may ever have said 'x is out.'

The Can't Substitute for Identicals Argument,

This argument has the same first premiss as the preceding argument. It then adds that if term $t_1$is coreferential with term t_2,viz., $t_1 = t_2$, and t_1 occurs in both the used and mentioned sentence, then t_2 should be able to be substituted for t_1 in both without changing truth-value. But consider: Cicero was a Roman orator and Mark said 'Cicero was a Roman orator,' and grant that Cicero = Tully. We may well change truth-value if we move to: Tully was a Roman orator and Mark said 'Tully was a Roman orator.

One reason for not taking these two arguments seriously is that we do not have to consider quantification and substitution for coreferential terms when we restrict our attention to formal sentential entailment. Even if we consider natural language instances of the variables we pay attention only to syntactic relations between sentences. So, reference does not interest us when discussing formal entailment. Perhaps this first reason is not too strong. The second reason for dismissing these two arguments is that their first premiss is not compelling. An indiscernibility of identicals principle does not require us to accept: If $e_1 = e_2$, then everything which is true of e_1 when employed for purpose P_1 is true of e_2 when e_2 is employed for purpose P_2. In particular, an indiscernibility of identicals principle does not require us to say that if a sentence is employed to assert a fact and employed to refer to a bit of language then everything which is true of it when employed to assert is true of it when employed to name. So, at least for the rest of this study we reject the first premiss of these two arguments. A major assumption of the remainder of this investigation is that one and the same expression may be used as a sentence and mentioned to make a term without any equivocation on the whole expression or any part of it.

With this major assumption we may use nested $\rightarrow$'s. The question now is: Should we use them? Of course we should! Entailments can be entailed. The best possible formal reasoning can, for instance, take us from $p \wedge q \rightarrow q$ and $q \rightarrow . q \vee r$ to $p \wedge q \rightarrow . q \vee r$. We should be able to assert that there is such a formally correct inference by asserting as a thesis: $(p \wedge q \rightarrow q) \wedge (q \rightarrow . q \vee r) \rightarrow . p \wedge q \rightarrow . q \vee r$. Even if someone would reject the preceding as a thesis we have to have it as a formula to discuss whether or not it should be a thesis. Also note that a mere fdf. language may not be adequate to mark crucial distinctions between theses. For instance, an adequate fdf. system would have both $(p \rightarrow q) \wedge \sim(p \rightarrow q) \supset . q \rightarrow r$ and $(p \rightarrow q) \wedge (q \rightarrow r) \supset . p \rightarrow r$ as theses. But a distinction should be marked between these two because the thesishood of the first depends upon being an instance of $p \wedge \sim p \supset r$ while the thesishood of the second depends upon the transitivity of $\rightarrow$. In an fdf. system both thesis are mere material implications. In a full entailment language we could mark the distinction by having $(p \rightarrow q) \wedge (q \rightarrow r) \rightarrow . p \rightarrow r$ as a thesis, $(p \rightarrow q) \wedge \sim(p \rightarrow q) \supset . q \rightarrow r$ as a thesis, but not having $(p \rightarrow q) \wedge \sim(p \rightarrow q) \rightarrow . q \rightarrow r$ as a thesis.

Hopefully, a case has been made that we can and should use a full entailment language as we do in the next part of this study. As a final argument for this case, let the author close with a phenomenological report. When I try to establish a thesis with nested $\rightarrow$'s I pay attention to the same kind of thing as when I try to establish a plain fde.. I simply pay attention to the subject matter of formal logic whatever that may be.

PART IV

IV.1 Introduction to Part IV, Syntactic development of system E, discussion of Assertion, Permutation, and Exportation.

In this section we present and begin to develop an axiom system for the entailment theses which we are recommending as the correct sentential logic. The system is Anderson's and Belnap's system E of entailment. In subsequent sections of this Part we develop, to compare them with system E, other full entailment systems. The main systems will be the Π systems of Ackermann, R,RM, NR or $R^{\Box}$, and system I. We briefly take note of an early entailment system of E. J. Nelson. We also touch upon the issue of defining modalities and consider how additional axioms collapse systems into mere modal logic or classical logic. The most difficult work in this Part is proving deduction theorems. This Part is syntactic. In Part V, we present model structure semantics for E and some of its extensions.

The following axiomatization of E was suggested in Anderson's and Belnap's abstract [1958]. This version of E is also the one presented by Belnap on pp. 82-83 of his monograph [1960a]. System E is a modification of Ackermann's Π' from his [1956]. Ackermann's first axiom schema $A \rightarrow A$ is replaced with E8 below and Ackermann's rules γ and δ are deleted. (There is discussion these two rules in this section and in the next.) There are several axiomatizations of system E. Another axiom set for E is readily available on pp. 231-232 of Anderson's and Belnap's [1975]. In the version below the axiom schemas are numbered so that E may be regarded as an extension of the fde. system TE. So, here, in one place, is a full axiom set for system E.

E1. $A \wedge B \rightarrow A$
E2. $A \wedge B \rightarrow B$
E3. $A \rightarrow . A \vee B$
E4. $B \rightarrow . A \vee B$
E5. $A \wedge (B \vee C) \rightarrow . B \vee (A \wedge C)$
E6. $A \rightarrow \sim\sim A$
E7. $\sim\sim A \rightarrow A$
E8. $((A \rightarrow A) \wedge (B \rightarrow B) \rightarrow C) \rightarrow C$
E9. $A \rightarrow B \rightarrow . B \rightarrow C \rightarrow . A \rightarrow C$
E10. $A \rightarrow B \rightarrow . C \rightarrow A \rightarrow . C \rightarrow B$
E11. $(A \rightarrow . A \rightarrow B) \rightarrow . A \rightarrow B$ Contraction
E12. $(A \rightarrow B) \wedge (A \rightarrow C) \rightarrow . A \rightarrow . B \wedge C$
E13. $(A \rightarrow C) \wedge (B \rightarrow C) \rightarrow . A \vee B \rightarrow C$
E14. $A \rightarrow B \rightarrow . \sim B \rightarrow \sim A$
E15. $A \wedge \sim B \rightarrow . \sim (A \rightarrow B)$

The rules of proof are MP, called α by Ackermann, and Adj. called β by Ackermann.

Most of the axioms have already been defended in I.6. While developing E we will try to motivate acceptance of E8 and E11. An exercise brings out that E10, Prefixing, is provable from E9, Suffixing, E11, T33, and rule α. Our first step in the development of E is to observe that we have rules r1, r2 r3, and r4 of system TE as derived rules from E9 or E10, E12, E13, and E14 respectively. Also r5 of system TEc is easily obtained from E15. We continue to label these five derived rules with r1,r2, etc., and also with the names given them in III. 2. Other derived rules and theorems are numbered as coming after those of TE and TEc. We also follow a useful labelling practice from Belnap's monograph. When a theorem or axiom is an $A \rightarrow B$, there is a corresponding rule $A \vdash B$; we label the rule rT_ or rA- where the blank is filled with the number of the theorem or axiom schema. Furthermore, if a theorem has a name such as Permutation, we cite uses of that theorem and its corresponding rule by use of the name or an abbreviation of the name. In this section $\vdash$ is always $\vdash_E$ But of more importance than notational matters is the observation that TE and TEc are subsystems of system E. Hence, from Theorem IV of III.4 and Lemma 1 below, we get the first theorem of this section.

Lemma 1 of IV.1: Matrix $\mathfrak{M}_0$ is suitable for E.

We do not give any details of the proof of Lemma 1. On p.26 of his monograph, Belnap acknowledges a debt to John Wallace and David Levin for establishing the details.

Theorem I of IV.1: The fde. theses of E are exactly the TE entailments.

All tautologous zdfs. are theorems of E because TEc is a subsystem of E. We can use the procedure of treating E's entailment arrow, $\rightarrow$, as $\supset$ and using classical truth-tables as we did for a proof of Theorem I of III.4 to show that no non-tautologous zdf. is a theorem of E. So, we have a second theorem.

Theorem II of IV.1: The zdf. theses of E are exactly the classical tautologies.

Because use of schemas gives uniform substitution for variables as an admissible rule, we draw the following corollary.

Corollary of II of IV.1: If A is a substitution instance of a classical tautology, then $\vdash$ A.

When we use this corollary to justify a claim that such-and-such is a theorem or theorem schema, we cite 'classical logic' or CL. A by-product of the procedure used to prove Theorem II gives a consistency proof for system E.

Theorem III of IV.1: E is consistent in the senses that no formula and its negation are both theorems, no single variable is a theorem, and some formula is not a theorem.

The enrichment of TE's language to get E's language does not significantly alter the strategy of the proofs of Theorems II and III of III.2. So, again without proof we state a Theorem.

Theorem IV of IV.1: General Commutativity and Associativity for $\wedge$ and v hold in E.

Because fdf. system TEf. has MD or Ackermann's rule γ, we defer any discussion of its relation to E until we discuss Ackermann's systems in the next section. Here we are interested in establishing a Replacement Theorem for E. Two easily establised derived rules are used.

Dr.8 (rE9) $A \rightarrow B \vdash B \rightarrow C \rightarrow . A \rightarrow C$ Suf.
Dr.9 (rE10) $A \rightarrow B \vdash C \rightarrow A \rightarrow . C \rightarrow B$ Prefix.

Theorem V of IV.1: If $A \leftrightarrow B$, then $F(A) \leftrightarrow F(B/A)$.

Let the following remarks suffice for a proof. The proof is by induction on the length of F(A). Most of the labor has already been done in the proof of Theorem I of III.2. The basis case from Theorem I of III.2 can readily be adapted for this proof. For the cases in which F(A) is more complex than a single variable, the only really new case is the case where F(A) is of the form $G(A) \rightarrow H(A)$. We want to show that we can get $(G(A) \rightarrow H(A)) \leftrightarrow (G(B/A) \rightarrow H(B/A))$. Here let there be no requirements that both G(A) and H(A) have to contain A or that there has to be a replacement of A with B in both G(A) and H(A) to get $G(B/A) \rightarrow H(B/A)$. An induction assumption would give: $G(A) \rightarrow G(B/A)$, $G(B/A) \rightarrow G(A)$, $H(A) \rightarrow H(B/A)$, and $H(B/A) \rightarrow H(A)$. We obtain $G(A) \rightarrow H(A) \rightarrow . G(B/A) \rightarrow H(B/A)$ as follows.

1) $G(B/A) \rightarrow G(A)$ Induction assumption
2) $G(A) \rightarrow H(A) \rightarrow . G(B/A) \rightarrow H(A)$ Suf. on (1).
3) $H(A) \rightarrow H(B/A)$ Induction assumption
4) $G(B/A) \rightarrow H(A) \rightarrow . G(B/A) \rightarrow H(B/A)$ Prefix. on (3)
5) $G(A) \rightarrow H(A) \rightarrow . G(B/A) \rightarrow H(B/A)$ Trans. (2),(4).

A similar combination of Suffixing and Prefixing establishes $G(B/A) \rightarrow H(B/A) \rightarrow . G(A) \rightarrow H(A)$, and completes a proof for this Replacement Theorem.

Theorem V has the following useful corollary. We label uses of Theorem V or its corollary with Repl..

Corollary of V of IV.1: $A \leftrightarrow B$, $F(A) \vdash F(B/A)$.

A by-product of the proof remarks forTheorem V should be motivation for acceptance of the Transitivity of $\rightarrow$ in the strong forms given by Suffixing and Prefixing.

We now borrow extensively from Belnap's monograph to establish some theorems and rules of E which are interesting for their own sake and useful for proving deduction theorems for E.

T33. $((A \rightarrow A) \rightarrow B) \rightarrow B$

Proof

1) $(A \rightarrow A) \wedge (B \rightarrow B) \rightarrow . A \rightarrow A$ — E1
2) $(A \rightarrow A) \rightarrow B \rightarrow . (A \rightarrow A) \wedge (B \rightarrow B) \rightarrow B$ — Suf. on (1)
3) $((A \rightarrow A) \wedge (B \rightarrow B) \rightarrow B) \rightarrow B$ — E8 with B for C
4) $((A \rightarrow A) \rightarrow B) \rightarrow B$ — Trans. (2),(3).

A system consisting of T33, E9-E11 and rule or MP is called the pure implicational system I by Belnap on pp. 48-49 of his monograph. It is interesting to note with Belnap that T33 with MP yields or T1: $A \rightarrow A$. Simply use the following two instances of T33.

$(A \rightarrow A \rightarrow . A \rightarrow A) \rightarrow . A \rightarrow A$

$((A \rightarrow A \rightarrow . A \rightarrow A) \rightarrow . A \rightarrow A) \rightarrow . A \rightarrow A$

So, in E we can prove $A \rightarrow A$ with pure implicational formulas, i.e., formulas whose only logical sign is $\rightarrow$. We don't need negation axioms although we used them to get T1 when we had only TE. Indeed we need only pure implication formulas to get all of the pure implicational theorems of E. A 1971 result of Meyer's, which is given as Corollary 3 of Theorem 2 in Meyer's and Routley's [1974] is that E is a conservative extension of the pure implicational fragment of E. We can, for definiteness' sake, consider the pure implicational fragment of E to be the theorems of I_3 of Anderson's, Belnap's, and Wallace's [1960]. The three independent axiom schemas of I_3 are T33, E9, and E11. MP is the sole rule of I_3.

The fact that T33 with E9 and E11 gives the pure implicational theorems of E suggests that T33 should be an axiom schema for E. However, because we have E8 in order to get a satisfactory modal logic within E we can, as we just saw, get T33 as a theorem from E8. Because E8 with an occurrence of yields the pure implicational T33, the result that E is a conservative extension of its pure implicational fragment suggests that we need more than $\rightarrow$ to express modal theses, if we need E8 to express adequately modal theses. Its role in expressing modal theses help to motivate E8.

There is a schema called the Law of Assertion; it is: $A \rightarrow . A \rightarrow B \rightarrow B$. In the last section of this part it is shown that Assertion is not a thesis schema of E. Actually system R is system E plus Assertion. There are two interesting aspects to the Law of Assertion. First, Assertion allows a non-entailment to entail an entailment. In particular, it allows a zdf. to entail an entailment. For example, acceptance of the Law of Assertion commits us to accepting that plain p entails the entailment $p \to q \to q$. Recall our arguments against accepting a thesis such as $p \to . p \to q \to q$ when we spoke about modal fallacies back in I.6. Secondly, in the presence of T33, the Law of Assertion precludes use of a very natural definition of 'it is necessary that A.' If we specify that $\Box A =_{df} (A \to A) \to A$, we get $\Box A \leftrightarrow A$ if we have both the Law of Assertion and T33. A version of T33 is: $(A \to A \to A) \to A$ and a version of Assertion is $A \to . A \to A \to A$. So, we do not want the Law of Assertion because of this "demodalizing" effect. We do, of course, want entailment claims to be necessarily true, if they are true. Furthermore, if we can assert necessity we want to be able to assert that entailment claims are necessarily true. So, there is no objection to having as a thesis schema: $(A \to B) \leftrightarrow \Box(A \to B)$. To be sure, given such an equivalance, the assertion $\Box(A \to B)$ gives no new information which $(A \to B)$ fails to give. Nevertheless, $\Box(A \to B)$ enables us to call attention to the modal status of entailments, i.e., we can express their necessity rather than let their thesishood indicate their necessity. We have, then, no objection to a restricted Law of Assertion in which the antecedent is required to be an entailment. Indeed, we positively want T34 below or so-called Restricted Assertion. There will be other theorems of E which are also restrictions of theorems of system R obtained by requiring certain formulas to have the $A \to B$ form.

T34: $A \to B \to . A \to B \to C \to C$ Rest. Assert.

Proof

1) $A \to B \to . A \to A \to A \to B$ Prefix. E10
2) $(A \to A \to . A \to B) \to . A \to B \to C \to . A \to A \to C$ E11 Suf.
3) $A \to A \to C \to C$ T33
4) $((A \to A \to C) \to C) \to .$
$((A \to B \to C) \to (A \to A \to C)) \to . A \to B \to C \to C$

Line (4) is a version of E10 where $A \to B \to C$ is Prefixed to antecedent $A \to A \to C$ and then to consequent C of $A \to A \to C \to C$.

5) $(A \to B \to C) \to (A \to A \to C) \to . A \to B \to C \to C$ MP 3,4
6) $(A \to A \to . A \to B) \to . A \to B \to C \to C$ Trans. 2,5
7) $A \to B \to . A \to B \to C \to C$ Trans. 1,6.

In his system Π', Ackermann has the following rule of proof which he called rule δ.

Ackermann's rule δ,

From A and $B \to . A \to C$ infer $B \to C$ provided A is necessarily true, i.e., "eine logische Identitat."

Certainly we should not use rule δ with an A which we are not prepared to accept as necessarily true, if we regard A's being entailed by $A \rightarrow A$ as sufficient for A's necessity. Ackermann notes how we can derive $A \rightarrow A \rightarrow A$ from plain A by use of δ . Rule δ takes us directly from $A \rightarrow A \rightarrow . A \rightarrow A$ to $A \rightarrow A \rightarrow A$. And if the $\rightarrow$ is to be interpreted as entailment, the claim that A is entailed by the necessary truth $A \rightarrow A$ should be taken as sufficient for claiming that A is necessarily true. Fortunately, for Ackermann's policy of restricting uses of δ , the theorem R4 of system R, viz., $A \wedge (B \rightarrow . A \rightarrow C) \rightarrow . B \rightarrow C$, is not a theorem schema of Π'. Fortunately, also, for our hope to have $\Box A \leftrightarrow . A \rightarrow A \rightarrow A$ but not to have $\Box A \leftrightarrow A$, R4 is not a theorem schema of E either, as we will see in the last section of this part. However, if we are prepared to accept entailment claims as necessarily true, if true, we should have no hesitation about using a version of δ in which "the A" is required to be of the form $C \rightarrow D$. So, there should be no objection to E's next theorem.

T35: $A \rightarrow B \rightarrow . (C \rightarrow . A \rightarrow B \rightarrow D) \rightarrow . C \rightarrow D$

To prove T35, start with T34 : $A \rightarrow B \rightarrow . (A \rightarrow B \rightarrow D) \rightarrow D$. By Prefixing , the consequent of this version of T34 entails $(C \rightarrow . A \rightarrow B \rightarrow D) \rightarrow . C \rightarrow D$. Then Trans. gives the theorem.

An immediate consequence of T35 is a useful rule which we label rT35 or Rest. δ .

rT35: $A \rightarrow B, C \rightarrow . A \rightarrow B \rightarrow D \vdash C \rightarrow D$ Rest. δ

We use rT35 to prove T36 and T36 is used to get T37 and rT37 both of which are called Importation.

T36: $A \rightarrow B \rightarrow . A \wedge C \rightarrow B$ Premiss Addition

Proof

1) $A \rightarrow B \rightarrow . A \wedge C \rightarrow A \rightarrow . A \wedge C \rightarrow B$ E10
2) $A \wedge C \rightarrow A$ E1
3) $A \rightarrow B \rightarrow . A \wedge C \rightarrow B$ Rest. δ,1,2.

We already have rT36 as Dr.6; and both the rule and the theorem are called Premiss Addition.

T37: $(A \rightarrow . B \rightarrow C) \rightarrow . A \wedge C \rightarrow C$ Importation

Proof

1) $(A \rightarrow . B \rightarrow C) \rightarrow . A \wedge B \rightarrow . B \rightarrow C$ T36
2) $(A \wedge B \rightarrow . B \rightarrow C) \rightarrow . (B \rightarrow C \rightarrow . A \wedge B \rightarrow C) \rightarrow . A \wedge B \rightarrow . A \wedge B \rightarrow C$
Line 2 is a version of E9.
3) $B \rightarrow C \rightarrow . A \wedge B \rightarrow C$ T36
4) $(A \wedge B \rightarrow . B \rightarrow C) \rightarrow . A \wedge B \rightarrow . A \wedge B \rightarrow C$ Rest. δ 2,3
5) $(A \rightarrow . B \rightarrow C) \rightarrow . A \wedge B \rightarrow . A \wedge B \rightarrow C$ Trans. 1,4
6) $(A \wedge B \rightarrow . A \wedge B \rightarrow C) \rightarrow . A \wedge B \rightarrow C$ E11
7) $(A \rightarrow . B \rightarrow C) \rightarrow . A \wedge B \rightarrow C$ Trans. 5,6.

rT37: $A \rightarrow . B \rightarrow C \vdash A \wedge B \rightarrow C$ Importation

Apply Importation to E9,E10, and T35 to get three more theorems.

T38: $(A \rightarrow B) \wedge (B \rightarrow C) \rightarrow . A \rightarrow C$ Simple Trans.
T39: $(A \rightarrow B) \wedge (C \rightarrow A) \rightarrow . C \rightarrow B$ Simple Trans.
T40: $(A \rightarrow B) \wedge (C \rightarrow . A \rightarrow B \rightarrow C) \rightarrow . C \rightarrow D$

If we had the Law of Assertion, the next theorem could be obtained by Importation. Because we don't have such a law you need to work a bit more to get the next theorem.

T41: $A \wedge (A \rightarrow B) \rightarrow B$ Law of MP.

Let us digress a bit to reflect upon the disastrous consequences of having the reverse of Importation, viz. Exportation. No serious candidate for an entailment system or even a relevant implication system has Eportation. Exportation does not even hold for strict implication. Exportation, merely as a rule, destroys the whole program of having a system without $p \wedge \sim p \rightarrow q$ as a thesis, if the system has a fairly reasonable set of axioms and rules. With an axiom such as E2 we have $\sim q \wedge p \rightarrow p$ as a theorem which with Exportation would give the variable sharing relevance condition violating $\sim q \rightarrow . p \rightarrow p$ as a theorem. In an MA system an axiom such as E15 which gives a material implication from an entailment $\sim q \rightarrow . p \rightarrow p$ gives $p \wedge \sim p \rightarrow q$. Obviously, Exportation gives the paradoxical $A \rightarrow . B \rightarrow A$ from $A \wedge B \rightarrow A$. With Contraposition, Double Negation, and Trans., Exportation gives the paradoxical $\sim A — . A \rightarrow B$ from $\sim A \wedge \sim B \rightarrow \sim A$. If Exportation were added to system E, system E would collapse into classical sentential logic in the sense that $(A \supset B) \leftrightarrow . A \rightarrow B$ would be a theorem schema. E15 already gives $A \rightarrow B \rightarrow . A \supset B$. As noted above Exportation in E would give both A---.B---A and $\sim A \rightarrow . A \rightarrow B$. So, use of r3 of TE would yield $\sim A \vee B \rightarrow . A \rightarrow B$, i.e., $A \supset B \rightarrow . A \rightarrow B$. So, unrestricted Exportation is a disaster.

Exportation is undesirable even if we restrict it to entailment claims. For instance, Exportation takes us immediately from the highly plausible Simplification thesis $(A \rightarrow A) \wedge (B \rightarrow B) \rightarrow . B \rightarrow B$ to the relevance rupture between antecedent and consequent revealed in $A \rightarrow A \rightarrow . B \rightarrow B \rightarrow . B \rightarrow B$.

Furthermore, we have normative intuitions against Exportation which can be brought to the surface by consideration of our acceptance of $A \wedge B \rightarrow A$ and rejection of $A \rightarrow . B \rightarrow A$. Merely because we can get A from A B by the best possible formal reasoning we should not think that from A alone we can conclude that we can go from B to A by the best possible formal reasoning from B. Actually reflection on the fact that we got A from A B suggests that B is irrelevant to getting A or at least unnecessary for getting A.

Indeed intuitions against Exportation are so strong, a bit of defense must be offered for Suffixing and Prefixing which are "Exported" versions of Transitivity. On p. 496 of their [1932], Lewis and Langford objected to these "Exported" forms of Transitivity for strict implication. Nevertheless the situation is different with simple Transitivity, viz., $(A \to B) \wedge (B \to C) \to . A \to C$, than it is with $A \wedge B \to A$. We use both $A \to B$ and $B \to C$ in Transitivity to get $A \to C$. So, we can consider $A \to B$ and conclude that now $B \to C$ suffices to give $A \to C$ by the best formal reasoning. The good formal reasoning is to use $B \to C$ with $A \to B$ to get $A \to C$ by Transitivity. A similar line of thought justifies Prefixing by revealing that, given $A \to B$, $C \to A$ alone suffices to yield $C \to B$. In the cases of Suffixing and Prefixing, we use the formal context, viz., $A \to B$, to get a result from $B \to C$ or $C \to A$. (Recall our discussion of Prefixing from II.9.) But, in general, we cannot assume that because we got C from $A \wedge B$ we use A as part of the formal context to get C from B.

Let us note here that we will see in Section IV.4, where we present the Kron Deduction Theorem, that we have a type of Exportation for an $A \wedge B \to C$ if we use both A and B to get C.

When we develop system R in Section IV.7 we will see that R has a theorem of Permutation: $(A \to . B \to C) \to . B \to . A \to C$. Permutation may appear to be a result of Importation and then Exportation. But Permutation cannot be such a result because we will see that R does not have Exportation. If we had Permutation in system E we could prove $A \to . A \to A \to A$. We would start with the following version of Permutation: $(A \to A \to . A \to A) \to . A \to . A \to A \to A$ and then use the version of T1: $A \to A \to . A \to A$ to get by MP $A \to \Box A$. However, we do have in E a restricted form of Permutation, viz., the middle antecedent permuted to be the leftmost antecedent is required to be an entailment claim. A useful derived rule should be proved first by Prefixing on $C \to D$ to get $B \to C \to . B \to D$ by use of the hypotheses of Dr.10.

Dr.10: $A \to . B \to C,\ C \to D \vdash A \to . B \to C$

T42: $(C \to . A \to B \to D) \to . A \to B \to . C \to D$ Rest. Perm.

We sketch the following proof. Start with a version of E9.

1) $(C \to . A \to B \to D) \to . (A \to B \to D \to . C \to D) \to . C \to . C \to D$
   Use E11 in form: $(C \to . C \to D) \to . C \to D$, Dr.10 and (1) to get (2).
2) $(C \to . A \to B \to D) \to . (A \to B \to D \to . C \to D) \to . C \to D$
   Prefix C to antecedent and consequent of the consequent of (2); then use (2) and Trans. with the result of the Prefixing to get (3).
3) $(C \to . A \to B \to D) \to . C \to (A \to B \to D \to . C \to D) \to . C \to . C \to D$
   Use E11 and Dr.10, as we did for line (2) to get (4) form (3).
4) $(C \to . A \to B \to C) \to . C \to (A \to B \to D \to . C \to D) \to . C \to D$
   By Suffixing $C \to D$ on T35 we get (5), which [illegible] (4) gives T4[illegible]
5) $((C \to . A \to B \to D \to . C \to D) \to . C \to D) \to . A$ [illegible] $\to . C \to D$.

rT42: $C \to . A \to B \to D \vdash A \to B \to . C \to D$ Rest. Perm.

As last theorems for this section we state the theorem corresponding to Dr. 3 and the theorem for Modus Tollens for the entailment $\to$.

T43: $(A \to B) \wedge (C \to D) \to . A \wedge C \to . B \wedge D$

T44: $(A \to B) \wedge \sim B \to \sim A$ MT Modus Tollens

rT44: $(A \to B), \sim B \vdash \sim A$. MT Modus Tollens

In the next section we continue our development of E by studying the modal logic which can be developed in E. This involves comparison and contrast of E with Ackermann's systems.

Exercises IV.1

1. Prove theorems 41, 43, and 44.

2. Prove Theorem III.

The next three exercises brong out results of Anderson's, Belnap's, and Wallace's [1960]. A significant result of this paper is that the pure implication theory of entailment I which was discussed after T33 has E10 as a redundant axiom. The independent axioms are those of I_3: T33, E9, and E11. So, E10 is, of course, redundant in our axiomatization of E.

3. Show that Rest. δ , i.e., rT35, can be proved in I_3.

4. Show that T42 can be proved in I_3.

5. Show how E10 can be proved in I_3 if T42 and Rest. δ are available.

IV.2 Ackermann's systems Π' and Π'', modalities in E.

Ackermann's system Π' of his [1956] can be obtained by replacing E8 with simple $A \rightarrow A$, which we would then label $\Pi'8$, and by adding rules γ and δ.

Rule γ : $A, \sim A \vee B \vdash_{\Pi'} B$ Rule γ is, of course, MD.

Rule δ : From $A \rightarrow . B \rightarrow C$ infer $A \rightarrow C$ if B is a logical truth.

Because we will assume theorems are logical truths and will not assume that hypotheses are logical truths, we present rule δ as δT below where $\vdash$ is to be understood a provability in the system being discussed.

Rule δT: From $A \rightarrow . B \rightarrow C$ and $\vdash B$ infer $A \rightarrow C$.

The first theorem of this section is not completely proved until we get Meyer's and Dunn's result about the admissibility of rule γ for E in Section V.3.

Theorem I of IV.2: $\vdash_{\Pi'} A$ iff. $\vdash_{E} A$.

A proof of Theorem I can be assembled primarily from the following lemmas.

Lemma 1 of IV.2: If $\vdash_{E} A$ and $\vdash_{E} \sim A \vee B$, then $\vdash_{E} B$ (Admissibility of γ for E.)

Lemma 2 of IV.2: If $\vdash_{E} B$ and $A \rightarrow . B \rightarrow C$, then $A \rightarrow C$. (δT for E.)

Lemma 3 of IV.2: $\vdash_{\Pi'} (A \rightarrow A) \wedge (B \rightarrow B) \rightarrow C \rightarrow C$

Proof

1) $(A \rightarrow A) \wedge (B \rightarrow B) \rightarrow C \rightarrow . (A \rightarrow A) \wedge (B \rightarrow B) \rightarrow C$ $\Pi'8$

2) $(A \rightarrow A) \wedge (B \rightarrow B)$ Adj. with two versions of $\Pi'8$.

3) $(A \rightarrow A) \wedge (B \rightarrow B) \rightarrow C \rightarrow C$ δT on (1) and (2).

Lemma 2 is proved later in this section. In light of Theorem I, we dispense with subscripts on $\vdash$ in this section. Of course, Π' and E are very different systems despite the fact that they have exactly the same theorems. Π' fails to meet condition C11 because γ is a non-normal rule. Also if we use Π' as the sentential logic for an axiom system with non-logical axioms, anything follows if these new axioms are inconsistent just as if a classical sentential logic had been used. With Π', because of rule γ , any claim can be derived from an explicit contradiction although Π' does not have $A \wedge \sim A \rightarrow B$ as a theorem schema. Nevertheless we do not want only a safe set of entailment theses. We also want to be able to use our sentential logic as the underlying logic of axiom systems; and when we so use it we do not want to allow derivations involving irrelevancies from those axioms even if those axioms are inconsistent. R.K. Meyer on pp.21-22 of his dissertation [1966] and in his witty [1971b] forcefully reminds us that we want to be able to say that a system has only a small inconsistency. But use of a logic which allows everything to be derived from a contradiction makes all inconsistencies equally disastrous. So, Ackermann's system Π' is not the system we are looking for.

Nevertheless it must be granted that $A \rightarrow A$ is more appleaing than E8. Of course, E8 is true. If a claim is entailed by a conjunction of logical truths, of which $A \rightarrow A$ is a paradigm, we can conclude from that fact that it has to be true.. Similar considerations, of course, show that T33 is acceptable. The trouble with E8 is simply that it does not seem to be a schema which we would immediately accept as an axiom. Consideration of E8's role in establishing theses about necessity may help us rest more easily with E8's axiomatic status. Mention of necessity brings us to the main topic of this section, viz., definition of $\Box A$ in Π' and in E and establishment of a modal logic within E.

Ackermann thought that his Π' had a defect which it did not have. He thought that to define $\Box A$ in Π' he had to augment the language of Π' with a sentential constant, which we label f and which is to be interpreted as making an absurd claim such as $1 \neq 1$. With this constant, he specified that $\Box A =_{df} \sim A \rightarrow f$. Then he added two new axiom schemas: $A \wedge \sim A \rightarrow f$, $A \rightarrow f \rightarrow \sim A$, and a new rule ε : From $\vdash A \rightarrow B$ and $\vdash (A \rightarrow B) \wedge C \rightarrow f$, infer $\vdash C \rightarrow f$, to get a new system Π''. We will not pursue Ackermann's development of a modal logic within Π''. The interested reader can consult Ackermann's [1958] as well as his original [1956] paper, Anderson's and Belnap's "Modalities in Ackermann's rigorous implication" of 1959, and R. K. Meyer's [1970a].

Here we want to criticize the introduction of such a sentential constant and repeat our claim from the discussion of C12 back in I.6 that $\Box A$ should be definable in terms of the $\rightarrow$ in an adequate entailment system. We add here the rather weak normative intuition that $\Box A$ should be definable without use of negation because having to be true seems to be a positive idea. The sentential constant allows relevance ruptures between antecedent and consequent. For instance, there is no meaning connection between $1 \neq 1$ and 'John goes but John does not go.' Whatever logically absurd claim is used to interpret the constant f, it will be totally irrelevant to some explicit contradiction. Unfortunately, we use Ackermann's $A \wedge \sim A \rightarrow f$ to get $\Box(A \vee \sim A)$. More generally, we can observe that if we introduce a sentential constant c and have it be either the antecedent or consequent of a schema: $c \rightarrow F$ or $F \rightarrow c$ where F does not contain c, there will be instances of the schema in which antecedent and consequent are irrelevant to one another in the sense of not sharing a variable. So, we do not want a system which uses sentential constants. However, one of the foremost investigators of entailment systems, viz., R.K. Meyer, is very fond of using sentential constants. So, in the next section we briefly consider the use of sentential constants and the fact that their use does not significantly alter entailment systems except for the relevance rupturing just noted.

Despite our weak normative intuitions that necessity is a positive idea, it is very natural to try to give $\Box A$ the negative definition: $\sim A \rightarrow A$. At least one suspects $\sim A \rightarrow A$ would be equivalent to $\Box A$. If $\sim A$ gives A, in the best possible formal way, there is no way to avoid having A. In both E and Π' we do get A from $\sim A \rightarrow A$.

T45: $\sim A \rightarrow A \rightarrow A$ also $A \rightarrow \sim A \rightarrow \sim A$ Self-abuse

To prove the first version of T45 start with E15 in the form: $A \wedge \sim A \rightarrow . \sim(\sim A \rightarrow A)$. Use the fact that $\sim A \leftrightarrow . \sim A \wedge \sim A$ and then Repl. and Contraposition to get the theorem.

If $\Box A$ were $\sim A \rightarrow A$, T45 would give the desirable theorem $\Box A \rightarrow A$. However, $\Box A$ cannot be satisfactorily defined in E or Π' as $\sim A \rightarrow A$. Belnap reminds us on p.80 of his monograph that we certainly want $\not\vdash \Box(A \rightarrow A)$. In the last section of this part, we will see that neither E nor Π' have any theorems of the form $\sim(A \rightarrow B) \rightarrow . C \rightarrow D$. So, obviously, neither system would have $\sim(A \rightarrow A) \rightarrow . A \rightarrow A$ as a theorem. So, in these systems we cannot even hope for $\Box A$ to be equivalent to $\sim A \rightarrow A$. With Belnap, let us note in passing that Ackermann had a mistaken idea of why $\Box A$ could not be identified with $\sim A \rightarrow A$ in Π'. Ackermann believed that a sufficient condition for $\Box \sim A$, i.e., A is impossible, is: $A \rightarrow . B \wedge \sim B$. But Ackermann did not think that he could go from $A \rightarrow . B \wedge \sim B$ to $A \rightarrow \sim A$, viz., $\Box \sim A$. Belnap notes that Π' has T46.

T46: $A \rightarrow B \wedge \sim B \rightarrow . A \rightarrow \sim A$

To prove T46 you can use T47 below. Start with E9 in the form: $A \rightarrow B \wedge \sim B \rightarrow . B \wedge \sim B \rightarrow \sim A \rightarrow . A \rightarrow \sim A$. Then prove T47 . After that you can get the theorem with Repl. and E11.

T47: $(A \rightarrow B \wedge \sim B) \leftrightarrow (B \wedge \sim B \rightarrow \sim A)$

We merely sketch a proof. To get $A \rightarrow B \wedge \sim B \rightarrow . B \wedge \sim B \rightarrow \sim A$ start with the easily proved $B \wedge \sim B \rightarrow . \sim(B \wedge \sim B)$ and Prefix to get $A \rightarrow B \wedge \sim B \rightarrow . A \rightarrow \sim(B \wedge \sim B)$; Contrapose the consequent. To get the other half, start again with $B \wedge \sim B \rightarrow \sim(B \wedge \sim B)$ but Suffix to get $\sim(B \wedge \sim B) \rightarrow \sim A \rightarrow . B \wedge \sim B \rightarrow \sim A$; Contrapose the antecedent.

It is desirable that $\Box A$ cannot be satisfactorily identified with $\sim A \rightarrow A$ in system E. If we could so identify it and had some entailment claims as necessary truths, we would have to have theses of the $\sim(A\rightarrow B)\rightarrow .C\rightarrow D$ form. But we really should not be able to draw any conclusions from an $\sim(A\rightarrow B)$. To keep faith with the idea that $\rightarrow$ is a primitive sign we should treat $\sim(A\rightarrow B)$ as a unit. In particular, we should not draw $A\wedge\sim B$ from $\sim(A\rightarrow B)$ because in the presence of E15 having $\sim(A\rightarrow B)$ entail $A\wedge\sim B$ would give: $(A\rightarrow B)\leftrightarrow .A\supset B$. Still, if we assume $\sim(A\rightarrow B)$ and think that we can get consequences from it, the most natural consequence we can think of is $A\wedge\sim B$. So, let us count E's constraints on reasoning from $\sim(A\rightarrow B)$ as blessings!

Anderson and Belnap in [1959b] show that Ackermann could have defined $\Box A$ as $A\rightarrow A\rightarrow A$ and for system E $\Box A$ is so defined. Let us call this <u>the positive definition of necessity</u>. It is certainly a reasonable definition because if A is entailed by a necessary truth A is certainly necessarily true, and $A\rightarrow A$ is necessarily true if any truth is necessarily true. So, let us make the following our official modal definitions for system E.

Def. 1: $\Box A =_{df} A\rightarrow A\rightarrow A$ Positive definiton of necessity

Def. 2: $\Diamond A =_{df} \sim(\sim A\rightarrow \sim A\rightarrow \sim A)$, i.e., $\sim\Box\sim A$.

Def. 3: $A \mathbin{-\!\!\!\supset} B =_{df} \sim(A\wedge\sim B)\rightarrow \sim(A\wedge\sim B)\rightarrow \sim(A\wedge\sim B)$,

i.e., $\Box\sim(A\wedge\sim B)$

We do not go into much detail in investigating modal notions in E. We prove a few theorems about necessity, show the role of E8 in establishing some crucial theorems about $\Box$, show that Necessitation is an admissible rule for E, establish Lemma 2 of this section, report Meyer's result that the modal logic in E is S4, and entertain the question of whether or not it should be S5.

We certainly want $\Box A\rightarrow A$ as a theorem. We already have $\Box A\rightarrow A$ as a special version of T33, viz., $A\rightarrow A\rightarrow A\rightarrow A$, although we label it T48. Recall that E8 was used to get T33.

T48: $\Box A\rightarrow A$

$\Box$ should distribute over $\wedge$. So, fortunately we have T49.

T49: $\Box(A\wedge B)\leftrightarrow(\Box A\wedge\Box B)$

To go from from right to left we sketch Belnap's proof using E8 from p.84 of his monograph. Start with a form of T43.

1) $(A\rightarrow A\rightarrow A)\wedge(B\rightarrow B\rightarrow B)\rightarrow .(A\rightarrow A)\wedge(B\rightarrow B)\rightarrow .A\wedge B$

Suffix $A\wedge B$ within the consequent of (1) so that you get with Trans. (2).

2) $(A\rightarrow A\rightarrow A)\wedge(B\rightarrow B\rightarrow B)\rightarrow .A\wedge B\rightarrow A\wedge B\rightarrow .(A\rightarrow A)\wedge(B\rightarrow B)\rightarrow .A\wedge B$

3) $(A\rightarrow A)\wedge(B\rightarrow B)\rightarrow A\wedge B\rightarrow A\wedge B$ E8.

With Dr.10 on (2) and (3) we get (4) which is $\Box A\wedge\Box B\rightarrow\Box(A\wedge B)$

4) $(A\rightarrow A\rightarrow A)\wedge(B\rightarrow B\rightarrow B)\rightarrow .A\wedge B\rightarrow A\wedge B\rightarrow A\wedge B$.

To get the second half we sketch a proof, using T33, of $A \land B \rightarrow A \land B \rightarrow A \land B \rightarrow . A \rightarrow A \rightarrow A$, viz., $\Box(A \land B) \rightarrow \Box A$.

1) $A \land B \rightarrow A$ — E1
2) $A \land B \rightarrow A \land B \rightarrow A \land B \rightarrow . A \land B \rightarrow A \land B \rightarrow A$ — Prefix on (1)
3) $A \land B \rightarrow A \land B \rightarrow A \rightarrow . A \rightarrow A \rightarrow . A \land B \rightarrow A \land B \rightarrow A$ — E9
4) $A \land B \rightarrow A \land B \rightarrow A \rightarrow A$ — T33
5) $A \land B \rightarrow A \land B \rightarrow A \rightarrow . A \rightarrow A \rightarrow A$ — Dr. 10 on (3),(4).
6) $A \land B \rightarrow A \land B \rightarrow A \land B \rightarrow . A \rightarrow A \rightarrow A$ — Trans. (2),(5).

A proof of $\Box(A \land B) \rightarrow \Box B$ could begin with $A \land B \rightarrow B$.

We, of course, want actuality to entail possibility as we have in T50. To prove T50 start with the $\Box \sim A \rightarrow \sim A$ version of T48 and Contrapose. We also want necessity to entail possibility as is claimed in T51 which comes immediately from T48 and T50.

T50: $A \rightarrow \Diamond A$

T51: $\Box A \rightarrow \Diamond A$

It is shown in the last section of this part, viz., IV.11, that we do not have the converses of T50 and T51. Certainly, if our A is to be a plausible assertion of necessity we do not want the converses of T50 and T51. To satisfy Belnap's C3 and C4 we want T57 below but not its converse. So, in IV.11, we need to show that $A \,-\!\!3\, B \rightarrow . A \rightarrow B$ is not a theorem of E.

Some other theorems, which are interesting for their own sake, help us prove that entailments entail strict implications. We do want entailments to be necessarily true and we want to be able to assert that they are necessarily true. Hence, T52 is desirable. T52 comes from Rest. Perm, i.e., rT42, applied to the following version of T1: $(A \rightarrow B \rightarrow . A \rightarrow B) \rightarrow . A \rightarrow B \rightarrow . A \rightarrow B$.

T52: $A \rightarrow B \rightarrow \Box(A \rightarrow B)$

With T48,T52, and Adj. we get T53.

T53: $A \rightarrow B \leftrightarrow \Box(A \rightarrow B)$

Given that entailments are necessarily true, if true, any claim entailed by a true entailment should be necessarily true. Certainly $A \rightarrow A$ is a true entailment. So, we should not be unhappy with T54.

T54: $A \rightarrow A \rightarrow B \rightarrow \Box B$

Proof

1) $A \rightarrow A \rightarrow B \rightarrow B$ — T33
2) $B \rightarrow B \rightarrow . A \rightarrow A \rightarrow B \rightarrow B$ — Suffix on (1).
3) $A \rightarrow A \rightarrow B \rightarrow . B \rightarrow B \rightarrow B$ — Rest. Perm. on (2)

We do not want to suggest that a claim is entailed by its being entailed by a claim of necessity, let alone that its necessity is entailed by its being entailed by a claim of necessity.

Thus we do not want either $\Box A \rightarrow B \rightarrow B$ or $\Box A \rightarrow B \rightarrow \Box B$ as thesis schemas. With T48 either of these two schemas would make E inconsistent in the sense that plain B would become a theorem schema. Nevertheless, we do want to be able to conclude that B is necessary from a claim that A is necessary if A entails B. In other words, we want T55.

T55: $A \rightarrow B \rightarrow . \Box A \rightarrow \Box B$

Proof

1)	$A \rightarrow B \rightarrow . A \rightarrow A \rightarrow A \rightarrow . A \rightarrow A \rightarrow B$	E10
2)	$A \rightarrow A \rightarrow B \rightarrow . B \rightarrow B \rightarrow B$	T54 with B defined.
3)	$A \rightarrow B \rightarrow . A \rightarrow A \rightarrow A \rightarrow . B \rightarrow B \rightarrow B$	Dr.10 on (1),(2).

By use of Rest. Perm., Dr.10, and T48 we get the following corollary of T55, which is a restricted Law of Assertion.

T56: $\Box A \rightarrow . A \rightarrow B \rightarrow B$

A proof that entailments entail strict implication now comes fairly easy.

T57: $A \rightarrow B \rightarrow . A -\!\!\exists B$

Proof

1)	$A \rightarrow B \rightarrow \sim(A \wedge \sim B)$	From E15
2)	$\Box(A \rightarrow B) \rightarrow \Box\sim(A \wedge \sim B)$	rT55 on (1).
3)	$A \rightarrow B \rightarrow . \Box\sim(A \wedge \sim B)$	Use T53 and Repl on (2).
4)	$A \rightarrow B \rightarrow . \Box\sim(A \wedge \sim B)$	Use Def. 3 on (3).

Consider $A -\!\!\exists B$ in its undefined form and the following version of T33: $\sim(A \wedge \sim B) \rightarrow \sim(A \wedge \sim B) \rightarrow \sim(A \wedge \sim B) \rightarrow \sim(A \wedge \sim B)$ to get a proof of T58 saying that strict implications entail material implications.

T58: $A -\!\!\exists B \rightarrow . A \supset B$

The next theorem, which is helpful for proving Lemma 4, permits distribution of $\Box$ over $\rightarrow$. It is provable from T48 and T55 with Trans..

T59: $\Box(A \rightarrow B) \rightarrow . \Box A \rightarrow \Box B$

Lemma IV of IV.2: For E, if $\vdash A$, then $\vdash \Box A$. Necessitation

Proof is by induction on the length of a proof of A. In the basis case A is an axiom. Because all axioms of E are of the $C \rightarrow D$ form rT52 gives $\Box(C \rightarrow D)$. Assume that the lemma holds for all proofs with less than n lines. Ignore the cases of the n-th line being an axiom or a repetition of an earlier line. There are two cases. In the first case the n-th line is A which was obtained from $\vdash B$ and $\vdash B \rightarrow A$ by MP. From the induction assumption we have $\vdash \Box B$ and $\vdash \Box(B \rightarrow A)$. Use of rT59 gives $\vdash \Box B \rightarrow \Box A$. So, by MP we get $\vdash \Box A$. In the second case the n-th line is a $C \wedge D$ obtained by Adj. The induction assumption gives $\vdash \Box C$ and $\vdash \Box D$ which by Adj. and T49 yields $\vdash \Box(C \wedge D)$.

Lemma 4 is, in effect, a sublemma for Lemma 2 which we now prove. Suppose we have $\vdash$ B and A$\longrightarrow$.B$\longrightarrow$C. By Lemma 4 we have $\vdash$ B$\longrightarrow$B$\longrightarrow$B. By Prefixing B$\longrightarrow$B into the consequent of A$\longrightarrow$.B$\longrightarrow$C we get A$\longrightarrow$.B$\longrightarrow$B$\longrightarrow$B$\longrightarrow$.B$\longrightarrow$B$\longrightarrow$C. Use rT35 to get A$\longrightarrow$.B$\longrightarrow$B$\longrightarrow$C. With $\vdash$B$\longrightarrow$B use rT35 to get A$\longrightarrow$B. So, we have δT for system E.

Necessitation is also a rule which holds for the modal system S4. Another special feature of S4 is having $\Box$A$\dashv$ $\Box\Box$A as a thesis schema. In E this characteristic S4 thesis is a theorem. Indeed the strict implication can be strengthened to an entailment. We have the S4-ish T60 as an immediate consequence of T52 because $\Box$A is a formula with the C$\longrightarrow$D form.

T60: $\Box$A$\longrightarrow$$\Box\Box$A.

The question now arises as to whether or not the $\Box$ of E works in accordance with the laws of S4. The answer is "yes." The answer is clarified here but it is not proved here. The reader is referred to R.K. Meyer's "E and S4" for a proof of and comment upon this significant result. What does it mean to say that the necessity of E is S4 necessity? Assume that we have a formulation of S4 with $\Box$ as the modal primitive and $\wedge$,v, and $\sim$ as the truth-functional connectives. Let there be the following translation t( ) of the language of this version of S4 into the language of E. Ignore sentential constants!

Translation of a modal language into E's language:

t(A) = A if A is a sentential variable
t(A$\wedge$B) = t(A)$\wedge$t(B)
t(A v B) = t(A) v t(B)
t($\sim$A) = $\sim$t(A)
t($\Box$A) = t(A)$\longrightarrow$t(A)$\longrightarrow$t(A)

The claim that the defined necessity of E is S4 necessity is explicated as: $\vdash_{E}$ t(A) iff. $\vdash_{S4}$ A.

On p. 76 of their modal logic text Hughes and Cresswell note the Carnapian position that the necessity of S5 is the most suitable formalization of what can be called logical necessity. The gist of this position is that in modal structure semantics for S5 A holds iff. A holds in all consistent descriptions;not in only some. Let us not quarrel here with the position that S5 necessity is logical necessity. Here let us at least start to consider that we should not want necessity in E to be full logical necessity. Given the equivalence of A$\longrightarrow$B with $\Box$(A$\longrightarrow$B) in T53, we should hesitate about saying that E's $\Box$ expresses logical necessity. We do not want to say that a true A$\longrightarrow$B is only logically necessary because logical necessity is not a sufficient condition for the truth of an entailment. When we assert the necessity of the truth of an entailment, shouldn't we be asserting something stricter than logical necessity?

We begin exercises for this section with two more theorems.

T61: $\sim A \rightarrow A \rightarrow . A \rightarrow A \rightarrow A$ I.e., $\sim A \rightarrow A \rightarrow \Box A$.

T62: $B \rightarrow . A \rightarrow C \rightarrow . \Box A \rightarrow . B \rightarrow C$

Exercises IV.2

1. Add $B \rightarrow . A \rightarrow A$ to E to get what Meyer's calls S4 in [1970a]. Show that this ssystem has $B \wedge \sim B \rightarrow A$ as a theorem schema.
2. Show that I_3 plus $\Box A \rightarrow B \rightarrow B$ as a new axiom schema is inconsistent.

IV.3 Use and elimination of a sentential constant,

The purpose of this section is to introduce and to appraise axiomatizations using a sentential constant. For reasons given in the preceding section we do not use such axiomatizations. Nevertheless, we want to see what such axiomatizations of a system are like and we want to show that they really add nothing new. There are at least two explications of the claim that sentential constants really add nothing new. The second explication, viz., the eliminability of constants, will reveal that an apparent advantage of the use of constants is illusory.

The following system which they call E and we call Et is from Meyer's and Routley's [197_b]. The language of Et is that of E augmented with all wffs. with a sententail constant t occurring as if it were a sentential variable. Below are the axioms of Et. The rules of proof are MP. and Adj.. On the right we frequently cite the label for Et schemas in E.

AEt0.	$t \rightarrow . A \rightarrow A$	
AEt1.	$t \rightarrow A \rightarrow A$	
AEt2.	$A \rightarrow B \rightarrow . B \rightarrow C \rightarrow . A \rightarrow C$	E9
AEt3.	$(A \rightarrow . A \rightarrow B) \rightarrow . A \rightarrow B$	E11
AEt4.	$A \wedge B \rightarrow A$	E1
AEt5.	$A \wedge B \rightarrow B$	E2
AEt6.	$(A \rightarrow B) \wedge (A \rightarrow C) \rightarrow . A \rightarrow B \wedge C$	E12
AEt7.	$A \rightarrow . A \vee B$	E3
AEt8.	$B \rightarrow . A \vee B$	E4
AEt9.	$(A \rightarrow C) \wedge (B \rightarrow C) \rightarrow . A \vee B \rightarrow C$	E13
AEt10.	$A \wedge (B \vee C) \rightarrow . A \wedge B \vee C$	E5
AEt11.	$A \rightarrow \sim A \rightarrow \sim A$	T45
AEt12.	$A \rightarrow \sim B \rightarrow . B \rightarrow \sim A$	
AEt13.	$\sim \sim A \rightarrow A$	E7.

The first goal is to show that if $\vdash_{E} A$ then $\vdash_{Et} A$. As a first step towards this goal let us note that the second axiom gives us both Trans. and Suffixing as rules for Et. If the constant t is to be interpreted as a logical truth just as Ackermann's f was supposed to be an absurdity, then plain t should be a theorem of Et.

Et1. t

To prove Et1 take AEt0 in the form $t \rightarrow . t \rightarrow t$, AEt1 in the form $t \rightarrow t \rightarrow t$, link by Trans. to get $t \rightarrow t$, and then use $t \rightarrow t$ with $t \rightarrow t \rightarrow t$ to get plain t by MP.

With Et1 and AEt1,MP immediately gives Et's next theorem.

Et2: A⟶A

The next theorem of Et is E's T33.

Et3: A⟶A⟶B⟶B

Proof

1)	t⟶.A⟶A	AEt0.
2)	A⟶A⟶B⟶.t⟶B	Suf. on (1)
3)	t⟶B⟶B	AEt1
4)	A⟶A⟶B⟶B	Trans. (2),(3).

With MP, AEt2,AEt3, and Et3 we have the pure implicational system I_3 discussed in IV.1 (See the exercises of IV.1.) In Section IV.1, we noted that all theorems of E containing only ⟶ as a logical sign are theorems of I_3. We also had the inelegant feature that in E we used an axiom with conjunction,viz., E8, to get T33 and hence we used an axiom with conjunction to get the pure implicational fragment of E. On the other hand, Et seems to have the advantage of getting the pure implicational fragment from pure implicational formulas. However, this apparent advantage of Et is illusory if we discover that constant t is implicitly conjunctive. But let us for awhile continue our efforts to get all axioms of E as theorems of Et.

With Et2 in the form ~A⟶~A and AEt12 in the form ~A⟶~A⟶.A⟶~~A we get E6 as an Et theorem.

Et4: A⟶~~A

We refer to the result, brought out in the exercises for IV.1, that Prefixing is a theorem of I_3 to prove the next theorem.

Et5: A⟶B⟶.C⟶A⟶.C⟶B E10 (Prefix.)

A proof of E8 is about the same as one for Et3 except that AEt6 is used to get t⟶(A⟶A)∧(B⟶B).

Et6: (A⟶A)∧(B⟶B)⟶C⟶C E8

Our version of Contraposition is also easily obtained.

Et7: A⟶B⟶.~B⟶~A E14

Proof

1)	B⟶~~B	Et4
2)	A⟶B⟶.A⟶~~B	Preix on (1).
3)	A⟶~~B⟶.~B⟶~A	AEt12
4)	A⟶B⟶.~B⟶~A	Trans (2), (3).

It remains only to show that E15 is an Et theorem. Observe that Et has all the axioms of TE of III.2. Hence, Et has all of the equivalences of an MA system. Also observe that we can carry our a proof of Repl. for Et because the proof of Theorem V of IV.1 does not use E15. Let us present this as Lemma 1.

Lemma 1 of IV.3: Et has the equivalences of an MA system and Repl. holds for Et.

Reconsider the proof of T36 back in IV.1 to note that E15 was not used in its proof. So, let us cite T36 as an Et theorem.

Et8: $A \rightarrow B \rightarrow . A \wedge C \rightarrow B$ T36 Premiss Add.

Et's next theorem brings us close to E15.

Et9: $A \rightarrow B \rightarrow . A \wedge \sim B \rightarrow \sim (A \wedge \sim B)$

Proof

1) $B \rightarrow . \sim A \vee B$	AEt9
2) $A \rightarrow B \rightarrow . A \rightarrow . \sim A \vee B$	Prefix on (1)
3) $(A \rightarrow . \sim A \vee B) \rightarrow . A \wedge \sim B \rightarrow . \sim A \vee B$	Et8
4) $(\sim A \vee B) \leftrightarrow \sim (A \wedge \sim B)$	By Lemma 1
5) $(A \rightarrow . \sim A \vee B) \rightarrow . A \wedge \sim B \rightarrow \sim (A \wedge \sim B)$	Repl. (3),(4)
6) $A \rightarrow B \rightarrow . A \wedge \sim B \rightarrow \sim (A \wedge \sim B)$	Trans (2),(5).

To prove Et10 connect, by Trans., AEt11 in the form $(A \wedge \sim B) \rightarrow \sim (A \wedge \sim B) \rightarrow \sim (A \wedge \sim B)$ with Et9. By use of Contraposition an easy corollary of Et10 is E15. So, our first theorem of this section can be stated after Et11.

Et10: $A \rightarrow B \rightarrow \sim (A \wedge \sim B)$

Et11: $A \wedge \sim B \rightarrow \sim (A \rightarrow B)$ E15

Theorem I of IV.3: If $\vdash_{E} A$, then $\vdash_{Et} A$.

In passing let us admit that there may be a reason for preferring AEt11 over our E15 as the crucial axiom for getting zdfs. from entailment formulas. E15 simply postulates the condition that an entailment gives a material implication. But AEt11 is a general principle about entailment and negation. Nevertheless we keep E15 as an axiom because it brings out the general principle that a necessary condition for an entailment are the conditions for a material implication.

Of most importance here, though, is the issue of whether or not Et has more significant theses than E has. Obviously, Et has theses which E does not have, eg., AEt0 and AEt1. But without an interpretation of t, it is not obvious that Et has any more significant theses than E has. If we regard the significant entailment theses as those stated using only variables because only these are fully general claims, the fact that Et is a conservative extension of E shows that Et does not really tell us more about entailment than E does. Recall that Et is a conservative extension of E if the theorems of Et without the constant t are all theorems of E. We follow Meyer's and Routley's first theorem of [197_b] to show that Et is in fact a conservative extension of E. Theorem I tells us that Et is an extension of E. So, it suffices to show that if we have a proof: $A_1, \ldots, A_n$ in Et where A_n is also a wff. of E, the proof can be transformed into a proof in E $A^*_1,\ldots,A^*_m$ where A^*_m is A_n. Each A_i is transformed into an A^*_i by replacing each occurrence of t with a conjunction of all of the $p_i \rightarrow p_i$ where p_i is a sentential variable occurring in the Et proof $A_1,\ldots,A_n$. We label this conjunction t*. By this replacement each of the A^*_i are in the language of E. Uses of MP and Adj. are not affected by replacement of the unti t with the larger unit t*. So, to show that the sequence $A^*_1,\ldots,A^*_m$, where m = n, can be transformed into a proof in E, it suffices to show that occurrences of AEto and AEt1 are E theorems when t is replaced with t*. The remarks upon Lemma 4 of II.8, the Atomic Components Lemma, tells us that $\vdash_E t^* \rightarrow .A \rightarrow A$. To show that $\vdash_E t^* \rightarrow A \rightarrow A$, let us cite a lemma which enables us to use E8. In the lemma $\bigwedge_{i=1}^{n} A_i$ means a conjunction $A_1 \wedge, \ldots, \wedge A_n$ and $\vdash$ means is provable in E.

Lemma 2 of IV.3: $\vdash \bigwedge_{i=1}^{n}(p_i \rightarrow p_i) \leftrightarrow (\bigwedge_{j=1}^{n-1} p_j \rightarrow \bigwedge_{j=1}^{n-1} p_j) \wedge (p_n \rightarrow p_n)$.

We leave an inductive proof of Lemma 2 as an exercise. We merely remind the reader that Dr.3 from III.2 is useful in the proof.

Now any t* is a $\bigwedge_{i=1}^{n}(p_i \rightarrow p_i)$. So, any $t^* \rightarrow A \rightarrow A$ is a $\bigwedge_{n=1}^{n}(p_i \rightarrow p_i) \rightarrow A \rightarrow A$. As a result of Lemma 2 and Repl., then, any $t^* \rightarrow A \rightarrow A$ can be replaced with the following version of E8. $(\bigwedge_{j=1}^{n-1} p_j \rightarrow \bigwedge_{j=1}^{n-1} p_j) \wedge (p_n \rightarrow p_n) \rightarrow A \rightarrow A$. Again we have occasion to appreciate E8! Hopefully, we have said enough to provide the ingredients for a proof of the second theorem of this section.

Theorem II of IV.3: Et is a conservative extension of E.

The preceding discussion shows how use of the constant t can be eliminated from Et and extensions of Et if the extensions are made without adding any new axioms for t. In any contexts where axioms are used, viz.,proofs, the t constant can always be replaced with a t* conjunction. We can take this contextual eliminability of t as another explication of the contention that use of t does not really involve the addition of anything new to E. (The first explication was that Et is a conservative extension of E.) In any context t can always be regarded as a familiar conjunction of $p_i \rightarrow p_i$ theorems. Observe, though, that we have now come to regard t as essentially a schema for conjunctions. Hence, the suggestion that in Et we get the pure implication theorems without conjunction is misleading. We suggest that $t \rightarrow A \rightarrow A$ is implicitly "more conjunctive" than E8, because in some contexts t becomes a very long conjunction.

With this last suggestion we leave the issue of using sentential constants. We refer the reader to pp.182-183 and fn.4

of Meyer's [1970a] for some defense of use of such constants and his [1974a] for the strategy of contextually eliminating constant t and expression of some hesitancy about use of t.

Exercises IV.3

1. Show for Et that $\vdash$A, then $\vdash$ t$\rightarrow$A. Is the modal logic for Et the same as that for E if $\Box A =_{df} t \rightarrow A$?
2. Show for Et that $(t\rightarrow A)\leftrightarrow(A\rightarrow A\rightarrow A)$.
3. Prove Lemma 2.

IV.4 The Entailment Theorem for E.

Our goal in this section is to state and to prove the Anderson and Belnap Entailment Theorem for E. We observe that the Entailment Theorem guarantees a type of rule normality for E and, of course, we use it to prove some theorems. Further we see how it can be proved for extensions of system E. The Entailment Theorem for E is now presented in section 23.6 of Anderson's and Belnap's [1975].

In order to state the Entailment Theorem, we have to introduce a notion of a restricted type of derivation. Basically we want to show that if there is a derivation of B from $A_1,\ldots,A_n$, then $\vdash A_1 \wedge ,\ldots, \wedge A_n \rightarrow B$ However, we would not want such a result if we stayed with the fundamental notion of a derivation of B as a sequence of wffs. $B_1,\ldots,B_m$ such that each B_j is an axiom, a hypothesis, or a consequence of predecessors by MP or Adj.. With such an unrestricted notion of derivation an entailment theorem would give, as a theorem $A \rightarrow . B \rightarrow B$; we would simply prove $B \rightarrow B$ without any use of the hypothesis A.

So, we want to restrict our attention to derivations in which at least some of the hypotheses are used to get the last line of the derivation. On p. 85 of his monograph, Belnap presents Anderson's and his restricted notion of derivation which safely allows us to go from $A_1,\ldots,A_n \vdash$ B to $\vdash A_1 \wedge \ldots, \wedge A_n \rightarrow B$. Occasionally we call these derivations some-premiss-using or some-hypotheses-using derivations to contrast them with derivations in which all hypotheses have to be used. In the next section, we study A. Kron's Deduction Theorem for all-premiss-using derivations. But usually we call these some-premiss-using derivations <u>starring derivations</u>.

A <u>starring derivation in E</u> of B from hypotheses $A_1,\ldots,A_n$ is a sequence of wffs. $B_1,\ldots,B_m$ such that B_m is B, each B_j is any axiom, an hypothesis A_i, a consequence of predecessors by MP or Adj., and the following starring conditions are met.

i) Stars * may be prefixed to the steps $B_1,\ldots,B_m$ so as to satisfy the following rules.
   a) If B_j is an hypothesis, then B_j is starred.
   b) If B_j is introduced as an axiom, then B_j is <u>not</u> starred.
   c) If B_j is a consequence by MP, then B_j is starred if wither premiss is starred; otherwise B_j is not starred.
   d) If B_j is a consequence of Adj., then B_j is starred if <u>both</u> premisses are starred but if neither premiss is starred B_j is not starred. Adj. is not applied to one starred line and one unstarred line.

ii) As a consequence of (i), the final step B_m, viz., B, is starred.

Before commenting upon these starring conditions, let us cite a lemma whose inductive proof we leave as an exercise.

Lemma 1 of IV.4: If B_j is an unstarred line of a starring derivation, then $\vdash B_j$.

Brief consideration of these conditions justifies the some-hypotheses-using label. We put in stars when we introduce a hypotheses, draw a conclusion from hypotheses, or conclusions from previous conclusions of hypotheses. So, a star on B_m is the result of using some hypotheses to get B_m. Here we comment only upon (ii) and (id). The other conditions pretty clearly carry out the intent of indicating use of some of the hypotheses in the derivation. If we did not have (ii), a theorem, eg., $B \rightarrow B$, could be the B_m of a derivation where a sole hypothesis A is listed, used a bit, and then $B \rightarrow B$ is deduced from axioms alone. If an entailment theorem applied to such a derivation we would get the relevance violating $A \rightarrow . B \rightarrow B$. In defense of forbidding Adjunction of a theorem not proved by use of any hypotheses -an unstarred line- and a formula derived by use of some hypotheses -a starred line-, Belnap makes the following type of observation. Let A be our sole hypothesis. Now A may be a theorem of E such as $C \rightarrow C$ even if we are here treating it as a hypothesis. In any derivation we can easily get an unstarred $B \rightarrow B$ where B has no variable in common with A. If we now, contrary to (id), apply Adj. to starred A and unstarred $B \rightarrow B$. it would be reasonable to star the result $A \wedge (B \rightarrow B)$ because a hypothesis has been used to get it. We could then put $A \wedge (B \rightarrow B) \rightarrow . B \rightarrow B$ into the derivation and get a starred $B \rightarrow B$ by use of MP. Then if we had an entailment theorem we could get $A \rightarrow . B \rightarrow B$

Maybe reflection on the easily proved T63 will help develop an appreciation of the restrictions on Adj. in "really good" derivations.

T63: $A \rightarrow B_1 \wedge B_2 \rightarrow . (A \rightarrow B_1) \wedge (A \rightarrow B_2)$

We can look at T63 as telling us that if the conjunction of B_1 and B_2 comes from a hypothesis A, or conjunction of hypotheses A, then each of the conjuncts comes from i.e, is separately entailed by, what they come from. So, if B_1 is starred while B_2 is unstarred, B_1 comes from the hypotheses while B_2 does not.

It needs to be emphasized that we are not restricting Adj.. Any two formulas may be conjoined in a derivation. We are simply going to pay especial attention to derivations in which Adj. has been restricted because such derivations meet a condition which helps insure that the hypotheses are relevant to the derived conclusion and such derivations have interesting properties, One of the interesting properties is expressed in the Entailment Theorem which we now prove following Belnap's proof from p. 87 of his monograph.

Theorem I of IV.4: If there is a starring derivation of B from hypotheses $A_1,\ldots,A_n$, then $\vdash A_1, \ldots, A_n \rightarrow B$.

In the proof we follow Belnap in using $A_1{}^n$ as an abbreviation for the conjunction of all of the hypotheses $A_1,\ldots,A_n$; except that we delete the subscript. Transform the starring derivation $B_1,\ldots,B_m$ into $B_1',\ldots,B_m'$ where B_j' is A^n---B_j if B_j is starred but B_j' is plain B_j if B_j is not starred. Because B_m is starred, B_m' is $A^n \rightarrow B_m$ or $A^n \rightarrow B$. We now show that the sequence $B_1',\ldots,B_m'$ can be transformed into a proof of B_m' in system E. We prove by induction on the number of lines in the $B_1',\ldots,B_m'$ sequence that any line in the sequence is a theorem.

In the basis case B_j' is B_1' and B_1' is either an axiom or a hypothesis. If B_1' is an axiom, of course, $\vdash B_1'$. If B_1' is a hypothesis A_i, then B_1 is a conjunct in A^n and consequently we have $\vdash A^n \rightarrow B_1$, i.e., $\vdash B_1'$. As an induction assumption, assume that if $h < j$, then $\vdash B_h'$. There are several cases at the inductive step. In case (i) B_j' is simply B_j; so, by Lemma 1 we have $\vdash B_j'$. In case (ii), B_j' is of the form $A^n \rightarrow B_j$ but B_j is one of the hypotheses. So, as in the basis case we have $\vdash A^n \rightarrow B_j$. Case(iii) in which B_j has come from B_h and B_k with $h < j$ and $k < j$ by MP because B_h is $B_k \rightarrow B_j$ breaks up into three subcases. In subcase (iiia) only B_k is starred. Here by induction assumption we have $\vdash A^n \rightarrow B_k$ and $\vdash B_k \rightarrow B_j$ which by Trans. give $\vdash A^n \rightarrow B_j$. In subcase (iiib) only $B_k \rightarrow B_j$ is starred. So, we have by induction assumption $\vdash B_k$ and $\vdash A^n \rightarrow . B_k \rightarrow B_j$, which by δT for E gives $\vdash A^n \rightarrow B_j$. (See Lemma 2 of IV.2 for δT.) In subcase (iiic) both B_k and $B_k \rightarrow B_j$ are starred; so, we have $\vdash A^n \rightarrow B_k$ and $\vdash A^n \rightarrow . B_k \rightarrow B_j$ which lead to $\vdash A^n \rightarrow B_j$ as the reader may verify. Case (iv) in which B_j comes from a B_h and a B_k by Adj. breaks up into two subcases: both B_h and B_k are starred and neither are starred. We leave consideration of these two subcases to the reader.

Belnap draws the following corollary of the Entailment Theorem.

Corollary of I of IV.4: If $\vdash A$ and B is a conjunction of the axioms used in a proof of A, then $\vdash B \rightarrow A$

We observe with Belnap that this corollary gives non-trivial news. In general, we do not have $\vdash_E A \rightarrow B$ if $\vdash_E A$ and $\vdash_E B$. As we will see we do not have $A \rightarrow A \rightarrow . B \rightarrow B$ as a theorem. But for material and strict implication, we do have $\vdash A \supset B$ and $\vdash A \multimap B$ if just B is a theorem.

Of course, the proof of the Entailment Theorem for E can be duplicated for extensions of E which are obtained by merely adding axiom schemas to E. If another rule is added we would need to consider whether the induction step could be carried out for that rule. Let us say that a <u>system S_1 is an axiomatic extension of system S_2</u> if S_1 is obtained by adding only axioms to S_2. We then let the preceding remarks suffice for a proof of the next theorem.

Theorem II of IV.4: If system S is an axiomatic extension of E, then an entailment theorem for starring derivations holds for S.

Does the Entailment Theorem guarantee rule normality for E? Certainly, if the hypotheses or premisses of the rule are minimally relevant to the conclusion of the rule. They are minimally relevant if we can use at least one of the premisses to get the conclusion. Admittedly, we can regard $A \vdash B \rightarrow B$ as a derived rule in system E even if we do not derive $B \rightarrow B$ from A. It is a good idea to restrict the notion of derived rule to rules in which there is a starring derivation from premisses to conclusion; and we do so. Or we could say that $A_1, \ldots, A_n \vdash B$ is a <u>genuine derived rule</u> only if there is a starring derivation from $A_1, \ldots, A_n$ to B. Thus, not only do we have a guarantee that we have rule normality for genuine derived rules; we also have another sense for saying that an $A \rightarrow B$ thesis in E requires relevance between A and B. A theorem reveals the sense in which $A \rightarrow B$ theorems of E have what can be called <u>minimal or starring derivational relevance between antecedent and consequent</u>.

Theorem III of IV.4: If there is not a starring derivation of B from $A_1, \ldots, A_n$, then it is not the case that $A_1 \wedge \ldots \wedge A_n \rightarrow B$ is a theorem of E. (Theorem III can also be expressed as: If $\vdash_E A \rightarrow B$, then there is minimal derivational relevance between A and B.)

To get a proof of Theorem III consider that if $A_1 \wedge \ldots \wedge A_n \rightarrow B$ is a theorem of E, we can get a derivation from the antecedent which stars B by listing all the hypotheses A_k, starring them, using Adj. to get a starred $A_1 \wedge \ldots \wedge A_n$, and then using MP with the assumed theorem $A_1 \wedge \ldots \wedge A_n \rightarrow B$.

As an illustration of a use of the Entailment Theorem, let us prove Self-distribution which is on use in the next section. We label uses of the Entailment Theorem Ent. Th..

T64: $A \rightarrow B \rightarrow C \rightarrow . A \rightarrow B \rightarrow . A \rightarrow C$ Self-distribution

Proof

1)	* $A \rightarrow . B \rightarrow C$	Hyp.
2)	$B \rightarrow C \rightarrow . A \rightarrow B \rightarrow . A \rightarrow C$	E10
3)	* $A \rightarrow . A \rightarrow B \rightarrow . A \rightarrow C$	Trans. (1),(2)
4)	* $A \rightarrow B \rightarrow . A \rightarrow . A \rightarrow C$	Rest. Perm. (3)
5)	$(A \rightarrow . A \rightarrow C) \rightarrow . A \rightarrow C$	E11
6)	* $A \rightarrow B \rightarrow . A \rightarrow C$	Trans.(4),(5)
7)	$A \rightarrow B \rightarrow . A \rightarrow B \rightarrow . A \rightarrow C$	Ent.Th. (1) to (6).

The proof of T64 brings out that we will use derived rules with the Entailment Theorem and, hence, raises the question of the propriety of using derived rules in starring derivations. We leave it to the interested and industrious reader to verify that each use of a derived rule from a starred premiss leads to a starred conclusion if the starred premiss is used in the derived rule. See exercises 3 and 4 below.

We close this section by citing two theorems whose proofs are facilitated by use of the Entailment Theorem and derived rules. But the third one is best proved by use of Ell and Restricted Permutation.

T65: $(A \rightarrow B) \wedge (C \rightarrow D) \wedge (A \vee C) \rightarrow . B \vee D$ Construct. Dilemma

T66: $(A \rightarrow B) \wedge (C \rightarrow D) \wedge (\sim B \vee \sim D) \rightarrow . \sim A \vee \sim B$ Destruct. Dilemma

T67: $A \rightarrow B \rightarrow . A \rightarrow . \sim B \rightarrow \sim A$

Exercises IV.4

1. Prove T63 without use of the Entailment Theorem.
2. Complete the subcases for (iv) in Theorem I.
3. Show that if $*(A \rightarrow B)$ and $B \rightarrow C$ are lines of a starring derivation, there is a continuation of this derivation which is also a starring derivation such that it ends with $*(A \rightarrow C)$ and that no lines of the original derivation except $*(A \rightarrow B)$ and $B \rightarrow C$ are used in the continuation.
4. Consider T42 and rT42, viz., Rest. Perm.. Show that if a starring derivation ends with $*(C \rightarrow . A \rightarrow B \rightarrow D)$ there is a continuation of this derivation which is also a starring derivation such that it ends with $*(A \rightarrow B \rightarrow . C \rightarrow D)$ and that no lines of the original derivation besides $*(C \rightarrow . A \rightarrow B \rightarrow D)$ are used.

The strategy for working exercises 3 and 4 reveals a strategy for justifying use of derived rules with the Entailment Theorem.

5. Recall Theorem VI of III.4 and now prove that neither MD nor DS are genuine derived rules of E. It may help to recall Theorem I of IV.1 which says that the fde. fragment of E is exactly the TE entailments.
6. Show that any axiomatic extension of E with exactly the same fde. fragment does not have MD or DS as genuine derived rules.

Recall the definition of 'genuine derived rule' given right after Theorem II.

IV.5 Kron's Deduction Theorem, brief remarks on system P, and system T of Ticket Entailment.

In this section we follow A. Kron's [1973] to show that for a restricted class of derivations E has a genuine Deduction Theorem of the form: If $A_1,\ldots,A_n \vdash^S_E B$, then $A_1,\ldots,A_{n-1} \vdash^S_E A_n \rightarrow B$, where the superscript on $\vdash$ indicates special restrictions on the derivation. We call these special derivations _all-hypotheses-using_ derivations or _Kron derivations_. We here deepen our understanding of how E requires the premisses in the best possible formal reasoning to be derivationally relevant to the conclusion in the sense that the conclusion is really gotten from the premisses. We have already attained some appreciation of this derivational relevance in the previous section. In the previous section we saw that E discriminates between derivations which use none of the hypotheses and those which use some by giving the some-hypotheses-using derivations the privilege of an entailment theorem. We here realize how biased E is towards using hypotheses to get the conclusion by seeing how E bestows the special privilege of a genuine deduction theorem to derivations using all of their hypotheses. Given that we share E's biases, we can regard E's awarding of privileges as revealing what derivational relevance really is. The main points of this section can be appreciated without laboring over the details of the proof of Lemma 1.

A _Kron-derivation_ in E of B from $A_1,\ldots A_n$ is a sequence of formulas $B_1,\ldots,B_m$ with $B_m=B$, which is a derivation in the standard sense defined in the Notational Preface, but which in addition satisfies conditions (i),(ii),(iii), and (iv) below.

i) Finite ordered t-tuples of non-zero integer numerals $\langle n_1,\ldots,n_t\rangle$ are prefixed to lines of the derivation so as to satisfy the following conditions. (If we have an ordered t-tuple of numerals as above we refer to an arbitrary member as n_t. We also use n_t to refer to the last member. The context will clarify the use.)

Kron-derivations are from ordered sets of hypotheses. The subscripts on the hypotheses indicate the order in which the hypotheses are used in the derivation by being cited as Hyp.. When a formula is cited as a hypothesis it is regarded as a new hypothesis even if an identical formula has already been cited as a hypothesis. So, for Kron-derivations there may be duplications in the $A_1,\ldots A_n$.

a) If B_i is the g-th hypothesis in the list $A_1,\ldots,A_n$, i.e., the g-th citing of a hypothesis, then $\langle g\rangle$ is prefixed to B_i.

b) If B_i is an axiom, which is not also a hypothesis, then the empty-tuple or, for simplicity's sake, nothing is prefixed to B_i

Axioms and theorems may be hypotheses! Axioms and theorems which are explicitly given as hypotheses are different from those which are only used for the logical manipulations in the construction of the derivation. Axioms explicitly given as hypotheses cannot be altered by uniform substitution for variables or for us: cannot be put into different versions by uniform substitution for basic schema letters. Axioms used for the logical manipulations function as genuine axioms and can be put into the derivation in any version. For instance, if $B \longrightarrow B \longrightarrow . B \longrightarrow B$ is given as a hypothesis which yields $B \longrightarrow B$, $B \longrightarrow B \longrightarrow . B \longrightarrow B$ has to be kept in this form. But E's first theorem, which is presented as $A \longrightarrow A$, may be inserted into the derivation as $B \longrightarrow B$.

c) If B_i is a consequence of and Adjunction applied to B_j and B_k, meets the conditions of (iii) below, and $\langle c_1, \ldots, c_r \rangle$ is prefixed to <u>both</u> B_j and B_k, then $\langle c_1, \ldots, c_r \rangle$ is prefixed to $B_j \wedge B_k$, viz., B_i.

d) If B_i is a consequence of MP on B_k and B_j where B_j is $B_k \longrightarrow B_i$, MP meets the conditions (iv) below, $\langle d_1, \ldots, d_p \rangle$ is prefixed to B_j and $\langle h_1, \ldots, h_q \rangle$ to B_k, then $\langle c_1, \ldots, c_r \rangle$ is prefixed to B_i and $\langle c_1, \ldots c_r \rangle$ is the d_p's and h_q's in numerical order.

ii) If $\langle a_1 \rangle$,..., $\langle a_g \rangle$,..., $\langle a_n \rangle$ are prefixed to the $A_1, \ldots, A_g, \ldots, A_n$ respectively, then $\langle a_1, \ldots, a_n \rangle$ is prefixed to B_m.

If a hypothesis is used it is used to get the conclusion B_m. Also condition (ii) forces all the hypotheses to be used to get the conclusion.

iii) Adjunction is not used to get $B_j \wedge B_k$ or $B_k \wedge B_j$ from B_j and B_k if B_j and B_k have different prefixes.

Condition (iii) is a generalization of the starring derivation restrictions on Adj.. Only formulas from the same source may be conjoined in Kron-derivations. One aspect of this condition is that it stops us from dishonestly saying that we use a hypothesis A_g by adjoining it with another hypothesis A_f, using $A_g \wedge A_f \longrightarrow A_f$ and MP to get A_f again, and then proceed to reason from A_f without using A_g again. Also an exercise which shows how Exportation could be proved by violating condition (iii) helps to motivate acceptance of (iii).

iv) Modus Ponens is <u>not</u> used to get B_i from B_k and $B_k \longrightarrow B_i$ if <u>all</u> the following four conditions are met. Here $\langle h_1, \ldots, h_q \rangle$ is prefixed to B_k and $\langle d_1, \ldots, d_p \rangle$ is prefixed to $B_k \longrightarrow B_i$.

e) $0 < p$ This means that $B_k \longrightarrow B_i$ is not an E theorem proved without any of the given hypotheses. Remember that a line of a derivation may be by fomr a theorem even if it has been derived by use of the hypotheses.

f) $0 < q$ B_k is not an E theorem derived without use of any of the hypotheses.

g) $h_q < d_p$ B_k is obtained before $B_k \rightarrow B_i$.

h) B_k is not of the form $F \rightarrow G$.

An example may motivate these restrictions on MP. Consider a derivation in which we intend to go from $A_1, A_2 \vdash B$ to $\vdash A_1 \rightarrow .A_2 \rightarrow B$. Let's say that the first hypothesis used is A and that the second hypothesis used is $A \rightarrow B$. We have the following derivation.

1) $\langle 1 \rangle$ A Hyp.
2) $\langle 2 \rangle$ $A \rightarrow B$ Hyp.
3) $\langle 1,2 \rangle$ B MP (1),(2).

There is nothing wrong with the preceding derivation if we leave it as it is. But if we try to go from it to $\vdash A \rightarrow .A \rightarrow B \rightarrow B$ we will have fallaciously proved the unrestricted Law of Assertion for E. Note that if we had used $A \rightarrow B$ before A nothing undesirable could be done by going from $A \rightarrow B, A \vdash B$ to $\vdash A \rightarrow B \rightarrow .A \rightarrow B$. Also note that if the first hypothesis used had the form $F \rightarrow G$, eg. $A \rightarrow A$, and the second one used were $A \rightarrow A \rightarrow B$, then use of a deduction theorem would only give a version of the Restricted Law of Assertion which is T34.

As his first lemma , Kron observes that if $\langle c_1, \ldots c_r \rangle$ is prefixed to any B_i each of the c_r have been originally prefixed to a unique occurrence of a hypothesis A_g. We have to talk of unique occurrences of a hypothesis because the same formula may be cited more than once as a hypothesis. We leave Kron's first lemma as an observation and split his first theorem into two lemmas. Let $\vdash^k_E$ mean Kron-derivation in E.

Lemma 1 of IV.5: Let $A_1, \ldots, A_n \vdash^k_E B$ and let B_i be a line of the given derivation. If $\langle c_1, \ldots, c_r \rangle$ is prefixed to B_i, $r \geq 1$, and $\langle c_1 \rangle, \ldots, \langle c_r \rangle$ are prefixed respectively to $C_1, \ldots, C_r$ occurring among the $A_1, \ldots A_n$, then $\vdash_E C_1 \rightarrow .,,, \rightarrow .C_r \rightarrow B_i$.

Lemma 2 of IV.5: Given the hypothesis of Lemma 1 except have r = 0, then $\vdash_E B_i$.

We leave a proof of Lemma 2 as an inductive exercise. Before we become immersed in the messy details of a proof of Lemma 1, let us see how it is used to get the two main theorems of this section. Both are called Kron Deduction Theorems.

Theorem I of IV.5: If there is a Kron-derivation of B from the hypotheses $A_1, \ldots, A_n$, then $\vdash_E A_1 \rightarrow .,,, \rightarrow .A_n \rightarrow B$.

To prove Theorem I note that condition (ii) for a Kron-derivation prefixes $\langle a_1, \ldots, a_n \rangle$ to B. So, the hypotheses $A_1, .., A_n$ may be regarded as the $C_1, \ldots, C_r$ of Lemma 1.

The next theorem is really a corollary of Theorem I. But it is significant enough to be ranked as a theorem.

Theorem II of IV.5: If there is a Kron-derivation of B from $A_1,\ldots,A_n$, then $A_1,\ldots,A_{n-1} \vdash_E A_n \rightarrow B$. (Note that there is no restriction on $\vdash_E$.)

To prove this second theorem observe that from the antecedent of the theorem and Theorem I, we have $\vdash_E A_1 \rightarrow .,,, \rightarrow .A_n \rightarrow B$. So, if we now have $A_1,\ldots,A_{n-1}$ as hypotheses, n-1 applications of MP yields $A_n \rightarrow B$.

Theorem II looks like a full-flegded deduction theorem such as we have in classical sentential logic. But it must be emphasized that it gives a deduction theorem only for a proper subclass of derivations in E, viz., certain all-hypotheses- using derivations.

We now follow Kron in the proof of Lemma 1. Many readers may wish to skip to the remarks on system P. In this proof $\vdash$ means 'theorem in E.' The proof is by induction on the length of the derivation. The basis case has B_1 as an axiom or as a hypothesis. If B_1 is an axiom, the case is covered by Lemma 2. If B_1 is a hypothesis, it is covered by the argument of inductive case (i) below. So, assume for derivations shorter than i, viz., for derivations with fewer than i lines, that Lemma 1 holds. Because Lemma 2 covers the case of r=0, we consider only the cases of $r \geq 1$, i.e., lines which are not presented as theorems of E. There are three main cases: B_i is a hypothesis, B_i is obtained by Kron-restricted Adj., and B_i is obtained by Kron-restricted MP.

Case (1) B_i is the g-th citation of the use of a hypothesis; so B_i is prefixed with $\langle g \rangle$. In this case, $C_1 \rightarrow .,,,. \rightarrow .C_r \rightarrow B$ is merely $C_g \rightarrow B_i$ with $C_g = B_i$ and, of course, $\vdash C_g \rightarrow C_g$.

Case(2) B_i is obtained by Kron-restricted Adjunction from B_j and B_k. Hence, the induction assumption gives (j) and (k) below which by r2 of III.2, viz., Comp., yield line (i) which is what we want.

j) $\vdash C_1 \rightarrow .,,, \rightarrow .C_r \rightarrow B_j$
k) $\vdash C_1 \rightarrow .,,, \rightarrow .C_r \rightarrow B_k$
i) $\vdash C_1 \rightarrow .,,, \rightarrow .C_r \rightarrow B_j\ B_k$. Comp. (j),(k).

Case (3) B_i is from B_j and B_k by Kron-restricted MP where B_j is $B_k \rightarrow B_i$. There are four main subcases to consider because whenever one of the four conditions collectively prohibiting use of MP fails we have a case where MP may be used. Subcases are labelled by use of the letter labelling the prohibiting condition which is assumed to have failed.

Subcase (3e) p=0. This means that B_j has no numerical prefix. So, by Lemma 2, $\vdash B_j$. Because B_j is $B_k \rightarrow B_i$ we have (j) below.

j) $\vdash B_k \rightarrow B_i$

Now the prefix of B_i will simply be the prefix $\langle h_1,\ldots,h_q\rangle$ of B_k. By letting h_q be c_r our induction assumption gives (k).

k) $\vdash C_1 \rightarrow .,,, \rightarrow . C_r \rightarrow B_k$

By use of Dr.10 we can go from this (j) and (k) to (i) which is what we want for this case.

i) $C_1 \rightarrow .,,, \rightarrow . C_r \rightarrow B_i$.

Subcase (3f) q=0, viz., B_k has no prefix. So, by Lemma 2 we have line (k) below.

k) $\vdash B_k$

So the prefix $\langle c_1,\ldots,c_r\rangle$ of B_i is simply the prefix $\langle d_1,\ldots,d_p\rangle$ of $B_k \rightarrow B_i$. By induction assumption we have line (j).

j) $\vdash C_1 \rightarrow .,,, \rightarrow . C_r \rightarrow . B_k \rightarrow B_i$

Rule δT with $\vdash B_k \rightarrow B_i \rightarrow . B_k \rightarrow B_i$ and (k) gives $\vdash B_k \rightarrow B_i \rightarrow B_i$. Prefix r-times to get line (k*) form $B_k \rightarrow B_i \rightarrow B_i$.

k*) $\vdash (C_1 \rightarrow .,,, \rightarrow . C_r \rightarrow . B_k \rightarrow B_i) \rightarrow . C_1 \rightarrow .,,, \rightarrow . C_r \rightarrow B_i$

Now MP with (j) and (k*) yields what we want for Subcase (3f).

There remain two messy subcases to work through.

Subcase (3g) $h_q \geq d_p$. Assume that $0 < p$ and $0 < q$ so that we have a pure case of only condition (g) failing. We have the following situation where $\langle c_1,\ldots,c_r\rangle = \{d_1,\ldots,d_p,h_1,\ldots,h_q\}$ in numerical order.

$\langle d_1,\ldots,d_p\rangle$ $B_k \rightarrow B_i$
$\langle h_1,\ldots,h_q\rangle$ B_k
$\langle c_1,\ldots,c_r\rangle$ B_i By MP from the two lines immediately above.

The induction assumption gives lines (j) and (k) below. (Remember that a D_p, an H_q, or a C_r is a hypothesis to which the d_p, h_q, or c_r has been prefixed.)

j) $\vdash D_1 \rightarrow .,,, \rightarrow . D_p \rightarrow . B_k \rightarrow B_i$

k) $\vdash H_1 \rightarrow .,,, \rightarrow . H_q \rightarrow B_k$

Assume the following sublemma in which T is as below.

FORMULA T

$D_1 \rightarrow .,,, \rightarrow . D_p \rightarrow . B_k \rightarrow B_i \rightarrow . H_1 \rightarrow .,,, \rightarrow H_q \rightarrow . H_q \rightarrow B_k \rightarrow . C_1 \rightarrow .,,, \rightarrow . C_r \rightarrow B_i$.

Sublemma 1 of IV.5: For D's, H's, and C's as in Subcase (3g), $\vdash$ T.

Because T is: $j \rightarrow . k \rightarrow . C_1 \rightarrow .,,, \rightarrow . C_r \rightarrow B_i$, two uses of MP with lines (j),(k), and T yields what is desired for this subcase.

A proof of Sublemma 1 is complicated. The following remarks on its proof give essentially the basis for an induction that such T formulas are theorems. Readers uninterested in syntactic details are urged to skip these remarks.

As preliminaries observe the following. Because $h_q \geq d_p$ and $c_r = \max(d_p, h_q)$, we have two cases: I and II.

Case I: $c_r = h_q$ and $c_r > d_p$; consequently C_r is H_q. Here $r \neq 1$ because then condition (e) on MP would be violated.

Case II: $c_r = h_q$ and $c_r = d_p$; consequently C_r, H_q, and D_p are the same formula. Here $r \neq 1$ because then B_k and $B_k \rightarrow B_i$ would be the same hypothesis!

We sketch how if $r > 1$ we get $\vdash$ T by inserting predecessors of C_i's.

Case I breaks down into three subcases for c_{r-1} with $r > 1$. The explanation of @theorems below tells why we begin with c_{r-1}.

Subcase (Ii): $c_{r-1} = dp$ and $h_{q-1} < d_p$. Here C_r is Hq while C_{r-1} is D_p.

Subcase (Iii): $c_{r-1} = h_{q-1}$ and $d_p < h_{q-1}$. Here C_r is H_q while C_{r-1} is H_{q-1}.

Subcase (Iiii): $c_{r-1} = d_p = h_{q-1}$. Here C_r is H_q while C_{r-1}, D_p, and H_{q-1} are the same formula.

In Subcase (Ii) proceed as follows.

1) $\vdash B_k \rightarrow B_i \rightarrow . H_q \rightarrow B_k \rightarrow . C_r \rightarrow B_i$ E10 because H_q is C_r.

2) $\vdash H_q \rightarrow B_k \rightarrow . B_k \rightarrow B_i \rightarrow . C_r \rightarrow B_i$ Rest. Perm. on (1).

3) $\vdash (B_k \rightarrow B_i \rightarrow . C_r \rightarrow B_i) \rightarrow . (D_p \rightarrow . B_k \rightarrow B_i) \rightarrow . C_{r-1} \rightarrow . C_r \rightarrow B_i$

Because D_p is C_{r-1} in this subcase line (3) is E10.

4) $\vdash H_q \rightarrow B_k \rightarrow . (D_p \rightarrow . B_k \rightarrow B_i) \rightarrow . C_{r-1} \rightarrow . C_r \rightarrow B_i$

Line (4) is obtained by Trans. from (2),(3).

@ 5) $\vdash (D_p \rightarrow . B_k \rightarrow B_i) \rightarrow . H_q \rightarrow B_k \rightarrow . C_{r-1} \rightarrow . C_r \rightarrow B_i$

Line (5) is obtained by Rest. Perm. on (4).

In Subcase (Iii) begin with (1) of Subcase (Ii). Because in Subcase (Iii) C_{r-1} is H_{q-1}, (2) is the following version of E10.

2) $\vdash (H_q \rightarrow B_k \rightarrow . C_r \rightarrow B_i) \rightarrow . (H_{q-1} \rightarrow . H_q \rightarrow B_k) \rightarrow . C_{r-1} \rightarrow . C_r \rightarrow B_i$

Trans. on (1) and (2) gives (3).

@ 3) $\vdash B_k \rightarrow B_i \rightarrow . (H_{q-1} \rightarrow . H_q \rightarrow B_k) \rightarrow . C_{r-1} \rightarrow . C_r \rightarrow B_i$

In Subcase (Iiii) again start with (1) of Subcase (Ii). In this subcase C_{r-1}, D_p, and H_q are the same formula; so Prefixing on (1) gives (2) below.

2) $\vdash (D_p \rightarrow . B_k \rightarrow B_i) \rightarrow . H_{q-1} \rightarrow H_q \rightarrow B_k \rightarrow . C_r \rightarrow B_i$

By Self-distribution, T64, on the consequent of (2) and Trans. get (3). In (3) remember that H_{q-1} is C_{r-1}.

@ 3) $\vdash (D_p \rightarrow . B_k \rightarrow B_i) \rightarrow . (H_{q-1} \rightarrow . H_q \rightarrow B_k) \rightarrow . C_{r-1} \rightarrow . C_r \rightarrow B_i$.

Case II also breaks down into three subcases when we consider c_{r-1}. In all subcases C_r, D_q, and H_q are the same formula.

Subcase (IIi): $c_{r-1} = d_{p-1}$ and $h_{q-1} < d_{p-1}$. So, C_{r-1} is D_{p-1}.

Subcase (IIii): $c_{r-1} = h_{q-1}$ and $d_{p-1} < h_{q-1}$. So, C_{r-1} is H_{q-1}.

Subcase (IIiii): $c_{r-1} = h_{q-1} = d_{p-1}$. So, not only are C_r, D_p, and H_q the same formula but also C_{r-1}, D_{p-1}, and H_{q-1} are the same formula. Of course, C_r need not be C_{r-1}.

For all three subcases line (1) is the following version of T64. Remember $C_r = D_p = H_q$.

1) $\vdash (D_p \rightarrow . B_k \rightarrow B_i) \rightarrow . H_q \rightarrow B_k \rightarrow . C_r \rightarrow B_i$

In Subcase (IIi), Rest. Perm. on (1) gives (2). Consider the consequent of (2); Prefix D_{p-1} to its antecedent and C_{r-1}, which is D_{p-1}, to its consequent. Use Trans. to get (3). Then use Rest. Perm. on (3) to get (4) which is a @ theorem.

2) $\vdash H_q \rightarrow B_k \rightarrow . (D_p \rightarrow . B_k \rightarrow B_i) \rightarrow . C_r \rightarrow B_i$

3) $\vdash H_q \rightarrow B_k \rightarrow . (D_{p-1} \rightarrow . D_p \rightarrow . B_k \rightarrow B_i) \rightarrow . C_{r-1} \rightarrow . C_r \rightarrow B_i$

@ 4) $\vdash (D_{p-1} \rightarrow . D_p \rightarrow . B_k \rightarrow B_i) \rightarrow . H_q \rightarrow B_k \rightarrow . C_{r-1} \rightarrow . C_r \rightarrow B_i$.

In Subcase (IIii) consider the whole of (1); Prefix H_{q-1} to its antecedent and C_{r-1}, which in this subcase is H_{q-1}, to its consequent. Use Trans. to get @ Theorem (2).

@ 2) $\vdash (D_p \rightarrow . B_k \rightarrow B_i) \rightarrow . (H_{q-1} \rightarrow . H_q \rightarrow B_k) \rightarrow . C_{r-1} \rightarrow . C_r \rightarrow B_i$

In Subcase (IIiii) consider again the whole of (1); Prefix D_{p-1} to its antecedent and H_{q-1}, which in this subcase is D_{p-1}, to its consequent to get (2).

2) $\vdash (D_{p-1} \rightarrow . D_p \rightarrow . B_k \rightarrow B_i) \rightarrow . H_{q-1} \rightarrow . H_q \rightarrow B_k \rightarrow . C_r \rightarrow B_i$

Consider the consequent of (2); Self-distribute the antecedent of (2)'s consequent, viz., H_{q-1}, and then use Trans. with (2) to get @ theorem (3). Here H_{q-1} is also C_{r-1}.

@ 3) $\vdash (D_{p-1} \rightarrow . D_p \rightarrow . B_k \rightarrow B_i) \rightarrow . (H_{q-1} \rightarrow . H_q \rightarrow B_k) \rightarrow . C_{r-1} \rightarrow . C_r \rightarrow B_i$.

Go back and reconsider the six @ theorems. Unless r = 2 none of these @ theorem schemas are formula T. But each is "on its way to being T." To expand any @ theorem into T consider next c_{r-2}. When c_{r-2} is considered, each @ theorem gives rise to three subcases. For instance, reconsider the @ theorem:

$(D_{p-1} \rightarrow . D_p \rightarrow . B_k \rightarrow B_i) \rightarrow H_q \rightarrow B_k \rightarrow . C_{r-1} \rightarrow . C_r \rightarrow B_i$,

from Subcase (IIi). Three subcases are: (i) $c_{r-2} = d_{p-2}$ and $h_{q-1} < d_{p-2}$, (ii) $c_{r-2} = h_{q-1}$ and $d_{p-2} < h_{q-1}$, or (iii) in which $c_{r-2} = d_{p-2} = h_{q-2}$. Then use the @ theorem as the first line in a deduction for each of the corresponding subcases. In the deduction you will Prefix formulas identical with C_{r-2} in the appropriate places to get a formula closer to T. In order to Prefix in the appropriate places you may need to use Rest. Perm. and Self-distribution. You thereby get more @ theorems, or approximations to T. Then consider c_{r-3} for each new @ theorem, then c_{r-4} for the resulting @ theorems and so on. Ultimately T is reached because r is finite. It is too complex notationally to prove that we can move from the c_{r-n} cases to the $c_{r-(n+1)}$ cases. But how we moved from the c_r to the c_{r-1} cases should have been instructive. So, let these heuristic remarks suffice as a proof for Sublemma 1.

Let us now return to the proof of Lemma 1 by considering its last subcase, viz., Subcase (3f). Assume that the first three restrictions on MP, viz., (e),(f), and (g), hold. But now assume that B_k has the form $F \longrightarrow G$. We have the same induction assumptions (j) and (k) as in Subcase (3g), except that we can now write them as below.

j) $\vdash D_1 \longrightarrow .,,, \longrightarrow .D_p \longrightarrow .F \longrightarrow G \longrightarrow B_i$

k) $\vdash H_1 \longrightarrow .,,, \longrightarrow .H_q \longrightarrow .F \longrightarrow G$

So, again, if we can show that T is a theorem schema we can prove $C_1 \longrightarrow .,,, \longrightarrow .C_r \longrightarrow B_i$ as in Subcase (3g). Again we only sketch how we can work towards getting $\vdash$ T. Observe that in this Subcase (3h) we have $h_q < d_p$ because condition (g) holds; and since $c_r = \max(h_q, d_p)$ we have $c_r = d_p$. Consequently, formula C_r is formula D_p. Consider a second sublemma.

Sublemma 2 for Lemma 1 of IV.5: For D's, H's, and C's as needed for Subcase (3h), $\vdash$ T with B_k as $F \longrightarrow G$.

Again we make only heuristic remarks by way of proof. But as opposed to Subcase (3g) we have only one main case because we have ruled out $c_r = h_q$. Let us label this one main case III. Nevertheless III breaks down into three subcases for $r > 1$. (We do not have $r = 1$ because then restriction (f) on MP would be violated.)

Subcase (IIIi): $c_{r-1} = d_p$ and $h_q < d_{p-1}$. Here, C_{r-1} is D_{p-1}.

Subcase (IIIii): $c_{r-1} = h_q$ and $d_{p-1} < h_q$. Here C_{r-1} is H_q.

Subcase (IIIiii): $c_{r-1} = d_{p-1} = h_q$. C_{r-1}, D_{p-1}, and H_q are identical.

Remember that in all three above subcases C_r is D_p.

The deduction of a @ theorem for each subcase has the following (1) as a first line, which is obtained from the following versions of T1 and T42.

$(F \longrightarrow G \longrightarrow .D_p \longrightarrow B_i) \longrightarrow .F \longrightarrow G \longrightarrow .C_r \longrightarrow B_i$ T1

$(D_p \longrightarrow .F \longrightarrow G \longrightarrow B_i) \longrightarrow .F \longrightarrow G \longrightarrow .D_p \longrightarrow B_i$ T42

1) $\vdash (D_p \rightarrow . F \rightarrow G \rightarrow B_i) \rightarrow . F \rightarrow G \rightarrow . C_r \rightarrow B_i$

In Subcase (IIIi), apply Rest. Perm. to (1) to get (2).

2) $\vdash F \rightarrow G \rightarrow . (D_p \rightarrow . F \rightarrow G \rightarrow B_i) \rightarrow . C_r \rightarrow B_i$

Prefix D_{p-1}, which is here C_{r-1}, to both antecedent and consequent of the consequent of (2). Use Trans. to get (3).

3) $\vdash F \rightarrow G \rightarrow . (D_{p-1} \rightarrow . D_p \rightarrow . F \rightarrow G \rightarrow B_i) \rightarrow . C_{r-1} \rightarrow C_r \rightarrow B_i$

Apply Rest. Perm. to (3) to get @ theorem (4).

@ 4) $\vdash (D_{p-1} \rightarrow . D_p \rightarrow . F \rightarrow G \rightarrow B_i) \rightarrow . F \rightarrow G \rightarrow . C_{r-1} \rightarrow . C_r \rightarrow B_i$.

In Subcase (IIIii), Prefix H_q, which is here C_{r-1}, to both antecedent and consequent of the consequent of (1). Then use Trans. with the result to get @ theorem (2).

@ 2) $\vdash (D_p \rightarrow . F \rightarrow G \rightarrow B_i) \rightarrow . (H_q \rightarrow . F \rightarrow G) \rightarrow . C_{r-1} \rightarrow . C_r \rightarrow B_i$.

In Subcase (IIIiii), consider the whole of (1); Prefix D_{p-1}, which is here also H_q, to both its antecedent and consequent to get (2).

2) $\vdash (D_{p-1} \rightarrow . D_p \rightarrow . F \rightarrow G \rightarrow B_i) \rightarrow . H_q \rightarrow . F \rightarrow G \rightarrow . C_r \rightarrow B_i$

Consider the consequent of this subcases' (2). Self-distribute H_q, which is here also C_{r-1}, through the consequent of (2). Use Trans. to get @ theorem (3).

@ 3) $\vdash (D_{p-1} \rightarrow . D_p \rightarrow . F \rightarrow G \rightarrow B_i) \rightarrow . (H_q \rightarrow . F \rightarrow G) \rightarrow . C_{r-1} \rightarrow . C_r \rightarrow B_i$.

As in the (3g) subcases the @ theorems provide a basis for going on to a proof in general that $\vdash$ T. So, let the preceding remarks suffice as a proof of Sublemma 2 and, hence, let us take Lemma 1 as proved.

It is interesting to note that Kron shows that a system P has a similar deduction theorem. Kron characterizes P as our version of E with $A \rightarrow A$ replacing E8. Belnap originally characterized P on p.81 of his monograph as, in effect, our version of E with $A \rightarrow A \rightarrow B \rightarrow B$, viz., T33, replacing E8.Don't take Kron as intending to characterize P as Belnap did. We are not able to get T33 from what, in effect, is Ackermann's Π' without rules γ and δ. In effect, Kron gave as system P the system **T** of ticket entailment which is given on p. 340 of Anderson and Belnap [1975]. On p. 48 a result of Chidgey that $A \rightarrow A \rightarrow A \rightarrow A$, an instance of T33, is not a theorem of the pure implication fragment of system T is proved. On p. 375 Meyer's result that T is a conservative extension of its implicational fragment is reported. So, we can conclude that T is not the system which we want because it does not have $\Box A \rightarrow A$ as a theorem for our defined sense of $\Box A$. Unfortunately, at the time of this writing, February 1977, the author does not have a proof that E8 cannot be derived in system P, where P is the system just like E except that T33 replaces E8. If E8 cannot be derived in P we do not want P because we want E8 and $\Box A \wedge \Box B \rightarrow \Box(A \wedge B)$. If E8 can be obtained in P, then we want P for the same reasons for which we want E. So, we do not give any especial consideration to system P.

Before illustrating use of Kron's Deduction Theorem for E, let us note with Kron that system R also has such a deduction theorem except that for system R restriction (g) on MP is not needed. Kron points out that Moh Shaw-Kwei had essentially obtained these results for R in [1950].

In the following proof of T68 by use of Kron's Deduction Theorem we see how all of the premisses are used. T68 is sometimes called "Replacement of the Middle."

T68: $D \rightarrow B \rightarrow .(A \rightarrow .B \rightarrow C) \rightarrow .A \rightarrow .D \rightarrow C$

Proof

1) $\langle 1 \rangle$, $D \rightarrow B$	Hyp.
2) $\langle 2 \rangle$, $A \rightarrow .B \rightarrow C$	Hyp.
3) $\langle 3 \rangle$, A	Hyp.
4) $\langle 4 \rangle$, D	Hyp.
5) $\langle 2,3 \rangle$, $B \rightarrow C$	MP (2),(3)
6) $\langle 1,4 \rangle$, B	MP (1),(4)
7) $\langle 1,2,3,4 \rangle$, C	MP (5),(6).

T68 now follows by Kron's Deduction Theorem.

The first three of the following four theorems are easily proved by use of Kron's Deduction Theorem. It helps to use T47 in a proof of T72.

T69: $C \rightarrow D \rightarrow .(A \rightarrow .B \rightarrow C) \rightarrow .A \rightarrow .B \rightarrow C$ Replacement of the Third,

T70: $(A \rightarrow B \rightarrow C) \rightarrow .A \rightarrow .D \rightarrow B \rightarrow .D \rightarrow C$ Prefixing in the Consequent.

T71: $(A \rightarrow .B \rightarrow C) \rightarrow .A \rightarrow .C \rightarrow D \rightarrow .B \rightarrow D$ Suffixing in the Consequent.

T72: $A \rightarrow B \rightarrow .A \rightarrow {\sim}B \rightarrow {\sim}A$.

Let us close by noting how Kron's restrictions block an attempt to prove Factor, viz., $A \rightarrow B \rightarrow .A \wedge C \rightarrow .B \wedge C$.

Proof Attempt

1) $\langle 1 \rangle$, $A \rightarrow B$	Hyp.
2) $\langle 2 \rangle$, $A \wedge C$	Hyp.
3) $A \wedge C \rightarrow A$	E1
4) $A \wedge C \rightarrow C$	E2
5) $\langle 2 \rangle$, A	MP (2),(3)
6) $\langle 2 \rangle$, C	MP (2),(4)
7) $\langle 2 \rangle$, $A \wedge C$	Adj. (5),(6)
8) $\langle 1,2 \rangle$, B	MP (1),(5).

We cannot, because of Kron's restrictions on Adjunction, conjoin lines (6) and (8). These restrictions can be appreciated in this case. The prefix of line (6) tells us that C has been obtained solely from the hypothesis A C. The prefix of line (8) tells us that we needed both $A \rightarrow B$ and $A \wedge C$ to get B. Thus, we should not say that $A \rightarrow B$ entails that we can get $B \wedge C$ from $A \wedge C$; we should only assert $(A \rightarrow B) \wedge (A \wedge C) \rightarrow . B\ C$.

Exercises IV.5

1. Explain how Kron-derivations require use of all hypotheses.
2. Explain how Kron's restrictions block an attempt to prove Exportation.
3. Can we assert: If $\vdash_{E} A \rightarrow B$, then there is a Kron-derivation of B from A?
4. Show that if we have aKron-derivation of $A_n \rightarrow B$ from $A_1, \ldots, A_{n-1}$, the prefix of $A_n \rightarrow B$ is $\langle 1, \ldots, n-1 \rangle$.
5. Prove Lemma 2.
6. Prove theorems 69 through 72.
7. Show that the Kron restriction $h_q < d_p$ on MP blocks an attempt to prove <u>via</u> his deduction theorem the special axiom for system EM: $\overline{A \rightarrow B} \rightarrow . A \rightarrow B \rightarrow . A \rightarrow B$.
8. Consider E8 in the form: $(A \rightarrow A) \wedge (B \rightarrow B) \rightarrow C \rightarrow C$, but not as an axiom, i.e., consider it as a hypothesis. In E do we have $E8^* \leftrightarrow . \Box A \wedge \Box B \rightarrow \Box (A \wedge B)$ where E8* is E8 in the form just above? Let E8 have the form $(A \rightarrow A) \wedge (B \rightarrow B) \rightarrow A \wedge B \rightarrow A \wedge B$; in this form do we have $E8 \leftrightarrow \Box A \wedge \Box B \rightarrow \Box (A \wedge B)$?

IV.6 A.R. Anderson's "subscripting" relevance protecting natural deductions, Fitch style versions of systems, system FE.

This section presupposes some familiarity with the Fitch subordinate proof natural deduction technique. See Fitch's [1952] or [1974] or any of several texts such as Thomason's [1970] or Leblanc's and Wisdom's [1972] for an exposition of this technique. See especially Anderson's and Belnap's [1975] for exposition of the Fitch style systems. Fitch style systems are labelled FX where X is replaced with the usual name for the system. We here present A.R. Anderson's so-called subscripting requirements for relevance preservation between hypotheses and conclusions by presenting system FE. We use primarily Anderson's [1960a]. The Fitch version of the pure implication fragment of E is presented in Anderson's and Belnap's [1962b]. Now, the Fitch style version of E, viz., FE, is presented in fragments in Anderson's and Belnap's [1975] on pp. 23,108, 271-74, and conveniently gathered together in 23.5. For typographical reasons, we use sets of numbers as prefixes to lines of derivations rather than subscripts on formulas as did Anderson. We submit that Anderson's use of subscripts and restrictions on derivations are the best devices for showing that for system E and $A \longrightarrow B$ is a thesis only if B is obtained in the best formal way from A. We let Anderson speak for himself and let his method show us that in E we get $A \longrightarrow B$ only if we get B from A without regard to the truth or modal status of A or B.

Anderson wrote the following on p. 203 of his [1960a].

> In the system E, which will constitute our principal topic, we intend to interpret the arrow in such a way that $A \longrightarrow B$ shall be true if and only if B "depends on the logical content of A." . . . What we shall do in this paper is to propose an explication of the notion "depends on the logical content of" which will be sufficiently precise to enable us to prove a completeness theorem for E: $A \longrightarrow B$ will be provable in E just in case B does depend on the logical content of A (in the sense to be explained). . . . Our aim, roughly speaking, is to alter the subordinate proof technique in such a way as to keep track of all the hypotheses which are actually <u>used</u> as premisses in the application of rules leading to a proposition A, and then to restrict the introduction rule for implication (which will be called "entailment introduction") in such a way that $A \longrightarrow B$ will be said to follow from a proof of B on the hypothesis A, only if A is used in arriving at B.

These ideas are given precision in the following natural deduction system labelled FE.

EXPOSITION OF SYSTEM FE

The prefixing rule: In constructing a proof or derivation, each new hypothesis receives a unit class $\{k\}$ as a prefix where k is a non-zero natural number. Do not assign two hypotheses the same prefix. Assign prefixes to hypotheses by assigning $\{1\}$ to the first hypothesis cited and then proceed to assign prefixes to hypotheses in standard numerical order. I.e., $\{2\}$ to the second hypothesis and so on.

In the following rules x,y, and z denote classes of numbers used as prefixes. We call them relevance markers. They may denote the empty class on occasion.

R1. Repetition (Rep) If x A is a line of a subproof SP, x A may be written as a later line of SP.

R2. Reiteration (Reit) If x A is of the form x $C \rightarrow D$ and x A is a line of subproof SP and SP' is a subproof subordinate to SP, x A may be written as a line of SP'.

The restriction of Reit to wffs. of the $C \rightarrow D$ form, together with R3, prevents having a non-entailment, eg., a zdf., entail an entailment. It helps in proofs about natural deductions if we regard a reiterated formula as reiterated into any subproof SP" between the one in which we want it,viz.,SP', and the one from which it is taken, viz., SP, if SP" is subordinate to SP.

R3. Entailment Introduction ($\rightarrow$ I) From a subproof SP_n of y B on hypothesis $\{k\}$ A, infer as a line of the subproof immediately subordinate to SP_n, viz., SP_{n-1}, y- $\{k\}$ $A \rightarrow B$ provided $k \in y$.

The provision that $k \in y$ is a requirement that $\{k\}$ A be used to get y B. We use y- $\{k\}$ to indicate that we are no longer using hypothesis $\{k\}$ A.

R4. Entailment Elimination ($\rightarrow$ E) From x A and y $(A \rightarrow B)$, infer $x \cup y$ B.

R5. Conjunction Introduction ($\wedge$ I) From x A and x B, infer x $A \wedge B$.

Note that the reference markers must be the same for A and B. We are familiar with, even if not totally reconciled to, such restrictions on Adjunction in starring-derivations and in Kron-deductions.

R6. Conjunction Elimination ($\wedge$ E) From x $(A \wedge B)$, infer x A, y B, or both.

R7. Distribution (Dist) From x $(A \wedge (B \vee C))$, infer x $((A \wedge B) \vee C)$.

Distribution seems a bit out of place as a pr[illegible]tive natural deduction rule. Nevertheless, we want to be [illegible]e to deduce $A \wedge (B \vee C) \rightarrow .(A \wedge B) \vee C$. Our attempts to deduce t[illegible] run afoul of the restrictions on Reiteration. nonetheless Dist. is an acceptable principle. So, let us not be too upset that we make it primitive rather than deriving it. See 23.3 of Anderson's and Belnap's [1975] for similar observations about Distribution.

R8. Negation Introduction (~I) From a subproof SP_n with hypothesis {k} A and lines x B and y ~B, infer as the next line of the subproof to which it is immediately subordinate, viz., SP_{n-1}, (x∪y)- {k} ~A, provided k∈x and k∈y.

The provision that k∈x and k∈y requires that both sides of the contradiction come from A.

R9. Negation Elimination (~E) From x ~B and y (A→B), infer x∪y ~A. We label (~E) MT for <u>Modus Tollens</u>.

The name for R9 is not the standard use of "Negation Elimination" in natural deduction theory. R9 is, of course, <u>Modus Tollens</u>. As in the case of Distribution, we are tempted to think that <u>Modus Tollens</u> should be a derived rule. Unfortunately, we cannot derive it. Still, we should accept it as a paradigm of a good inference. Also we can regard accepting MT as accepting an axiom for Contraposition just as we regarded accepting R7 as accepting Distribution as an axiom

R10. Double Negation Introduction (~~I) From x A, infer x ~~A.

R11. Double Negation Elimination (~~E) From x ~~A, infer x A.

In FE A v B is defined in the usual way as ~(~A∧~B). So, system FE has (v I) and (v E) as derived rules. We leave their derivations as exercises.

R12. Disjunction Introduction (v I) From x A, infer x (A v B).

R13. Disjunction Elimination (v E) From x (A→C), x (B→C), and y (A v B), infer x∪y C.

We'll find that (v E) is not as useful as we would like because A→C and B→C need to have the same reference markers.

We say that A is a theorem of FE if there is a proof of A from no hypotheses.

END OF THE EXPOSITION OF SYSTEM FE

As our first theorem, we note that E is contained in FE.

Theorem I of IV.6: if $\vdash_{E}$ A, then $\vdash_{FE}$ A.

We have MP from R4 and Adj. from R5. So a proof of Theorem I is obtained by showing that all E axioms are theorems of FE. We will only show how E8 is an FE theorem to illustrate the techniques of FE. (No reference marker means the null class.)

1	$\{1\}\ (A \rightarrow A) \wedge (B \rightarrow B) \rightarrow C$	Hyp
2	$\{2\}\ A$	Hyp
3	$\{2\}\ A$	Rep 2
4	$A \rightarrow A$	$\rightarrow$ I 2,3
5	$\{3\}\ B$	Hyp
6	$\{3\}\ B$	Rep 5
7	$B \rightarrow B$	$\rightarrow$ I 5,6
8	$(A \rightarrow A) \wedge (B \rightarrow B)$	$\wedge$ I 4,7
9	$\{1\}\ C$	$\rightarrow$ E 8,1
10	$(A \rightarrow A) \wedge (B \rightarrow B) \rightarrow C \rightarrow C$	$\rightarrow$ I 1 through 9

Observe that the prefix on the first hypothesis in the above proof of E8 could have contained any number k and we would still have had the null class as reference marker by line 10. Let these considerations suffice as hints on how to prove our first lemma.

Lemma 1 of IV.6: In an FE subproof, E theorems with the null class a reference marker may be used as a line of the proof.

We label the listing of an E theorem "Theorem Introduction" or Th. Intro. . We call an FE deduction in which an E theorem is listed by citing Th. Intro. a <u>quasi proof</u>. When the goal of an FE derivation is to end up with an FE theorem we may call it a deduction.

We now want to sketch the main lines of Anderson's argument that FE is included in E. We will spare many of the details.

Theorem II of IV.6: If $\vdash_{FE}$ A, then $\vdash_{E}$ A.

By way of proof we make only the following remarks. There are two main cases. The first case occurs when neither R3 nor R8 were used. The second case occurs when either R3 or R8 is used. If neither R3 nor R8 were used and we have $\vdash_{FE}$ A, we have a proof of A with no hypotheses and no subordinate proofs. This single proof of A is an E proof because all the other rules of FE are derived E rules. So, the only interesting case occurs when R3 or R8 are used. Anderson proves the following theorem which we label a lemma. Its statement is complicated.

Lemma 2 of IV.6: Let P be a proof or quasi-proof in FE, let SP_n be a rightmost subproof of P with lines $y_1\ B_1, \ldots, y_m\ B_m$ of which the first line is the hypothesis $\{k\}$ A, let SP_{n-1} be the subproof to which SP_n is an immediate subproof, and let D be the formula of SP_{n-1} obtained by use of SP_n. Let $z_i\ C_i$ be $y_i\ B_i$ or $y_i - \{k\}\ (A \rightarrow B_i)$ according as k is not or is in y_i, and let $SP_n{}'$ be the result of replacing SP_n by the sequence of lines $z_i\ C_i$. Under these conditions E theorems can be introduced into $SP_n{}'$ to form $SP_n{}''$ and $SP_n{}''$ can be placed into SP_{n-1} itself to fill the lines taken by subordinate proof SP_n in SP_{n-1} so that SP_{n-1} down through D has now no subproof where SP_n was and there is an FE quasi-proof of D using only R4,R5, and lines repeated into the SP_n" lines from the part of SP_{n-1} above the line at which SP_n started.

The proof remarks for Lemma 2 sketch how to give an inductive proof that for SP_n' there is an SP_n" such that each line of SP_n" is a line of SP_{n-1} prior to the start of SP_n, a theorem of E, or a consequence of predecessors by R4 (MP) or R5 (Adj.). Before we get into any details of the induction, let us note how the induction gives Lemma 2 and how Lemma 2 gives Theorem II. The D proved by use of SP_n is going to be $y_m - \{k\}\ (A \rightarrow B_m)$ if rule ($\rightarrow$ I) is used while D is going to be a $y_h \cup y_j\ \sim A$ if rule ($\sim$I) is used. If it were rule ($\rightarrow$ I) which has been used, then the last line of SP_n" is already what we want. If it were rule ($\sim$I) which has been used, then SP_n" has a line $y_h - \{k\}\ (A \rightarrow B_h)$ and a line $y_j - \{k\}\ (A \rightarrow \sim B_j)$. A version of T72 can now be introduced which yields, by two uses of R4, $\sim A$ with appropriate reference markers. Lemma 2 gives Theorem II because it shows how rightmost subproofs can be eliminated beginning with the uppermost one on the right. There are only finitely many subproofs; so we ultimately get an assumptionless proof, a quasi-proof, consisting of E theorems and consequents by R4 (MP) and R5 (Adj.), viz., a proof of an E theorem.

Let us now sketch how to give an inductive proof on the $y_i B_i$ that there is such an SP_n". The basis case is taken care of because $z_1\ C_1$ is the E theorem $A \rightarrow A$. Assume each $z_g\ C_g$, $g < i$, is a reiterated formula from SP_{n-1}, an E theorem, or a consequence by R4 or R5 from earlier members of SP_n' together with theorems of E. At the inductive step, the twelve primitive FE rules give twelve cases of $z_i\ C_i$ to consider. We ignore most of the cases. We are certainly entitled to ignore ($\rightarrow$ I) and ($\sim$I) because we are considering a rightmost subproof. Reit. can be ignored because there is nothing to proof of a line obtained by Reit. . We consider, in some detail, only the case that R4 ($\rightarrow$ E) has been used to get $y_i\ B_i$. If R4 has been used to get $y_i\ B_i$, there are four subcases because $y_i\ B_i$ was obtained from a $y_g\ (B_j \rightarrow B_i)$ and $y_j\ B_j$ with $g < i$ and $j < i$. There are four ways k can be in or out of y_g and y_j. We characterize the subcases but leave it as an exercise to uncover which E theorems need to be introduced to get $z_i\ C_i$ from $z_g\ C_g$ and $z_j\ C_j$.

Subcase (R4a) $k \in y_g$ and $k \in y_j$. So, we have the following.

$z_g\ C_g$ is: $y_g - \{k\}\ A \rightarrow .B_j \rightarrow B_i$

$z_j\ C_j$ is: $y_j - \{k\}\ A \rightarrow B_j$

$z_i\ C_i$ is: $y_g \cup y_j - \{k\}\ A \rightarrow B_i$

Subcase (R4b) $k \in y_j$ but $k \notin y_g$. So, we have the following.

z_g C_g is: y_g $B_j \rightarrow B_i$

z_j C_j is: $y_j - \{k\}$ $A \rightarrow B_j$

z_i C_i is: $y_g \cup y_j - \{k\}$ $A \rightarrow B_i$

For subcase (R4c), and for an analogous subcase in the treatment of R9, viz., ($\sim$E), the following sublemma is helpful.

> Sublemma 1 of IV.6: In a rightmost subproof SP_n as characterized in Lemma 2, if $k \notin y_i$ then E theorems can be added to SP_n so that y_i $\Box B_i$ is obtained from y_i B_i by using only R4 and R5.

In regard to a proof of the sublemma, observe that such a y_i B_i has been reiterated into SP_n because $k \notin y_i$. Consequently, B has the $C \rightarrow D$ form. Use of T53 will get y_i $B_i \rightarrow B_i \rightarrow B_i$, Viz., $\Box B_i$.

Subcase (R4c) $k \in y_g$ but $k \notin y_j$. So, we have the following.

z_g C_g is: $y_g - \{k\}$ $A \rightarrow .B_j \rightarrow B_i$

z_j C_j is: y_j B_j Remember that B_j has the $C \rightarrow D$ form.

z_i C_i is: $y_g \cup y_j - \{k\}$ $A \rightarrow B_i$

Use of the sublemma gives y_i $B_i \rightarrow B_i \rightarrow B_i$ which with rT62 helps give $A \rightarrow B_i$ with the appropriate reference marker.

Subcase (R4d) k belongs to neither y_g nor y_j. Here z_i C_i is simply y_i B_i which is an R4 consequence of y_g $B_j \rightarrow B_i$ and y_j B_j with $y_i = y_g \cup y_j$.

If we consider R5, we have two subcases, viz., $k \in y_j$ and $k \notin y_j$. But let us not pursue examination of cases any further. The interested reader may consult Anderson's paper for hints on how to handle the remaining cases. Of more interest is use of this natural deduction technique. The technique serves to block natural ways of trying to prove two non-theorems of E, viz., MD and a formula which we will call the Maksimowa formula. Of course, failure of a natural deduction does not show that the formula, which failed to be proved, is a non-theorem. Nevertheless such a failure helps us see why the formula is not a theorem.

Let us see how an attempt to prove $A \wedge (\sim A \vee B) \rightarrow B$ is blocked. The attempted proof uses the or-elimination technique. But, since one half of the attempted proof contains two violations, we present only the half which contains the violations.

1	$\{1\}\ A \wedge (\sim A \vee B)$	Hyp
2	$\{1\}\ A \wedge \sim A \vee A \wedge B$	Obtainable from (1) by Dist.
3	$\{2\}\ A \wedge \sim A$	Hyp for ($\vee$ E)
4	$\{3\}\ \sim B$	Hyp for R8, <u>reductio</u> hyp.
5	$\{2\}\ A \wedge \sim A$	Reit3 WRONG!
6	$\{2\}\ A$	$\wedge$E 5
7	$\{2\}\ \sim A$	$\wedge$E 5
	$\{3\}\ \sim\sim B$	($\sim$I) 4 - 7 WRONG! $3 \notin \{2\}$
9	$\{3\}\ B$	($\sim\sim$E) on 8

First we see how the restriction on Reit saves us from reasoning from "just any old assumption" once we have made the <u>reductio</u> assumption of B. To be sure, we have assumed $A \wedge \sim A$. Nevertheless, even if we have assumed $A \wedge \sim A$, it is not clear that we have assumed that it can be used in any argument. If we had assumed A A as a principle of logic we would have assumed that it can be used in any argument. But in general we cannot use our assumptions can be used in any of our reasoning. For instance, if we assume that we have a contradiction in our political beliefs there is no reason for thinking that such a contradiction can be used as a premiss in our physical reasoning. Second we can see how the restriction on ($\sim$I) saves us from indicating that we got a contradiction from $\sim B$ when we did not use $\sim B$ in getting A and $\sim A$.

We call: $(A \rightarrow . B \rightarrow C) \wedge (B \rightarrow . A \vee C) \rightarrow . B \rightarrow C$, Maksimowa's formula; it serves to distinguish system E from system NR. Let us see how a natural attempt to prove it is blocked.

1	$\{1\}\ A \rightarrow . B \rightarrow C$	Hyp and $\wedge$E
2	$\{1\}\ B \rightarrow . A \vee C$	
3	$\{2\}\ B$	Hyp
4	$\{1\}\ B \rightarrow . A \vee C$	Reit 2
5	$\{1,2\}\ A \vee C$	($\rightarrow$E) 3,4
6	$\{3\}\ A$	Hyp for ($\vee$ E)
7	$\{1\}\ A \rightarrow . B \rightarrow C$	Reit 1
8	$\{1,3\}\ B \rightarrow C$	($\rightarrow$ E) 6,7
9	$\{2\}\ B$	Reit 3 WRONG!
10	$\{1,2,3\}\ C$	($\rightarrow$ E) 8,9

Again we see how the restriction on Reit prevents us from using an assumption in any argument made "after we make the assumption" unless we have assumed that it is a logical truth, viz., an entailment.

With these remarks we leave system E for awhile to consider systems R and NR.

Exercises IV.6

1. Show that E9 through E15 are FE theorems.
2. Prove Sublemma 1.
3 Complete the reasoning for some subcases for the induction step in Lemma 2.

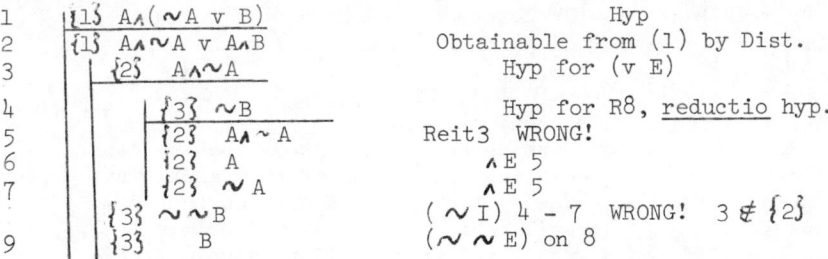

IV.7 Systems R and NR ($R^{\Box}$), proof of Maksimowa's formula in NR, argument for E instead of NR, matrices $\mathfrak{N}$r and Ackermann's $\mathfrak{A}$.

A main goal of this section is to present the systems R and NR. These systems are developed enough so that we can make a case for accepting E instead of one of them as the system for entailment. Actually the system R has not been offered as a system for entailment; so we develop R primarily to show its difference from E and to facilitate development of NR. System NR has been offered as a candidate for the system of entailment; see Meyer's [1966],[1968a], and Meyer's and Routley's [1972b]. We develop NR enough to show that is has a Maksimowa formula: $(A \Longrightarrow .B \Longrightarrow C) \wedge (B \Longrightarrow .A \vee C) \Longrightarrow .B \Longrightarrow C$, as a thesis, where $\Longrightarrow$ is the connective in NR for representing entailment. In IV.11 we will find that the Maksimowa formula using the $\rightarrow$ of E is not a theorem of E. So, we make a case that the Maksimowa formula should not be a thesis about entailment. We also argue that NR's use of a defined connective for entailment is less desirable than E's use of a primitive connective for entailment. Nevertheless, we must admit that NR has many pleasing features. At the close we use matrices to call attention to some nice properties of NR.

System R is obtainable from system E by adding to E an unrestricted Law of Assertion as an axiom schema. Let us call this schema R1.

R1: $A \rightarrow .A \rightarrow B \rightarrow B$

We retain the labelling of E axioms and the theorems of E from previous sections. We label with R theorems whose proof requires R1. Hopefully, the context will make it clear whether we are discussing formulas with E's $\rightarrow$ or the $\rightarrow$ of some system other than E such as R.

Of course, a version of R1 is: $A \rightarrow .A \rightarrow A \rightarrow A$, which is $A \rightarrow \Box A$ as $\Box A$ is defined for system E in IV.2. Hence, our modal distinctions in E are lost when we extend E to R. In E we could distinguish entailments from many non-entailments by virtue of modality. T53 told us that an $A \rightarrow B$ is equivalent to $\Box(A \rightarrow B)$. But in general an A is not equivalent to $\Box A$. In particular, we will see in IV.11 that no zdf. thesis of E is equivalent to an assertion of its necessity. We may regard E as telling us that all formulas equivalent to an assertion of their necessity are, in effect, entailments because they are thus entailment equivalent to an entailment. Because not all formulas are equivalent to an assertion of their necessity in E, there is a significant distinction in E between entailments and non-entailments. However, this distinction is lost in R because with R1 and T33 we get R2.

R2: $A \leftrightarrow . A \rightarrow A \rightarrow A$

We certainly do not want to admit that every formula is equivalent to an entailent. But if the $\rightarrow$ in R2 is not supposed to symbolize entailment, R2 may not be too objectionable.

Citation of T53 gives occasion to observe that T53 reveals both a merit and a demerit of E. The merit is that we have to use the $\rightarrow$ of E to represent if___then___ sentences which are necessarily true in the sense of 'necessity' definable in E. Under pain of distorting what we symbolize, we are forced to use the $\rightarrow$ of E to symbolize if___then___ sentences which are at least logical truths. This is a merit because we are trying to discover an $\rightarrow$ to symbolize the best kind of logical if___then___. Of course, the corresponding demerit is that we cannot use the $\rightarrow$ of E to symbolize non-necessary if___then___ sentences; let alone non-logical ones. But because of the paradoxes of material and strict implication, it is desirable to have a better representation for many if___then___ sentences than either $\supset$ or ⥽. In particular, it would be desirable to have an $\rightarrow$ for representing if___then___'s which did not have such undesirable features as: $A \rightarrow . B \rightarrow A$, $\sim A \rightarrow . A \rightarrow B$, $A \wedge \sim A \rightarrow B$, and $A \rightarrow . B \vee \sim B$. The $\rightarrow$ of R has these desirable features. See Meyer's dissertation [1966] pp. 74-94 and Barker's [1969] for arguments on the value of R's $\rightarrow$ for representing a relevance preserving non-logical if___then___. After a suggestion of J. Bacon, R's $\rightarrow$ has been called relevant implication rather than entailment. So, the demerit of E is a merit in R while the merit of E becomes a demerit of R. R's $\rightarrow$ may be best for symbolizing many non-necessary if___then___'s, but unsuitable for symbolizing necessary if___then___'s and hence unsuitable for symbolizing entailment. So, E and R are not competitors. On the contrary, we want both the $\rightarrow$ of E and the $\rightarrow$ of R. At least there is a <u>prima facie</u> case that we should have something like the $\rightarrow$ of R over and above strict and material implication. The system NR developed below is a very, very tempting suggestion on how to have both!

But before presenting NR, we prove two more theorems of R, note how R could collapse into classical logic, and state some theorems about R. System R has unrestricted Permutation (Perm).

R3: $(A \rightarrow . B \rightarrow C) \rightarrow . B \rightarrow . A \rightarrow C$

Start a proof of R3 with the following version of R1.

1) $B \rightarrow . B \rightarrow C \rightarrow C$

Prefixing on the consequent of (1) and Trans. gives (2)

2) $B \rightarrow . (A \rightarrow . B \rightarrow C) \rightarrow . A \rightarrow C$

Now Rest. Perm. on (2) gives (3).

3) $(A \rightarrow . B \rightarrow C) \rightarrow . B \rightarrow . A \rightarrow C$.

Use Permutation and Importation on R3 to get R4 which gives what we could call an unrestricted rule δ for R. (See IV.1 for a discussion of rule $\mathcal{E}$.)

R4: $A \wedge (B \rightarrow . A \rightarrow C) \rightarrow . B \rightarrow C$

Note that with Permutation the addition of $B \rightarrow . A \rightarrow A$ as an axiom schema would collapse R into classical sentential logic. By use of Perm we would get $A \rightarrow . B \rightarrow A$. As can be seen on p.82 of Thomason's [1970] $A \rightarrow . B \rightarrow A$, Contraposition, and Self-distribution (T64) with MP would give all classical sentential logic theorems with $\rightarrow$ replacing $\supset$.

Theorems I through of IV.1, for system E, can readily be altered to apply to system R. We state here only the content of theorems I and II.

Theorem I of IV.7: The zdf. theses of R are exactly the classical tautologies and the fde. theses are exactly the TE entailments.

Of course, it has to be argued by those who advance R as being a system for representing some non-logical if___then___'s that the fde. fragment should be exactly the TE entailments.

We can also conclude from the fact that R is an axiomatic extension of E and Theorem II of IV.4 that R has an Entailment Theorem. But let us rush on to presentsystem NR because it is a competitor with E for being the entailment system. We will get an "Entailment Theorem" as a lemma about NR.

We can obtain NR by augmenting the language of E with a primitive $\Box$ sign for necessity, by adding the following four axiom schemas to those of R, and the following axiom generating rule NR5. Our axiomatization is adapted from Meyer's and Routley's [1973a] It seems that R. Meyer is the inventor of NR and that he first presented it in his [1966]. In Anderson's and Belnap's [1975], NR is relabelled as $R^{\Box}$. There is no claim that the following is a set of independent axioms. Let us label these new axioms with NR and theorems proved by use of them with TNR.

NR1: $\Box A \rightarrow A$
NR2: $\Box A \rightarrow \Box \Box A$
NR3 $\Box (A \rightarrow B) \rightarrow . \Box A \rightarrow \Box B$
NR4: $\Box A \wedge \Box B \rightarrow . \Box (A \wedge B)$
NR5: If A is an axiom, then $\Box$A is an axiom.

At first glance, NR5 seems inelegant because it gives infinitely many axioms by use of our natural language rather than by the efficient device of presenting a schema. However, for the purpose of proving theorems about NR, NR5 is very desirable because it makes NR an axiomatic extension of E. Thus by Theorem II of IV.4 we have an entailment theorem for NR as a lemma. Because the $\rightarrow$ of R rather than the $\Rightarrow$ of NR is the connective in the lemma, it may be more appropriate to talk of "a relevant implication theorem" than of " an entailment theorem." Nevertheless, we use 'entailment.'

Lemma 1 of IV.7: Let 'starring-derivation' be defined as in IV.4. If there is a NR starring derivation of B from $A_1,\ldots,A_n$, then $\vdash_{NR} A_1,\ldots,A_n \rightarrow B$.

It should be emphasized that the $\rightarrow$ of NR is the $\rightarrow$ of system R. NR's primitive $\rightarrow$ is not NR's symbol for representing entailment. We can regard NR as adding to R what was lost in the move from E to R, viz., a S4-ish modal subsystem. As a result of having $\Box$ in NR we can distinguish two implication signs.

Definition of $A \Rightarrow B$ in NR

$A \Rightarrow B =_{df} \Box(A \rightarrow B)$.

Thus $A \Rightarrow B$ stands to $A \rightarrow B$ in NR as $A \prec B$ stands to $A \supset B$ in the Lewis modal systems. $A \Rightarrow B$ is, if you will, strict relevant implication. _Prima facie_ it seems that, by having these two kinds of implication, NR has the merits of E and R while cancelling out their demerits. When we want to symbolize a necessarily true if___then___, we can use $A \Rightarrow B$, or even $A \prec B$ when we do not care about relevance between A and B. When we do not want to be forced to symbolize the if___then___ sentence as if it were necessarily true, we can use $\rightarrow$ and even $\supset$. So, in our search for the right entailment system, it is now crucial that we consider whether or not we should use the $\rightarrow$ of E or the $\Rightarrow$ of NR to symbolize entailment.

Even if we had $\vdash_E A \rightarrow B$ iff. $\vdash_{NR} A \Rightarrow B$, we would still have to decide which system to choose since they have different primtives. For instance, we may choose E over NR because necessity should not be a primitive concept but be definable in terms of entailment. However, if we do not have $\vdash_E A \rightarrow B$ iff. $\vdash_{NR} A \Rightarrow B$, part of the basis for our choice between systems would certainly be that an $A \Rightarrow B$ theorem of NR, for which the corresponding $A \rightarrow B$ is not an E theorem, does not agree with our normative intuitions about entailment. So, to force ourselves to make a choice on the basis of theorems we are going to show that although we have: If $\vdash_E A \rightarrow B$ then $\vdash_{NR} A \Rightarrow B$ we do not have the converse in a significant sense. (The converse fails trivially if we have an A or B in the language of NR with primitive $\Box$'s in them.)

Let us first, then, give a translation t() of the language of E into the language of NR. We can then significantly ask whether or not $\vdash_E A$ iff. $\vdash_{NR} t(A)$.

Translation of E's language into NR's language

$t(A) = A$ if A is a sentential variable.
$t(A \wedge B) = t(A) \wedge t(B)$
$t(A \vee B) = t(A) \vee t(B)$
$t(\sim A) = \sim t(A)$
$t(A \rightarrow B) = t(A) \Rightarrow t(B)$, i.e., $\Box(t(A) \rightarrow t(B))$.

In effect, the translation is carried out by simply going through an E formula and replacing $\rightarrow$ with $\Rightarrow$.

Two lemmas now facilitate a proof that if $\vdash_{E} A$ then $\vdash_{NR} t(A)$

Lemma 2 of IV.7: Necessitation is an admissible rule of NR. I.e., if $\vdash_{NR} A$, then $\vdash_{NR} \Box A$.

Lemma 2 is readily provable by an induction on the length of proof in NR. NR5 takes care of the basis case. The induction step is easily handled by use of Adj., MP, NR4, and NR3.

The third lemma is also readily provable by adding a case to the proof of the Replacement Theorem for E, i.e., Theorem V of IV.1.

Lemma 3 of IV.7: If $\vdash_{NR} A \leftrightarrow B$, $\vdash_{NR} F(A) \leftrightarrow F(B/A)$.

For proof we consider only the inductive step case in which F(A) has the form $\Box G(A)$. For this case, the induction assumption would give $\vdash G(A) \leftrightarrow G(B/A)$. Necessitation gives $\vdash \Box(G(A) \leftrightarrow G(B/A))$. Now by use of NR3, primarily, we get $\vdash \Box G(A) \leftrightarrow \Box G(B/A)$.

Maybe Lemma 3 could be said to show only that NR has Repl. for relevant equivalents. But a corollary of Lemma 3 gives a Replacement Theorem for entailment equivalents in NR. We leave proof of this corollary as an exercise.

Corollary of Lemma 3 of IV.7: If $\vdash A \Leftrightarrow B$, then $\vdash F(A) \Leftrightarrow F(B/A)$, where $A \Leftrightarrow B$ is $(A \Rightarrow B) \wedge (B \Rightarrow A)$.

We follow Meyer's [1966], pp. 151-153 and his [1968a] in giving hints on how to prove the following theorem.

Theorem II of IV.7: If $\vdash_{E} A$, then $\vdash_{NR} t(A)$.

The proof proceeds by showing that if A is an E-axiom then t(A) is an NR theorem and by showing that NR has the following two derived rules. An induction is then used on the length of the proof of A in E.

rNR1: $A, A \Rightarrow B \vdash B$
rNR2: $\Box A, \Box B \vdash \Box(A \wedge B)$.

We leave proof of the rules and the induction as exercises. We only remark on the basis case of showing that E-axioms are translated into NR theorems. For the first seven axioms, one application of Necessitation to the corresponding axiom in the R fragment of NR gives the E-axiom as an NR theorem. We have to work harder for the other axioms. Let us consider only E8 and E11. The formula t(E8) is:

$\Box(\Box(\Box(A \rightarrow A) \wedge \Box(B \rightarrow B) \rightarrow C) \rightarrow C)$.

In t(E8) the $\rightarrow$ is that of system R.

TNR1: $\vdash_{NR}$ t(E8).

Proof sketch

1) $\Box(A\rightarrow A)\wedge\Box(B\rightarrow B)\rightarrow.(\Box(A\rightarrow A)\wedge\Box(B\rightarrow B)\rightarrow C)$---C R1

2) $\Box(A\rightarrow A)\wedge\Box(B\rightarrow B)$ T1, Necessitation, Adj.

3) $\Box(A\rightarrow A)\wedge\Box(B\rightarrow B)\rightarrow C\rightarrow C$ MP (1),(2)

4) $\Box(\Box(A\rightarrow A)\wedge\Box(B\rightarrow B)\rightarrow C\rightarrow C)$ Necessitation on (3)

Use NR3 on (4) and then Trans. to get (5).

5) $\Box(\Box(A\rightarrow A)\wedge\Box(B\rightarrow B)\rightarrow C)\rightarrow\Box C$

Use NR1 on (5) and then Trans. to get (6).

6) $\Box(\Box(A\rightarrow A)\wedge\Box(B\rightarrow B)\rightarrow C)\rightarrow C$

Now Necessitation applied to (6) gives the theorem.

t(E11) is: $\Box(\Box(A\rightarrow\Box(A\rightarrow B))\rightarrow\Box(A\rightarrow B)$.

TNR2: $\vdash_{NR}$ t(E11).

Proof sketch

1) $\Box(A\rightarrow B)\rightarrow.A\rightarrow B$ NR1

2) $(A\rightarrow\Box(A\rightarrow B))\rightarrow.A\rightarrow.A\rightarrow B$ Prefixing on (1)

3) $(A\rightarrow.A\rightarrow B)\rightarrow.A\rightarrow B$ E11 (R11,if you prefer)

4) $(A\rightarrow\Box(A\rightarrow B)\rightarrow.A\rightarrow B$ Trans. (2),(3).

5) $\Box((A\rightarrow\Box(A\rightarrow B))\rightarrow.A\rightarrow B)$ Necessitation on (4)

Use of NR3 and Trans. will now get the theorem from (5).

Theorem II is of tremendous significance for our search for the right entailment system. If we find that NR is to be preferred over E, our labor with E is not in vain. To move to a better entailment system we need only add the axioms and notation required to get NR from E. All of our E theorems are convertible into NR theorems by merely changing E's $\rightarrow$ to NR's $\Rightarrow$.

Before we deal with the major theorem of this section, which is that the converse of Theorem II fails, let us consider two areas in which E and NR agree. By treating $\Box$ as an identity operator on classical truth tables we can use the technique of Theorem II of IV.1 to prove the following.

Theorem III of IV.7: The zdf. theorems of NR are exactly the classical tautologies.

Of more interest than agreement on zdf. theses is agreement on fde. entailments in the following sense.

Theorem IV of IV.7: Let $A\rightarrow B$ be an fde. formula, $\vdash_{E} A\rightarrow B$ iff. $\vdash_{NR}$ t$(A\rightarrow B)$

Of course, Theorem II gives us half of the proof. We get the other half by noticing that t$(A\rightarrow B)$ is $\Box(A\rightarrow B)$ for the $\rightarrow$ of R. By NR1 we get $\vdash_{NR} A\rightarrow B$ and then by Theorem I of this section we have $\vdash_{E} A\rightarrow B$.

Thus if we switched to NR the arguments for the fde. system of E would be arguments for the "fde system" of NR where the fde entailments are really the higher degree formulas $\Box(A \rightarrow B)$ where $A \rightarrow B$ is properly an fde. .

But let us now see a theorem divergence between E and NR. We first cite the following lemma which we do not prove until IV.11. Larisa Maksimowa proved it in her [1972].

Lemma 4 of IV.7: The Maksimowa formula in the language of E: $(A \rightarrow . B \rightarrow C) \wedge (B \rightarrow . A \vee C) \rightarrow . B \rightarrow C$, is not a theorem of E.

As would be expected our next lemms says that the t() translation of the Maksimowa formula is an NR theorem. Maksimowa credits G.E. Minc with proving it. The t() translation is: $(A \Rightarrow . B \Rightarrow C) \wedge (B \Rightarrow . A \vee C) \Rightarrow . B \Rightarrow C$; but we will prove it in NR in an unabbreviated version. The following two trivial theorems are useful in its proof.

TNR3: $\Box A \wedge \Box B \leftrightarrow \Box(A \wedge B)$
TNR4: $\Box\Box A \leftrightarrow \Box A$

Lemma 5 of IV.7: $\Box(\Box(A \rightarrow \Box(B \rightarrow C) \wedge \Box(B \rightarrow . A \vee C) \rightarrow \Box(B \rightarrow C))$ is a theorem of NR. We will call this TNR5.

We prove Lemma 5 by giving an entailment theorem proof of TNR5.

1)* $\Box(A \rightarrow \Box(B \rightarrow C))$ Hyp.
2)* $\Box(B \rightarrow . A \vee C)$ Hyp.
Use of rNR1 and Trans. gives (3) and (4).
3)* $A \rightarrow . B \rightarrow C$
4)* $B \rightarrow . A \vee C$
5)* $B \rightarrow . A \rightarrow C$ Perm on (3).
6)* $B \rightarrow . (A \vee C) \wedge (A \rightarrow C)$ From (4),(5) mainly by use of E12.
7) $(A \vee C) \wedge (A \rightarrow C) \rightarrow . A \wedge (A \rightarrow C) \vee C \wedge (A \rightarrow C)$ Dist.
8) $A \wedge (A \rightarrow C) \rightarrow C$ T41
9) $C \wedge (A \rightarrow C) \rightarrow C$ E1
10) $A \wedge (A \rightarrow C) \vee C \wedge (A \rightarrow C) \rightarrow C$ From (8),(9) mainly by use of E13.
11)* $B \rightarrow C$ Trans. (6),(7), and (10).
12) $\Box(A \rightarrow \Box(B \rightarrow C)) \wedge \Box(B \rightarrow . A \vee C) \rightarrow . B \rightarrow C$ From 1 - 11 by use of Lemma 1 (Entailment Theorem for NR.)

Apply Necessitation to (12) and use NR3 and MP to get:
13) $\Box(\Box(A \rightarrow \Box(B \rightarrow C) \wedge \Box(B \rightarrow . A \vee C)) \rightarrow \Box(B \rightarrow C)$

Use TNR3 and Repl. to make the antecedent of (13): $\Box\Box(A \rightarrow \Box(B \rightarrow C) \wedge \Box\Box(B \rightarrow . A \vee C)$. Now use TNR4 and Repl. to eliminate the double $\Box$'s in the above new antecedent for (13) to get (14)
14) $\Box(A \rightarrow \Box(B \rightarrow C) \wedge \Box(B \rightarrow . A \vee C) \rightarrow \Box(B \rightarrow C)$

Now a single application of Necessitation gives TNR5.

Lemmas 4 and 5 give the theorem which we will call Maksimowa's Theorem.

Theorem V of IV.7: There is a formula A of the C⟶D form in the language of E such that it is not the case that $\vdash_{E}$ A but it is the case that $\vdash_{NR}$ t(A), where t() is the translation defined earlier in this section.

We now have to make a choice between E and NR.

Our first reason for preferring E has been suggested in our discussion of Belnap's adequacy condition C12 back in I.6. Entailment should be taken as a primitive notion. We will understand that kind of necessity which holds between antecedent and consequent of the proper subset of the logical implications which we call entailments only when we isolate that proper subset. Hence, we find NR's way of defining entailment as unsatisfying. It is assumed by users of NR that we already have that sense of necessity which holds in entailments.

A second reason for being suspicious of NR's approach to entailment is that it seems to identify entailments with necessarily true empirical conditionals. At least a prima facie mark in favor of NR was that its ⟶, viz., R's ⟶, van be used to symbolize, without any relevance paradoxes, certain empirically true conditionals. It may be the case that some empirically true conditionals are necessarily true in some sense of 'necessary' and that we would want to assert that they are necessary. But for this purpose of asserting empirical or natural necessity we should frankly acknowledge that we are introducing a sign for natural necessity and be suspicious of having a single necessity sign turn A⟶B into an assertion of an entailment and an assertion of natural necessity.

Perhaps a defender of NR may reply that not every true A⟶B is turned into an assertion of entailment by prefixing □ to it. Only A⟶B which are logically true are converted to assertions of entailment by prefixing of □. The most reasonable cnadidate for what it means to be a logically true A⟶B is to be a thesis of some specified system. Hence, this suggestion can be taken as saying □(A⟶B) is an entailment when A⟶B is a thesis of a system such as R. As Meyer puts it in his [1968a]: prior to being augmented to NR an A⟶B of R could only indicate entailment by virtue of being a theorem of R. In NR we can express that an A⟶B is an entailment by converting it to A⟹B if A⟶B is an R theorem.

As a reply to the suggestion of the preceding paragraph, we can point out that entailment is not really being represented by A⟹B. The A⟹ B are ambiguous. An A⟹ B is an entailment if the □ is prefixed onto A⟶B by Necessitation. But if the □ is not prefixed by Necessitation, then □(A⟶B), i.e. $A \Longrightarrow B$, may only assert a naturally necessary connection. There is circularity as well as ambiguity involved in the suggestion. Before we can confidently accept the $A \rightarrow B$ of a system as indicating entailment by virtue of being theorems of the system we have to know that the $A \rightarrow B$ theorems of that system are the entailments. In other words, we need the entailment system we are looking for before we apply Necessitation to its theorems to assert that they are entailments.

Let us illustrate the charge of circularity with an example. Systems E and R may be looked at as competitors for being the entailment system whose $A \rightarrow B$ theorems indicate entailment. We ask ourselves if the NR analogue of R1, viz., $A \Longrightarrow .A \Longrightarrow B \Longrightarrow B$, is a thesis when we can express entailment. Try as hard as you will, you will prove only $\Box A \Longrightarrow .A \Longrightarrow B \Longrightarrow B$ but not the NR analogue of R1. In an exercise we will see that $A \Longrightarrow .A \Longrightarrow B \Longrightarrow B$ is not a theorem of NR. Very likely we would reconcile ourselves to the non-theoremhood of the NR analogue of R1 by arguing that it is not really a thesis about entailment. Possibly we would point out that in a system where $\rightarrow$ indicates entailment, viz., E, $A \rightarrow .A \rightarrow B \rightarrow B$ is not a thesis. It does not help to observe that NR has as a thesis $A \Longrightarrow .A \rightarrow B \rightarrow B$ because this reveals the ambiguity imposed upon R's $\rightarrow$ in NR. If $\rightarrow$ were not used ambiguously so that it can represent an empirical conditional and entailment, all of the $\rightarrow$ in $A \rightarrow .A \rightarrow B \rightarrow B$ could be converted to $\Longrightarrow$.

Finally, we can take the failure of the "natural" or-elimination natural deduction of the E-version of Maksimowa's formula, which we considered at the end of the previous section as evidence that the formula should not be a theorem. Recall that that attempted deduction involved trying to treat all hypotheses as necessary truths and hence as usable in all subsequent arguments.

Nevertheless, despite the polemics against NR, it may be a better system than E. So, we close by using a matrix to exhibit some nice properties of NR. The matrix is from Meyer's [1968a]; we label it $\mathfrak{N}$r. We use $\{+3,+2,+1,-1,-2,-3\}$ instead of $\{+3,+2,+t,-f,-2,-3\}$. In $\mathfrak{N}$r, plus values are designated. The and v tables may be read off from the lattice diagram below. The $\Longrightarrow$ table is obtained by applying $\Box$ to the values of the $\rightarrow$ table.

Lattice diagram for $\mathfrak{N}$r

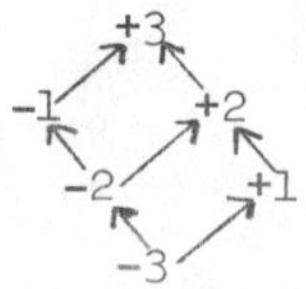

The $\sim$, $\Box$, $\rightarrow$, and $\Rightarrow$ tables for $\mathcal{N}$r,

A	$\sim$A	$\Box$A
+3	-3	+1
+2	-2	+1
+1	-1	+1
-1	+1	-3
-2	+2	-3
-3	+3	-3

$\rightarrow$	+3	+2	+1	-1	-2	-3
+3	+3	-3	-3	-3	-3	-3
+2	+3	+2	-3	-2	-2	-3
+1	+3	+2	+1	-1	-2	-3
-1	+3	-3	-3	+1	-3	-3
-2	+3	+2	-3	+2	+2	-3
-3	+3	+3	+3	+3	+3	+3

$\Rightarrow$	+3	+2	+1	-1	-2	-3
+3	+1	-3	-3	-3	-3	-3
+2	+1	+1	-3	-3	-3	-3
+1	+1	+1	+1	-3	-3	-3
-1	+1	-3	-3	+1	-3	-3
-2	+1	+1	-3	+1	+1	-3
-3	+1	+1	+1	+1	+1	+1

Characterization of Ackermann's matrix $\mathcal{A}$,

It is useful to observe here that the $\wedge$, v, $\sim$, and $\Rightarrow$ tables of $\mathcal{N}$r are essentially Ackermann's matrix from his [1956] for showing that Π' has no theorem of the form A$\rightarrow$.B$\rightarrow$C where A is a zdf.. So, we call a matrix with the above tables for $\wedge$, v, $\sim$, and $\Rightarrow$ where the $\Rightarrow$ table becomes the $\rightarrow$ table Ackermann's matrix $\mathcal{A}$. We will use $\mathcal{A}$ in our work in IV.11.

To prove the sixth lemma we only point out that v(A$\rightarrow$B)$\in$D iff. v(A)$\leq$v(B) where the lattice diagram shows the order of the elements. Then use Theorem II of I.7. There is still, of course, considerable labor involved in showing that NR is sound on $\mathcal{N}$r.

Lemma 6 of IV.7: $\mathcal{N}$r is suitable for NR.

Because entailments in NR are formulas of the $\Box$A form, viz., of the $\Box$(C$\rightarrow$D) form, if we show that NR has no theorems of the form A$\Rightarrow$.B$\Rightarrow$C where A contains no $\Box$ and no theorems of the form $\sim\Box$A$\Rightarrow\Box$B, we will show that in NR non-entailments do not entail entailments and, in particular, negations of entailments do not entail entailments. For the reasons given in discussion of C6 in I.6 while discussing modal fallacies and in IV.2 while discussing what we should get from $\sim$(A$\rightarrow$B) in E, we regard these as nice properties for an entailment system candidate. There is the following theorem.

Theorem VI of IV.7: NR has no theorems of the forms: A$\Rightarrow$.B$\Rightarrow$ C where A contains no $\Box$ and $\sim\Box$A$\Rightarrow\Box$B.

We make the following remarks by way of a proof. It is easy to show that no $\sim\Box$A$\Rightarrow\Box$B is $\mathcal{N}$r valid because only two values are involved and hence only four cases need consideration: v($\Box$A)=+1 and v($\Box$B)=+1, v($\Box$A)=+1 and v($\Box$B)=-3, etc.. The other form requires an induction which can be adapted from Ackermann's proof in [1956] that Π' has no A$\rightarrow$.B$\rightarrow$C theorem with A as a zdf.. The induction is used to show that if A has no occurrence of $\Box$ there is some v() such that v(A)=+2 or v(A)=-2. We will not give the induction here. Once we have the induction, and remind ourselves that B$\Rightarrow$C is $\Box$(B$\rightarrow$C), we see that v(B$\Rightarrow$ C) is +1 or -3 for all v().

But $+2 \Longrightarrow +1$, $+2 \Longrightarrow -3$, $-2 \Longrightarrow +1$, and $-2 \Longrightarrow -3$ all equal -3. So, let us take Theorem VI as proved.

We touch on NR again in Part V when we consider model structure semantics for it. But for now we move on under the hypothesis that E is the right system of entailment. Still, we are prepared to be persuaded that NR is better than E.

Exercises IV.7

1. Show that R and NR are consistent.

2. Add $B \longrightarrow . A \longrightarrow A$ as an axiom schema to NR. Is the resulting system modal system S4?

3. Assume Belnap's result about fdf's. from his [1967a] that for fdf. formula A $\vdash_E$ A iff. $\vdash_R$ A. Get the following result of pp. 154-55 of Meyer's dissertation: for fdf. formula A in the language of E, if $\vdash_{NR}$ t(A) then $\vdash_E$ A.

   Hint: consider an NR proof $B_1, \ldots, B_n$ of t(A). Transform it into $B'_1, \ldots, B'_n$ by deleting all . Show that $\vdash_{NR}$ (t(A))'.

4. For E10 or E9 show that its t() translation is an NR theorem.

5. Show that the following R-analogues are not NR theorems. $A \Longrightarrow . A \Longrightarrow B \Longrightarrow C$ and $(A \Longrightarrow . B \Longrightarrow C) \Longrightarrow . B \Longrightarrow . A \Longrightarrow C$.

6. Complete the missing induction from the proof of Theorem VI.

IV.8 Formal intensional disjunction and conjunction or contenability, many results about non-theorems of E and R.

Our goal in this section is to introduce so-called formal intensional disjunction A+B and formal intensional conjunction A∘B for systems E and R. Several philosophers have discussed non-truth functional 'or' in natural languages. For instance, C.I. Lewis in [1918], Belnap on pp.38-42 of his 1960 monograph, Anderson and Belnap in their [1962a], and Meyer on pp. 217-234 of his dissertation discuss non-truth functional disjunction. J. Woods in[1967] criticizes the notion of a non-truth functional 'and.' But see J. Barker [1969] for a careful development and defense of an intensional, or non-truth functional, 'and' which can be represented by the A∘B of system R. We do not take part in the important task of surveying natural language to uncover uses of 'or' and 'and' which are not adequately symbolized by $\wedge$ and $\vee$. Our procedure is to present some formal properties of the intensional disjunction A+B and A∘B in both E and R.

Definitions of A+B and A∘B in E and in R,

A+B abbreviates $\sim A \longrightarrow B$. Frequently A+B is symbolized as $A \cup B$.
A∘B abbreviates $\sim(A \longrightarrow \sim B)$.

We presume that the associated A+B and A∘B have some application if the $A \longrightarrow B$ has application. Of course, if $A \longrightarrow B$ has application to natural language we do not thereby have a guarantee that the associated A+B is suitable for symbolizing some sense of 'or'; it may only be suitable for symbolizing what is more explicitly symbolized by $\sim A \longrightarrow B$. Nevertheless, despite our formal concerns, we occasionally cite annecdotal evidence to suggest applications for the formal notions. Because in E and R $(A \longrightarrow B)$ is not truth-functional on its intended interpretation, neither are A+B and A∘B. So, we clearly have formal intensional disjunction and conjunction even if their existence in natural language is doubted, and even if their charcterization as disjunctions and conjunctions is regarded as misleading.

In listing properties of systems, we use T if a theorem of E, R if a theorem of R, and X( ) to indicate being a non-theorem. In the parentheses after X we list the names of the systems in which the schema fails to be a theorem schema. On the right of non-theorems, we frequently cite a matrix valuation or a Theorem of IV.11 which justifies the charge of non-theoremhood.

The most striking feature of A+B in E is the number of features of A $\vee$ B in E which A+B lacks. Let us first list some of A+B's properties in E; both positive and negative.

T73: $A+B \leftrightarrow B+A$
T74: $A+\sim A$
T75: $A+A \rightarrow A$
T76: $A+B \rightarrow .A \vee B$
T77: $\sim A \wedge (A+B) \rightarrow B$ Intensional Disjunctive Syllogism,
X1(E,R): $A \rightarrow .A+A$ Use $\mathcal{M}_0$ of III.4, set $v(A)=+0$.
X2(E,R): $A \rightarrow .A+B$ Use $\mathcal{M}_0$, set $v(A)=v(B)=+0$
X3(E): $(A+B)+C \rightarrow A+(B+C)$ Use $\mathcal{A}$ of IV.7 and set $v(A)=-2, v(B)=-1$, and $v(C)=+3$.
X4(E): $A+(B+C) \rightarrow .(A+B)+C$ Use $\mathcal{A}$ with $v(A)=+3, v(B)=-1$, and $v(C)=-2$.
X5(E,R): $A \vee B \rightarrow .A+B$ Use $\mathcal{M}_0$; set $v(A)=v(B)=+0$.

These results show that E's intensional disjunction is not extremely odd or undesirable as a disjunction. Still, they do not help make a case that we should symbolize most, let alone all, uses of 'or' with A+B in E. We simply have an alternatie symbolization for some uses of 'or.' Because of T74, this intensional disjunction is not suitable for symbolizing Intuitionists' use of 'or.' We do not pursue efforts to get a disjunction in E suitable for Intuitionists. See Meyer's [1973c] for efforts to get an intuitionistically acceptable disjunction.

Some observations can be made to suggest that E's A+B may have application. Certainly it is nice to have a disjunction for which Disjunctive Syllogism holds. The failures of Addition: The failures of $A \rightarrow .A+A$ and $A \rightarrow .A+B$, offer us something desirable for some uses of 'or.' If we assert 'J. Carter is the U.S.A. President in 1977,' we do not want to be committed to 'If J. Carter is not the U.S.A. President in 1977, then J. Carter is the U.S.A. President in 1977.' Similarly, we do not want to be committed to 'If J. Carter is not the U.S.A. President in 1977, the his wife is.' Even a non-associative disjunction may be desirable to avoid mixing-up cases. The two cases:A or B, C are not <u>prima facie</u> the two cases:A,B or C. For an example, suppose that we have the two cases that the solution to an equation is a positive integer or a complex number. The positive integer case breaks down into two subcases of being odd or being even. So, we have: x is a complex number or (x is an odd integer or x is an even integer). We cannot intelligibly re-associate the preceding disjunction to: (x is a complex number or x is an odd integer) or x is an even integer; we especially cannot get this re-association if its first disjunction is regarded as an abbreviation of: If x is not a complex number, then x is an odd integer.

Before considering R's intensional conjunction, let us consider what may be called E's intensional conjunction. 'It is not the case that not-A or not-B' seems to be a way of asserting both A and B together. It is natural to take denial of a disjunction as asserting a conjunction. With Double Negation $A \circ B$, i.e., $\sim(A \rightarrow \sim B)$, is equivalent to $\sim(\sim A + \sim B)$.

In so far as A+B can be regarded as a disjunction, we take the equivalence of AoB to $\sim(\sim A + \sim B)$ as grounds for calling AoB some kind of conjunction. Nevertheless, it is doubtful that any natural language use of 'and' is well symbolized with E's AoB as it is defined in this section. It may be better to read AoB as ' A is consistent with B' or 'A is cotenable with B.' Remember,though, that to say that A is consistent with B is not to say that either is consistent just as saying that A is cotenable with B is not saying that either is tenable. Let us list some properties of E's AoB.

T78: $A \circ B \leftrightarrow \sim(\sim A + \sim B)$
T79: $A+B \leftrightarrow \sim(\sim A \circ \sim B)$
T80: $A \circ B \leftrightarrow B \circ A$
T81: $\sim(A \circ \sim A)$ A Law of non-Contradiction?
T82: $A \rightarrow . A \circ A$
T83: $A \wedge B \rightarrow . A \circ B$
rT83: $A, B \vdash A \circ B$ A type of Adjunction for $\circ$.

X6(E,R): $A \circ A \rightarrow A$ Use $\mathcal{M}_o$ with v(A)=-0.
X7(E,R): $A \circ B \rightarrow B$ Use $\mathcal{M}_o$ with v(A)=v(B)=-0.
X8(E,R): $A \circ B \rightarrow . A+B$ Use same valuation as for X7.
X9(E,R): $A+B \rightarrow . A \circ B$ Treat $\rightarrow$ as $\supset$ and use classical truth tables.
X10 (E,R): $A \circ B \rightarrow . A \wedge B$ Exercise.
X11 (E,R): $A+(B \circ C) \rightarrow . (A+B) \circ (A+C)$ Use $\mathcal{M}_o$ with v(A)=+1, v(B)=+2. and v(C)=-1.
X12 (E): $A \circ (B+C) \rightarrow . (A \circ B)+(A \circ C)$ See Theorem III of IV.11.
X13 (E,R): $(A \circ B)+(A \circ C) \rightarrow . A \circ (B+C)$ Use the valuation of X11.
X14 (E): $(A+B) \circ (A+C) \rightarrow . A+(B \circ C)$ Treat same as X12.
X15 (E): $A \circ (B \circ C) \rightarrow . (A \circ B) \circ C$ Use $\mathcal{A}$ with v(A)=+2,v(B)=+1,v(C)=-3.
X16 (E): $(A \circ B) \circ C \rightarrow . A \circ (B \circ C)$ Use $\mathcal{A}$ with v(A)=-3,v(B)=+1,v(C)=+2.
X17 (E,R): $A \rightarrow B \rightarrow . A \circ C \rightarrow B$ Use $\mathcal{M}_o$ with v(A)=v(B)=+1 and v(C)=-3.
X18 (E): $A \circ B \rightarrow C \rightarrow . A \circ \sim C \rightarrow \sim B$ Use $\mathcal{A}$ with v(A)=+2,v(B)=-1, and v(C)=+3.
X19(E): $A \circ B \rightarrow C \rightarrow . A \rightarrow . B \rightarrow C$ Use $\mathcal{A}$ with v(A)=+2,v(B)=+1, and v(C)=+3.
X20(E): $(A \rightarrow . B \rightarrow C) \rightarrow . A \circ B \rightarrow C$ Treat same as X16.
X21(E,R): $(A \circ C \rightarrow B) \rightarrow . A \rightarrow B$ Treat same as X9.
X22(E,R): $A \rightarrow B \rightarrow . A \circ B$ Boethius' thesis Treat same as X9.
X23(E,R): $A \circ A$ Aristotle's thesis. Treat same as X9.
X24(E,R): $\sim((A \wedge \sim A) \circ (B \wedge \sim B))$ Use $\mathcal{M}_o$ with v(A)=+2 and v(B)=+3.

It should be emphasized that a claim that a certain schema is not a theorem schema of E where no claim is made about R is not to say indirectly that the schema is a theorem schema of R. For instance, we do not know whether or not X12 and X14 are theorems of R.

There are many more properties of + and o in E which we

could consider. For instance, do we have the following analogues of E12 and E13?

$(A \rightarrow B) \wedge (A \rightarrow C) \rightarrow . A \rightarrow . B \circ C$

$(A \rightarrow C) \wedge (B \rightarrow C) \rightarrow . A + B \rightarrow C$

Nevertheless, we have seen enough to appreciate E's intensional conjunction as a connective for asserting cotenability even if it is not suitable for symbolizing any natural language use of 'and.' Perhaps we should say that we start to develop a concept of cotenability by study of the formal intensional conjunctions. We find from T81 that it is provably wrong to assert that a sentence and its negation can both be held together; but from X24 we find that it is not provably (demonstratively) wrong to assert that two explicit contradictions can be held together. Fortunately, even if we can truly assert that two explicit contradictions can be held together with one another, the failure of Simplification for $\circ$ brought out by X7 reassures us that such an assertion does not commit us to a contradiction. From X23 we discover that we cannot, in general, assert that a sentence is cotenable with itself. For instance, we have $\vdash_E p \wedge \sim p \rightarrow \sim(p \wedge \sim p)$, i.e., $\vdash_E \sim((p \wedge \sim p) \circ (p \wedge \sim p))$. But for more complex illogical assertions than $p \wedge \sim p$ such as $\sim(A \rightarrow A)$ we can, consistently with our theses, assert self-cotenability. In particular X25 below tells us that we can assert $\sim(A \rightarrow A) \circ \sim(A \rightarrow A)$.

X25(E,R): $\sim(A \rightarrow A) \rightarrow . A \rightarrow A)$ Use $\mathfrak{M}_0$ with v(A)=+0.

Recall from IV.2 that a result such as X25 persuaded us not to define in E $\Diamond A$ as $\sim(A \rightarrow \sim A)$ because we would not thereby get the impossibility of $\sim(A \rightarrow A)$ as a theorem. The self-cotenability of the impossible $\sim(A \rightarrow A)$ suggest that in E the notion of cotenability is broader than possibility. T84 and T85 together with X26 and X27 show us that the suggestion is correct. The theorems tell us that compossibility gives cotenability while the X formulas tell us that the converses fail. $\Diamond(A \wedge B)$ says that A and B are compossible or co-possible.

T84: $\Diamond(A \wedge B) \rightarrow . A \circ B$

With Contraposition and Double Negation it suffices to prove: $A \rightarrow \sim B \rightarrow . \sim(A \wedge B) \rightarrow \sim(A \wedge B) \rightarrow \sim(A \wedge B)$. Use Kron's deduction theorem or Anderson's natural deduction technique.

T 85 is a corollary of T84.

T85: $\Diamond A \rightarrow . A \circ A$

X26 (E,R): $A \circ B \rightarrow \Diamond(A \wedge B)$ Use $\mathfrak{M}_0$ with v(A)=+1 and v(B)=-2.

X27 (E,R): $A \circ A \rightarrow \Diamond A$ Use $\mathfrak{M}_0$ with v(A)=-0.

Incidentally, note that X26 tells us we do not have in E $A \rightarrow\!\!\!\!\exists\, B \rightarrow . A \rightarrow B$.

Since one of the insights which has stimulated this search

has been the normative intuition that inconsistencies can be held without total logical disaster, eg., every sentence being entailed, our preceding results suggest that cotenability could be our basic notion instead of entailment. We could then define $A \longrightarrow B$ as $\sim(A \circ \sim B)$. Indeed R.K.Meyer in [1974a] remarks that intensional conjunction, which he calls fusion., is the fundamental notion in the search for entailment. But we shall not pursue treating $A \circ B$ as the fundamental notion. Formally such a treatment would be essentailly a notational switch. In regard to interpreting formulas such a treatment would make formulas difficult to read. There would be a great temptation to read $A \circ B$ as $A \wedge B$. Furthermore, we do not have many normative intuitions about $A \circ B$. In fact, we may only develop our concept of what $A \circ B$ is supposed to be able to symbolize by getting properties of it from a system for $A \longrightarrow B$. We shall, though, see how R's intensional disjunction and conjunction come a bit closer to being suitable symbols for some kind of 'or' and 'and.' Still, our aim is not to try to find some more suitable symbols for 'or' and 'and' than $\wedge$ and $\vee$. We are satisfied with $\wedge$ and $\vee$ for most purposes. It is not at all clear that natural language disjunctions and conjunctions, awkwardly symbolized by $\wedge$ and $\vee$, will be better symbolized by $+$ and $\circ$ in E. And we are accepting E. But what about R?

Our interest in R here is somewhat historical. The earliest system to avoid the Lewis paradoxical derivations treated conjunction in a way which gave it some features in common with R's intensional conjunction. So to gain some appreciation of E.J.Nelson's pioneering work we observe some features of $A+B$ and $A \circ B$ in R. J. Barker in Ch.IV of his [1969] offers an extensive development of $A+B$ and $A \circ B$ in a system SIR-system of intensional relations- whose sentential logic contains R. SIR is basically system R with Ackermann's rule γ. (In Part V when we see that γ is an admissible rule for R, we will see that R and SIR agree on theorems.) Unrestricted Permutation,R3, provides the major differences between E's $+$ and $\circ$ and R's; it is used to prove most of the following.

R5: $A+(B+C) \longleftrightarrow (A+B)+C$ — $+$ Associativity for R
R5: $A \circ (B \circ C) \longleftrightarrow (A \circ B) \circ C$ — $\circ$ Associativity for R
R7: $A \circ B \longrightarrow C \longrightarrow . A \longrightarrow . B \longrightarrow C$ — $\circ$ Exportation for R
R8: $(A \longrightarrow . B \longrightarrow C) \longrightarrow . A \circ B \longrightarrow C$ — $\circ$ Importation for R
R9: $A \circ B \longrightarrow C \longrightarrow . A \circ \sim C \longrightarrow \sim B$ — $\circ$ Antilogism for R
R10: $A \circ (A \longrightarrow B) \longrightarrow B$
R11: $(A \longrightarrow B) \circ (B \longrightarrow C) \longrightarrow . A \longrightarrow C$

The preceding R theorems with X7 suggest that R's $\circ$ functions as a conjunction for which Simplification fails while Antilogism holds. Such a conjunction is reminiscient of the conjunction of E.J. Nelson's pioneering system which we briefly survey in the next section.

Exercises IV.8

1. Prove R5 through R11.
2. Show that R10 and R11 are not theorems of E. $\mathcal{A}$ may be useful.
3. Prove T84.
4. System RM is R plus $A \rightarrow . A \rightarrow A$. Show that if X27 were added to R as an axiom schema, $A \rightarrow . A \rightarrow A$ would be a theorem of the new system. So, RM is contained in R plus X27. Does the converse hold?
5. In RM what properties of truth-functional $A \wedge B$ which $A \circ B$ lacks in R does $A \circ B$ pick up?
6. Try to prove X12 and X14 in R. Try to prove them in RM.

IV.9 E.J. Nelson's system NE: an attempt to show that Nelson's restriction on conjunction may be regarded as insights into the special place of all-premiss-using derivations,

The brevity of this section should not obscure the significance of E.J. Nelson's pioneering attack upon using strict implication as the representative for the best type of formal logical implication. Although E.J. Nelson and W.T. Parry were ahead of their time, their early challenges to strict implication showed that its use could be challenged by systematic development of an alternative implication stricter than Lewis' modal notion of strict implication, viz., $\Box(A \supset B)$. In this section, we merely present Nelson's system, argue that his conjunction $A \wedge B$ cannot be interpreted as the intensional conjunction of R, viz., R's $A \circ B$, note that Nelson's system is consistent, and make a case that Nelson's rejection of Simplification is motivated by a valuable insight into what makes a formal derivation into the best possible kind of formal dervation.

We present Nelson's system from his [1930],[1933a], and [1933b]. We call it NE. In NE $\wedge$, $\sim$, and $\circ$ are the primitive signs. $A \rightarrow B$ is defined as $\sim(A \circ \sim B)$. In the presentation below, we use $A \rightarrow B$ in the axioms. We use axiom schemas instead of particular axioms. Nelson gives MP and Repl. as the rules. We assume that Adj. is also a rule. Since we are going to consider translating $A \wedge B$ in NE into $A \circ B$ of system R, we will not use $\circ$ in formulas of NE. But let us note that Nelson reads his $A \circ B$ as 'A is consistent with B.' However, because he allows impossible propositions to be consistent with one another, it may be best to regard $A \circ B$ as asserting cotenability as discussed in the previous section.

SYSTEM NE

NE1: $A \rightarrow A$
NE2: $A \rightarrow \sim B \rightarrow . B \rightarrow \sim A$
NE3: $A \rightarrow \sim\sim A$
NE4: $A \rightarrow B \rightarrow . \sim(A \rightarrow \sim B)$
NE5: $(A \rightarrow B) \wedge (B \rightarrow C) \rightarrow . A \rightarrow C$, provided $A \neq B$ and $B \neq C$.
NE6: $A \wedge B \leftrightarrow B \wedge A$
NE7: $A \wedge B \rightarrow C \rightarrow . A \wedge \sim C \rightarrow \sim B$.

The proviso on NE5 deserves comment before we eliminate it. The restriction on NE5 is to avoid theorems of the forms: $(A \rightarrow A) \wedge (A \rightarrow C) \rightarrow . A \rightarrow C$ and $(A \rightarrow B) \wedge (B \rightarrow B) \rightarrow . A \rightarrow B$, which would also be versions of the Simplification schemas. Nelson not only thought that Simplification sometimes failed. He also rejected Simplification almost as totally as we reject $A \wedge \sim A$ because he thought that every instance of Simplification was objectionable. However, the Angell matrix $\mathcal{A}n$, which is presented below, shows that NE does not have $\sim(A \wedge B \rightarrow B)$ as a theorem schema. So, his rejection of Simplification is not quite as total as our rejection of $A \wedge \sim A$; the system can consistently tolerate theorems which happen to have the Simplification forms. We can, then, eliminate the clumsy proviso in NE5 by following a procedure of Geach from Section II.16. We will accept as theorems of NE formulas of the forms: $A \wedge B \rightarrow A$ and $A \wedge B \rightarrow B$ provided that they are substitution instances of theorem schemas which are not of these Simplification forms. $\mathcal{A}$n shows that Simplification is not a theorem.

In light of X7,i.e., failure of Simplification for R's AoB, T80,R9, and R11, it is reasonable to conjecture that NE's $A \wedge B$ can be translated into R's $A \circ B$. However, the following "natural" translation t() on the wffs. of NE into those of R is unsatisfactory.

Suggested translation t() of NE into R,

$t(A) = A$ if A is a sentential variable
$t(A \wedge B) = t(A) \circ t(B)$
$t(\sim A) = \sim t(A)$
$t(A \rightarrow B) = t(A) \rightarrow t(B)$

This natural translation of NE into R translates all NE axioms, except NE4, into theorems of R. Nevertheless, even if we ignore NE4, this translation is unsatisfactory because it translates non-theorems of NE into theorems of R. For instance, $t(A \wedge B \rightarrow C \rightarrow . A \rightarrow . B \rightarrow C)$ is R7. But Exportation is not an NE theorem.

With this claim of non-theoremhood about Exportation, we have to present a matrix for supporting such claims. We use the following matrix of B. Angell from his [1962]. We call it $\mathcal{A}$n. The set of designated values is $\{0,1\}$.

Matrix $\mathcal{A}$n

A	$\sim$A
0	3
1	2
2	1
3	0

$\wedge$	0	1	2	3
0	1	0	3	2
1	0	1	2	3
2	3	2	3	2
3	2	3	2	3

$\rightarrow$	0	1	2	3
0	1	2	3	2
1	2	1	2	3
2	1	2	1	2
3	2	1	2	1

Lemma 1 of IV.9: Angell's $\mathcal{A}$n is suitable for NE.

As usual we leave the reader the task of verifying that a matrix is suitable for a system. But, given Lemma 1, we can show that Exportation is not an NE theorem by setting $v(A)=0$, $v(B)=2$, and $v(C)=1$. To show that $A \wedge B \rightarrow A$ is not a theorem schema, set $v(A)=0$ and $v(B)=2$.

Also with Lemma 1 we can establish the consistency of NE in the senses that no variable is a theorem of NE and that if A is a theorem then A is not a theorem. Due to NE4, a proof of the consistency of NE is not as trivial as typical consistency proofs for sentential logics. If we replace the $\longrightarrow$ in NE4 with $\supset$ we do not get a classical tautology. Indeed, if we add Boethius' thesis, with $\supset$ replacing $\longrightarrow$, as an axiom schema to classical logic we get an inconsistent system. Furthermore, if we add Boethius' thesis to E we get an inconsistent system, as we will show at the end of the next section. So, in the presence of Boethius' thesis, i.e., NE4, the consistency of NE is significant enough to warrant theorem status.

Theorem I of IV.9: Nelson's NE is consistent.

There may be some translation t'() such that t'(A$\wedge$B) = t'(A)$\circ$t'(B) and $\vdash_{NE}$ A iff. $\vdash_{R'}$ t'(A), where R' is an extension of R. But we will not pursue this topic. It is distorting to try to represent Nelson's as R's intensional conjunction. Nelson did distinguish A$\wedge$B from $\sim$(A$\longrightarrow\sim$B), i.e., A$\circ$B, in his system. So for him A$\wedge$B was not a type of cotenability; he had his own A$\circ$B for asserting cotenability. It would be distorting, then, to translate his $\wedge$ into a type of cotenability which is not too different from his own cotenability logical sign. Perhaps we can regard his restrictions on $\wedge$ as reflections of insights into the function of ordinary extensional 'and' in the premisses of the best possible fromal arguments. Here it is useful to quote from p.444 of his [1930].

> I do not take pq to mean "p is true and q is true," but simply "p and q", which is a unit or whole, not simply an aggregate, and expresses the joint force of p and q. I day that pq is not a simple aggregate composed of pa dn q because, for example in asserting that pq entails r, I am not asserting something simply about p and about q, but about them taken together, i.e., their joint force. pq does not entail r unless both p and q function together in entailing r. It is this functioning together or joint force that gives conjunction a unity which a mere aggregate or collection does not have. And this unity of conjunction is in a sense relational:, e.g., the propositions "All men are mortal" and "Socrates is a man" form a conjunction in relation to "Socrates is mortal", for "Socrates is mortal" expresses their joint force; but they do not form such a conjunction in relation to "Socrates is a man." However, if pq alone be asserted, then the mere aggregate of p and q is asserted;, i.e., p is asserted and q is asserted. In such a case the unity of the conjunction is lost, and the mere assertion of each component remains.

On p. 448 he added the following.

> Though "p and q entail p" cannot be asserted on logical grounds, I do not deny that from "pis true and q is true" we can pass to "p is true." All I deny is that such a passage is in virtue of an entailment relation holding between "p is true and q is true" and "p is true."

We will not concede that Simplification fails to be an entailment. In the simplest, and best possible formal way a conjunction brings along its conjuncts. Nevertheless, we should concede that it is odd to say that a conclusion is derived from a specified set of premisses or hypotheses when some of these hypotheses are not used in the derivation. For instance, it would be odd to say that an elementary computational truth such as 2+3=5 was derived from the axioms for a system of arithmetic where these axioms contain axioms for arithmetical addition and an axiom schema for mathematical induction. (Consider a system such as Mendelson's S in his [1964].) Such a claim is odd! Upon reflection we realize that the induction axiom was not used at all; and so, in a sense, we did not get 2+3=5 from the axioms as a whole. Of course, the oddity can be removed by pointing out that not all of the axioms were used but that the axiom system was used by using a part. But then a reply may be "But really you used only those axioms to get 2+3=5 and so it is those axioms which really entail 2+3=5."

Here the difference between entailment theses and derivations should be noted. Theses are truths about entailment which can be used in any derivation or deduction. The Simplification axioms E1 and E2 are truths; not deductions. These axioms can be used in any derivation or deduction to separate conjunctions into their conjuncts. When we use a Simplification axiom to get A from $A \wedge B$, we take premiss $A \wedge B$ with $A \wedge B \longrightarrow A$ and use MP to get A. In this simple derivation we did use both premisses,where the premisses are $A \wedge B$ and $A \wedge B \longrightarrow A$. All theses are equally good; they are all truths. However, there can be discrimination amongst deductions and derivations, e.g., ordinary derivations, starring-derivations, and Kron-derivations.

Let us regard Nelson's insights which are expressed in the preceding quotations as telling us that the best possible formal derivations are those which use all of their hypotheses or premisses. Derivations which use all of their premisses or hypotheses deserve special recognition; and not only because they are efficient. They do not mislead us to think that certain premisses are relevant to getting a conclusion when they are really not relevant to getting it. Such derivations also seem to be the derivations which fulfill our rather inchoate normative intuitions that a deduction theorem holds and that Exportation holds. If we derive B from $A_1,\ldots,A_n$, we tend to think that we have shown that under the assumption of $A_1,\ldots,A_{n-1}$ there is a formally correct inference from A_n to B. But,unfortunately, in an ordinary derivation A_n may not have been used at all to get B. Formula A_n may be totally irrelevant to getting B as it is in the derivation of B from $\{A_n, B\}$. We do not want to go from B, $A_n \vdash B$ to $B \vdash A_n \to B$. This is the way to paradoxical theses. But if all the A_i are used to get B, it is not odd to say that $A_1, \ldots, A_{n-1}$ entitle us to go from A_n to B in the best possible formal way because A_n is relevant to getting B and all that A_n needs is the help of $A_1, \ldots, A_{n-1}$. We are tempted to accept Exportation because we tend to read $A \to . B \to C$ as a variant of $A \wedge B \to C$; especially if we read $\to$ as if__then___. Exportation, though, is patently bad reasoning if, with it, we go from '$A \wedge B$ gives us B' to 'A gives us that B gives us B.' However, Exportation seems plausible if both A and B are used to get C. Hopefully, the preceding remarks have brought out a bias in favor of all premiss using derivations.

Our presentation of Kron-derivations and Kron's Deduction Theorem in IV.5 shows that E gives a preeminent place to derivations using all premisses. So, we take E's possession of a Kron Deduction Theorem as showing that E preserves Nelson's valuable insights.

Because we accept Simplification we reject Antilogism. Antilogism with $A \wedge B \to A$ immediately gives $A \wedge \sim A \to \sim B$. However, if we use both A and B, in Kron's way, to get C we do have both $\vdash_E A \wedge B \to C$ and $\vdash_E A \wedge \sim C \to \sim B$. This fact that when all premisses are used E has a type of Antilogism helps support our interpretation of Nelson's remarks on conjunction. He favored using all premisses and he had Antilogism.

Let us close this brief treatment of Nelson's work by seeing how we can appreciate his acceptance of Boethius' thesis. E preserves the insight behind acceptance of Boethius' thesis by having the following restricted version.

T86: $A \wedge (A \to B) \to . \sim(A \to \sim B)$

R has an even less restricted Boethius-thesis. The mere assumption that A is cotenable with itself entails, with R's $\to$, a Boethius-thesis.

R12: $A \circ A \to . A \to B \to . \sim(A \to \sim B)$.

For more literature on systems with Boethius' thesis, see Angell's [1962], Bode [1973], MaCall [1966], Montgomery and R. Routley [1968], and section 29.8 of Anderson's and Belnap's [1975].

Exercises IV.9

1. Prove T86 and R12.
2. Show that $\sim(A \wedge B \to A)$ and $A \wedge A \to A$ are not NE theses.
3. Can NE have a thesis of the form $A \to B$ where A is a thesis?
4. Does NE have $A \circ A$ as a thesis? Should $\Diamond A$ be defined as $A \circ A$?
5. What happens if Exportation is added as an axiom schema to NE?

IV.10 Some extensions of system E, some which are clearly unacceptable but some which are still candidates, systems I, RM, those with Boethius' Thesis, E plus Maksimowa's formula, E plus A⟶C⟶.B⟶C⟶.A v B⟶C, E plus A⟶.A⟶A, and EM,

Beneath the results and observations of this section, lies a severe disappointment of the author. He would have liked to have shown that E is the right system by showing that tempting extensions of E are clearly defective. A clear way of showing that a system is defective for our purposes is to show that it has theses which violates Belnap's variable sharing relevance condition C7. Unfortunately, of the systems cited in the above section description, we have proofs only that systems I and RM violate variable sharing condition C7. So we have to resort to making a case that we should not accept the other systems cited above except for those which contain Boethius' Thesis because they are inconsistent.

Let us first consider system I. System I is developed in R. Routley in [1972a]. For our purposes we can consider I as E plus the Factor axiom schema which we label I1 here. Formula X28 of the next section shows that I1 is not a theorem schema of E,R, or NR.

I1 A⟶B⟶.A∧C⟶.B∧C

Routley shows that I and E agree on fdf. theorems. So system I does not have either A∧~A⟶B or A⟶.B v~B as theorem schemas. Unfortunately for system I, it has relevance rupturing: B⟶C⟶.A⟶A as a theorem schema. Indeed Routley has B⟶C⟶.A⟶A as an axiom schema for I. But we are interested in seeing how the plausible principle of Factor damages E. To survey this damage we prove five theorems of system I. We are assuming that we have Repl. for these extensions of E; there would really be no significant changes in a proof of Repl. for E needed to extend Repl. to these extensions.

I 2: A⟶B⟶.A⟶A

To prove I 2 start with I1 in the form: A⟶B---.A∧A⟶.B∧A and use Repl. to replace A∧A with A to get:A⟶B⟶.A⟶.B∧A. Now Dr.10 with B∧A⟶A gives the theorem.

I 3: A⟶B⟶.B⟶B

To prove I 3 start with the version of I 2 of the form: ~B⟶~A⟶.~B⟶~B and use Repl. with the two E theorems: B⟶B ⟷ ~B⟶~B and A⟶B ⟷ ~B⟶~A.

With I 2,I 3, and r2 (comp.) we get I 4.

I 4: A⟶B⟶.(A⟶A)∧(B⟶B).

With I 1, A∧C⟶C, and Dr.10 we get I 5.

I 5: $A \rightarrow B \rightarrow . A \wedge C \rightarrow C$

I 6: $A \rightarrow B \rightarrow C \rightarrow C$

Proof

1)	$A \rightarrow B \rightarrow . A \wedge C \rightarrow C$	I 5
2)	$A \wedge C \rightarrow C \rightarrow . (A \wedge C \rightarrow A \wedge C) \wedge (C \rightarrow C)$	I 4
3)	$(A \wedge C \rightarrow A \wedge C) \wedge (C \rightarrow C) \rightarrow . C \rightarrow C$	E2
4)	$A \rightarrow B \rightarrow . C \rightarrow C$	Trans. used twice (1)to (:

In [197_c] Meyer and Routley also show that system I, as we have presented it, has I 6. I 6, of course, tells us that C7 violating $p \rightarrow p \rightarrow . q \rightarrow q$ is an I theorem. So, implicational system I is not the system we are looking for. It is, nevertheless, at first glance surprising that the plausible principle of Factor leads to fallacies of relevance while Suffixing and Prefixing do not. But observe that in Suffixing and in Prefixing the C linked with A and B in the consequent is linked with an entailment sign whereas in Factor the link is only a conjunction. With an entailment there has to be a connection between the two formulas connected by the entailment sign; but a conjunction can hold together two totally disconnected sentences. Thus we can have 'Four is an even number and Nixon was the first U.S. president to resign' but cannot have either entailing the other. So, rejection of Factor saves us from having to say 'Four is an even number and Nixon was the first U.S. president to resign entails four is divisible by two and Nixon was the first U.S. president to resign.' It is nice to be saved from saying this because it is not the first conjunction which entails the second conjunction; we have only the conjuncts of the first conjunction separately entailing the conjuncts of the second conjunction. Here, again, we see how E reflects some of E.J. Nelson's insights, which we discussed in IV.9, about reasoning from conunctions. Of course, those who are not moved by the preceding remarks designed to stimulate normative intuitions against Factor can rely on the appeal of E's axioms, C7, and I 6 to build a case against Factor.

The principle $A \rightarrow . B \rightarrow B$ is not at all plausible for those who demand relevance between antecedent and consequent in a thesis. But $A \rightarrow . A \rightarrow A$ has <u>prima facie</u> appeal. Once we are given the subject matter discussed in A, we may, it seems, assume that we are thereby given the most elementary logical truths about that subject matter. However, this apparently plausible principle leads to fallacies of relevance in R.

Consider the addition of what we here label RM 1 to system R to get the system RM.

RM 1: $A \rightarrow . A \rightarrow A$

X30 in the next section shows that RM 1 is not a theorem of E,R, or NR.

We now turn to proving enough theorems of RM to show that RM contains violations of the variable sharing relevance condition C7.

RM 2: $\sim A \rightarrow . A \rightarrow \sim A$.

To prove RM 2 start with $A \rightarrow . A \rightarrow A$, contrapose the consequent to get $A \rightarrow . \sim A \rightarrow \sim A$ and then use Perm,rR3, to get the theorem.

The next theorem is easily obtained from RM 2 with Dbl. Neg..

RM 3: $A \rightarrow . \sim A \rightarrow A$

In his [1970], Dunn attributes the next proof to R.K. Meyer.

RM 4: $\sim(A \rightarrow A) \rightarrow . B \rightarrow B$

Proof sketch

1) $(A \rightarrow A) \wedge (B \rightarrow B)$ T1, Adj.

Use RM3 with (1) as the A and then use MP.

2) $\sim((A \rightarrow A) \wedge (B \rightarrow B)) \rightarrow . (A \rightarrow A) \wedge (B \rightarrow B)$

3) $\sim(A \rightarrow A) \vee \sim(B \rightarrow B) \rightarrow . (A \rightarrow A) \wedge (B \rightarrow B)$ De. M. on (2).

4) $\sim(A \rightarrow A) \vee \sim(B \rightarrow B) \rightarrow . B \rightarrow B$ Dr. 1 on (3)

5) $\sim(A \rightarrow A) \rightarrow . B \rightarrow B$ Dr. 2 On (4).

In light of the completeness theorem of RM with respect to Sugihara matrices, Theorem V of II.21, and Theorem VII of II.21, which told us that the negation of any Sugihara thesis entailed any Sugihara thesis, RM4 should be no surprise. Still it is illuminating to see the relevance violation pulled out of a plausible principle by acceptable syntactic techniques.

So we reject RM as an entailment system. The three theorems below show that RM's $\rightarrow$ would not even be satisfactory to represent an empirical conditional.

RM 5: $\sim A \rightarrow . B \rightarrow . A \rightarrow B$

RM 6: $\sim(A \rightarrow B) \rightarrow . B \rightarrow A$

RM 7: $A \rightarrow B \vee B \rightarrow A$

It would be nice to be able to reject E plus RM1 as a candidate for the entailment system. But the author does not know how to mimic a proof of RM 4, or RM 4 restricted to entailment formulas, in E plus RM1. So he has not been able to show that system EM violates adequacy condition C7. EM is E plus EM 1 below.

EM 1: $A \rightarrow B \rightarrow . A \rightarrow B \rightarrow . A \rightarrow B$

Still we reject RM1 and EM 1 because they involve derivational irrelevance between antecedent and consequent. An attempt to obtain either RM1 or EM 1 in the natural deduction system FE of IV.6 reveals that in neither do we get the conseque[illegible] in any clear way from the antecedent; we get the consequ[illegible] simply because they are theorems.

It seems as if it would be nice to have an v-elimination in system FE which is not hampered by Anderson's restrictions on Adjunction or R5. If the exported form of v-elimination: $A \rightarrow C \rightarrow . B \rightarrow C \rightarrow . A \vee B \rightarrow C$ were a theorem, then there could be a more typical v-elimination. However, we do not accept this exported form as an additional axiom for E because it leads to EM 1 as a theorem. X 29 of the next section shows that EM 1 is not a theorem of E or R; hence X29 shows that this exported form of v-elimination is not a theorem of E or R or NR.

But what about accepting Maksimowa's formula as a new axiom schema for E? We reject with suggestion because it seems that acceptance of it would bring with it the breakdown of the barrier between E and R because the "natural" way to get the Maksimowa formula in a natural deduction system such as FE is to allow Reit. of non-entailments. Nevertheless, we must admit that there is not a very strong case for rejecting the addition of the Maksimowa formula as a new axiom schema.

Our final point is that the additon of Boethius' thesis to extensions of E leads to inconsistency is a point which is easily made. E has $p \wedge \sim p \rightarrow . \sim(p \wedge \sim p)$ as a theorem and of course $p \wedge \sim p \rightarrow . p \wedge \sim p$. But if we have Boethius' thesis $p \wedge \sim p \rightarrow . p \wedge \sim p$ would give $\sim(p \wedge \sim p \rightarrow \sim(p \wedge \sim p))$.

Exercises IV.10

1. In I prove Factor by starting with E plus $B \rightarrow C \rightarrow . A \rightarrow A$.
2. Trace out some oddities of R plus Factor. See Bacon [1965a] to see that it gives classical logic.
3. Work out some of the theorems for A+B and A∘B in RM.
4. Prove RM5,6,& 7.
5. If we add to E as an axiom a formula which is not a classical tautology when $\rightarrow$ is preplace with $\supset$, do we get an inconsistent system?
6. See if you can show that EM violates C7.

IV.11 Section on non-theorems of E,R,RM, and NR, Use of Maksimowa's matrix $\mathfrak{M}$a to show that NR theses do not translate into E theses,

This section continues IV.8 since we continue to show that formulas are not theorems of systems under consideration. Hence, we use the same notation for designating non-theorems. Again we use X( ), where the names of the systems for which we claim the formula is not a theorem are listed between the parentheses. The most significant result of this section is a proof that system E lacks, as a theorem, Maksimowa's formula, as asserted in Theorem V of IV.7. The methodology of this section is primarily semantical because we use matrices. It would be useful to recall matrix $\mathfrak{M}$o from III.4. Still, we are not wholly finished with syntax; we close with some E theorems which are useful for Part V and interesting for their own sake.

If the □ of NR is treated as an identity operator, the proof that $\mathfrak{M}$o is suitable for NR is the same as a proof that it is suitable for R. Assume, then, that it has been established that $\mathfrak{M}$o is suitable for E, Π', R, and NR. Our first theorem shows us that the systems we take most seriously meet adequacy condition C7 of variable sharing relevance. Furthermore, Theorem I enables us to use inspection to tell at a glance that many formulas are non-theorems of E, Π', R, and NR.

Theorem I of IV.11: If a B⟶C is a theorem of E, Π', R, or NR, then B and C share a sentential variable.

The crucial step in the proof of Theorem I is an inductive proof on the length of A to get Lemma 1. We leave the induction as an exercise.

Lemma 1 of IV.11: If A is a wff. of the languages of the systems cited in Theorem I, then if every variable of A is assigned +1 on $\mathfrak{M}$o, v(A)=±1; and if every variable is assigned +2, v(A)=±2.

With Lemma 1, the theorem is proved by noting that if B and C in B⟶C share no variable, there is an assignment on $\mathfrak{M}$o such that v(B)=±1 and v(C)=±2. Inspection of $\mathfrak{M}$o's ⟶ table shows: +1⟶+2 = +1⟶ -2 = -1⟶+2 = -1⟶ -2 = -3.

While we have $\mathfrak{M}$o under consideration, let us use it to show that E,R, and NR all lack the special axioms of I, EM, and RM. Note that since □ of NR is being interpreted as an identity operator on $\mathfrak{M}$o, the ⟶'s of the formulas below can be looked at as ⟹'s when we want to consider the formula as an NR formula.

X28(E,R,NR): A⟶B⟶.A∧C⟶.B∧C Set v(A)=+1,v([illegible] , and v(C)=+2.

X29(E,R,NR): A⟶B⟶.A⟶B⟶.A⟶B Set v(A [illegible] and v(B)=-0.

X30 (E,R,NR): A⟶.A⟶A   Set v(A)=-0.

Consider now Ackermann's matrix 𝒜 given with Meyer's 𝒩r at the end of IV 7. As usual we state without details of proof the following soundness result from Ackermann's [1956].

Lemma 2 of IV.11: 𝒜 is suitable for E.

The next two theorems about E can be proved by following the hints given for Theorem VI of IV.7, except use 𝒜 instead of 𝒩r. These theorems enable us to tell by inspection that certain formulas are not E theorems.

Theorem II of IV.11: E has no theorem of the form A⟶.B⟶C, where A is a zdf..

Theorem III of IV.11: E has no theorem of the form ~(A⟶B)⟶.C⟶D.

For the reasons given back in IV.2, Theorem III is highly desirable. An immediate result of Theorem III is that in E AoB entails no entailments. An immediate result of Theorem II is that R is not contained in E.

X31(E): A⟶.A⟶B⟶B

While we have 𝒜 under consideration, let us use it to verify that E does not have Permutation.

X32 (E): (A⟶.B⟶C)⟶.B⟶.A⟶C   Set v(A)=-3,v(B)=+2, and v(C)=-1.

We now turn to a consideration of E,R, NR, and RM and their interpretations on Sugihara matrices. Again treat NR's □ as an identity operation. If you completed a proof of Theorem V of II.21, you have proved the next lemma.

Lemma 3 of IV.11: Sugihara matrices are suitable for E, R, NR, and RM.

Before using Sugihara matrices to show that certain formulas are not theses of specified systems, let us note that Lemma 3 together with Theorem IV of III.6 give us a theorem about the lack of finite characteristic matrices. For the reasons given at the end of III.6, it is desirable that a system does not have a finite characteristic matrix.

Theorem IV of IV.11: E,R,RM, and NR have no finite characteristic matrices.

Since RM is a rather weak system inasmuchas it admits many formulas as theses which are unacceptable as entailments, it is interesting to note that RM lacks the appealing principle of Factor. To verify that RM lacks Factor use the denumerable but inconsistent Sugihara matrix of Example 1 of II.21; set v(A)=+1, v(B)=+2, and v(C)=0.

Systems E, R, NR, and RM do satisfy Belnap's C2 by distinguishing material implication from entailment.

X33(E,R, NR, RM): $A \supset B \rightarrow . A \rightarrow B$ Use $\mathcal{S}_{\bar{1}}$ of Example 4 of II.21 and set $v(A)=+1$ and $v(B)=0$.

So even system RM_3 distinguishes $A \supset B$ from $A \rightarrow B$!

Because only E has a significant definition of $\Box A$ in terms of $A \rightarrow A \rightarrow A$, X34 really only shows that in E strict implication does not entail an entailment.

X34(E,R,NR,RM): $\sim(A \wedge \sim B) \rightarrow \sim(A \wedge \sim B) \rightarrow \sim(A \wedge \sim B) \rightarrow . A \rightarrow B$
Use $\mathcal{S}_2$ of Example 3 of II.21 and set $v(A)=-1$ and $v(B)=-2$.

In X35, where $\Box$ is the primitive $\Box$ of NR is, of course, significant only for NR. Nevertheless, we must not overlook the fact that X3 and X35 show that both E and NR satisfy Belnap's C4.

X35(NR): $\Box(A \supset B) \rightarrow . A \Rightarrow B$ Proceed as for X34 but treat as an identity operator.

X36, X37, and X38 show us that these systems satisfy C16 by not having rules of Exportation, Antilogism, and Suppression of Necessary Truths. (The remarks at the end of the preceding section show us that these systems could not have a rule corresponding to Boethius' thesis.) X36 would come form $A \wedge B \rightarrow B$ by Exportation, X37 would come from $A \wedge \sim B \rightarrow A$ by Antilogism, and X38 from $A \wedge (B \vee \sim B) \rightarrow . B \vee \sim B$ by Suppression of Necessary Truths. Again use $\mathcal{S}_{\bar{1}}$. So, again note that even RM_3 lacks these rules.

X36(E,R, NR, RM): $A \rightarrow . B \rightarrow B$ Set $v(A)=+1$ and $v(B)=0$.
X37(E,R, NR, RM): $A \wedge \sim A \rightarrow B$ Set $v(A)=0$ and $v(B)=-1$.
X38(E,R, NR, RM): $A \rightarrow . B \vee \sim B$ Set $v(A)=+1$ and $v(B)=0$.

We now come to the most important part of this section. This is a proof of Lemma 4 of IV.7 which we can restate here as X39.

X39(E): $(A \rightarrow . B \rightarrow C) \wedge (B \rightarrow . A \vee C) \rightarrow . B \rightarrow C$ Use $\mathfrak{M}$a below and set $v(A)=-6, v(B)=-5$, and $v(C)=-5$.

Of course, we need Lemma 4 below for the valuation given after X39 to show that the Maksimowa formula is not an E theorem. The proof of this lemma may be eased considerably when we discuss in V.5 how $\mathfrak{M}$a is developed from a model structure for E. It has been verified by TESTER;see end of section.

Lemma 4 of IV.11: $\mathfrak{M}$a is suitable for the positive fragment of E.

Lemma 4 suffices because X39 is in the positive fragment

of E and system E is a conservative extension of its positive fragment. (For the result that E is a conservative extension of its positive fragment see p. 245 Fact 11 of Meyer's and Routley's [1974] and Maksimowa's [1971]. Furthermore, as an exercise will bring out, it is easy enough to add a negation table to $\mathfrak{M}$a so that the matrix with a negation table is suitable for all of E.)

The matrix $\mathfrak{M}$a is taken from the E model structure of Maksimowa's [1972] and presented in V.4. Since there are four points in this model structure, $\mathfrak{M}$a is a world-matrix for four worlds. The worlds are labelled w0, w1, w2, and w3. Consequently, there are 16 elements for the matrix; they are interpreted as on Table I below. The positive elements are the designated elements. The lattice diagram gives the order of the elements and enables us to read-off the $\wedge$ and $\vee$ tables by finding meets below and joins above. View the diagram as looking down into a pit with the lowest level being:

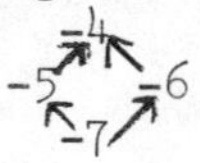

Table I

	w0	w1	w2	w3
+7	T	T	T	T
+6	T	T	T	F
+5	T	T	F	T
+4	T	T	F	F
+3	T	F	T	T
+2	T	F	T	F
+1	T	F	F	T
+0	T	F	F	F
-0	F	T	T	T
-1	F	T	T	F
-2	F	T	F	T
-3	F	T	F	F
-4	F	F	T	T
-5	F	F	T	F
-6	F	F	F	T
-7	F	F	F	F

Lattice Diagram for $\mathfrak{M}$a,

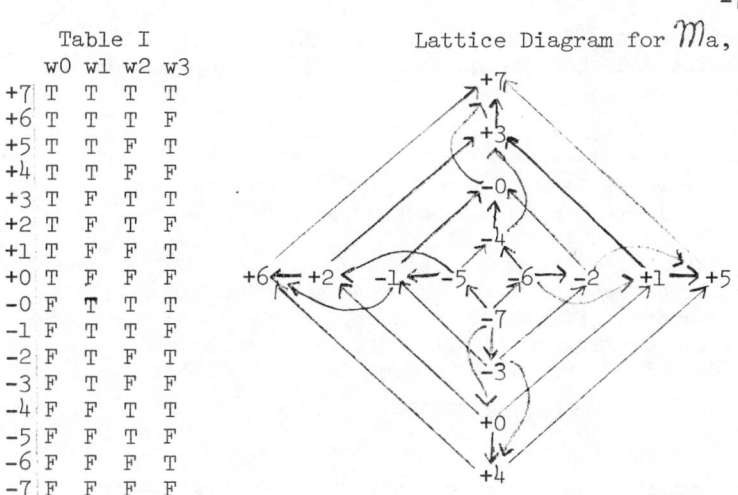

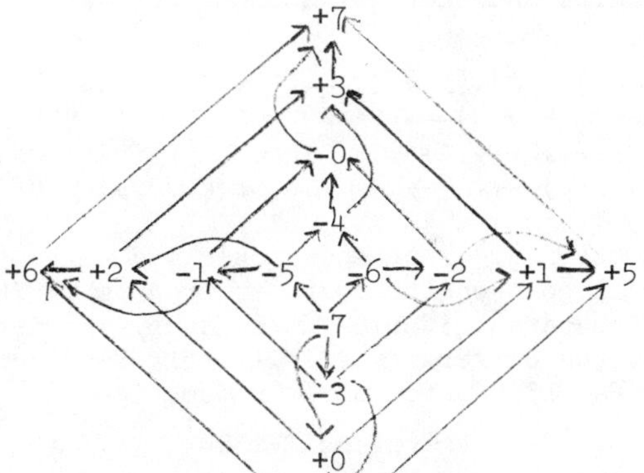

It may be helpful for understanding this matrix and for proving Lemma 4 to reconsider the discussion of world-matrices from I.7. Verify that $+3 \wedge +4 = +1$, that $+3 \wedge -2 = -6$, and that $-5 \vee +1 = +3$.

N.D. Belnap Jr. with the computer program TESTER helped the author correct some errors on the following $\longrightarrow$ table for $\mathfrak{M}$a.

Table II, the ⟶ table for $\mathfrak{M}$a,

⟶	+7	+6	+5	+4	+3	+2	+1	+0	-0	-1	-2	-3	-4	-5	-6	-7
+7	+7	-7	-6	-7	-4	-7	-6	-7	-0	-7	-6	-7	-4	-7	-6	-7
+6	+7	+0	-6	-7	-4	-7	-6	-7	-0	-7	-6	-7	-4	-7	-6	-7
+5	+7	-7	+1	-7	-4	-7	-6	-7	-0	-7	-6	-7	-4	-7	-6	-7
+4	+7	+0	+1	+0	-4	-7	-6	-7	-0	-7	-6	-7	-4	-7	-6	-7
+3	+7	-7	-6	-7	+3	-7	-6	-7	-0	-7	-6	-7	-4	-7	-6	-7
+2	+7	+0	-6	-7	+3	+0	-6	-7	-0	-7	-6	-7	-4	-7	-6	-7
+1	+7	-7	+1	-7	+3	-7	+1	-7	-0	-7	-6	-7	-4	-7	-6	-7
+0	+7	+0	+1	+0	+3	+0	+1	+0	-0	-7	-6	-7	-4	-7	-6	-7
-0	+7	-7	-6	-7	-4	-7	-6	-7	+7	-7	-6	-7	-4	-7	-6	-7
-1	+7	+1	-6	-6	-4	-6	-6	-6	+7	+1	-6	-6	-4	-6	-6	-6
-2	+7	-7	+7	-7	-4	-7	-4	-7	+7	-7	+7	-7	-4	-7	-4	-7
-3	+7	+7	+7	+7	-4	-4	-4	-4	+7	+7	+7	+7	-4	-4	-4	-4
-4	+7	-7	-6	-7	+7	-7	-6	-7	+7	-7	-6	-7	+7	-7	-6	-7
-5	+7	+1	-6	-6	+7	+1	-6	-6	+7	+1	-6	-6	+7	+1	-6	-6
-6	+7	-7	+7	-7	+7	-7	+7	-7	+7	-7	+7	-7	+7	-7	+7	-7
-7	+7	+7	+7	+7	+7	+7	+7	+7	+7	+7	+7	+7	+7	+7	+7	+7

Let us conclude Part IV on syntax for relevance preserving logics and their extensions with a bit of syntactical work.

T87: ((A⟶B) v C)∧(A v C)⟶.B v C
T88: (A v C)∧(B v C)⟶.(A∧B) v C
T89: (A v B)⟶C⟶.A⟶C   Theorem version of Dr.2.
T90: (A⟶.B∧C)⟶.A⟶B   Theorem version of Dr.1.

In section 8.4.1 of Anderson's and Belnap's [1975] there is a brief report on the computer program TESTER for verifying that matrices are suitable for systems. Readers are invited to contact the University of Pittsburg Computer Center, Pittsburg Pa. 15260, for more information on TESTER.

Exercises IV.11

1. Prove T87 - 90.

2. Does R have any theorem of the form ∼(A⟶B)⟶.C⟶D?

3. Trace out some consequences of RM plus Factor.

4. Show that Weakening, X40 below, is not a theorem of E,R, NR, or RM.

X40(E,R, NR,RM): A⟶B⟶.A⟶.A⟶B.

5. Make a negation table for $\mathfrak{M}$a with classical negation. Then make a negation table as follows. v(∼A) is T at w0 iff. v(A) is F at w0. v(∼A) is T at w1 iff. v(A) is F at w1. v(∼A) is T at w2 iff. v(A) is F at w3. Finally,

Exercises IV.11 continued

v(∼A) is T at w3 iff. v(A) is F at w2. (Here w2 and w3 are imperfect complements of one another. See I.7.) Relabel elements so that ∼+a = -a and ∼-a = +a. Show that $\mathfrak{M}_a$ with either negation table is suitable for E. (See exercise 5 of V.4.)

PART V

V.1 Introduction to Part V on model structure semantics, the E model structures of Meyer/Routley and L. Maksimowa, Soundness Theorem for E,

This part will be more accessible to those familiar with model structure or "possible worlds" semantics for modal logic. Cresswell's and Hughes' introductory text,[1968], provides a lucid introduction to model structure semantics for modal systems. Also, Part V presupposes familiarity with deduction techniques for first-order predicate logic presentend in typical logic texts. Yes! We use classical logic in our reasoning about model structures. Someone versed in standard predicate logic, but without prior acquaintance with model structure semantics can follow the arguments of this Part; but the converse is not true.

A value of model structure semantics is that they enable us to explicate what it means to say that theses of a system are necessarily true. We can say that all, but only all, of the theses of a system hold at all points of all model structures of a certain type.Of course, if such an explication is to lend any support to the system 'hold,''points in a model structure,' and 'model structure' have to be interpreted. If 'hold' meant true, points were interpreted as possible worlds, and model structures were regarded as sets of possible worlds; then such an explication of the necessity of theses would say that they are true in all possible worlds. We, though, are going to allow inconsistencies to hold at points; so we will not use 'true' and 'possible world' in our efforts to interpret model structure results. In fact, we will not say much about interpretations of model structures until the last section. Discussion about such interpretations and creation of interpretations is philosophical activity which should be stimulated by presentation of the semantics. We hope to provide some of that stimulus. Nevertheless, we regard having a well interpreted model structure semantics, or even a matrix semantics, as only an auxiliary support for a system. The ultimate test for a system is conformity of its theses to our developed normative intuitions.

In this first section of Part V, we present Larisa Maksimowa's characterization of E model structures, Ems., from her [1972]. The characterization is essentially that of Meyer's and Routley's [197-b] except that we do not use a 0-point. Remarks and exercises of Part V bring out the essential identity of the two characterizations; see especially exercises 1 and 2 of V.3. In this section, our goal is to characterize Ems., define 'validity' on an Ems., and show that all E theorems are valid on all Ems., viz., establish a Soundness Theorem for E on Ems. We use underlined capital letters, with subscripts and superscripts, to designate Ems., and we will continue to use Ems. for both the singular and plural of 'E model structure.'

An Ems. M is an ordered 4-tuple $\langle K,P,R,*\rangle$, where K is a non-empty set of points, P is a unary predicate of K's, R is a ternary relation amongst the K's, and * is a unary operation on the K's into the K's; and the following postulates hold for all a,b,c,d in K. The a,b,c,d can be regarded as implicitly universally quantified, free variables, or individual parameters in the sense of Thomason [1970]. If a member of K is a P, we call it a P-point and designate it with a subscripted 0. Three other definitions are useful, although D3 is rarely used here. Meyer and Routley use D3 in their several presentations of model structure semantics.

D1: $a \preccurlyeq b =_{df} (\exists x)(Px \wedge Rxab)$

D2: $R^2abcd =_{df} (\exists x)(Rabx \wedge Rxbd)$

D3: $R^2a(bc)d =_{df} (\exists x)(Rbcx \wedge Raxd)$

POSTULATES for Ems.

$\mathcal{E}1$: $(\exists x)(Px \wedge Rxaa)$
$\mathcal{E}2$: $(x)((Px \wedge Rxab) \supset (\exists y)(Py \wedge Rayb))$
$\mathcal{E}3$: $(x)((Rabx \wedge Rxcd) \supset (\exists y)(Racy \wedge Rbyd))$ or $R^2abcd \supset R^2b(ac)d$
$\mathcal{E}4$: $Rabc \supset (\exists x)(Rabx \wedge Rxbc)$ or $Rabc \supset R^2abbc$
$\mathcal{E}5$: $(x)((Px \wedge Rxab) \wedge Rbcd \supset .Racd)$
$\mathcal{E}6$: $(x)((Px \wedge Rxab) \wedge Rcbd \supset .Rcad)$
$\mathcal{E}7$: $a^{**} = a$
$\mathcal{E}8$: $Rabc \supset Rac^*b^*$
$\mathcal{E}9$: Raa^*a

Numbers 3,4,7,8 and 9 above are respectively postulates 3,4,7,8 and 9 of Meyer and Routley. Theorem $\mathcal{T}1$ is Meyer's and Routley's first postulate, but for them $a \preccurlyeq b$ is R0ab for a selected P-point 0.

$\mathcal{T}1$: $a \preccurlyeq a$

A proof comes immediately from $\mathcal{E}1$ and D1.

$\mathcal{T}2$: $a \preccurlyeq b \wedge b \preccurlyeq c \supset .a \preccurlyeq c$

Proof sketch:
1) $Px \wedge Rxab$ — hyp. of $a \preccurlyeq b$
2) $Py \wedge Rybc$ — hyp. of $b \preccurlyeq c$
3) $(Px \wedge Rxab) \wedge Rybc$ — Predicate logic, PL, (1),(2).
4) $(Px \wedge Rxab) \wedge Rybc \supset .Ryac$ — from $\mathcal{E}6$
5) $Ryac$ — MD (3),(4)!
6) $Py \wedge Ryac$ — PL (2),(5)
7) $(\exists y)(Py \wedge Ryac)$, $a \preccurlyeq c$ — Existential Generalization, EG, on (6).

$\mathcal{T}3$ is postulate 5 of Meyer and Routley; its proof is readily obtained from $\mathcal{E}1$ and $\mathcal{E}2$. But we will sketch a proof of $\mathcal{T}4$.

$\mathcal{T}3$: $(\exists y)(Py \wedge Raya)$

$\mathcal{T}4$: (y)(Py∧Ryaa ⊃ (∃x)((Py∧Ryax)∧Rxaa)

Proof sketch

1) Ryaa⊃(∃x)(Ryax∧Rxaa)   from $\mathcal{E}4$
2) Py∧Ryaa⊃(∃x)(Py∧Ryax∧Rxaa)   PL on (1)
3) (y)(Py∧Ryaa ⊃ (∃x)(Py∧Ryax∧Rxaa)   Universal Generalization,UG, on a logical consequence of a postulate.

$\mathcal{T}5$: Raaa

Proof sketch

1) Po_1∧Ro_1aa   From $\mathcal{E}1$
2) (∃x)(Po_1∧Ro_1ax)∧Rxaa   from (1) and $\mathcal{T}4$
3) (Po_1∧Ro_1ax)∧Rxaa   Existential Instantiation,EI, on (2)
4) (∃y)((Py∧Ryax)∧Rxaa   EG on (3)
5) (∃y)((Py∧Ryax)∧Rxaa)⊃.Raaa   from $\mathcal{E}5$
6) Raaa   MD (4),(5).

$\mathcal{T}6$: Rabc⊃(∃x)(Rabx∧Raxc)

Proof sketch

1) Raaa∧Rabc   Assume Rabc and use $\mathcal{T}5$.
2) (∃y)(Raay∧Rybc)   EG on (1)
3) (∃y)(Raay∧Rybc)⊃(∃x)(Rabx∧Raxc)   A PL equivalent of $\mathcal{E}3$
4) (∃x)(Rabx∧Raxc)   MD on (2),(3)

A proof of $\mathcal{T}7$ comes easily from $\mathcal{E}9$,D1, and peculiar properties of ⊃. Use $\mathcal{E}6$, $\mathcal{E}7$, and $\mathcal{E}8$ for $\mathcal{T}8$.

$\mathcal{T}7$: (x)(Px⊃.x*≼ x)

$\mathcal{T}8$: (x)((Px∧Rxcd)∧Rabc ⊃.Rabd)

In the proof of $\mathcal{T}9$ we finally have to pay the price of taking the E-provable E-10(Prefixing) as an axiom. Recall exercise 2 of IV.1. A special semantic postulate is not given for validating Prefixing. So, instead of proving a theorem of Prefixing in E, we prove a theorem in the formal semantics for E which serves to validate Prefixing in Ems..

$\mathcal{T}9$: (x)(Rabx∧Rxcd⊃(∃y)(Rbcy∧Rayd)),   Prefixing theorem,

Proof

1) Rabx∧Rxcd   Hyp.
2) (∃y)(Py∧Rxyx) $\mathcal{T}3$
3) Po_1∧Rxo_1x EI (2) to o_1
4) Rabx∧Rxo_1x PL (1),(3)
5) Rao_1z∧Rbzx   From (4) with $\mathcal{E}3$ and EI to z
6) Rbzx∧Rxcd   PL (1),(5)
7) Rbcu∧Rzud   From (6) with $\mathcal{E}3$ and EI to u
8) Rao_1z∧Rzud   PL (5),(7)
9) Rauw∧Ro_1wd From (8) with $\mathcal{E}3$ and EI to w

Proof of $\mathcal{T}$9 continued

10) $(Po_1 \wedge Ro_1wd) \wedge Rauw \supset .Raud$	From 8
11) $(Po_1 \wedge Ro_1wd) \wedge Rauw$	PL (9),(3)
12) Raud	MD (10,(11)
13) $Rbcu \wedge Raud$	PL (7(,(12)
14) $(\exists y)(Rbcy \wedge Rayd)$	EG u in (13).

Isn't it somewhat surprising that we have to do so much syntactical manipulation to present semantics for E? However, the preceding theorems about Ems. are crucial for showing that E-axioms are valid in all Ems.. To talk of validity we need to talk of interpretations of E's language and to talk of formulas "holding" at points, or "holding" at some crucial points, of Ems.. Here, it is only fair to warn readers that the following presentation of formulas holding at points of an Ems. is somewhat non-standard amongst presentation of model structure semantics. We do not talk of formulas, in general, of being assigned a value from $\{1,0\}$ or $\{T,F\}$ at points of an Ems.. Instead we talk of formulas being forced into or not being forced into sets of formulas constructed at points of an Ems.. This approach enables us to use a style reminiscient of Hintikka's model-set technique in arguments that formulas are valid, does not suggest that points of model structures represent worlds or some situations at which sentences are true or false, and opens the possibility of interpreting points of an Ems. as the kind of thing at which sets of sentences are constructed, eg., sources and recipients of messages. The term 'forcing' is borrowed from Maksimowa although we do not use it as she does.

A <u>forcing on an Ems. M</u> is obtained by an assignment of each variable at each point of K, definition of a set w_a at each a,a$\in$K, and a forcing of formulas into the w_a's to get a set-up Ha at each point a,a$\in$K. (The notion of set-up is borrowed from the Routley's [1972].) An <u>assignment of variables</u> is a function f() on K $\times$ V, where V is the set of variables, into $\{1,0\}$ subject to the following restriction called the Inclusion Condition.

INCLUSION CONDITION on assignments f( )

If $(\exists x)(Px \wedge Rxab)$ and f(p,a)=1, then f(p,b)=1

Given an assignment f(), $w_a = \{p / f(p,a)=1\}$. Formulas are then forced into the w_a to get set-ups Ha. A <u>set-up Ha</u> is the smallest set of formulas obtained from w_a by forcing formulas into w_a by the following procedures.

FORCING PROCEDURES

i) If A is a variable, A $\in$ Ha iff. A $\in w_a$.
ii) $A \wedge B \in$ Ha iff. A $\in$ Ha and B $\in$ Ha. $\wedge$-normality
iii) $(A \vee B) \in$ Ha iff. A $\in$ Ha or B $\in$ Ha. $\vee$-normality

FORCING PROCEDURES continued

iv) $\sim A \in Ha$ iff. $A \notin Ha^*$, where Ha^* is the set-up built at $w_a{}^*$ and $w_a{}^*$ is the set of variables at a^* under assignment function f(). Let us call (iv) Imperfect Consistency.

v) $A \longrightarrow B$ Ha iff. $(x)(y)(Raxy \wedge A \in Hx \supset . B \in Hy)$. We call this rule the Triad Rule.

These forcing, or set-up building, procedures can easily be regarded as valuation functions or interpretation functions on the formulas into $\{T, F\}$ or $\{1, 0\}$. Where we have $A \in Ha$ others, such as Meyer and Routley in their several works on semantics of entailment, would have I(A,a)=T, i.e., A is true or holds at point a. Our set-ups can be regarded as the set of formulas or the theory which consists of exactly the formulas assigned T or 1 at a point of an Ems.. Also note the similarity of the first four forcing procedures and the structural meaning rules developed in III.5. This similarity may help those who want to have some interpretation of Ems. instead of merely working formally with them as we are doing.

We say that a formula A is valid on an Ems. $\underline{M}$ if for any assignment f() of variables on K, $K \in \underline{M}$, $A \in Hx$ for all x such that Px. In terms of truth, a formula A is valid on $\underline{M}$ if A is true at all P-points for any assignment of True and False to variables at the points of $\underline{M}$. A formula is E-valid if it is valid on all Ems..

We can now start moving towards the main goal of this section which is a proof of the following Soundness Theorem.

Theorem I of V.1: If $\vdash_E A$, then A is E-valid.

The remainder of this section is devoted primarily to proving Theorem I by showing that E's axioms are E-valid and that E's rules preserve E-validity. We close with some remarks about Ems. and world-matrices.

We start with three lemmas on procedural rules. We call use of Lemma 1 the Inclusion Condition and use of Lemma 2 the Elimination Argument or EA. Lemma 3 gives a Rule of Identity.

Lemma 1 of V.1: If $(\exists x)(Px \wedge Rxab)$, i.e., $a \leq b$, and $A \in Ha$, then $A \in Hb$.

The proof of Lemma 1 is by induction on the length of A. The basis step is readily taken by noting the Inclusion Condition for assignments of variables and forcing procedure (i). So, assume that the Inclusion condition holds for B and C shorter than A. We consider only the cases in which A has the form $\sim B$ and A has the form $B \longrightarrow C$. Assume for both cases that we have Po_1 and Ro_1ab. Consider the $\sim B$ case. If $\sim B \in Ha$, then, by Imperfect Consistency, $B \notin Ha^*$. From $\varepsilon 8$ we get $Ro_1b^*a^*$ from Ro_1ab. So, the induction assumption tells us that $B \notin Hb^*$; because if B were in Hb^* we would have $B \in Ha^*$ from the induction assumption and $Ro_1b^*a^*$. Imperfect Consistency now gets us $\sim B \in Hb$ from $B \notin Hb^*$. For the $B \rightarrow C$ case, consider the following <u>reductio</u>.

1)	$B \rightarrow C \in Ha$ with Ro_1ab	
2)	$B \rightarrow C \notin Hb$	<u>reductio</u> hypothesis
3)	a) $B \in Hc$ with $Rbcd$	Triad Rule on (2).
	b) $C \notin Hd$	
4)	$Ro_1ab \wedge Rbcd$	PL from (1) and (2)
5)	$Ro_1ab \wedge Rbcd \supset (\exists y)(Ro_1cy \wedge Rayd)$	From $\mathcal{E}3$
6)	a) Ro_1cy	From (5) by MD and EI
	b) $Rayd$	
7)	$B \in Hy$	From the induction assumption on (3a) and (6a)
8)	$C \in Hd$	Triad Rule on (1),(7), and (6b).

Since (8) and (3b) are inconsistent we have Lemma 1 by <u>reductio</u>.

Note that Lemma 1 tells us that the $\leqslant$-relation on points of an Ems. corresponds to an inclusion relation between set-ups at points. We leave an argument for Lemma 2 as an exercise.

Lemma 2 of V.1: If $B \in Ha$ or $C \in Ha$ but $B \notin Ha$, then $C \in Ha$.

The next lemma suggests that some set-ups may lack such basic logical truths as $A \rightarrow A$!

Lemma 3 of V.1: For any x, if $x \in K$ and $K \in \underline{M}$ of Ems. $\underline{M}$, then if Px, $A \rightarrow A \in Hx$.

To prove this lemma assume that $A \rightarrow A \notin Hx$ with Px. By the Triad Rule we have Ro_1ab, $A \in Ha$, $A \notin Hb$ with $x = o_1$. But with $a \leqslant b$, viz., Ro_1ab, and the Inclusion Condition we get $A \in Hb$. So, by <u>reductio</u> we have the lemma.

We call use of Lemma 3 use of the Rule of Identity. We now turn to a lemma with as many sublemmas as E has axiom schemas. We do not prove all of the sublemmas. Hopefully, we show enough to make clear how the Ems. postulates are used and which ones are crucial for validating certain axioms.

Lemma 4 of V.1: If A is an axiom of E, then A is E-valid.

The sublemmas will be proved by <u>reductio</u> by assuming that the axiom schema does not belong to Ho for some P-point o of some Ems.. Because all axioms are of the $A \rightarrow B$ form, our <u>reductio</u> assumptions and the Triad Rule always give us: Po, Roab, $A \in Ha$, but $B \notin Hb$ for some a,b in the Ems.. So, proofs of the sublemmas can begin with $A \in Hb$ and $B \notin Hb$ by use of the Inclusion Condition, where A is the antecedent and B is the consequent of the axiom being considered.

Sublemma 1 of V.1: E1 is E-valid.

Proof

1 a) $A \wedge B \in Hb$ with Roab and Po

b) $A \notin Hb$

Now $\wedge$-normality immediately tells us that we have a contradiction.

Sublemmas 2 and 3 of V.1: E2 and E3 are E-valid.

Sublemma 4 of V.1: E4 is E-valid.

Proof

1 a) $B \in Hb$ with Po and Roab

b) $A \vee B \notin Hb$

Now $\vee$-normality immediately tells us that we have a contradiction.

Sublemma 5 of V.1: E5 is E-valid.

Proof

1 a) $A \wedge (B \vee C) \in Hb$ with Po and Roab

b) $B \vee (A \wedge C) \notin Hb$

2 a) $A \in Hb$ — $\wedge$-normality on (1a)

b) $B \vee C \in Hb$

3 a) $B \notin Hb$ — $\vee$-normality on (1b)

b) $A \wedge C \notin Hb$

4) $B \in Hb$ or $C \in Hb$ — $\vee$-normality on (2b)

5) $C \in Hb$ — EA (3a),(4)

6) $A \notin Hb$ or $C \notin Hb$ — $\wedge$-normality on (3b)

7) $A \notin Hb$ — EA (5),(6)

Since (7) and (2a) are inconsistent we have validated the Distribution axiom by a <u>reductio</u> argument.

Sublemmas 6 and 7 of V.1: E6 and E7 are E-valid.

We consider only E7 in our proof.

1 a) $\sim\sim A \in Hb$ — with Po and Roab

b) $A \notin Hb$

2) $\sim A \notin Hb$* — Imperfect Consistency on (1a)

3) $A \in Hb$** Imperfect Consistency on (2)

4) $A \in Hb$ — $\mathcal{E}7$ on (3)

The proof is finished because (4) and (1b) conflict.

Sublemma 8 of V.1: E8 is E-valid.

Proof

1 a) $(A \rightarrow A) \wedge (B \rightarrow B) \rightarrow C$ Hb — with Po and Roab

b) $C \notin Hb$

2) Po_1 and Rbo_1b — From $\mathcal{T}3$

3) $(A \rightarrow A) \wedge (B \rightarrow B) \in Ho_1$ — Rule of Identity on (2)

4) $C \in Hb$ — Triad Rule (3),(2), and (1a).

The proof is finished because (4) and (1b) conflict.

Sublemma 9 of V.1: E9 is E-valid.

Proof

1 a) $A \rightarrow B \in Hb$ with Po and Roab

b) $B \rightarrow C \rightarrow . A \rightarrow C \notin Hb$

2 a) $B \rightarrow C \in Hc$ with Rbcd By Triad Rule on (1b)

b) $A \rightarrow C \notin Hd$

3 a) $A \in He$ with Rdef By Triad Rule on (2b)

b) $C \notin Hf$

By PL we get $(\exists x)(Rbcx \wedge Rxef)$ from Rbcd and Rdef. By the Suffixing postulate $\mathcal{E}3$ we get $(\exists x)(Rbex \wedge Rcxf)$ which gives:

4) Rbex and Rcxf.

The Triad Rule with Rbex,(1a),and (3a) gives:

5) $B \in Hx$.

The Triad Rule with Rcxf,(2a), and (5) gives:

6) $C \in Hf$.

Since (6) and (3b) are inconsistent we have the sublemma by <u>reductio</u>.

Sublemma 10 of V.1: E10 is E-valid.

Proof

1 a) $A \rightarrow B \in Hb$ with Po and Roab

b) $C \rightarrow A \rightarrow . C \rightarrow B \notin Hb$

2 a) $C \rightarrow A \in Hc$ with Rbcd By Triad Rule on (1b)

b) $C \rightarrow B \notin Hd$

3 a) $C \in He$ with Rdef By Triad Rule on (2b)

b) $B \notin Hf$

By PL we get $Rbcd \wedge Rdef$ from (2) and (3). By use of the Prefixing theorem $\mathfrak{T}9$ we get $(\exists y)(Rcey \wedge Rbyf)$ which, in turn, yields:

4) Rcey and Rbyf.

The Triad Rule with Rcey,(2a), and (3a) gives:

5) $A \in Hy$.

The Triad Rule with Rbyf,(5), and (1a) gives:

6) $B \in Hf$.

Since (6) and (3b) are inconsistent we have the sublemma by <u>reductio</u>.

Sublemma 11 of V.1: E11 is E-valid.

Proof

1 a) $A \rightarrow . A \rightarrow B \in Ha$ with Po and Roab Note: we use Ha.

b) $A \rightarrow B \notin Hb$

2 a) $A \in Hc$ with Rbcd By Triad Rule on (1b)

b) $B \notin Hd$

From (1) and (2) we have $(Po \wedge Roab) \wedge Rbcd$ which by $\mathcal{E}5$ gives:

3) Racd.

By use of $\mathcal{E}4$ with Racd we get:

4) Racx and Rxcd.

The Triad Rule with Racx,(1a), and (2a) gives:

Proof of Sublemma 11 continued,

5) $A \longrightarrow B \in Hx$.

The Triad Rule with Rxcd,(5), and (2a) gives:

6) $B \in H_d$ which conflicts with (2b).

After the preceding three sublemmas, the validation of E12 and E13 is delightfully easy.

Sublemmas 12 and 13 of V.1: E12 and E13 are E-valid.

Sublemma 14 of V.1: E14 is E-valid.

Proof

1 a) $A \longrightarrow B \in Hb$ with Po and Roab
  b) $\sim B \longrightarrow \sim A \notin Hb$

2 a) $\sim B \in Hc$ with Rbcd — By Triad Rule on (1b)
  b) $\sim A \notin Hd$

3) $B \notin Hc^*$ — Imperfect Consistency on (2a)

4) $A \in Hd^*$ — Imperfect Consistency on (2b)

From Rbcd of (2) by $\mathcal{E}8$ we get:

5) Rbd*c*

The Triad Rule with (5),(1a), and (4) gives:

6) $B \in H_c^*$ which conflicts with (3).

Sublemma 15 of V.1: E15 is E-valid.

Proof

1 a) $A \wedge \sim B \in Hb$ with Po and Roab
  b) $\sim(A \longrightarrow B) \notin Hb$

2) $A \longrightarrow B \in Hb^*$ — Imperfect Consistency on (1b)

3 a) $A \in Hb$ — $\wedge$-normality on (1a)
  b) $\sim B \in Hb$

4) $B \notin Hb^*$ — Imperfect Consistency on (3b)

By $\mathcal{E}9$ we have Rb*b**b* which by $\mathcal{E}7$ is:

5) Rb*bb*.

The Triad Rule with (5),(2), and (3a) gives:

6) $B \in Hb^*$ which conflicts with (4).

To complete the proof of Theorem I we now need only to verify that E's rules of proof preserve E-validity.

Lemma 5 of V.1: MP and Adj. preserve E-validity.

The Adjunction case is an immediate consequence of $\wedge$-normality. For MP consider the following <u>reductio</u>. We assume that $A \longrightarrow B$ and A are in every Ho_i, where Po_i, but that for some o, such that Po, $B \notin Ho$.

1 a) $A \longrightarrow B \in Ho$
  b) $A \in Ho$
  c) $B \notin Ho$

2) Rooo — By $\mathcal{X}5$

The Triad Rule with (2),(1a), and (1b) gives:

3) $B \in Ho$ which conflicts with (1c).

So E-theorems are all E-valid.

Just before Lemma 1 of I.7 and just before Theorem V of I.7 a promise was made. The promise was to motivate the requirement that on world-matrices whose D is the set of P-positive elements: $\underset{\sim}{a} \rightarrow \underset{\sim}{b} \in D$ iff. $\underset{\sim}{a} \leq \underset{\sim}{b}$. Here we can regard forcing A so that $A \in Hx$ as assigning A the value 1 or T at Ems. point x. A review of the I.7 discussion of world-matrices brings out that the requirement that $\underset{\sim}{a} \rightarrow \underset{\sim}{b} \in D$ iff. $\underset{\sim}{a} \leq \underset{\sim}{b}$ corresponds with the Ems. forcing requirement: for all P-points o of an Ems. $A \rightarrow B \in Ho$ iff. for all Ems. points x, if $A \in Hx$ then $B \in Hx$. Let us make this Ems. requirement a theorem.

Theorem II of V.1: On an Ems. and for a forcing on it, $A \rightarrow B \in Ho$ for all P-points o iff. for all x $A \in Hx$ then $B \in Hx$.

We certainly want Theorem II. If we accept $A \rightarrow B$, i.e., hold it at all P-points, we want $A \rightarrow B$ never to fail. A way of representing the failure of $A \rightarrow B$ is to have A belong to a set-up Hx while B fails to be in Hx. On the other hand, if $A \rightarrow B$ never fails, we want to accept it. So, Theorem II justifies the requirement on world-matrices. The question is: Is it really a theorem? We sketch a proof.

First, suppose that $A \rightarrow B \in Ho$, for all P-points o, but suppose that for some x $A \in Hx$ while $B \notin Hx$. $\mathscr{T}1$ tells us that there is a o_i such that Po_i and Ro_ixx. So, with $A \rightarrow B \in Ho_i$, Ro_ixx, and the Triad Rule, we have $B \in Hx$ if $A \in Hx$, which conflicts with our reductio assumption that $A \in Hx$ but $B \notin Hx$.

Second, suppose that for all x: if $A \in Hx$ then $B \in Hx$, but that for some o_i, Po_i, and $A \rightarrow B \notin Ho_i$. We have, then, for some x and y, Ro_ixy with $A \in Hx$ but $B \notin Hy$. Now the Inclusion Condition with Ro_ixy tells us that $A \in Hy$. But we cannot have $A \in Hy$ but $B \notin Hy$ if for all x A's belong to Hx implies B's belonging to Hx. So, we have, by reductio, the second part of the theorem.

Exercises V.1

1. Show that each of the Ems. postulates is used at least once in showing that the E axioms are E-valid.
2. Prove $\mathscr{T}8$.
3. Complete Lemma 1 for the cases of $B \wedge C$ and $B \vee C$.
4. Prove Sublemmas 6, 12, and 13.
5. Let us say that a set-up Ha is zdf.-normal if Ha = Ha*. Show that a zdf.-normal set-up is consistent, complete, and prime. I.e., show (i) For no A do $A \in Ha$ and $\sim A \in Ha$, (ii) for any A either $A \in Ha$ or $\sim A \in Ha$, and (iii) if $A \vee B$ is in Ha, then either $A \in Ha$ or $B \in Ha$.

Exercises V.1 continued,

6. If Ha is zdf.-normal, does $A \rightarrow A \in Ha$ for all a? Consider an Ems. with four points {o, a, b, c}, have Rabc, let a* = a, and have an interpretation such that f(p,a) = f(p,b) = 1 while f(p,c) = 0. Can this Ems. be developed so that $A \rightarrow A \notin Ha$?

7. Go through the Forcing Rules and replace $A \in Hx$ with I(A,x) = T. Show (i):if $a \leqslant b$ and I(A,a) = T, then I(B,a) = T and (ii): {A: I(A,a) = T} = Ha.

   This exercise shows that our set-up approach is, for technical purposes, the same as Meyer's and Routley's. However, the approaches may differ in regard to interpretation possibilities. The set-up approach does not even suggest that there should be talk of formulas being true at points of an Ems..

8. This exercise uses Meyer's notion of metavaluation which is presented on p. 270 of Anderson's and Belnap's [1975] and in several other works by Meyer. A metavaluation on E is a function on the formulas of E into {1,0} satisfying the following conditions.

   i) $v(A \rightarrow B) = 1$ iff. $\vdash_E A \rightarrow B$.

   ii) $v(A \vee B) = 1$ iff. $v(A) = 1$ or $v(B) = 1$.

   iii) $v(A \wedge B) = 1$ iff. $v(A) = 1$ and $v(B) = 1$.

   iv) $v(\sim A) = 1$ iff. $v(A) = 0$.

   He calls a formula <u>metavalid</u> if it is 1 on all metavaluations. He calls a system <u>coherent</u> if all of its theorems are metavalid. Show that E is metavalid. Make the appropriate changes in the above so that in clause (i) you talk of classical logic and S5 instead of E. Show that neither classical logic nor S5 are coherent. What is the significance of being coherent?

V.2: Completeness Theorem for E relative to validity on Ems., use of the Zorn's Lemma strategy,

Our goal in this section is to show that all E-valid formulas are theorems of E. This completeness goal is reached by showing that if a formula A is not an E-theorem, then there is an Ems. M such that for some forcing or interpretation on M there is a o, o $\in$ K, K $\in$ M, Po, but A $\notin$ Ho. We borrow extensively from Meyer's and Routley's "Semantics of Entailment" I,II,III, and IV. We are especially indebted to them for the Zorn's Lemma strategy. In this, and in subsequent sections, we refer to this sequence of papers with SEI, SEII, etc..

We begin with several definitions of Meyer, Routley, and Dunn. These definitions characterize sets of formulas of the full entailment language which we call theories.

Def. 1: A <u>intensional E-theory T</u> is a non-empty set of formulas closed under Adj. and E-entailment, i.e., if A $\in$ T and B $\in$ T then A$\wedge$B $\in$ T and if $\vdash_E$ A$\rightarrow$B and A $\in$ T then B $\in$ T.

Def.2: An intensional E-theory T is <u>prime</u> if whenever A $\vee$ B $\in$ T, A $\in$ T or B $\in$ T.

Def. 3: An intensional E-theory T is <u>regular</u> if all theorems of E are in T. Regular intensional E-theories are called simply <u>E-theories</u>.

Def. 4: An intensional E-theory T is <u>consistent</u> if for no A do both A and $\sim$A belong to T.

Def.5: An intensional E-theory T is <u>negation complete</u> if for every A either A $\in$ T or $\sim$A $\in$ T.

Def.6: An intensional E-theory T is <u>normal</u> if T is prime, regular, and consistent.

Def.7: $\vdash_E^T$A iff. there is an E-derivation of A from hypotheses T. In this section we use $\vdash^T$ A instead of $\vdash_E^T$ A, and sometimes T$\vdash$ A. Of course, S$\vdash^T$ A is S $\cup$ T $\vdash$ A, where S is a set of formulas. Note that B$\vdash^T$ A is $\vdash^{T \cup \{B\}}$ A. When we extend E to get a new logic we subscript the name of the new logic to $\vdash$ instead of using $\vdash_E$.

Theories must be distinguished from logics.

Def.8: An <u>E-logic</u> is an E-theory which is also closed under uniform substitution for variables. (In effect, for us this means uniform substitution for basic schema letters.)

Because E itself is an E-theory, systems E, R, and RM are E-logics in the sense of definition 8. If we add a single variable p to system E but do not allow uniform substitution for variables in p we have a regular theory $E \cup \{p\}$. If we allow uniform substitution for this p we have an inconsistent logic.

We talk of intensional E-theories because in these theories we have only the consequences of members of the theory by us of E, a non-extensional logic. These theories differ from theories as characterized by R. Thomason on p. 272 of his [1970] as a set of formulas closed under classically valid consequence. Intensional E-theories need not even contain all logical truth, i.e., theorems of E. Even if they are regular but inconsistent they may not contain every formula. The crucial feature of intensional E-theories is that we look to E to see whether A in the theory puts B into the theory; we look to see whether $A \rightarrow B$ is an E theorem. We will have occasion to look to a larger set of entailments than those of E to see whether A in the set or theory gives B in the set. So, we develop the notion of intensional T-theory. In intensional T-theories we can draw more consequences than in E-theories but the logic is still that of E.

Def.9: If T is an E-theory a set of formulas T' is <u>an intensional T-theory</u> if T' is closed under Adj. and T-entailment, i.e., if $A \rightarrow B \in T$ while $A \in T'$, then $B \in T'$.

Def.10: An intensional T-theory T' is <u>prime</u> if whenever $A \vee B \in T'$, then $A \in T'$ or $B \in T'$.

Def.11: An intensional T-theory T' is <u>regular</u> if all theorems of E are in T'. We call regular intensional T-theories simply <u>T-theories</u>.

Def.12: An intensional T-theory T' is <u>consistent</u> if for no A do both A and $\sim A$ belong to T'.

Def.13: An intensional T-theory T' is <u>negation complete</u> if for every A, $A \in T'$ or $\sim A \in T'$.

Def.14: An intensional T-theory T' is <u>normal</u> if it is prime, regular, and consistent.

Let us draw some corollaries from these definitions. Most of the proofs are left as exercises.

Corollary 1 of V.2: If T is an intensional E-theory (an E-theory), the $T \cup S$ is an intensional E-theory (an E-theory) for any set of formulas S. In particular, if T is an intensional E-theory or an E-theory, then $T \cup \{B\}$ is an intensional E-theory, and an E-theory if T is also an E-theory.

Corollary 2 of V.2: If T is an intensional E-theory and $A \rightarrow B \in T$ and $A \in T$, then $B \in T$. (Use T41.)

Corollary 3 of V.2: If T is an intensional E-theory, then $T\vdash A$ iff. $A\in T$.

Remember $T\vdash A$ is $\vdash^{T} A$; $B\vdash^{T} C$ is $T\cup\{B\}\vdash C$.

Corollary 4 of V.2: If T is an intensional E-theory, then $A\vdash^{T} A$.

Corollary 5 of V.2: If T is an intensional E-theory, then $\vdash^{T} A$ and $A\vdash^{T} B$ yield $\vdash^{T} B$.

Corollary 6 of V.2: If T is an intensional E-theory, then if $\vdash^{T} B$, then $A\vdash^{T} B$.

Corollary 7 of V.2: If T is an intensional E-theory, then $A\vdash^{T} B$ and $B\vdash^{T} C$ yield $A\vdash^{T} C$.

Corollary 8 of V.2: If T is an intensional E-theory, then $A\vdash^{T} A \vee B$ and $B\vdash^{T} A \vee B$.

Corollary 9 of V.2: A normal E-theory is negation complete.

The next batch of corollaries brings out connections between intensional E-theories and the set-ups defined in V.1.

Corollary 10 of V.2: If $a\in K$ and $K\in \underline{M}$ of Ems. $\underline{M}$, then Ha is a prime intensional E-theory.

By way of proof consider the following. $\wedge$-normality gives closure under Adj. while $\vee$-normality gives primeness. We get from $\mathcal{E}1$: Po and Roaa. If we have $\vdash_{E} A\longrightarrow B$, then by Po and the Soundness Theorem of V.1 we have $A\longrightarrow B\in$ Ho. If we also have $A\in$ Ha, then Roaa and the Triad rule give us $B\in$ Ha. So, Ha is closed under E-entailment.

The Soundness Theorem of V.1 and the definition of E-validity as being in all set-ups at all P-points of all Ems. give us our next corollary.

Corollary 11 of V.2: If o is a P-point of an Ems., then Ho is a prime regular intensional E-theory.

By use of the Inclusion Condition and Corollary 11, we get our next corollary.

Corollary 12 of V.2: If $b\in K$ and $K\in \underline{M}$, where $\underline{M}$ is an Ems., and $(\exists x)(Px\wedge Rxxb)$, then Hb is regular.

From exercise 5 of V.1 we have that Ha=Ha* suffices for the consistency of Ha. This fact helps in a proof of our next corollary.

Corollary 13 of V.2: If o is a P-point of an Ems. and $o\leqslant o^*$, then Ho is normal.

As a proof for Corollary 13, consider the following. As an instance of $\mathcal{E}9$ we have Roo*o, i.e., $o^* \preccurlyeq o$. The Inclusion Condition gives us $Ho^* \subseteq Ho$ from $o^* \preccurlyeq o$. From the hypothesis $o \preccurlyeq o^*$, the Inclusion condition gives us $Ho \subseteq Ho^*$. So we have $Ho = Ho^*$ which suffices for the consistency of Ho. Corollary 11 gives the other conditions for normality.

Our next corollary is from p.462 of Dunn's and Meyer's important paper [1969]. Its proof is complicated enough to class it as a theorem. In this section it is really a lemma for our first lemma. But we class it as a corollary because it is on the same topics as the preceding corollaries.

Corollary 14 of V.2: If T is an E-theory, $A \overset{T}{\vdash} C$ and $B \overset{T}{\vdash} C$, then $A \lor B \overset{T}{\vdash} C$.

The proof is obtained by use of Corollary 7 and (a),(b), and (c) below.

(a) $A \lor B \overset{T}{\vdash} C \lor B$, (b) $C \lor B \overset{T}{\vdash} C \lor C$, (c) $C \lor C \overset{T}{\vdash} C$.
In the rest of this proof we delete subscript E and superscript T on $\vdash$. We readily get (c) from the facts that $C \lor C \rightarrow C$ is a theorem of E and that, by Corollary 1, $T \cup \{C\}$ is closed under E-entailment. We follow Meyer and Dunn in proving only (a) from $A \vdash C$ because the proof of (b) from $B \vdash C$ would be similar. $A \vdash C$ tells us that there is a derivation: $A_1, \ldots, A_n$, where each A_i is a member of T, A, or a consequence of predecessors by MP or Adj., and A_n is C. (Since T is a E-theory and thereby contains all E-theorems we do not consider the case of being an E-theorem over and above the case of being a member of T.) We prove by induction on the length of the derivation that $A \lor B \vdash A_i \lor B$. For the basis we have two cases depending upon whether $A_1 \in T$ or A_1 is A.

Basis case 1: If $A_1 \in T$, then $\vdash A_1$ by Corollary 3. By Corollary 8 we have $A_1 \vdash A_1 \lor B$. By Corollary 5 we get $\vdash A_1 \lor B$ from $\vdash A_1$ and $A_1 \vdash A_1 \lor B$. By Corollary 6 we get $A \lor B \vdash A_1 \lor B$ from $\vdash A_1 \lor B$.

Basis case 2: If A_1 is A, then $A \lor B \vdash A_1 \lor B$ is $A \lor B \vdash A \lor B$ which we have by Corollary 4.

Assume that for all $i < j$ in $A_1, \ldots, A_n$ we have $A \lor B \vdash A_i \lor B$. There are four cases to consider depending upon whether $A_j \in T$, A_j is A, A_j is obtained from A_h and $A_h \rightarrow A_j$ by MP, or A_j is obtained from an A_g and A_h by Adj.. We consider only the MP and Adj. cases since the other two cases were considered in the basis case.

Induction case 3, for MP: By induction assumption we have $A \lor B \vdash A_h \lor B$ and $A \lor B \vdash (A_h \rightarrow A_j) \lor B$. Now by Adj. in the

(proof of Corollary 14 continued)

E-theory $T \cup \{A \vee B\}$ we can get $A \vee B \vdash ((A_h \rightarrow A_j) \vee B) \wedge (A_h \vee B)$. Use the appropriate version of T87 at the end of IV.11 and T's closure under E-entailment to get $A \vee B \vdash A_j \vee B$.

Induction case 4, for Adj.: By induction assumption we have $A \vee B \vdash A_h \vee B$ and $A \vee B \vdash A_g \vee B$. By Adj. in the E-theory $T \cup \{A \vee B\}$ we get $A \vee B \vdash (A_h \vee B) \wedge (A_g \vee B)$. Use the appropriate version of T88 and T's closure under E-entailment to get $A \vee B \vdash A_j \vee B$ where $A_j = A_h \wedge A_g$.

We are now in a position to work more directly towards a Henkin style proof of the main theorem of this section. This is the completeness of E with respect to the E-valid formulas. (Remember we use not-$\vdash$ for 'is not a theorem.')

Theorem I of V.2: If not-$\vdash_E$ A, then there is an Ems. M such that A is not valid in M.

We need to struggle through several lemmas and sub-lemmas on our way to Theorem I. Our first lemma tells us that any non-theorem of E fails to belong to some E-theory which can be a set-up at a P-point of some Ems. This first lemma is also the first lemma of Meyer's and Dunn's [1969].

Lemma 1 of V.2: If not-$\vdash_E$ A, then there is a prime E-theory T such that $A \notin T$ but $\sim A \in T$, and $E \subseteq T$.

The first step of the proof is to define T as the union of the following series of E-theories. To get the series we start with some enumeration of the formulas of E: F_1, F_2, etc.. We get the series of E-theories as follows.

(1) $T_o = E$
(2) a) $T_i = T_{i-1}$ if $A \in (T_{i-1} \cup \{F_i\})$, i.e., if $F_i \vdash^{T_{i-1}} A$.
   b) $T_i = T_{i-1} \cup \{F_i\}$ otherwise.

Corollary 1 and the fact that $T_o = E$ guarantees that each member of the series and its union T are E-theories. It remains to show that T is prime, lacks A but contains $\sim$A. If T were not prime, we would have $\vdash^T B \vee C$ but lack both $\vdash^T B$ and $\vdash^T C$ for some B and C. If neither B nor C are in T, then $B \vdash^T A$ and $C \vdash^T A$;otherwise B and C would have been put into some T_i. By Corollary 14 $B \vdash^T A$ and $C \vdash^T A$ give $B \vee C \vdash^T A$. But by Corollary 5, $B \vee C \vdash^T A$ and $\vdash^T B \vee C$ give $\vdash^T A$ which is impossible because T has been constructed with A excluded. Because A is not a theorem of E, $A \notin T_o$ and A would not be placed in any other T_i. So, we have to accept that T is prime. Since T is an E-theory, it has the E-theorem $A \vee \sim A$. Now because T is prime, lacks A but $(A \vee \sim A) \in T$, we have $\sim A \in T$.

It is a good idea to pause to take stock of what we are doing. We want to show that non-theorem A does not belong to a set-up Ho for some P-point o of an Ems. We have just shown that such an A does not belong to some prime E-theory. Corollary 11 tells us that an Ho is a prime E-theory. So, if we could take the T proved to exist in Lemma 1 as an Ho, we would have a proof of Theorem I. And we will take the T of Lemma 1 as an Ho; but in so taking T we give T two roles. First we give T the role of being a P-point in an Ems. Secondly, we give T the role of being a set-up at itself in the Ems. in which it is a P-point. We give T its first role by placing it in a system of T-intensional theories and showing that the set of theories in this system can be the K of an Ems. It is difficult to show that T can play the first role. Once it is shown that T can play the first role, it is not difficult to show that T can play its second role. To show that T and the T-intensional theories making up the K of an Ems. can be set-ups at themselves we give the so-called canonical interpretation: $f(p,T_i)=1$ iff. p T_i, where T_i is one of the T-intensional theories in K.

Before we become immersed in the details of showing that T can play the first role, note that Lemma 1 does not guarantee us that T is consistent. Still T lacks A; and that is all we need. But because T may be inconsistent it would be very misleading to think of T as representing the actual world even if T is going to be a zero point, a P-point, in an Ems..

Because we are working on a proof of Theorem I, we are working with the hypothesis that not-$\vdash$A. Lemma 1 has given us a prime E-theory T without A. With this T we now construct a model structure which we label M_T. M_T is the following ordered four-tuple $\langle K_T, P_T, R_T, * \rangle$ characterized below.

Model Structure M_T

i) K_T is the class of T-intensional theories.

ii) For any $a \in K$, $P_T a$ iff. for any wff. B, if $B \longrightarrow B \longrightarrow B \in T$ then $B \in a$.

iii) For any a,b,and c in K_T, $R_T abc$ iff. whenever $B \longrightarrow C \in a$ and $B \in b$, then $C \in c$.

iv) For any $a \in K$, $a^* = \{B : \sim B \notin a\}$.

We can immediately observe that T is a P-point of M_T. As an E-theory $B \longrightarrow B \in T$. Hence, if $B \longrightarrow B \longrightarrow B$, viz., $\Box B$, is in T, then $B \in T$ by Corollary 2. For M_T, P-points are T-intensional theories which contain all claims asserted to be necessarily true in T. Note further that E is a subset of all P-points of M_T. By Lemma 4 of IV.2 we have Necessitation for E. So, for any B, if $\vdash_E$ B then $\vdash_E$ B$\rightarrow$B$\rightarrow$B and thus B$\rightarrow$B$\rightarrow$B $\in$ T; hence by definition of P_T,B is in any P-point. It is important to note that clause (iii) gives a Triad Rule for M_T, viz., if not-Rabc then there is a B$\rightarrow$C $\in$ a such that B $\in$ b but C $\notin$ c.

Notice, though, that we have not called M_T an Ems.. We have only called M_T a model structure because we are not going to prove that M_T is an Ems.. We are interested in only the prime intensional T-theories of K_T because we want to consider theories also as set-ups; and set-ups are prime because of **v**-normality. We want really to talk of a structure we label $\underline{M}'_T$:$\langle K'_T, P'_T, R'_T, *' \rangle$, where the parts are characterized as for M_T except that they are restricted to prime intensional T-theories. Unfortunately, proof that $\mathcal{E}2$, $\mathcal{E}3$, and $\mathcal{E}4$ are true of $\underline{M}'_T$ seems extremely difficult, if not impossible, by direct consideration of $\underline{M}'_T$. So, following the strategy of Meyer and Routley from SEI,III, and IV, we first show that these Ems. postulates are true of M_T and then use the so-called Zorn's Lemma strategy to show that they are true of $\underline{M}'_T$. We also prove that the other positive postulates are true of both M_T and M'_T. (The positive postulates are those with no occurrences of *.) So, it will be shown that $M+_T$ which is $\langle K_T, P_T, R_T \rangle$ is a positive Ems.. (See SEIII for treatment of positive model structures.) Also be aware that we will drop the T subscripts from K, P, and R because PT and RTxy will be used to say that T has the predicate P and stands in the R-relation. We frequently delete the T subscripts on M_T and $\underline{M}'_T$.

We now turn to the task of verifying the Ems. postulates for $\underline{M}'$.

Lemma 2 of V.2: $\mathcal{E}1$, $(\exists x)(Px \wedge Rxaa)$, is true of M and $\underline{M}'$.

To start the proof recall that we already observed that PT holds. Because T-intensional theories are closed under T-entailment we have C $\in$ a if B$\rightarrow$C $\in$ T and B $\in$ a. So, PT$\wedge$RTaa which gives,by EG on T: $(\exists x)(Px \wedge Rxaa)$. Since Lemma 1 tells us that T is prime, the proof would be the same if we gave it for $\underline{M}'_T$.

We defer the complex proofs involving the Zorn's Lemma strategy until we verify $\mathcal{E}5$ through $\mathcal{E}9$. A sublemma helps with the verification of $\mathcal{E}5$ and $\mathcal{E}6$. This sublemma also shows that members of K' meet the Inclusion Condition when they are considered as set-ups.

Sublemma 1 of V.2: If $(\exists x)(Px \wedge Rxab)$ for points a,b of K or K', then a $\subseteq$ b.

To prove this recall our observation that E is a subset of P-points. So, B$\rightarrow$B $\in$ x if Px. Rxab tells us that B $\in$ b if B $\in$ a, given that B$\rightarrow$B $\in$ x.

Lemma 3 of V.2: $\mathcal{E}5$, $(x)((Px \wedge Rxab) \wedge Rbcd \supset .Racd)$, is true of M and $\underline{M}'$.

To prove Lemma 3 assume Px Rxab. With Px∧Rxab, Sublemma 1 gives $a \subseteq b$. Rbcd tells us that if $B \rightarrow C \in a$ and $B \in c$, then $C \in d$. So, because $a \subseteq b$, if some $B \rightarrow C \in a$ and $B \in c$, then $C \in d$; and this suffices for Racd. Notice that nothing except superscripts would have to be added if we wanted to deal explicitly with members of K'.

We leave a proof of our fourth lemma as an exercise because it is similar to a proof of Lemma 3.

Lemma 4 of V.2: $\mathcal{E}6$, $(x)((Px \wedge Rxab) \wedge Rcbd \supset .Rcad)$, is true of M and $\underline{M}'$.

Before we verify the negation postulates, i.e., those containing a * operation sign, we need to show that *' is indeed a unary operation on K' into K' to establish that $\underline{M}'_T$ is a genuine Ems.. We make this fact about *' the content of a second sublemma. We failed to get a similar proof for the * of M_T. Thus we verify $\mathcal{E}7$, $\mathcal{E}8$, and $\mathcal{E}9$ only for $\underline{M}'_T$. Thus, since we won't deal with the * operation of M_T, let us delete the prime sign ' from *' to get plain *.

Sublemma 2 of V.2: If $a \in K'$, then $a^* \in K'$, where $a^* = \{B: \sim B \notin a\}$.

To prove this sublemma we want to show that a* is a prime intensional T-theory given that a is a prime intensional T-theory. So, we show that a* is closed under T-entailment, Adj., and is prime.

i) a* is closed under T-entailment. Assume for reductio that a* is not closed under T-entailment. We have, then, $B \rightarrow C \in T$, $B \in a^*$ but $C \notin a^*$. $B \in a^*$ gives $\sim B \notin a$ while $C \notin a^*$ gives $\sim C \in a$. Because T is closed under E-entailment, $B \rightarrow C \in T$ gives $\sim C \rightarrow \sim B \in T$. Because a is closed under T-entailment $\sim C \in a$ and $\sim C \rightarrow \sim B \in T$ give $\sim B \in a$; and thus gives a contradiction from the reductio assumption that a* is not closed under T-entailment.

ii) a* is closed under Adj. if a is prime. Assume for reductio that a* is not closed under Adj.. We have, then, $B \in a^*$, $C \in a^*$, but $B \wedge C \notin a^*$; these yield respectively: $\sim B \notin a$, $\sim C \notin a$, but $\sim(B \wedge C) \in a$. Because a is an intensional T-theory with $E \subseteq T$ we get $\sim B \vee \sim C \in a$ from $\sim(B \wedge C) \in a$. But because we assumed that a is prime we cannot have $\sim B \vee \sim C \in a$, $\sim B \notin a$, and $\sim C \notin a$. (It is this use of the primeness of a which stops us from proving this sublemma for M_T.)

Proof of Sublemma 2 continued

iii) a^* is prime. Assume for *reductio* that $B \vee C \in a^*$ but that $B \notin a^*$ and $C \notin a^*$. These give respectively: $\sim(B \vee C) \notin a$, $\sim B \in a$, and $\sim C \in a$. Now, because theory a is an intensional T-theory with $E \subseteq T$, $\sim(B \vee C) \notin a$ gives $\sim B \wedge \sim C \notin a$. But $\sim B \wedge \sim C \notin a$ while $\sim B \in a$ and $\sim C \in a$ conflicts with a's closure under Adj..

Lemma 5 of V.2: $\mathcal{E}7$, $a^{**} = a$, is true of $\underline{M}'_T$.

For a proof consider the following sequence.

1)	$B \in a^{**}$ iff. $\sim B \notin a^*$	Def. of *
2)	$\sim\sim B \notin a$ iff. $\sim B \in a^*$	Def. of *
3)	$\sim B \notin a^*$ iff. $\sim\sim B \in a$,	Classical Logic, CL, on (2).
4)	$B \in a^{**}$ iff. $\sim\sim B \in a$	CL on (1),(3)

Because a is an intensional T-theory with $E \subseteq T$, we have:

5) $\sim\sim B \in a$ iff. $B \in a$

6) $B \in a^{**}$ iff. $B \in a$, i.e., $a^{**} = a$, CL on (4),(5).

Lemma 6 of V.2: $\mathcal{E}8$, $Rabc \supset Rac^*b^*$, is true of $\underline{M}'_T$.

Assume we have Rabc, $B \rightarrow C \in a$, and $B \in c^*$. We prove the lemma if we show that $C \in b^*$. From $B \in c^*$ we get $\sim B \notin c$. Because a is an intensional T-theory with $E \subseteq T$ we get $\sim C \rightarrow \sim B \in a$ from $B \rightarrow C \in a$. Rabc tells us that we have $\sim B \in c$ if $\sim C \rightarrow \sim B \in a$ and $\sim C \in b$. From: If $\sim C \rightarrow \sim B \in a$ and $\sim C \in b$, then $\sim B \in c$, we get by Classical Logic: If $\sim C \rightarrow \sim B \in a$ and $\sim B \notin c$, then $\sim C \notin b$. We have both $\sim C \rightarrow \sim B \in a$ and $\sim B \notin c$; so we get $\sim C \notin b$. But $\sim C \notin b$ gives $C \in b^*$, which completes this proof of Lemma 6.

Lemma 7 of V.2: $\mathcal{E}9$, Raa^*a, is true of $\underline{M}'_T$.

To prove Lemma 7 it suffices to show that we get $C \in a$ from the assumptions that $B \rightarrow C \in a$ and $B \in a^*$. Because a is an intensional T-theory with $E \subseteq T$, $B \rightarrow C \in a$ gives $\sim B \vee C \in a$. $B \in a^*$ tells us that $\sim B \notin a$. Now because a is prime by virtue of being in K', $\sim B \vee C \in a$ and $\sim B \notin a$ give us $C \in a$.

We turn now to the difficult jobs of verifying that $\mathcal{E}2$, $\mathcal{E}3$, and $\mathcal{E}4$ hold for $\underline{M}'_T$. It is not too difficult to verify that they hold for M_T. The difficulties lie in showing that the existential quantifiers in their consequents can be instantiated to prime intensional T-theories. The Meyer and Routley Zorn's Lemma strategy is first to verify the postulates for plain M_T and then to show indirectly that the postulates would still hold for $\underline{M}'_T$. We work through the strategy in detail for $\mathcal{E}2$. We adapt Meyer's and Routley's treatment of their fifth postulate, $(\exists x)(Px \wedge Raxa)$ from SEIV.

Lemma 8 of V.2: $\mathcal{E}2$, $(x)(Px \wedge Rxab \supset .(\exists y)(Py \wedge Rayb)$, is true of M_T .

Proof of Lemma 8

Assume Px Rxab, which Sublemma 1 tells us is an assumption that $a \subseteq b$. With the assumption of $a \subseteq b$, we can prove $(\exists y)(Py \wedge Rayb)$ by finding an intensional T-theory o such that Po and Rbob because $\mathcal{E}5$ is true of M_T. Let o be: $\{D: D \rightarrow D \rightarrow D \in T\}$. In light of this definition of o we need only show: (i) o is closed under T-entailment, (ii) o is closed under Adj. to show that o is a P-point of M_T.

i) Assume $B \rightarrow C \in T$ and $B \in o$. To show that o is closed under T-entailment work to get $C \in o$. $B \in o$ tells us that $B \rightarrow B \rightarrow B \in T$. Since T is closed under E-entailment, we can get $B \rightarrow C \rightarrow . B \rightarrow B \rightarrow C$ by Suffixing which with $B \rightarrow C \in T$ by Corollary 2 gives $B \rightarrow B \rightarrow C \in T$. By T54, viz., $B \rightarrow B \rightarrow C \rightarrow . C \rightarrow C \rightarrow C$, and T's closure under E-entailment we get $C \rightarrow C \rightarrow C \in T$. But $C \rightarrow C \rightarrow C \in T$ gives $C \in o$.

ii) We leave development of an argument that o is closed under Adj. as an exercise after hinting that use of T49 facilitates a proof.

To show Rbob assume $B \rightarrow C \in b$, $B \in o$, and get $C \in b$. As in (i) just above, $B \in o$ gives $B \rightarrow C \rightarrow . B \rightarrow B \rightarrow C \in T$. With $B \rightarrow C \in b$ and the fact that b is an intensional T-theory we, then, get $B \rightarrow B \rightarrow C \in b$. Because $E \subseteq T$ we have T33, viz., $B \rightarrow B \rightarrow C \rightarrow C \in T$; so we get $C \in b$ by the fact that b is an intensional T-theory. And so we have Lemma 8.

It would be delightful if we could go on to prove that the o theory of Lemma 8 is prime. Unfortunately, we have not been able to prove that this o is prime. An assumption that this o is not prime seems only to have the consequence thatprime theory T has $B \vee C$ while lacking both $\Box B$ and $\Box C$. However, the labor of proving Lemma 8 has not been in vain. Observe that we can take the proof of Lemma 8 as showing us that if there are x,a,b in K' meeting the condition $P'x \wedge R'xab$, there is a $o \in K$, but not necessarily in K', such that $Po \wedge Raob$. Nothing in the proof of Lemma 8 would have to be changed if we restricted our attention to prime intensional T-theories a,b such that $a \subseteq b$. So, the proof of Lemma 8 gives us the valuable information that for any a,b in K' such that $a \subseteq b$ the set $\Gamma(a,b)$ is non-empty.

$$\Gamma(a,b) = \{y: y \in K, Py, \text{ and } Rayb\}.$$

Henceforth we delete the (a,b) after Γ and assume that the a,b are in K', i.e., are prime. If we could show that any such Γ contained a member of K', we would complete a verification that $\mathcal{E}2$ is true of M'_T. It is the Zorn's Lemma strategy which is used to show that such Γ's contain a prime intensional T-theory. We now outline this strategy. In our outline of the strategy we dispense with predominantly set-theoretic arguments by leaving them as observations.

Outline of the Zorn's Lemma Strategy

The first step in application of this strategy is to note that Γ is partially ordered by set-inclusion: $\subseteq$. We can use van Fraassen's definition from p.15 of his [1971].

Relation $\preccurlyeq$ partially orders a set G iff. for x,y in G (a) $\preccurlyeq$ is reflexive, (b) $\preccurlyeq$ is transitive, and (c) is anti-symmetric, i.e., if $x \preccurlyeq y \wedge y \preccurlyeq x$, then x = y.

The second step is to observe that in partially ordered there are so-called chains. A chain in partially ordered Γ is a non-empty subset $C\Gamma$ such that if $x \in C\Gamma$ and $y \in C\Gamma$, then $x \preccurlyeq y$ or $y \preccurlyeq x$.

Observe, in the third place, that each $C\Gamma$ has the union, $\bigcup C\Gamma$, of all its members, as an upper bound in Γ. I.e., for any $x \in C\Gamma$, $x \subseteq \bigcup C\Gamma$. Despite the need to use properties of intensional T-theories to establish this third observation, we still leave this third observation to be supported by an exercise. The fifth step involves enough work.

The fourth step is to apply Zorn's Lemma to Γ. We adapt a formulation from p.15 of van Fraassen's [1971].

> Zorn's Lemma: If every chain in a partially ordered system under $\preccurlyeq$ has an upper bound, the system has a maximal member under $\preccurlyeq$.

A maximal member for Γ is a member x of Γ such that for any $y \in \Gamma$, if $x \subseteq y$ then x = y. Hence, Zorn's Lemma guarantees us that Γ has a maximal member which we label o'.

The fifth step is to show that o' is prime, i.e., o' $\in$ K'. We use a sublemma to take the fifth step. The sublemma is adapted from p.215 of SEI, p.65 of SEII, and p.205 of SEIII; it is all that we need to get a lemma that $\mathcal{E}$·2 is true of $\underline{M}'_T$.

Sublemma 3 of V.2: o' $\in$ K'.

To start the *reductio* proof assume B $\vee$ C $\in$ o' but B $\notin$ o' and C $\notin$ o'. Define [B,o'] and [C,o'] as follows

[B,o'] = {D: ($\exists$F)(F $\in$ o' and B$\wedge$F$\longrightarrow$D $\in$ T)}. abbreviated as b.
[C,o'] = {D: ($\exists$F)(F $\in$ o' and C$\wedge$F$\longrightarrow$D $\in$ T)}. abbreviated as c.

Let us observe that o' $\subseteq$ [B,o'] and o' $\subseteq$ [C,o']. To show that o' $\subseteq$ [B,o'], assume D $\in$ o'. With D $\in$ o' and the fact that E $\subseteq$ T we get D $\in$ [B,o'] because the F can be D itself. Similarly, o' $\subseteq$ [C,o'] can be established. Moreover, both are intensional T-theories. Let us show that [B,o'] is closed under T-entailment and Adj.. Assume that D$\longrightarrow$G $\in$ T and that D $\in$ [B,o'],i.e., ($\exists$F)(F $\in$ o' and B$\wedge$F$\longrightarrow$D $\in$ T). We want: ($\exists$F)(F $\in$ o' and B$\wedge$F$\longrightarrow$G $\in$ T). With D$\longrightarrow$G $\in$ T, B$\wedge$F$\longrightarrow$D $\in$ T, and E $\subseteq$ T, we get B$\wedge$F$\longrightarrow$G $\in$ T, which readily gives that [B,o'] is closed under T-entailment. Consideration of the fact that if B$\wedge F_1\longrightarrow$D $\in$ T and B$\wedge F_2\longrightarrow$D $\in$ T, where F_1 and F_2 are in o', then B$\wedge(F_1\wedge F_2)\longrightarrow$D $\in$ T, helps show

Proof of Sublemma 3 continued

that [B,o'] is closed under Adj.. Similarly, it can be shown that [C,o'] is an intensional T-theory. By virtue of having o' as a subset both [B,o'] and [C.o'] have formulas D such that $D \rightarrow D \rightarrow D \in T$. So, both [B,o'] and [C,o'] are P-points for M_T. We have now shown that both [B,o'] and [C,o'] are in K and satisfy the P-predicate; so if they fail to be in Γ it is because they do not stand in the appropriate R-relation with a,b. We now turn to showing that neither are in Γ.

Because both $B \wedge F_1 \rightarrow B \in T$ and $C \wedge F_2 \rightarrow C \in T$ for some F_1 and F_2 we have both $B \in [B,o']$ and $C \in [C,o']$. Hence, with our reductio assumption that neither B nor C are in o' and our first observation that o' is a subset of both [B,o'] and [C,o'], we conclude that o' is a proper subset of both [B,o'] and [C,o']. But, then, because o' is a maximal member of Γ under $\subseteq$, neither [B,o'] nor [C,o'] is in Γ.

Hence, because neither [B,o'] nor [C,o'] is in Γ, we have not-Ra[B,o']b and not-Ra[C,o']b which we abbreviate as: not-Ra$\underline{b}$b and not-Ra$\underline{c}$b. From not-Ra$\underline{b}$b we get that there is a $D \rightarrow G$ such that $D \rightarrow G \in a$, $D \in \underline{b}$, but $G \notin b$. From $D \in \underline{b}$ we get, for some F_1, $F_1 \in o'$ and $B \wedge F_1 \rightarrow D \in T$. From not-Ra$\underline{c}$b we get that there is a $H \rightarrow J$, such that $H \rightarrow J \in a$, that for some F_2 both $F_2 \in o'$ and $C \wedge F_2 \rightarrow H \in T$, but that $J \notin b$. By use of theorems of E we get: $(B \vee C) \wedge F_1 \wedge F_2 \rightarrow . D \vee H \in T$. By our reductio assumption that $B \vee C \in o'$ and the closure of o' under Adj., we get: $(B \vee C) \wedge F_1 \wedge F_2 \in o'$. Because o' is closed under T-entailment, we get $D \vee H \in o'$. From $D \rightarrow G \in a$ and $H \rightarrow J \in a$ and the fact that a is an intensional T-theory, we get: $D \vee H \rightarrow . J \vee H \in a$. Now, because $o' \in \Gamma$, we have Rao'b; hence $D \vee H \rightarrow . G \vee H \in a$ and $D \vee H \in o'$ give $G \vee H \in b$. Recall, though, that we have assumed that b is prime; so we cannot have $G \vee H \in b$ with $G \notin b$ and $J \notin b$. So, at last we have reached a contradiction which gives a proof of Sublemma 3.

With Sublemma 3 we have a proof of our ninth lemma.

Lemma 9 of V.2: $\mathcal{E}2$ is true of $\underline{M}'_T$.

We go into less detail to verify that $\mathcal{E}3$ and $\mathcal{E}4$ are true of $\underline{M}'_T$. In both cases we start by showing that they are true of M_T.

Lemma 10 of V.2: $\mathcal{E}3$, $(x)(Rabx \wedge Rxcd \supset .(\exists y)(Racy \wedge Rbyd))$, is true of M_T.

In the proof, we first show that $\mathcal{E}3$ is true of M_T but realize that the argument would be the same if we specified that the points a,b,c,d, and x of K_T be prime, viz., members of K'_T; so we explicitly restrict ourselves to members of K'. Secondly, we show by use of Zorn's Lemma that there is a maximal y' in K such that Racy'$\wedge$Rby'd. Thirdly, we show, in a fashion similar to that used in the proof of Sublemma 3, that y'$\in$ K' given that a,b,c,d, and x are in K'. We, consequently, organize our proof that $\mathcal{E}3$ is true of M' under three sublemmas. The first sublemma of this triad gives Lemma 10.

Sublemma 4 of V.2: For a,b,c,d,x, in K', there is a z, z$\in$K, although z does not necessarily belong to K', such that Racz$\wedge$Rbzd if Rabx$\wedge$Rxcd.

A proof is adapted from Meyer's and Routley's verification of their third postulate in SEIV. Assume that we have Rabx and Rxcd. Let z = $\{D: (\exists F)(F \rightarrow D \in a \text{ and } F \in c\}$. We show that z$\in$K by showing (i) and (ii) below.

i) z is closed under T-entailment. Assume that H$\rightarrow$J$\in$T and that H$\in$z. H$\in$z gives F$\rightarrow$H$\in$a and F$\in$c for some F. We want J$\in$z, i.e., $F_1 \rightarrow J \in a$ and $F_1 \in c$ for some F_1. By Prefixing we get F$\rightarrow$H$\rightarrow$.F$\rightarrow$J$\in$T from H$\rightarrow$J$\in$T. Because point a is closed under T-entailment, we get F$\rightarrow$J$\in$a from F$\rightarrow$H$\rightarrow$.F$\rightarrow$J$\in$T and F$\rightarrow$H$\in$a; and by taking F as F_1 we get J$\in$z.

ii) z is closed under Adj.. Here the crucial step involves seeing that ($F_1 \rightarrow H \in a$ and $F_1 \in c$) and ($F_2 \rightarrow J \in a$ and $F_2 \in c$), viz., H$\in$z and J$\in$z, give $F_1 \wedge F_2 \rightarrow .H \wedge J \in a$ and $F_1 \wedge F_2 \in c$, viz., H$\wedge$J$\in$z.

The definition of z guarantees that Racz. So, it remains only to show that Rbzd. Assume that D$\rightarrow$G$\in$b and D$\in$z. D$\in$z gives F$\rightarrow$D$\in$a and F$\in$c for some F. We want G$\in$d. Because E$\subseteq$T and point a is an intensional T-theory, Suffixing can take us from F$\rightarrow$D$\in$a to D$\rightarrow$G$\rightarrow$.F$\rightarrow$G$\in$a. Because we have assumed that Rabx and that D$\rightarrow$G$\in$b, the Triad Rule gives F$\rightarrow$G$\in$x. Because we also assumed that Rxcd and F$\in$c, the Triad Rule gives G$\in$d, which is what we wanted to complete the proof of this fourth sublemma.

Now use of the Zorn's Lemma strategy is in order.

Sublemma 5 of V.2: If $\Gamma = \{y: y \in K, z \subseteq y, \text{ and } Rbyd\}$, where z is the z of Sublemma 4, there is a maximal member y' of Γ.

We omit a proof of Sublemma 5 since it is basically observing that Zorn's Lemma applies to Γ. It may be helpful to note that a more natural defintion of Γ by using Racy$\wedge$Rbyd instead of only Rbyd would only complicate a proof of our next sublemma. As [B,y'] and [C,y'] will be defined below both Rac[B,y'] and Rac[C,y'] hold. Thus when we would argue that neither [B,y'] nor [C,y'] are in Γ we would have to verify that they do not fail to be in Γ by virtue of Rac[B,y'] and Rac[C,y'] failing.

Sublemma 6 of V.2: Let y' be as in Sublemma 5 and let b and d be in K', viz., prime, as in Sublemma 4. Under these conditions $y' \in K'$, viz., y' is prime.

We only sketch a proof of this sixth sublemma. Assume for <u>reductio</u> that $B \vee C \in y'$ but that $B \notin y'$ and $C \notin y'$. Define [B,y'] and [C,y'] as follows.

$[B,y'] = \{D: (\exists F)(F \in y' \text{ and } B \wedge F \longrightarrow D \in T)\}$. abbreviated as <u>b</u>'
$[C,y'] = \{D: (\exists F)(F \in y' \text{ and } C \wedge F \longrightarrow D \in T)\}$. abbreviated as <u>c</u>'.

We leave as exercises arguments that $[B,y'] \in K$, $[C,y'] \in K$, that $y' \subset [B,y']$, and that $y' \subset [C,y']$. The facts that y' is maximal in Γ while being a proper subset of both [B,y'] and [C,y'] preclude both [B,y'] and [C,y'] from being in Γ. Since both [B,y'] and [C,y'], i.e., <u>b</u>'and <u>c</u>', fail to be in Γ while being in K, both Rb<u>b</u>'d and Rb<u>c</u>'d fail. So we have: $D_1 \longrightarrow G_1 \in b$, $B \wedge F_1 \longrightarrow D_1 \in T$, $F_1 \in y'$, $D_2 \longrightarrow G_2 \in b$, $C \wedge F_2 \longrightarrow D_2 \in T$, $F_2 \in y'$, but $G_1 \notin d$ and $G_2 \notin d$. We now get $(B \vee C) \wedge F_1 \wedge F_2 \longrightarrow . D_1 \vee D_2 \in T$ from $B \wedge F_1 \longrightarrow D_1 \in T$ and $C \wedge F_2 \longrightarrow D_2 \in T$. We assumed that $B \vee C \in y'$ and have now $F_1 \in y'$ and $F_2 \in y'$. So, $(B \vee C) \wedge F_1 \wedge F_2 \in y'$. Consequently, because $y' \in K$, we have $D_1 \vee D_2 \in y'$. Further we have, from the facts that b is closed under T-entailment and $E \subseteq T$, the result that $D_1 \vee D_2 \longrightarrow . G_1 \vee G_2 \in b$ from $D_1 \longrightarrow G_1 \in b$ and $D_2 \longrightarrow G_2 \in b$. We have Rby'd because y' is in Γ ; hence by the Triad Rule for M_T, $G_1 \vee G_2 \in d$. Since we assumed $d \in K'$, viz., that d is prime, we cannot have $G_1 \vee G_2 \in d$ but $G_1 \notin d$ and $G_2 \notin d$. So we cannot assume that $y' \notin K'$; and as a result we have both Sublemma 6 and Lemma 10.

Our fourth and sixth sublemmas now give us our eleventh lemma.

Lemma 11 of V.2: $\mathcal{E}3$ is true of M'_T.

We will be even more sparing on details in showing that $\mathcal{E}4$ is true of M_T and $\underline{M}'_T$. We merely state the sublemmas because a statement of the sublemmas gives the crucial definition of the point of K which instantiates the existential quantifier in the consequent of $\mathcal{E}4$ and the definition of the Γ from which we select a maximal point and show it to be prime. The proofs for the previous lemmas should show that the definitions really give the proof. The following about $\mathcal{E}4$ is adapted from Meyer's and Routley's proof of their fourth Ems. postulate in SEIV.

Lemma 12 of V.2: $\mathcal{E}4$, $Rabc \supset (\exists x)(Rabx \wedge Rxbc)$, is true of M_T and $\underline{M}'_T$.

Sublemma 7 of V.2: If a,b,c are in K', Rabc, ar
$z = \{C: B \longrightarrow C \in a \text{ and } B \in b\}$, then $z \in K$ and Rab oc.

For those interested in M_T as a positive Ems., note that a proof of Sublemma 7 works if we assume only that a,b,c are in K, i.e., simply intensional T-theories.

Sublemma 8 of V.2: If $\Gamma = \{y: z \subseteq y,\ y \in K, \text{ and } Rybc\}$, where z is as in Sublemma 7, there is a maximal member of Γ labelled y'.

Sublemma 9 of V.2: y'$\in$ K', where y' is as in Sublemma 8.

For Sublemma 9, define [B,y'] and [C,y'] as in Sublemma 6.

Lemmas 2 through 12 may now be summed up in a thirteenth lemma.

Lemma 13 of V.2: $\underline{M}'_T$ is an Ems. with T as a P-point.

We will complete the proof of Theorem I if we show that the canonical interpretation f() gives a set-up at each point of K' identical with the point. This proves Theorem I because we are working under the assumption that non-theorem A does not belong to the P-point T of $\underline{M}'$. The canonical interpretation of E's variables on M' is as follows.

For any point b in K', f(p,b) = 1 iff. p$\in$b.

Sublemma 1 of this section tells us that the canonical interpretation is a genuine interpretation because it meets the Inclusion Condition for interpretations. So with one more lemma we can secure Theorem I. Unfortunately, the need for some logical labor still lies ahead.

Lemma 14 of V.2: For the canonical interpretation on $\underline{M}'_T$ Hb = b for all b in K'.

Proof is by induction on the length of formula B because we want to show that B$\in$Hb iff. B$\in$b. The basis case is readily settled by the definition of the canonical interpretation. So, we assume for C,D shorter than B that for any x in K' C$\in$Hx iff. C$\in$x and D$\in$Hx iff. D$\in$x. Let us consider the cases. Case 1) B has the form C $\vee$ D. If C $\vee$ D$\in$Hb, then C$\in$Hb or D$\in$Hb by $\vee$-normality for Hb. By induction assumption we, then, get C$\in$b or D$\in$b, which by virtue of the fact that b is an intensional T-theory containing E gives C $\vee$ D$\in$b. On the other half, we get a payoff from our labor with the Zorn's Lemma strategy. Because b is prime, if C $\vee$ D$\in$b then C$\in$b or D$\in$b which by induction assumption is equivalent to C$\in$Hb or D$\in$Hb. By $\vee$-normality C$\in$Hb or D$\in$Hb gives C $\vee$ D$\in$Hb.

Case 2) B has the form C$\wedge$D. A proof is left as an exercise.

Case 3) B has the form $\sim$C. $\sim$C$\in$Hb iff. C$\notin$ Hb*. By induction assumption: C$\notin$ Hb* iff. C$\notin$ b. Now $b^* = \{C: \sim C \notin b\}$. So, C$\notin$ b* iff. $\sim$C$\in$b. Hence, from these equivalences we get: $\sim$C$\in$Hb iff. $\sim$C$\in$b.

Proof of Lemma 14 continued

Case 4) B has the form $C \rightarrow D$. Assume first that $C \rightarrow D \in b$. From the third clause of the definition of M_T we get: $(x)(y)(x \in K' \wedge y \in K' \wedge Rbxy \wedge C \in x \supset . D \in y)$, from $C \rightarrow D \in b$. And this formula begining with (x)(y) gives the conditions for saying that $C \rightarrow D \in Hb$.

To complete this fourth case we want to show that if $C \rightarrow D \notin b$ then there is an x' and z' from K' such that Rbx'z', $C \in x'$, but $D \notin z'$. Here is where we have to labor a bit. Again we have to establish existential claims about prime theories; so again we have to employ the Zorn's Lemma strategy. We follow the suggestions of Theorem 2 of Meyer's and Routley's SEIII.

Assume that $C \rightarrow D \notin b$ and consider the definitions below.

$u = \{F: C \rightarrow F \in T\}$.

$w = \{F: (\exists G)(G \rightarrow F \in b \text{ and } G \in u\}$.

Sublemma 10 of V.2: For u, w as defined above the following hold: (i) Rbuw, (ii) u and w are in K, viz., closed under T-entailment and Adj., (iii) $C \in u$, but (iv) $D \notin w$.

We leave (ii) as an exercise and merely point out that w has been defined so that it meets the minimal conditions for having Rbuw, as given in the third clause of the definition of M_T. Because T contains E, $C \rightarrow C \in T$; so we have (iii). If $D \in w$, we have $G_1 \rightarrow D \in b$ and $C \rightarrow G_1 \in T$. Then by Suffixing on $C \rightarrow G_1$ we get $G_1 \rightarrow D \rightarrow . C \rightarrow D \in T$. Then the closure of b under T-entailment gives $C \rightarrow D \in b$ contrary to the assumptions that $C \rightarrow D \notin b$. So, we have (iv).

Unfortunately, we cannot stop here because we are not guaranteed that u and w are prime. So we define two sets and apply Zorn's Lemma. Note that you need to prove that they are non-empty before you can apply Zorn's Lemma.

$\Gamma w = \{z: z \in K_T, Rbuz, \text{ but } D \notin z\}$.

By Zorn's Lemma there is a maximal member z' of Γw.

$\Gamma u = \{x: x \in K_T, u \subseteq x, Rbxz', \text{ and } C \in x\}$.

By Zorn's Lemma there is a maximal member x' of Γu.

So we have: Rbx'z', $C \rightarrow D \notin b$, $C \in x'$, but $D \notin z'$. But are z' and x' prime?

Sublemma 11 of V.2: z' is prime, viz., $z' \in K'$.

As proof consider the following argumentthat i[illegible] is not prime we can extend it to a bigger member of [illegible]lled z". Assume for <u>reductio</u> that $H \vee J \in z'$ but that neith[illegible]nor H are in z'. We want to argue that either J or H c[illegible] added

Proof of Sublemma 11 for Lemma 14 continued,

to z' to get a bigger z". Let's say that we try to add H. When we add H to z' to get z" we also close z' plus H under T-entailment and Adj.; so $z'' \in K_T$. Of course, $w \subseteq z''$ and adding formulas to z' to get z" does not stop conditions for Rbuz" to be true. (To falsify Rbuz" we would have to put an $\longrightarrow$ formula in b, its antecedent in u, but leave its consequent out of z".) In regard to having z" in Γw we worry only about putting D into z". If we have to put D into z" by adding H, it is because $H \longrightarrow D \in T$. If it happens that $H \longrightarrow D \in T$, then add J to z' to get z" instead of adding H. If $J \longrightarrow D \in T$ then the addition of J to z' would put D into z" and force z" out of Γw. But we cannot have both $H \longrightarrow D \in T$ and $J \longrightarrow D \in T$ because if both $H \longrightarrow D$ and $J \longrightarrow D$ were in T, then D would be in z' by the facts that $H \vee J \in z'$, $E \subseteq T$, and z' is closed under T-entailment. But because z' is a maximal member of Γw, $D \notin z'$. So, we can add either H or J to z' to get z" if z' is not prime and this z" will be a larger member of Γw. So, by <u>reductio</u> we have Sublemma 11.

The next, and final, sublemma can now be established in the way that Sublemma 6 was established because x' is a maximal member "between" two prime theories in Rbx'z'.

Sublemma 12 of V.2: x' is prime, viz., $x' \in K'$.

For proof we give only the following hints. For <u>reductio</u> assume $H \vee J \in x'$ but $H \notin x'$ and $J \notin x'$. Define the following two sets.

$[H,x'] = \{F: (\exists G)(G \in x' \text{ and } H \wedge G \longrightarrow F \in T)\}$. abbreviate it as <u>h</u>.

$[J,x'] = \{F: (\exists G)(G \in x' \text{ and } J \wedge G \longrightarrow F \in T)\}$. abbreviate it as <u>j</u>.

You need to develop arguments that $x' \in [H,x']$, $x' \in [J,x']$, and that both [H,x'] and [J,x'] are closed under T-entailment and Adj.. We only point out that for formula C used in Lemma 14 we have $C \in [H,x']$ because $C \in x'$; hence, there is a G in x', viz., C itself, such that $H \wedge G \longrightarrow C \in T$. Similarly, $C \in [J,x']$. Thus, since neither [H,x'] nor [J,x'] belong to Γu, because they are bigger than Γu's maximal member x', both Rb<u>h</u>z' and Rb<u>j</u>z' fail. Note that both <u>h</u> and <u>j</u> belong to K, contain u, and have C as a member. Now proceed as in the proof of Sublemma 6.

With Sublemma 12, we have secured Lemma 14 and thereby have completed a proof of Theorem I. By contraposition of Theorem I we get a result significant enough to be labelled as a theorem.

Theorem II of V.2: If A is E-valid, then $\vdash_E A$.

The third theorem is simply a corollary of the Soundness

Theorem, i.e., Theorem I of V.2, and the Completeness Theorem just above.

Theorem III of V.2: $\vdash_{E}$ A iff. A is E-valid.

Next we want to show that a rule of MD, i.e., rule γ, is admissible in E. Unfortunately, we do not get a contradiction by assuming that $A \in Ho$, $\sim A \vee B \in Ho$, but that $B \notin Ho$, where o is a P-point of an Ems.. We have no guarantee that P-points are consistent. So, to establish the admissibility of MD, we have to alter slightly the notion of an Ems.. This is the task of the next section.

The body of this section leaves many, almost too many, exercises for the reader. Nevertheless, we add a few more.

Exercises V.2

1. Prove Corollaries 1 - 9,11, and 12.

2. Show that Ho for P-point o is normal if o* = o.

3. See if you can prove an analog of Lemma 1 by specifying that $T_i = T_{i-1}$ if either $F_i \vdash^{T_{i-1}} A$ or $F_i \vdash^{T_{i-1}} D \wedge \sim D$. Consider how we showed that T was prime. If T could have been defined in this way, we would not need another section to show the admissibility of MD.

   Observe also that we would have difficulty showing that T is prime if we started with $E \cup \{\sim A\}$ and added F_i iff. $T_{i-1} \cup \{F_i\}$ did not yield, via E's rules, an explicit contradiction. We would put in $A \vee B \wedge \sim B$, where A and B share no variables; but we would not put in either A or $B \wedge \sim B$.

4. Call: $(x)(Rabx \wedge Rxcd \supset .(\exists y)(Rbcy \wedge Rayd)$, $\mathcal{E}10$. Show that $\mathcal{E}10$ is true of M'_T.

5. Show that Γw and Γu for Sublemma 12 are non-empty.

V.3 The E-admissibility of MD or Rule γ ,Normal Ems, argument that Ackermann's Π' has E's semantics,

The major goal of this section is to establish the admissibility of Rule γ for E. However, this result is not of interest primarily for the practical purpose of proving theoems in E. For us its admissibility has two significant consequences. First, it allows us to complete the proof of Theorem I of IV.2 that Ackermann's Π' and system E have the same theorems. Secondly, it allows us to recognize and accommodate, to some extent, the strong normative intuitions in favor of MD and Disjunctive Syllogism. The admissibility of Rule γ was one of the open problems for system E listed by A.R. Anderson in his [1963]. The problem was orginally solved by algebraic means by Dunn and Meyer in their [1969]. The arguments of this section are adapted from section 5 of SEIV and section 8 of SEI.

A crucial notion is that of normal Ems: and Emsn.. So, some definitions are in order.

Def. 1: A <u>normal Ems</u>., an Emsn., is an Ems. <u>Mn</u> such that $\overline{(\exists x)(Px \wedge x = x^*)}$ is true of it.

Def. 2: A <u>normal P-point</u> of an Ems. is a P-point o such that $o = o^*$.

Def. 3: Formula A is <u>normal E-valid</u>, En-valid, iff. A is a member of all set-ups Ho at all normal P-points o in all normal Ems..

In light of Theorem III of V.2 we have the following two corollaries. from the definitions.

Corollary 1 of V.3: If A is E-valid, then A is En-valid.

Corollary 2 of V.3: If $\vdash_E$ A, then A is En-valid.

The first theorem of this section is the converse of Corollary 1.

Theorem I of V.3: If A is En-valid, then A is E-valid.

Most of the work of this section is concerned with proving the contrapositive of Theorem I. But we defer its proof until we use it to establish the admissibility of Rule γ. With Theorem I and Corollary 1, we get the co-extensionality of E-validity and En-validity.

Theorem II of V.3: A is E-valid iff. A is En-valid.

Theorem III of V.2 and Theorem II give us our third theorem of E's completeness with respect to En-validity.

Theorem III of V.3: $\vdash_E$ A iff. A is En-valid.

The admissibility of Rule γ is, in effect, a corollary of Theorem I. Nevertheless it is significant to be labelled a theorem.

Theorem IV of V.3: If $\vdash_E$ A and $\vdash_E \sim A \vee B$, then $\vdash_E$ B.

To prove Theorem IV by <u>reductio</u> assume that $\vdash_E$ A, $\vdash_E \sim A \vee B$, but not-$\vdash_E$ B. Theorem I of V.2 and the contrapositive of Theorem I of this section tell us that B $\notin$ Ho where o is a normal P-point in an Emsn.. Corollary 2 and Def. 3 tell us that A $\in$ Ho and $\sim A \vee B \in$ Ho. With B $\notin$ Ho we have to have $\sim A \in$ Ho from $\sim A \vee B \in$ Ho because, by Corollary 11 of V.2, Ho is prime. But, since o = o*, we cannot have both A $\in$ Ho and $\sim A \in$ Ho, as we saw from exercise 5 of V.1. So, to avoid inconsistency, we accept the admissibility of Rule γ.

Theorem IV is, of course, Lemma 1 of IV.2. Finally, then, we have completed the proof of Theorem I of IV.2, viz., $\vdash_E$ A iff. $\vdash_{\Pi'}$ A. As a result we have E's model structure semantics for Ackermann's Π'.

Thereom V of V.3: a) $\vdash_{\Pi'}$ A iff. A is E-valid.
b) $\vdash_{\Pi'}$ A iff. A is En-valid.

We now turn to the labor of proving the contrapositive of Theorem I. Readers uninterested in purely formal work with model structures may omit the remainder of this section. How will we show: If A is not E-valid, then A is not En-valid? We will show that if A $\notin$ Ho, where o is a P-point of an Ems. <u>M</u>, there is associated with <u>M</u> a normal Ems. <u>Mn</u> such that for some normal P-point o_n of <u>Mn</u> A $\notin$ Ho_n for some forcing on <u>Mn</u>. We show the preceding by showing how to extend an Ems. <u>M</u> to an Emsn. <u>Mn</u> by adding a normal P-point o_n and then by giving a forcing on <u>Mn</u> such that $Ho_n \subseteq$ Ho, where o is an arbitrarily selected P-point of <u>M</u>. In particular, the arbitrarily selected P-point of <u>M</u> could be the one such that A $\notin$ Ho.

Two more definitions are crucial here.

Def. 4: A <u>normalization of an Ems. M</u> $\langle K,P,R,*\rangle$ <u>with respect to P-point</u> o is a structure <u>Mn</u> $\langle K_n, P_n, R_n, *_n\rangle$

obtained in the following way. Select a P-point of <u>M</u> and label it o. Extend <u>M</u>'s components as follows. $K_n = K \cup \{o_n\}$ where $o_n \notin K$. $P_n x$ iff. Px or x = o_n.

$*_n$ is * except that $o_n^{*_n} = o_n$; so use plain * for $*_n$. (For simplicity's sake let us also use <u>K</u> for K_n, <u>P</u> for P_n, and <u>R</u> for R_n. Use <u>o</u> for o_n.)

Extend R to <u>R</u> by making the following specifications where a,b,c,o, and o* are all members of K.

i) <u>R</u>abc iff. Rabc, ii) <u>R</u> <u>o</u> <u>o</u> <u>o</u>, iii) <u>R</u> <u>o</u>ab iff. Roab
iv) <u>R</u> <u>o</u> <u>o</u> a iff. Rooa, v) <u>R</u>ab<u>o</u> iff. Rabo*

Def. 4 continued

vi) Rao o iff. Raoo*, vii) R o a o iff. Roao*
vii) Ra o b iff. Raob.
Call these eight conditions R-normalizing conditions.

Def. 5: A normalized forcing I_n is a forcing on an Mn which is a normalization of Ems. M with respect to P-point o and which is based on the following assignment fn() on Mn. For all a in K, fn(p,a) = f(p,a) and fn(p,o) = f(p,o) where f() is an assignment on M.

To show that I_n is a genuine forcing it suffices, in light of Lemma 1 of V.1, to show that fn() meets the Inclusion Condition for assignments.

Lemma 1 of V.3: A normalized forcing I_n is a genuine forcing.

We want to show that if $(\exists x)(Px \wedge Rxab)$ and fn(p,a) = 1, then fn(p,b) = 1. As a preliminary for the proof, note that from $\mathfrak{X}7$ back in V.1 we have $o^* \preccurlyeq o$; so on M f(p,o*) = 1 gives f(p,o) = 1. There are several cases to consider. We merely list the cases and discuss three. From the assumption that $Px \wedge Rxab$ we have two general cases depending upon whether the P-point x is in K or is o. For all cases below a,b,o, and o* are in K of M.

I) $x \in K$. There are four subcases: (i) Rxab, (ii) Rxob, (iii) Rxao, (iv) Rxo o . Here we have Px from Px.

II) x = o. Again there are four subcases: (i) R oab, (ii) R o o b, (iii) R o a o, (iv) R o o o .

Consider case (Ii). By the R-normalizing conditions Rxab gives Rxab and here Px gives Px; so here fn() is plain f() which already meets the Inclusion Condition. Consider case (Iiii). The R-normalizing conditions give Rxao* from Rxao. In this case fn(p,a) = 1 gives f(p,a) = 1 which with Raxo* gives f(p,o*) = 1 which, by the preliminary observation, gives f(p,o) = 1. But fn(p,o) = f(p,o). So, Rxao and fn(p,a) = 1 gives fn(p,o) = 1 as desired. Consider case (IIii). Assume fn(p,o) = 1 and show f(p,b) = 1. By R-normalizing conditions R o o b gives Roob. Because fn(p,o) = f(p,o) we have f(p,b) = 1 which with Roob gives f(p,b) = 1 which because $b \in K$, gives fn(p,b) = 1. Hopefully, the above illustrations serve to show how to complete a proof of Lemma 1.

To make our next point we are going to assume that the normalized Mn obtained from Ems. M is itself a Ems.. This assumption will not be question-begging in the proof of Lemma 3 as you may verify. Let us use Ha for the set-up at point a, $a \in K$, based on the forcing I_n from fn(). Use plain Ha for the set-up at point a, $a \in K$, based on the forcing from assignment f(). Observe that if Mn is an Ems., $H o \subseteq Ho$. Why?

From 5 we have Rooo which by the R-normalizing condition (viii) gives $\underline{R}o\underline{o}o$. Because $\underline{P}o$ and $\underline{H}$ is a genuine forcing, Lemma 1 of V.1, viz., the Inclusion Condition for forcings, gives us $\underline{H}\ \underline{o} \subseteq \underline{H}o$. (We needed to assume that $\underline{Mn}$ is an Ems. to use Lemma 1 of V.1.) If we can show that for $a \in K$ we have $\underline{H}a = Ha$, we will have $\underline{H}\ \underline{o} \subseteq Ho$. Recall from the discussion immediately before Def. 4 why we want to show that $\underline{H}\ \underline{o} \subseteq Ho$ in order to prove Theorem I.

> Lemma 2 of V.3: Let I_n be a normalized forcing on $\underline{Mn}$ based on fn( ) associated with assignment f( ) on $\underline{M}$ as specified before Lemma 1. Under these conditions under I_n $\underline{H}a = Ha$ for all a in K.

The proof is by induction on the length of formula B. The basis case is readily settled by the way fn( ) is defined in terms of f( ). So, for C and D shorter than B we assume: $C \in \underline{H}a$ iff. $C \in Ha$ and $D \in \underline{H}a$ iff. $D \in Ha$. At the induction step we consider only the case that B has the form $C \longrightarrow D$. We want to show that $C \longrightarrow D \notin \underline{H}a$ iff. $C \longrightarrow D \notin Ha$. The first R-normalizing condition makes it easy to get $C \longrightarrow D \notin \underline{H}a$ if $C \longrightarrow D \notin Ha$. So, we consider only the cases coming from the assumption that $C \longrightarrow D \notin \underline{H}a$. From this assumption we have: $\underline{R}abc$, $C \in \underline{H}b$, but $D \notin \underline{H}c$; and we want to get Rade, $C \in Hd$, but $D \notin He$. for some points d and e from K. We ignore the case where both b and c are from K. We list the interesting cases below.

(i) $\underline{R}a\underline{o}b$, $C \in \underline{H}\ \underline{o}$, $D \notin \underline{H}b$, with $a \in K$, and $b \in K$.

(ii) $\underline{R}ab\underline{o}$, $C \in \underline{H}b$, $D \notin \underline{H}\ \underline{o}$, with $a \in K$, and $b \in K$.

(iii) $\underline{R}a\ \underline{o}\ \underline{o}$, $C \in \underline{H}\ \underline{o}$, $D \notin \underline{H}\ \underline{o}$, with $a \in K$.

We consider cases (ii) and (iii). In case (ii) $\underline{R}ab\underline{o}$ gives by R-normalization condition (v):Rabo*.(Here b and o* will be the points d and e from K.) The induction assumption gives $C \in Hb$ from $C \in \underline{H}b$. The preliminary observation that $\underline{H}\ \underline{o} \subseteq \underline{H}o$ gives $D \notin \underline{H}o$ from $D \notin \underline{H}\ \underline{o}$; and,then, the induction assumption gives $D \notin Ho$. Recall from the preliminary remarks in the proof of Lemma 1 that $Ho^* \subseteq Ho$; so we get $D \notin Ho^*$ from $D \notin Ho$. In case (iii) $\underline{R}a\ \underline{o}\ \underline{o}$ gives Raoo* by R-normalizing condition (vi). Treat $D \notin \underline{H}\ \underline{o}$ as in the previous case to get $D \notin Ho^*$. The fact that $\underline{H}\ \underline{o} \subseteq \underline{H}o$ gives $C \in \underline{H}o$ from $C \in \underline{H}\ \underline{o}$; and, then, the induction assumption gives $C \in Ho$.

Let the above suffice for a proof of Lemma 2. We complete a proof of Theorem I with a sketch of how to show that $\underline{Mn}$ is an Ems..

> Lemma 3 of V.3: $\underline{Mn}$ is an Emsn., i.e., the normalization of an Ems. is a normal Ems..

A proof consists of sublemmas asserting that the Ems. postulates are true of $\underline{Mn}$ after we note that $\underline{Mn}$ has been construted so that the normality postulate: $(\exists x)(Px \wedge x = x^*)$ is tru of $\underline{Mn}$. Verfification that these postulates hold is lengthy.

So we are very sparing on details of how to show that they hold.

Sublemma 1 of V.3: $(\exists x)(\underline{P}x \wedge \underline{R}xaa)$ holds of $\underline{Mn}$.

The fact that $(\exists x)(Px \wedge Rxaa)$ holds of $\underline{M}$ and the definitions of $\underline{P}$ and $\underline{R}$ take care of the case where $a \neq \underline{o}$. The case of $a = \underline{o}$ is taken care of by R-normalizing condition (ii).

Sublemma 2 of V.3: $(x)(\underline{P}x \wedge \underline{R}xab \supset (\exists y)(\underline{P}y \wedge \underline{R}ayb)$ holds of $\underline{Mn}$.

We illustrate several cases here to indicate the labor involved. If x,a,and b are in K, $\mathcal{E}2$ holds by virtue of holding for $\underline{M}$. So let us consider some of the cases when at least one of x,a, and b are $\underline{o}$.

i) $x = a = b = \underline{o}$. We have $\underline{P}\ \underline{o}$ by definition of $\underline{P}$ and $\underline{R}\ \underline{o}\ \underline{o}\ \underline{o}$ by R-normalizing condition (ii). So EG gives $(\exists y)(\underline{P}y \wedge \underline{R}\ \underline{o}\ y\ \underline{o})$.

ii) Only $x = \underline{o}$. The antecedent for this instance of $\mathcal{E}2$ is $\underline{P}\ \underline{o} \wedge \underline{R}\ \underline{o}ab$. By R-normalizing condition (iii) $\underline{R}\ \underline{o}ab$ gives Roab. Because we have Po, we have $Po \wedge Roab$ which, because $\mathcal{E}2$ holds of $\underline{M}$, gives $(\exists y)(Py \wedge Rayb)$ which, in turn, gives $Py \wedge Rayb$. By the definition of $\underline{P}$ and R-normalizing condition (i) we get $\underline{P}y \wedge \underline{R}ayb$ from $Py \wedge Rayb$ where $y \in K$. Now EG gives the desired consequent: $(\exists y)(\underline{P}y \wedge \underline{R}ayb)$.

iii) $x = a = \underline{o}$. The antecedent is $\underline{P}\ \underline{o} \wedge \underline{R}\ \underline{o}\ \underline{o}\ b$. R-normalizing condition (iv) gives Roob. So we have Po Roob which, by $\mathcal{E}2$ for $\underline{M}$, gives $(\exists y)(Py \wedge Royb)$. We have, then, Py and Royb with $y \in K$. R-normalizing condition (iii) gets us $\underline{R}\ \underline{o}yb$ from Royb; Classical Logic gets us, then, $(\exists y)(\underline{P}y \wedge \underline{R}\ \underline{o}yb)$.

iv) $x = b = \underline{o}$. The antecedent is $\underline{P}\ \underline{o} \wedge \underline{R}\ \underline{o}\ a\ \underline{o}$. $\underline{R}\ \underline{o}\ a\ \underline{o}$ gives Roao* with Po. We thus have $Po \wedge Roao^*$ which by $\mathcal{E}2$ for $\underline{M}$ gives a $Py \wedge Rayo^*$. Py gives $\underline{P}y$ and Rayo* gives $\underline{R}ay\underline{o}$. The rest is easy.

v) $a = \underline{o}$. The antecedent is $\underline{P}x \wedge \underline{R}x\ \underline{o}\ b$. $\underline{R}x\ \underline{o}\ b$ gives Rxob. Now $\mathcal{E}2$ for $\underline{M}$ gives a $Py \wedge Royb$. Py gives $\underline{P}y$ and Royb gives $\underline{R}\ \underline{o}yb$. The rest is easy.

vi) $b = \underline{o}$. The antecedent is $\underline{P}x \wedge \underline{R}xa\underline{o}$. $\underline{R}xa\underline{o}$ gives Rxao* and $\underline{P}x$ gives Px, as it also did in case (v). Again $\mathcal{E}2$ for $\underline{M}$ gives a Py and a Rayo*. Py gives $\underline{P}y$ and Rayo* gives $\underline{R}ay\underline{o}$. The rest is easy.

vii) We leave this whole case as an exercise. $a = b = \underline{o}$.

The preceding illustration of cases of Sublemma 2 indicates the character of the strategy for proving the other sublemmas. It is a routine consideration of cases. There is no need to employ the Zorn's Lemma strategy. So in the remaining proofs we are even more sparing on details. At most we discuss a single case.

Sublemma 3 of V.3: $(x)(\underline{R}abx \wedge \underline{R}xcd \supset (\exists y)(\underline{R}acy \wedge \underline{R}byd)$ holds of $\underline{Mn}$.

In a proof we would assume $\underline{R}abx \wedge Rxcd$ and worry about the cases where at least one of: a,b,c,d, and x, referred to $\underline{o}$.

Proof of Sublemma 3 continued,

Consider only the case in which we have $\underline{R}ab\underline{o} \wedge \underline{R}\,\underline{o}cd$. $\underline{R}ab\underline{o}$ gives $Rabo^*$ and $\underline{R}\,\underline{o}cd$ gives $Rocd$. By $\mathfrak{X}7$ we have Roo^*o. By $\mathfrak{X}8$ $(Po \wedge Roo^*o) \wedge Rabo^*$ gives $Rabo$. With $Rabo \wedge Rocd$, $\mathcal{E}3$ for plain $\underline{M}$ gives $(\exists y)(Racy \wedge Rbyd)$. R-normalizing condition (i) will gives us the desired consequent.

Sublemma 4 of V.3: $\underline{R}abc \supset (\exists x)(\underline{R}abx \wedge \underline{R}xbc)$ holds of $\underline{Mn}$.

Consider only the case where the antecedent is $\underline{R}ab\underline{o}$. $\underline{R}ab\underline{o}$ gives $Rabo^*$ and $\mathcal{E}4$ for $\underline{M}$ gives $(\exists x)(Rabx \wedge Rxbo^*)$. Use R-normalizing condition (i) to get the desired consequent.

Sublemma 5 of V.3: $(x)((\underline{P}x \wedge \underline{R}xab) \wedge \underline{R}bcd \supset . \underline{R}acd)$ is true of $\underline{Mn}$.

Consider only the case where the antecedent is $(\underline{P}x \wedge \underline{R}xa\underline{o}) \wedge \underline{R}\,\underline{o}cd$. $\underline{P}x$ gives Px, $\underline{R}xa\underline{o}$ gives $Rxao^*$, and $\underline{R}\,\underline{o}cd$ gives $Rocd$. As in the illustration of a case for Sublemma 3, $Rxao^*$ gives $Rxao$. By applying $\mathcal{E}5$ to $(Px \wedge Rxao) \wedge Rocd$ we get $Racd$ which by R-normalizing condition (i) gives $\underline{R}acd$.

Sublemma 6 of V.3: $(x)((\underline{P}x\ \underline{R}xab) \wedge \underline{R}cbd \supset . \underline{R}cad)$ is true of $\underline{Mn}$.

Consider the case where the antecedent is $(\underline{P}x \wedge \underline{R}xa\underline{o}) \wedge \underline{R}c\underline{o}d$. $\underline{P}x$ gives Px, $\underline{R}xa\underline{o}$ gives $Rxao^*$, and $\underline{R}c\underline{o}d$ gives $Rcod$. As in the previous sublemma $Rxao^*$ gives $Raxo$. $\mathcal{E}6$ for $\underline{M}$ now gives $Rcad$ from Px, $Rxao$, and $Rcod$; and $Rcad$ iff. $\underline{R}cad$.

Remember that we are deleting the subscript from $*_1$ since $*_1$ alters $*$ so little. We do not bother to illustrate cases from proofs of Sublemmas 7 and 9; we consider only one case under Sublemma 8.

Sublemma 7 of V.3: $a^{**} = a$ is true of $\underline{Mn}$.

Sublemma 8 of V.3: $\underline{R}abc \supset \underline{R}ac^*b^*$

Consider the case where the antecedent is $\underline{R}ab\underline{o}$. $\underline{R}ab\underline{o}$ gives $Rabo^*$. $\mathcal{E}8$ on $\underline{M}$ gives $Rao^{**}b^*$ from $Rabo^*$. By $\mathcal{E}7$ on $\underline{M}$ $Rao^{**}b^*$ gives $Raob^*$ which by R-normalizing condition (viii) gives $\underline{R}a\underline{o}b^*$. The definition requirement that $\underline{o} = \underline{o}^*$ gives $\underline{R}a\underline{o}^*b^*$ as desired.

Sublemma 9 of V.3: $\underline{R}aa^*a$ is true of $\underline{Mn}$.

We let the preceding lemmas, sublemmas, and accompanying remarks serve as a proof of Theorem I. In light of Corollary 13 of V.2 we close with a theorem about set-ups at normal P-points.

Theorem VI of V.3: Set-ups at a normal P-point in an Emsn. are normal E-theories in the sense of V.2.

Exercises V.3 on the next page

Exercises V.3

1. Consider the following alteration of our notion of Ems.. An Ems. is a quintuple ⟨o,K, P,R, *⟩ where o ∈ K and Po. Replace our ℰ1 with Roaa. The other postulates can remain the same and forcings can be defined in the same way. Say that A is E-valid iff. A ∈ Ho for all forcings on all Ems.. Call this <u>Meyer/Routley E-validity</u>. Show that A is Meyer/Routley E-valid iff. A is E-valid in our sense. Hint: recall from V.2 that if A is not E-valid A ∉ T where T can be a suitable Ho for a Meyer/Routley Ems.. See SEIV.

2. Alter the notion of Emsn. to conform to the Meyer/Routley notion of having a specific o as a P-point. Show that there is no disagreement on which formulas are normally-E-valid.

3. Investigate the consequences of adding (x)(Px⊃Raxa) as a postulate. Or, if you prefer Meyer/Routley semantics with a o-point, add Raoa.

4. Show that the system TEf of Section III.6 is contained in the fdf. theorems of E.

5. Complete another case for each of the sublemmas.

V.4 The value of P-points in Ems., Two E-matrices developed from Ems., explanation of the ⟶ table for Maksimowa's $\mathfrak{M}$a.

Our main goal in this section is to gain some appreciation of the need for a plurality of P-points in Ems.. We accomplish this by showing that if we have only one P-point in an Ems., a single o-point, we validate $A \supset \Box A$, viz., $A \supset .A \rightarrow A \rightarrow A$. We then develop a matrix which shows that $A \supset \Box A$ is not a theorem of E. While we are developing a matrix from an Ems. we find it appropriate to close with an explanation of how the ⟶ table of Maksimowa's $\mathfrak{M}$a, which was presented in IV.11, was computed.

A way to obtain the effect of having only one P-point in an Ems. is to replace postulate $\mathcal{E}2$: $(x)((Px \wedge Rxab \supset (\exists y)(Py \wedge Rayb))$, with a postulate we label $\mathcal{R}$m 1: $(x)(Px \supset Raxa)$. Let us label model structures satisfying $\mathcal{R}$m 1 and all Ems. postulates except $\mathcal{E}2$ mRms. for 'material R model structures' because they validate the material implication consequence of the R-theorem: $A \rightarrow \Box A$.

Theorem I of V.4: In an Ems. transformed into an mRms. no two P-points x,y are distinguishable because in it Rxab iff. Ryab, Raxb iff. Rayb, and Rabx iff. Raby.

We give no details of proof because the theorem states exactly what needs to be done. We merely suggest that $\mathcal{E}5$, $\mathcal{E}6$, and $\mathfrak{X}7$ are useful in a proof.

Let us label the discernible P-point of an mRms. with o. So, in effect, $\mathcal{R}$m 1 gives us Raoa. In her [1972], Maksimowa observes that Raoa with o as the single P-point validates $A \supset \Box A$. We make this observation our next theorem.

Theorem II of V.4: $\sim A \vee .A \rightarrow A \rightarrow A$ is mRms.-valid.

The proof is the typical <u>reductio</u> type used in V.1.

1) $\sim A \vee .A \rightarrow A \rightarrow A \notin Ho$, where o is the sole P-point.	
2 a) $\sim A \notin Ho$	
b) $A \rightarrow A \rightarrow A \notin Ho$	By v-normality from (1),
3 a) $A \rightarrow A \in Hb$	Triad Rule gives an Roab and
b) $A \notin Hb$	Inclusion Condition allows us to work with Robb.
4) $A \in Ho^*$	Imperfect Consistency on (2a),
5) $A \in Ho$	From (4) by use of $\mathfrak{X}7$ and Inclusion Condition, see preliminary remarks for Lemma 1 of V.3.
6) $A \in Hb$	Triad Rule on (3a),(5), and $\mathcal{R}$m 1's result that Rbob.

The contradiction between (3b) and (6) gives the theorem.

Observe that the proof of Theorem II involved use of the Ems. postulates for negation, viz. postulates for *. The significance of this observation comes from Meyer's and Routley's result in SEIII that the positive fragment of E is complete with respect to Ems. with a single P-point o and Raoa. It is negation which requires us to have a plurality of P-points in Ems.. Here we need to note also that although Meyer's and Routley's E model structures have a selected P-point o they do not have Raoa for full E model structures; they have only $(\exists y)(Py \wedge Raya)$ which is our $\mathfrak{X}3$. The result is that in all Ems. there cannot be only one P-point which satisfies $(\exists y)(Py \wedge Raya)$ for all points a in the Ems.. At least there cannot be such single P-points in all Ems. if $A \supset \Box A$ is not an E-theorem. This is our next theorem.

Theorem III of V.4: $\sim A \vee . A \longrightarrow A \longrightarrow A$ is not a theorem of E.

We get a proof of Theorem III from two lemmas although we offer two choices for the second lemma.

To avoid subscripting o's we use i and j for P-points.

Lemma 1 of V.4: The following is an Ems. which we label $\underline{M_3}$. $\underline{M_3} = \langle K,P,R,*\rangle$ where $K = \{i,j,k\}$, $P = \{i,j\}$, we have Rikk, Rijj, Riii, Rjkk, Rjjj, Rkjk, Rkkj, and Rkkk, and also $i^* = i$, $j^* = j$, and $k^* = k$.

A proof of Lemma 1 is a laborious process of checking that each of the Ems. postulates is true of $\underline{M_3}$. It is laborious primarily because of $\mathcal{E}3$ and $\mathcal{E}4$. Here we merely show how to handle some cases under $\mathcal{E}6$, $\mathcal{E}5$, $\mathcal{E}4$, and $\mathcal{E}3$. The basic idea in these cases is to verify that if the given stipulations about the R-relation satisfy the antecedent we do not have to add stipulations to satisfy the consequent of the postulate in question. Consider the following instance of $\mathcal{E}6$: $(Pj \wedge Rjkk) \wedge Rkkk \supset Rkkk$. For this instance of $\mathcal{E}6$, we have the antecedent and also the consequent. Consider the following instance of $\mathcal{E}5$: $(Pi \wedge Rijj) \wedge Rjkk \supset Rjkk$ to see again that having the antecedent does not require us to make further stipulations about the R-relation in $\underline{M_3}$. Consider the following instance of $\mathcal{E}4$: $Rkjk \supset (\exists y)(Rkjy \wedge Ryjk)$. In this instance of $\mathcal{E}4$ if we instantiate y to k we do not get any new claims about the R-relation; we merely get Rkjk twice. Consider the following instance of $\mathcal{E}3$: $Rjkk \wedge Rkjk \supset (\exists y)(Rjjy \wedge Rkyk)$. In this instance of $\mathcal{E}3$, y may be safely instantiated to j to get Rjjj and Rkjk. Hopefully, the above suggestion of the kinds of cases to consider suffice for hints on how to prove Lemma 1.

Lemma 2 of V.4: There is a forcing on $\underline{M_3}$ such that $\sim p \vee . p \longrightarrow p \longrightarrow p \notin Hi$.

The proof amounts to showing that (1) below is consistent.

1) $\sim p \vee . p \longrightarrow p \longrightarrow p \notin Hi$

2 a) $\sim p \notin Hi$

b) $p \longrightarrow p \longrightarrow p \notin Hi$ — $\vee$-normality on (1) proof of Lemma 2 continued,

3) $p \in Hi$ — Imperfect Consistency on (2a) with i = i*.

4 a) $p \rightarrow p \in Hk$ — Triad Rule on (2b) using Rikk,
   b) $p \notin Hk$

Now we do not have Rkik although we have Rkjk for the sake of 1. Because we do not have Rkik, lines (4a) and (3) do not require us to contradict ourselves at line (4b) by putting p into Hk. Thus $\sim p \vee .p \rightarrow p \rightarrow p$ is not in the set-up at a P-point of some Ems. under some forcing; and because $\sim p \vee .p \rightarrow p \rightarrow p$ is not E-valid, $\sim A \vee .A \rightarrow A \rightarrow A$ is not an E theorem schema.

However, the proof of Lemma 2 may not be as convincing as we would like. You may fear that some "tricks" could be played with Ems. postulates to get a contradiction from (1). Those who have worked a bit on trying to show a formula is valid by getting a contradiction from an assumption that it does not belong to Hx where Px holds will appreciate how hidden the contradiction may be. So, let us develop a world-matrix refutation of $\sim A \vee .A \rightarrow A \rightarrow A$ as an E-theorem. This development also indicates how to get a world-matrix from an Ems..

The matrix which we label $\mathfrak{M}e8$ is an ordered six-tuple: $\langle B8, D, \vee, \wedge, \bar{\ }, \rightarrow \rangle$, where B8 = $\{+3,+2,+1,+0,-0,-1,-2,-3\}$ and D is the set of designated elements $\{+3,+2\}$. As usual for matrices $\vee$, $\wedge$, $\bar{\ }$, and $\rightarrow$ are operations on B8 which interpret logical $\vee, \wedge, \sim$, and $\rightarrow$. $\mathfrak{M}e8$ is a world-matrix built on the three worlds or points of $\underline{M_3}$. The eight elements of B8 are interpreted as on the following chart where 1 means 'holds at the point' and 0 means 'does not hold at the point.' You can also interpret 1 as 'belongs to the set-up at the point under some forcing' and 0 as 'does not belong to the set-up at the point under the forcing.' Because of $\underline{M_3}$'s conditions that i = i*, j = j*, and k = k*, negation on $\mathfrak{M}e8$ will be classical negation as discussed back in I.7.

Interpretation of $\mathfrak{M}e8$'s values relative to $\underline{M_3}$,

	+3	+2	+1	+0	-0	-1	-2	-3
i	1	1	1	1	0	0	0	0
j	1	1	0	0	1	1	0	0
k	1	0	1	0	1	0	1	0

Let us see how the above matrix values are related to some forcing on $\underline{M_3}$. For a variable p, v(p) = +2 means $p \in Hi$, $p \in Hj$ but $p \notin Hk$; and v(p) = +2 also means that for the interpretation f() from which the forcing is developed f(i,p) = 1, f(j,p) = 1, but f(k,p) = 0. More generally, we can regard assigning A a value a from $\mathfrak{M}e8$ as assigning A a series of three values from $\{1, 0\}$ where 1 in the first place means $A \in Hi$,

0 in the first place means A $\notin$ Hi, 1 in the second place means that A $\in$ Hj, etc.. So, in general, the $\mathfrak{M}$e8 values assigned to formulas represent set-ups at points of $\underline{M}_3$ to which they belong under some forcing. So, if v(A) = +3 or v(A) = +2 for all assignments to its variables then for all possible forcings on $\underline{M}_3$, which make an assignment to A's variables, A belongs to the set-ups at both P-points i and j. Thus formula A would be valid on Ems. $\underline{M}_3$ if v(A) = +3 or v(A) =+2 for all assignments to its variables. And, hence, +3 and +2 are naturally taken as designated elements.

If we now construct **v**, $\wedge$, $\bar{\ }$, and $\longrightarrow$ tables appropriately we will have the suitability of $\mathfrak{M}$e8 for E. The appropriate way is to have the matrix values be assigned to formulas iff. the forcing rules would put the formulas in the set-ups in the way in which the matrix values represent the formulas being put into set-ups. In this way, because +3 and +2 are designated, the $\mathfrak{M}$e8 valid formulas will be valid on Ems. $\underline{M}_3$; the Completeness Theorem II of V.2 tells us that the formulas valid on $\underline{M}_3$ contain the theorems of E. The following are the appropriate ways. Give A$\wedge$B the value 1 at a point iff. both A and B had matrix values which gave them 1 at the point in question. Give A **v** B the value 1 at a point iff. either A or B got the value 1 at the point. We give $\sim$A the value 1 at a point x iff. we gave A the value 0 at the point. We should pause here to note that these guidelines for assigning matrix values to conjunctions, disjunctions, and negations are exactly those for a world-matrix as discussed in I.7 except here we use 1 instead of T. So, because we have three points or worlds and negation is treated classically, the $\wedge$, **v**, and $\bar{\ }$ tables for $\mathfrak{M}$e8 are those following the lattice diagram D5 in I.7. But remember that for $\mathfrak{M}$e8 only +3,+2 are designated. The guidelines for A$\longrightarrow$B are a bit more elaborate because of the Triad Rule. We give A$\longrightarrow$B the value 1 at a point x iff. whenever Rxyz and A is given 1 at y then B is given 1 at z. This is better expressed negatively. We give A$\longrightarrow$B the value 0 at a point x iff. Rxyz and A is given 1 at y while B is given 0 at z. Consequently we assign values to A$\longrightarrow$B on $\mathfrak{M}$e8 as follows.

For the P-point i we have Riii, Rijj, and Rikk. So, we have that A$\longrightarrow$B gets 0 at point i iff. A is 1 at i but B is 0 at i or A is 1 at j but B is 0 at j or A is 1 at k but B is 0 at k.

For the P-point j we have Rjjj and Rjkk. So, we have that A$\longrightarrow$B gets 0 at j iff. A is 1 at j but B is 0 at j or A is 1 at k but B is 0 at k.

For the non-P-point k we have Rkkj,Rkjk, and Rkkk. So, we have that A$\longrightarrow$B gets 0 at k iff. A gets 1 at k but B gets 0 at j or A gets 1 at j but B gets 0 at k or A gets 1 at k but B gets 0 at k.

Below is presented the → table for $\mathcal{M}$e8. Two forms of the matrix values are given so that readers may readily check that the table has been constructed according to the preceding specifications.

→	111 +3	110 +2	101 +1	100 +0	011 -0	010 -1	001 -2	000 -3
111 +3	111 +3	000 -3	000 -3	000 -3	011 -0	000 -3	000 -3	000 -3
110 +2	111 +3	110 +2	001 -2	000 -3	011 -0	010 -1	001 -2	000 -3
101 +1	111 +3	000 -3	110 +2	000 -3	011 -0	000 -3	010 -1	000 -3
100 +0	111 +3	111 +3	111 +3	111 +3	011 -0	011 -0	011 -0	011 -0
011 -0	111 +3	000 -3	000 -3	000 -3	111 +3	000 -3	000 -3	000 -3
010 -1	111 +3	110 +2	001 -2	000 -3	111 +3	110 +2	001 -2	000 -3
001 -2	111 +3	000 -3	110 +2	000 -3	111 +3	000 -3	110 +2	000 -3
000 +3	111 +3	111 +3	111 +3	111 +3	111 +3	111 +3	111 +3	111 +3

We can now state our third lemms; it may be used instead of Lemma 2, with Lemma 1, to prove Theorem III.

Lemma 3 of V.4: Matrix $\mathcal{M}$e8 is suitable for E and on it ~A v .A→A→A is invalidated by setting v(A) = +0.

In light of the preceding observations on how to construct $\mathcal{M}$e8 to guarantee that $\mathcal{M}$e8 is suitable for E we can make some observations about the construction of $\mathcal{M}$a which will help prove Lemma 4 of IV.11, viz., the suitability of $\mathcal{M}$a for the positive fragment of E. In her [1972], L. Maksimowa gave the following model structure for the negation free fragment of E, and Ems.+ A Ems.+ is an ordered triple ⟨K,P,R⟩ which satisfies the first six $\mathcal{E}$ postulates. In her's, which we label <u>M4</u>+, K={o,a,b,c}, P ={o}, and R is as follows. Rooo,Roaa,Robb,Rocc; Raaa,Raoa, Raob,Raoc,Rabc,Rabb,Racc; Rbbb,Rbob,Rboc,Rbbc,Rbcc; Rccc,Rcoc.

To relate this to the discussion of IV.11 regard o as w0, a as w1,b as w2, and c as w3. The world-matrix treatment of ∧ and v guarantees that A∧B gets 1 at a point x iff. both A and B get 1 at x; and,thus, the matrix rule for A∧B corresponds to the forcing rule whereby A∧B ε Hx iff. A ε Hx and B ε Hx. Similarly, the matrix rule for A v B will correspond to the forcing rule. To guarantee that A→B gets 1 at a point x iff. A→B ε Hx we compute $\mathcal{M}$a's → table as follows.

i) A→B gets 0 at w0 iff. A gets 1 at w0 and B gets 0 at w0 because of Rooo or A gets 1 at w1 and B gets 0 at w1 because of Roaa or A gets 1 at w2 and B gets 0 at w2 because of

Robb or A gets 1 at w3 and B gets 0 at w3 because of Rocc.

ii) A⟶B gets 0 at w1 iff. A gets 1 at w1 and B gets 0 at w1 because of Raaa or A gets 1 at w0 and B gets 0 at w1 because of Raoa or A gets 1 at w0 and B gets 0 at w2 because of Raob or A gets 1 at w0 and B gets 0 at w3 because of Raoc or A gets 1 at w2 and B gets 0 at w3 because of Rabc or A gets 1 at w2 and B gets 0 at w2 because of Rabb or A gets 1 at w3 and B gets 0 at w3 because of Racc.

iii) A⟶B gets 0 at w2 iff. A gets 1 at w2 and B gets 0 at w2 because of Rbbb or A gets 1 at w0 and B gets 0 at w2 because of Rbob or A gets 1 at w0 and B gets 0 at w3 because of Rboc or A gets 1 at w2 and B gets 0 at w3 because of Rbbc or A gets 1 at w3 and B gets 0 at w3 because of Rbcc.

iv) A⟶B gets 0 at w3 iff. A gets 1 at w3 and B gets 0 at w3 because of Rccc or A gets 1 at w0 and B gets 0 at w3 because of Rcoc.

Hopefull these remarks will help in the verification that $\mathfrak{M}$a is suitable for the negation free fragment of E.

Exercises V.4

1. Show that $\mathcal{E}$2 follows from $\mathcal{R}$m 1 and the other $\mathcal{E}$ postulates.
2. Complete a proof of Theorem I.
3. Show that ~A v . A⟶A⟶A is m$\mathcal{R}$ms. valid.
4. By use of the rules for developing the ⟶ tables for $\mathfrak{M}$e8 and $\mathfrak{M}$a, compute the values for -2⟶+1 on each.
5. Reconsider exercise 5 of IV.11 on adding two different negation tables to $\mathfrak{M}$a. Now consider adding both kinds of negation to $\underline{M}$4+: (a) Classical negation x** = x and x* = x for all x and (b) Negation of Imperfect Consistency x** = x for all x, 0* = 0, a* = a, b* = c, and c* = b.

   For each kind of negation consider how $\mathcal{E}$8 and $\mathcal{E}$9 are going to require extension of relation R. For instance, $\mathcal{E}$8 with Classical Negation is going to require addition of Racb because of Rabc ⊃ Rac*b*; and $\mathcal{E}$9 with negation of Imperfect Consistency will require Rcbc to get Rcc*c. For each kind of negation recompute the ⟶ table and see if the resulting matrix is still suitable for E. The new matrices should still be suitable because no new way of making A⟶B 0 at w0 will be introduced.

V.5 Model structure semantics for R,RM,S4, Classical Logic, and EDS, explanation of the $\rightarrow$ table for Belnap's $\mathcal{M}_0$,

Our goal in this section is to present model structure semantics using the three-placed R-relation for some extensions of E. We hope, thereby, to start to gain some understanding of what this R-relation could be by seeing how different conditions on it validate different crucial formulas. The systems which we consider are: R, RM, versions of S4 and Classical Logic (CL) and EDS which is a system we have not yet considered. There will be remarks on how to modify E's completeness proof to get completeness proofs for R,RM, S4, and EDS. In passing, we point out how the $\rightarrow$ table for Belnap's $\mathcal{M}_0$ can be computed from an R model structure, an Rms.. In general, if S is the name of a system Sms. reads as 'S model structure.' Correct results presented in this section are obtained from Meyer and Routley; mistakes and awkward arguments are the fault of the author.

When we develop model structures for system R and its extensions, there is no need to block validation of the characteristic R-axiom: $A \rightarrow .A \rightarrow A \rightarrow A$; let alone $A \supset .A \rightarrow A \rightarrow A$. So, we can dispense with P-points in model structures for R and its extensions. In this section, then, model structures are ordered quadruples $\langle o,K,R,* \rangle$ where $o \in K$ while K,R, and * are as in V.1 except for having different postulates about them. We build on the set of $\mathcal{P}$-postulates below. These $\mathcal{P}$-postulates are obtained by replacing $Px \wedge Rxab$ contexts in the $\mathcal{E}$-postulates of V.1 with Roab. We drop $\mathcal{E}9$ and add $\mathcal{P}9$ as the special postulate for system R.

$\mathcal{P}1$: Roaa
$\mathcal{P}2$: $Roab \supset Raob$
$\mathcal{P}3$: $(x)(Rabx \wedge Rxcd \supset (\exists y)(Racy \wedge Rbyd))$
$\mathcal{P}4$: $Rabc \supset (\exists x)(Rabx \wedge Rxbc)$
$\mathcal{P}5$: $Roab \wedge Rbcd \supset Racd$ i.e., $a \leq b \wedge Rbcd \supset Racd$
$\mathcal{P}6$: $Roab \wedge Rcbd \supset Rcad$ i.e., $a \leq b \wedge Rcbd \supset Rcad$
$\mathcal{P}7$: $a^{**} = a$
$\mathcal{P}8$: $Rabc \supset Rac^*b^*$
$\mathcal{P}9$: $Rabc \supset Rbac$

We now define $a \leq b$ merely as Roab. Remember that in the above postulates the letters a,b,c,d, are free variables ranging over members of K and that they can be regarded as universally bound. Let us derive some theorems from these postulates to see that they are equivalent to a set of postulates known to characterize the model structures for system R.

$\mathcal{P}t$ 1: $a \leq b \wedge b \leq c \supset .a \leq c$ Simply an instance of $\mathcal{P}6$

To prove $\mathcal{P}t$ 2 start with the instance of $\mathcal{P}2$: $Roaa \supset Raoa$.

ρt 2: Raoa

ρt 3: Raaa

Proof

1) $Roaa \supset (\exists x)(Roax \wedge Rxaa)$	ρ4
2) $Roaa$	ρ1
3) $(\exists x)(Roax \wedge Rxaa)$	MD on (1) and (2),
4) $Roax \wedge Rxaa$	EI on (3),
5) $Roax \wedge Rxaa \supset Raaa$	ρ5
6) $Raaa$	MD on (4) and (5).

ρt 4: Raa*a

Proof

1) $Ra^*a^*a^*$	ρt 3
2) $Ra^*a^*a^* \supset Ra^*a^{**}a^{**}$	ρ8
3) $Ra^*a^{**}a^{**}$	MD on (1) and (2),
4) Ra^*aa	ρ7 on (3),
5) $Ra^*aa \supset Raa^*a$	ρ9
6) Raa^*a	MD on (4) and (5).

ρt 5: $o^* \leqslant o$, viz., Roo^*o, Immediate from ρt 4,

ρt 6: $(x)(Rabx \wedge Rxcd \supset (\exists y)(Racy \wedge Rybd)$ "Pasch's Law"

Proof

1) $Rabx \wedge Rxcd$	Hyp.
2) $Rabx \wedge Rxcd \supset (\exists y)(Racy \wedge Rbyd)$	From ρ3,
3) $(\exists y)(Racy \wedge Rbyd)$	MD on (1) and (2),
4) $Racy \wedge Rbyd$	EI on (3),
5) $Rbyd$	Simplify (4),
6) $Rbyd \supset Rybd$	ρ9 the "R postulate,"
7) $Rybd$	MD on (5) and (6),
8) $Racy \wedge Rybd$	Classical Logic (4),(7),
9) $(\exists y)(Racy \wedge Rybd)$	EG on (8),

Now the Deduction Theorem for classical predicate logic gives ρt 6.

ρt 7: $Rabc \supset (\exists x)(Rabx \wedge Raxc)$

To prove this assume Rabc and use ρt 3: Raaa. Then use ρ3 in the form: $Raaa \wedge Rabc \supset (\exists x)(Rabx \wedge Raxc)$.

ρt 8: $Rocd \wedge Rabc \supset Rabd$, i.e, $c \leqslant d \wedge Rabc \supset Rabd$

To prove this assume Rocd and Rabc and use ρ8 to get $Rod^*c^* \wedge Rac^*b^*$. Use the appropriate version of ρ6 to get Rad^*b^* which by ρ8 gives $Rab^{**}d^{**}$ which by ρ7 gives Rabd.

ρt 9: $(x)(Rabx \wedge Rxcd \supset (\exists y)(Rbcy \wedge Rayd))$.

This is $\mathfrak{X}$9 of V.1. So we dispense with proving it in this context. You may consult the proof of $\mathfrak{X}$9 to see how to prove ρt 9 from the ρ-postulates.

We label SEI the following set of postulates.

SEI = $\{\rho 1, \rho t3, \rho t6, \rho 5, \rho 7, \rho 8\}$

The set of postulates which we just labelled SEI were shown by Meyer and Routley in SEI to be necessary and sufficient to characterize Rms.. Our first theorem tells us that the ρ-postulates are deductively equivalent with the SEI set.

Theorem I of V.5: A model structure is characterized by the ρ-postulates iff. it is characterized by the SEI postulates.

By way of proof we note that we have already shown that all model structures characterized by the ρ-postulates have the SEI postulates true of them. So, we need only to show that all model structures characterized by the SEI postulates have the ρ-postulates true of them. Here we show only how to derive $\rho 9$ and $\rho 4$ from the SEI postulates. To obtain $\rho 9$ assume Rabc. Use Roaa$\wedge$Rabc with ρt6 to get Robx$\wedge$Rxac. Now $\rho 5$ gives Rbac. To obtain $\rho 4$ assume Rabc and use the just obtained $\rho 9$ to commute the first two terms of Rabc to get Rbac. Take Rbbb$\wedge$Rbac and use ρt6 to get a Rabx$\wedge$Rxbc. Again by using $\rho 9$ to commute terms of the R-relation we get Rabx$\wedge$Rxbc which by EG gives $(\exists x)$(Rabx$\wedge$Rxbc). We leave derivation of $\rho 3$ and $\rho 6$ from SEI as exercises.

In light of Meyer's and Routley's result from SEI and Theorem I, we draw the following corollary.

Corollary of I of V.5: A model structure which has the ρ-postulates true of it is a Rms..

As the proof of Theorem I reveals ρt6 or Pasch's Law, as it has been called by J.Dunn, is quite powerful. We would not want Pasch's Law to hold for Ems. because it would allow us to commute the first two terms of the R-relation. We will see shortly that such commutativity validates the R axiom $A \longrightarrow .A \longrightarrow B \longrightarrow B$.

Since we mentioned Ems. it is convenient to consider here the relation between Ems. and Rms.. Because $E \subseteq R$ we would expect that all Ems. are Rms.. If we alter the notion of Rms. so that we have Po$\wedge$(y)(Py $\supset$ .y = o) true of all Rms., we get the expected result. We can easily regard the o point of the model structures of this section as the unique P-point for the structures. We can have Po$\wedge$(y)(Py $\supset$ .y = o) true of all of them. We do not even need to introduce a new predicate because Px can be defined as x = o. So, since all model structures we consider in this section will be obtained by adding to the ρ-postulates or $\mathcal{E}$-postulates, we have the following theorem.

Theorem II of V.5: If <u>M</u> is an Ems., then <u>M</u> is an Rms..

The proof consists of showing that the $\mathcal{E}$-postulates are ρt theorems when a P-predicate applying only to o is introduced. For instance, consider $\mathcal{E}2$. Assume Px$\wedge$Rxab.

Proof remarks on Theorem II continued,

Since Px is x = o, Px∧Rxab gives Roab. ρ2 with Roab gives Raob; so we have Po∧Raob which gives $(\exists y)(Py \wedge Rayb)$.

It is also interesting to note that in SEIII Meyer and Routley showed that the postulate set consisting of: ρ1, ρt1, ρ5, ρt3, ρ4, ρ3, ρt9, ρt7, ρt2, and ρ9 characterize model structures for the positive fragment of system R. In SEIII they were not concerned with picking a minimal set of postulates. They added postulates one-by-one to validate formulas added one-by-one to a basic system. In this way it becomes apparent which properties of the R-relation are crucial for validation of specified formulas.

In this section we can use the semantic notions of V.1 with only slight changes. The notion of interpretation is the same except that now the Inclusion Condition is stated simply in terms of Roab, i.e., $a \preccurlyeq b$. The forcing rules are unchanged. We say that <u>A is valid in a particular Sms. S</u> if $A \in Ho$ for all forcings on <u>S</u>. We say that <u>A is S-valid</u> if A is valid in all Sms..

Let us, at least, report some of SEI's semantic results about system R. The first is R's Soundness on Rms..

Theorem III of V.5: If A is a theorem of R, then A is R-valid.

For proof we show only that the special R axiom is R-valid.

1) $A \longrightarrow .A \longrightarrow B \longrightarrow B \notin Ho$		Assume for <u>reductio</u>.
2 a) $A \in Hb$		Triad Rule on (1) gives an Roab and
b) $A \longrightarrow B \longrightarrow B \notin Hb$		the Inclusion Condition allows us to consider only Hb.
3 a) $A \longrightarrow B \in Hc$	Rbcd	Triad Rule on (2b),
b) $B \notin Hd$		

From Rbcd we get, by ρ9, Rcbd. With (2a),(3a), and Rcbd the Triad Rule gives (4) which contradicts (3b) and completes the <u>reductio</u>.

4) $B \in Hd$.

We also do little by way of actually proving Rms. Completeness for system R.

Theorem IV of V.5: If A is R-valid, then A is a theorem of R.

A proof can be obtained by modifying the completeness proof for E in V.5. We would talk of R-intensional theories instead of E-intensional theories. Especially in the analog of Lemma 1 of V.2 we would prove that if A is not a theorem of R, then there is a prime intensional R-theory T such that $R \subseteq T$, $A \notin T$ but $\sim A \in T$; the proof would hardly change. As in the proof of E's completeness, we would define two model structures: $\langle T, K_T, R, * \rangle$ and $\langle T, K_T', R', *' \rangle$ where K_T is the set of T-intensional theories and K_T' is the set of prime T-intensional theories.

proof discussion of Theorem IV continued,

Of course, we would not need to define P-points; we would let T be the o point. We would then proceed as in the proof of E's completeness. The only significant difference would be the verification that $\rho 9$ holds of both model structures. Because $\rho 9$ has no existential quantifiers, its verification does not require use of the Zorn's Lemma strategy. We can, in the case of $\rho 9$, directly consider the model structure restricted to prime intensional T-theories. Assume R'abc. We want R'bac. R'abc tells us that whenever $A \rightarrow B \in a$ and $A \in b$, then $B \in c$. (Remember that here a,b,and c are prime intensional T-theories.) To get R'bac we want to get that whenever $A \rightarrow B \in b$ and $A \in a$, then $B \in c$. So assume that $A \rightarrow B \in b$ and $A \in a$. Because T contains system-R, $A \rightarrow . A \rightarrow B \rightarrow B \in T$. Because theory a is closed under T-entailment, $A \in a$ gives $A \rightarrow B \rightarrow B \in a$. But now R'abc and $A \rightarrow B \in b$ gives $B \in c$, which is what we want to verify $\rho 9$.

You may study Theorem 4 of SEI to develop arguments that Rms. validity is co-extensive with normal Rms. validity where normal Rms. have o = o*. Indeed our arguments for the admissibility of Rule γ in V.3 have been adapted from this theorem of Meyer and Routley. So, we present the admissibility of Rule γ in R as a theorem.

Theorem V of V.5: If $\vdash_R A$ and $\vdash_R \sim A \vee B$, then $\vdash_R B$.

Before we consider model structure postulates which give model structures for other extensions of E let us look at a particular Rms. from which Belnap's matrix $\mathfrak{M}$o can be developed. This model structure is presented in SEI and called Ko; it is noted that Urquhart also discovered it. Of course, $\mathfrak{M}$o was not developed from Ko since $\mathfrak{M}$o was developed long before these model structures were even thought of. However, Ko does enable us to understand how tables for $\mathfrak{M}$o could have been computed.

Model structure Ko for matrix $\mathfrak{M}$o,

Ko is the structure $\langle o, \{o,a,b\}, R, * \rangle$ where R and * are as follows. o* = o, a* = b, and b* = a. For relation R we have: Rooo,Roaa, Robb,Raoa,Raaa, Raba,Rabb, Rabo, Rbob, Rbbb, Rbab, Rbaa, and Rbao.

Recall that the $\rightarrow$ table for $\mathfrak{M}$o is given in III.4 and that the $\wedge$, $\vee$, and $\bar{\ }$ tables are given in I.7 in relation to diagram D6. Also the values of $\mathfrak{M}$o are interpreted as world-matrix values on the $\bar{\ }$ table back in I.7. To relate the I.7 interpretation of $\mathfrak{M}$o values to Ko regard w0 as o, w1 as a, and w2 as b; and regard T as 1 and F as 0 to conform with our development of matrices in V.4. Here it may be helpful to recall from V.4 how matrix values may represent results of a forcing.

We can now appreciate the significance of such features of $\mathfrak{M}o$ as: If v(A) = +2(110), then v(~A) = -2(010). At first we wonder why the values of A and ~A are here identical in the last two places. Now we see that v(A) = +2 represents: A $\in$ Ho, A $\in$ Ha, but A $\notin$ Hb. By the forcing rules, if A $\in$ Ho and o* = o, then ~A $\notin$ Ho; if A $\in$ Ha and a* = b, then ~A $\notin$ Hb; and if A $\notin$ Hb and b* = a, then ~A $\in$ Ha.

We can also explain how the $\rightarrow$ table for $\mathfrak{M}o$ is developed in the way in which we explained the $\rightarrow$ tables for $\mathfrak{M}e8$ and $\mathfrak{M}a$ in the previous section.

Explanation of $\rightarrow$ table for $\mathfrak{M}o$

i) A$\rightarrow$B gets 0 at w0 iff. A gets 1 at w0 and B gets 0 at w0 because of Rooo or A gets 1 at w1 and B gets 0 at w1 because of Roaa or A gets 1 at w2 and B gets 0 at w2 because of Robb.

ii) A$\rightarrow$B gets 0 at w1 iff. A gets 1 at w0 and B gets 0 at w1 because of Raoa or A gets 1 at w1 and B gets 0 at w1 because of Raaa or A gets 1 at w2 and B gets 0 at w1 because of Raba or A gets 1 at w2 and B gets 0 at w2 because of Rabb.

iii) A$\rightarrow$B gets 0 at w2 iff. A gets 1 at w0 and B gets 0 at w2 because of Rbob or A gets 1 at w2 and B gets 0 at w2 because of Rbbb or A gets 1 at w1 and B gets 0 at w2 because of Rbab or A gets 1 at w1 and B gets 0 at w1 because of Rbaa or A gets 1 at w1 and B gets 0 at w0 because of Rbao.

We now turn to a brief consideration of model structure semantics for system RM. Let us say that an RMms. is an Rms. of which ρ10 is true.

ρ10: Rabc $\supset$.Roac **v** Robc   The RM semantic postulate,

In section 13 of their SEIV, Meyer and Routley suggest adding ρ10 to get RMms.. In section 9 of their SEI, they gave p7: Rooa **v** Rooa* as the additional postulate, to be added to what we earlier called the SEI set, to characterize RMms.. In [197_a], Dunn argues that ρ10 is adequate to characterize RMms.. Dunn also points out that ρ10 is better than p7 because p7 is a postulate for negation by virtue of containing *; and we should not need to invoke ideas underlying negation to validate the negation free A$\rightarrow$.A$\rightarrow$A. Let us state a Soundness theorem for RM.

Theorem VI of V.5: If $\vdash_{RM}$ A, then A is RM valid.

For proof we show only that the special RM axiom: A$\rightarrow$.A$\rightarrow$A, is RM valid. This shows use of ρ10.

1) A$\rightarrow$.A$\rightarrow$A $\notin$ Ho   Assume for <u>reductio</u>.
2 a) A $\in$ Hb
   b) A$\rightarrow$A $\notin$ Hb   Triad Rule on (1),

a case under Theorem VI continued,

3 a) $A \in Hc$ with Rbcd — Triad Rule on (2b),
b) $A \notin Hd$

4) Robd v Rocd — From Rbcd of (3) by use of $\rho 10$,

Now Robd, (2a), and the Inclusion Condition give $A \in Hd$. On the other hand, Rocd, (3a), and the Inclusion Condition give $A \in Hd$. So, v-elimination on (4) gives (5) which contradicts (3b) and completes the reductio.

5) $A \in Hd$.

Again we give little by way of proof for an RM-completeness theorem. We again leave it to the interested reader to make the appropriate changes in the completeness proof for system E. As in the case of completeness for system-R most of the changes involve replacing the name E with RM. So, for RM's completeness proof we only argue that $\rho 10$ is true of a model structure $\langle T, K_T', R', *' \rangle$ where T is a prime intensional RM-theory such that $RM \subseteq T$, K_T' is the set of prime intensional T-theories and R' and *' are as in V.2. We adapt our argument from section 13 of SEI.

We assume R'abc and not-R'oac; and we want to get R'obc. Since T is the o-point here we have not-R'Tac and are trying to get R'Tbc. We leave as an exercise establishing R'Txy iff. $x \subseteq y$ where x and y are in K_T'. So we have assumed that there is a B such that $B \in a$ but $B \notin c$ by assuming not-R'Tac. Now to show R'Tbc, viz., $b \subseteq c$, we assume that some formula A belongs to B and show that this arbitrarily selected $A \in c$. Because theory a is closed under T-entailment and $B \rightarrow .A \vee B \in T$, $B \in a$ gives $A \vee B \in a$. The version of the RM axiom: $A \vee B \rightarrow .A \vee B \rightarrow .A \vee B$ belongs to T; and so with $A \vee B \in a$ we get $A \vee B \rightarrow .A \vee B \in a$. The fact that theory a is closed under RM-entailment gets us $A \rightarrow .A \vee B \in a$ from $A \vee B \rightarrow .A \vee B \in a$. Now $A \in b$, $A \rightarrow .A \vee B \in a$, and R'abc gives us $A \vee B \in c$. But c is a prime theory; so we have $A \in c$ or $B \in c$. We, however, assumed that $B \notin c$. So we have $A \in c$, which is what we wanted finally to verify $\rho 10$ for $\langle T, K_T', R', *' \rangle$.

Observe, though, that the preceding argument required us to be talking about prime intensional T-theories. The above argument did not verify $\rho 10$ for a structure $\langle T, K_T, R, * \rangle$ where K_T is simply the intensional T-theories. We would use such a model structure with plain K_T to employ the Zorn's Lemma strategy. However, we do not need the Zorn's Lemma strategy to verify $\rho 10$. So we are not troubled by the fact that $\rho 10$ may not hold for plain $\langle T, K_T, R, * \rangle$. Still, this makes $\rho 10$ a bit like negation postulates after all. Recall that back in V.2 we could not verify $\mathcal{E}7$, $\mathcal{E}8$, and $\mathcal{E}9$ for the plain $\langle T, K_T, P, R, * \rangle$.

Enough hints on its proof have been dropped to entitle us to present the completeness of RM as a theorem.

Theorem VII of V.5: If A is RM-valid, then $\vdash_{RM}$ A.

Let us briefly consider the consequences of adding some other postulates to the ρ and $\mathcal{E}$-postulates. First consider adding ρ11 to the Rms. postulates. ρ10 is a classical logical consequence of ρ11.

11: Rabc $\supset$ Robc

Let us call model structures characterized by ρ1 - ρ9 and ρ11 Cms. for classical model structures. We call Cms. classical model structures because A$\rightarrow$B $\leftrightarrow$ A$\supset$B is C-valid. There is a syntactic way and a semantic way to show this. The syntactic way is to use ρ11 to validate B$\rightarrow$.A$\rightarrow$A. Then prove the desired equivalence in R plus B$\rightarrow$.A$\rightarrow$A. In the semantic way, use ρt2 with ρ11 to get Rooa,i.e., o$\preccurlyeq$a. Now the Inclusion Condition on forcings gives A $\in$ Ha iff. A $\in$ Ho. So, in effect, in a Cms. we have only the o-point. We leave it as an exercise to show the equivalence of A$\rightarrow$B and A $\supset$ B in model structures with only one "world" or point. The preceding semantic argument is from p.223 of SEI where Rooa was used as a postulate for collapsing Rms. into Cms..

We now wish to consider adding postulates to the -postulates. First we consider adding $\mathcal{E}$10 below because it is analogous to ρ11.

$\mathcal{E}$10: Rabc $\supset$ $(\exists x)$(Px$\wedge$Rxbc)

Let us note some of the parallels between $\mathcal{E}$10 and ρ11, and some of the differences. When Meyer and Routley add a postulate to their Ems. postulates to get S4ms. they add Rabc $\supset$ Robc because they use a selected P-point as a o-point in Ems.. Nevertheless Rabc $\supset$ Robc does not do quite the damage to their Ems. that ρ11 does to Rms; for them Rabc$\supset$ Robc does not collapse Ems. to Cms.. This semantical fact corresponds to the syntactical fact that E plus B$\rightarrow$.A$\rightarrow$A does not collapse to classical logic whereas R plus B$\rightarrow$.A$\rightarrow$A does collapse to classical logic.

Our interest, however, lies in $\mathcal{E}$10. We call a model structure characterized by $\mathcal{E}$1 - $\mathcal{E}$10 an S4ms.. An exercise will help justify the use of the S4 label. Our immediate interest is to show that B$\rightarrow$.A$\rightarrow$A is S4-valid.

1) B$\rightarrow$.A$\rightarrow$A $\notin$ Ho Po	Assume for <u>reductio</u>.
2 a) B $\in$ Hb	
b) A$\rightarrow$A $\notin$ Hb	Triad Rule on (1),
3 a) A $\in$ Hc	
b) A $\notin$ Hd Rbcd	Triad Rule on (2b)

From Rbcd by 10 we get R$o_1$cd with Po_1. R$o_1$cd, A$\in$ Hc and the Inclusion Condition gives (5) which contradicts (3b)

5) A $\in$ Hd.

If we label as S4 as system consisting of E plus $B \rightarrow . A \rightarrow A$, the above argument entitles us to state a Soundness Theorem for this S4.

Theorem VIII of V.5: If $\vdash_{S4} A$, then A is S4-valid.

We drop only a few hints on how to prove completeness for this S4 and add some comments on an assumption that we deal with non-empty intensional T-theories. The hints are from section 5 of SEV. The crucial step is to show that $\mathcal{E}10$ is true of a $\langle T, K_T', P', R', *' \rangle$ where T is an intensional S4-theory and K_T' is a set of non-empty intensional T-theories. We leave it as an exercise to show that for b,c in K_T' $b \subseteq c$ iff. $(\exists x)(Px \wedge Rabc)$. So, to show that $\mathcal{E}10$ holds, we want to show that if R'abc then $b \subseteq c$. So, assume an arbitrarily selected A belongs to b, i.e., $A \in b$. Now because theory a is non-empty there is some formula D such that $D \in a$. Because $S4 \subseteq T$ and theory a is closed under T-entailment, $A \rightarrow A \in a$ since $D \rightarrow . A \rightarrow A \in T$. So, R'abc with $A \rightarrow A \in a$ and $A \in b$ gives us $A \in c$, which is what we want for $b \subseteq c$.

As is apparent, the preceding argument used the assumption that we are dealing with non-empty intensional T-theories. This assumption prevents us from saying that a completeness proof for S4 can be adapted from that for E back in V.2 by merely changing some labels. The problem is whether the other Ems. postulates hold for a $\langle T, K_T', P', R', *' \rangle$ when K_T' is restricted to non-empty intensional T-theories. They do hold. But to prove that they hold we need to use a broader notion of non-degenerate theory. Go back to Def. 9 of V.2 to modify first the notion of intensional T-theory by replacing E with the name of the system under consideration, eg., S4 or EDS. Then add a definition that an intensional T-theory is <u>non-degenerate</u> if it is neither empty nor the set of all formulas. Then focus attention on a $\langle T, K_T', P', R', *' \rangle$ where K_T' is the set of prime non-degenerate intensional T-theories. The remaining task is to work through the lemmas of V.2 to confirm that the proofs that the first nine $\mathcal{E}$-postulates still hold for K_T' so restricted.

Lemma 1 of V.2 guarantees that T will be non-degenerate. Sublemma 2 of V.2 goes through if it is assumed that the theory is non-degenerate. So the negation postulates still hold. The postulates whose verification did not involve use of Zorn's Lemma are verified as before, viz., show that they hold of all intensional T-theories, let alone non-degenerate ones. The serious work lies in re-working the verification of $\mathcal{E}2$, $\mathcal{E}3$, and $\mathcal{E}4$. Many theories are defined in the course of the verification of these postulates. So we have to go through the relevant lemmas and sublemmas to prove that the defined theories are non-degenerate if the theories in terms of which they are defined are non-degenerate. Here we remark only on the easy case of Lemma 8 of V.2. Consider the o theory defined in that Lemma 8. Because the theory T lacks at least one formula, viz., the A in question, the theory o lacks A because we can't have $A \longrightarrow A \longrightarrow A \notin T$ because $A \longrightarrow A \in T$. Since T contains $B \longrightarrow B \longrightarrow B$ for all theorems B theory o is non-empty.

Despite the sketchiness of the above hints we feel entitled to present the following Completeness Theorem for S4.

Theorem IX of V.2: If A is S4-valid, then $\vdash_{S4}$ A.

Let us close this section by calling attention to a system which Meyer and Routley label EDS for 'E with Disjunctive Syllogism.' Semantically EDS is the theses, the valid formulas, of the model structures characterized by $\mathcal{E}1$ - $\mathcal{E}9$ and $\mathcal{E}11$.

$\mathcal{E}11$: $(\exists x)(Px \wedge Rxa^*a)$, $a^* \preceq a$.

Syntactically EDS is E plus $\sim A \wedge (A \vee B) \longrightarrow B$.

A soundness proof for syntactic EDS relative to EDS-validity we leave to the reader because it merely involves getting a contradiction from $\sim A \wedge (A \vee B) \longrightarrow B \notin Ho$ using $\mathcal{E}11$.

Theorem X of V.5: If A is an EDS theorem, then A is EDS-valid.

We drop only the briefest hints on a completeness proof for EDS. The crucial step is to show that $a^* \subseteq a$ for a and a* in a K_T' where K_T' is a non-empty set of prime intensional T-theories based on an EDS theory T. Assume $A \in a^*$; this gives $\sim A \notin a$. Theory a is non-empty; so for some B, $B \in a$. Hence, $A \vee \sim A \in a$ because $B \longrightarrow .A \vee \sim A$ is an EDS theorem. Theory a is also prime; so $\sim A \notin a$ gives $A \in a$ which is what we want for $a^* \subseteq a$. So we state a Completeness Theorem for EDS.

Theorem XI of V.5: If A is EDS-valid, then A is an EDS theorem.

From $\mathcal{E}11$ and the Inclusion Condition on forcings it is easy to get that Ha = Ha* for all forcings on an EDSms.. With this fact we state the following result from the Routley's [1972] as a theorem. Its proof is an exercise.

Theorem XII of V.5: If $A \longrightarrow B$ is an fde., then $A \longrightarrow B$ is EDS-valid iff. $A \supset B$ is a classical tautology.

Now EDS is certainly not the system which we are looking for; it has, as we just used, $B \longrightarrow .A \vee \sim A$ as a thesis. EDS nevertheless does have interest because it separates concern with fde. theses from concern with higher order theses. We do not get system R from EDS let alone collapsing EDS's $\longrightarrow$ into $\supset$ despite the fact that in fdes. EDS's $\longrightarrow$ collapses into $\supset$. To support these claims consider $\mathfrak{M}$e8 of the previous section. Because $\mathfrak{M}$e8 has classical negation, it is readily established that $\mathfrak{M}$e8 is suitable for EDS by validiating

$\sim A \wedge (A \vee B) \longrightarrow B$. But the following are not EDS theorems, as valuations on $\mathcal{M}e8$ show.

$A \longrightarrow . A \longrightarrow B \longrightarrow B$	$v(A) = v(B) = +0$
$\sim A \vee B \longrightarrow . A \longrightarrow B$	$v(A) = +3$, $v(B) = +0$
$A \longrightarrow . B \longrightarrow A$	$v(A) = +0$, $v(B) = +3$
$B \longrightarrow . A \longrightarrow A$	$v(A) = +1$, $v(B) = +3$.

Exercises V.5

1. Derive $\rho 3$ and $\rho 6$ from the postulate set called SEI.

2. By use of the methods of this section compute $+1 \longrightarrow -1$ and $-2 \longrightarrow +0$ on $\mathcal{M}o$.

3. a) Derive Rooa v Rooa* from the RMms. postulates.
   b) Derive $\rho 10$ from the Rms. postulates plus Rooa v Rooa*.

4. Derive a = a* or $(\exists x)(Px \wedge Rxaa^*) \wedge (\exists y)(Py \wedge Rya^*a)$ from the postulates for an S4ms.. So, the * operation is unnecessary in S4ms..

5. Show that we can dispense with P-points in an S4ms.. Hint: show that an arbitrarily selected point of an S4ms. can serve as a o-point. Show that if $A \notin Ha$ then for some P-point o_i $A \notin Ho_i$. Thus if A is not in the set-up at an arbitrarily selected point A is not valid in the original sense of being in all set-ups at all P-points. To get this, show $(\exists x)(Px \wedge x \leq a)$.

6. For S4ms. show Rabc $\supset$ Rabb.

7. Restrict attention to S4ms.. Define Sab as Rabb. Show that relation S is reflexive and transitive.

8. Show that $A \longrightarrow B \in Ha$ iff. if $A \in Ha$ and Sab, then $B \in Hb$

   In light of exercises (4) - (8) an S4ms. can be presented as a triple $\langle o, K, S \rangle$ where $o \in K$ and S is a reflexive and transitive relation on K. See pp. 105 - 115 of Hughes' and Cresswell's text for proof that such model structures characterize modal system S4.

V.6 Model structure semantics for system NR

The goal of this section is very modest. We merely present model structure semantics for system NR and illustrate their use in the validation of some formulas and in showing that some formulas are not theses of NR. We follow Meyer's and Routley's SEII which is devoted to development of model structure semantics for NR.

A value of presenting NR's semantics is that it helps build our case, begun in IV.7, that E is to be preferred over NR. We will see here that NR is not to be preferred over E because NR's model structure semantics is somehow simpler or more natural than E's. The complexity of having P-points in Ems. is balanced by having a special binary accessibility relation in NRms.. And a primitive one-place predicate is simpler than a primitive binary predicate. To those familiar with model structure semantics for modal logics, an accessibility relation may be quite natural by now. But it must be admitted that there are differences over what postulates should be true of an accessibility relation. (See pp.77-80 of Hughes' and Cresswell's text for an introduction to talk of accessibility relations.) So, it cannot be held that we have a perfectly clear idea of what an accessibilty relation is. On the other hand, because of its novelty, we can say that we have a clear idea of what the P-predicate is; it is what it is said to be by the Ems. postulates. Unfortunately, the last mentioned advantage of the P-predicate vanishes as soon as people start considering additions to the Ems. postulates. Hopefully, some remarks in the last section will show that P-points can get a reasonable interpretation.

An NRms. is an ordered quintuple $\langle o,K,R,S,*\rangle$, where $o \in K$, K is a set of points at which we force formulas into sets to make set-ups, R is a triadic relation on K, S is a binary relation on K, and * is a unary operation on K. The following postulates hold for NRms..

NRms. postulates,

$\mathfrak{n}$r 1: $Roaa$
$\mathfrak{n}$r 2: $Raaa$
$\mathfrak{n}$r 3: $(x)(Rabx \wedge Rxcd \supset (\exists y)(Racy \wedge Rybd))$
$\mathfrak{n}$r 4: $Roab \wedge Rbcd \supset .Racd$
$\mathfrak{n}$r 5: $Rabc \supset Rac^*b^*$
$\mathfrak{n}$r 6: $a = a^{**}$
$\mathfrak{n}$r 7: Saa
$\mathfrak{n}$r 8: $(x)(Sax \wedge Sxb \supset Sab)$
$\mathfrak{n}$r 9: $Roab \wedge Sbc \supset .Sac$
$\mathfrak{n}$r10: $(x)(Rabx \wedge Sxc \supset .(\exists y)(\exists z)((Say \wedge Sbz) \wedge Ryzc))$

We note that the first six NRms. postulates are those for an Rms. which we labelled SEI in the previous section. Consequently we can use the P-postulates for an Rms. and the Pt theorems of the previous section as theorems about NRms..

Given an interpretation which meets the Inclusion Condition for interpretations, forcings can be defined as in V.1 except for one new clause to handle the primitive $\Box$ of NR. So we add (vi) to the five forcing rules in V.1. We call this sixth forcing rule the Alethic Rule.

vi) $\Box A \in Ha$ iff. whenever Sab then $A \in Hb$. Alethic Rule,

Intuitively, Sab says that whatever holds necessarily at a point a holds at point b. Does this Alethic Rule alter the character of forcings in any serious way?

Lemma 1 of V.6: The Inclusion Condition for set-ups holds for forcings on NRms., i.e., if Roab and $A \in Ha$, then $A \in Hb$.

For proof we only extend the inductive argument of Lemma 1 of V.1 to cover the case in which A has the form $\Box B$. Assume that $\Box B \in Ha$, Roab, but $\Box B \notin Hb$. By the new forcing rule (vi) we get Sbx and $B \notin Hx$ from $\Box B \notin Hb$. With $\mathfrak{N}$r9, Roab, and Sbx we get Sax. So, by rule (vi) we get $B \in Hx$ from $\Box B \in Ha$. The lemma follows by <u>reductio</u>.

It is also interesting to note that all Rms. can be regarded as NRms.. We extend Rms. to include a binary relation S where this added S relation is not really a genuine extension of Rms. because the new binary relation is the identity relation. So, we present the following as a theorem whose proof is simply a matter of checking that the NRms. postulates hold when S is =.

Theorem I of V.6: All Rms. are NRms..

For proof regard Rms. as quintuples $\langle o,K,R,=,* \rangle$.

NR-validity can be defined as R-validity was in V.5. Here we simply note the major result of Meyer's and Routley's SEII, and then close with some applications of the semantics. The applications show the roles of the $\mathfrak{N}$r-postulates.

Theorem II of V.6: $\vdash_{NR}$ A iff. A is NR-valid.

As our first application we verify that NR 3 is NR-valid.

1) $\Box(A \rightarrow B) \rightarrow . \Box A \rightarrow \Box B \notin Ho$		Assume for <u>reductio</u>.
2 a) $\Box(A \rightarrow B) \in Hb$ b) $\Box A \rightarrow \Box B \notin Hb$		Triad Rule on (1),
3 a) $\Box A \in Hc$ b) $\Box B \notin Hd$	Rbcd	Triad Rule on (2b),
4) $B \notin He$	Sde	Alethic Rule on (3b)
5) Sby, Scz, Ryze for some y and z		$\mathfrak{N}$r10 applied to Rbcd and Sde
6) $A \in Hz$		Alethic Rule with Scz and (3a),
7) $A \rightarrow B \in Hy$		Alethic Rule with Sby and (2a),
8) $B \in He$		Triad Rule with Ryze, (6), and (7),

The inconsistency of (4) and (8) completes the <u>reductio</u>.

On p.69 of SEII, they point out that □(A ⊃ B) ⊃ .□A ⊃ □B is not NR-valid. Thus, despite the fact that system NR has an S4-ish □, a genuine S4 formulated with truth-functional connectives and □ or ◇ is not contained in NR. Let us corroborate their observation.

1) ∼□(∼A v B) v. ∼□A v □B ∉ Ho — Assume for attempted *reductio*.

2 a) ∼□(∼A v B) ∉ Ho
  b) ∼□A v □B ∉ Ho — v-normality on (1),

3 a) ∼□A ∉ Ho
  b) □B ∉ Ho — v-normality on (2b),

(2a) and (3a) give □(∼A v B) ∈ Ho* and □A ∈ Ho*. But because Roo*o we also get (4a) and (4b) by Inclusion Condition.

4 a) □(∼A v B) ∈ Ho
  b) □A ∈ Ho

5) B ∉ Hx Sox — Alethic Rule on (3b),

6 a) ∼A v B ∈ Hx
  b) A ∈ Hx — Alethic Rule on (4a) and (4b) with Sox from (5).

7) ∼B ∈ Hx* — Imperfect Consistency on (5),

8) ∼A ∈ Hx — v-normality (5) and (6a),

Of course, Hx has an inconsistency in it. But Hx's inconsistency is not our inconsistency. So our attempted *reductio* has reached an impasse. To be sure, a matrix proof of non-theoremhood would be more satisfying; but development of an NR suitable matrix from an NRms. is difficult. We will not struggle with that difficulty here. Instead we look at the kind of modal logic system E contains. According to Meyer's "E and S4," system E does have t(□(A ⊃ B) ⊃ .□A ⊃ □B) as a theorem where t( ) is the translation of S4 into E given in IV.2. So, here we see that without even having a primitive system E has a better modal logic than system NR, assuming that it is good to get S4.

Exercises V.6

1. Show that if A is NR-valid, then so is □A.
2. Show that the Maksimowa formula using ⟹ is NR-valid.
3. Add a postulate to validate □(A ⊃ B) ⊃ .□A ⊃ □B.
4. Validate NR1 to NR5 of IV.7.
5. Show that A ⟹ .A ⟹ B ⟹ B is not NR-valid.

V.7 Halldén reasonableness of E, gist of strategy for showing Halldén reasonableness of extensions of E,

In this section our goal is to sketch they Meyer and Routley technique for showing that E and several of its extensions are Halldén complete or Halldén reasonable. A system is <u>Halldén reasonable</u> iff. whenever A **v** B is a theorem and A and B share no variables then either A is a theorem or B is a theorem. (See Halldén [1951a] and pp. 268-70 of Hughes' and Cresswell for some discussion of Halldén reasonableness.) Hallden reasonableness is certainly desirable for systems which are complete with respect to validity in certain kinds of model structures or which are complete on certain kinds of matrices. If we have $\vdash$ A **v** B but lack both $\vdash$ A and $\vdash$ B, then we would have model structure 1, msl., in which A is invalidated and ms2 in which B is invalidated. But if A and B share no variables it seems that we should somehow be able to get a single model structure ms3. which combines msl. and ms2. and which invalidates A in the way msl. did and invalidates B in the way ms2. did. But if both A and B are invalidated in an ms3., we would not have $\vdash$ A **v** B. The oddity is even more vivid if we assume a system has a characteristic type of matrix. A Halldén unreasonable system suggests also that there is some type of connection between formulas which share no variables. Why else can we not simultaneously invalidate both A and B? We have throughout held that variable sharing is a necessary condition for relevance. So we should require Hallden reasonableness of the right logic. Another value of the proof of Hallden reasonableness is that it makes it clear that we have to take the members of the K of a model structure as objects which can be manipulated. For simplicity's sake it would have been nice to think of them as nothing but the sets of formulas constituting set-ups at them

In the remainder of this section we borrow extensively from section 7 of SEIV and pp.71-72 of SEII.

The strategy of the proof of E's Halldén reasonableness is as follows. Assume that $\vdash_E$ A v B where A and B share no variables. For <u>reductio</u> assume that not-$\vdash_E$ A and not-$\vdash_E$ B. By the completeness of E with respect to Ems.-validity the <u>reductio</u> assumption tells us that there is an Ems. <u>1M</u> such that A is invalid in <u>1M</u> and an Ems. <u>2M</u> such that B is invalid in <u>2M</u>. The labor of the proof is involved in showing that there is a way of combining <u>1M</u> and <u>2M</u> into an Ems. <u>3M</u> in which both A and B are invalid; and, hence, contrary to the assumption that A v B is a theorem of E, A v B is not valid.

We first define the product <u>3M</u> of two Ems. <u>1M</u> and <u>2M</u>. If <u>1M</u> is $\langle$1K, 1R,1P, 1*$\rangle$, and <u>2M</u> is $\langle$2K, 2R, 2P, 2*$\rangle$ their <u>product</u> is <u>3M</u> whose components are as follows.

Definition of a product ms.,

3K is the set of ordered pairs $\langle 1a,2a \rangle$ where $1a \in 1K$ and $2a \in 2K$.
3P $\langle 1a,2a \rangle$ iff. 1P1a and 2P2a.
3R $\langle 1a,2a \rangle$ $\langle 1b,2b \rangle$ $\langle 1c,2c \rangle$ iff. 1R1a1b1c and 2R2a2b2c.
$\langle 1a,2a \rangle$ 3* is $\langle 1a1^*,2a2^* \rangle$.

The numerical prefixes make formulas difficult to read; so let us adopt the following conventions. Use a,b,c and x to refer to members of 1K, d,e,f, and y to refer to members of 2K, and g,h,i, and z to refer to members of 3K. Use o for a P-point of 1K and o̲ for a P-point of 2K. With these conventions we may delete the numerical prefixes from R, P, and * because 1R applies only to a,b,c,x, 1P only to a,b,c, x, etc..

In a similar way we could define products for Rms. RMms. etc.. Of course, and unfortunately, we cannot simply define the structure 3M̲ as an Ems.. In a general study of model structures a result that products of Sms. are also Sms. would be a significant theorem. Here we have only a lemma on the way to asserting the Halldén reasonableness of E.

Lemma 1 of V.7: The product 3M̲ of Ems. 1M̲ and 2M̲ is an Ems..

The proof consists of nine sublemmas showing that the nine Maksimowa postulates hold of 3M̲. We, however, present proofs for only two of these sublemmas. The sublemmas would be numbered according to the numbering of the postulates in V.1.

Sublemma 1 of V.7: $(\exists z)(Pz \wedge Rzgg)$.

Consider the following argument. Let g be any element of 3K. So, by definition $g = \langle a,d \rangle$. Because 1M̲ and 2M̲ are Ems., we have Px, Rxaa, Py,and Rydd. There is, by definition of 3K, a z in 3K such that $z = \langle x,y \rangle$. By definition of 3P we get, then, that Pz. Also by definition of 3R we get Rzgg from Rxaa and Rydd. So, classical predicate logic gives this sublemma.

Sublemma 4 of V.7: $Rghi \supset (\exists z)(Rghz \wedge Rzhi)$.

Consider the following argument. Assume Rghi which by definition gives a Rabc and a Rdef. From $\mathcal{E}$-4 and the fact that 1M̲ and 2M̲ are assumed to be Ems. we get from Rabc and Rdef: Rabx,Rxbc, Rdey, and Ryef. By definition of 3R, Rabx and Rdey gives: R $\langle a,d \rangle$ $\langle b,e \rangle$ $\langle x,y \rangle$. Similarly, Rxbc and Ryef gives: R $\langle x,y \rangle$ $\langle b,e \rangle$ $\langle c,f \rangle$. Now from the way Rabc and Rdef were obtained from Rghi, we can say: $g = \langle a,d \rangle$, $h = \langle b,e \rangle$, and $i = \langle c,f \rangle$. So we have Rghz and Rzhi with $z = \langle x,y \rangle$. EG completes the proof.

Proofs of the other sublemmas are similar in as much as the proofs consist primarily on seeing how the results of the appropriate postulate applied to 1M and 2M can be put together to prove that the postulate holds for 3M . Frequently, the major complexity is notational. So let us move to the theorem.

Theorem I of V.7: If $\vdash_E$ A v B, then $\vdash_E$ A or $\vdash_E$ B if A and B share no variables. E is Halldén reasonable.

For *reductio* assume that A v B is a theorem of E but that neither A nor B are theorems of E despite the fact that they share no variables. Completeness of E gives us that A $\notin$ Ho for some forcing on an Ems. 1M where o is a P-point of 1M and that B $\notin$ Ho for some forcing on an Ems. 2M where o is a P-point of 2M. We now get the product of 1M and 2M which, by Lemma 1, is an Ems. 3M. The strategy of the proof is to given an interpretation on 3M which leads to a forcing which invalidates both A and B by uniting those forcings which invalidated A and B on 1M and 2M respectively. The forcing which invalidated A on 1M was based on an interpretation 1f() just as the forcing which invalidated B on 2M was based on an interpretation 2f(). The first step in getting a suitable interpretation 3f() on 3M is to select some variable from A and label it p_a. Let the element g of 3K be $\langle a,d \rangle$, with a $\in$ 1K and d $\in$ 2K. Let 3f() be as follows.
If p is a variable of A, 3f(p,e) = 1 iff. 1f(p,a) = 1.
If q is a variable of B, 3f(q,e) = 1 iff. 2f(q,d) = 1.
If r is a variable of neither A nor B, 3f(r,e) = 1 iff. 1f(p_a,a) = 1.
To be guaranteed that 3f() is a genuine interpretation we need to know that the Inclusion Condition holds for it, i.e., that Pz, Rzgh, 3f(p,g) = 1, give 3f(p,h) = 1. Pz gives a Px and a Py. Rzgh gives a Rxab and a Ryde. (Remember our conventions about lower case letters and the members of the various K's.) To show that the Inclusion Condition holds for 3f() there are three cases to consider from the three ways in which a variable may be in or out of A and B. Let us consider only the case of a variable r which is in neither A nor B. Assume 1f(p_a,a) = 1 for the a forming half of g; so 3f(r,g) = 1. Here g = $\langle a,d \rangle$ and h = $\langle b,e \rangle$. The Inclusion Condition for 1f() gives 1f(r,b) = 1. Since b is the 1K element forming the left half of h, 3f(r,h) = 1. Let these remarks suffice to show that 3f() meets the Inclusion Condition for interpretations.

So 3f() leads to a genuine forcing on 3M which we label simply H because tags on H's will indicate which Ems. they are built on. (When we talk of an H on 1M it is the one based on 1f() and similarly an H on 2M is the one base 2f().) To show that this H based on 3f() invalidates A n 3M we proceed as follows. We consider formulas wh ntain only variable from A and use A# to refer to such formulas. Similarly, we use B# to refer to formulas containing only variables from B. We now show: A# $\in$ Hg iff. A# $\in$ Ha and B# $\in$ Hg iff. B# $\in$ Hd where again g = $\langle a,d \rangle$. This will invalidate A v B on <u>3M</u> because there will be a z in 3K such that z = $\langle o,\underline{o} \rangle$. The facts that Po and P$\underline{o}$ give Pz. A $\notin$ Ho and B $\notin$ H$\underline{o}$ will give that A v B $\notin$ Hz. So we finish this proof and this section by an inductive argument that A# $\in$ Hg iff. A# $\in$ Ha. (We focus our attention on A because the argument is identical for the B case.) The basis is settled by the definition of 3f() and the first forcing rule of V.1. So we assume for C and D shorter than A# and containing only variables from A: C $\in$ Hg iff. C $\in$ Ha and D $\in$ Hg iff. D $\in$ Ha. We consider only two of the inductive cases.

Case 1. A# is $\sim$C. Suppose $\sim$C $\in$ Hg. By Imperfect Consistency C $\notin$ Hg* where g* = $\langle a^*,d^* \rangle$. The induction assumption gives C $\notin$ Ha* which by Imperfect Consistency gives $\sim$C $\in$ Ha. On the other hand, suppose $\sim$C $\notin$ Hg. Imperfect Consistency gives C $\in$ Hg* where g* = $\langle a^*,d^* \rangle$. The induction assumption gives C $\in$ Ha* which by Imperfect Consistency gives $\sim$C $\notin$ Ha.

Case 2. A# is C $\rightarrow$ D. Suppose C $\rightarrow$ D $\notin$ Hg. The Triad Rule gives Rghi, C $\in$ Hh, D $\notin$ Hi with g = $\langle a,d \rangle$, h = $\langle b,e \rangle$, and i = $\langle c,f \rangle$. The induction assumption gives: C $\in$ Hb and D $\notin$ Hc. Rghi gives us Rabc; so the Triad Rule with C $\in$ Hb and D $\notin$ Hc gives us C $\rightarrow$ D $\notin$ Ha. On the other hand, suppose that C $\rightarrow$ D $\notin$ Ha. So we have an Rabc with C $\in$ Hb but D $\notin$ Hc. We also have Rddd. So with Rabc and Rddd we have Rghi where again g = $\langle a,d \rangle$, but now h = $\langle b,d \rangle$, and i = $\langle c,d \rangle$. The induction assumption gives us: C $\in$ Hh but D $\notin$ Hi. So by the Triad Rule we have C $\rightarrow$ D $\notin$ Hg. This completes our proof of Theorem I.

To adapt this argument to other systems is primarily a task of verifying that the model structure postulates for the new system hold of the appropriately defined model structure.

Exercises V.7

1. Why isn't it odd, in general, to have A v B as a theorem without having either A or B as theorems?

2. Verify two more Ems. postulates under Lemma 1.

V.8 Ems. for fdes. and fdfs., interpretation of Ems. for fdes., and interpretation of the Smiley matrix,

In this section we take a first step towards interpreting model structure semantics for E. We find that the forcing rules used for the Ems. needed to interpret fdes. are exactly the structural meaning rules of the structural meaning theory of Section III.5. Hence, for this restricted class of Ems., we suggest regarding the pairs of Ems. points consisting of a point b and its b* as sources or recipients of messages. We also provide an interpretation for the values of the Smiley matrix which was shown to be characteristic for system TE (E_{fde}) back in III.3. A value of interpreting the Smiley matrix is that we can then say that the fde. fragment of Parry's systems is not better than the TE entailments because Parry's fde. fragment has a finite characteristic matrix with interpreted values. Recall from II.10 the interpretation of the values of Parry's original o.

Let us characterize the restricted classes of Ems. sufficient for validating fde. and fdf. formulas.

Consider first the validation of fde. formulas. If we test fde. A⟶B for E-validity we start by assuming that A⟶B ∉ Ho for some point o with Po where Ho is obtained by some forcing. We immediately, by use of the Inclusion Condition for forcings, move to consideration of A ∈ Hb and B ∉ Hb. All of the subsequent work is an application of the ∧, ∨, and ∼ forcing rules on Hb and Hb* because A and B are zdfs.. So, all that we really consider from an Ems. when testing an fde. is a pair of points (b,b*). Let us say that <u>a pure fdems.</u> is simply such a pair of points. An interpretation on a pure fdems. is a function f(,) such that f(p,b) = 1 or 0 and f(p,b*) = 1 or 0 for all variables p. Given an interpretation, we define a forcing as in Section V.1 except that we do not give rules for saying that A⟶B belongs to a set-up because we are not going to put entailment formulas into set-ups. We say <u>fde. A⟶B is valid</u> on a pure fdems. iff. whenever A ∈ Hb then B ∈ Hb. Here we define 'validity' only for fdes.. Observe that we really only need one pure fdems. because prior to interpretations and forcings there is nothing to distinguish a (c,c*) from a (b,b*). And we need use only one fdems. at a time. So, we can identify pure fdems.-validity with validity on a (b,b*).

From the preceding it is not hard to develop a proof of the following which is suggested by R. Routley's [1972a].

Theorem I of V.8: For fde. A⟶B, A⟶B is E-valid iff. A⟶B is pure fdems.-valid.

We can now profit by recognizing that the structural meaning rules of III.5 are the set-up rules for pure fdems. and that the III.5 definition of 'entailment' is that of pure fdems.-validity. Consequently, we can regard the model structure semantics for the fde. fragment of E as the structural theory of meaning of III.5. In response to the question: What are the points b and b*? we reply that they can be regarded as the giver or receiver of messages. We find it most natural to interpret (b,b*) here as the sender of messages. In the next section we change.

We can also get an interpretation for the values of Smiley's matrix $\mathcal{S}$m. For zdf. A, v(A) = +1 means A $\in$ Hb and A $\in$ Hb*, v(A) = +0 means A $\in$ Hb but A $\notin$ Hb*, v(A) = -1 means A $\notin$ Hb but A $\in$ Hb*, and v(A) = -0 means that A $\notin$ Hb and A $\notin$ Hb*. For fde. A $\rightarrow$ B, v(A $\rightarrow$ B) = +1 then means that we do not have either A $\in$ Hb but B $\notin$ Hb or A $\in$ Hb* but B $\notin$ Hb*. And '$\in$ Hx' can here be interpreted as in the structural meaning theory.

Let us briefly focus attention on the restricted language of the system TEc of III.4. Recall that it consisted only of zdfs. and fdes.. We want to select as valid on the classical tautologies and TE entailments because we know by Theorems I and II of IV.1 and II of V.2 that these are the E-valid formulas of the language of TEc. We can proceed as follows. For zdf. A we can prove that A is a classical tautolgy iff. A must belong to every set-up at a point c such that c = c*. Theorem I specified conditions for selecting the TE entailments semantically. The problem is now to put these two conditions together. If we try to invalidate a wff. A from TEc we assume A $\notin$ Ho where Po. If A is a zdf. we do not consider any other set-up except possibly Ho*. If o = o* we consider, of course, only Ho. If A is an fde. B $\rightarrow$ C the assumption that B $\rightarrow$ C $\notin$ Ho where Po leads immediately to B $\in$ Hb but C $\notin$ Hb; and we stay with Hb or Hb*. So, we say that a TEcms. is a triple (o,b,b*) where o* = o. We define interpretation and forcing as we did for pure fdems. except now we give the following rule for fdes. B $\rightarrow$ C.

> If x is a point of a TEcms. and x $\neq$ o B $\rightarrow$ C $\in$ Hx iff. B $\supset$ C $\in$ Hx and B $\rightarrow$ C $\in$ Ho iff. for all points x if B $\in$ Hx then C $\in$ Hx.

We say that A is TEcms.-valid iff. A $\in$ Ho for all forcings on (o,b,b*).

TEcms. have been designed to validate TEc theorems. If a zdf. or fde. is not a TEc theorem, it is not an E theorem. Why? If it is not an E theorem it can be invalidated on an Ems. using no more of that Ems. than is needed to make a TEcms. So, if a zdf. or fde. is not a TEc theorem it is not TEcms.-valid. Let these heuristic remarks suffice to assert the following theorem.

> Theorem II of V.8: If A is a zdf. or fde., then A is E-valid iff. A is TEcms.-valid.

To dismiss worries about stipulating that o* = o consider the result of V.3 that we can restrict attention to normal Ems. and to the following. In any Ems. if Pó then Roo*o. So for any forcing Ho*   Ho. So, if we do not stipulate that o* = o Ho* can be a proper subset of Ho. Now if $B \in Ho$ but $B \notin Ho^*$ we have $B \wedge \sim B \in Ho$. So the effect of not stipulating that $o = o^*$ is that contradictions can be in Ho. But these contradictions won't be tolerated as valid because they will always be invalidated by the interpretation which assigns the same variables to o and to o^*. So no valid formulas are lost by the stipulation.

Hopefully, the preceding discussion will help motivate the following characterization of model structures for fdfs. which is given in section 6 of SEIV.

A fdfms. is an ordered triple $\langle o, K, * \rangle$ where $o \in K$, $o^* = o$. and for all $a \in K$ $a^{**} = a$.

An interpretation on a fdfms. is an assignment of variables to members of K. The forcing rules are as usual except for $B \rightarrow C$ formulas.

$B \rightarrow C \in Ho$ iff for all $x \in K$ if $B \in Hx$ then $C \in Hx$ and if $x \neq o$ then $B \rightarrow C \in Hx$ iff. $B \supset C \in Hx$.

We say that fdf. A is fdfms.-valid iff. for all fdfms. and all forcings on them $A \in Ho$. Observe that for fdfms.-validity we had to talk of a whole class of model structures. In the cases of pure fdems.-validity and TEcms.-validity we could talk of a single structure, viz., (b,b^*) and (o,b,b^*). This disparity corresponds to the facts that systems TE and TEc have finite characteristic matrices whereas full fdf. systems do not.

We make only heuristic remarks in support of the next theorem. See Routley [1972a] theorem 12 for details.

Theorem III of V.8: For fdf. A, A is Ems.-valid iff. A is fdfms.-valid.

The idea behind the proof is to show first that if fdf. A is not an E-theorem no more than is in a fdfms. need be used to invalidate it. The second half requires showing that if fdf. A is not valid in a fdfms. it is not valid in an Ems..

In light of the Claim about TEf and E_{fdf} made back in III.6 we close with the following Claim which is a kind of corollary of Theorem III.

Claim A is a theorem of TEf iff. A is fdfms.-valid.

Exercises V.8

1. Show that if $a = a^*$ and A is a zdf. $A \in Ha$ iff. A is a classical tautology.
2. Show that if A is a zdf. there is a forcing on (b,b^*) such that $A \in Hb$. Routleys' [1972].
3. Show that if A is a zdf. there is a forcing on (b,b^*) such that $A \in Hb$. Routleys' [1972].

V.9 On interpreting model structure semantics, why it is not too bad that we have no well-developed interpretation for Ems.,

This section will be a disappointment to those who expect to be told what model structures with the now familiar triadic R-relation are supposed to represent and who hope to hear a case that the Ems. postulates are truths about what is so represented. The author is disappointed. The work with model structure semantics has been even more formal than the previous syntactic development of systems. There has not even been a reading interpretation for the predicate signs in model structure postulates, except for the following artificial interpretation. Points of an Ems. are simply points at which we build sets of formulas by the forcing rules. P-points and R-triples of points are simply selections of the points which we make to satisfy the Ems. postulates. Have we been keeping a secret throughout the preceding eight sections on model structure semantics? No secret has been kept; we do not have any significant interpretation of model structures, let alone, Ems.. Interpretation of these model structures is a field wide-open for discovery and invention; perhaps only for invention. We close with only a hint on how one may start work in this field. Before we drop this hint we explain why we do so little towards getting an interpretation and then note why it is still significant that a system has a model structure semantics.

To provide a satisfactory interpretation of Ems. we have to do at least the following. Find some subject matter in which there are at least denumerably many objects. We do not want to have to set a finite limit on the size of K in an Ems.. This subject matter would have to be divisible into systems because we want a plurality of Ems.. We would have to find a one-place predicate of these objects which can be the interpretation of the P-predicate and a triadic relation amongst these objects to interpret the R-relation.

Leave aside the task of inventing a sense to assigning formulas to these objects and consider only the problem of discovering truths about this subject matter amongst which must be the postulates for Ems.. We have taken this book to make a case that system E gives the truths about sentential entailment. It is reasonable to expect that discovery of truths about some subject matter, yet to be identified, will take at least as much work. This is one reason why we do not undertake the task of interpreting Ems. in any serious way. Also the interpretation task constantly faces the danger that one will invent a subject matter so that it does satisfy the postulates for the model structures of a previously selected system. There is nothing objectionable about selecting a system prior to developing a model structure semantics for it, as long as it was selected for good reasons. But it is unnecessary labor to invent a subject matter simply to tell "a story," i.e., satisfy postulates, which is supposed to provide additional evidence for the system. Of course, such a story is not evidence at all since it is developed on the assumption that the system in question is to be accepted. The author of this text has found that all his efforts to find a satisfactory interpretation of Ems. have been nothing but attempts to invent subject matters satisfying the Ems. postulates. So, he is not here psychologically competent to undertake an honest investigation of interpreting model structures. Hopefully, though, a good case has been made for the selection of system prior to development of model structure semantics for it.

Nevertheless it is significant that a system has model structure semantics despite the fact that in [197_i] and [197_j] Meyer and Routley make it clear that model structure semantics can be developed for almost any sentential logic system anyone is likely to consider. Model structure semantics, first of all, opens up the opportunity of investigating a system with mathematical techniques different from those suitable for dealing with syntax. For instance, without some semantics, be it model structure or algebraic (matrix) semantics, it would be difficult if not impossible to prove the admissibility of Rule-γ. Secondly, possession of model structure semantics opens up the possibility of providing an interpretation of validity which will support a system by showing that being valid in its kind of model structures is real or significant validity. Actually, though, it is not so much that a system of logic needs more support than is provided by its syntactic features, viz., its theses, which makes the possibility of interpreting its model structure semantics so desirable. The desirable feature is that logic may thereby be related to other areas; especially metaphysics. Perhaps the model structures could be interpreted in terms of some metaphysical subject matter such as systems of possible worlds. Then the model structure postulates would be truths about fundamental reality or whatever it is that metaphysics is about. Possibly, then, being valid and hence being a thesis of the system would be linked with the fundamental nature of reality. Obviously, however, such a metaphysical interpretation is beyond the competence of this author and most likely of our century. A third value of model structure semantics, and especially the kind considered in this work, is heuristic. They teach us forcefully that in regard to interpreting a system work with model structure semantics is as formal as work with matrix semantics. They make it clear that interpretation of a language on a model structure does not give meaning to the signs. A least they do not give a meaning in the clear way in which we give the logical signs their intended reading and replace variables with natural language sentences. Indeed, model structure semantics gives us another formal system, viz., predicate logic, to interpret in addition to the original sentential logic system.

Before we give our hint on how to interpret Ems. it is well to remind ourselves that we cannot interpret the points of an Ems. as possible worlds, even if there are possible worlds. The possible worlds interpretation is precluded because, as we pointed out at the beginning of Part V and have illustrated throughout, contradictions may hold at points of Ems..

We close with the following suggestion on interpreting Ems.. We recommend trying to continue the interpretation of fdems. suggested in the previous section. Regard pairs of points (a,a*) as recipients of messages from a single source. Set-ups with formulas are interpreted as forms of messages. We take these pairs as recipients because,in general, a recipient does not get a complete and consistent message for the reasons given in III.5. However, each (b,b*) and (a,a*) need not be regarded as different individuals; they could be the same individual getting different meassages. In the theory of structural meaning we already discussed what is structurally meant by sentences of forms other than the A⟶B form. So, here we extend the theory of structural meaning to cover A⟶B's in messages.

What is meant by an assertion of A⟶B? To answer we adopt the perspective of standing outside a situation of a single message giver giving different messages to different parties. We do not regard ourselves as the source or as a recipient. If A⟶B were asserted as a principle of logic it would say that whenever A then B. But an A⟶B may not always be asserted as a principle of logic. Nevertheless, it seems that we should be guaranteed of this much from any assertion of an A⟶B in a message Ha. There are messages of two groups related to Ha in such a way that when A is in one member of the first group B is in a member of the second group connected with the one containing A. There has to be at least some restricted assertion of: Whenever A then B. The Triad Rule really does seem to express the minimal meaning of a conditional asserted by some single source giving a plurality of messages. (You may regard giving a plurality of messages as developing a plurality of theories.)

So, we accept the Triad forcing rule as a structural meaning rule. This acceptance interprets the R-relation. Rabc means that if A⟶B is asserted in the Ha component of a message to (a,a*) and A is asserted in the Hb component of a message to (b,b*), then B is asserted in the Hc component of a message to (c,c*). In the preceding interpretation of the R-relation, all the messages should be regarded as being in the same emission of messages from the source. An emission of messages corresponds to an interpretation of the language for a forcing, i.e., an assignment of variables to the points.

The problem now is to interpret P-points and at least suggest how the Ems. postulates may be justified.

A point x is a P-point if the recipient (x,x*) is such that the source gives all logical truths in all messages to (x,x*), and in addition gives all necessary truths in which the source may be interested, if there are, or believed to be, non-logical necessary truths. For instance, mathematicians, philosophical-logicians, and metaphysicians are interested in getting all logical truths in their messages. I.e., in their theories they want the underlying logic to be explicitly given, However, these three fields may also have some special principles which are necessarily true although not logically true. Hence, the messages to (x,x*)'s, where x is a P-point, will not be all the same. For instance, if there are three P-points: x_1 for a mathematician, x_2 for a philosophical-logician, and x_3 for a metaphysician, the source may put different necessary truths in Hx_1, Hx_2, and Hx_3 but there will be a common core. They will all contain a common core, viz., the logically necessary truths. So far there is no specification of what constitutes the logical truths. There is only the platitude that the logical truths are the principles of reasoning common to all disciplines. So, the notion of validity on an Ems., viz., in all set-ups at all P-points, has now, upon interpretation, become a platitude. However, the serious question is: What will be in this common core of messages to (x,x*) where x is a P-point? I.e., what are the logical truths? Exercise 3 of V.8 reveals that the structural meaning rules of III.5 do not even guarantee that classical tautologies belong to all Hx. The mere Triad Rule adds nothing until we specify what stands in the R-relation. So, we need postulates to get all logical truths into some messages. But which postulates should be laid down?

The temptation in selecting or justifying postulates is to select them on the basis of their need to get all logical truths into all Hx where x is a P-point. But, of course, such a procedure presupposes that you already have and are aware of the correct logic; hence the semantics provides no support for the choice of logic. The author finds himself in this predicament of justifying postulates by their role in validating formulas which he thinks ought to be validated. However, let us close with the suggestion that the postulates be justified as rules for rational message giving. Consider only $\mathcal{E}1$: $(\exists x)(Px \wedge Rxaa)$. This postulate can be looked at as a requirement that all messages be closed under entailment whatever the entailments may be. Again, though, the danger is that we may regard giving our favorite system of logic in all P-point messages as a rule for rational message giving.

So, on this pessimistic note about the capability of formal semantics to justify a system of logic, we close. But we close optimistically. We believe we have made a strong case that the theses of system E give the truths about entailment, viz., about the best possible formal connection between premisses and conclusion. For those who are not persuaded by our case the negative results about the justificatory role of formal semantics gives positive guidance on how to continue the debate. Return to the formal systems with the intended interpretations in natural language for the logical signs and argue whether or not particular formulas should be theses. Such arguments are open to all; not only to those with some highly technical training and skills.

Bibliography

There is no claim that this bibliography is complete. There is only the hope that it will be useful. A complete bibliography is being prepared by Robert G. Wolf for the second volume of Anderson, Belnap, *et al.* on Entailment.

Some abbreviations which are used are as follows.

AJP	*Australasian Journal of Philosophy*
JP	*Journal of Philosophy*
JPL	*Journal of Philosophical Logic*
JSL	*Journal of Symbolic Logic*
LA	*Logique et Analyse*
MA	*Mathematische Annalen*
MR	*Mathematical Reviews*
NDJFL	*Notre Dame Journal of Formal Logic*
PAS	*Proceedings of the Aristotelian Soceity*
PS	*Philosophical Studies*
RLC	Proceedings of the International Conference on Relevance Logic, St. Louis 1974 (forthcoming)
ZML	*Zeitschrift für mathematische und Grundlagen der Mathematik*

Abraham, Leo
1933 "Implication, modality, and intension in symbolic logic" *The Monist* 43(1933), 119-53

Ackermann, Whilhelm
1956 "Begründung einer strenge Implikation" JSL 21(1956) 113-28
Reviewed by A. Robinson MR 18(1957) p.271

1958 "Über die Beziehung zwischen strickter und strenger Implikation" *Dialectica* 12(1958) 213-22
Also: *Logica, studia, Paul Bernays dedicata*, Nechatel(Editions du Griffon) 1959, 9-16.

Allen, Laymon E.
1974 "The Concept of Legal Right Defined in Terms of a Variant of Anderson-Belnap Relevance Logic" RLC

Ambrose, Alice
1955 "On entailment and logical necessity" PAS 56(1955) 241-58

Anderson, Alan Ross
1951 "A note on subjunctive and counterfactual conditionals" *Analysis* 12(1951) 35-38

1955 Review of Sugihara [1955], JSL 20(1955) 303

Anderson, A.R. continued

1957 Review of Ackermann [1956] JSL 22(1957) 327-28

1960a "Completeness theorems for the system E of entailment and EQ of entailment with quantification" ZML 6(1960) 201-16. Originally: Technical Report No. 6 Contract No. SAR/Nonr-609(16), Office of Naval Research, New Haven 1959

1960b "Entailment shorn of modality" (abstract) JSL 25(1960) 388

1962 "A problem concerning entailment"(abstract) JSL 27(1962) 382

1963 "Some open problems concerning the system E of entailment" _Acta Philosophica Fennica_ 16(1963) 7 - 18

1966 Review of Belnap & Wallace [1965] MR#4714 31(1966)

1967a Review of D. Makinson [1965] MR #5460 33(1967)

1967b Review of Hockney & Wilson [1965] MR #5472 33(1967)

1967c "Some nasty problems in the formal logic of ethics" _Nous_ 1 (1967) 345-60

1967d Review of Maksimowa [1967b] JSL 33(1967) 608-10

1969 "Completeness and Decidability of a Fragment of the System E of Entailment"(abstract) JSL 34(1969) 541

1970 "An intensional interpretation of truth-functions"(abstract) JSL 35(1970) 361-62

1972a "Negative implication formulas"(abstract) JSL 37(1972) 442

1972b "An intensional interpretation of truth-values" _Mind_ 81(1972) 348-71. Reprinted in _Logic, language, and probability_, ed. R.J. Bogdan and I. Niiniluoto, Dordrecht(Reidel) 1973 3-28.

1974 "Meaning and implication" _Idealistic Studies_ 4(1974) 79-88

with Nuel D. Belnap Jr.

1958 "A modification of Ackermann's 'rigorous implication' " (abstract) JSL 23(1958) 457-58

1959a "A simple treatment of truth-functions" JSL 24(1959) 301-02

Anderson A.R. & N.D. Belnap Jr. continued

1959b "Modalities in Ackermann's 'rigorous implication' " JSL 24(1959) 107-11

1961 "Enthymemes" JP 58(1961) 713-23

1962a "Tautological entailments" PS 13(1962) 9-24 Reviewed by D. Makinson JSL 33(1968) p.608 See 15 and 15.1 of Anderson's and Belnap's [1975] for similar material.

1962b "The pure calculus of entailment" JSL 27(1962) 19-52. See the first five sections of Anderson's and Belnap's [1975] for similar material.

1963 "First Degree Entailments" MA 149(1963) 302-19. Originally: Technical Report No 10, Contract No SAR/Nonr - 609(616), Office of Naval Research, New Haven. See section 17 of Anderson's and Belnap's [1975] for similar material.

1965 "Entailment with negation" ZML 11(1965) 277-89

1968 "Entailment" A composite of parts of their [1962a] and [1962b] in Logic and Philosophy, ed. by G. Iseminger, New York (Appleton-Century Crofts) 1968 76-110

1975 Entailment, The logic of relevance and necessity Princeton U. Press, Princeton N.J. 1975

Anderson & Belnap with J.R. Wallace

1960 "Independent axiom schemata for the pure theory of entailment" ZML 6(1960) 93-95.

A.R. Anderson with R.K. Meyer

197_ "Open problems II" RLC

Angell, Richard B.

1962 "A propositional logic with subjunctive conditionals" JSL 27(1962) 327-43

1971 "Connexive Implication, Modal Logic, and Subjunctive Conditionals"(abstract) JSL 36(1971) 367-68

197_ "Entailment as Analytic Containment"(A copy has been received from R.G. Wolf) RLC

Austin, J.L.

1961 "If's and Can's" Philosophical Papers, ed. J.O. Urmson and G.J. Warnock, Oxford, Oxford U. Press 1961 153-180

Ashby, R.W.

1963 "Entailment and Modality" PAS 63(1963) 203-16

1967 "Linguistic Theory of the Apriori" vol. 4 Encyclopedia of Philosophy, ed. P. Edwards Macmillan, pp. 479-85

Bacon, John B.

1965a Review of M. Fisk [1964] JSL 30(1965) 87-88

1965b "Entailment and the Modal Fallacy" Review of Metaphysics 18(1964/65) 566-71

1971 "The Subjunctive Conditional as Relevant Implication" Philosophia 1(1971) 61-80

197_ "Categorical Propositions in Relevance Logic" RLC

Barker, John A.

1969 A Formal Analysis of Conditionals, Southern Illinois University Monographs, Carbondale Ill.

1975 "Relevance Logic, Classical Logic, and Disjunctive Syllogism" PS 27(1975) No.6 361-76

Bayart, A.

1969a "Pour Une Logique de L《Entailment》" LA 12 (1969) 353-60

1969b Reviews of Anderson and Belnap [1959a] and Belnap's [1960b] JSL 34(1969) 120

Baylis, C. 1931 "Implication and subsumption" Monist 41(1931) 392-99

Belnap, Nuel D. Jr. see also Anderson & Belnap

1959a The formalization of entailment, Ph.D. dissertation, Yale 1959

1959b "Pure Rigorous Implication as a 'Sequenzen Kalkul' "(abstract) JSL 24(1959) 282

1959c "Tautological entailments"(abstract) JSL 24(1959) 316

1960a A formal analysis of entailment, Technical Report No 7, Contract SAR/Nonr-609(616), Yale University, New Haven 1960

Belnap entries continued,

1960b "Entailment and Relevance" JSL 25(1960) 144-46

1960c "EQ and the First Order Functional Calculus" ZML 6(1960) 217-18.

1962 "Tonk, Plonk, and Plink" Analysis22(1962) 130-34. Also Philosophical Logic, ed. P.F.Strawson, Oxford 1967, 132-37

1967a "Intensional Models for First Degree Formulas" JSL 32(1967) 1-22

1967b "Special Cases of the Decision Problem for Entailment and Relevant Implication"(abstract) JSL 32(1967) 431-32

1970 "Conditional Assertion and Restricted Quantification" Nous 4(1967) 1 - 3, with abstracts of critical remarks by W.V. Quine and J.M. Dunn

1975 "Grammatical Propaedeutic" The Logical Enterprise
eds. eds. A.R. Anderson,R.B. Marcus, R.M. Martin 143-65 Yale 1975, Also Appendix to Anderson & Belnap [1975].

with Wallace J.R.

1965 " A decision procedure for the system $E_{\overline{I}}$ of entailment with negation" ZML 11(1965) 277-89

with Spencer J. H.

1966 "Intensionally complemented distributive lattices" Portugaliae Mathematica 25(1966) 99-104

with Dunn, J.M.

1968a "The substitution interpretation of quantifiers" Nous 2(1968) 28-38

1968b "Homomorphisms of intensionally complemented distributive lattices" MA 176(1968) 28-38

with Dunn and Anil Gupta

197_ "A Consecution Calculus for Positive Relevant Implication with Necessity"(abstract) RLC

Bennett, Jonathan F.

1954 "Meaning and Implication" Mind 63(1954) 451-63

1959 "On a Recent Account of Entailment" Mind 68(1959) 393-95

1965 Reviews of Anderson"s & Belnap's [1962b] and T. Smiley's [1959], JSL 30(1965) 240-41

1969 "Entailment" Philosophical Review 78(1969) 197-236

Birkhoff, G
1948,1967 Lattice Theory, Providence R.I. 1967 3rd ed.

Blanshard, Brand
1939 The Nature of Thought, Vol. II, London 1939 p. 309 f
1962 Reason and Analysis, Open court, 1962
1974 "A reply to my critics" Idealistic Studies 4(1974) 107-130

Bode, James R.
1973 A logic for conditional statements, Ph.D. dissertation, Ohio State University, Ann Arbor Microfilms 1973

Briskman, L.
1975 "Classical semantics and entailment" Analysis 35 no. 4, Mar. 1975 118-26

Bronstein, D.J.
1936 "The meaning of Implication" Mind45(1936) 157-80
1937 "Mr. Nelson's Conception of Entailment" Mind 46(1937) 127-29

Burrell, David B.
1964 "Entailment,'E' and Aristotle" LA 7(1964) 111-29

Carnap, R.
1947 Meaning and Necessity, U. Chi. Press 2nd. enlarged ed. 1956

Chidgey, John R.
1973 "A Note on Transitivity" NDJFL 14(1973) 273-75
1974 On Entailment Ph.D. dissertation, U. of Manchester
197_ "A 'Real' logic of sanction" Xerox copy of a typescript sent to the author.
197_ "On the non-availability of Dawson-modelling into certain relevance alethic modal logics" Xerox copy of a typescript sent to the author.

with Z. Parks
1972 "Necessity and Ticket Entailment" NDJFL 13(1972) 224-26

Christensen, Niels Egmont
19 1973 "Is There A 'Logic" of Formal System Based on the Concept of a Truth Determinant?" Danish Yearbook of Philosophy10(1973) 77-85

Church, Alonzo

1951a "The weak theory of implication" Kontrolliertes Denken, Untersuchungen zum Logikkalkul und zur Logik der Einzelwissenschaften ed. by A. Menne, A. Wilhelmy, and H. Angsil Munich 1951 22-27

1951b "The weak positive implicational propositional calculus"(abstract) JSL 16(1951) 238

1951c "Minimal logic"(abstract) JSL 16(1951) 238

1956 Introduction to mathematical logic, 2nd. ed. Vol. I Princeton N.J. 1956

Cleave, John P.

1974 "An Account of Entailment Based On Classical Semantics" Analysis 34(Mar. 1974) 118-122

Coffa, J. Alberto

1970 "Fallacies of modality"(abstract) JSL 36(1970) 369-70 This material is elaborated in 22.1.2 of Anderson's and Belnap's [1975].

Collier, Kenneth W.

1973 "Physical Modalities and the System E" NDJFL 14(1973) 185-194

with Ann Gaspar and R.G. Wolf eds.

197_ Proceedings of the international conference on relevance logics in St. Louis 1974

Copi, I

1967 Symbolic Logic, 3rd. ed. Macmillan 1967

Corcoran, John

1972 "Strange Arguments" NDJFL 13(1972) 206-10

Cresswell, M.J. with Hughes G.E.

1968 An Introduction to Modal Logic, Methuen, London 1968

Curly, E.M.

1972 "Lewis and Entailment" PS 23(1972) 198-204

Curry, Haskell, B

1963 Foundations of mathematical logic, McGraw-Hill N.Y. 1963

Dale, A.J

1972 "The Transitivity of 'If,then' " LA 15(1972) 439-41

1973 "Geach on Entailment" Philosophical Review 82(1973) 215-19

Dawson, E.E. 1973 — Revies of Ashby [1963], Bacon[1965b], and J.O. Nelson[1965] JSL 38(1973) 668-70 (deals with the so-called modal fallacy)

Donchenko, V.V.
1963 — In Russian, "Some questions connected with the decision problem for Ackermann's system of Rigorous Implication" Problems of Logic 1963 18-24

Dubish, Roy 1964 — Lattices to Logic, New York(Blaisdel Pub. Co)

Dugundji, J.
1940 — "Note on a property of matrices for Lewis' and Langford's calculi of propositions" JSL 5(1940) 150-51

Duncan-Jones, A.E.
1935 — "Is strict implication the same as entailement?" Analysis 2(1935) 70-78

Dunn, Jon Michael Look also under the Belnap entries
1966 — The algebra of intensional logic, Ph.D. dissertation U. of Pittsburgh, Ann Arbor Microfilms. See sections 18 and 28.2 of Anderson's and Belnap's [1975] for Dunn's further development of the algebra of intensional logic.

1967 — "An intuitive semantics for first degree relevant implications"(abstract) JSL 36 (1971) 362-63

1970 — "Algebraic Completeness Results for R-Mingle and Its Extensions" JSL 35(1970) 1 - 13. See section 29.4 of Anderson's and Belnap's [1975] for further treatment of this material by Dunn.

1972 — "A Modification of Parry's Analytic Implication"NDJFL 13(1972) 195-205

197_ a — "Intuitive Semantics for First-Degree Entaliments on 'Coupled Trees' " Forthcoming in PS. Xerox copy received from R.G. Wolf in 1975

197_b — "R-Mingle and Beneath, Extensions of the Routley-Meyer Semantics for R" Xerox copy received from R.G. Wolf in 1975.

with R.K. Meyer

1969 — "E,R, and γ " JSL 34(1969) 460-74. A version of this is in sections 25.3 and 25.4 of Anderson's and Belnap's [1975].

Edelstein, Roy
1976 "A decision procedure for Cleave's system CK" A copy may be obtained from the author of this text.

Emch, Arnold F.
1936a "Implication and Deducibility" JSL 1(1936) 26-35

1936b Addendum to [1936a] JSL 1(1936) p.58

1936c "Consistency and independence in postulation technique" _Philosophy of Science_ 3(1936) 188-96

1937 "Deducibility as to Necessary and Impossible Propositions" JSL 2(1937) 78-81

Fine, Kit
1974 "Models for Entailment" JPL 3(1974) 347-72

197_ "Analytic Implication" RLC, The author of this text worked from a ditto copy obtained from R.G. Wolf in 1975.

Feys, Robert
1956 "Un systeme de l'implication rigoreuse" LA 7(1956) 3-18

Fisk, Milton
1964 _A Modern Formal Logic_, Prentice-Hall 1964

Fitch, Benton F.
1933 "Note on Leo Abraham's transformations of strict implication" _Monist_ 43(1933) 297-98

1952 _Symbolic Logic_, New York (Ronald Press) 1952

1974 _Elements of Combinatory Logic_, Yale U. Press New Haven 1974

Gabbay, Dov. M
1972 "A General Theory of the Conditional in Terms of a Ternary Operator" _Theoria_ 38(1972) 97-104

Geach, Peter T.
1948 "Necessary Propositions and Entailment Statements" _Mind_ 57(1948) 491-93. Parts of this are on pp. 201-03 of _Logic Matters_ by P.T. Geach U. Calif. Press 1972.

1958 "Entailment" PAS supp.vol. 32(1958). Also on pp. 174-86 of _Logic Matters_.

1970 "Entailment Again" _Philosophical Review_ 79(.970) 237-39 and pp. 186-88 of _Logic Matters_

Geach. P.T.
1971 "Reply to Myro's "A Note on Strict Implication and Entailment" " Analysis 32(1971) 56

Goddard, L. with R. Routley
1966 "Use, mention, and quotation" AJP 44(1966) 1 - 49

1972 The Logic of Significance and Content, Scottish Academic Press

Grover, D.L
1960 Entailment: A critical study of system E and a critical bibliography of the subject in general, MA thesis, Victoria U., Wellington New Zealand

Haack, Susan
1976 "The Justification of Deduction" Mind 85 Jan. 1976 112-119

Hacking, J.
1963 "What is strict implication?" JSL 28(1963) 51-71

Halldén, Sőren
1948a "A note concerning the paradoxes of strict implication and Lewis' system S1" JSL 13(1948) 138-39

1948b "A question concerning a logical calculus related to Lewis' system of strict implication which is of special interest for the study of entailment" Theoria 14(1948) 265-69

1951a "On the semantic non-completeness of certain Lewis calculi" JSL 16(1951) 127-29

1951b Review of Yonemitsu [1951] JSL 16(1951) 278

Hampshire, Stuart N.
1948 "Mr. Strawson on Necessary Propositions and Entailment Statements" Mind 57(1948) 354-57 (A critique of Strawson [1948])

Heyting, A.
1956 Intuitionism: An Introduction, Amsterdam 1956

Hilbert, D. and Ackermann, W.
1928(1950) Mathematical Logic, Chelsea 1950 (German 1928)

Hintikka, J.
1962 Knowledge and Belief, Cornell 1962

Hockney, Donald J.
1968 "A Vindication of System E" LA 11(1968) 480-91

D.J. Hockney with K. Wilson
1965 "In Defense of a Relevance Condition" LA 8(1965) 211-220

Isiki, Kiyoshi
1967 "On the classical propositional calculus of A.R. Anderson and N.D. Belnap" Proc. Japan Academy 43(1967) 202-03

Jeffrey, Harold
1942 "Does a Contradiction Entail Every Proposition?" Mind 51(1942) p.90

Jeffrey, Richard
1967 Formal Logic: Its Scope and Limits, McGraw-Hill 1967

Johnson, Fred
1976 "A three-valued Interpretation for a Paradox Free Entailment Calculus" Relevance Logic Newsletter 1(1976) 123-28

Kane, R.H.
1972 "Presupposition and Entailment" Mind 81(1972) 401-04

Kanger, Stig
1965 Natural Deduction: a proof theoretic inquiry, Stockholm 1965

1973 "Entailment" Modality, Morality, and Nonsense Essays dedicated to Sören Halldén, Lund Sweden CWK Gleerup 1973 167-99

Kielkopf, Charles F.
1970 Strict Finitism, Mouton & Co. The Hague 1970

1972 "The Binary Operation called "material Implication" Soberly Understood" Mind 81(1972) 338-47

1974 "Critique of the Routleys' First Degree Semantics" AJP 52(Aug. 1974) 105-120

1975a "Adjunction and Paradoxical Derivations" Analysis 33(Mar. 1975) 127-29

1975b "My Critique of the Routleys' Semantics: A Correction" AJP 53(Aug.1975) 165-66

1976 "Two E matrices"(abstract) JSL 41(1976) 554 Presented to 1975 ASL meeting Chicago

197_b "A favorable mark for strict implication" LA

Kielkopf, C.F.
197_c "Classical Logic of Relevant Logicians" RLC

197_d "Intuition as the cause of necessity" International Logic Review

Kleene, S.C.
1950 Introduction to Metamathematics, Van Nostrand North-Holland, Amsterdam 1950

Kneale, William
1946 "Truths of Logic" PAS 46(1946) 207-34

1947 "Are necessary truths True by Conventions?" PAS supp. vol. 21(1947) 118-33

with Martha Kneale
1962 Development of Logic, Oxford 1962

Koningsveld, H.
1973 "What does 'p entails q' mean?" Mind 82(1973) 118-22

Korner, Stephen
1947 "On Entailment" PAS 47(1946/47) 143-62

1949 "Entailment and the Meaning of Words" Analysis 10(1949) 89-62

1955 Conceptual Thinking, CAmbridge U. Press 1955

Kripke, Saul
1959a "Distinguished Constituents"(abstract) JSL 24(1959) 323

1959b "The Problem of Entailment"(abstract) JSL 24(1959) 324

Kron, Alexsander
1972 "A note on E" NDJFL 13(1972) 424-26

1973 "Deduction theorems for relevant logics" ZML 19(1973) 85-92

Langford, Harold
1936 Review of Bronstein [1936] JSL 1(1936) p.65
See Lewis,C.I.

Leblanc, H.
1973 Truth, Syntax, and Modality, North-Holland 1973 editor
with Wisdom, W.A.
1972 Deductive Logic, Allyn & Bacon, Boston 1972

with J.M. Dunn and R.K. Meyer
1974 "Completeness of Relevant Quantification Theories" NDJFL 15(1974) 97-121

Lehrer, Keith
1973 "Relevant Deduction and Minimally Inconsistent Sets" Philosophia 3(1973) 153-65

Lewis, C.I. See the bibliography of Schilpp [1968]
1918 A survey of symbolic logic, Berkeley 1918

1936 "Emch's calculus and strict implication" JSL 1 (1936) 77-86

with H.C. Langford
1932, 1959 Symbolic Logic N.Y./London 1932
2nd. ed. Dover Pub. Co. N.Y. 1959

Lewy, Casmir
1946 "Entailment and Empirical Propositions" Mind 55(1946) 74-78

1950 "Entailment and necessary propositions" Philosophical Analysis, ed. M.Black Cornell 1950 195-210

1958 "Entailment" PAS supp. vol. 32(1958) 123-42

1963 "Entailment and propositional identity" PAS 64(1963/64) 107-122

MaCall, Storrs,
1966 "Connexive Implication" JSL 31(1966) 415-33

1967a "Connexive class logic" JSL 32(1967) 83-90

1967b "Connexive Implication and the Syllogism" Mind 76(1967) 346-56

1975 Section 29.8 of Anderson's and Belnap's [1975] which elaborates on connexive logic.

MacColl, H.
1905 "Symbolic Reasoning VIII" Mind 15(1906) 504-18

McKinsey, J.C.C.
1934 "A note on Bronstein's and Tarter's definition of strict implication" Philosophical Review 43(1934) 518-20

1939a "Proof of the independence of primitive sybols of Heyting's claculus of propositions" JSL 4(1939) 155-58

1939b Review of Vredenduin's [1939] JSL 4(1939) 124

1941 "A solution to the decision problem for the Lewis systems S2 and S4 with an application to topology" JSL 6(1941) 117-134

with A. Tarski
1948 "Some theorems about the sentential calculus of Lewis and Heyting" JSL 13(1948) 1 - 15.

MacLachlan, D.L.C.
1970 "The Pure Hypothetical Syllogism and Entailment" _Philosophical Quarterly_ 20(1970) 26-40

Makinson, D.
1965 "An Alternative Characterisation of First Degree Entailment" LA 8(1965) 308-11

Maksimowa, Larisa L. Works of her's not seen by the author are cited to indicate some of the work on entailment being done in the Soviet Union.
1964 "On a Set of Axioms for the System of Rigorous Implication" _Algébra i Logika_, Séminar 3(1964) 59-68 (Russian)

1966 "Formal Deductions in the calculus of strict entailment" _Algébra i Logika_ Sem. 5(1966) 33-39 (Russian)

1967a "On models of the system E" _Algébra i Logika_ Sem. 6(1967) 5 -20
Reviewed by B. Veglong MR #2585 37(1969)

1967b "Some problems on the Ackermann Calculus" _Soviet Mathematics_ (English translation) 8(1967) 997-99
Reviewed by H. Rasiowa MR #4956, 36(1968)

1968 "On the Calculus of Strict Entailment" _Algebra and Logic_ 7(1968) 102-16 (English translation)

1970 "E-theories " _Algebra and Logic_ 9(1970) 320-25 (English translation)

1971 "An Interpretation and Separation Theorems for the Logical Systems E and R" _Algebra and Logic_ 10(1971) 232-41 (English trans.)

1973 "A Semantics for the Calculus E of Entailment" _Bulletin of the Section of Logic_, Polish Academy of Philosophy and Sociology, vol. 2 18-21

1974 "Relevance Principles and Formal Deducibility" Dittoed copy was available at RLC St. Louis 1974

Malcolm, Norman
1940a "Are Necessary Propositions Really Verbal" _Mind_ 49(1940 189-203

1940b "The Nature of Entailment" _Mind_ 49(1940) 337-47

Martin, R.M.
1972 "On Stevenson's If-iculties" _Philosophy of Science_ 39(1972) 515-21

Mendelson, E.
1964 _Introduction to Mathematical Logic_, Van-Nostrand 1964

Meyer, Robert K.
1966 _Topics in Modal and Many-valued Logic_, Ph.D. dissertation, U. of Pittsburgh 1966, Ann Arbor Microfilms

1968a "Entailment and Relevant Implication" LA 10(1968) 472-79

1968b "An undecidability result in the theory of relevant implication" ZML 14(1968) 255-62 Reviewed by A. Oberschelp MR #4287 38(1969)

1970a "E and S4" NDJFL 11(1970) 181-99

1970b "R_I -The Bounds of finitude" ZML 16(1970) 385-87

1970c "Some problems no longer open for E and related logics"(abstract) JSL 35(1970) 353 Presented at 1969 New Orleans ASL meeting

1971a "Coherence in Modal Logics" LA 14(1971) 658-68 See also section 22.3 in Anderson's and Belnap's [1975].

1971b "Entailment" JP 68(1971) 808-18

1971c "Logics contained in R"(abstract) JSL 36(1971) pp. 365-66, presented at 1967 ASL Chicago meeting

1971d "R-mingle and relevant disjunction"(abstract) JSL 36(1971) 366, presented at 1967 Chicago ASL meeting, See now section 29.3 of Anderson's and Belnap's [1975].

1972a "On Relevantly Derivable Disjunctions" NDJFL 13(1972) 476-79

1972b "Negation Disarmed")abstract) JSL 37(1972) 445 Presented at 1971 New York ASL meeting

1972c "Canonical Metavaluations"(abstract) JSL 37(1972) 445-46, Presented at 1971 New York ASL meeting,

1973a "On Conserving Positive Logics" NDJFL 14(1973) 224-236, See now 24.4.2 of Anderson's and Belnap's [1975].

R.K. Meyer entries continued

1973b — "Conservative Extension in Relevant Implication" *Studia Logica* 31(1973) 39-46

1973c — "Intuitionism, Entailment, Negation" 168-98 of Leblance [1973]

1973d — "Simple Belnap lattices and their implicative extensions"(abstract) JSL 38(1973) 350-51 Presented at 1969 New York ASL meeting,

1974a — "New Axiomatics for Relevant Logics I" JPL 3(1974) 53-86

1974b — "Entailment is Not Strict Implication" AJP 52 no.3(1974) 212-31, See now 29.12 of Anderson's and Belnap's [1975].

See joint papers with A.R. Anderson, J.M. Dunn, and H. Leblanc

with Richard Routley

1972a — "A Kripke Semantics for Entailment"(abstract) JSL 37(1972) 442-43, Presentend at 1973 New York ASL meeting,

1972b SEII — "The Semantics of Entailment II" JPL 1(1972) 53-73

1972c SEIII — "The Semantics of Entailment III" JPL 1(1972) 192-208

1972d — "Algebraic Analysis of Entailment I" LA 15(1972) 407-28

1973a SEI — "The Semantics of Entailment I" 200-243 of Leblanc [1973]

1973b — "An undecidable relevant logic" ZML 19(1973) 389-97

1973c — "Classical Relevant Logics I" *Studia Logica* 32(1973) 51-68

1974 — "E is a Conservative Extension of $E_{\bar{I}}$ " *Philosophica* 4(1974) 223-49

197_a — "Classical Relevant Logics II" Mimeograph copy from R.G. Wolf

197_b SEIV — "The Semantics of Entailment IV" JSL(forthcoming) Xerox copy received from R.G. Wolf in 1975

197_c SEV — "The Semantics of Entailment V" Xerox copy received from R.G. Wolf

The next three entries are possible papers by Meyer and Routley

197_d "The SEmantics of Entailment VI"

197_e "The Semantics of Entailment VII"

197_f "The Semantics of Entailment VIII"

197_g "Towards a general theory of implication and conditionals" Reports on Mathematical Logic

197_h "Algebraic Analysis of Entailment II"

197_i "Every Sentential Logic has a Two-Valued Worlds Semantics" memeograph copy from R.G. Wolf

197_j "Dialectical Logic, Classical Logic, and the Consistency of the World" mimeograph copy from R. Routley 1976

with R.G. Wolf
197_ "Two Criteria for Entailment Logics" ditto copy received from R.G. Wold in 1976

Moh Shaw-Kwei
1950 "The deduction theorem and two new logical systems" Methodos 2(1950) 56-75

Montgomery and R. Routley
1968 "On Systems Containing Aristotle's Thesis" JSL 33(1968) 82-96

Moore, G.E.
1920 "External and Internal Relations" PAS 20 (1919/1920), Reprinted in G.E. Moore's Philosophical Studies International Lib. Psychology, Phil. and Scientific Method 276-309

1944 "Russell's Theory of Descriptions" The Philosophy of Bertrand Russell, ed. P.A. Schlipp, Open Court 1944. Also 149-92 of Moore's Philosophical Papers, Allen and Unwin 1959

Morscher, Edgar
1972 "From 'Is' to 'Ought' via Knowing" Ethics 83(1972) 84-86

Myhill, John
197_ "Relevance" RLC

Myro, George
1971 "A Note on Strict Implication and Entailment" Analysis 32(Dec.1971) 55-56

Nelson, Everett J.
1929 "An Intensional Logic of Propositions" Ph.D. thesis, Harvard Library

1930 "Intensional Relations" _Mind_ 39(1930) 440-53

1933a "Deductive Systems and the Absoluteness of Logic" _Mind_ 42(1933) 31-34

1933b "On Three Logical Principles in Intension" _Monist_ 43(1933) 268-84

1936a "To the Editor of Mind" _Mind_ 45(1936) 551

1936b Review of Emch [1936c] JSL 1(1936) 66

1936c Review of Emch [1936a,b] JSL 1(1936) 67-68

Nelson, J.O.
1964 "A Question of Entailment" _Review of Metaphysics_ 18(1964) 364-77

1966 "Is material implication inferentially harmless?" _Mind_ 75(1966) 542-55

Pap, Arthur
1950 "Logic and the concept of entailment" JP 47(1950) 378-87

1955 "Strict Implication, Entailment, and Modal Iteration" _Philosophical Review_ 64(1955) 604-13

Parks, Zane See also Chidgey
1972 "A Note on R-Mingle and Sobocinski's Three-Valued Logic" NDJFL 13(1972) 227-28

Parry, W.T.
1931 _Implication_, Ph.D. thesis, Harvard Library

1933 "Ein Axiomsystem für eine neuw Art von Implikation(analytische Implikation)" _Ergebnisse eines mathematischen Kolloquiums_ 4(1933) 5 - 6

1968 "The Logic of C.I. Lewsi" 115-154 of _The Philosophy of C.I. Lewis_ Schlipp [1968]

1972 "Comparison of entailment theories"(abstract) JSL 37(1972) 441-42, Present 1971 N.Y. ASL meeting,

197_ "Analytic Entailment: History, Motivation, and Varieties" RLC

Pollock, John
1965 "Implication and Analyticity" JP 62(1965) 150-57

Pollock, J.
1966 "The Paradoxes of Strict Implication" LA 9(1966) 180-96

1967 "Basic Modal Logic" JSL 32(1967) 355-65

Popper, Karl
1943 "Are contradictions embracing?" Mind 52(1943) 47-50

Prior, A.N.
1948 "Facts, Propositions, and Entailment" Mind 57(1948) 62-68

1955 Formal Logic, Oxford 1955, 1961

Putnam, Hilary
1963 Review of von Wright's [1957], Philosophical Review72(1963) 242-49

Quine, W.V.
1953 "Three grades of modal involvement" Proceedings XIV Internat. Cong. Phil, Brussels 1953 vol. 14 pp. 65-81

1960 Word and Object, MIT Press, Cambridge Mass. 1960

1966 Ontological Relativity and Other Essays, New York 1969

1970 Philosophy of Logic, Prentic-Hall 1970

Rescher, N.
1962 Review of Anderson's & Belnap's [1961] JSL 27(1962) 115-16

1969 Many-valued Logic, McGraw-Hill 1969

Routley, Richard See especially the Meyer and Routley entries
1972a "A semantical analysis of implicational system I and the first degree of entailment" MA 196(1972) 58-84

1972b "Vredenduin's System of Strict Implication" LA 15(1972) 435-57

1974 "A Rival Account of Logical Consequence" Reports on Mathematical Logic No.3(1974) 41-52

197_ "Semantics Unlimited: The Synthesis of Relevant Implication and Entailment with Non-transmissible Functors such as Belief, Assertion, and Perception" RLC

with Valerie Routley
1969 "A Fallacy of Modality" Nous 3(1969) 129-53

1972 "The Semantics of First Degree Entailment" Nous 6(1972) 335-59

See Goddard and Montgomery for other work of R. Routley.

Schillp, Paul A. ed.
1968 *The Philosophy of C.I. Lewis*, Open Court 1968

Smiley, Timothy
1959 "Entailment and Deducibility" PAS 59(1959) 233-54
1970 Review of von Wright [1959] JSL 35(1970) 462

Stephenson, G.H.
1975 "Entailment, Negation, and Disjunctive Syllogism" PS 27(1975) 377-87

Stevenson, Charles L.
1970 "If-iculties" *Philosophy of Science* 37(1970) 27-49

Strawson, P.F.
1948 "Necessary Propositions and Entailment Statements" *Mind* 57(1948) 184-200
1958 Review of von Wright [1957], *Phil. Quarterly* 8(1958) 372-76

Sugihara, Takeo
1955 "Strict Implication Free from Implicational Paradoxes" *Memoirs of the Faculty of Liberal Arts, Fukui University*, Series I(1955) 55-59

Synder, Paul D.
1960 "Models for Logical Entailments" LA9(1960) 344-59
1971 *Modal Logic and its applications*, Ch. VII, van Nostrand 1971

Szász, G.
1963 Introduction to Lattice Theory, N.Y. Academic Press 1963

Thomason, R.
1970 *Symbolic Logic*, MacMillan 1970

Toms, E.
1940 "Facts and Entailment" *Mind* 49(1940) 451-54
A critique of Malcolm [1940b],

Urquhart, Alasdair
1972 "Semantics for relevant logics" JSL 37(1972) 159-69
1973 "A Semantical Theory of Analytic Implication" JPL 2(1973) 212-19

van Fraassen, Bas C.
1967 "Meaning Relations among Predicates" [illegible] 1(1967) 161-79

van Fraassen, B.C.
1969 "Facts and Tautological Entailments" JP 66(1969) 477-87 See also 20.3 of Anderson's and Belnap's [1975].

1971 Formal Semantics, MacMillan 1971

von Wright, G.H.
1957a Logical Studies, London 1957

1957b "A New System of Modal Logic" 89-126 of [1957a]

1957c "On Conditionals" 127-65 of [1957a]

1957d "The Concept of Entailment" 166-91 of [1957a]

1959 "A Note on Entailment" Phil.Quarterly 9(1959) 363-65

Vredenduin, P.G. J.
1939 "A system of strict implication" JSL 4(1939) 73-76

Watling, J.
1958 "Entailment" PAS supp. vol. 32(1958) 143-46

Woods, John
1964 "Relevance" LA 7(1964) 130-37

1965 "On how not to invalidate disjunctive syllogism" LA 8(1965) 312-20

1966 "Relevance Revisited: A Reply to Hockney and Wilson" LA 9(1966) 364-371

1967a "Non-paradoxical paradoxes" NDJFL 8(1967) 346-52

1967b "Is there a relation of intensional conjunction?" Mind 76(1967) 357-68

Index of Names and Subjects

Rarely is every occurrence of a term listed; the author has listed only what he judged to be an especially informative or interesting occurrence. Unfortunately, many significant terms are not listed. Because A.R. Anderson, N.D. Belnap Jr., J.M. Dunn, R.K. Meyer, and R. Routley have made such large contributions to the search for entailment their names occur in the text in far more places than those listed below. The bibliography provides names of many people who have contributed to the search. The first few pages of the Notational Preface provides a list of the symbols used in formulas and the Table of Contents can be a type of index to systems presented.